P9-AGM-029

RAINBOW SIX

ALSO BY TOM CLANCY

FICTION

THE HUNT FOR RED OCTOBER

RED STORM RISING

PATRIOT GAMES

THE CARDINAL OF THE KREMLIN

CLEAR AND PRESENT DANGER

THE SUM OF ALL FEARS

WITHOUT REMORSE

DEBT OF HONOR

EXECUTIVE ORDERS

NONFICTION

SUBMARINE
A GUIDED TOUR INSIDE A NUCLEAR WARSHIP

ARMORED CAV
A GUIDED TOUR OF AN ARMORED CAVALRY REGIMENT

FIGHTER WING
A GUIDED TOUR OF AN AIR FORCE COMBAT WING

MARINE
A GUIDED TOUR OF A MARINE EXPEDITIONARY UNIT

AIRBORNE
A GUIDED TOUR OF AN AIRBORNE TASK FORCE

INTO THE STORM
A STUDY IN COMMAND
WITH GENERAL FRED M. FRANKS, JR. (RET.)

RAINBOW SIX

TOM CLANCY

G. P. PUTNAM'S SONS
NEW YORK

G. P. Putnam's Sons
Publishers Since 1838
a member of
Penguin Putnam Inc.
375 Hudson Street
New York, NY 10014

This is a work of fiction. The events described here are imaginary; the settings and characters are fictitious and not intended to represent specific places or living persons.

Published simultaneously in Canada

Library of Congress Cataloging-in-Publication Data

Clancy, Tom, date.
Rainbow Six / by Tom Clancy.
p. cm.
ISBN 0-399-14390-4
ISBN 0-399-14413-7 (Limited edition)
I. Title.
PS3553.L245R35 1998 98-22301 CIP
813'.54—dc21

Printed in the United States of America

1 3 5 7 9 10 8 6 4 2

This book is printed on acid-free paper. ♾

BOOK DESIGN BY LOVEDOG STUDIO

For Alexandra Maria

lux mea mundi

There are no compacts between lions and men, and wolves and lambs have no concord.

HOMER

RAINBOW SIX

PROLOGUE

SETTING UP

JOHN CLARK HAD MORE TIME IN AIRPLANES THAN most licensed pilots, and he knew the statistics as well as any of them, but he still didn't like the idea of crossing the ocean on a twin-engine airliner. Four was the right number of engines, he thought, because losing one meant losing only 25 percent of the aircraft's available power, whereas on this United 777, it meant losing *half*. Maybe the presence of his wife, one daughter, and a son-in-law made him a little itchier than usual. No, that wasn't right. He wasn't itchy at all, not about flying anyway. It was just a lingering . . . what? he asked himself. Next to him, in the window seat Sandy was immersed in the mystery she'd started the day before, while he was trying to concentrate on the current issue of *The Economist,* and wondering what was putting the cold-air feeling on the back of his neck. He started to look around the cabin for a sign of danger but abruptly stopped himself. There wasn't anything wrong that he could see, and he didn't want to seem like a nervous flyer to the cabin crew. He sipped at his glass of white wine, shook his shoulders, and went back to the article on how peaceful the new world was.

Right. He grimaced. Well, yes, he had to admit that things were a hell of a lot better than they'd been for nearly all of his life. No more swimming out of a submarine to do a collection on a Russian beach, or flying into Tehran to do something the Iranians wouldn't like much, or swimming up a fetid river in North Vietnam to rescue a downed aviator. Someday maybe Bob Holtzman would talk him into a book on his career. Problem was, who'd believe it—and would CIA ever allow him to tell his tales except on his own deathbed? He was not in a hurry for that, not with a grandchild on the way. Damn. He grimaced, unwilling to contemplate that development. Patsy must have caught a silver bullet on their wedding night, and Ding glowed more about it than she did. John looked back to business class—the curtain wasn't in place yet—and there they were, holding hands while the stewardess did the safety lecture. *If the airplane hit the water at 400 knots, reach under your seat for the life-preserver and inflate it by pulling* . . . he'd heard that one before. The bright yellow life-jackets would make it somewhat easier for search aircraft to find the crash site, and that was about all they were good for.

Clark looked around the cabin again. He still felt that draft on his neck. Why? The flight attendant made the rounds, removing his wine glass as the aircraft taxied out to the end of the runway. Her last stop was by Alistair over on the left side of the first-class cabin. Clark caught his eye and got a funny look back as the Brit put his seat back in the upright position. Him, too? Wasn't that something? Neither of the two had ever been accused of nervousness.

Alistair Stanley had been a major in the Special Air Service before being permanently seconded to the Secret Intelligence Service. His position had been much like John's—the one you called in to take care of business when the gentler people in the field division got a little too skittish. Al and John had hit it off right away on a job in Romania eight years before, and the American was pleased to be working with him again on a more regular basis, even if they were both too old now for the fun stuff. Administration wasn't exactly John's idea of what his job should be, but he had to admit he wasn't twenty anymore . . . or thirty . . . or even forty. A little old to run down alleys and jump over walls. . . . Ding had said that to him only a week before in John's office at Langley, rather more respectfully than usual, since he was trying to make a logical point to the grandfather-presumptive of his first child. What the hell, Clark told himself, it was remarkable enough that he was still alive to gripe about being old—no, not old, old*er*. Not to mention he was respectable now as Director of the new agency. Director. A polite term for a REMF. But you didn't say no to the President, especially if he happened to be your friend.

The engine sounds increased. The airliner started moving. The usual sensation came, like being pressed back into the seat of a sports car jumping off a red light, but with more authority. Sandy, who hardly traveled at all, didn't look up from the book. It must have been pretty good, though John never bothered reading mysteries. He never could figure them out, and they made him feel stupid, despite the fact that in his professional life he'd picked his way through real mysteries more than once. A little voice in his head said *rotate,* and the floor came up under his feet. The body of the aircraft followed the nose into the sky, and the flight began properly, the wheels rising up into the wells.

Instantly, those around him lowered their seats to get some sleep on the way to London Heathrow. John lowered his, too, but not as far. He wanted dinner first.

"On our way, honey," Sandy said, taking a second away from the book.

"I hope you like it over there."

"I have three cookbooks for after I figure this one out."

John smiled. "Who done it?"

"Not sure yet, but probably the wife."

"Yeah, divorce lawyers are so expensive."

Sandy chuckled and went back to the story as the stews got up from their seats to resume drink service. Clark finished *The Economist* and started *Sports Illustrated.* Damn, he'd be missing the end of the football season. That was one thing he'd always tried to keep track of, even off on a mission. The Bears were coming back, and he'd grown up with Papa Bear George Halas and the Monsters of the Midway—had often wondered if he might have made it as a pro himself. He'd been a pretty good linebacker in high school, and Indiana University had shown some interest in him (also for his swimming). Then he'd decided to forgo college and join the Navy, as his father had before him, though Clark had become a SEAL, rather than a skimmer-sailor on a tin can . . .

"Mr. Clark?" The stew delivered the dinner menu. "Mrs. Clark?"

One nice thing about first class. The flight crew pretended you had a name. John had gotten an automatic upgrade—he had frequent-flyer miles up the yingyang, and from now on he'd mainly fly British Airways, which had a very comfortable understanding with the British government.

The menu, he saw, was pretty good, as it usually was on international flights, and so was the wine list . . . but he decided to ask for bottled water instead of wine, thank you. Hmph. He grumbled to himself, settled back, and rolled up the sleeves of his shirt. These damned flights always seemed overheated to him.

The captain got on next, interrupting all the personal movies on their mini-screens. They were taking a southerly routing to take advantage of the jet stream. That, Captain Will Garnet explained, would cut their time to Heathrow by forty minutes. He didn't say that it would also make for a few bumps. Airlines tried to conserve fuel, and forty-five minutes' worth would put a gold star in his copybook . . . well, maybe just a silver one . . .

The usual sensations. The aircraft tilted, more to the right than the left, as it crossed over the ocean at Sea Isle City in New Jersey for the three-thousand-mile flight to the next landfall, somewhere on the Irish coast, which they'd reach in about five and a half hours, John thought. He had to sleep for some of that time. At least the captain didn't bother them with the usual tour-director crap—*we are now at forty thousand feet, that's almost eight miles to fall if the wings come off and* . . . They started serving dinner. They'd be doing the same aft in tourist class, with the drink and dinner carts blocking the aisles.

It started on the left side of the aircraft. The man was dressed properly, wearing a jacket—that was what got John's attention. Most people took them off as soon as they sat down but—

—it was a Browning automatic, with a flat-black finish that said "military" to Clark, and, less than a second later, to Alistair Stanley. A moment later, two more men appeared on the right side, walking right next to Clark's seat.

"Oh, shit," he said so quietly that only Sandy heard him. She turned and looked, but before she could do or say anything, he grabbed her hand. That was enough to keep her quiet, but not quite enough to keep the lady across the aisle from screaming—well, almost screaming. The woman with her covered her mouth with a hand and stifled most of it. The stewardess looked at the two men in front of her in total disbelief. This hadn't happened in years. How could it be happening now?

Clark was asking much the same question, followed by another: Why the hell had he packed his sidearm in his carry-on and stowed it in the overhead? What was the point of having a gun on an airplane, you idiot, if you couldn't get to it? What a dumbass rookie mistake! He only had to look to his left to see the same expression on Alistair's face. Two of the most experienced pros in the business, their guns less than four feet away, but they might as well be in the luggage stored below. . . .

"John . . ."

"Just relax, Sandy," her husband replied quietly. More easily said than done, as he well knew.

John sat back, keeping his head still, but turned away from the window and toward the cabin. His eyes moved free. Three of them. One, probably the leader, was taking a stew forward, where she unlocked the door to the flight deck. John watched the two of them go through and close the door behind them. Okay, now Captain William Garnet would find out what was going on. Hopefully he would be a pro, and he'd be trained to say *yes, sir—no, sir—three-bags-full, sir* to anybody who came forward with a gun. At best he'd be Air Force- or Navy-trained, and therefore he'd know better than to do anything stupid, like trying to be a goddamned hero. His mission would be to get the airplane on the ground, somewhere, anywhere, because it was a hell of a lot harder to kill three hundred people in an airplane when it was sitting still on the ramp with the wheels chocked.

Three of them, one forward in the flight deck. He'd stay there to keep an eye on the drivers and to use the radio to tell whomever he wanted to talk to what his demands were. Two more in first class, standing there, forward, where they could see down both aisles of the aircraft.

"Ladies and gentlemen, this is the captain speaking. I've got the seat-belt sign on. There's a little chop in the air. Please stay in your seats for the time being. I'll be back to you in a few minutes. Thank you."

Good, John thought, catching Alistair's eye. The captain sounded cool, and the bad guys weren't acting crazy—yet. The people in back probably didn't know anything was wrong—yet. Also good. People might panic . . . well, no, not necessarily, but so much the better for everyone if nobody knew there was anything to panic about.

Three of them. Only three? Might there be a backup guy, disguised as a passenger? That was the one who controlled the bomb, if there was a bomb, and a bomb was the worst thing there could be. A pistol bullet might punch a hole in the skin of the aircraft, forcing a rapid descent, and that would fill some barf bags and cause some soiled underwear, but nobody died from that. A bomb would kill everyone aboard, probably . . . better than even money, Clark judged, and he hadn't gotten old by taking that sort of chance when he didn't have to. Maybe just let the airplane go to wherever the hell these three wanted to go, and let negotiations start, by which time people would know that there were another three very special people inside. Word would be going out now. The bad guys would have gotten onto the company radio frequency and passed along the bad news of the day, and the Director of Security for United—Clark knew him, Pete Fleming, former Deputy Assistant Director of the FBI—would call his former agency and get *that* ball rolling, to include notification of CIA and State, the FBI Hostage Rescue Team in Quantico, and Little Willie Byron's Delta Force down at Fort Bragg. Pete would also pass along the passenger list, with three of them circled in red, and *that* would get Willie a little nervous, plus making the troops at Langley and Foggy Bottom wonder about a security leak—John dismissed that. This was a random event that would just make people spin wheels in the Operations Room in Langley's Old Headquarters Building. Probably.

It was time to move a little. Clark turned his head very slowly, toward Domingo Chavez, just twenty feet away. When eye contact was established, he touched the tip of his nose, as though to make an itch go away. Chavez did the same . . . and Ding was still wearing his jacket. He was more used to hot weather, John thought, and probably felt cold on the airplane. Good. He'd still have his Beretta .45 on . . . probably . . . Ding preferred the small of his back, though, and that was awkward for a guy strapped into an airliner seat. Even so,

Chavez knew what was going down, and had the good sense to do nothing about it . . . yet. How might Ding react with his pregnant wife sitting next to him? Domingo was smart and as cool under pressure as Clark could ever ask, but under that he was still Latino, a man of no small passion—even John Clark, experienced as he was, saw flaws in others that were perfectly natural to himself. He had *his* wife sitting next to him, and Sandy was frightened, and Sandy wasn't supposed to be frightened about her own safety. . . . It was her husband's self-assigned job to make certain of that. . . .

One of the bad guys was going over the passenger list. Well, that would tell John if there had been a security leak of some sort. But if there were, he couldn't do anything about it. Not yet. Not until he knew what was going on. Sometimes you just had to sit and take it and—

The guy at the head of the left-side aisle started moving, and fifteen feet later, he was looking down at the woman in the window seat next to Alistair.

"Who are you?" he demanded in Spanish.

The lady replied with a name John didn't catch—it was a Spanish name, but from twenty feet away he couldn't hear it clearly enough to identify it, mainly because her reply had been quiet, polite . . . cultured, he thought. Diplomat's wife, maybe? Alistair was leaning back in his seat, staring with wide blue eyes up at the guy with the gun and trying a little too hard not to show fear.

A scream came from the back of the aircraft. "Gun, that's a gun!" a man's voice shouted—

Shit, John thought. Now everybody would know. The right-aisle guy knocked on the cockpit door and stuck his head in to announce this good news.

"Ladies and gentlemen . . . this is Captain Garnet . . . I, uh, am instructed to tell you that we are deviating from our flight plan. . . . We, uh, have some guests aboard who have told me to fly to Lajes in the Azores. They say that they have no desire to hurt anyone, but they are armed, and First Officer Renford and I are going to do exactly what they say. Please remain calm, stay in your seats, and just try to keep things under control. I will be back to you later." Good news. He had to be military trained; his voice was as cool as the smoke off dry ice. Good.

Lajes in the Azores, Clark thought. Former U.S. Navy base . . . still active? Maybe just caretakered for long over-water flights flying there—as a stop and refueling point for somewhere else? Well, the left-side guy had spoken in Spanish, and been replied to in Spanish. Probably not Middle Eastern bad guys. Spanish speakers . . . Basques? That was still perking over in Spain. The woman, who was she? Clark looked over. Everyone was looking around now, and it was safe for him to do so. Early fifties, well turned out. The Spanish ambassador to Washington was male. Might this be his wife?

The left-side man shifted his gaze a seat. "Who are you?"

"Alistair Stanley" was the reply. There was no sense in Alistair's lying, Clark knew. They were traveling openly. Nobody knew about their agency. They hadn't even started it up yet. Shit, Clark thought. "I'm British," he added in a quaky voice. "My passport's in my bag up in the—" He reached up and had his hand slapped down by the bad guy's gun.

Nice play, John thought, even if it hadn't worked. He might have gotten the bag down, produced the passport, and then had his gun in his lap. Bad luck that the gunman had believed him. That was the problem with accents. But Alistair was up to speed. The three wolves didn't know that the sheep herd had three dogs in it. Big ones.

Willie would be on the phone now. Delta kept an advance team on round-the-clock standby, and they'd be prepping for a possible deployment now. Colonel Byron would be with them. Little Willie was that kind of soldier. He had an XO and staff to follow things up while he led from the front. A lot of wheels were spinning now. All John and his friends really had to do was sit tight . . . so long as the bad guys kept their cool.

More Spanish from the left side. "Where is your husband?" he demanded. He was pretty mad. Made sense, John thought. Ambassadors are good targets. But so were their wives. She was too sharp-looking to be the wife of just a diplomat, and Washington had to be a premier post. Senior guy, probably aristocracy. Spain still had that. High-profile target, the better to put pressure on the Spanish government.

Blown mission was the next thought. They wanted him, not her, and they would not be happy about that. *Bad intelligence, guys,* Clark thought, looking at their faces and seeing their anger. *Even happens to me once in a while.* Yeah, he thought, like about half the fucking time in a good year. The two he could see were talking to each other . . . quietly, but the body language said it all. They were pissed. So, he had three (or more?) angry terrorists with guns on a two-engine airplane over the North Atlantic at night. Could have been worse, John told himself. Somehow. Yeah, they might have had Semtex jackets with Primacord trim.

They were late twenties, Clark thought. Old enough to be technically competent, but young enough to need adult supervision. Little operational experience, and not enough judgment. They'd think they knew it all, think they were real clever. That was the problem with death. Trained soldiers knew the reality of it better than terrorists did. These three would want to succeed, and wouldn't really consider the alternative. Maybe a rogue mission. The Basque separatists hadn't ever messed with foreign nationals, had they? Not Americans anyway, but this was an *American* airliner, and that was a big black line to step over. Rogue mission? Probably. Bad news.

You wanted a degree of predictability in situations like this. Even terrorism had rules. There was almost a liturgy to it, steps everyone had to take before something really bad happened, which gave the good guys a chance to talk to the bad guys. Get a negotiator down to establish rapport with them, negotiate the little stuff at first—*come on, let the children and their mothers off, okay? No big deal, and it looks bad for you and your group on TV, right?* Get them started giving things up. Then the old people—who wants to whack grandma and grandpa? Then the food, maybe with some Valium mixed in with it, while the response team's intel group started spiking the aircraft with microphones and miniature lenses whose fiber-optic cables fed to TV cameras.

Idiots, Clark thought. This play just didn't work. It was almost as bad as kidnapping a child for money. Cops were just too good at tracking those fools, and Little Willie was sure as hell boarding a USAF transport at Pope Air Force Base right now. If they really landed at Lajes, the process would start real soon, and the only variable was how many good guys would bite the big one before the bad guys got to do the same. Clark had worked with Colonel Byron's boys and girls. If they came into the aircraft, at least three people would not be leaving it alive. Problem was, how much company would they have in the hereafter? Hitting an airliner was like having a shoot-out in a grammar school, just more crowded.

They were talking more, up front, paying little attention to anything else, the rest of the aircraft. In one sense, that was logical. The front office was the most important part, but you always wanted to keep an eye on the rest. You never knew who might be aboard. Sky marshals were long in the past, but cops traveled by air, and some of them carried guns . . . well, maybe not on international flights, but you didn't get to retire from the terrorist business by being dumb. It was hard enough to survive if you were smart. Amateurs. Rogue mission. Bad intelligence. Anger and frustration. This was getting worse. One of them balled his left hand into a fist and shook it at the entire adverse world they'd found aboard.

Great, John thought. He turned in the seat, again catching Ding's eye and shaking his head side to side ever so slightly. His reply was a raised eyebrow. Domingo knew how to speak proper English when he had to.

It was as though the air changed then, and not for the better. Number 2 went forward again into the cockpit and stayed for several minutes, while John and Alistair watched the one on the left side, staring down the aisle. After two minutes of frustrated attention, he switched sides as though in a spasm, and looked aft, leaning his head forward as though to shorten the distance, peering down the aisle while his face bounced between expressions of power and impotence. Then, just as quickly, he headed back to port, pausing only to look at the cockpit door in anger.

There's only the three of them, John told himself then, just as #2 reappeared from the front office. Number 3 was too hyped. Probably just the three? he wondered. Think through it, Clark told himself. If so, that really made them amateurs. *The Gong Show* might be an amusing thought in another context, but not at 500 knots, 37,000 feet over the North Atlantic. If they could just be cool about everything, let the driver get the twin-engine beast on the ground, maybe some common sense would break out. But they wouldn't be very cool, would they?

Instead of taking his post to cover the right-side aisle, #2 went back to #3 and they spoke in raspy whispers which Clark understood in context if not content. It was when #2 pointed to the cockpit door that things became worst of all—

—*nobody's really in charge,* John decided. That was just great, three free-agents with guns in a friggin' airplane. It was time to start being afraid. Clark was not a stranger to fear. He'd been in too many tight places for that, but in every other case he'd had an element of control over the situation—or if not that, at least over his own actions, such as the ability to run away, which was a far more comforting thought now than he'd ever realized. He closed his eyes and took a deep breath.

Number 2 headed aft to look at the woman sitting next to Alistair. He just stood there for a few seconds, staring at her, then looking at Alistair, who looked back in a subdued way.

"Yes?" the Brit said finally, in his most cultured accent.

"Who are you?" Number 2 demanded.

"I told your friend, old man, Alistair Stanley. I have my passport in my carry-on bag if you wish to see it." The voice was just brittle enough to simulate a frightened man holding it together.

"Yes, show it to me!"

"Of course, sir." In elegantly slow movements, the former SAS major slipped out of his seat belt, stood, opened the overhead bin, and extracted his black carry-on bag. "May I?" he asked. Number 2 replied with a nod.

Alistair unzipped the side compartment and pulled the passport out, handed it over, then sat down, his trembling hands holding the bag in his lap.

Number 2 looked at the passport and tossed it back into the Brit's lap while John watched. Then he said something in Spanish to the woman in 4A. "Where is your husband?" it sounded like. The woman replied in the same cultured tones that she'd used just a few minutes earlier, and #2 stormed away to speak with #3 again. Alistair let out a long breath and looked around the cabin, as though for security, finally catching John's eye. There was no movement from his hands or face, but even so John knew what he was thinking. Al was not happy with this situation either, and more to the point, he'd seen both #2 and #3 close up, looked right in their eyes. John had to factor that into his thought processes. Alistair Stanley was worried, too. The slightly junior officer reached up as though to brush his hair back, and one finger tapped the skull above the ear twice. It might even be worse than he'd feared.

Clark reached his hand forward, enough to shield it from the two in the front of the cabin, and held up three fingers. Al nodded half an inch or so and turned away for a few seconds, allowing John to digest the message. He agreed that there were only three of them. John nodded with appreciation at the confirmation.

How much the better had they been smart terrorists, but the smart ones didn't try stuff like this anymore. The odds were just too long, as the Israelis had proven in Uganda, and the Germans in Somalia. You were safe doing this only so long as the aircraft was in the air, and they couldn't stay up forever, and when they landed the entire civilized world could come crashing in on them with the speed of a thunderbolt and the power of a Kansas tornado—and the real problem was that not all that many people truly wanted to die before turning thirty. And those who did used bombs. So, the smart ones did other things. For that reason they were more dangerous adversaries, but they were also predictable. They didn't kill people for recreation, and they didn't get frustrated early on because they planned their opening moves with skill.

These three were dumb. They had acted on bad intelligence, hadn't had an intel team in place to give them a final mission check, to tell them that their primary target hadn't made the flight, and so here they were, committed to a dumb mission that was already blown, contemplating death or life-long imprisonment . . . for nothing. The only good news, if you could call it that, was that their imprisonment would be in America.

But they didn't want to contemplate life in a steel cage any more than they wished to face death in the next few days—*but* soon they'd start to realize that there was no third alternative. And that the guns in their hands were the only power they had, and that they might as well start using them to get their way . . .

. . . and for John Clark, the choice was whether or not to wait for that to start. . . .

No. He couldn't just sit here and wait for them to start killing people.

Okay. He watched the two for another minute or so, the way they looked at each other while trying to cover both aisles, as he figured out how to do it. With both the dumb ones and the smart ones, the simple plans were usually the best.

It took five minutes more until #2 decided to talk some more with #3. When he did, John turned enough to catch Ding's eye, swiping one finger across his upper lip, as though to stroke a mustache he'd never grown. Chavez cocked his head as though to reply *you sure?* but took the sign. He loosened his seat belt and reached behind his back with his left hand, bringing his pistol out before the alarmed eyes of his six-week wife. Domingo touched her right hand with his to reassure her, covered the Beretta with a napkin in his lap, adopted a neutral expression, and waited for his senior to make the play.

"You!" Number 2 called from forward.

"Yes?" Clark replied, looking studiously forward.

"Sit still!" The man's English wasn't bad. Well, European schools had good language programs.

"Hey, look, I, uh, had a few drinks, and—well, you know, how about it? *Por favor,"* John added sheepishly.

"No, you will stay in your seat!"

"Hey, whatcha gonna do, shoot a guy who needs to take a leak? I don't know what your problem is, okay, but I gotta go, okay? Please?"

Number 2 and #3 traded an oh-shit look that just confirmed their amateur status one last time. The two stews, strapped in their seats forward, looked very worried indeed but didn't say anything. John pressed the issue by unbuckling his seat belt and starting to stand.

Number 2 raced aft then, gun in front, stopping just short of pressing it against John's chest. Sandy's eyes were wide now. She'd never seen her husband do anything the least bit dangerous, but she knew this wasn't the husband who had slept next to her for twenty-five years—and if not that one, then he had to be the other Clark, the one she knew about but had never seen.

"Look, I go there, I take a leak, and I come back, okay? Hell, you wanna watch," he said, his voice slurred now from the half glass of wine he'd drunk alongside the terminal. "That's okay, too, but please don't make me wet my pants, okay?"

What turned the trick was Clark's size. He was just under six-two, and his forearms, visible with the rolled-up sleeves, were powerful. Number 3 was smaller by four inches and thirty pounds, but he had a gun, and making bigger people do one's wishes is always a treat for bullies. So #2 gripped John by the left arm, spun him around and pushed him roughly aft toward the right-side lavatory. John cowered and went, his hands above his head.

"Hey, *gracias, amigo,* okay?" Clark opened the door. Dumb as ever, #2 actually allowed him to close it. For his part, John did what he'd asked permission to do, then washed his hands and took a brief look in the mirror.

Hey, Snake, you still got it? he asked himself, without so much as a breath.

Okay, let's find out.

John slid the locking bar loose, and pulled the folding door open with a grateful and thoroughly cowed look on his face.

"Hey, uh, thanks, y'know."

"Back to your seat."

"Wait, let me get you a cuppa coffee, okay, I—" John took a step aft, and #2 was dumb enough to follow in order to cover him, then reached for Clark's shoulder and turned him around.

"Buenas noces," Ding said quietly from less than ten feet away, his gun up and aimed at the side of #2's head. The man's eyes caught the blue steel that had to be a gun, and the distraction was just right. John's right hand came around, his forearm snapping up, and the back of his fist catching the terrorist in the right temple. The blow was enough to stun.

"How you loaded?"

"Low-velocity," Ding whispered back. "We're on an airplane, 'mano," he reminded his director.

"Stay loose," John commanded quietly, getting a nod.

"Miguel!" Number 3 called loudly.

Clark moved to the left side, pausing on the way to get a cup of coffee from the machine, complete with saucer and spoon. He then reappeared in the left-side aisle and moved forward.

"He said to bring you this. Thank you for allowing me to use the bathroom," John said, in a shaky but grateful voice. "Here is your coffee, sir."

"Miguel!" Number 3 called again.

"He went back that way. Here's your coffee. I'm supposed to sit down now, okay?" John took a few steps forward and stopped, hoping that this amateur would continue to act like one.

He did, coming toward him. John cowered a little, and allowed the cup and saucer to shake in his hand, and just as #3 reached him, looking over to the right side of the aircraft for his colleague, Clark dropped both of them on the floor and dove down to get them, about half a step behind Alistair's seat.

Number 3 automatically bent down as well. It would be his last mistake for the evening.

John's hands grabbed the pistol and twisted it around and up into its owner's belly. It might have gone off, but Alistair's own Browning Hi-Power crashed down on the back of the man's neck, just below the skull, and #3 went limp as Raggedy Andy.

"You impatient bugger," Stanley rasped. "Bloody good acting, though." Then he turned, pointed to the nearest stewardess, and snapped his fingers. She came out of her seat like a shot, fairly running aft to them. "Rope, cord, anything to tie them up, quickly!"

John collected the pistol and immediately removed the magazine, then jacked the action to eject the remaining round. In two more seconds, he'd field stripped the weapon and tossed the pieces at the feet of Alistair's traveling companion, whose brown eyes were wide and shocked.

"Sky marshals, ma'am. Please be at ease," Clark explained.

A few seconds after that, Ding appeared, dragging #2 with him. The stewardess returned with a spool of twine.

"Ding, front office!" John ordered.

"Roge-o, Mr. C." Chavez moved forward, his Beretta in both hands, and stood by the cockpit door. On the floor, Clark did the wrapping. His hands remembered the sailor knots from thirty years earlier. Amazing, he thought, tying them off as tight as he could. If their hands turned black, too damned bad.

"One more, John," Stanley breathed.

"You want to keep an eye on our two friends."

"A pleasure. Do be careful, lots of electronics up there."

"Tell me about it."

John walked forward, still unarmed. His junior was still at the door, pistol aimed upward in both hands, eyes on the door.

"How we doing, Domingo?"

"Oh, I was thinking about the green salad and the veal, and the wine list ain't half bad. Ain't a real good place to start a gunfight, John. Let's invite him aft."

It made good tactical sense. Number 1 would be facing aft, and if his gun went off, the bullet was unlikely to damage the aircraft, though the people in Row 1 might not like it all that much. John hopped aft to retrieve the cup and saucer.

"You!" Clark gestured to the other stewardess. "Call the cockpit and tell the pilot to tell our friend that Miguel needs him. Then stand right here. When the door opens, if he asks you anything, just point over to me. Okay?"

She was cute, forty, and pretty cool. She did exactly as she was told, lifting the phone and passing along the message.

A few seconds later, the door opened, and #1 looked out. The stewardess was the only person he could see at first. She pointed to John.

"Coffee?"

It only confused him, and he took a step aft toward the large man with the cup. His pistol was aimed down at the floor.

"Hello," Ding said from his left, placing his pistol right against his head.

Another moment's confusion. He just wasn't prepared. Number 1 hesitated, and his hand didn't start to move yet.

"Drop the gun!" Chavez said.

"It is best that you do what he says," John added, in his educated Spanish. "Or my friend will kill you."

His eyes darted automatically around the cabin, looking for his colleagues, but they were nowhere to be seen. The confusion on his face only increased. John took a step toward him, reached for the gun, and took it from an unresisting hand. This he placed in his waistband, then dropped the man to the floor to frisk him while Ding's gun rested at the back of the terrorist's neck. Aft, Stanley started doing the same with his two.

"Two magazines . . . nothing else." John waved to the first stew, who came up with the twine.

"Fools," Chavez snarled in Spanish. Then he looked at his boss. "John, you think that was maybe just a little precipitous?"

"No." Then he stood and walked into the cockpit. "Captain?"

"Who the hell are you?" The flight crew hadn't seen or heard a thing from aft.

"Where's the nearest military airfield?"

"RCAF Gander," the copilot—Renford, wasn't it?—replied immediately.

"Well, let's go there. Cap'n, the airplane is yours again. We have all three of them tied up."

"Who are you?" Will Garnet asked again rather forcefully, his own tension not yet bled off.

"Just a guy who wanted to help out," John replied, with a blank look, and the message got through. Garnet was ex-Air Force. "Can I use your radio, sir?"

The captain pointed to the fold-down jump-seat, and showed him how to use the radio.

"This is United Flight Niner-Two-Zero," Clark said. "Who am I talking to, over?"

"This is Special Agent Carney of the FBI. Who are you?"

"Carney, call the director, and tell him Rainbow Six is on the line. Situation is under control. Zero casualties. We're heading for Gander, and we need the Mounties. Over."

"Rainbow?"

"Just like it sounds, Agent Carney. I repeat, the situation is under control. The three hijackers are in custody. I'll stand by to talk to your director."

"Yes, sir," replied a very surprised voice.

Clark looked down to see his hands shaking a little now that it was over. Well, that had happened once or twice before. The aircraft banked to the left while the pilot was talking on the radio, presumably to Gander.

"Niner-Two-Zero, Niner-Two-Zero, this is Agent Carney again."

"Carney, this is Rainbow." Clark paused. "Captain, is this radio link secure?"

"It's encrypted, yes."

John almost swore at himself for violating radio discipline. "Okay, Carney, what's happening?"

"Stand by for the Director." There was a click and a brief crackle. "John?" a new voice asked.

"Yes, Dan."

"What gives?"

"Three of them, Spanish-speaking, not real smart. We took them down."

"Alive?"

"That's affirmative," Clark confirmed. "I told the pilot to head for RCAF Gander. We're due there in—"

"Niner-zero minutes," the copilot said.

"Hour and a half," John went on. "You want to have the Mounties show up to collect our bad boys, and call Andrews. We need transport on to London."

He didn't have to explain why. What ought to have been a simple commercial flight of three officers and two wives had blown their identities, and there was little damned sense in having them hang around for everyone aboard to see their faces—most would just want to buy them drinks, but that wasn't a good idea. All the effort they'd gone to, to make Rainbow both effective and secret, had been blown by three dumbass Spaniards—or whatever they were. The Royal Canadian Mounted Police would figure that one out before handing them over to the American FBI.

"Okay, John, let me get moving on that. I'll call René and have him get things organized. Anything else you need?"

"Yeah, send me a few hours of sleep, will ya?"

"Anything you want, pal," the FBI Director replied with a chuckle, and the line went dead. Clark took the headset off and hung it on the hook.

"Who the hell are you?" the captain demanded again. The initial explanation hadn't been totally satisfactory.

"Sir, my friends and I are air marshals who just happened to be aboard. Is that clear, sir?"

"I suppose," Garnet said. "Glad you made it. The one who was up here was a little loose, if you know what I mean. We were damned worried there for a while."

Clark nodded with a knowing smile. "Yeah, so was I."

THEY'D been doing it for some time. The powder-blue vans—there were four of them—circulated throughout New York City, picking up homeless people and shuttling them to the dry-out centers run by the corporation. The quiet, kindly operation had made local television over a year ago, and garnered the corporation a few dozen friendly letters, then slid back down below the horizon, as such things tended to do. It was approaching midnight, and with dropping autumn temperatures, the vans were out, collecting the homeless throughout central and lower Manhattan. They didn't do it the way the police once had. The people they helped weren't compelled to get aboard. The volunteers from the corporation asked, politely, if they wanted a clean bed for the night, free of charge, and absent the religious complications typical of most "missions," as they were traditionally called. Those who declined the offer were given blankets, used ones donated by corporate employees who were home sleeping or watching TV at the moment—participation in the program was voluntary for the staff as well—but still warm, and waterproofed. Some of the homeless preferred to stay out, deeming it to be some sort of freedom. More did not. Even habitual drunkards liked beds and showers. Presently there were ten of them in the van, and that was all it could hold for this trip. They were helped aboard, sat down, and seat-belted into their places for safety purposes.

None of them knew that this was the *fifth* of the four vans operating in lower Manhattan, though they found out something was a little different as soon as it started moving. The attendant leaned back from the front seat and handed out bottles of Gallo burgundy, an inexpensive California red, but a better wine than they were used to drinking, and to which something had been added.

By the time they reached their destination, all were asleep or at least stuporous. Those who were able to move were helped from one truck into the back of another, strapped down in their litter beds, and allowed to fall asleep. The rest were carried and strapped down by two pairs of men. With that task done, the first van was driven off to be cleaned out—they used steam to make sure that whatever residue might be left was sterilized and blasted out of the van. The second truck headed uptown on the West Side Highway, caught the curling ramp for the George Washington Bridge, and crossed the Hudson River. From there it headed north through the northeast corner of New Jersey, then back into New York State.

IT turned out that Colonel William Lytle Byron was already in the air in a USAF KC-10 on a course track almost identical to, and only an hour behind, the United 777. It altered course northward for Gander as well. The former P-3 base had to wake up a few personnel to handle the inbound jumbos, but that was the least of it.

The three failed hijackers were blindfolded, hog-tied, and laid on the floor just forward of the front row of first-class seats, which John, Ding, and Alistair appropriated. Coffee was served, and the other passengers kept away from that part of the aircraft.

"I rather admire the Ethiopians' approach to situations like this," Stanley observed. He was sipping tea.

"What's that?" Chavez asked tiredly.

"Some years ago they had a hijacking attempt on their national flag carrier. There happened to be security chaps aboard, and they got control of the situation. Then they strapped their charges in first-class seats, wrapped towels around their necks to protect the upholstery, and cut their throats, right there on the aircraft. And you know—"

"Gotcha," Ding observed. *Nobody* had messed with that airline since. "Simple, but effective."

"Quite." He set his cup down. "I hope this sort of thing doesn't happen *too* often."

The three officers looked out the windows to see the runway lights just before the 777 thumped down at RCAF Gander. There was a muted series of cheers and a smattering of applause from aft. The airliner slowed and then taxied off to the military facilities, where it stopped. The front-right door was opened, and a scissors-lift truck moved to it, slowly and carefully.

John, Ding, and Alistair unsnapped their seat belts and moved toward the door, keeping an eye on the three hijackers as they did so. The first aboard the aircraft was a RCAF officer with a pistol belt and white lanyard, followed by three men in civilian clothes who had to be cops.

"You're Mr. Clark?" the officer asked.

"That's right." John pointed. "There's your three—suspects, I think the term is." He smiled tiredly at that. The cops moved to deal with them.

"Alternate transport is on the way, about an hour out," the Canadian officer told him.

"Thank you." The three moved to collect their carry-on baggage, and in two cases, their wives. Patsy was asleep and had to be awakened. Sandy had gotten back into her book. Two minutes later, all five of them were on the ground, shuffling into one of the RCAF cars. As soon as they pulled away, the aircraft started moving again, taxiing to the civilian terminal so that the passengers could get off and stretch while the 777 was serviced and refueled.

"How do we get to England?" Ding asked, after getting his wife bedded down in the unused ready room.

"Your Air Force is sending a VC-20. There will be people at Heathrow to collect your bags. There's a Colonel Byron coming for your three prisoners," the senior cop explained.

"Here are their weapons." Stanley handed over three airsick bags with the disassembled pistols inside. "Browning M-1935s, military finish. No explosives. They really were bloody amateurs, Basques, I think. They seem to have been after the Spanish ambassador to Washington. His wife was in the seat next to mine. Señora Constanza de Monterosa—the wine family. They bottle the most marvelous clarets and Madeiras. I think you will find that this was an unauthorized operation."

"And who exactly are you?" the cop asked. Clark handled it.

"We can't answer that. You're sending the hijackers right back?"

"Ottawa has instructed us to do that under the Hijacking Treaty. Look, I have to say something to the press."

"Tell them that three American law enforcement officers happened to be aboard and helped to subdue the idiots," John told him.

"Yeah, that's close enough," Chavez agreed with a grin. "First arrest I ever made, John. Damn, I forgot to give them their rights," he added. He was weary enough to think that enormously funny.

THEY were beyond filthy, the receiving team saw. That was no particular surprise. Neither was the fact that they smelled bad enough to gag a skunk. That would have to wait. The litters were carried off the truck into the building, ten miles west of Binghamton, New York, in the hill country of central New York State. In the clean room, all ten were sprayed in the face from a squeeze bottle much like that used to clean windows. It was done one at a time to all of them, then half were given injections into the arm. Both groups of five got steel bracelets, numbered 1 to 10. Those with even numbers got the injections. The odd-numbered control group did not. With this task done, the ten homeless were carried off to the bunk room to sleep off the wine and the drugs. The truck which had delivered them was already gone, heading west for Illinois and a return to its regular duties. The driver hadn't even known what he'd done, except to drive.

CHAPTER 1

MEMO

THE VC-20B FLIGHT WAS SOMEWHAT LACKING IN amenities—the food consisted of sandwiches and an undistinguished wine—but the seats were comfortable and the ride smooth enough that everyone slept until the wheels and flaps came down at RAF Northholt, a military airfield just west of London. As the USAF G-IV taxied to the ramp, John remarked on the age of the buildings.

"Spitfire base from the Battle of Britain," Stanley explained, stretching in his seat. "We let private business jets use it as well."

"We'll be back and forth outta here a lot, then," Ding surmised at once, rubbing his eyes and wishing for coffee. "What time is it?"

"Just after eight, local—Zulu time, too, isn't it?"

"Quite," Alistair confirmed, with a sleepy grunt.

Just then the rain started, making for a proper welcome to British soil. It was a hundred-yard walk to the reception building, where a British official stamped their passports and officially welcomed them to his country before going back to his breakfast tea and newspaper.

Three cars waited outside, all of them black Daimler limousines, which headed off the base, then west, and south for Hereford. This was proof that he was a civilian bureaucrat, Clark told himself in the lead car. Otherwise they'd have used helicopters. But Britain wasn't entirely devoid of civilization. They stopped at a roadside McDonald's for Egg McMuffins and coffee. Sandy snorted at the cholesterol intake. She'd been chiding John about it for months. Then she thought about the previous night.

"John?"

"Yes, honey?"

"Who were they?"

"Who, the guys on the airplane?" He looked over and got a nod. "Not sure, probably Basque separatists. It looked like they were after the Spanish ambassador, but they screwed up big-time. He wasn't aboard, just his wife."

"They were trying to hijack the airplane?"

"Yep, they sure were."

"Isn't that scary?"

John nodded thoughtfully. "Yes, it is. Well, would have been scarier if they were competent, but they weren't." An inner smile. *Boy, did they ever pick the wrong flight!* But he couldn't laugh about it now, not with his wife sitting next to him, on the wrong side of the road—a fact that had him looking up in some irritation. It felt very wrong to be on the left side of the road, driving along at . . . eighty miles per hour? *Damn.* Didn't they have speed limits here?

"What'll happen to them?" Sandy persisted.

"There's an international treaty. The Canadians will ship them back to the States for trial—Federal Court. They'll be tried, convicted, and imprisoned for air piracy. They'll be behind bars for a long time." And they were lucky at that, Clark didn't add. Spain might well have been a little more unpleasant about it.

"First time in a long time something like that happened."

"Yep." Her husband agreed. You had to be a real dolt to hijack airplanes, but dolts, it appeared, were not yet an endangered species. That was why he was the Six of an organization called Rainbow.

THERE *is good news and there is bad news,* the memo he'd written had begun. As usual, it wasn't couched in bureaucratese; it was a language Clark had never quite learned despite his thirty years in CIA.

With the demise of the Soviet Union and other nation states with political positions adverse to American and Western interests, the likelihood of a major international confrontation is at an all-time low. This, clearly, is the best of good news.

But along with that we must face the fact that there remain many experienced and trained international terrorists still roaming the world, some with lingering contacts with national intelligence agencies—plus the fact that some nations, while not desirous of a direct confrontation with American or other Western nations, could still make use of the remaining terrorist "free agents" for more narrow political goals.

If anything, this problem is very likely to grow, since under the previous world situation, the major nation states placed firm limits on terrorist activity—these limits enforced by controlled access to weapons, funding, training, and safe-havens.

It seems likely that the current world situation will invert the previous "understanding" enjoyed by the major countries. The price *of support, weapons, training, and safe-havens might well become actual terrorist activity, not the ideological purity previously demanded by sponsoring nation states.*

The most obvious solution to this—probably—increasing problem will be a new multinational counterterrorist team. I propose the code name Rainbow. I further propose that the organization be based in the United Kingdom. The reasons for this are simple:

- *The U.K. currently owns and operates the Special Air Service, the world's foremost—that is, most experienced—special-operations agency.*
- *London is the world's most accessible city in terms of commercial air travel—in addition to which the SAS has a very cordial relationship with British Airways.*
- *The legal environment is particularly advantageous, due to press restrictions possible under British law but not American.*
- *The long-standing "special relationship" between American and British governmental agencies.*

For all of these reasons, the proposed special-operations team, composed of U.S., U.K., and selected NATO personnel, with full support from national-intelligence services, coordinated at site. . . .

And he'd sold it, Clark told himself with a wispy smile. It had helped that both Ed and Mary Pat Foley had backed him up in the Oval Office, along with General Mickey Moore and selected others. The new agency, Rainbow, was blacker than black, its American funding directed through the Department of the Interior by Capitol Hill, then through the Pentagon's Office of Special Projects, with no connection whatsoever to the intelligence community. Fewer than a hundred people in Washington knew that Rainbow existed. A far smaller number would have been better, but that was about the best that could be expected.

The chain of command was a little baroque. No avoiding that. The British influence would be hard to shake—fully half of the field personnel were Brits, and nearly that many of the intel weenies, but Clark was the boss. That constituted a major concession from his hosts, John knew. Alistair Stanley would be his executive officer, and John didn't have a problem with that. Stanley was tough, and better yet, one of the smartest special-operations guys he'd ever met—he knew when to hold, when to fold, and when to play the cards. About the only bad news was that he, Clark, was now a REMF—worse, a *suit.* He'd have an office and two secretaries instead of going out to run with the big dogs. Well, he had to admit to himself, that had to come sooner or later, didn't it?

Shit. He wouldn't run with the dogs, but he would play with them. He *had* to do that, didn't he, to show the troops that he was worthy of his command. He would be a *colonel,* not a general, Clark told himself. He'd be with the troops as much as possible, running, shooting, and talking things over.

Meanwhile, *I'm a captain,* Ding was telling himself in the next car behind, while eagerly taking in the countryside. He'd only been through Britain for layovers at Heathrow or Gatwick, and never seen the land, which was as green as an Irish postcard. He'd be under John, Mr. C, leading one of the strike teams, and in effective rank, that made him a captain, which was about the best rank to have in the Army, high enough that the NCOs respected you as worthy of command, and low enough that you weren't a staff puke and you played with the troops. He saw Patsy was dozing next to him. The pregnancy was taking it out of her, and doing so in unpredictable ways. Sometimes she bubbled with activity. Other times, she just vegetated. Well, she was carrying a new little Chavez in her belly, and that made everything okay—better than okay. A miracle. Almost as great as the miracle that here he was back doing what he'd originally been trained for—to be a soldier. Better yet, something of a free agent. The bad news was that he was subject to more than one government—suits that spoke multiple languages—but that couldn't be helped, and he'd volunteered for this to stay with Mr. C. Someone had to look after the boss.

The airplane had surprised him quite a bit. Mr. C hadn't had his weapon handy—what the hell, Ding thought, you bother to get a permit that allows you to carry a weapon on a civilian airliner (about the hardest thing you can wish to have) and then you stash your weapon where you can't get at it? *Santa Maria!* even John Clark was getting old. Must have been the first operational mistake he'd made in a long time, and then he'd tried to cover it by going cowboy on the takedown. Well, it had been nicely done. Smooth and cool. But overly fast, Ding thought, overly fast. He held Patsy's hand. She was sleeping a lot now. The little guy was sapping her strength. Ding leaned over to kiss her lightly on the cheek, softly enough that she didn't stir. He caught the driver's eye in the mirror and stared back with a poker expression. Was the guy just a driver or a team member? He'd find out soon enough, Chavez decided.

SECURITY was tougher than Ding had expected. For the moment Rainbow HQ was at Hereford, headquarters of the British Army's 22nd Special Air Service Regiment. In fact, security was even tougher than it looked, because a man holding a weapon just looked like a man holding a weapon—from a distance you couldn't tell the difference between a rent-a-cop and a trained expert. On eyeballing one close, Ding decided these guys were the latter. They just had different eyes. The man who looked into his car earned himself a thoughtful nod, which was dutifully returned as he waved the car forward. The base looked like any other—the signs were different as was some of the spelling, but the buildings had closely trimmed lawns, and things just looked neater than in civilian areas. His car ended up in officer country, by a modest but trim house, complete with a parking pad for a car Ding and Patsy didn't have yet. He noticed that John's car kept going another couple of blocks toward a larger house—well, colonels lived better than captains, and you couldn't beat the rent in any case. Ding opened the door, twisted out of the car, and headed for the trunk—excuse me, he thought, *boot*—to get their luggage moved in. Then came the first big surprise of this day.

"Major Chavez?" a voice asked.

"Uh, yeah?" Ding said, turning. *Major?* he wondered.

"I'm Corporal Weldon. I'm your batman." The corporal was much taller than Ding's five-feet-seven, and beefy-looking. The man bustled past his assigned officer and manhandled the bags out of the trunk/boot, leaving Chavez with nothing more to do or say than, "Thanks, Corporal."

"Follow me, sir." Ding and Patsy did that, too.

Three hundred meters away, it was much the same for John and Sandy, though their staff was a sergeant and a corporal, the latter female, blond, and pretty in the pale-skinned English way. Sandy's first impression of the kitchen was that British refrigerators were tiny, and that cooking in here would be something of an exercise in contortion. She was a little slow to catch on—a result of the air travel—that she'd touch an implement in this room only at the sufferance of Corporal Anne Fairway. The house wasn't quite as large as their home in Virginia, but would be quite sufficient.

"Where's the local hospital?"

"About six kilometers away, mum." Fairway hadn't been briefed in on the fact that Sandy Clark was a highly trained ER nurse and would be taking a position in the hospital.

John checked out his study. The most impressive piece of furniture was the liquor cabinet—well stocked, he saw, with Scotches and gins. He'd have to figure a way to get some decent bourbons. The computer was in place, tempested, he was sure, to make sure that people couldn't park a few hundred yards away and read what he was typing. Of course, getting that close would be a feat. The perimeter guards had struck John as competent. While his batman and -woman got his clothes squared away, John hopped into the shower. This would be a day of work for him. Twenty minutes later, wearing a blue pinstripe suit, a white shirt, and a striped tie, he appeared at the front door, where an official car waited to whisk him off to his headquarters building.

"Have fun, honey," Sandy said, with a kiss.

"You bet."

"Good morning, sir," his driver said. Clark shook his hand and learned that his name was Ivor Rogers, and that he was a sergeant. The bulge at his right hip probably made him an MP. Damn, John thought, the Brits take their security seriously. But, then, this was the home of the SAS, probably not the most favorite unit of terrorists both inside and outside the UK. And the real professionals, the truly dangerous ones, were careful, thorough people. *Just like me,* John Clark told himself.

"WE have to be careful. Extremely careful every step of the way." That was no particular surprise to the others, was it? The good news was that they understood about caution. Most were scientists, and many of them routinely trafficked in dangerous substances, Level-3 and up, and so caution was part of their way of looking at the world. And that, he decided, was good. It was also good that they understood, really understood the importance of the task at hand. A holy quest, they all thought—knew—it to be. After all, they were dealing in human life, the taking thereof, and there were those who didn't understand their quest and never would. Well, that was to be expected, since it was their lives which would be forfeited. It was too bad, but it couldn't be helped.

With that, the meeting broke up, later than usual, and people left, to walk out to the parking lot, where some—fools, he thought—would ride bicycles home, catch a few hours of sleep, and then bike back to the office. At least they were True Believers, if not overly practical ones—and, hell, they rode *airplanes* on long trips, didn't they? Well, the movement had room for people of differing views. The whole point was to create a big-tent movement. He walked out to his own vehicle, a very practical Hummer, the civilian version of the military's beloved HMMWV. He flipped on the radio, heard Respighi's *The Pines of Rome,* and realized that he'd miss NPR and its devotion to classical music. Well, some things couldn't be helped.

SHOWERED, shaved, and dressed in a Brooks Brothers suit and an Armani tie purchased two days beforc, Clark walked out of his official residence, toward his official car, the driver standing there to hold the door open. The Brits were really into status symbols, and John wondered how quickly he might become addicted to them.

It turned out that his office was less than two miles from his house, in a two-story brick building surrounded by workers. Another soldier was at the front door, a pistol tucked away in a white canvas holster. He snapped to and saluted when Clark got within ten feet.

"Good morning—*Sahr!*"

John was sufficiently startled that he returned the salute, as though crossing onto the quarter-deck of a ship. "Morning, soldier," John replied, almost sheepishly, and thinking he'd have to learn the kid's name. The door he managed to open for himself, to find Stanley inside, reading a document and looking up with a smile.

"The building won't be finished for another week or so, John. It was unused for some years, rather old, I'm afraid, and they've only been working on it for six weeks. Come, I'll take you to your office."

And again Clark followed, somewhat sheepishly, turning right and heading down the corridor to the end office—which was, it turned out, all finished.

"The building dates back to 1947," Alistair said, opening the door. There John saw two secretaries, both in their late thirties, and probably cleared higher than he was. Their names were Alice Foorgate and Helen Montgomery. They stood when the Boss came in, and introduced themselves with warm and charming smiles. Stanley's XO office was adjacent to Clark's, which contained a huge desk, a comfortable chair, and the same kind of computer as in John's CIA office—tempested here, too, so that people couldn't monitor it electronically. There was even a liquor cabinet in the far right corner, doubtless a British custom.

John took a breath before trying out the swivel chair and decided to doff his jacket first. Sitting in a chair with a suit coat on was something he'd never really learned to enjoy. That was something a "suit" did, and being a "suit" wasn't John's idea of fun. He waved Alistair to the seat opposite the desk.

"Where are we?"

"Two teams fully formed. Chavez will have one. The other will be commanded by Peter Covington—just got his majority. Father was colonel of the 22nd some years ago, retired as a Brigadier. Marvelous lad. Ten men per team, as agreed. The technical staff is coming together nicely. We have an Israeli chap on that, David Peled—surprised they let us have him. He's a bloody genius with electronics and surveillance systems—"

"And he'll report back to Avi ben Jakob every day."

A smile. "Naturally." Neither office was under any illusions about the ultimate loyalty of the troops assigned to Rainbow. But, were they not capable of such loyalty, what good would they be? "David's worked with SAS on and off for a decade. He's quite amazing, contacts with every electronics corporation from San Jose to Taiwan."

"And the shooters?"

"Top drawer, John. As good as any I've ever worked with." Which was saying something.

"Intel?"

"All excellent. The chief of that section is Bill Tawney, a 'Six' man for thirty years, supported by Dr. Paul Bellow—Temple University, Philadelphia, was a professor there until your FBI seconded him. Bloody smart chap. Mind-reader, he's been all over the world. Your chaps lent him to the Italians for the Moro job, but he refused to take an assignment to Argentina the next year. Principled, also, or so it would seem. He flies in tomorrow."

Just then Mrs. Foorgate came in with a tray, tea for Stanley, coffee for Clark. "Staff meeting starts in ten minutes, sir," she told John.

"Thanks, Alice." *Sir,* he thought. Clark wasn't used to being addressed like that. Yet another sign he was a "suit." Damn. He waited until the heavy soundproofed door closed to ask his next question. "Al, what's my status here?"

"General officer—brigadier at least, maybe a two-star. I seem to be a colonel—chief of staff, you see," Stanley said, sipping his tea. "John, you know that there must be protocol," he went on reasonably.

"Al, you know what I really am—was, I mean?"

"You were a navy chief boatswain's mate, I believe, with the Navy Cross, Silver Star with a repeat cluster. Bronze star with Combat-V and three repeats, and three Purple Hearts. And all that's before the Agency took you in and gave you no less than four Intelligence Stars." Stanley said all this from memory. "Brigadier's the least we can do, old man. Rescuing Koga and taking Daryei out were bloody brilliant jobs, in case I never told you. We do know a little bit about you, and your young Chavez—the lad has enormous potential, if he's as good as I've heard. Of course, he'll need it. His team is composed of some real stars."

"YO, Ding!" a familiar voice called. Chavez looked to his left in genuine surprise.

"*Oso!* You son of a bitch! What the hell are you doing here?" Both men embraced.

"The Rangers were getting boring, so I shipped up to Bragg for a tour with Delta, and then this came up on the scope and I went after it. You're the boss for Team Two?" First Sergeant (E-8) Julio Vega asked.

"Sorta-kinda," Ding replied, shaking the hand of an old friend and comrade. "Ain't lost no weight, man, Jesu Christo, Oso, you *eat* barbells?"

"Gotta keep fit, sir," replied a man for whom a hundred morning push-ups didn't generate a drop of sweat. His uniform blouse showed a Combat Infantryman's Badge and the silver "ice-cream cone" of a master parachutist. "You're looking good, man, keeping up your running, eh?"

"Yeah, well, running away is an ability I want to keep, if you know what I mean."

"Roge-o." Vega laughed. "Come on, I'll intro you to the team. We got some good troops, Ding."

Team Two, Rainbow, had its own building—brick, single-story, and fairly large, with a desk for every man, and a secretary named Katherine Moony they'd all share, young and pretty enough, Ding noticed, to attract the interest of any unattached member of his team. Team Two was composed exclusively of NCOs, mainly senior ones, four Americans, four Brits, a German, and a Frenchman. He only needed one look to see that all were fit as hell—enough so that Ding instantly worried about his own condition. He had to lead them, and that meant being as good as or better than all of them in every single thing the team would have to do.

Sergeant Louis Loiselle was the nearest. Short and dark-haired, he was a former member of French parachute forces and had been detailed to DGSE some years before. Loiselle was vanilla, a utility infielder, good in everything but a nonspecialist specialist—like all of the men, a weapons expert, and, his file said, a brilliant marksman with pistol and rifle. He had an easy, relaxed smile with a good deal of confidence behind it.

Feldwebel Dieter Weber was next, also a paratrooper and a graduate of the German army's *Burger Führer* or Mountain Leader school, one of the physically toughest schools in any army in the world. He looked it. Blond-haired and fair-skinned, he might have been on an SS recruiting poster sixty years earlier. His English, Ding learned at once, was better than his own. He could have passed for American—or English. Weber had come to Rainbow from the German GSG-9 team, which was part of the former Border Guards, the Federal Republic's counterterror team.

"Major, we have heard much about you," Weber said from his six-three height. A little tall, Ding thought. Too large a target. He shook hands like a German. One quick grab, vertical jerk, and let go, with a nice squeeze in the middle. His blue eyes were interesting, cold as ice, interrogating Ding from the first. The eyes were usually found behind a rifle. Weber was one of the team's two long-riflemen.

SFC Homer Johnston was the other. A mountaineer from Idaho, he'd taken his first deer at the age of nine. He and Weber were friendly competitors. Average-looking in all respects, Johnston was clearly a runner rather than an iron-pumper at his six-feet-nothing, one-sixty. He'd started off in the 101st Air-Mobile at Fort Campbell, Kentucky, and rapidly worked his way into the Army's black world. "Major, nice to meet you, sir." He was a former Green Beret and Delta member, like Chavez's friend, Oso Vega.

The shooters, as Ding thought of them, the guys who went into the buildings to do business, were Americans and Brits. Steve Lincoln, Paddy Connolly, Scotty McTyler, and Eddie Price were from the SAS. They'd all been there and done that in Northern Ireland and a few other places. Mike Pierce, Hank Patterson, and George Tomlinson mainly had not, because the American Delta Force didn't have the experience of the SAS. It was also true, Ding reminded himself, that Delta, SAS, GSG-9, and other crack international teams cross-trained to the point that they might as well have married one another's sisters. Every one of them was taller than "Major" Chavez. Every one was tough. Every one was smart, and with this realization came an oddly deflating feeling that, despite his own field experience, he'd have to earn the respect of his team and earn it fast.

"Who's senior?"

"That's me, sir," Eddie Price said. He was the oldest of the team, forty-one, and a former color sergeant in the 22nd Special Air Service Regiment, since spot-promoted to sergeant major. Like the rest in the bullpen, he was wearing nonuniform clothes, though they were all wearing the *same* nonuniform things, without badges of rank.

"Okay, Price, have we done our PT today?"

"No, Major, we waited for you to lead us out," Sergeant Major Price replied, with a smile that was ten percent manners and ninety percent challenge.

Chavez smiled back. "Yeah, well, I'm a little stiff from the flight, but maybe we can loosen that up for me. Where do I change?" Ding asked, hoping his last two weeks of five-mile daily runs would prove to be enough—and he *was* slightly wasted by the flight.

"Follow me, sir."

"MY name's Clark, and I suppose I'm the boss here," John said from the head of the conference table. "You all know the mission, and you've all asked to be part of Rainbow. Questions?"

That startled them, John saw. Good. Some continued to stare at him. Most looked down at the scratch pads in front of them.

"Okay, to answer some of the obvious ones, our operational doctrine ought to be little different from the organizations you came from. We will establish that in training, which commences tomorrow. We are supposed to be operational right now," John warned them. "That means the phone could ring in a minute, and we will have to respond. Are we able to?"

"No," Alistair Stanley responded for the rest of the senior staff. "That's unrealistic, John. We need, I would estimate, three weeks."

"I understand that—but the real world is not as accommodating as we would like it to be. Things that need doing—do them, and quickly. I will start running simulations on Monday next. People, I am not a hard man to work with. I've been in the field, and I know what happens out there. I don't expect perfection, but I *do* expect that we will always work for it. If we screw a mission up, that means that people who deserve to live will not live. That is going to happen. You know it. I know it. *But* we will avoid mistakes as much as possible, and we will learn the proper lessons from every one we make. Counterterrorism is a Darwinian world. The dumb ones are already dead, and the people out there we have to worry about are those who've learned a lot of lessons. So have we, and we're probably ahead of the game, tactically speaking, but we have to run hard to stay there. We will run hard.

"Anyway," he went on, "intelligence, what's ready and what's not?"

Bill Tawney was John's age, plus one or two, John estimated, with brown, thinning hair and an unlit pipe in his mouth. A "Six" man—meaning he was a former (well, current) member of Britain's Secret Intelligence Service, he was a field spook who'd come inside after ten years working the streets behind the Curtain. "Our communications links are up and running. We have liaison personnel to all friendly services either here or in the corresponding capitals."

"How good are they?"

"Fair," Tawney allowed. John wondered how much of that was Brit understatement. One of his most important but most subtle tasks would be to decode what every member of his staff said when he or she spoke, a task made all the more difficult by linguistic and cultural differences. On inspection, Tawney looked like a real pro, his brown eyes calm and businesslike. His file said that he'd worked directly with SAS for the past five years. Given SAS's record in the field, he hadn't stiffed them with bad intel very often, if at all. Good.

"David?" he asked next. David Peled, the Israeli chief of his technical branch, looked very Catholic, rather like something from an El Greco painting, a Dominican priest, perhaps, from the fifteenth century, tall, skinny, hollow of cheek and dark of hair (short), with a certain intensity of eye. Well, he'd worked a long time for Avi ben Jakob, whom Clark knew, if not well then well enough. Peled would be here for two reasons, to serve as a senior Rainbow staffer, thus winning allies and prestige for his parent intelligence service, the Israeli Mossad, and also to learn what he could and feed it back to his boss.

"I am putting together a good staff," David said, setting his tea down. "I need three to five weeks to assemble all the equipment I need."

"Faster," Clark responded at once.

David shook his head. "Not possible. Much of our electronics items can be purchased off the shelf, as it were, but some will have to be custom-made. The orders are all placed," he assured his boss, "with high-priority flags—from the usual vendors. TRW, IDI, Marconi, you know who they are. But they can't do miracles, even for us. Three to five weeks for some crucial items."

"SAS are willing to hire anything important to us," Stanley assured Clark from his end of the table.

"For training purposes?" Clark asked, annoyed that he hadn't found out the answer to the question already.

"Perhaps."

DING cut the run off at three miles, which they'd done in twenty minutes. Good time, he thought, somewhat winded, until he turned to see his ten men about as fresh as they'd been at the beginning, one or two with a sly smile for his neighbors at their wimpy new leader.

Damn.

The run had ended at the weapons range, where targets and arms were ready. Here Chavez had made his own change in his team's selection. A longtime Beretta aficionado, he'd decided that his men would use the recent .45 Beretta as their personal sidearms, along with the Hechler & Koch MP-10 submachine gun, the new version of the venerable MP-5, chambered instead for the 10-mm Smith & Wesson cartridge developed in the 1980s for the American FBI. Without saying anything, Ding picked up his weapon, donned his ear-protectors, and started going for the silhouette targets, set five meters away. *There,* he saw, all eight holes in the head. But Dieter Weber, next to him, had grouped his shots in one ragged hole, and Paddy Connolly had made what appeared to be one not-so-ragged hole less than an inch across, all between the target's eyes, without touching the eyes themselves. Like most American shooters, Chavez had believed that Europeans didn't know pistols worth a damn. Evidently, training corrected that, he saw.

Next, people picked up their H&Ks, which just about anyone could shoot well because of the superb diopter sights. Ding walked along the firing line, watching his people engage pop-up steel plates the size and shape of human heads. Driven up by compressed air, they fell back down instantly with a metallic *clang*. Ding ended up behind First Sergeant Vega, who finished his magazine and turned.

"Told you they were good, Ding."

"How long they been here?"

"Oh, 'bout a week. Used to running five miles, sir," Julio added with a smile. "Remember the summer camp we went to in Colorado?"

Most important of all, Ding thought, was the steady aim despite the run, which was supposed to get people pumped up, and simulate the stress of a real combat situation. But these bastards were as steady as fucking bronze statues. Formerly a squad leader in the Seventh Light Infantry Division, he'd once been one of the toughest, fittest, and most effective soldiers in his country's uniform, which was why John Clark had tapped him for a job in the Agency—and in *that* capacity he'd pulled off some tense and tough missions in the field. It had been a very long time indeed since Domingo Chavez had felt the least bit inadequate about anything. But now quiet voices were speaking into his ear.

"Who's the toughest?" he asked Vega.

"Weber. I heard stories about the German mountain school. Well, they be true, 'mano. Dieter isn't entirely human. Good in hand-to-hand, good pistol, damned good with a rifle, and I think he could run a deer down if he had to, then rip it apart barehanded." Chavez had to remind himself that being called "good" in a combat skill by a graduate of Ranger school *and* Fort Bragg's special-operations schools wasn't quite the same as from a guy in a corner bar. Julio was about as tough as they came.

"The smartest?"

"Connolly. All those SAS guys are tops. Us Americans have to play a little catchup ball. But we will," Vega assured him. "Don't sweat it, Ding. You'll keep up with us, after a week or so. Just like it was in Colorado."

Chavez didn't really want to be reminded of that job. Too many friends lost in the mountains of Colombia, doing a job that their country had never acknowledged. Watching his men finish off their training rounds told him much about them. If anyone had missed a single shot, he failed to notice it. Every man fired off exactly a hundred rounds, the standard daily regimen for men who fired five hundred per working week on routine training, as opposed to more carefully directed drill. That would start tomorrow.

"OKAY," John concluded, "we'll have a staff meeting every morning at eight-fifteen for routine matters, and a more formal one every Friday afternoon. My door is always open—including the one at home. People, if you need me, there's a phone next to my shower. Now, I want to get out and see the shooters. Anything else? Good. We stand adjourned." Everyone stood and shuffled out the door. Stanley remained.

"That went well," Alistair observed, pouring himself another cup of tea. "Especially for one not accustomed to bureaucratic life."

"Shows, eh?" Clark asked with a grin.

"One can learn anything, John."

"I hope so."

"When's morning PT around here?"

"Oh-six-forty-five. You plan to run and sweat with the lads?"

"I plan to try," Clark answered.

"You're too old, John. Some of those chaps run marathons for recreation, and you're closer to sixty than to fifty."

"Al, I can't command those people without trying, and you know that."

"Quite," Stanley admitted.

THEY awoke late, one at a time, over a period of about an hour. For the most part they just lay there in bed, some of them shuffling off to the bathroom, where they also found aspirin and Tylenol for the headaches they all had, along with showers, which half of them decided to take and the other half to forgo. In the adjoining room was a breakfast buffet that surprised them, with pans full of scrambled eggs, pancakes, sausage and bacon. Some of them even remembered how to use napkins, the people in the monitoring room saw.

They met their captor after they'd had a chance to eat breakfast. He offered all of them clean clothes, after they got cleaned up.

"What is this place?" asked the one known to the staff only as #4. It sure as hell wasn't any Bowery mission he was familiar with.

"My company is undertaking a study," the host said from behind a tightly fitting mask. "You gentlemen will be part of that study. You will be staying with us for a while. During that time, you will have clean beds, clean clothes, good food, good medical care, *and*"—he pulled a wall panel back—"whatever you want to drink." In a wall alcove which the guests remarkably had not yet discovered were three shelves of every manner of wine, beer, and spirit that could be purchased at the local liquor store, with glasses, water, mixes, and ice.

"You mean we can't leave?" Number 7 asked.

"We would prefer that you stay," the host said, somewhat evasively. He pointed to the liquor cabinet, his eyes smiling around the mask. "Anyone care for a morning eye-opener?"

It turned out that it wasn't too early in the morning for any of them, and that the expensive bourbons and ryes were the first and hardest hit. The additional drug in the alcohol was quite tasteless, and the guests all headed back to their alcove beds. Next to each was a TV set. Two more decided to make use of the showers. Three even shaved, emerging from the bathroom looking quite human. For the time being.

IN the monitoring room half a building away, Dr. Archer manipulated the various TV cameras to get close-ups on every "guest."

"They're all pretty much on profile," she observed. "Their blood work ought to be a disaster."

"Oh, yeah, Barb," Dr. Killgore agreed. "Number Three looks especially unwell. You suppose we can get him slightly cleaned up before . . . ?"

"I think we should try," Barbara Archer, M.D., thought. "We can't monkey with the test criteria too much, can we?"

"Yeah, and it'd be bad for morale if we let one die too soon," Killgore went on.

" 'What a piece of work is man,' " Archer quoted, with a snort.

"Not all of us, Barb." A chuckle. "Surprised they didn't find a woman or two for the group."

"I'm not," replied the feminist Dr. Archer, to the amusement of the more cynical Killgore. But it wasn't worth getting all worked up over. He looked away from the battery of TV screens, and picked up the memo from corporate headquarters. Their guests were to be treated as guests—fed, cleaned up, and offered all the drink they could put away consistent with the continuance of their bodily functions. It was slightly worrisome to the epidemiologist that all their guest-test-subjects were seriously impaired street alcoholics. The advantage of using them, of course, was that they wouldn't be missed, even by what might have passed for friends. Few had any family members who would even know where to look for them. Fewer still would have any who would be surprised by the inability to locate them. And none, Killgore judged, had so much as one who would notify proper authorities on the inability to find them—and even if *that* happened, would the New York City Police care? Not likely.

No, all their "guests" were people written off by their society, less aggressively but just as finally as Hitler had written off his Jews, though with somewhat more justice, Archer and Killgore both thought. What a piece of work was man? These examples of the self-designated godlike species were of less use than the laboratory animals they were now replacing. And they were also far less appealing to Archer, who had feelings for rabbits and even rats. Killgore found that amusing. He didn't much care about them either, at least not as individual animals. It was the species as a whole that mattered, wasn't it? And as far as the "guests" were concerned, well, they weren't even good examples of the substandard humans whom the species didn't need. Killgore was. So was Archer, her goofy political-sexual views notwithstanding. With that decided, Killgore returned to making a few notes and doing his paperwork. Tomorrow they'd do the physical examinations. That would be fun, he was sure.

CHAPTER 2

SADDLING UP

THE FIRST TWO WEEKS STARTED OFF PLEASANTLY enough. Chavez was now running five miles without any discomfort, doing the requisite number of push-ups with his team, and shooting better, as well as about half of them, but not as well as Connolly and the American Hank Patterson, both of whom must have been born with pistols in their cribs or something, Ding decided after firing three hundred rounds per day to try to equal them. Maybe a gunsmith could play with his weapon. The SAS based here had a regimental armorer who might have trained with Sam Colt himself, or so he'd heard. A little lighter and smoother on the trigger, perhaps. But that was mere pride talking. Pistols were secondary weapons. With their H&K MP-10s, every man could put three quick aimed rounds in a head at fifty meters about as fast as his mind could form the thought. These people were awesome, the best soldiers he'd ever met—or heard about, Ding admitted to himself, sitting at his desk and doing some hated paperwork. He grunted. Was there anyone in the world who didn't hate paperwork?

The team spent a surprising amount of time sitting at their desks and reading, mainly intelligence stuff—which terrorist was thought to be where, according to some intelligence agency or police department or money-grubbing informer. In fact the data they pored over was nearly useless, but since it was the best they had, they pored over it anyway as a way of breaking the routine. Included were photos of the world's surviving terrorists. Carlos the Jackal, now in his fifties, and now settled into a French maximum-security prison, was the one they'd all wanted. The photos of him were computer-manipulated to simulate his current-age appearance, which they then compared with real-life photos from the French. The team members spent time memorizing all of them, because some dark night in some unknown place, a flash of light might reveal one of these faces, and you'd have *that long* to decide whether or not to double-tap the head in question—and if you had the chance to bag another Carlos Il'ych Ramirez Sanchez, you wanted to take it, 'cuz then, Ding's mind went on, you'd never be able to buy a beer in a cop or special-ops bar again anywhere in the world, you'd be so famous. The real hell of it was, this pile of trash on his desk wasn't really trash after all. If they ever bagged the next Carlos, it would be because some local cop, in São Paolo, Brazil, or Bumfuck, Bosnia, or wherever, heard something from some informant or other, then went to the proper house and took a look, and then had his brain go *click* from all the flyers that filled cophouses around the world, and then it would be up to the street savvy of that cop to see if he might arrest the bastard on the spot—or, if the situation looked a little too tense, to report back to his lieutenant, and just maybe a special team like Ding's Team-2 would deploy quietly, and take the fucker down, the easy way or the hard way, in front of whatever spouse or kids there might be, ignorant of daddy's former career . . . and then it would make CNN with quite a splash. . . .

That was the problem with working at a desk. You started daydreaming. Chavez, simulated Major, checked his watch and rose, headed out into the bullpen, and handed off his pile of trash to Miss Moony. He was about to ask if everyone was ready, but they must have been, because the only other person to ask was halfway to the door. On the way, he drew his pistol and belt. The next stop was what the Brits called a robing room, except there were no robes, but instead coal-black fatigue clothes, complete with body armor.

Team-2 was all there, mostly dressed a few minutes early for the day's exercise. They were all loose, relaxed, smiling, and joking quietly. When all had their gear on, they went to the arms room to draw their SMGs. Each put the double-looped sling over his head, then checked to see that the magazine was full, sliding each into the proper port on the bottom of the weapon, and working the bolt back to the safe position, then snugging the weapon to make sure that each fitted to the differing specifications of each individual shooter.

The exercises had been endless, or as much so as two weeks could make them. There were six basic scenarios, all of which could be played out in various environments. The one they hated most was inside the body of a commercial aircraft. The only good thing about that was the confinement forced on the bad guys—they wouldn't be going anywhere. The rest was entirely bad. Lots of civilians in the fire arcs, good concealment for the bad guys—and if one of them really did have a bomb strapped to his body—they almost always claimed to—well, then all he had to have was the balls to pull the string or close the switch, and then, if the bastard was halfway competent, everyone aboard was toast. Fortunately, few people chose death in that way. But Ding and his people couldn't think like that. Much of the time terrorists seemed to fear capture more than death—so your shooting had to be fast *and* perfect, and the team had to hit the aircraft like a Kansas tornado at midnight, with your flash-bangs especially important to stun the bastards into combat-ineffectiveness so that the double-taps were aimed at nonmoving heads, and hope to God that the civilians you were trying to rescue didn't stand up and block the shooting range that the fuselage of the Boeing or Airbus had suddenly become.

"Team-2, we ready?" Chavez asked.

"Yes, sir!" came the chorused reply.

With that, Ding led them outside and ran them half a mile to the shooting house, a hard run, not the fast jog of daily exercises. Johnston and Weber were already on the scene, on opposite corners of the rectangular structure.

"Command to Rifle Two-Two," Ding said into his helmet-mounted microphone, "anything to report?"

"Negative, Two-Six. Nothing at all," Weber reported.

"Rifle Two-One?"

"Six," Johnston replied, "I saw a curtain move, but nothing else. Instruments show four to six voices inside, speaking English. Nothing else to report."

"Roger," Ding responded, the remainder of his team concealed behind a truck. He took a final look at the layout of the inside of the building. The raid had been fully briefed. The shooters knew the inside of the structure well enough to see it with their eyes closed. With that knowledge, Ding waved for the team to move.

Paddy Connolly took the lead, racing to the door. Just as he got there, he let go of his H&K and let it dangle on the sling while he pulled the Primacord from the fanny-pack hanging down from his body armor. He stuck the explosive to the door frame by its adhesive and pushed the blasting cap into the top-right corner. A second later, he moved right ten feet, holding the detonator control up in his left hand, while his right grabbed the pistol grip of his SMG and brought it up to point at the sky.

Okay, Ding thought. Time to move. "Let's go!" he shouted at the team.

As the first of them bolted around the truck, Connolly thumbed the switch, and the door frame disintegrated, sending the door flying inward. The first shooter, Sergeant Mike Pierce, was less than a second behind it, disappearing into the smoking hole with Chavez right behind him.

The inside was dark, the only light coming through the shattered doorway. Pierce scanned the room, found it empty, and then lodged himself by the doorway into the next room. Ding ran into that first, leading his team—

—there they were, four targets and four hostages—

Chavez brought his MP-10 up and fired two silenced rounds into the left-most target's head. He saw the rounds hit, dead-center in the head, right between the blue-painted eyes, then traversed right to see that Steve Lincoln had gotten his man just as planned. In less than a second, the overhead lights came on. It was all over, elapsed time from the Primacord explosion, seven seconds. Eight seconds had been programmed for the exercise. Ding safed his weapon.

"Goddamnit, John!" he said to the Rainbow commander.

Clark stood, smiling at the target to his left, less than two feet away, the two holes drilled well enough to ensure certain, instant death. He wasn't wearing any protective gear. Neither was Stanley, at the far end of the line, also trying to show off, though Mrs. Foorgate and Mrs. Montgomery were, in their center seats. The presence of the women surprised Chavez until he reminded himself that they were team members, too, and probably eager to show that they, too, belonged with the boys. He had to admire their spirit, if not their good sense.

"Seven seconds. That'll do, I guess. Five would be better," John observed, but the dimensions of the building pretty much determined the speed with which the team could cover the distance. He walked across, checking all the targets. McTyler's target showed one hole only, though its irregular shape proved that he'd fired both rounds as per the exercise parameters. Any one of these men would have earned a secure place in 3rd SOG, and every one was as good as he'd ever been, John Clark thought to himself. Well, training methods had improved markedly since his time in Vietnam, hadn't they? He helped Helen Montgomery to her feet. She seemed just a little shaky. Hardly a surprise. Being on the receiving end of bullets wasn't exactly what secretaries were paid for.

"You okay?" John asked.

"Oh, quite, thank you. It *was* rather exciting. My first time, you see."

"My third," Alice Foorgate said, rising herself. "It's always exciting," she added with a smile.

For me, too, Clark thought. Confident as he'd been with Ding and his men, still, looking down the barrel of a light machine gun and seeing the flashes made one's blood turn slightly cool. And the lack of body armor wasn't all that smart, though he justified it by telling himself he'd had to see better in order to watch for any mistakes. He'd seen nothing major, however. They were damned good.

"Excellent," Stanley said from his end of the dais. He pointed "You—uh—"

"Patterson, sir," the sergeant said. "I know, I kinda tripped coming through." He turned to see that a fragment of the door frame had been blasted through the entrance to the shooting room, and he'd almost stumbled on it.

"You recovered nicely, Sergeant Patterson. I see it didn't affect your aim at all."

"No, sir," Hank Patterson agreed, not quite smiling.

The team leader walked up to Clark, safing his weapon on the way.

"Mark us down fully mission-capable, Mr. C," Chavez said with a confident smile. "Tell the bad guys they better watch their asses. How'd Team-1 do?"

"Two-tenths of a second faster," John replied, glad to see the diminutive leader of -2 deflate a little. "And thanks."

"What for?"

"For not wasting your father-in-law." John clapped him on the shoulder and walked out of the room.

"Okay, people," Ding said to his team, "let's police up the brass and head back for the critique." No fewer than six TV cameras had recorded the mission. Stanley would be going over it frame by frame. That would be followed by a few pints at the 22nd's Regimental NCO club. The Brits, Ding had learned over the previous two weeks, took their beer seriously, and Scotty McTyler could throw darts about as well as Homer Johnston could shoot a rifle. It was something of a breach of protocol that Ding, a simulated major, hoisted pints with his men, all sergeants. He had explained that away by noting that he'd been a humble staff sergeant squad leader himself before disappearing into the maw of the Central Intelligence Agency, and he regaled them with stories of his former life in the Ninjas—stories that the others listened to with a mixture of respect and amusement. As good as the 7th Infantry Division had been, it wasn't *this* good. Even Domingo would admit to that after a few pints of John Courage.

"OKAY, Al, what do you think?" John asked. The liquor cabinet in his office was open, a single-malt Scotch for Stanley, while Clark sipped at a Wild Turkey.

"The lads?" He shrugged. "Technically very competent. Marksmanship is just about right, physical fitness is fine. They respond well to obstacles and the unexpected, and, well, they didn't kill us with stray rounds, did they?"

"But?" Clark asked with a quizzical look.

"But one doesn't know until the real thing happens. Oh, yes, they're as good as SAS, but the best of them *are* former SAS. . . ."

Old-world pessimism, John Clark thought. That was the problem with Europeans. No optimism, too often they looked for things that would go wrong instead of right.

"Chavez?"

"Superb lad," Stanley admitted. "Almost as good as Peter Covington."

"Agreed," Clark admitted, the slight on his son-in-law notwithstanding. But Covington had been at Hereford for seven years. Another couple of months and Ding would be there. He was pretty close already. It was already down to how many hours of sleep one or the other had had the night before, and pretty soon it would be down to what one or the other had eaten for breakfast. All in all, John told himself, he had the right people, trained to the right edge. Now all he had to do was keep them there. Training. Training. Training.

Neither knew that it had already started.

"SO, Dmitriy," the man said.

"Yes?" Dmitriy Arkadeyevich Popov replied, twirling his vodka around in the glass.

"Where and how do we begin?" the man asked.

They'd met by a fortunate accident, both thought, albeit for very different reasons. It had happened in Paris, at some sidewalk café, tables right next to each other, where one had noted that the other was Russian, and wanted to ask a few simple questions about business in Russia. Popov, a former KGB official, RIF'ed and scouting around for opportunities for entering the world of capitalism, had quickly determined that this American had a great deal of money, and was therefore worthy of stroking. He had answered the questions openly and clearly, leading the American to deduce his former occupation rapidly—the language skills (Popov was highly fluent in English, French, and Czech) had been a giveaway, as had Popov's knowledge of Washington, D.C. Popov was clearly not a diplomat, being too open and forthright in his opinions, which factor had terminated his promotion in the former Soviet KGB at the rank of Colonel—he still thought himself worthy of general's stars. As usual, one thing had led to another, first the exchange of business cards, then a trip to America, first class on Air France, as a security consultant, and a series of meetings that had moved ever so subtly in a direction that came more as a surprise to the Russian than the American. Popov had impressed the

American with his knowledge of safety issues on the streets of foreign cities, then the discussion had moved into very different areas of expertise.

"How do you know all this?" the American had asked in his New York office.

The response had been a broad grin, after three double vodkas. "I know these people, of course. Come, you must know what I did before leaving the service of my country."

"You actually worked with terrorists?" he'd asked, surprised, and thinking about this bit of information, even back then.

It was necessary for Popov to explain in the proper ideological context: "You must remember that to us they were not terrorists at all. They were fellow believers in world peace and Marxism-Leninism, fellow soldiers in the struggle for human freedom—and, truth be told, useful fools, all too willing to sacrifice their lives in return for a little support of one sort or another."

"Really?" the American asked again, in surprise. "I would have thought that they were motivated by something important—"

"Oh, they are," Popov assured him, "but idealists are foolish people, are they not?"

"Some are," his host admitted, nodding for his guest to go on.

"They believe all the rhetoric, all the promises. Don't you see? I, too, was a Party member. I said the words, filled out the bluebook answers, attended the meetings, paid my Party dues. I did all I had to do, but, really, I was KGB. I traveled aboard. I *saw* what life was like in the West. I much preferred to travel abroad on, ah, 'business' than to work at Number Two Dzerzhinsky Square. Better food, better clothes, better everything. Unlike these foolish youths, I knew what the truth was," he concluded, saluting with his half-full glass.

"So, what are they doing now?"

"Hiding," Popov answered. "For the most part, hiding. Some may have jobs of one sort or another—probably menial ones, I would imagine, despite the university education most of them have."

"I wonder . . ." A sleepy look reflected the man's own imbibing, so skillfully delivered that Popov wondered if it were genuine or not.

"Wonder what?"

"If one could still contact them . . ."

"Most certainly, if there were a reason for it. My contacts"—he tapped his temple—"well, such things do not evaporate." *Where was this going?*

"Well, Dmitriy, you know, even attack dogs have their uses, and every so often, well"—an embarrassed smile—"you know . . ."

In that moment, Popov wondered if all the movies were true. Did American business executives *really* plot murder against commercial rivals and such? It seemed quite mad . . . but maybe the movies were not entirely groundless. . . .

"Tell me," the American went on, "did you actually work with those people—you know, plan some of the jobs they did?"

"Plan? No," the Russian replied, with a shake of the head. "I provided some assistance, yes, under the direction of my government. Most often I acted as a courier of sorts." It had not been a favored assignment; essentially he'd been a mailman tasked to delivering special messages to those perverse children, but it was duty he'd drawn due to his superb field skills and his ability to reason with nearly anyone on nearly any topic, since the contacts were so difficult to handle once they'd decided to do something. Popov had been a spook, to use the Western vernacular, a really excellent field intelligence officer who'd never, to the best of his knowledge, been identified by any Western counterintelligence service. Otherwise, his entry into America at JFK International Airport would hardly have been so uneventful.

"So, you actually know how to get in touch with those people, eh?"

"Yes, I do," Popov assured his host.

"Remarkable." The American stood. "Well, how about some dinner?"

By the end of dinner, Popov was earning $100,000 per year as a special consultant, wondering where this new job would lead and not really caring. One hundred thousand dollars was a good deal of money for a man whose tastes were actually rather sophisticated and needed proper support.

It was ten months later now, and the vodka was still good, in the glass with two ice cubes. "Where and how? . . ." Popov whispered. It amused him where he was now, and what he was doing. Life was so very strange, the paths you took, and where they led you. After all, he'd just been in Paris that afternoon, killing time and waiting for a meet with a former "colleague" in DGSE. "When is decided, then?"

"Yes, you have the date, Dmitriy."

"I know whom to see and whom to call to arrange the meeting."

"You have to do it face-to-face?" the American asked, rather stupidly, Popov thought.

A gentle laugh. "My dear friend, yes, face-to-face. One does not arrange such a thing with a fax."

"That's a risk."

"Only a small one. The meet will be in a safe place. No one will take my photograph, and they know me only by a password and codename, and, of course, the currency."

"How much?"

Popov shrugged. "Oh, shall we say five hundred thousand dollars? In cash, of course, American dollars, Deutschmarks, Swiss francs, that will depend on what our . . . our friends prefer," he added, just to make things clear.

The host scribbled a quick note and handed the paper across. "That's what you need to get the money." And with that, things began. Morals were always variable things, depending on the culture, experiences, and principles of individual men and women. In Dmitriy's case, his parent culture had few hard-and-fast rules, his experiences were to make use of that fact, and his main principle was to earn a living—

"You know that this carries a certain degree of danger for me, and, as you know, my salary—"

"Your salary just doubled, Dmitriy."

A smile. "Excellent." A good beginning. Even the Russian Mafia didn't advance people as quickly as this.

THREE times a week they practiced zip-lining from a platform, sixty feet down to the ground. Once a week or so they did it for-real, out of a British Army helicopter. Chavez didn't like it much. Airborne school was one of the few things he'd avoided in his Army service—which was rather odd, he thought, looking back. He'd done Ranger school as an E-4, but for one reason or other, Fort Benning hadn't happened.

This was the next best or worst thing. His feet rested on the skids as the chopper approached the drop-site. His gloved hands held the rope, a hundred feet long in case the pilot misjudged something. Nobody trusted pilots very much, though one's life so often depended on them, and this one seemed pretty good. A little bit of a cowboy—the final part of the simulated insertion took them through a gap in some trees, and the top leaves brushed Ding's uniform, gently to be sure, but in his position, any touch was decidedly unwelcome. Then the nose came up on a powerful dynamic-braking maneuver. Chavez's legs went tight, and when the nose came back down, he kicked himself free of the skid and dropped. The tricky part was stopping the descent just short of the ground—and getting there quickly enough so as not to present yourself as a dangling target . . . done, and his feet hit the ground. He tossed the rope free, snatched up his H&K in both hands, and headed off toward the objective, having survived his fourteenth zip-line deployment, the third from a chopper.

There was a delightfully joyous aspect to this job, he told himself as he ran along. He was being a physical soldier again, something he'd once learned to love and that his CIA duties had mainly denied him. Chavez was a man who liked to sweat, who enjoyed the physical exertion of soldiering in the field, and most of all loved being with others who shared his likes. It was hard. It was dangerous: every member of the team had suffered a minor injury or other in the past month—except Weber, who seemed to be made of steel—and sooner or later, the statistics said, someone would have a major one, most probably a broken leg from zip-lining. Delta at Fort Bragg rarely had a complete team fully mission-capable, due to training accidents and injuries. But hard training made for easy combat. So ran the motto of every competent army in the world. An exaggeration, but not a big one. Looking back from his place of cover and concealment, Chavez saw that Team-2 was all down and moving—even Vega, remarkably enough. With Oso's upper-body bulk, Chavez always worried about his ankles. Weber and Johnston were darting to their programmed perches, each carrying his custom-made scope-sighted rifle. Helmet-mounted radios were working, hissing with the digitized encryption system so that only team members could understand what was being said . . . Ding turned and saw that everyone was in his pre-briefed position, ready for his next move-command . . .

THE Communications Room was on the second floor of the building whose renovations had just been completed. It had the usual number of teletype machines for the various world news services, plus TV sets for CNN, and Sky News, and a few other broadcasts. These were overseen by people the Brits called "minders," who were overseen in turn by a career intelligence officer. The one on this shift was an American from the National Security Agency, an Air Force major who usually dressed in civilian clothes which didn't disguise his nationality or the nature of his training at all.

Major Sam Bennett had acclimated himself to the environment. His wife and son weren't all that keen on the local TV, but they found the climate agreeable, and there were several decent golf courses within easy driving distance. He jogged three miles every morning to let the local collection of snake-eaters know he wasn't a total wimp, and he was looking forward to a little bird-shooting in a few weeks. Otherwise, the duty here was pretty easy. General Clark—that's how everyone seemed to think of him—seemed a decent boss. He liked it clean and fast, which was precisely how Bennett liked to deliver it. Not a screamer, either. Bennett had worked for a few of those in his twelve years of uniformed service. And Bill Tawney, the British intelligence team boss, was about the best Bennett had ever seen—quiet, thoughtful, and smart. Bennett had shared a few pints of beer with him over the past weeks, while talking shop in the Hereford Officers' Club.

But duty like this was boring most of the time. He'd worked the basement Watch Center at NSA, a large, low-ceiling room of standard office sheep-pens, with mini-televisions and computer printers that gave the room a constant low buzz of noise that could drive a man crazy on the long nights of keeping track of the whole fucking world. At least the Brits didn't believe in caging all the worker bees. It was easy for him to get up and walk around. The crew was young here. Only Tawney was over fifty, and Bennett liked that, too.

"Major!" a voice called from one of the news printers. "We have a hostage case in Switzerland."

"What service?" Bennett asked on the way over.

"Agence France-Press. It's a bank, a bloody bank," the corporal reported, as Bennett came close enough to read—but couldn't, since he didn't know French. The corporal could and translated on the fly. Bennett lifted a phone and pushed a button.

"Mr. Tawney, we have an incident in Bern, unknown number of criminals have seized the central branch of the Bern Commercial Bank. There are some civilians trapped inside."

"What else, Major?"

"Nothing at the moment. Evidently the police are there."

"Very well, thank you, Major Bennett." Tawney killed the line and pulled open a desk drawer, to find and open a very special book. Ah, yes, he knew that one. Then he dialed the British Embassy in Geneva. "Mr. Gordon, please," he told the operator.

"Gordon," a voice said a few seconds later.

"Dennis, this is Bill Tawney."

"Bill, haven't heard from you in quite a while. What can I do for you?" the voice asked pleasantly.

"Bern Commercial Bank, main branch. There seems to be a hostage situation there. I want you to evaluate the situation and report back to me."

"What's our interest, Bill?" the man asked.

"We have an . . . an understanding with the Swiss government. If their police are unable to handle it, we may have to provide some technical assistance. Who in the embassy liases with the local police?"

"Tony Armitage, used to be Scotland Yard. Good man for financial crimes and such."

"Take him with you," Tawney ordered. "Report back directly to me as soon as you have something." Tawney gave his number.

"Very well." It was a dull afternoon in Geneva anyway. "It will be a few hours."

And it will probably end up as nothing, they both knew. "I'll be here. Thank you, Dennis." With that, Tawney left his office and went upstairs to watch TV.

Behind the Rainbow Headquarters building were four large satellite dishes trained on communications satellites hovering over the equator. A simple check told them which channel of which bird carried Swiss television satellite broadcasts—as with most countries, it was easier to go up and back to a satellite than to use coaxial land-lines. Soon they were getting a direct newsfeed from the local station. Only one camera was set up at the moment. It showed the outside of an institutional building—the Swiss tended to design banks rather like urban castles, though with a distinctly Germanic flavor to make them appear powerful and forbidding. The voice was that of a reporter talking to his station, not to the public. A linguist stood by to translate.

" 'No, I have no idea. The police haven't talked to us yet,' " the translator said in a dull monotone. Then a new voice came on the line. "Cameraman," the translator said. "Sounds like a cameraman—there's something—"

—with that the camera zoomed in, catching a shape, a human shape wearing something over his head, a mask of sorts—

"What kind of gun is that?" Bennett asked.

"Czech Model 58," Tawney said at once. "So it would seem. Bloody good man on the camera."

" 'What did he say?' That was the studio to the reporter," the translator went on, hardly looking at the picture on the TV screen. " 'Don't know, couldn't hear with all the noise out here. He shouted something, didn't hear it.' Oh, good: 'How many people?' 'Not sure, the *Wachtmeister* said over twenty inside, bank customers and employees. Just me and my cameraman here outside, and about fifteen police officers that I can see.' 'More on the way, I imagine,' reply from the station." With that the audio line went quiet. The camera switched off, and shuffling on the audio line told them that the cameraman was moving to a different location, which was confirmed when the picture came back a minute later from a very different angle.

"What gives, Bill?" Tawney and Bennett turned to see Clark standing there behind them. "I came over to talk to you, but your secretary said you had a developing situation up here."

"We may," the Intelligence section chief replied. "I have the 'Six' station in Geneva sending two men over now to evaluate it. We do have that arrangement with the Swiss government, should they decide to invoke it. Bennett, is this going out on commercial TV yet?"

Bennett shook his head. "No, sir. For the moment they're keeping it quiet."

"Good," Tawney thought. "Who's the go-team now, John?"

"Team-2, Chavez and Price. They're just finishing up a little exercise right now. How long before you think we declare an alert?"

"We could start now," Bill answered, even though it was probably nothing more than a bank robbery gone bad. They had those in Switzerland, didn't they?

Clark pulled a mini-radio from his pocket and thumbed it on. "Chavez, this is Clark. You and Price report to communications right now."

"On the way, Six" was the reply.

"I wonder what this is about," Ding observed to his command sergeant major. Eddie Price, he'd learned in the past three weeks, was as good a soldier as he was ever likely to meet: cool, smart, quiet, with plenty of field experience.

"I expect we'll find out, sir," Price responded. Officers felt the need to talk a lot, he knew. Proof of that came at once.

"How long you been in, Eddie?"

"Nearly thirty years, sir. I enlisted as a boy soldier—age fifteen, you see. Parachute Regiment," he went on, just to avoid the next question. "Came over to SAS when I was twenty-four, been here ever since."

"Well, sar major, I'm glad to have you with me," Chavez said, getting in the car for the drive to the Headquarters Building.

"Thank you, sir," the sergeant major replied. A decent chap, this Chavez, he thought, perhaps even a good commander, though that remained to be seen. He could have asked his own questions, but, no, that wasn't done, was it? Good as he was, Price didn't know much about the American military yet.

You oughta be an officer, Eddie, Ding didn't say. In America this guy would have been ripped from his unit, kicking and screaming or not, and shipped off to OCS, probably with a college degree purchased by the Army along the way. Different culture, different rules, Chavez told himself. Well, it gave him a damned good squad sergeant to back him up. Ten minutes later, he parked in the back lot and walked into the building, following directions up to Communications.

"Hey, Mr. C, what gives?"

"Domingo, there's a chance we may have a job for you and your team. Bern, Switzerland. Bank robbery gone bad, hostage situation. All we know

now." Clark pointed both of them at the TV screens. Chavez and Price stole swivel chairs and moved them close.

If nothing else, it was good as a practice alert. The pre-planned mechanisms were now moving. On the first floor, tickets had already been arranged on no fewer than four flights from Gatwick to Switzerland, and two helicopters were on the way to Hereford to ferry his men to the airport with their equipment. British Airways had been alerted to accept sealed cargo—inspecting it for the international flight would just have gotten people excited. If the alert went further, Team-2 members would change into civilian clothes, complete with ties and suit jackets. Clark thought that a little excessive. Making soldiers look like bankers was no easy task, was it?

"Not much happening now," Tawney said. "Sam, can you roll the tapes from earlier?"

"Yes, sir." Major Bennett keyed one up and hit the play button on the remote.

"Czech 58," Price said immediately. "No faces?"

"Nope, that's the only thing we have on the subjects," Bennett replied.

"Odd weapon for robbers," the sergeant major noted. Chavez turned his head. That was one of the things he had yet to learn about Europe. Okay, hoods here didn't use assault rifles.

"That's what I thought," Tawney said.

"Terrorist weapon?" Chavez asked his squad XO.

"Yes, sir. The Czechs gave away a lot of them. Quite compact, you see. Only twenty-five inches long, manufactured by the Uhersky Broad works. Seven-point-six-two/thirty-nine Soviet cartridge. Fully automatic, selector switch. Odd thing for a Swiss bandit to use," Price said once more for emphasis.

"Why?" Clark asked.

"They make far better weapons in Switzerland, sir, for their territorials—their citizen soldiers stow them in their closets, you see. Should not be all that difficult to steal several."

The building shook then with the sound of helicopters landing not too far away. Clark checked his watch and nodded approval at the timing.

"What do we know about the neighborhood?" Chavez asked.

"Working on that now, old boy," Tawney answered. "So far, just what the TV feed shows."

The TV screen showed an ordinary street, devoid of vehicular traffic at the moment because the local police had diverted cars and buses away from the bank. Otherwise, they saw ordinary masonry buildings bordering an ordinary city street. Chavez looked over at Price, whose eyes were locked on the pictures they were getting—two now, because another Swiss TV station had dispatched a camera team there, and both signals were being pirated off the satellite. The translator continued to relay the remarks of the camera crews and reporters on the scene to their respective stations. They said very little, about half of it small-talk that could have been spoken from one desk to another in an office setting. One camera or the other occasionally caught the movement of a curtain, but that was all.

"The police are probably trying to establish communications with our friends on a telephone, talk to them, reason with them, the usual drill," Price said, realizing that he had more practical experience with this sort of thing than anyone else in the room. They knew the theory, but theory wasn't always enough. "We shall know in half an hour if this is a mission for us or not."

"How good are the Swiss cops?" Chavez asked Price.

"Very good indeed, sir, but not a great deal of experience with a serious hostage event—"

"That's why we have an understanding with them," Tawney put in.

"Yes, sir." Price leaned back, reached into his pocket, and took out his pipe. "Anyone object?"

Clark shook his head. "No health Nazis here, Sergeant Major. What do you mean by a 'serious' hostage event?"

"Committed criminals, terrorists." Price shrugged. "Chaps stupid enough to put their lives behind the chips on the gaming table. The sort who kill hostages to show their resolve." *The sort we go in after and kill,* Price didn't have to add.

It was an awful lot of brain-power to be sitting around doing nothing, John Clark thought, especially Bill Tawney. But if you had no information, it was difficult to make pontifical pronouncements. All eyes were locked on the TV screens, which showed little, and Clark found himself missing the inane drivel that one expected of TV reporters, filling silence with empty words. About the only interesting thing was when they said that they were trying to talk to the local cops, but that the cops weren't saying anything, except that they were trying to establish contact with the bad guys, so far unsuccessfully. That had to be a lie, but the police were supposed to lie to the media and the public in cases like this—because any halfway competent terrorist would have a TV set with him, and would have somebody watching it. You could catch a lot by watching TV, else Clark and his senior people would not be watching it either, would they?

The protocol on this was both simple and complex. Rainbow had an understanding with the Swiss government. If the local police couldn't handle it, they'd bump it up to the canton—state—level, which would then decide whether or not to bump it one more step to the central national government, whose ministerial-level people could then make the Rainbow call. That entire mechanism had been established months before as part of the mandate of the agency that Clark now headed. The "help" call would come through the British Foreign Office in Whitehall, on the bank of the Thames in central London. It seemed like a hell of a lot of bureaucracy to John, but there was no avoiding it, and he was grateful that there was not an additional level or two. Once the call was made, things got easier, at least in the administrative sense. But until the call was made, the Swiss would tell them nothing.

One hour into the TV vigil, Chavez left to put Team-2 on Alert. The troops, he saw, took it calmly, readying gear that needed to be seen to, which was not very much. The TV feed was routed to their individual desktop sets, and the men settled back in their swivel chairs to watch quietly as their boss went back to Communications, while the helicopters sat idle on the pad outside Team-2's area. Team-1 went on standby alert as well, in case the helicopters taking -2 to Gatwick crashed. The procedures had been completely thought through—except, John thought, by the terrorists.

On the TV screen, police milled about, some at the ready, most just standing and watching. Trained police or not, they were little trained for a situation like this, and the Swiss, while they had considered such an event—everyone in the civilized world had—had taken it no more seriously than, say, the cops in Boulder, Colorado. This had never happened before in Bern, and until it did, it would not be part of the local police department's corporate culture. The facts were too stark for Clark and the rest to discount. The German police—as competent as any in the world—had thoroughly blown the hostage rescue at Fürstenfeldbrück, not because they had been bad cops, but because it had been their first time, and as a result some Israeli athletes hadn't made it home from the 1972 Munich Olympiad. The whole world had learned from that, but how much had they learned? Clark and the rest all wondered at the same time.

The TV screens showed very little for another half hour beyond an empty city street, but then a senior police officer walked into the open, holding a cellular phone. His body language was placid at first, but it started to change, and then he held the cell phone close to his ear, seeming to lean into it. His free hand came up about then, placatingly, as though in a face-to-face conversation.

"Something's wrong," Dr. Paul Bellow observed, which was hardly a surprise to the others, especially Eddie Price, who tensed in his chair, but said nothing as he puffed on his pipe. Negotiating with people like those controlling the bank was its own little art form, and it was one this police superintendent—whatever his rank was—had yet to learn. Bad news, the sergeant major thought, for one or more of the bank customers.

" 'Was that a shot?' " the translator said, relaying the words of one of the reporters on the scene.

"Oh, shit," Chavez observed quietly. The situation had just escalated.

Less than a minute later, one of the bank's glass doors opened, and a man in civilian clothes dragged a body onto the sidewalk. It seemed to be a man, but his head, as both the cameras zoomed in on the scene from different angles, was a red mass. The civilian got the body all the way outside and froze the moment he set it down.

Move right, go to your right, Chavez thought as loudly as he could from so far away. Somehow the thought must have gotten there, for the unnamed man in his gray overcoat stood stock-still for several seconds, looking down, and then—furtively, he thought—went to the right.

" 'Somebody's shouting from inside the bank,' " the translator relayed.

But whatever the voice had shouted, it hadn't been the right thing. The civilian dove to his right, away from the double glass doors of the bank and below the level of the plate-glass bank windows. He was now on the sidewalk, with three feet of granite block over his head, invisible from the interior of the building.

"Good move, old man," Tawney observed quietly. "Now, we'll see if the police can get you into the clear."

One of the cameras shifted to the senior cop, who'd wandered into the middle of the street with his cell phone, and was now waving frantically for the civilian to get down. Brave or foolish, they couldn't tell, but the cop then walked slowly back to the line of police cars—astonishingly, without being shot for his troubles. The cameras shifted back to the escaped civilian. Police had edged to the side of the bank building, waving for the man to crawl, keep low, to where they were standing. The uniformed cops had submachine guns out. Their body language was tense and frustrated. One of the police faces looked to the body on the sidewalk, and the men in Hereford could easily translate his thoughts.

"Mr. Tawney, a call for you on Line Four," the intercom called. The intelligence chief walked to a phone and punched the proper button.

"Tawney . . . ah, yes, Dennis . . ."

"Whoever they are, they've just murdered a chap."

"We just watched it. We're pirating the TV feed." Which meant that Gordon's trip to Bern was a waste of time—but no, it wasn't, was it? "You have that Armitage chap with you?"

"Yes, Bill, he's going over to talk to their police now."

"Excellent. I will hold for him."

As though on cue, a camera showed a man in civilian clothes walking to the senior cop on the scene. He pulled out an ID folder, spoke briefly with the police commander, and walked away, disappearing around the corner.

"This is Tony Armitage, who's this?"

"Bill Tawney."

"Well, if you know Dennis, I expect you're a 'Six' chap. What can I do for you, sir?"

"What did the police tell you?" Tawney hit the speaker switch on the phone.

"He's out of his depth by several meters or so. Said he's sending it up to the canton for advice."

"Mr. C?" Chavez said from his chair.

"Tell the choppers to spool up, Ding, you're off to Gatwick. Hold there for further instructions."

"Roger that, Mr. C. Team-2 is moving."

Chavez walked down the stairs with Price behind him, then jumped into their car, which had them at Team-2's building in under three minutes.

"People, if you're watching the *telly,* you know what's happening. Saddle up, we're choppering to Gatwick." They'd just headed out the door when a brave Swiss cop managed to get the civilian to safety. The TV showed the civilian being hustled to a car, which sped off at once. Again the body language was the important thing. The assembled police, who had been standing around casually, were standing differently now, mainly crouched behind the cover of their automobiles, their hands fingering their weapons, tense but still unsure of what they ought to do.

"It's going out live on TV now," Bennett reported. "Sky News will have it on in a few."

"I guess that figures," Clark said. "Where's Stanley?"

"He's at Gatwick now," Tawney said. Clark nodded. Stanley would deploy with Team-2 as field commander. Dr. Paul Bellow was gone as well. He'd chopper out with Chavez and advise him and Stanley on the psychological aspects of the tactical situation. Nothing to be done now but order coffee and solid food, which Clark did, taking a chair and sitting in front of the TVs.

CHAPTER 3

GNOMES AND GUNS

THE HELICOPTER RIDE WAS TWENTY-FIVE MINUTES exactly, and deposited Team-2 and its attachments in the general-aviation portion of the international airport. Two vans waited, and Chavez watched his men load their gear into one of them for movement to the British Airways terminal. There, some cops, who were also waiting, supervised the van's handling into a cargo container—which would be first off the flight when the plane arrived at Bern.

But first they had to wait for the go-mission order. Chavez pulled out his cellular phone, flipped it open, and thumbed speed-dial number one.

"Clark," the voice said after the encryption software clicked through.

"Ding here, John. The call come from Whitehall yet?"

"Still waiting, Domingo. We expect it shortly. The canton bumped it upstairs. Their Justice Minister is considering it now."

"Well, tell the worthy gentleman that this flight leaves the gate in two-zero minutes, and the next one after that is ninety minutes, 'less you want us to travel Swissair. One of those in forty minutes, and another in an hour fifteen."

"I hear you, Ding. We have to hold."

Chavez swore in Spanish. He knew it. He didn't have to like it. "Roger, Six, Team-2 is holding on the ramp at Gatwick."

"Roger that, Team-2, Rainbow Six, out."

Chavez closed his phone and tucked it in his shirt pocket. "Okay, people," he said to his men over the shriek of jet engines, "we hold here for the go-ahead." The troops nodded, as eager to get it going as their boss, but just as powerless to make it happen. The British team members had been there before and took it better than the Americans and the others.

■ ■ ■

"BILL, tell Whitehall that we have twenty minutes to get them off the ground, after that over an hour delay."

Tawney nodded and went to a phone in the corner to call his contact in the Foreign Ministry. From there it went to the British Ambassador in Geneva, who'd been told that the SAS was offering special mission assistance of a technical nature. It was an odd case where the Swiss Foreign Minister knew more than the man making the offer. But, remarkably, the word came back in fifteen minutes: *"Ja."*

"We have mission approval, John," Tawney reported, much to his own surprise.

"Right." Clark flipped open his own phone and hit the speed-dial #2 button.

"Chavez," a voice said over considerable background noise.

"We have a go-mission," Clark said. "Acknowledge."

"Team-2 copies go-mission. Team-2 is moving."

"That's affirmative. Good luck, Domingo."

"Thank you, Mr. C."

CHAVEZ turned to his people and pumped his arm up and down in the speed-it-up gesture known to armies all over the world. They got into their designated van for the drive across the Gatwick ramp. It stopped at the cargo gate for their flight, where Chavez waved a cop close, and let Eddie Price pass the word to load the special cargo onto the Boeing 757. That done, the van advanced another fifty yards to the stairs outside the end of the jetway, and Team-2 jumped out and headed up the stairs. At the top, the control-booth door was held open by another police constable, and from there they walked normally aboard the aircraft and handed over their tickets to the stewardess, who pointed them to their first-class seats.

The last man aboard was Tim Noonan, the team's technical wizard. Not a wizened techno-nerd, Noonan had played defensive back at Stanford before joining the FBI, and took weapons training with the team just to fit in. Six feet, two hundred pounds, he was larger than most of Ding's shooters but, he'd be the first to admit, was not as tough. Still, he was a better-than-fair shot with pistol and MP-10, and was learning to speak the language. Dr. Bellow settled into his window seat with a book extracted from his carry-on bag. It was a volume on sociopathy by a professor at Harvard under whom he'd trained some years before. The rest of the team members just leaned back, skimming through the onboard magazines. Chavez looked around and saw that his team didn't seem tense at all, and was both amazed at the fact, and slightly ashamed that he was so pumped up. The airline captain made his announcements, and the Boeing backed away from the gate, then taxied out to the runway. Five minutes later, the aircraft rotated off the ground, and Team-2 was on its way to its first mission.

"IN the air," Tawney reported. "The airline expects a smooth flight and an on-time arrival in . . . an hour fifteen minutes."

"Great," Clark observed. The TV coverage had settled down. Both Swiss stations were broadcasting continuous coverage now, complete with thoughts from the reporters at the scene. That was about as useful as an NFL pre-game show, though police spokesmen were speaking to the press now. No, they didn't know who was inside. Yes, they'd spoken to them. Yes, negotiations were ongoing. No, they couldn't really say any more than that. Yes, they'd keep the press apprised of developments.

Like hell, John thought. The same coverage was reported on Sky News, and soon CNN and Fox networks were carrying brief stories about it, including, of course, the dumping of the first victim and the escape of the one who'd dragged the body out.

"Nasty business, John," Tawney said over his tea.

Clark nodded. "I suppose they always are, Bill."

"Quite."

Peter Covington came in then, stole a swivel chair and moved it next to the two senior men. His face was locked in neutral, though he had to be pissed, Clark thought, that his team wasn't going. But the team-availability rotation was set in stone here, as it had to be.

"Thoughts, Peter?" Clark asked.

"They're not awfully bright. They killed that poor sod very early in the affair, didn't they?"

"Keep going," John said, reminding all of them that he was new in this business.

"When you kill a hostage, you cross a large, thick line, sir. Once across it, one cannot easily go backwards, can one?"

"So, you try to avoid it?"

"I would. It makes it too difficult for the other side to make concessions, and you bloody need the concessions if you want to get away—unless you know something the opposition does not. Unlikely in a situation like this."

"They'll ask for a way out . . . helicopter?"

"Probably." Covington nodded. "To an airport, commercial aircraft waiting, international crew—but to *where?* Libya, perhaps, but will Libya allow them in? Where else might they go? Russia? I think not. The Bekaa Valley in Lebanon is still possible, but commercial aircraft don't land there. About the only sensible thing they've done is to protect their identities from the police. Would you care to wager that the hostage who got out has not seen their faces?" Covington shook his head.

"They're not amateurs," Clark objected. "Their weapons point to some measure of training and professionalism."

That earned John a nod. "True, sir, but not awfully bright. I would not be overly surprised to learn that they'd actually stolen some currency, like common robbers. Trained terrorists, perhaps, but not good ones."

And what's a "good" terrorist? John wondered. Doubtless a term of art he'd have to learn.

THE BA flight touched down two minutes early, then taxied to the gate. Ding had spent the flight talking to Dr. Bellow. The psychology of this business was the biggest blank spot in his copybook, and one he'd have to learn to fill in—and soon. This wasn't like being a soldier—the psychology of that job was handled at the general-officer level most of the time, the figuring out of what the other guy was going to do with his maneuver battalions. This was squad-level combat, but with all sorts of interesting new elements, Ding thought, flipping his seat belt off before the aircraft stopped moving. But it still came down to the least common denominator—steel on target.

Chavez stood and stretched, then headed aft to the doorway, his game-face now on all the way. Out the jetway, between two ordinary civilians who probably thought him a businessman, with his suit and tie. Maybe he'd buy a nicer suit in London, he thought idly, exiting the jetway, the better to fit the disguise he and his men had to adopt when traveling. There was a chauffeur sort of man standing out there holding a sign with the proper name on it. Chavez walked up to him.

"Waiting for us?"

"Yes, sir. Come with me?"

Team-2 followed him down the anonymous concourse, then turned into what seemed a conference room that had another door. In it was a uniformed police officer, a senior one, judging by the braid on his blue blouse.

"You are . . ." he said.

"Chavez." Ding stuck his hand out. "Domingo Chavez."

"Spanish?" the cop asked in considerable surprise.

"American. And you, sir?"

"Roebling, Marius," the man replied, when all the team was in the room and the door closed. "Come with me, please." Roebling opened the far door, which led outside to some stairs. A minute later, they were in a minibus heading past the park aircraft, then out onto a highway. Ding looked back to see another truck, doubtless carrying their gear.

"Okay, what can you tell me?"

"Nothing new since the first murder. We are speaking with them over the telephone. No names, no identities. They've demanded transport to this airport and a flight out of the country, no destination revealed to us as of yet."

"Okay, what did the guy who got away tell you?"

"There are four of them, they speak German, he says they sound as though it is their primary language, idiomatic, pronunciation, and so forth. They are armed with Czech weapons, and it would seem they are not reluctant to make use of them."

"Yes, sir. How long to get there, and will my men be able to change into their gear?"

Roebling nodded. "It is arranged, Major Chavez."

"Thank you, sir."

"Can I speak with the man who got out?" Dr. Bellow asked.

"My orders are to give you full cooperation—within reason, of course."

Chavez wondered what that qualification meant, but decided he'd find out in due course. He couldn't blame the man for being unhappy to have a team of foreigners come to his country to enforce the law. But these were the proverbial pros from Dover, and that was that—his own government had said so. It also occurred to Ding that the credibility of Rainbow now rested on his shoulders. It would be a hell of a thing to embarrass his father-in-law and his team and his country. He turned to look at his people. Eddie Price, perhaps reading his mind, gave a discreet thumbs-up. *Well,* Chavez thought, *at least one of us thinks we're ready.* It was different in the field, something he'd learned in the jungles and mountains of Colombia years before, and the closer you got to the firing line, the more different it got. Out here there were no laser systems to tell you who'd been killed. Real red blood would announce that. But his people were trained and experienced, especially Sergeant Major Edward Price.

All Ding had to do was lead them into battle.

■ ■ ■

THERE was a secondary school a block from the bank. The minibus and truck pulled up to it, and Team-2 walked into the gymnasium area, which was secured by ten or so uniformed cops. The men changed into their gear in a locker room, and walked back into the gym, to find Roebling with an additional garment for them to wear. These were pullovers, black like their assault gear. POLIZEI was printed on them, front and back, in gold lettering rather than the usual bright yellow. A Swiss affectation? Chavez thought, without the smile that should have gone with the observation.

"Thanks," Chavez told him. It was a useful subterfuge. With that done, the men and their gear reboarded the minibus for the remainder of their drive. This put them around the corner from the bank, invisible both to the terrorists and the TV news cameras. The long-riflemen, Johnston and Weber, were walked to pre-selected perches, one overlooking the rear of the bank building, the other diagonally facing the front. Both men settled in, unfolded the bipod legs on their gunstocks, and started surveying the target building.

Their rifles were as individual as the shooters. Weber had a Walther WA2000, chambered for the .300 Winchester Magnum cartridge. Johnston's was custom made, chambered for the slightly smaller but faster 7-mm Remington Magnum. In both cases, the sharpshooters first of all determined the range to target and dialed it into their telescopic sights, then lay down on the foam mattresses they'd brought. Their immediate mission was to observe, gather information, and report.

Dr. Bellow felt very strange in his black uniform, complete with body armor and POLIZEI pullover, but it would help prevent his identification by a medical colleague who caught this event on TV. Noonan, similarly dressed, set up his computer—an Apple PowerBook laptop—and started looking over the building blueprints so that he could input them into his system. The local cops had been efficient as hell. Over a period of thirty minutes, he had a complete electronic map of the target building. Everything but the vault combination, he thought with a smile. Then he erected a whip antenna and transmitted the imagery to the other three computers the team had brought along.

Chavez, Price, and Bellow walked to the senior Swiss policeman on the scene. Greetings were exchanged, hands shaken. Price set up his computer and put in a CD-ROM disk with photos of every known and photographed terrorist in the world.

The man who'd dragged the body out was one Hans Richter, a German national from Bonn who banked here for his Swiss-based trading business.

"Did you see their faces?" Price asked.

"Yes." A shaky nod. Herr Richter'd had a very bad day to this point. Price selected known German terrorists and started flashing photos.

"Ja, ja, that one. He is the leader."

"You are quite sure?"

"Yes, I am."

"Ernst Model, formerly of Baader-Meinhof, disappeared in 1989, whereabouts unknown." Price scrolled down. "Four suspected operations to date. Three were bloody failures. Nearly captured in Hamburg, 1987, killed two policemen to make his escape. Communist-trained, last suspected to be in Lebanon, that sighting report is thin—very thin, it would seem. Kidnapping was his specialty. Okay." Price scrolled down some more.

"That one . . . possibly."

"Erwin Guttenach, also Baader-Meinhof, last spotted 1992 in Cologne. Robbed a bank, background also kidnapping and murder—oh, yes, he's the chappie who kidnapped and killed a board member of BMW in 1986. Kept the ransom . . . four million D-marks. Greedy bugger," Price added.

Bellow looked over his shoulder, thinking as fast as he could. "What did he say to you on the phone?"

"We have a tape," the cop replied.

"Excellent! But I require a translator."

"Doc, a profile on Ernst Model, quick as you can." Chavez turned. "Noonan, can we get some coverage on the bank?"

"No problem," the tech man replied.

"Roebling?" Chavez said next.

"Yes, Major?"

"Will the TV crews cooperate? We have to assume the subjects inside have a TV with them."

"They will cooperate," the senior Swiss cop replied with confidence.

"Okay, people, let's move," Chavez ordered. Noonan went off to his bag of tricks. Bellow headed around the corner with Herr Richter and another Swiss cop to handle the translation. That left Chavez and Price alone.

"Eddie, am I missing anything?"

"No, Major," Sergeant Major Price replied.

"Okay, number one, my name is Ding. Number two, you have more experience in this than I do. If you have something to say, I want to hear it *right now,* got it? We ain't in no fuckin' wardroom here. I need your brains, Eddie."

"Very well, sir—Ding." Price managed a smile. His commander was working out rather nicely. "So far, so good. We have the subjects contained, good perimeter. We need plans of the building and information on what's happening inside—Noonan's job, and he seems a competent chappie. And we need an idea of what the opposition is thinking—Dr. Bellow's job, and he is excellent. What's the plan if the opposition just starts shooting out of hand?"

"Tell Louis, two flash-bangs at the front door, toss four more inside, and we blow in like a tornado."

"Our body armor—"

"Won't stop a seven-six-two Russian. I know," Chavez agreed. "Nobody ever said it was safe, Eddie. When we know a little more, we can figure a real assault plan." Chavez clapped him on the shoulder. "Move, Eddie."

"Yes, sir." Price moved off to join the rest of the team.

POPOV hadn't known that the Swiss police had such a well-trained counterterrorist squad. As he watched, the commander was crouching close to the front of the bank building, and another, his second-in-command, probably, was heading around the corner to the rest of the team. They were speaking with the escaped hostage—someone had walked him out of sight. Yes, these Swiss police were well trained and well-equipped. H&K weapons, it appeared. The usual for this sort of thing. For his own part, Dmitriy Arkadeyevich Popov stood in the crowd of onlookers. His first impression of Model and his little team of three others had been correct. The German's IQ was little more than room temperature—he'd even wanted a discussion of Marxism-Leninism with his visitor! The fool. Not even a young fool. Model was into his forties now and couldn't use youthful exuberance as an excuse for his ideological fixation. But not entirely impractical. Ernst had wanted to see the money, $600,000 in D-marks. Popov smiled, remembering where it had been stashed. It was unlikely that Ernst would ever see it again. Killing the hostage so early—foolish, but not unexpected. He was the sort who'd want to show his resolve and ideological purity, as though anyone cared about that today! Popov grunted to himself and lit a cigar, leaning back against yet another bank building to relax and observe the exercise, his hat pulled down and collar turned up, ostensibly to protect himself from the gathering evening chill, but also to obscure his face. One couldn't be too careful—a fact lost on Ernst Model and his three *Komraden*.

DR. Bellow finished his review of the taped phone conversations and the known facts about Ernst Johannes Model. The man was a sociopath with a distinct tendency for violence. Suspected in seven murders personally committed and a few more in the company of others. Guttenach, a less bright individual of the same ilk, and two others, unknown. Richter, the escapee, had told them, unsurprisingly, that Model had killed the first victim himself, shooting him in the back of his head from close range and ordering Richter to drag him out. So, both the shooting and the demonstration of its reality to the police had been ill-considered . . . it all fit the same worrisome profile. Bellow keyed his radio.

"Bellow for Chavez."

"Yeah, doc, this is Ding."

"I have a preliminary profile on the subjects."

"Shoot—Team, you listening?" There followed an immediate cacophony of overlapping responses. "Yeah, Ding." "Copying, leader." *"Ja."* And the rest. "Okay, doc, lay it out," Chavez ordered.

"First, this is not a well-planned operation. That fits the profile for the suspected leader, Ernst Model, German national, age forty-one, formerly of the Baader-Meinhof organization. Tends to be impetuous, very quick to use violence when cornered or frustrated. If he threatens to kill someone, we have to believe he's not kidding. His current mental state is very, repeat, *very* dangerous. He knows he has a blown operation. He knows that his likelihood of success is slim. His hostages are his only assets, and he will regard them as expendable assets. Do *not* expect Stockholm Syndrome to set in with this case, people. Model is too sociopathic for that. Neither would I expect negotiations to be very useful. I think that it is very likely that an assault resolution will be necessary tonight or tomorrow."

"Anything else?" Chavez asked.

"Not at this time," Dr. Bellow replied. "I will monitor further developments with the local cops."

NOONAN had taken his time selecting the proper tools, and now he was creeping along the outside wall of the bank building, below the level of the windows. At every one of them, he raised his head slowly and carefully to see if the interior curtains allowed any view of the inside. The second one did, and there Noonan affixed a tiny viewing system. This was a lens, roughly the shape of a cobra's head, but only a few millimeters across, which led by fiber-optic cable to a TV camera set in his black bag around the corner. He placed another at the lower corner of the bank's glass door, then worked his way back, crawling feet first, slowly and laboriously, to a place where he could stand. That done, he walked all the way around the block to repeat the procedure from the other side of the building, where he was able to make three placements, one again on the door, and two on windows whose curtains were a touch shorter than they ought to have been. He also placed microphones in order to pick up whatever sound might be available. The large plate-glass windows ought to resonate nicely, he thought, though this would apply to extraneous exterior sounds as well as to those originating inside the building.

All the while, the Swiss TV crews were speaking with the senior on-site policeman, who spent a great deal of time saying that the terrorists were serious—he'd been coached by Dr. Bellow to speak of them with respect. They were probably watching television inside, and building up their self-esteem worked for the team's purposes at the moment. In any case, it denied the terrorists knowledge of what Tim Noonan had done on the outside.

"Okay," the techie said in his place on a side street. All the video displays were up and running. They showed little. The size of the lenses didn't make for good imagery, despite the enhancement program built into his computer. "Here's one shooter . . . and another." They were within ten meters of the front of the building. The rest of the people visible were sitting on the white marble floor, in the center for easy coverage. "The guy said four, right?"

"Yeah," Chavez answered. "But not how many hostages, not exactly anyway."

"Okay, this is a bad guy, I think, behind the teller-places . . . hmph, looks like he's checking the cash drawers . . . and that's a bag of some sort. You figure they visited the vault?"

Chavez turned. "Eddie?"

"Greed," Price agreed. "Well, why not? It *is* a bank, after all."

"Okay." Noonan switched displays on the computer screen. "I got blueprints of the building, and this is the layout."

"Teller cages, vault, toilets." Price traced his finger over the screen. "Back door. Seems simple enough. Access to the upper floors?"

"Here," Noonan said. "Actually outside the bank itself, but the basement is accessible to them here, stairs down, and a separate exit to the alley in back."

"Ceiling construction?" Chavez asked.

"Rebarred concrete slab, forty centimeters thick. That's solid as hell. Same with the walls and floor. This building was made to last." So, there would be no explosives-forced entry through walls, floor, or ceiling.

"So, we can go in the front door or the back door, and that's it. And that puts number four bad guy at the back door." Chavez keyed his radio. "Chavez for Rifle Two-Two."

"Ja, Weber here."

"Any windows in the back, anything in the door, peep-hole, anything like that, Dieter?"

"Negative. It appears to be a heavy steel door, nothing in it that I can see," the sniper said, tracing his telescopic sight over the target yet again, and again finding nothing but blank painted steel.

"Okay, Eddie, we blow the rear door with Primacord, three men in that way. Second later, we blow the front glass doors, toss flash-bangs, and move in when they're looking the wrong way. Two and two through the front. You and me go left. Louis and George go right."

"Are they wearing body armor?" Price asked.

"Nothing that Herr Richter saw," Noonan responded, "and nothing visible here— but there ain't no head-protection anyway, right?" It would be nothing more than a ten-meter shot, an easy distance for the H&K shoulder weapons.

"Quite." Price nodded. "Who leads the rear-entry team?"

"Scotty, I think. Paddy does the explosives." Connolly was the best man on the team for that, and both men knew it. Chavez made an important mental note that the subteams had to be more firmly established. To this point he'd kept all his people in the same drawer. That he would have to change as soon as they got back to Hereford.

"Vega?"

"Oso backs us up, but I don't think we'll have much use for him on this trip." Julio Vega had become their heavy-machine gunner, slinging a laser-sighted M-60 7.62-mm machine gun for really serious work, but there wasn't much use for that now—and wouldn't be, unless everything went totally to hell.

"Noonan, send this picture to Scotty."

"Right." He moved the mouse-pointer and started transmitting everything to the team's various computers.

"The question now is when." Ding checked his watch. "Back to the doc."

"Yes, sir."

BELLOW had spent his time with Herr Richter. Three stiff shots had calmed him down nicely. Even his English had improved markedly. Bellow was walking him through the event for the sixth time when Chavez and Price showed up again.

"His eyes, they are blue, like ice. Like ice," Richter repeated. "He is not a man like most men. He should be in a cage, with the animals at the *Tiergarten*." The businessman shuddered involuntarily.

"Does he have an accent?" Price asked.

"Mixed. Something of Hamburg, but something of Bavaria, too. The others, all Bavarian accents."

"The Bundes Kriminal Amt will find that useful, Ding," Price observed. The BKA was the German counterpart to the American FBI. "Why not have the local police check the area for a car with German license plates—from Bavaria? Perhaps there's a driver about."

"Good one." Chavez left and ran over to the Swiss cops, whose chief got on his radio at once. Probably a dry hole, Chavez thought. But you didn't know until you drilled it. They had to have come here one way or another. Another mental note. Check for that on every job.

Roebling came over next, carrying his cell phone. "It is time," he said, "to speak with them again."

"Yo, Tim," Chavez said over his radio. "Come to the rally point."

Noonan was there in under a minute. Chavez pointed him to Roebling's phone. Noonan took it, popped the back off, and attached a small green circuit board with a thin wire hanging from it. Then he pulled a cell phone from a thigh pocket and handed it over to Chavez. "There. You'll hear everything they say."

"Anything happening inside?"

"They're walking around a little more, a little agitated, maybe. Two of them were talking face-to-face a few minutes ago. Didn't look real happy about things from their gestures."

"Okay. Everybody up to speed on the interior?"

"How about audio?"

The techie shook his head. "Too much background noise. The building has a noisy heating system—oil-fired hot water, sounds like—that's playing hell with the window mikes. Not getting anything useful, Ding."

"Okay, keep us posted."

"You bet." Noonan made his way back to his gear.

"Eddie?"

"Were I to make a wager, I'd say we have to storm the place before dawn. Our friend will begin losing control soon."

"Doc?" Ding asked.

"That's likely," Bellow agreed with a nod, taking note of Price's practical experience.

Chavez frowned mightily at that one. Trained as he was, he wasn't really all that eager to take this one on. He'd seen the interior pictures. There had to be twenty, perhaps thirty, people inside, with three people in their immediate vicinity holding fully automatic weapons. If one of them decided *fuck it* and went rock-and-roll on his Czech machine gun, a lot of those people wouldn't make it home to the wife and kiddies. It was called the responsibility of command, and while it wasn't the first time Chavez had experienced it, the burden never really got any lighter—because the price of failure never got any smaller.

"Chavez!" It was Dr. Bellow.

"Yeah, doc," Ding said, heading over toward him with Price in attendance.

"Model's getting aggressive. He says he'll kill a hostage in thirty minutes unless we get him a car to a helicopter pad a few blocks from here, and from there to the airport. After that, he kills a hostage every fifteen minutes. He says he has enough to last more than a few hours. He's reading off a list of the important ones now. A professor of surgery at the local medical school, an off-duty policeman, a big-time lawyer . . . well, he's not kidding, Ding. Thirty minutes from—okay, he shoots the first one at eight-thirty."

"What are the cops saying back?"

"What I told them to say, it takes time to arrange all of that, give us a hostage or two to show good faith—but that's what prompted the threat for eight-thirty. Ernst is coming a little unglued."

"Is he serious?" Chavez asked, just to make sure he understood.

"Yeah, he sounds serious as hell. He's losing control, very unhappy with how things turned out. He's barely rational now. He's not kidding about killing somebody. Like a spoiled kid with nothing under the tree on Christmas morning, Ding. There's no stabilizing influence in there to help him out. He feels very lonely."

"Super." Ding keyed his radio. Not unexpectedly, the decision had just been made by somebody else. "Team, this is Chavez. Stand to. I say again, stand to."

He'd been trained in what to expect. One ploy was to deliver the car—it'd be too small for all the hostages, and you could take the bad guys down on the way out with aimed rifle fire. But he had only two snipers, and their rifle bullets would blast through a terrorist's head with enough leftover energy to waste two of three people beyond him. SMG or pistol fire was much the same story. Four bad guys was too many for that play. No, he had to take his team in, while the hostages were still sitting down on the floor, below the line of fire. These bastards weren't even rational enough to want food which he might drug—or maybe they were smart enough to know about the Valium-flavored pizza.

It took several minutes. Chavez and Price crawled to the door from the left. Louis Loiselle and George Tomlinson did the same from the other side. At the rear, Paddy Connolly attached a double thickness of Primacord to the door frame, inserted the detonator, and stood away, with Scotty McTyler and Hank Patterson nearby.

"Rear team in place, Leader," Scotty told them over the radio.

"Roger that. Front team is in place," Chavez replied quietly into his radio transmitter.

"Okay, Ding," Noonan's voice came over the command circuit, "TV One shows a guy brandishing a rifle, walking around the hostages on the floor. If I had to bet, I'd say it's our friend Ernst. One more behind him, and a third to the right side by the second wood desk. Hold, he's on the phone now . . . okay, he's talking to the cops, saying he's getting ready to pick a hostage to whack. He's going to give out his name first. Nice of him," Noonan concluded.

"Okay, people, it's gonna go down just like the exercises," Ding told his troops. "We are weapons-free at this time. Stand by." He looked up to see Loiselle and Tomlinson trade a look and a gesture. Louis would lead, with George behind. It would be the same for Chavez, letting Price take the lead with his commander immediately behind.

"Ding, he just grabbed a guy, standing him up—on the phone again, they're going to whack the doctor first, Professor Mario Donatello. Okay, I have it all on Camera Two, he's got the guy stood up. I think it's show time," Noonan concluded.

"Are we ready? Rear team check in."

"Ready here," Connolly replied over the radio. Chavez could see Loiselle and Tomlinson. Both nodded curtly and adjusted their hands on their MP-10s.

"Chavez to team, we are ready to rock. Stand by. Stand by. Paddy, hit it!" Ding ordered loudly. The last thing he could do was cringe in expectation of the blast of noise sure to come.

The intervening second seemed to last for hours, and then the mass of the building was in the way. They heard it even so, a loud metallic *crash* that shook the whole world. Price and Loiselle had placed their flash-bangs at the brass lower lining of the door, and punched the switches on them as soon as they heard the first detonation. Instantly the glass doors disintegrated into thousands of fragments, which mainly flew into the granite and marble lobby of the bank in front of a blinding white light and end-of-the-world noise. Price, already standing at the edge of the door, darted in, with Chavez right behind, and going to his left as he entered.

Ernst Model was right there, his weapon's muzzle pressed to the back of Dr. Donatello's head. He'd turned to look at the back of the room when the first explosion had happened, and, as planned, the second one, with its immense noise and blinding flash of magnesium powder, had disoriented him.

The physician captive had reacted, too, dropping away from the gunman behind him with his hands over his head, and giving the intruders a blessedly clear shot. Price had his MP-10 up and aimed, and depressed the trigger for a quick and final three-round burst into the center of Ernst Model's face.

Chavez, immediately behind him, spotted another gunman, standing and shaking his head as though to clear it. He was facing away, but he still held his weapon, and the rules were the rules. Chavez double-tapped his head as well. Between the suppressors integral with the gun-barrels and the ringing from the flash-bangs, the report of the weapons was almost nil. Chavez traversed his weapon right, to see that the third terrorist was already on the floor, a pool of red streaming from what had been a head less than two seconds before.

"Clear!" Chavez shouted.

"Clear!" "Clear!" "Clear!" the others agreed. Loiselle raced to the back of the building, with Tomlinson behind him. Before they'd gotten there, the black-clad figures of McTyler and Patterson appeared, their weapons immediately pointing up at the ceiling: *"Clear!"*

Chavez moved farther left to the teller cages, leaping over the barrier to check there for additional people. None. "Clear here! Secure the area!"

One of the hostages started to rise, only to be pushed back down to the floor by George Tomlinson. One by one, they were frisked by the team members while another covered them with loaded weapons—they couldn't be sure which was a sheep and which a goat at this point. By this time, some Swiss cops were entering the bank. The frisked hostages were pushed in that direction, a shocked and stunned bunch of citizens, still disoriented by what had happened, some bleeding from the head or ears from the flash-bangs and flying glass.

Loiselle and Tomlinson picked up the weapons dropped by their victims, cleared each of them, and slung them over their shoulders. Only then, and only gradually, did they start to relax.

"What about the back door?" Ding asked Paddy Connolly.

"Come and see," the former SAS soldier suggested, leading Ding to the back room. It was a bloody mess. Perhaps the subject had been resting his head against the door frame. It seemed a logical explanation for the fact that no head was immediately visible, and only one shoulder on the corpse, which had been flung against an interior partition, the Czech M-58 rifle still grasped tightly in its remaining hand. The double thickness of Primacord had been a little too powerful . . . but Ding couldn't say that. A steel door and a stout steel frame had demanded it.

"Okay, Paddy, nice one."

"Thank you, sir." The smile of a pro who'd gotten the job well and truly done.

THERE were cheers on the street outside as the hostages came out. So, Popov thought, the terrorists he'd recruited were dead fools now. No real surprise there. The Swiss counterterror team had handled the job well, as one would expect of Swiss policemen. One of them came outside and lit a pipe—how very Swiss! Popov thought. The bugger probably climbs mountains for personal entertainment, too. Perhaps he was the leader. A hostage came up to him.

"Danke schön, danke schön!" the bank director said to Eddie Price.

"Bitte sehr, Herr Direktor," the Brit answered, just about exhausting his knowledge of the German language. He pointed the man off to where the Bern police had the other hostages. They probably needed a loo more than anything else, he thought, as Chavez came out.

"How'd we do, Eddie?"

"Rather well, I should say." A puff on his pipe. "An easy job, really. They were proper wallies, picking this bank and acting as they did." He shook his head and took another puff. The IRA were far more formidable than this. Bloody Germans.

Ding didn't ask what a "wally" was, much less a proper one. With that decided, he pulled his cell phone out and hit speed-dial.

"CLARK."

"Chavez. Did you catch it on TV, Mr. C?"

"Getting the replay now, Domingo."

"We got all four, down for the count. No hostages hurt, except for the one they whacked earlier today. No casualties on the team. So, boss, what do we do now?"

"Fly on home for the debrief, lad. Six, out."

"Bloody good," Major Peter Covington said. The TV showed the team gathering up their equipment for the next thirty or so minutes, then they disappeared around the corner. "Your Chavez does seem to know his business—and so much the better his first test was an easy one. Confidence builder."

They looked over at the computer-generated picture that Noonan had uploaded to them on his cellular phone system. Covington had predicted how the take-down would go, and made no mistakes.

"Any traditions I need to know about?" John asked, settling down, finally, and hugely relieved that there were no unnecessary casualties.

"We take them to the club for a few pints, of course." Covington was surprised that Clark didn't know about that one.

POPOV was in his car, trying to navigate the streets of Bern before police vehicles blocked everything on their way back to their stations. Left there . . . two traffic lights, right, then through the square and . . . there! Excellent, even a place for him to park. He left his rented Audi on the street right across from the half-baked safe house Model had set up. Defeating the lock was child's play. Upstairs, to the back, where the lock was just as easily dealt with.

"*Wer sind sie?*" a voice asked.

"Dmitriy," Popov replied honestly, one hand in his coat pocket. "Have you been watching the television?"

"Yes, what went wrong?" the voice asked in German, seriously downcast.

"It does not matter now. It is time to leave, my young friend."

"But my friends—"

"Are dead, and you cannot help them." He saw the boy in the dark, perhaps twenty years of age, and a devoted friend of the departed fool, Ernst Model. A homosexual relationship, perhaps? If so, it would make things easier for Popov, who had no love for men of that orientation. "Come, get your things. We must leave and leave quickly." There, there it was, the black-leather-clad suitcase with the D-marks inside. The lad—what was his name? Fabian something? Turned his back and went to get his parka, which the Germans called a *Joppe*. He never turned back. Popov's silenced pistol came up and fired once, then again, quite unnecessarily, from three meters away. Making sure the boy was indeed dead, he lifted the suitcase, opened it to verify the contents, and then walked out the door, crossed the street, and drove to his downtown hotel. He had a noon flight back to New York. Before that he had to open a bank account in a city well suited for the task.

THE team was quiet on the trip back, having caught the last flight back to England—this one to Heathrow rather than Gatwick. Chavez availed himself of a glass of white wine, again sitting next to Dr. Bellow, who did the same.

"So, how'd we do, doc?"

"Why don't you tell me, Mr. Chavez," Bellow responded.

"For me, the stress is bleeding off. No shakes this time," Ding replied, surprised at the fact that his hand was steady.

" 'Shakes' are entirely normal—the release of stress energy. The body has trouble letting it go and returning to normal. But training attenuates that. And so does a drink," the physician observed, sipping his own glass of a nice French offering.

"Anything we might have done differently?"

"I don't think so. Perhaps if we'd gotten involved earlier, we might have prevented or at least postponed the murder of the first hostage, but that's never really under our control." Bellow shrugged. "No, what I'm curious about is the motivation of the terrorists in this case."

"How so?"

"They acted in an ideological way, but their demands were—not ideological. I understand they robbed the bank along the way."

"Correct." He and Loiselle had looked at a canvas bag on the bank's floor. It had been full of notes, perhaps twenty-five pounds of money. That seemed to Chavez an odd way to count money, but it was all he had. Follow-up work by the Swiss police would count it up. The after-action stuff was an intelligence function, supervised by Bill Tawney. "So . . . were they just robbers?"

"Not sure." Bellow finished off his glass, holding it up then for the stewardess to see and refill. "It doesn't seem to make much sense at the moment, but that's not exactly unknown in cases like this. Model was not a very good terrorist. Too much show, and not enough go. Poorly planned, poorly executed."

"Vicious bastard," Chavez observed.

"Sociopathic personality—more like a criminal than a terrorist. Those—the good ones, I mean—are usually more judicious."

"What the hell is a good terrorist?"

"He's a businessman whose business is killing people to make a political point . . . almost like advertising. They serve a larger purpose, at least in their own minds. They believe in something, but not like kids in catechism class, more like reasoned adults in Bible study. Crummy simile, I suppose, but it's the best I have at the moment. Long day, Mr. Chavez," Dr. Bellow concluded, while the stew topped off his glass.

Ding checked his watch. "Sure enough, doc." And the next part, Bellow didn't have to tell him, was the need for some sleep. Chavez hit the button to run his seat back and was unconscious in two minutes.

CHAPTER 4

AAR

CHAVEZ AND MOST OF THE REST OF TEAM-2 WOKE up when the airliner touched down at Heathrow. The taxi to the gate seemed to last forever, and then they were met by police, who escorted them to the helo-pad for the flight back to Hereford. On the way through the terminal, Chavez caught the headline on an evening tabloid saying that Swiss police had dealt with a robbery-terrorist incident in the Bern Commercial Bank. It was somewhat unsatisfying that others got the credit for his successful mission, but that was the whole point of Rainbow, he reminded himself, and they'd probably get a nice thank-you letter from the Swiss government—which would end up in the confidential file cabinet. The two military choppers landed on their pad, and vans took the troops to their building. It was after eleven at night now, and all the men were tired after a day that had started with the usual PT and ended with real mission stress.

It wasn't rest time yet, though. On entering the building, they found all the swivel chairs in the bullpen arranged in a circle, with a large-screen TV to one side. Clark, Stanley, and Covington were there. It was time for the after-action review, or AAR.

"Okay, people," Clark said, as soon as they'd sat down. "Good job. All the bad guys are gone, and no good-guy casualties as part of the action. Okay, what did we do wrong?"

Paddy Connolly stood. "I used too much explosives on the rear door. Had there been a hostage immediately inside, he would have been killed," the sergeant said honestly. "I assumed that the door frame was stouter than it actually was." Then he shrugged. "I do not know how to correct for that."

John thought about that. Connolly was having an attack of over-scrupulous honesty, one sure mark of a good man. He nodded and let it go. "Neither do I. What else?"

It was Tomlinson who spoke next, without standing. "Sir, we need to work on a better way to get used to the flash-bangs. I was pretty wasted when I went through the door. Good thing Louis took the first shot on the inside. Not sure I could have."

"How about inside?"

"They worked pretty well on the subjects. The one I saw," Tomlinson said, "was out of it."

"Could we have taken him alive?" Clark had to ask.

"No, *mon general.*" This was Sergeant Louis Loiselle, speaking emphatically. "He had his rifle in hand, and it was pointing in the direction of the hostages." There would be no talk about shooting a gun out of a terrorist's hands. The assumption was that the terrorist had more than one weapon, and the backup was frequently a fragmentation grenade. Loiselle's three-round burst into the target's head was exactly on policy for Rainbow.

"Agreed. Louis, how did you deal with the flash-bangs? You were closer than George was."

"I have a wife," the Frenchman replied with a smile. "She screams at me all the time. Actually," he said, when the tired chuckles subsided, "I had my hand over one ear, the other pressed against my shoulder, and my eyes closed. I also controlled the detonation," he added. Unlike Tomlinson and the rest, he could anticipate the noise and the flash, which seemed a minor advantage, but a decisive one.

"Any other problems going in?" John asked.

"The usual," Price said. "Lots of glass on the floor, hinders one's footing—maybe softer soles on our boots? That would also make our steps quieter."

Clark nodded, and saw that Stanley made a note.

"Any problems shooting?"

"No." This was Chavez. "The interior was lighted, and so we didn't need our NVGs. The bad guys were standing up like good targets. The shots were easy." Price and Loiselle nodded agreement.

"Riflemen?" Clark asked.

"Couldn't see shit from my perch," Johnston said.

"Neither could I," Weber said. His English was eerily perfect.

"Ding, you sent Price in first. Why?" This was Stanley.

"Eddie's a better shot, and he has more experience. I trust him a little more than I trust myself—for now," Chavez added. "It seemed to be a simple mission all the way around. Everyone had the interior layout, and it was an easy one. I split the objective into three areas of responsibility. Two I could see. The third only had one subject in it—that was something of a guess on my part, but all of our information supported it. We had to move in fast because the principal subject, Model, was about to kill a hostage. I saw no reason to allow him to do that," Chavez concluded.

"Anyone take issue with that?" John asked the assembled group.

"There will be times when one might have to allow a terrorist to kill a hostage," Dr. Bellow said soberly. "It will not be pleasant, but it will occasionally be necessary."

"Okay, doc, any observations?"

"John, we need to follow the police investigation of these subjects. Were they terrorists or robbers? We don't know. I think we need to find out. We were not able to conduct any negotiations. In this case it probably did not matter, but in the future it will. We need more translators to work with. My language skills are not up to what we need, and I need translators who speak my language, good at nuance and stuff." Clark saw Stanley make a note of that, too. Then he checked his watch.

"Okay. We'll go over the videotapes tomorrow morning. For now, good job, people. Dismissed."

Team-2 walked outside into a night that was starting to fog up. Some looked in the direction of the NCO Club, but none headed that way. Chavez walked toward his house. On opening the door, he found Patsy sitting up in front of the TV.

"Hi, honey," Ding told his wife.

"You okay?"

Chavez managed a smile, lifting his hands and turning around. "No holes or scratches anywhere."

"It was you on the TV—in Switzerland, I mean?"

"You know I'm not supposed to say."

"Ding, I've known what daddy does since I was twelve," Dr. Patricia Chavez, M.D., pointed out. "You know, Secret Agent Man, just like you."

There was no sense in concealment, was there? "Well, Patsy, yeah, that was me and my team."

"Who were they—the bad guys, I mean?"

"Maybe terrorists, maybe bank robbers. Not sure," Chavez said, stripping off his shirt on the way to the bedroom.

Patsy followed him inside. "The TV said they were all killed."

"Yep." He took his slacks off and hung them in the closet. "No choice. They were about to kill a hostage when it went down. So . . . we had to go in and stop that from happening."

"I'm not sure if I like that."

He looked up at his wife. "I *am* sure. I don't like it. Remember that guy when you were in medical school, the leg that got amputated, and you assisted in the surgery? You didn't like it, did you?"

"No, not at all." It had been an auto accident, and the leg just too mangled to save.

"That's life, Patsy. You don't like all the things you have to do." With that, Chavez sat down on the bed and tossed his socks at the open-top hamper. *Secret Agent Man,* he thought. *Supposed to have a vodka martini, shaken not stirred, now, but the movies never showed the hero going to bed to get* sleep, *did they? But who wants to get laid right after killing somebody?* That was worth an ironic chuckle, and he lay back on top of the covers. *Bond. James Bond. Sure.* As soon as he closed his eyes, he saw again the sight-picture from the bank, and relived the moment, bringing his MP-10 to bear, lining up the sights on whoever the hell it was—Guttenach was his name, wasn't it? He realized he hadn't checked. Seeing the head right there in the ringed sight, and squeezing off the burst as routinely as zipping his pants after taking a leak. Puff puff puff. That fast, that quiet with the suppresser on the gun, and *zap,* whoever the hell he was, was dead as yesterday's fish. He and his three friends hadn't had much of a chance—in fact, they'd had no chance at all.

But the guy they'd murdered earlier hadn't had a chance, either, Chavez reminded himself. Some poor unlucky bastard who'd happened to be in the bank, making a deposit, or talking to a loan officer, or maybe just getting change for a haircut. *Save your sympathy for that one,* Ding told himself. And the doctor Model had been ready to kill was now in his home, probably, with his wife and family, probably half-wasted on booze, or maybe a sedative, probably going through a really bad case of the shakes, probably thinking about spending some time with a shrink friend to help get him through the delayed stress. Probably feeling pretty fucking awful. But you had to be alive to feel something, and that beat the shit out of having his wife and kids sitting in the living room of their house outside Bern, crying their eyes out and asking why daddy wasn't around anymore.

Yeah. He'd taken a life, but he'd redeemed another. With that thought, he revisited the sight-picture, remembering now the sight of the first round hitting the asshole just forward of the ear, knowing then that he was dead, even before rounds #2 and #3 hit, in a circle of less than two inches across, blowing his brains ten feet the other way, and the body going down like a sack of beans. The way the man's gun had hit the floor, muzzle angled up, and thankfully it hadn't gone off and hurt anyone, and the head shots hadn't caused his fingers to spasm closed and pull the trigger from the grave—a real hazard, he'd learned in training. But still it was unsatisfactory. Better to get them alive and pick their brains for what they knew, and why they acted the way they did. That way you could learn stuff you could use the next time—or, just maybe—go after someone else, the bastard who gave the orders, and fill his ass with ten-millimeter hollowpoints.

The mission hadn't been perfect, Chavez had to admit to himself, but, ordered in to save a life, he'd saved that life. And that, he decided, would have to do for now. A moment later he felt the bed move as his wife lay beside him. He reached over for her hand, which she moved immediately to her belly. So, the little Chavez was doing some more laps. That, Ding decided, was worth a kiss, which he rolled over to deliver.

POPOV, too, was settled into his bed, having knocked back four stiff vodkas while watching the local television news, followed by an editorial panegyric to the efficiency of the local police. As yet they weren't giving out the identity of the robbers—that was how the crime was being reported, somewhat to Popov's disappointment, though on reflection he didn't know why. He'd established his bona fides for his employer . . . and pocketed a considerable sum of money in the bargain. A few more performances like this one and he could live like a king in Russia, or a prince in many other countries. He could know for himself the comfort he'd so often seen and envied while he was a field intelligence officer with the former KGB, wondering then how the hell his country could ever defeat nations which spent billions on amusement in addition to billions more on military hardware, all of which was better than anything his nation had produced—else why would he have so often been tasked to discovering their technical secrets? That was how he'd worked during the last few years of the Cold War, knowing even then who would win and who would lose.

But defection had never been an option. What was the point in selling out his country for a minor stipend and an ordinary job in the West? Freedom? That was the word the West still pretended to worship. What was the good of being able to wander around at liberty when you didn't have a proper automobile in which to do it? Or a good hotel in which to sleep when one got there? Or the money to buy the food and drink one needed to enjoy life properly? No, his first trip to the West as an "illegal" field officer without a diplomatic cover had been to London, where he'd spent much of his time counting the expensive cars, and the efficient black taxis one took when too lazy to walk—his important movement had been in the "tube," which was convenient, anonymous, and cheap. But "cheap" was a virtue for which he had little affection. No, capitalism had the singular virtue of rewarding people who had chosen the correct parents, or had been lucky in business. Rewarding them with luxury, convenience, and comfort undreamed of by the czars themselves. And *that* was what Popov had instantly craved, and wondered even then how he might get it. A nice expensive car—a Mercedes was the one he'd always desired—and a proper large flat close to good restaurants, and money to travel to places where the sand was warm and the sky blue, the better to attract women to his side, as Henry Ford must have done, he was sure. What was the point of having that sort of power without the will to use it?

Well, Popov told himself, he was closer than ever to realizing it. All he had to do was set up a few more jobs like this one in Bern. If his employer was willing to pay that much money for fools—well, a fool and his money were soon parted; a Western aphorism he found delightfully appropriate. And Dmitriy Arkadeyevich was no fool. With that satisfied thought, he lifted his remote and turned his TV off. Tomorrow, wake up, breakfast, make his bank deposit, and then take a cab to the airport for the Swissair flight to New York. First class. Of course.

"WELL, Al?" Clark asked over a pint of dark British beer. They were sitting in the rear-corner booth.

"Your Chavez is all he was reported to be. Clever of him to let Price take the lead. He doesn't let ego get in the way. I like that in a young officer. His timing was right. His division of the floor plan was right, and his shots were bang on. He'll do. So will the team. So much the better that the first time out was an easy one. This Model chappie wasn't a rocket scientist, as you say."

"Vicious bastard."

Stanley nodded. "Quite. The German terrorists frequently were. We should get a nice letter from the BKA about this one, as well."

"Lessons learned?"

"Dr. Bellow's was the best. We need more and better translators if we're to get him involved in negotiations. I'll get to work on that tomorrow. Century House ought to have people we can use. Oh, yes, that Noonan lad—"

"A late addition. He was a techie with the FBI. They used him on the Hostage Rescue Team for technical backup. Sworn agent, knows how to shoot, with some investigative experience," Clark explained. "Good all-around man to have with us."

"Nice job planting his video-surveillance equipment. I've looked at the videotapes already. They're not bad. On the whole, John, full marks for Team-2." Stanley saluted with his jar of John Courage.

"Nice to see that everything works, Al."

"Until the next one."

A long breath. "Yeah." Most of the success, Clark knew, was due to the British. He'd made use of their support systems, and their men had actually led the takedown—two-thirds of it. Louis Loiselle was every bit as good as the French had claimed. The little bastard could shoot like Davy Crockett with an attitude, and was about as excitable as a rock. Well, the French had their own terrorist experiences, and once upon a time Clark had gone out into the field with them. So, this one would go into the records as a successful mission. Rainbow was now certified. And so, Clark knew, was he.

THE Society of Cincinnatus owned a large house on Massachusetts Avenue that was frequently used for the semi-official dinners that were so vital a part of the Washington social scene, and allowed the mighty to cross paths and validate their status over drinks and small talk. The new President made that somewhat difficult, of course, with his . . . eccentric approach to government, but no person could really change that much in this city, and the new crop in Congress needed to learn how Washington Really Worked. It was no different from other places around America, of course, and to many of them the gatherings at this former dwelling of somebody rich and important was merely the new version of the country club dinners where they'd learned the rules of polite-power society.

Carol Brightling was one of the new important people. A divorcée for over ten years who'd never remarried, she had no less than three doctorates, from Harvard, CalTech, and the University of Illinois, thus covering both coasts and three important states, which was an important accomplishment in this city, as that guaranteed her the instant attention, if not the automatic affection, of six senators and a larger number of congressmen, all of whom had votes and committees.

"Catch the news," the junior senator from Illinois asked her over a glass of white wine.

"What do you mean?"

"Switzerland. Either a terrorist thing or a bank robbery. Nice takedown by the Swiss cops."

"Boys and their guns," Brightling observed dismissively.

"It made for good TV."

"So does football," Brightling noted, with a gentle, nasty smile.

"True. Why isn't the President supporting you on Global Warming?" the senator asked next, wondering how to crack her demeanor.

"Well, he isn't *not* supporting me. The President thinks we need some additional science on the issue."

"And you don't?"

"Honestly, no, I think we have all the science we need. The top-down and bottom-up data are pretty clear. But the President isn't convinced himself, and does not feel comfortable with taking measures that affect the economy until he is personally sure." *I have to work on him some more,* she didn't add.

"Are you happy with that?"

"I see his point," the Science Advisor replied, surprising the senator from the Land of Lincoln. So, he thought, everyone who worked in the White House toed the line with this president. Carol Brightling had been a surprise appointment to the White House staff, her politics very different from the President's, respected as she was in the scientific community for her environmental views. It had been an adroit political move, probably engineered by Chief of Staff Arnold van Damm, arguably the most skillful political operator in this city of maneuvering, and had secured for the President the (qualified) support of the environmental movement, which had turned into a political force of no small magnitude in Washington.

"Does it bother you that the President is out in South Dakota slaughtering geese?" the senator asked with a chuckle, as a waiter replaced his drink.

"*Homo sapiens* is a predator," Brightling replied, scanning the room for others.

"But only the men?"

A smile. "Yes, we women are far more peaceful."

"Oh, that's your ex-husband over there in the corner, isn't it?" the senator asked, surprised at the change in her face when he said it.

"Yes." The voice neutral, showing no emotion, as she turned to face in another direction. Having spotted him, she needed to do no more. Both knew the rules. No closer than thirty feet, no lengthy eye contact, and certainly no words.

"I had the chance to put money into Horizon Corporation two years ago. I've kicked myself quite a few times since."

"Yes, John has made quite a pile for himself."

And well after their divorce, so she didn't get a nickel out of it. Probably not a good topic for conversation, the senator thought at once. He was new at the job, and not the best at politic conversation.

"Yes, he's done well, twisting science the way he has."

"You don't approve?"

"Restructuring DNA in plants and animals—no. Nature has evolved without our assistance for two billion years at least. I doubt that it needs help from us."

" 'There are some things man is not meant to know'?" the senator asked with a chuckle. His professional background was in contracting, in gouging holes in the ground and erecting something that nature didn't want there, though his sensitivity on environmental issues, Dr. Brightling thought, had itself evolved from his love of Washington and his desire to remain here in a position of power. It was called Potomac Fever, a disease easily caught and less easily cured.

"The problem, Senator Hawking, is that nature is both complex and subtle. When we change things, we cannot easily predict the ramifications of the changes. It's called the Law of Unintended Consequences, something with which the Congress is familiar, isn't it?"

"You mean—"

"I mean that the reason we have a federal law about environmental impact statements is that it's far easier to mess things up than it is to get them right. In the case of recombinant DNA, we can more easily change the genetic code than we can evaluate the effects those changes will cause a century from now. That sort of power is one that should be used with the greatest possible care. Not everyone seems to grasp that simple fact."

Which point was difficult to argue with, the senator had to concede gracefully. Brightling would be making that case before his committee in another week. Had that been the thing that had broken up the marriage of John and Carol Brightling? How very sad. With that observation, the senator made his excuses and headed off to join his wife.

"THERE'S nothing new in that point of view." John Brightling's doctorate in molecular biology came from the University of Virginia, along with his M.D. "It started with a guy named Ned Ludd a few centuries ago. He was afraid that the Industrial Revolution would put an end to the cottage-industry economy in England. And he was right. That economic model was wrecked. But what replaced it was better for the consumer, and that's why we call it *progress!*" Not surprisingly, John Brightling, a billionaire heading for number two, was holding court before a small crowd of admirers.

"But the complexity—" One of the audience started to object.

"Happens every day—every second, in fact. And so do the things we're trying to conquer. Cancer, for example. No, madam, are you willing to put an end to our work if it means no cure for breast cancer? That disease strikes five percent of the human population worldwide. Cancer is a *genetic* disease. The key to curing it is in the human genome. And my company is going to find that key! Aging is the same thing. Salk's team at La Jolla found the kill-me gene more than fifteen years ago. If we can find a way to turn it off, then human immortality can be real. Madam, does the idea of living forever in a body of twenty-five years' maturity appeal to you?"

"But what about overcrowding?" The congresswoman's objection was somewhat quieter than her first. It was too vast a thought, too surprisingly posed, to allow an immediate objection.

"One thing at a time. The invention of DDT killed off huge quantities of disease-bearing insects, and *that* increased populations all over the world, didn't it? Okay, we are a little more crowded now, but who wants to bring the anopheles mosquito back? Is malaria a reasonable method of population control? Nobody here wants to bring war back, right? We used to use that, too, to control populations. We got over it, didn't we? Hell, controlling populations is no big deal. It's called birth control, and the advanced countries have already learned how to do it, and the backward countries can, too, *if* they have a good reason for doing so. It might take a generation or so," John Brightling mused, "but is there anyone here who would not want to be twenty-five again—*with* all the things we've learned along the way, of course. It damned well appeals to me!" he went on with a warm smile. With sky-high salaries and promises of stóck options, his company had assembled an incredible team of talent to look at that particular gene. The profits that would accrue from its control could hardly be estimated, and the U.S. patent was good for seventeen years! Human immortality, the new Holy Grail for the medical community—and for the first time, it was something for serious investigation, not a topic of pulp science-fiction stories.

"You think you can do it?" another congresswoman—this one from San Francisco—asked. Women of all sorts found themselves drawn to this man. Money, power, good looks, and good manners made it inevitable.

John Brightling smiled broadly. "Ask me in five years. We know the gene. We need to learn how to turn it off. There's a whole lot of basic science in there we have to uncover, and along the way we hope to discover a lot of very useful things. It's like setting off with Magellan. We aren't sure what we're going to find, but we know it'll all be interesting." No one pointed out that Magellan hadn't made it home from that particular trip.

"And profitable?" a new senator from Wyoming asked.

"That's how our society works, isn't it? We pay people for doing useful work. Is this area useful enough?"

"If you bring it off, I suppose it is." This senator was himself a physician, a family practitioner who knew the basics but was well over his head on the deep-scientific side. The concept, the objective of Horizon Corporation, was well beyond breathtaking, but he would not bet against them. They'd done too well developing cancer drugs and synthetic antibiotics, and were the leading private company in the Human Genome Project, a global effort to decode the basics of human life. Himself a genius, John Brightling had found it easy to attract others like himself to his company. He had more charisma than a hundred politicians, and unlike the latter, the senator had to admit to himself, he really had something to back up the showmanship. It had once been called "the right stuff" for pilots. With his movie star looks, ready smile, superb listening ability, and dazzlingly analytical mind, Dr. John Brightling had the knack. He could make anyone near him feel interesting—and the bastard could *teach,* could apply his lessons to everyone nearby. Simple ones for the unschooled and highly sophisticated ones for the specialists in his field, at the top of which he reigned supreme. Oh, he had a few peers. Pat Reily at Harvard-Mass General. Aaron Bernstein at Johns Hopkins. Jacques Elisé at Pasteur. Maybe Paul Ging at U.C. Berkeley. But that was it. What a fine clinician Brightling might have made, the senator-M.D. thought, but, no, he was too good to be wasted on people with the latest version of the flu.

About the only thing in which he'd failed was his marriage. Well, Carol Brightling was also pretty smart, but more political than scientific, and perhaps her ego, capacious as everyone in this city knew it to be, had quailed before the greater intellectual gifts of her husband. Only room in town for one of us, the doctor from Wyoming thought, with an inner smile. That happened often enough in real life, not just on old movies. And Brightling, John, seemed to be doing better in that respect than Brightling, Carol. At the former's elbow was a very pretty redhead drinking in his every word, while the latter had come alone, and would be leaving alone for her apartment in Georgetown. Well, the senator-M.D. thought, that's life.

Immortality. Damn, all the pronghorns he might take, the doctor from Cody thought on, heading over to his wife. Dinner was about to start. The chicken had finished the vulcanization process.

THE Valium helped. It wasn't actually Valium, Killgore knew. That drug had become something of a generic name for mild sedatives, and this one had been developed by SmithKline, with a different trade name, with the added benefit that it made a good mix with alcohol. For street people who were often as contentious and territorial as junkyard dogs, this group of ten was remarkably sedate. The large quantities of good booze helped. The high-end bourbons seemed the most popular libations, drunk from cheap glasses with ice, along with various mixers for those who didn't care to drink it neat. Most didn't, to Killgore's surprise.

The physicals had gone well. They were all healthy-sick people, outwardly fairly vigorous, but inwardly all with physical problems ranging from diabetes to liver failure. One was definitely suffering from prostate cancer—his PSA was off the top of the chart—but that wouldn't matter in this particular test, would it? Another was HIV+, but not yet symptomatic, and so that didn't matter either. He'd probably gotten it from drug use, but strangely, liquor seemed all he needed to keep himself regulated here. How interesting.

Killgore didn't have to be here, and it troubled his conscience to look at them so much, but they were *his* lab rats, and he was supposed to keep an eye on them, and so he did, behind the mirror, while he did his paperwork and listened to Bach on his portable CD player. Three were—claimed to be—Vietnam veterans. So they'd killed their share of Asians—"gooks" was the word they'd used in the interview—before coming apart and ending up as street drunks. Well, *homeless people* was the current term society used for them, somewhat more dignified than *bums,* the term Killgore vaguely remembered his mother using. Not the best example of humanity he'd ever seen. Yet the Project had managed to change them quite a bit. All bathed regularly now and dressed in clean clothes and watched TV. Some even read books from time to time—Killgore had thought that providing a library, while cheap, was an outrageously foolish waste of time and money. But always they drank, and the drinking relegated each of the ten to perhaps six hours of full consciousness per day. And the Valium calmed them further, limiting any altercations that his security staff would have to break up. Two of them were always on duty in the next room over, also watching the group of ten. Microphones buried in the ceiling allowed them to listen in to the disjointed conversations. One of the group was something of an authority on baseball and talked about Mantle and Maris all the time to whoever would listen. Enough of them talked about sex that Killgore wondered if he should send the snatch team back out to get some female "homeless" subjects for the experiment—he would tell Barb Archer that. After all, they needed to know if gender had an effect on the experiment. She'd *have* to buy into that one, wouldn't she? And there'd be none of the sisterly solidarity with them. There couldn't be, even from the feminazi who joined him in running this experiment. Her ideology was too pure for that. Killgore turned when there came a knock at the door.

"Hey, doc." It was Benny, one of the security guys.

"Hey, how's it going?"

"Falling asleep," Benjamin Farmer replied. "The kids are playing pretty nice."

"Yeah, they sure are." It was *so* easy. Most had to be prodded a little to leave the room and go out to the courtyard for an hour of walking around every afternoon. But they had to be kept fit—which was to say, to simulate the amount of exercise they got on a normal day in Manhattan, staggering from one dreary corner to another.

"Damn, doc, I never knew *anybody* could put it away the way these guys do! I mean, I had to bring in a whole case of Grand-Dad today, and there's only two bottles left."

"That their favorite?" Killgore asked. He hadn't paid much attention to that.

"Seems to be, sir. I'm a Jack Daniel's man myself—but with me, maybe two a night, say, for Monday Night Football, if it's a good game. I don't drink *water* the way the kids drink hard booze." A chuckle from the ex-Marine who ran the night security shift. A good man, Farmer. He did a lot of things with injured animals at the company's rural shelter. He was also the one who'd taken to calling the test subjects *the kids*. It had caught on with the security staff and from them to the others. Killgore chuckled. You had to call them something, and lab rats just wasn't respectful enough. After all, they were human beings, after a fashion, all the more valuable for their place in this test. He turned to see one of them—#6—pour himself another drink, wander back to his bed, and lie down to watch some TV before he passed out. He wondered what the poor bastard would dream about. Some did, and talked loudly in their sleep. Something to interest a psychiatrist, perhaps, or someone doing sleep studies. They *all* snored, to the point that when all were asleep it sounded like an old steam-powered railroad yard in there.

Choo choo, Killgore thought, looking back down at his last bit of paperwork. Ten more minutes, and he could head home. Too late to put his kids to bed. Too bad. Well, in due course they would awaken to a new day and a new world, and wouldn't that be some present to give them, however heavy and nasty the price for it might be. Hmph, the physician thought, I could use a drink myself.

▪ ▪ ▪

"THE future has never been so bright as this," John Brightling told his audience, his demeanor even more charismatic after two glasses of a select California Chardonnay. "The bio-sciences are pushing back frontiers we didn't even know existed fifteen years ago. A hundred years of basic research are coming to bloom even as we speak. We're building on the work of Pasteur, Ehrlich, Salk, Sabin, and so many others. We see so far today because we stand on the shoulders of giants.

"Well," John Brightling went on, "it's been a long climb, but the top of the mountain is in sight, and we *will* get there in the next few years."

"He's smooth," Liz Murray observed to her husband.

"Very," FBI Director Dan Murray whispered back. "Smart, too. Jimmy Hicks says he's the top guy in the world."

"What's he running for?"

"God, from what he said earlier."

"Needs to grow a beard then."

Director Murray nearly choked at that, then he was saved by the vibrating of his cellular phone. He discreetly left his seat to walk into the building's large marble foyer. On flipping his phone open, it took fifteen seconds for the encryption system to synchronize with the base station calling him—which told him that it was FBI Headquarters.

"Murray."

"Director, this is Gordon Sinclair in the Watch Center. So far the Swiss have struck out on ID-ing the other two. Prints are on their way to the BKA so they can take a look." But if they hadn't been printed somewhere along the line, that, too, would be a dry hole, and it would take a while to identify Model's two pals.

"No additional casualties on the takedown?"

"No, sir, all four bad guys down for the count. All hostages safe and evacuated. They should all be back home now. Oh, Tim Noonan deployed on this operation, electronics weenie for one of the go-teams."

"So, Rainbow works, eh?"

"It did this time, Director," Sinclair judged.

"Make sure they send us the write-up on how the operation went down."

"Yes, sir. I already e-mailed them about that." Less than thirty people in the Bureau knew about Rainbow, though quite a few would be making guesses. Especially those HRT members who'd taken note of the fact that Tim Noonan, a third-generation agent, had dropped off the face of the earth. "How's dinner going?"

"I prefer Wendy's. More of the basic food groups. Anything else?"

"The OC case in New Orleans is close to going down, Billy Betz says. Three or four more days. Aside from that, nothing important happening."

"Thanks, Gordy." Murray thumbed the END button on his phone and pocketed it, then returned to the dining room after a look and a wave at two members of his protective detail. Thirty seconds later, he slid back into his seat, with a muted thump from his holstered Smith & Wesson automatic against the wood.

"Anything important?" Liz asked.

A shake of the head. "Routine."

The affair broke up less than forty minutes after Brightling finished his speech and collected his award plaque. He held court yet again, albeit with a smaller group of fans this time, while drifting toward the door, outside of which waited his car. It was only five minutes to the Hay-Adams Hotel, across Lafayette Park from the White House. He had a corner suite on the top floor, and the hotel staff had thoughtfully left him a bottle of the house white in an ice bucket next to the bed, for his companion had come along. It was sad, Dr. John Brightling thought, removing the cork. He'd miss things like this, really miss them. But he had made the decision long before—not knowing when he'd started off that it could possibly work. Now he thought that it would, and the things he'd miss were ultimately of far less value than the things he'd get. And for the moment, he thought, looking at Jessica's pale skin and stunning figure, he'd get something else that was pretty nice.

IT was different for Dr. Carol Brightling. Despite her White House job, she drove her own car without even a bodyguard to her apartment off Wisconsin Avenue in Georgetown, her only companion there a calico cat named Jiggs, who, at least, came to the door to meet her, rubbing his body along her pantyhosed leg the moment the door was closed, and purring to show his pleasure at her arrival. He followed her into the bedroom, watching her change in the way of cats, interested and detached at the same time, and knowing what came next. Dressed only in a short robe, Carol Brightling walked into the kitchen, opened a cupboard, and got a treat, which she bent down to feed to Jiggs from her hand. Then she got herself a glass of ice water from the refrigerator door, and drank it down with two aspirin. It had all been her idea. She knew that all too well. But after so many years, it was still as hard as it had been at first. She'd given up so much more. She'd gotten the job she'd craved—somewhat to her surprise, as things had turned out, but she had the office in the right building, and now played a role in making policy on the issues that were important to her. Important policy on important topics. But was it worth it?

Yes! She had to think that, and, truly, she believed it, but the price, the price of it, was often so hard to bear. She bent down to lift up Jiggs, cradling him like the child she'd never had and walking to the bedroom where, again, he'd be the only one to share it with her. Well, a cat was far more faithful than a man could ever be. She'd learned that lesson over the years. In a few seconds, the robe was on the chair next to the bed, and she under the covers, with Jiggs atop them and between her legs. She hoped sleep would come a little more quickly tonight than it usually did. But she knew it would not, for her mind would not stop thinking about what was happening in another bed less than three miles away.

CHAPTER 5

RAMIFICATIONS

DAILY PT STARTED AT 0630 AND CONCLUDED WITH the five-mile run, timed to last exactly forty minutes. This morning it ended at thirty-eight, and Chavez wondered if he and his team had an additional spring in their step from the successful mission. If so, was that good or bad? Killing fellow human beings wasn't supposed to make you feel good, was it? A deep thought for a foggy English morning.

By the end of the run, everyone had a good sweat, which the hot showers took care of. Oddly, hygiene was a little more complicated for his team than for uniformed soldiers. Nearly everyone had longer hair than their respective armies permitted, so that they could look like grown-up, if somewhat shabby, businessmen when they donned their coats and ties for their first-class flights to wherever. Ding's hair was the shortest, since at CIA he'd tried to keep it not too different from his time as staff sergeant in the Ninjas. It would have to grow for at least another month before it would be shaggy enough. He grunted at that thought, then stepped out of the shower. As Team-2 leader, he rated his own private facility, and he took the time to admire his body, always an object of pride for Domingo Chavez. Yeah, the exercise that had been so tough the first week had paid off. He hadn't been much tougher than this in Ranger School at Fort Benning—and he'd been, what? Twenty-one then, just an E-4 and one of the smallest men in the class. It was something of an annoyance to Ding that, tall and rangy like her mom, Patsy had half an inch on him. But Patsy only wore flats, which kept it respectable—and nobody messed with him. Like his boss, he had the look of a man with whom one did not trifle. Especially this morning, he thought, while toweling off. He'd zapped a guy the previous night, just as fast and automatic an action as zipping his zipper. Tough shit, Herr Guttenach.

Back home, Patsy was already dressed in her greens. She was on an OB/GYN rotation at the moment, scheduled to perform—well, to assist on—a Cesarean section this morning at the local hospital where she was completing what in America would have been her year of internship. Next would be her pediatric rotation, which struck both of them as totally appropriate. Already on the table for him was bacon and eggs—the eggs in England seemed to have brighter yolks. He wondered if they fed their chickens differently here.

"I wish you'd eat better," Patsy observed, again.

Domingo laughed, reaching for his morning paper, the *Daily Telegraph*. "Honey, my cholesterol is one-three-zero, my resting heart-rate is fifty-six. I am a lean, mean fighting machine, doctor!"

"But what about ten years from now?" Patricia Chavez, M.D., asked.

"I'll have ten complete physicals between now and then, and I will adjust my lifestyle according to how those work out," Domingo Chavez, Master of Science (International Relations), answered, buttering his toast. The bread in this country, he'd learned over the past six weeks, was just fabulous. Why did people knock English food? "Hell, Patsy, look at your dad. That old bastard is still in great shape." Though he hadn't run this morning—and at his best was hard-pressed to finish the five miles at the pace Team-2 set. Well, he was well over fifty. His shooting, however, hadn't suffered very much at all. John had worked to make that clear to the go-team members. One of the best pistoleros Chavez had ever seen, and better still with a sniper rifle. He was dead-level with Weber and Johnston out to 400 meters. Despite the suit he wore to work, Rainbow Six was on everyone's don't-fuck-with list.

The front page had a story on the previous day's events in Bern. Ding raced through it and found most of the details right. Remarkable. The *Telegraph*'s correspondent must have had good contacts with the cops . . . whom he gave credit for the takedown. Well, that was okay. Rainbow was supposed to remain black. No comment from the Ministry of Defense on whether the SAS had provided support to the Swiss police. That was a little weak. A flat "no" would have been better . . . but were that to be said, then a "no comment" spoken at some other time would be taken as a "yes." So, yeah, that probably made sense. Politics was not a skill he'd acquired yet, at least not on the instinctive level. Dealing with the media frightened him more than facing loaded weapons—he had training for the latter but not for the former. His next grimace came when he realized that while CIA had an office of public affairs, Rainbow sure as hell didn't. Well, in this business it probably didn't pay to advertise. About that time, Patsy put on her jacket and headed for the door. Ding hurried after her to deliver the goodbye kiss, watched his wife walk to the family car, and hoped she did better driving on the left side of the road than he did. It made him slightly nuts and required steady concentration. The really crazy part was that the gearshift was in the middle, the wrong side of the car, but the pedals were the same as in American autos. It made Chavez a little schizophrenic, driving left-handed and right-footed. The worst part was the traffic circles the Brits seemed to like better than real interchanges. Ding kept wanting to turn right instead of left. It would be a hell of a stupid way to get killed. Ten minutes later, dressed in his day uniform, Chavez walked over to the Team-2 building for the second AAR.

POPOV tucked his passbook in his coat pocket. The Swiss banker hadn't even blinked at seeing the suitcase full of cash. A remarkable machine had counted the bills, like mechanical fingers riffling through a deck of playing cards, even checking the denominations as it did the counting. It had taken a total of forty-five minutes to get things fully arranged. The number on the account was his old KGB service number, and tucked in the passbook was the banker's business card, complete with his Internet address for making wire transfers—the proper code-phrase had been agreed upon and written into his bank file. The topic of Model's failed adventure of the previous day hadn't come up. Popov figured he'd read the press reports in the *International Herald Tribune,* which he'd get at the airport.

His passport was American. The company had arranged to get him resident-alien status, and he was on his way to citizenship, which he found amusing, as he still had his Russian Federation passport, and two others from his previous career—with different names but the same photo—which he could still use if needed. Those were stashed in his travel briefcase, in a small compartment that only a very careful customs examiner would ever find, and then only if told ahead of time that there was something strange about the incoming traveler.

Two hours before his flight was scheduled to depart, he turned in his rental car, rode the bus to the international terminal, went through the usual rigmarole of checking in, and headed off to the first-class lounge for coffee and a croissant.

BILL Henriksen was a news junkie of the first order. On waking up, early as always, he immediately flipped his TV to CNN, often flipping to Fox News with his remote while he did his morning treadmill routine, frequently with a paper on the reading board as well. The front page on the *The New York Times* covered the event in Bern, as did Fox news—oddly, CNN talked about it but didn't show much. Fox did, using the feed from Swiss television, which allowed him to watch what could be seen of the takedown. Pure vanilla, Henriksen thought. Flash-bangs on the front doors—made the cameraman jump and go slightly off-target, as usual when they were that close—shooters in right behind them. No sounds of gunfire—they used suppressed weapons. In five seconds, it was all over. So, the Swiss had a properly trained SWAT team. No real surprise there, though he hadn't really known about it. A few minutes later, one guy came out and lit a pipe. Whoever that was, probably the team commander, he had a little style, Henriksen thought, checking the mileage on the treadmill. The team dressed as such people usually did, in coal-gray fatigues, with Kevlar body armor. Uniformed cops went in to get the hostages out after about the right amount of time. Yeah, nicely and smoothly done—another way of saying that the criminals/terrorists—the news wasn't clear on whether they were just robbers or political types—weren't real smart. Well, whoever said they were? They'd have to choose better ones the next time if this thing were going to work. The phone would ring in a few minutes, he was sure, summoning him to do a brief TV spot. A nuisance but a necessary one.

That happened when he was in the shower. He'd long since had a phone installed just outside the door.

"Yeah."

"Mr. Henriksen?"

"Yeah, who's this?" The voice wasn't familiar.

"Bob Smith at Fox News New York. Have you seen coverage of the incident in Switzerland?"

"Yeah, matter of fact I just saw it on your network."

"Any chance you could come in and give us some commentary?"

"What time?" Henriksen asked, knowing the response, and what his answer would be.

"Just after eight, if you could."

He even checked his watch, an automatic and wasted gesture that nobody saw. "Yeah, I can do that. How long will I be on this time?"

"Probably four minutes or so."

"Okay, I'll be down there in about an hour."

"Thank you, sir. The guard will be told to expect you."

"Okay, see you in an hour." The kid must be new, Henriksen thought, not to know that he was a regular commentator—why else would his name have been in the Fox rolodex?—and that the security guards all knew him by sight.

A quick cup of coffee and a bagel got him out the door, into his Porsche 911, and across the George Washington Bridge to Manhattan.

DR. Carol Brightling awoke, patted Jiggs on the top of his head, and stepped into the shower. Ten minutes later, a towel wrapped around her head, she opened the door and got the morning papers. The coffee machine had already made its two cups of Mountain-Grown Folger's, and in the refrigerator was the plastic box full of melon sections. Next she switched on the radio to catch the morning edition of *All Things Considered,* beginning her news fix, which started here and would go on through most of the day. Her job in the White House was mainly reading . . . and today she had to meet with that bozo from the Department of Energy who still thought it important to build H-bombs, which she would advise the President against, which advice he would probably decline without direct comment to her.

Why the hell had she been taken in by this administration? Carol wondered. The answer was simple and obvious: politics. This president had tried valiantly to avoid such entanglements in his year and a half of holding office. And she was female, whereas the President's team of insiders was almost entirely male, which had caused some comment in the media and elsewhere, which had befuddled the President in his political innocence, which had amused the press even more and given them a further tool to use, which had worked, after a fashion. And so she had been offered the appointment, and taken it, with the office in the Old Executive Office Building instead of the White House itself, with a secretary and an assistant, and a parking place on West Executive Drive for her fuel-efficient six-year-old Honda—the *only* Japanese-made car on that particular block, which *nobody* had said anything about, of course, since she was female, and she'd forgotten more about Washington politics than the President would ever learn. That was astounding when she thought about it, though she warned herself that the President was a notoriously quick learner. But not a good listener, at least as far as she was concerned.

The media let him get away with it. The lesson of that was that the media was nobody's friend. Lacking convictions of its own, it just published what people said, and so she had to speak, off the record, on deep background, or just casually, to various reporters. Some, those who covered the Environment regularly, at least understood the language, and for the most part could be trusted to write their pieces the proper way, but they always included the other side's rubbish science—*yes, maybe your position has merit, but the science isn't firm enough yet and the computer models are* not *accurate enough to justify this sort of action,* the other side said. As a result of which, the public's opinion—as measured in polls—had stagnated, or even reversed a little bit. The President was anything but an Environmental President, but the bastard was getting away with it—at the same time using Carol Brightling as political camouflage, or even political *cover!* That appalled her . . . or would have under other circumstances. But here she was, Dr. Brightling thought, zipping up her skirt before donning the suit-jacket, a senior advisor to the President of the United States. *That* meant she saw him a couple of times per week. It meant that he *read* her position papers and policy recommendations. It meant that she had *access* to the media's top-drawer people, free to pursue her own agenda . . . within reason.

But she was the one who paid the price. Always, it was she, Carol thought, reaching down to scratch Jiggs's ears as she made her way to the door. The cat would pass the day doing whatever it was that he did, mainly sleeping in the sun on the windowsill, probably waiting for his mistress to come home and feed him his Frisky treat. Not for the first time, she thought about stopping by a pet store and getting Jiggs a live mouse to play with and eat. A fascinating process to watch, predator and prey, playing their parts . . . the way the world was supposed to be; the way it had been for unnumbered centuries until the last two or so. Until Man had started changing everything, she thought, starting the car, looking at the cobblestoned street—still real cobbles for this traditional Georgetown address, with streetcar tracks still there, too—and brick buildings which had covered up what had probably been a pretty hardwood forest less than two hundred years before. It was even worse across the river, where only Theodore Roosevelt Island was still in its pristine state—and that was interfered with by the screech of jet engines. A minute later, she was on M Street, then around the circle onto Pennsylvania Avenue. She was ahead of the daily rush-hour traffic, as usual, heading the mile or so down the wide, straight street before she could turn right and find her parking place—they weren't reserved *per se,* but everyone had his or her own, and hers was forty yards from the West Entrance—and as a regular, she didn't have to submit to the dog search. The Secret Service used Belgian Malinois dogs—like brown German shepherds—keen of nose and quick of brain, to sniff at cars for explosives. Her White House pass got her into the compound, then up the steps into the OEOB, and right to her office. It was a cubbyhole, really, but larger than those of her secretary and assistant. On her desk was the *Early Bird,* with its clips of articles from various national newspapers deemed important to those who worked in this building, along with her copy of *Science Weekly, Science,* and, today, *Scientific American,* plus several medical journals. The environmental publications would arrive two days later. She hadn't yet sat down when her secretary, Margot Evans, came in with the codeword folder on nuclear-weapons policy, which she'd have to review before giving the President advice that he'd reject. The annoying part of that, of course, was that she'd have to think to produce the position paper that the President would not think about before rejecting. But she couldn't give him an excuse to accept, with great public reluctance, her resignation—rarely did anyone at this level ask to leave *per se,* though the local media had the mantras down and fully understood. Why not take it a step further than usual, and recommend the closure of the dirty reactor at Hanford, Washington? The only American reactor of the same design as Chernobyl—less a power reactor than one designed to produce plutonium—Pu^{239}—for nuclear weapons, the worst gadget the mind of war-like *men* had ever produced. There were new problems with Hanford, new leaks from the storage tanks there, discovered before the leakage could pollute ground water, but still a threat to the environment, expensive to fix. The chemical mix in those tanks was horribly corrosive, *and* lethally toxic, *and* radioactive . . . and the President wouldn't listen to that bit of sound advice either.

The science of her objections to Hanford was real, even Red Lowell worried about it—but *he* wanted a *new* Hanford built! Even this President wouldn't countenance that!

With that reassuring thought, Dr. Brightling poured herself a cup of coffee and started reading the *Early Bird,* while her mind pondered how she'd draft her doomed recommendation to the President.

"SO, Mr. Henriksen, who were they?" the morning anchor asked.

"We don't know much beyond the name of the purported leader, Ernst Model. Model was once part of the Baader-Meinhof gang, the notorious German communist terrorist group from the '70s and '80s. He dropped out of sight about ten years ago. It will be interesting to learn exactly where he's been hiding out."

"Did you have a file on him during your time with the FBI Hostage Rescue Team?"

A smile to accompany the terse reply. "Oh, yeah. I know the face, but Mr. Model will now transfer to the inactive files."

"So, was this a terrorist incident or just a bank robbery?"

"No telling as yet from press reports, but I would not entirely discount robbery as a motive. One of the things people forget about terrorists is that they have to eat, too, and you need money to do that. There is ample precedent for supposedly political criminals to break the law just to make money to support themselves. Right here in America, the CSA—the Covenant, the Sword and the Arm of the Lord, as they called themselves—robbed banks to support themselves. Baader-Meinhof in Germany used kidnappings to extort money from their victims' corporate and family ties."

"So, to you they're just criminals?"

A nod, and a serious expression. "Terrorism is a crime. That's dogma at the FBI, where I came up. And these four who got killed yesterday in Switzerland were criminals. Unfortunately for them, the Swiss police have assembled and trained what appears to be an excellent, professional special-operations team."

"How would you rate the takedown?"

"Pretty good. The TV coverage shows no errors at all. All the hostages were rescued, and the criminals all were killed. That's par for the course in an incident like this. In the abstract, you would like to take the criminals down alive if possible, but it is not always possible—the lives of the hostages have absolute priority in a case like this one."

"But the terrorists, don't they have rights—"

"As a matter of principle, yes, they do have the same rights as other criminals. We teach that at the FBI, too, and the best thing you can do as a law enforcement officer in a case like this one is to arrest them, put them in front of a judge and jury, and convict them, *but* remember that the hostages are innocent victims, and their lives are at risk *because of* the criminals' actions. Therefore, you try to give them a chance to surrender—really, you try to disarm them if you can.

"But very often you do not have that luxury," Henriksen went on. "Based on what I saw on TV from this incident, the Swiss police team acted no differently than what we were trained to do at Quantico. You only use deadly force when necessary—but when it's necessary, you do use it."

"But who decides when it's necessary?"

"The commander on the scene makes that decision, based on his training, experience, and expertise." *Then,* Henriksen didn't go on, *people like you second-guess the hell out of him for the next couple of weeks.*

"Your company trains local police forces in SWAT tactics, doesn't it?"

"Yes, it does. We have numerous veterans of the FBI HRT, Delta Force, and other 'special' organizations, and we could use this Swiss operation as a textbook example of how it's done," Henriksen said—because his was an international corporation, which trained foreign police forces as well, and being nice to the Swiss wouldn't hurt his bottom line one bit.

"Well, Mr. Henriksen, thanks for joining us this morning. International terrorism expert William Henriksen, CEO of Global Security, Inc., an international consulting firm. It's twenty-four minutes after the hour." In the studio, Henriksen kept his calm, professional face on until five seconds after the light on the nearest camera went out. At his corporate headquarters, they would have already taped this interview to add to the vast library of such things. GSI was known over most of the world, and their introductory tape included snippets from many such interviews. The floor director walked him off the set to the makeup room, where the powder was removed, then let him walk himself out to where his car was parked.

That had gone well, he thought, going through the mental checklist. He'd have to find out who'd trained the Swiss. He made a mental note to have one of his contacts chase that one down. If it were a private company, that was serious competition, though it was probably the Swiss army—perhaps even a military formation disguised as policemen—maybe with some technical assistance from the German GSG-9. A couple of phone calls should run that one down.

POPOV'S four-engine Airbus A-340 touched down on time at JFK International. You could always trust the Swiss to do everything on time. The police team had probably even had a schedule for the previous night's activities, he thought whimsically. His first-class seat was close to the door, which allowed him to be the third passenger out, then off to claim his bags and go through the ordeal of U.S. Customs. America, he'd long since learned, was the most difficult country to enter as a foreigner—though with his minimal baggage and nothing-to-declare entry, the process was somewhat easier this time. The customs clerks were kind and waved him right through to the cabstand, where, for the usual exorbitant fee, he engaged a Pakistani driver to take him into town, making him wonder idly if the cabbies had a deal with the customs people. But he was on an expense account—meaning he had to get a receipt—and, besides, he had ensured that day that he could afford such things without one, hadn't he? He smiled as he gazed at the passing urban sprawl. It got thicker and thicker on the way to Manhattan.

The cab dropped him off at his apartment house. The flat was paid for by his employer, which made it a tax-deductible business expense for them—Popov was learning about American tax law—and free for him. He spent a few minutes dumping his dirty laundry and hanging up his good clothes before heading downstairs and having the doorman flag a cab. From there it was another fifteen minutes to the office.

"So, how did it go?" the boss asked. There was an odd buzz in the office, designed to interfere with any listening devices that a corporate rival might place. Corporate espionage was a major factor in the life of this man's company, and the defenses against it were at least as good as those the KGB had used. And Popov had once believed that governments had the best of everything. That was certainly *not* true in America.

"It went much as I expected. They were foolish—really rather amateurish, despite all the training we gave them back in the eighties. I told them to feel free to rob the bank as cover for the real mission—"

"Which was?"

"To be killed," Dmitriy Arkadeyevich replied at once. "At least, that is what I understood your intentions to be, sir." His words occasioned a smile of a sort Popov wasn't used to. He made a note to check the stock value of the bank. Had the intention of this "mission" been to affect the standing of the bank? That didn't seen very likely, but though he didn't *need* to know why he was doing these things, his natural curiosity had been aroused. This man was treating him like a mercenary, and though Popov knew that was precisely what he'd become since leaving the service of his country, it was vaguely and distantly annoying to his sense of professionalism. "Will you require further such services?"

"What happened to the money?" the boss wanted to know.

A diffident reply: "I'm sure the Swiss will find a use for it." Certainly his banker would. "Surely you did not expect me to recover it?"

A shake of the boss's head. "No, not really, and it was a trivial sum anyway."

Popov nodded his understanding. *Trivial sum?* No Soviet-employed agent had ever gotten so much in a single payment—the KGB had always been niggardly in its payments to those whom it gave money, regardless of the importance of the information that had earned it—nor had the KGB ever been so casual in disposing of cash in any amount. Every single ruble had to be accounted for, else the bean-counters at Number 2 Dzerzhinsky Square would bring down the devil's own wrath on the field officer who'd been so lax in his operations! The next thing he wondered about was how his employer had laundered the cash. In America if you deposited or withdrew so little as ten *thousand* dollars in cash, the bank was required to make a written record of it. It was supposedly an inconvenience for drug dealers, but they managed to work with it nevertheless. Did other countries have similar rules? Popov didn't know. Switzerland did not, he was sure, but that many banknotes didn't just materialize in a bank's vaults, did they? Somehow his boss had handled that, and done it well, Popov reminded himself. Perhaps Ernst Model had been an amateur, but this man was not. Something to keep in mind, the former spy told himself in large, red, mental letters.

There followed a few seconds of silence. Then: "Yes, I will require another operation."

"What, exactly?" Popov asked, and got the answer immediately. "Ah." A nod. He even used the correct word: *operation.* How very strange. Dmitriy wondered if he'd be well advised to check up on his employer, to find out more about him. After all, his own life was now in pawn to him—and the reverse was true as well, of course, but the other man's life was not an immediate concern to Popov. How hard would it be? To one who owned a computer and a modem, it was no longer difficult at all . . . if one had the time. For now, it was clear, he'd have but one night in his apartment before traveling overseas again. Well, it was an easy cure for jet lag.

THEY looked like robots, Chavez saw, peering around a computer-generated corner. The hostages, too, but in this case the hostages were computer-generated children, all girls in red-and-white striped dresses or jumpers—Ding couldn't decide which. It was clearly a psychological effect programmed into the system by whoever had set up the parameters for the program, called SWAT 6.3.2. Some California-based outfit had first produced this for Delta Force under a DOD contract overseen by RAND Corporation.

It was expensive to use, mainly because of the electronic suit he wore. It was the same weight as the usual black mission suit—lead sheets sewn into the fabric had seen to that—and everything down to the gloves was filled with copper wires and sensors that told the computer—an old Cray YMP—exactly what his body was doing, and in turn projected a computer-generated image into the goggles he wore. Dr. Bellow gave the commentary, playing the roles of bad-guy leader and good-guy advisor in this particular game. Ding turned his head and saw Eddie Price right behind him and Hank Patterson and Steve Lincoln across the way at the other simulated corner—robotic figures with numbers on them to let him know who was who.

Chavez pumped his right arm up and down three times, calling for flash-bangs, then peered around the corner one more time—

—at his chair, Clark saw the black line appear on the white corner, then hit the 7 key on his computer keyboard—

—bad-guy #4 trained his weapon on the gaggle of schoolgirls—

"Steve! Now!" Chavez ordered.

Lincoln pulled the pin on the flash-bang. It was essentially a grenade simulator, heavy in explosive charge to produce noise and magnesium powder for a blinding flash—simulated for the computer program—and designed to blind and disorient through the ear-shattering blast, which was loud enough to upset the inner ear's mechanism for balance. That sound, though not quite as bad, came through their earphones as well, along with the white-out of their VR goggles. It still made them jump.

The echo hadn't even started to fade when Chavez dived into the room, weapon up and zeroing in on Terrorist #1, the supposed enemy leader. Here the computer system was faulty, Chavez thought. The European members of his team didn't shoot the way the Americans did. They pushed their weapons forward against the double-looped sling, actually extending their H&Ks before firing them. Chavez and the Americans tended to tuck them in close against the shoulder. Ding got his first burst off before his body hit the floor, but the computer system didn't always score this as a hit—which pissed Ding off greatly. He didn't *ever* miss, as a guy named Guttenach had discovered on finding St. Peter in front of him without much in the way of warning. Hitting the floor, Chavez rolled, repeated the burst, and swung the MP-10 for another target. His earphones produced the too-loud report of the shots (the SWAT 6.3.2 program for some reason didn't allow for suppressed weapons). To his right, Steve Lincoln and Hank Patterson were in the room and shooting at the six terrorists. Their short, controlled bursts rang in his ears, and in his VR goggles, heads exploded into red clouds quite satisfactorily—

—but bad guy #5 depressed his trigger, not at the rescuers, but rather at the hostages, which started going down until at least three of the Rainbow shooters took him out at once—

—"Clear!" Chavez shouted, jumping to his feet and going to the images of the bad guys. One, the computer said, was still residually alive, albeit bleeding from the head. Ding kicked his weapon loose, but by that time #4's shade had stopped moving.

"Clear!" "Clear!" shouted his team members.

"Exercise concluded," Clark's voice told them. Ding and his men removed their Virtual Reality goggles to find a room about double the size of a basketball court, and entirely absent of objects, empty as a high-school gym at midnight. It took a little getting used to. The simulation had been of terrorists who'd taken a kids' school—evidently a girls' school, for greater psychological effect.

"How many did we lose?" Chavez asked the ceiling.

"Six killed and three wounded, the computer says." Clark entered the room.

"What went wrong?" Ding asked, suspecting he knew what the answer was.

"I spotted you looking around the corner, boy," Rainbow Six answered. "That alerted the bad guys."

"Shit," Chavez responded. "That's a program glitch. In real life I'd use the mirror rig, or take this Kevlar hat off, but the program doesn't let us. The flash-bangs would have gone in clean."

"Maybe," John Clark allowed. "But your score on this one is a B-minus."

"Gee, thanks, Mr. C," the Team-2 leader groused. "Next you gonna say our shooting was off?"

"Yours was, the machine says."

"God *damn* it, John! The program doesn't simulate marksmanship worth a damn, and I will *not* train my people to shoot in a way the machine likes instead'a doing it the way that puts steel on target!"

"Settle down, Domingo. I know your troops can shoot. Okay, follow me. Let's watch the replay."

"Chavez, why did you take this way in?" Stanley asked when everyone was seated.

"This doorway is wider, and it gives a better field of fire—"

"For *both* sides," Stanley observed.

"Battlefields are like that," Ding countered. "But when you have surprise and speed going for you, that advantage conveys also. I put my backup team on the back door, but the configuration of the building didn't allow them to participate in the takedown. Noonan had the building spiked. We had good coverage of the bad guys, and I timed the assault to catch them all in the gym—"

"With all six guns colocated with the hostages."

"Better that than to have to go looking for them. Maybe one of them could flip a grenade around a corner and kill a bunch of the Barbie dolls. No, sir, I thought about coming in from the back, or doing a two-axis assault, but the distances and timing factors didn't look good to me. Are you saying I'm wrong, sir?"

"In this case, yes."

Bullshit, Chavez thought. "Okay, show me what you think."

It was as much a matter of personal style as right and wrong, and Alistair Stanley had been there and done that as much as any man in the world, Ding knew. So he watched and listened. Clark, he saw, did much the same.

"I don't like it," Noonan said, after Stanley concluded his presentation. "It's too easy to put a noisemaker on the doorknob. The damned things only cost ten bucks or so. You can buy one in any airport gift shop—people use them on hotel doors in case somebody tries to come in uninvited. We had a case in the Bureau when a subject used one—nearly blew the whole mission on us, but the flash-bang on the outside window covered the noise pretty well."

"And what if your spikes didn't give us positions on all the subjects?"

"But they did, sir," Noonan countered. "We had time to track them." In fact the training exercise had compressed the time by a factor of ten, but that was normal for the computer simulations. "This computer stuff is great for planning the takedowns, but it falls a little flat on other stuff. I think we did it pretty well." His concluding sentence also announced the fact that Noonan wanted to be a full member of Team-2, not just their techno-weenie, Ding thought. Tim had been spending a lot of time in the shooting range, and was now the equal of any member of the team. Well, he'd worked the FBI's Hostage Rescue Team under Gus Werner. He had the credentials to join the varsity. Werner had been considered for the Six job on Rainbow. But then, so had Stanley.

"Okay," Clark said next, "let's roll the tape."

That was the nastiest surprise of all. Terrorist #2, the computer said, had taken his head shot and spun around with his finger depressed on the trigger of his AK-74, and one of his rounds had neatly transfixed Chavez's head. Ding was dead, according to the Cray computer, because the theoretical bullet had gone under the brim of his Kevlar helmet and transited right through his brain. The shock of it to Chavez had surprising magnitude. A random event generated by the computer program, it was also quite real, because real life did include such random events. They'd talked about getting Lexan visors for their helmets, which might or might not stop a bullet, but had decided against it because of the distortion it would impose on their sight, and therefore their shooting . . . maybe we need to re-think that one, Chavez told himself. The bottom line of the computer's opinion was simple: if it was possible, then it *could* happen, and if it could, sooner or later, it *would,* and somebody on the team would have to drive to a house on post and tell a wife that she'd just become a widow. Because of a random event—bad luck. A hell of a thing to tell somebody who'd just lost a husband. Cause of death, bad luck. Chavez shivered a little at the thought. How would Patsy take it? Then he shook it off. It was a very low order of probability, mathematically right down there with being hit by lightning on a golf course or being wasted in a plane crash, and life *was* risk, and you avoided the risks only by being dead. Or something like that. He turned his head to look at Eddie Price.

"Unforgiving things, dice," the sergeant major observed with a wry smile. "But I got the chappie who killed you, Ding."

"Thanks, Eddie. Makes me feel a lot better. Shoot faster next time?"

"I shall make a point of it, sir," Price promised.

"Cheer up, Ding," Stanley observed, noting the exchange. "Could have been worse. I've yet to see anyone seriously harmed by an electron."

And you're supposed to learn from training exercises, Ding added for himself. But learn what from this one? Shit happens? Something to think about, he supposed, and in any case, Team-2 was now on standby, with Peter Covington's Team-1 on the ready line. Tomorrow they'd do some more shooting, aimed at getting the shots off a little faster, maybe. Problem was, there just wasn't any room for improvement—not much anyway—and pushing too hard might have the effect of dulling the sharp edge already achieved. Ding felt as though he were the head coach of a particularly good football team. The players were all excellent, and hard-working . . . just not quite perfect. But how much of that could be corrected by training, and how much merely reflected the fact that the other side played to win, too? The first job had been too easy. Model and his bunch had cried aloud to be killed. It wouldn't always be that easy.

CHAPTER 6

TRUE BELIEVERS

THE PROBLEM WAS ENVIRONMENTAL TOLERANCE. They knew the baseline organism was as effective as it needed to be. It was just so delicate. Exposed to air, it died far too easily. They weren't sure why, exactly. It might have been temperature or humidity, or too much oxygen—that element so essential to life was a great killer of life at the molecular level—and the uncertainty had been a great annoyance until a member of the team had come up with a solution. They'd used genetic-engineering technology to graft cancer genes into the organism. Specifically, they'd used genetic material from colon cancer, one of the more robust strains, and the results had been striking. The new organism was only a third of a micron larger and far stronger. The proof was on the electron microscope's TV screen. The tiny strands had been exposed to room air and room light for ten hours before being reintroduced into the culture dish, and already, the technician saw, the minute strands were active, using their RNA to multiply after eating, replicating themselves into millions more little strands, which had only one purpose—to eat tissue. In this case it was kidney tissue, though liver was just as vulnerable. The technician—who had a medical degree from Yale—made the proper written notations, and then, because it was her project, she got to name it. She blessed the course in comparative religion she'd taken twenty years before. You couldn't just call it anything, could you?

Shiva, she thought. Yes, the most complex and interesting of the Hindu gods, by turns the Destroyer and the Restorer, who controlled poison meant to destroy mankind, and one of whose consorts was Kali, the goddess of death herself. Shiva. *Perfect.* The tech made the proper notations, including her recommended name for the organism. There would be one more test, one more technological hurdle to hop before all was ready for execution. Execution, she thought, a proper word for the project. On rather a grand scale.

For her next task, she took a sample of Shiva, sealed in a stainless-steel container, and walked out of her lab, an eighth of a mile down the corridor, and into another.

"Hi, Maggie," the head of that lab said in greeting. "Got something for me?"

"Hey, Steve." She handed the container over. "This is the one."

"What are we calling it?" Steve took the container and set it on a countertop.

"Shiva, I think."

"Sounds ominous," Steve observed with a smile.

"Oh, it is," Maggie promised him. Steve was another M.D., Ph.D., both of his degrees from Duke University, and the company's best man on vaccines. For this project he'd been pulled off AIDS work that had begun to show some promise.

"So, the colon cancer genes worked like you predicted?"

"Ten hours in the open, it shows good UV tolerance. Not too sure about direct sunlight, though."

"Two hours of that is all we need," Steve reminded her. And really one hour was plenty, as they both knew. "What about the atomization system?"

"Still have to try it," she admitted, "but it won't be a problem." Both knew that was the truth. The organism should easily tolerate passage through the spray nozzles for the fogging system—which would be checked in one of the big environmental chambers. Doing it outside would be better still, of course, but if Shiva was as robust as Maggie seemed to think, it was a risk better not run.

"Okay, then. Thanks, Maggie." Steve turned his back, and inserted the container into one of the glove-boxes to open it, in order to begin his work on the vaccine. Much of the work was already done. The baseline agent here was well-known, and the government had funded his company's vaccine work after the big scare the year before, and Steve was known far and wide as one of the best around for generating, capturing, and replicating antibodies to excite a person's immune system. He vaguely regretted the termination of his AIDS work. Steve thought that he might have stumbled across a method of generating broad-spectrum antibodies to combat that agile little bastard—maybe a 20 percent change, he judged, plus the added benefit of leading down a new scientific pathway, the sort of thing to make a man famous . . . maybe even good enough for a flight to Stockholm in ten years or so. But in ten years, it wouldn't matter, would it? Not hardly, the scientist told himself. He turned to look out the triple-windows of his lab. A pretty sunset. Soon the night creatures would come out. Bats would chase insects. Owls would hunt mice and voles. Cats would leave their houses to prowl on their own missions of hunger. He had a set of night-vision goggles that he often used to observe the creatures doing work not so very different from his own. But for now he turned back to his worktable, pulled out his computer keyboard, and made some notations for his new project. Many used notebooks for this, but the Project allowed only computers for record-keeping, and all the notes were electronically encrypted. If it was good enough for Bill Gates, then it was good enough for him. The simple ways were not always best. That explained why he was here, part of the newly named Shiva Project, didn't it?

THEY needed guys with guns, but they were hard to find—at least the right ones, with the right attitudes—and the task was made more difficult by government activities with similar, but divergent aims. It helped them keep away from the more obvious kooks, though.

"Damn, it's pretty out here," Mark observed.

His host snorted. "There's a new house right the other side of that ridge line. On a calm day, I can see the smoke from their chimney."

Mark had to laugh. "There goes the neighborhood. You and Dan'l Boone, eh?"

Foster adopted a somewhat sheepish look. "Yeah, well, it *is* a good five miles."

"But you know, you're right. Imagine what it looked like before the white man came here. No roads 'cept for the river banks and deer trails, and the hunting must have been pretty spectacular."

"Good enough you didn't have to work that hard to eat, I imagine." Foster gestured at the fireplace wall of his log cabin, covered with hunting trophies, not all of them legal, but here in Montana's Bitterroot Mountains, there weren't all that many cops, and Foster kept pretty much to himself.

"It's our birthright."

"Supposed to be," Foster agreed. "Something worth fighting for."

"How hard?" Mark asked, admiring the trophies. The grizzly bear rug was especially impressive—and probably illegal as hell.

Foster poured some more bourbon for his guest. "I don't know what it's like back East, but out here, if you fight—you fight. All the way, boy. Put one right 'tween the running lights, generally calms your adversary down a mite."

"But then you have to dispose of the body," Mark said, sipping his drink. The man bought only cheap whiskey. Well, he probably couldn't afford the good stuff.

A laugh: "Ever hear of a backhoe? How 'bout a nice fire?"

It was believed by some in this part of the state that Foster had killed a fish-and-game cop. As a result, he was leery of local police—and the highway patrol people didn't like him to go a mile over the limit. But though the car had been found—burned out, forty miles away—the body of the missing officer had not, and that was that. There weren't many people around to be witnesses in this part of the state, even with a new house five miles away. Mark sipped his bourbon and leaned back in the leather chair. "Nice to be part of nature, isn't it?"

"Yes, sir. It surely is. Sometimes I think I kinda understand the Indians, y'know?"

"Know any?"

"Oh, sure. Charlie Grayson, he's a Nez Percé, hunting guide, got my horse off o' him. I do that, too, to make some cash sometimes, mainly take a horse into the high country, really, meet people who get it. And the elk are pretty thick up there."

"What about bear?"

"Enough," Foster replied. "Mainly blacks, but some grizz'."

"What do you use? Bow?"

A good-natured shake of the head. "No, I admire the Indians, but I ain't one myself. Depends on what I'm hunting, and what country I'm doing it in. Bolt-action .300 Winchester Mag mainly, but in close country, a semiauto slug shotgun. Nothing like drillin' three-quarter-inch holes when you gotta, y'know?"

"Handload?"

"Of course. It's a lot more personal that way. Gotta show respect for the game, you know, keep the gods of the mountains happy."

Foster smiled at the phrase, in just the right sleepy way, Mark saw. In every civilized man was a pagan waiting to come out, who really believed in the gods of the mountains, and in appeasing the spirits of the dead game. And so did he, really, despite his technical education.

"So, what do you do, Mark?"

"Molecular biochemistry, Ph.D., in fact."

"What's that mean?"

"Oh, figuring out how life happens. Like how does a bear smell so well," he went on, lying. "It can be interesting, but my real life is coming out to places like this, hunting, meeting people who really understand the game better than

I do. Guys like you," Mark concluded, with a salute of his glass. "What about you?"

"Ah, well, retired now. I made some of my own. Would you believe geologist for an oil company?"

"Where'd you work?"

"All over the world. I had a good nose for it, and the oil companies paid me a lot for finding the right stuff, y'know? But I had to give it up. Got to the point—well, you fly a lot, right?"

"I get around," Mark confirmed with a nod.

"The brown smudge," Foster said next.

"Huh?"

"Come on, you see it all over the damned world. Up around thirty thousand feet, that brown smudge. Complex hydrocarbons, mainly from passenger jets. One day I was flying back from Paris—connecting flight from Brunei, I came the wrong way 'round 'cuz I wanted to stop off in Europe and meet a friend. Anyway, there I was, in a fuckin' 747, over the middle of the fucking Atlantic Ocean, like four hours from land, y'know? First-class window seat, sitting there drinking my drink, lookin' out the window, and there it was, the smudge—that goddamned brown shit, and I realized that I was helpin' make it happen, dirtyin' up the whole fuckin' atmosphere.

"Anyway," Foster went on, "that was the moment of my . . . conversion, I guess you'd call it. I tendered my resignation the next week, took my stock options, cashed in half a mil worth, and bought this place. So, now, I hunt and fish, do a little guide work in the fall, read a lot, wrote a little book about what oil products do to the environment, and that's about it."

It was the book that had attracted Mark's attention, of course. The brown-smudge story was in its poorly written preface. Foster was a believer, but not a screwball. His house had electricity and phone service. Mark saw his high-end Gateway computer on the floor next to his desk. Even satellite TV, plus the usual Chevy pickup truck with a gun-rack in the back window . . . and a diesel-powered backhoe. So, maybe he believed, but he wasn't too crazy about it. That was good, Mark thought. He just had to be crazy enough. Foster was. Killing the fish-and-game cop was proof of that.

Foster returned the friendly stare. He'd met guys like this during his time in Exxon. A suit, but a clever one, the kind who didn't mind getting his hands dirty. Molecular biochemistry. They hadn't had that major at the Colorado School of Mines, but Foster also subscribed to *Science News,* and knew what it was all about. A meddler with life . . . but, strangely, one who understood about the deer and elk. Well, the world was a complex place. Just then, his visitor saw the Lucite block on the coffee table. Mark picked it up.

"What's this?"

Foster grinned over his drink. "What's it look like?"

"Well, it's either iron pyrite or it's—"

"Ain't iron. I do know my rocks, sir."

"Gold? Where from?"

"Found it in my stream, 'bout three hundred yards over yonder." Foster pointed.

"That's a fair-sized nugget."

"Five and a half ounces. About two thousand dollars. You know, people—white people—been living right on this ranch on this spot for over a hundred years, but nobody ever saw that in the creek. One day I'll have to backtrack up, see if it's a good formation. Ought to be, that's quartz on the bottom of the big one. Quartz-and-gold formations tend to be pretty rich, 'cuz of the way the stuff bubbled up from the earth's core. This area's fairly volcanic, all the hot springs and stuff," he reminded his guest. "We even get the occasional earth tremor."

"So, you might own your own gold mine?"

A good laugh. "Yep. Ironic, ain't it? I paid the going rate for grazing land—not even that much 'cuz o' the hills. The last guy to ranch around here bitched that his cattle lost every pound they gained grazin' by climbing up to where the grass was."

"How rich?"

A shrug. "No tellin', but if I showed that to some guys I went to school with, well, some folks would invest ten or twenty million finding out. Like I said, it's a quartz formation. People gamble big-time on those. Price of gold is depressed, but if it comes out of the ground pretty pure—well, it's a shitload more valuable than coal, y'know?"

"So, why don't you? . . ."

"'Cuz I don't need it, and it's an ugly process to watch. Worse 'n drilling oil, even. You can pretty much clean that up. But a mine—no way. Never goes away. The tailing don't go away. The arsenic gets into the ground water and takes forever to leach out. Anyway, it's a pretty coupla rocks in the plastic, and if I ever need the money, well, I know what to do."

"How often you check the creek?"

"When I fish—brown trout here, see?" He pointed to a big one hanging on the log wall. "Every third or fourth time, I find another one. Actually, I figure the deposit must have been uncovered fairly recently, else folks would have spotted it a long time ago. Hell, maybe I should track it down, see where it starts, but I'd just be tempting myself. Why bother?" Foster concluded. "I might have a weak moment and go against my principles. Anyway, not like it's gonna run away, is it?"

Mark grunted. "Guess not. Got any more of these?"

"Sure." Foster rose and pulled open a desk drawer. He tossed a leather pouch over. Mark caught it, surprised by the weight, almost ten pounds. He pulled the drawstring and extracted a nugget. About the size of a half-dollar, half gold, half quartz, all the more beautiful for the imperfection.

"You married?" Foster asked.

"Yeah. Wife, two kids."

"Keep it, then. Make a pendant out of it, give it to her for her birthday or something."

"I can't do that. This is worth a couple of thousand dollars."

Foster waved his hand. "Shit, just takin' up space in my desk. Why not make somebody happy with it? 'Sides, you understand, Mark. I think you really do."

Yep, Mark thought, this was a recruit. "What if I told you there was a way to make that brown smudge go away? . . ."

A quizzical look. "You talking about some organism to eat it or something?"

Mark looked up. "No, not exactly . . ." How much could he tell him now? He'd have to be very careful. It was only their first meeting.

"GETTING the aircraft is your business. Where to fly it, that we can help with," Popov assured his host.

"Where?" the host asked.

"The key is to become lost to air-traffic-control radar and also to travel far enough that fighter aircraft cannot track you, as you know. Then if you can land in a friendly place, and dispose of the flight crew upon reaching your destination, repainting the aircraft is no great task. It can be destroyed later, even dismantled for sale of the important parts, the engines and such. They can easily disappear into the international black market, with the change of a few identity plates," Popov explained. "This has happened more than once, as you know. Western intelligence and police agencies do not advertise the fact, of course."

"The world is awash with radar systems," the host objected.

"True," Popov conceded, "but air-traffic radars do not see aircraft. They see the return signals from aircraft radar transponders. Only military radars see the aircraft themselves, and what African country has a proper air-defense network? Also, with the addition of a simple jammer to the aircraft's radio systems, you can further reduce the ability of anyone to track you. Your escape is not a problem, *if* you get as far as an international airport, my friend. That," he reminded them, "is the difficult part. Once you disappear over Africa—well, that is your choice then. Your country of destination can be selected for ideological purity or for a monetary exchange. Your choice. I recommend the former, but the latter is possible," Popov concluded. Africa was not yet a hotbed of international law and integrity, but it did have hundreds of airports capable of servicing jetliners.

"A pity about Ernst," the host said quietly.

"Ernst was a fool!" his lady friend countered with an angry gesture. "He should have robbed a smaller bank. All the way in the middle of Bern. He was trying to make a statement," Petra Dortmund sneered. Popov had known her only by reputation until today. She might have been pretty, even beautiful, once, but now her once-blond hair was dyed brown, and her thin face was severe, the cheeks sunken and hollow, the eyes rimmed in dark circles. She was almost unrecognizable, which explained why European police hadn't snatched her up yet, along with her long-time lover, Hans Fürchtner.

Fürchtner had gone the other way. He was a good thirty kilos overweight, his thick dark hair had either fallen out or been shaved, and the beard was gone. He looked like a banker now, fat and happy, no longer the driven, serious, committed communist he'd been in the '70s and '80s—at least not visibly so. They lived in a decent house in the mountains south of Munich. What neighbors they had thought them to be artists—both of them painted, a hobby unknown to their country's police. They even sold the occasional work in small galleries, which was enough to feed them, though not to maintain their lifestyle.

They must have missed the safe houses in the old DDR and Czechoslovakia, Dmitriy Arkadeyevich thought. Just get off the aircraft and get taken away by car to comfortable if not quite lavish quarters, leave there to shop in the "special" stores maintained for the local Party elite, get visited frequently by serious, quiet intelligence officers who would feed them information with which to plan their next operation. Fürchtner and Dortmund had accomplished several decent operations, the best being the kidnapping and interrogation of an American sergeant who serviced nuclear artillery shells—this mission had been assigned them by the Soviet GRU. Much had been learned from that, most of it still useful, as the sergeant had been an expert on the American PAL—permissible action link—safety systems. His body had later been discovered in the snowy mid-winter mountains of southern Bavaria, apparently the result of a nasty traffic accident. Or so GRU thought, based on the reports of its agents within the NATO high command.

"So, what is it that you want to learn?" she asked.

"Electronic access codes to the international trading system."

"So, you, too, are a common thief now?" Hans asked, before Petra could sneer.

"A very uncommon thief, my sponsor is. If we are to restore a socialist, *progressive* alternative to capitalism, we need both funding and to instill a certain lack of confidence in the capitalist nervous system, do we not?" Popov paused for a second. "You know who I am. You know where I worked. Do you think I have forgotten my Motherland? Do you think I have forsaken my beliefs? My father fought at Stalingrad and Kursk. He knew what it was to be pushed back, to suffer defeat—and yet not give up, ever!" Popov said heatedly. "Why do you think I risk my life here? The counterrevolutionaries in Moscow would not look kindly upon my mission . . . but they are not the only political force in Mother Russia!"

"Ahhh," Petra Dortmund observed. Her face turned serious. "So, you think all is not lost?"

"Did you ever think the forward march of humanity would be absent of setbacks? It is true we lost our way. I saw it myself in KGB, the corruption in high places. That is what defeated us—not the West! I saw it myself as a captain, Brezhnev's daughter—looting the Winter Palace for her wedding reception. As though she were the Grand Duchess Anastasia herself! It was my function in KGB to learn from the West, learn their plans and secrets, but our *nomenklatura* learned only their corruption. Well, we have learned that lesson, in more ways than one, my friends. You are a communist or you are not. You believe or you do not. You act in accordance with those beliefs or you do not."

"You ask us to give up much," Hans Fürchtner pointed out.

"You will be properly provided for. My sponsor—"

"Who is that?" Petra asked.

"This you may not know," Popov replied quietly. "You suppose that *you* take risks here? What about me? As for my sponsor, no, you may not know his identity. Operational security is paramount. You are supposed to know these things," he reminded them. They took the mild rebuke well, as he'd expected. These two fools were true believers, as Ernst Model had been, though they were somewhat brighter and far more vicious, as that luckless American sergeant had learned, probably staring with disbelief into the still-lovely blue eyes of Petra Dortmund as she'd used the hammer on his various body parts.

"So, Iosef Andreyevich," Hans said—they knew Popov by one of his many cover names, in this case I. A. Serov. "When do you wish us to act?"

"As quickly as possible. I will call you in a week, to see if you are indeed willing to take this mission and—"

"We are willing," Petra assured him. "We need to make our plans."

"Then I shall call you in a week for your schedule. I will need four days to activate my part of the operation. An additional concern, the mission depends on the placement of the American navy carrier in the Mediterranean. You may not execute the mission if it is in the western Mediterranean, because in such a case their aircraft might track your flight. We wish this mission to succeed, my friends." Then they negotiated the price. It didn't prove hard. Hans and Petra knew Popov from the old days and actually trusted him personally to make the delivery.

Ten minutes later, Popov shook hands and took his leave, this time driving a rented BMW south toward the Austrian border. The road was clear and smooth, the scenery beautiful, and Dmitriy Arkadeyevich wondered again about his hosts. The one bit of truth he'd given them was that his father was indeed a veteran of the Stalingrad and Kursk campaign, and had told his son much about his life as a tank commander in the Great Patriotic War. There was something odd about the Germans, he'd learned from his professional experience in the Committee for State Security. Give them a man on a horse, and they'd follow him to the death. It seemed that the Germans craved someone or something to follow. How very strange. But it served his purposes, and those of his sponsor, and if these Germans wanted to follow a red horse—a *dead* red horse, Popov reminded himself with a smile and a grunt—well, that was their misfortune. The only really innocent people involved were the bankers whom they would attempt to kidnap. But at least they wouldn't be subjected to torture, as that black American sergeant had been. Popov doubted that Hans and Petra would get that far, though the capabilities of the Austrian police and military were largely unknown to him. He'd find out, he was sure, one way or another.

IT was odd the way it worked. Team-1 was now the Go-Team, ready to depart Hereford at a moment's notice while Chavez's Team-2 stood down, but it was the latter that was running complex exercises while the former did little but morning PT and routine marksmanship training. Technically, they were worried about a training accident that could hurt or even cripple a team member, thus breaking up a field team at a delicate moment.

Master Chief Machinist's Mate Miguel Chin belonged to Peter Covington's team. A former U.S. Navy SEAL, he'd been taken from Norfolk-based SEAL Team Six for Rainbow. The son of a Latino mother and a Chinese father, he, like Chavez, had grown up in East L.A. Ding spotted him smoking a cigar outside the Team-1 building and walked over.

"Hey, Chief," Chavez said from ten feet away.

"Master Chief," Chin corrected. "Like being a CSM in the army, sir."

"Name's Ding, 'mano."

"Mike." Chin extended a hand. Chin's face could have passed for damned near anything. He was an iron-pumper like Oso Vega, and his rep was of a guy who'd been around the block about a hundred times. Expert with all types of weapons, his handshake announced his further ability to tear a man's head right off his shoulders.

"Those are bad for you," Chavez noted.

"So's what we do for a livin', Ding. What part of L.A.?"

Ding told him.

"No kiddin'? Hell, I grew up half a mile from there. You were *Banditos* country."

"Don't tell me—"

The master chief nodded. *"Piscadores,* till I grew out of it. A judge suggested that I might like enlisting better 'n jail, and so I tried for the Marines, but they didn't want me. Pussies," Chin commented, spitting some tobacco off his cigar. "So, went through Great Lakes, they made me a machinist . . . but then I heard about the SEALs, an', well, ain't a bad life, y'know? You're Agency, I hear."

"Started off as an Eleven-Bravo. Took a little trip to South America that went totally to shit, but I met our Six on the job and he kinda recruited me. Never looked back."

"Agency send you to school?"

"George Mason, just got my master's. International relations," Chavez replied with a nod. "You?"

"Yeah, shows, I guess. Psychology, just a bachelor's, Old Dominion University. The doc on the team, Bellow. Smart son of a bitch. Mind-reader. I got three of his books at my place."

"How's Covington to work for?"

"Good. He's been there before. Listens good. Thoughtful kinda guy. Good team here, but as usual, not a hell of a lot to do. Liked your takedown at the bank, Chavez. Fast and clean." Chin blew smoke into the sky.

"Well, thank you, Master Chief."

"Chavez!" Peter Covington came out the door just then. "Trying to steal my number-one?"

"Just found out we grew up a few blocks apart, Peter."

"Indeed? That's remarkable," the Team-1 commander said.

"Harry's aggravated his ankle some this morning. No big deal, he's chewing some aspirin," Chin told his boss. "He banged it up two weeks ago zip-lining down from the helo," he added for Ding's benefit.

Damn training accidents, the chief didn't have to add. That was the problem with this sort of work, they all knew. The Rainbow members had been selected for many reasons, not the least of which was their brutally competitive nature. Every man deemed himself to be in competition with every other, and each one of them pushed himself to the limit in everything. It made for injuries and training accidents—and the miracle was that they'd yet to place one of the team into the base hospital. It was sure to happen soon. The Rainbow members could no more turn that aspect of their personalities off than they could stop breathing. Olympic team members hardly had a tougher outlook on what they did. Either you were the very best, or you were nothing. And so every man could run a mile within thirty or forty seconds of the world record, wearing boots instead of track shoes. It did make sense in the abstract. Half a second could easily be the difference between life and death in a combat situation—worse, not the death of one of their own, but of an innocent party, a hostage, the person whom they were sworn to protect and rescue. But the really ironic part was that the Go-Team was not allowed heavy training for fear of a training accident, and so their skills degraded slightly over time—in this case, the two weeks of being stood-to. Three more days to go for Covington's Team-1, and then, Chavez knew, it would be his turn.

"I hear you don't like the SWAT program," Chin said next.

"Not all that much. It's good for planning movement and stuff, but not so good for the takedowns."

"We've been using it for years," Covington said. "Much better than it used to be."

"I'd prefer live targets and MILES gear," Chavez persisted. He referred to the training system the U.S. military often used, in which every soldier had laser-receivers mounted on his body.

"Not as good at close range as at long," Peter informed his colleague.

"Oh, never used it that way," Ding had to admit. "But as a practical matter, once we get close, it's decided. Our people don't miss many targets."

"True," Covington conceded. Just then came the *crack* of a sniper rifle. Rainbow's long-riflemen were practicing over on the thousand-yard range, competing to see who could fire the smallest group. The current leader was Homer Johnston, Ding's Rifle Two-One, an eighth of an inch better than Sam Houston, Covington's leading long-rifleman, at five hundred yards—at which range either could put ten consecutive shots inside a two-inch circle, which was considerably smaller than the human head both men practiced exploding with their hollow-point match rounds. The fact of the matter was that two misses from any of the Rainbow shooters in a given week of drills was remarkable, and usually explained by tripping on something in the shooting house. The riflemen had yet to miss *anything,* of course. The problem with their mission wasn't shooting. It was getting in close enough—more than that, making a well-timed decision to move and take down the subjects, for which they most often depended on Dr. Paul Bellow. The shooting part, which they practiced daily, was the tensest part, to be sure, but also technically and operationally the easiest. It seemed perverse in that respect, but theirs was a perverse business.

"Anything on the threat board?" Covington asked.

"I was just heading over, but I doubt it, Peter." Whatever bad guys were still thinking about making mischief somewhere in Europe had seen TV coverage of the Bern bank, and that would have calmed them down some, both team leaders thought.

"Very good, Ding. I have some paperwork to do," Covington said, heading back inside his building. On that cue, Chin tossed his cigar into the smokers' bucket and did the same.

Chavez continued his walk to the headquarters building, returning the salute of the door guard as he went inside. The Brits sure saluted funny, he thought. Once inside, he found Major Bennett at his desk.

"Hey, Sam,"

"Good morning, Ding. Coffee?" The Air Force officer gestured to his urn.

"No, thanks. Anything happening anywhere?"

A shake of the head. "Quiet day. Not even much in the way of crime."

Bennett's primary sources for normal criminal activity were the teleprinters for the various European news services. Experience showed that the services notified those who were interested about illegal activity more quickly than the official channels, which generally sent information via secure fax from the American or British embassies across Europe. With that input source quiet, Bennett was working on his computerized list of known terrorists, shifting through the photos and written summaries of what was positively known about these people (generally not much) and what was suspected (not much more).

"What's this? Who's that?" Ding asked, pointing at the computer.

"A new toy we're using. Got it from the FBI. It ages the subject photos. This one is Petra Dortmund. We only have two photos of her, both almost fifteen years old. So, I'm aging her by fifteen years, playing with hair color, too. Nice thing about women—no beards," Bennett observed with a chuckle. "And they're usually too vain to pork up, like our pal Carlos did. This one, check out the eyes."

"Not a girl I'd try to pick up in a bar," Chavez observed.

"Probably a bad lay anyway, Domingo," Clark said from behind. "That's impressive stuff, Sam."

"Yes, sir. Just set it up this morning. Noonan got it for me from Headquarters Division Technical Services. They invented it to help ID kidnap victims years after they disappeared. It's been pretty useful for that. Then somebody figured that if it worked on children growing up, why not try it on grown-up hoods. Helped 'em find a top-ten bank robber earlier this year. Anyhow, here's what Fräulein Dortmund probably looks like now."

"What's the name of her significant other?"

"Hans Fürchtner." Bennett played with his computer mouse to bring up that photo. "Christ, this must be his high-school yearbook pictorial." Then he scanned the words accompanying the photo. "Okay, likes to drink beer . . . so, let's give him another fifteen pounds." In seconds, the photo changed. "Mustache . . . beard . . ." And then there were four photos for this one.

"These two must get along just great," Chavez noted, remembering his file on the pair. "Assuming they're still together." That started a thought moving, and Chavez walked over to Dr. Bellow's office.

"Hey, doc."

Bellow looked up from his computer. "Good morning, Ding. What can I do for you?"

"We were just looking at photos of two bad guys, Petra von Dortmund and Hans Fürchtner. I got a question for you."

"Shoot," Bellow replied.

"How likely are people like that to stay together?"

Bellow blinked a little, then leaned back in his chair. "Not a bad question at all. Those two . . . I did the evaluation for their active files. . . . They're probably still together. Their political ideology is probably a unifying factor, an important part of their commitment to each other. Their belief system is what brought them together in the first place, and in a psychological sense they took their wedding vows when they acted out on it—their terrorist jobs. As I recall, they are suspected to have kidnapped and killed a soldier, among other things, and activity like that creates a strong interpersonal bond."

"But most of the people, you say, are sociopaths," Ding objected. "And sociopaths don't—"

"Been reading my books?" Bellow asked with a smile. "Ever hear the one about how when two people marry they become as one?"

"Yeah. So?"

"So in a case like this, it's real. They *are* sociopaths, but ideology gives their deviance an ethos—and *that* makes it important. Because of that, sharing the ideology makes them one, and their sociopathic tendencies merge. For those two, I would suspect a fairly stable married relationship. I wouldn't be surprised to learn that they were formally married, in fact, but probably not in a church," he added with a smile.

"Stable marriage . . . kids?"

Bellow nodded. "Possible. Abortion is illegal in Germany—the Western part, I think, still. Would they choose to have kids? . . . That's a good question. I need to think about that."

"I need to learn more about these people. How they think, how they see the world, that sort of thing."

Bellow smiled again, rose from his chair, and walked to his bookcase. He took one of his own books and tossed it to Chavez. "Try that for starters. It's a text at the FBI academy, and it got me over here a few years ago to lecture to the SAS. I guess it got me into this business."

"Thanks, doc." Chavez hefted the book for weight and headed out the door. *The Enraged Outlook: Inside the Terrorist Mind* was the title. It wouldn't hurt to understand them a little better, though he figured the best thing about the inside of a terrorist's mind was a 185-grain 10-mm hollow-point bullet entering at high speed.

POPOV could not give them a phone number to call. It would have been grossly unprofessional. Even a cellular phone whose ownership had been carefully concealed would give police agencies a paper—even deadlier today, an electronic—trail that they could run down, much to his potential embarrassment. And so he called them every few days at their number. They didn't know how that was handled, though there were ways to step a long-distance call through multiple instruments.

"I have the money. Are you prepared?"

"Hans is there now, checking things out," Petra replied. "I expect we can be ready in forty-eight hours. What of your end?"

"All is in readiness. I will call you in two days," he said, breaking the connection. He walked out of the phone booth at Charles De Gaulle International Airport and headed toward the taxi stand, carrying his attaché case, which was largely full of hundred D-mark banknotes. He found himself impatient for the currency change in Europe. The equivalent amount of euros would be much easier to obtain than the multiple currencies of Europe.

CHAPTER 7

FINANCE

IT WAS UNUSUAL FOR A EUROPEAN TO WORK OUT OF his home, but Ostermann did. It was large, a former baronial *schloss* (translated as "castle," though in this case "palace" would have been more accurate) thirty kilometers outside Vienna. Erwin Ostermann liked the *schloss;* it was totally in keeping with his stature in the financial community. It was a dwelling of six thousand square meters divided into three floors, on a thousand hectares of land, most of which was the side of a mountain steep enough to afford his own skiing slopes. In the summer, he allowed local farmers to graze their sheep and goats there . . . not unlike what the peasants once indentured to the *schloss* had done for the *graf,* to keep the grass down to a reasonable height. Well, it was far more democratic now, wasn't it? It even gave him a break on the complex taxes put in place by the left-wing government of his country, and more to the point, it looked good.

His personal car was a Mercedes stretch—two of them, in fact—and a Porsche when he felt adventurous enough to drive himself to the nearby village for drinks and dinner in the outstanding *Gasthaus* there. He was a tall man, one meter eighty-six centimeters, with regal gray hair and a trim, fit figure that looked good on the back of one of his Arabian horses—you couldn't live in a home such as this one without horses, of course. Or when holding a business conference in a suit made in Italy or on London's Savile Row. His office, on the second floor had been the spacious library of the original owner and eight of his descendants, but it was now aglow with computer displays linked to the world's financial markets and arrayed on the credenza behind a desk.

After a light breakfast, he headed upstairs to his office, where three employees, two female and one male, kept him supplied with coffee, breakfast pastry, and information. The room was large and suitable for entertaining a group of twenty or so. The walnut-paneled walls were covered with bookshelves filled with books that had been conveyed with the *schloss,* and whose titles Ostermann had never troubled himself to examine. He read the financial papers rather than literature, and in his spare time caught movies in a private screening room in the basement—a former wine-cellar converted to the purpose. All in all, he was a man who lived a comfortable and private life in the most comfortable and private of surroundings. On his desk when he sat down was a list of people to visit him today. Three bankers and two traders like himself, the former to discuss loans for a new business he was underwriting, and the latter to seek his counsel on market trends. It fed Ostermann's already sizable ego to be consulted on such things, and he welcomed all manner of guests.

POPOV stepped off his airliner and walked onto the concourse alone, like any other businessman, carrying his attaché case with its combination lock, and not a single piece of metal inside, lest some magnetometer operator ask him to open it and so reveal the paper currency inside—terrorists had really ruined air travel for everyone, the former KGB officer thought to himself. Were someone to make the baggage-scanners more sophisticated, enough to count money inside carry-on baggage, for example, it would further put a dent in the business affairs of many people, including himself. Traveling by train was *so* boring.

Their tradecraft was good. Hans was at his designated location, sitting there, reading *Der Spiegel* and wearing the agreed-upon brown leather jacket, and he saw Dmitriy Arkadeyevich, carrying his black attaché case in his left hand, striding down the concourse with all the other business travelers. Fürchtner finished his coffee and left to follow him, trailing Popov by about twenty meters, angling off to the left so that they took different exits, crossing over to the parking garage by different walkways. Popov allowed his head to turn left and right, caught Hans on the first sweep and observed how he moved. The man had to be tense, Popov knew. Betrayal was how most of the people like Fürchtner got caught, and though Dmitriy was known and trusted by them, you could *only* be betrayed by someone whom you trusted, a fact known to every covert operator in the world. And though they knew Popov both by sight and reputation, they couldn't read minds—which, of course, worked quite well for Popov in this case. He allowed himself a quiet smile as he walked into the parking garage, turned left, stopped as though disoriented, and then looked around for any overt signs that *he* was being followed before finding his bearings and moving on his way. Fürchtner's car proved to be in a distant corner on the first level, a blue Volkswagen Golf.

"Grüss Gott," he said, on sitting in the right-front seat.

"Good morning, Herr Popov," Fürchtner replied in English. It was American in character and almost without accent. He must have watched a lot of television, Dmitriy thought.

The Russian dialed the combinations into the locks of the case, opened the lid, and placed it in his host's lap. "You should find everything in order."

"Bulky," the man observed.

"It is a sizable sum," Popov agreed.

Just then suspicion appeared in Fürchtner's eyes. That surprised the Russian, until he thought about it for a moment. The KGB had never been lavish in their payments to their agents, but in this attaché case was enough cash to enable two people to live comfortably in any of several African countries for a period of some years. Hans was just realizing that, Dmitriy saw, and while part of the German was content just to take the money, the smart portion of his brain suddenly wondered where the money had come from. Better not to wait for the question, Dmitriy thought.

"Ah, yes," Popov said quietly. "As you know, many of my colleagues have outwardly turned capitalist in order to survive in my country's new political environment. But we are still the Sword and Shield of the Party, my young friend. That has not changed. It is ironic, I grant you, that now we are better able to compensate our friends for their services. It turns out to be less expensive than maintaining the safe houses which you once enjoyed. I personally find that amusing. In any case, here is your payment, in cash, in advance, in the amount you specified."

"Danke," Hans Fürchtner observed, staring down into the attaché case's ten centimeters of depth. Then he hefted the case. "It's heavy."

"True," Dmitriy Arkadeyevich agreed. "But it could be worse. I might have paid you in gold," he joked, to lighten the moment, then decided to make his own play. "Too heavy to carry on the mission?"

"It *is* a complication, Iosef Andreyevich."

"Well, I can hold the money for you and come to you to deliver it upon the completion of your mission. That is your choice, though I do not recommend it."

"Why is that?" Hans asked.

"Honestly, it makes me nervous to travel with so much cash. The West, well, what if I am robbed? This money is *my* responsibility," he replied theatrically.

Fürchtner found that very amusing. "Here, in Österreich, robbed on the street? My friend, these capitalist sheep are very closely regulated."

"Besides, I do not even know where you will be going, and I really do not need to know—at this time, anyway."

"The Central African Republic is our ultimate destination. We have a friend there who graduated Patrice Lumumba University back in the sixties. He trades in arms to progressive elements. He will put us up for a while, until Petra and I can find suitable housing."

They were either very brave or very foolish to go to that country, Popov thought. Not so long before it had been called the Central African Empire, and had been ruled by "Emperor Bokassa I," a former colonel in the French colonial army, which had once garrisoned this small, poor nation. Bokassa had killed his way to the top, as had so many African chiefs of state, before dying, remarkably enough, of natural causes—so the papers said, anyway; you could never really be sure, could you? The country he'd left behind, a small diamond producer, was somewhat better off economically than was the norm on the dark continent, though not by much. But then, who was to say that Hans and Petra would ever get there?

"Well, my friend, it is your decision," Popov said, patting the attaché case still open in Fürchtner's lap.

The German considered that for half a minute or so. "I have seen the money," he concluded, to his guest's utter delight. Fürchtner lifted a thousand-note packet of the cash and riffled it like a deck of cards before putting it back. Next he scribbled a note and placed it inside the case. "There is the name. We will be with him starting . . . late tomorrow, I imagine. All is ready on your end?"

"The American aircraft carrier is in the eastern Mediterranean. Libya will allow your aircraft to pass without interference, but will not allow overflights of any NATO aircraft following you. Instead, their air force will provide the coverage and will lose you due to adverse weather conditions. I will advise you not to use more violence than is necessary. Press and diplomatic pressure has more strength today than it once did."

"We have thought that one through," Hans assured his guest.

Popov wondered briefly about that. But he'd be surprised if they even boarded an aircraft, much less got it to Africa. The problem with "missions" like this one was that no matter how carefully most of its parts had been considered, this chain was decidedly no stronger than its weakest link, and the strength of *that* link was all too often determined by others, or by chance, which was even worse. Hans and Petra were believers in their political philosophy, and like earlier people who'd believed so much in their religious faith so as to take the most absurd of chances, they would pretend to plan this "mission" through with their limited resources—and when you got down to it, their only resource was their willingness to apply violence to the world; and lots of people had that—and substitute hope for expectations, belief for knowledge. They would accept random chance, one of their deadliest enemies, as a neutral element, when a true professional would have sought to eliminate it entirely.

And so their belief structure was really a blindfold, or perhaps a set of blinkers, which denied the two Germans the ability to look objectively at a world that had passed them by, and to which they were unwilling to adapt. But for Popov the real meaning of this was their willingness to let him hold the money. Dmitriy Arkadeyevich had adapted himself quite well to changing circumstances.

"Are you sure, my young friend?"

"Ja, I am sure." Fürchtner closed the case, re-set the locks, and passed it over to Popov's lap. The Russian accepted the responsibility with proper gravity.

"I will guard this carefully." *All the way to my bank in Bern.* Then he extended his hand. "Good luck, and please be careful."

"Danke. We will get you the information you require."

"My employer needs that badly, Hans. We depend on you." Dmitriy left the car and walked back in the direction of the terminal, where he'd get a taxi to his hotel. He wondered when Hans and Petra would make their move. Perhaps today? Were they *that* precipitous? No, he thought, they would say that they were that *professional.* The young fools.

SERGEANT First Class Homer Johnston extracted the bolt from his rifle, which he lifted to examine the bore. The ten shots had dirtied it some, but not much, and there was no erosion damage that he could see in the throat forward of the chamber. None was to be expected until he'd fired a thousand or so rounds, and he'd only put five hundred forty through it to this point. Still, in another week or so he'd have to start using a fiber-optic instrument to check, because the 7-mm Remington Magnum cartridge did develop high temperatures when fired, and the excessive heat burned up barrels a little faster than he would have preferred. In a few months, he'd have to replace the barrel, a tedious and fairly difficult exercise even for a skilled armorer, which he was.

The difficulty was in matching the barrel perfectly with the receiver, which would then require fifty or so rounds on the known-distance range to make sure that it delivered its rounds as accurately as it was intended to do. But that was in the future. Johnston sprayed a moderate amount of Break-Free onto the cleaning patch and ran it through the barrel, back to front. The patch came out dirty. He removed it from the cleaning rod, then put a new one on the tip, and repeated the motion six times until the last patch came through totally clean. A final clean patch dried the bore of the select-grade Hart barrel, though the Break-Free cleaning solvent left a thin—not much more than a molecule's thickness—coating of silicon on the steel, which protected against corrosion without altering the microscopic tolerances of the barrel. Finished and satisfied, he replaced the bolt, closing it on an empty chamber with the final act of pulling the trigger, which de-cocked the rifle as it dropped the bolt into proper position.

He loved the rifle, though somewhat surprisingly he hadn't named it. Built by the same technicians who made sniper rifles for the United States Secret Service, it was a 7-mm Remington Magnum caliber, with a Remington match-quality receiver, a select-grade Hart barrel, and Leupold ten-power Gold Ring telescopic sight, all married to an ugly Kevlar stock—wood would have been much prettier, but wood warped over time, whereas Kevlar was dead, chemically inert, unaffected by moisture or time. Johnston had just proven, again, that his rifle could fire at about one quarter of a minute of angle's accuracy, meaning that he could fire three consecutive rounds inside the diameter of a nickel at one hundred yards. Someday somebody might design a laser weapon, Johnston thought, and maybe that could improve on the accuracy of this hand-made rifle. But nothing else could. At a range of one thousand yards, he could put three consecutive rounds into a circle of four inches—that required more than a rifle. That meant gauging the wind for speed and direction to compensate for drift-deflection. It also meant controlling his breathing and the way his finger touched the two-and-a-half-pound double-set trigger. His cleanup tasks done, Johnston lifted the rifle and carried it to its place in the gun vault, which was climate-controlled, and nestled it where it belonged before going back to the bullpen. The target he'd shot was on his desk.

Homer Johnston lifted it. He'd shot three rounds at 400 meters, three at 500, two at 700, and his last two at 900. All ten were inside the head-shape of the silhouette target, meaning that all ten would have been instantly fatal to a human target. He shot only cartridges that he'd loaded himself: Sierra 175-grain hollow-point boat-tailed match bullets traveling in front of 63.5 grains of IMR 4350 smokeless powder seemed to be the best combination for that particular rifle, taking 1.7 seconds to reach a target 1,000 yards downrange. That was an awfully long time, especially against a moving target, Sergeant Johnston thought, but it couldn't be helped. A hand came down on his shoulder.

"Homer," a familiar voice said.

"Yeah, Dieter," Johnston said, without looking up from the target. He was in the zone, all the way in. Shame it wasn't hunting season.

"You did better than me today. The wind was good for you." It was Weber's favorite excuse. He knew guns pretty well for a European, Homer thought, but guns were American things, and that was that.

"I keep telling you, that semiautomatic action doesn't headspace properly." Both of Weber's 900-meter rounds were marginal. They would have incapacitated the target, but not definitely killed it, even though they scored as hits. Johnston was the best rifle in Rainbow, even better than Houston, by about half a cunt hair on a good day, Homer admitted to himself.

"I like to get my second round off more quickly than you," Weber pointed out. And that was the end of the argument. Soldiers were as loyal to their firearms as they were to their religions. The German was far better in rate of fire with his golliwog Walther sniper rifle, but that weapon didn't have the inherent accuracy of a bolt-action and also fired a less-speedy cartridge. The two riflemen had debated the point over many a beer already, and neither would ever move the other.

In any case, Weber patted his holster. "Some pistol, Homer?"

"Yeah." Johnston stood. "Why not?" Handguns were not serious weapons for serious work, but they were fun, and the rounds were free here. Weber had him faded in handguns by about one percent or so. On the way to the range, they passed Chavez, Price and the rest, coming out with their MP-10s, joking with one another as they passed. Evidently everyone had had a good morning on the range.

"Ach," Weber snorted, "anyone can shoot at five meters!"

"Morning, Robert," Homer said to the rangemaster. "Want to set up some Qs for us?"

"Quite so, Sergeant Johnston," Dave Woods replied, grabbing two of the American-style targets—called "Q targets" for the letter Q in the middle, about where the heart would be. Then he got a third for himself. A lavishly mustached color sergeant in the British Army military police regiment, he was pretty damned good with a 9-mm Browning. The targets motored down to the ten-meter line and turned sideways while the three sergeants donned their ear-protectors. Woods was, technically, a pistol instructor, but the quality of the men at Hereford made that a dull job, and as a result he himself fired close to a thousand rounds per week, perfecting his own skills. He was known to shoot with the men of Rainbow, and to challenge them to friendly competition, which, to the dismay of the shooters, was almost a break-even proposition. Woods was a traditionalist and held his pistol in one hand, as Weber did, though Johnston preferred the two-hand Weaver stance. The targets turned without warning, and three handguns came up to address them.

THE home of Erwin Ostermann was magnificent, Hans Fürchtner thought for the tenth time, just the sort of thing for an arrogant class-enemy. Their research into the target hadn't revealed any aristocratic lineage for the current owner of this *schloss,* but he doubtless thought of himself in those terms. For now, Hans thought, as he turned onto the two-kilometer driveway of brown gravel and drove past the manicured gardens and bushes arranged with geometric precision by workers who were at the moment nowhere to be seen. Pulling up close to the palace, he stopped the rented Mercedes and turned right, as though looking for a parking place. Coming around the rear of the building, he saw the Sikorsky S-76B helicopter they'd be using later, sitting on the usual asphalt pad with a yellow circle painted on it. Good. Fürchtner continued the circuit around the *schloss* and parked in front, about fifty meters from the main entrance.

"Are you ready, Petra?"

"Ja" was her terse, tense reply. It had been years since either had run an operation, and the immediate reality of it was different from the planning they'd spent a week to accomplish, going over charts and diagrams. There were things they did not yet know for certain, like the exact number of servants in the building. They started walking to the front door when a delivery truck came up, arriving there just as they did. The truck doors opened, and two men got out, both carrying large boxes in their arms. One waved to Hans and Petra to go up the stone steps, which they did. Hans hit the button, and a moment later the door opened.

"Guten Tag," Hans said. "We have an appointment with Herr Ostermann."

"Your name?"

"Bauer," Fürchtner said. "Hans Bauer."

"Flower delivery," one of the other two men said.

"Please come in. I will call Herr Ostermann," the butler—whatever he was—said.

"Danke," Fürchtner replied, waving for Petra to precede him through the or-

nate door. The deliverymen came in behind, carrying their boxes. The butler closed the door, then turned to walk left toward a phone. He lifted it and started to punch a button. Then he stopped.

"Why don't you take us upstairs?" Petra asked. There was a pistol in her hand aimed right into his face.

"What is this?"

"This," Petra Dortmund replied with a warm smile, "is my appointment." It was a Walther P-38 automatic pistol.

The butler swallowed hard as he saw the deliverymen open their boxes and reveal light submachine guns, which they loaded in front of him. Then one of them opened the front door and waved. In seconds, two more young men entered, both similarly armed.

Fürchtner ignored the new arrivals, and took a few steps to look around. They were in the large entrance foyer, its high, four-meter walls covered with artwork. Late Renaissance, he thought, noteworthy artists, but not true masters, large paintings of domestic scenes in gilt frames, which were in their way more impressive than the paintings themselves. The floor was white marble with black-diamond inserts at the joins, the furniture also largely gilt and French-looking. More to the point, there were no other servants in view, though he could hear a distant vacuum cleaner working. Fürchtner pointed to the two most recent arrivals and pointed them west on the first floor. The kitchen was that way, and there would doubtless be people there to control.

"Where is Herr Ostermann?" Petra asked next.

"He is not here, he—"

This occasioned a movement of her pistol, right against his mouth. "His automobiles and helicopter are here. Now, tell us where he is."

"In the library, upstairs."

"Gut. Take us there," she ordered. The butler looked into her eyes for the first time and found them far more intimidating than the pistol in her hand. He nodded and turned toward the main staircase.

This, too, was gilt, with a rich red carpet held in place with brass bars, sweeping on an elegant curve to the right as they climbed to the second floor. Ostermann was a wealthy man, a quintessential capitalist who'd made his fortune trading shares in various industrial concerns, never taking ownership in one, a string-puller, Petra Dortmund thought, a *Spinne,* a spider, and this was the center of his web, and they'd entered it of their own accord, and here the spider would learn a few things about webs and traps.

More paintings on the staircase, she saw, far larger than anything she'd ever done, paintings of men, probably the men who'd built and lived in this massive edifice, this monument to greed and exploitation . . . she already hated its owner who lived so well, so opulently, so publicly proclaiming that he was better than everyone else while he built up his wealth and exploited the ordinary workers. At the top of the staircase was a huge oil portrait of the Emperor Franz Josef himself, the last of his wretched line, who'd died just a few years before the even more hated Romanovs. The butler, this worker for the evil one, turned right, leading them down a wide hall into a doorless room. Three people were there, a man and two women, better dressed than the butler, all working away at computers.

"This is Herr Bauer," the butler said in a shaky voice. "He wishes to see Herr Ostermann."

"You have an appointment?" the senior secretary asked.

"You will take us in *now,*" Petra announced. Then the gun came into view, and the three people in the anteroom stopped what they were doing and looked at the intruders with open mouths and pale faces.

Ostermann's home was several hundred years old, but not entirely a thing of the past. The male secretary—in America he would have been called an executive assistant—was named Gerhardt Dengler. Under the edge of his desk was an alarm button. He thumbed this hard and long while he stared at the visitors. The wire led to the *schloss*'s central alarm panel, and from there to the alarm company. Twenty kilometers away, the employees at the central station responded to the buzzer and flashing light by immediately calling the office of the *Staatspolizei.* Then one of them called the *schloss* for confirmation.

"May I answer it?" Gerhardt asked Petra, who seemed to him to be in charge. He got a nod and lifted the receiver.

"Herr Ostermann's office."

"HIER *ist Traudl,*" the alarm company's secretary said.

"Guten Tag, Traudl. Hier ist Gerhardt," the executive assistant said. "Have you called about the horse?" That was the phrase for serious trouble, called a duress code.

"Yes, when is the foal due?" she asked, carrying on to protect the man on the other end, should someone be listening in on the line.

"A few more weeks, still. We will tell you when the time comes," he told her brusquely, staring at Petra and her pistol.

"Danke, Gerhardt. *Wiederseh'n."* With that, she hung up and waved to her watch supervisor.

■ ■ ■

"IT is about the horses," he explained to Petra. "We have a mare in foal and—"

"Silence," Petra said quietly, waving for Hans to approach the double doors into Ostermann's office. So far, she thought, so good. There was even some cause for amusement. Ostermann was right through those double doors, doing the work he did as though things were entirely normal, when they decidedly were not. Well, now it was time for him to find out. She pointed to the executive assistant. "Your name is? . . ."

"Dengler," the man replied. "Gerhardt Dengler."

"Take us in, Herr Dengler," she suggested, in a strangely childlike voice.

Gerhardt rose from his desk and walked slowly to the double doors, head down, his movements wooden, as though his knees were artificial. Guns did that to people, Dortmund and Fürchtner knew. The secretary turned the knobs and pushed, revealing Ostermann's office.

The desk was huge, gilt like everything else in the building, and sat on a huge red wool rug. Erwin Ostermann had his back to them, head down examining some computer display or other.

"Herr Ostermann?" Dengler said.

"Yes, Gerhardt?" was the reply, delivered in an even voice, and when there was no response, the man turned in his swivel chair—

—"What is this?" he asked, his blue eyes going very wide when he saw the visitors, and then wider still when he saw the guns. "Who—"

"We are commanders of the Red Workers' Faction," Fürchtner informed the trader. "And you are our prisoner."

"But—what is this?"

"You and we will be taking a trip. If you behave yourself, you will come to no harm. If you do not, you and others will be killed. Is that clear?" Petra asked. To make sure it was, she again aimed her pistol at Dengler's head.

What followed then could have been scripted in a movie. Ostermann's head snapped left and right, looking for something, probably help of some sort, which was not to be seen. Then he looked back at Hans and Petra and his face contorted itself into shock and disbelief. *This* could not be happening to *him*. Not *here,* not in *his own office.* Next came the outraged denial of the facts he could see before him . . . and then, finally, came fear. The process lasted five or six seconds. It was always the same. She'd seen it before, and realized that she'd forgotten how pleasurable it was to behold. Ostermann's hands balled into fists on the leather surface of his desk, then relaxed as his body realized how powerless it was. Trembling would start soon, depending on how much courage he might have. Petra didn't anticipate a great deal of that. He looked tall, even sitting down, thin—regal, even, in his white shirt with the starched collar and striped tie. The suit was clearly expensive, Italian silk, probably, finely tailored just for him. Under the desk would be custom-made shoes, polished by a servant. Behind him she could see lines of data marching upward on the computer screens. Here Ostermann was, in the center of his web, and scarcely a minute before he'd been totally at ease, feeling himself invincible, master of his fate, moving money around the world, adding to his fortune. Well, no more of that for a while—probably forever, though Petra had no intention of telling him that until the last possible second, the better to see the shock and terror on his regal face just before the eyes went blank and empty.

She had forgotten how it was, Petra realized, the sheer joy of the power she held in her hands. How had she ever gone so long without exercising it?

THE first police car to arrive on the scene had been only five kilometers away on getting the radio call. Reversing direction and racing to the *schloss* had only taken three minutes, and now it parked behind a tree, almost totally concealed from the house.

"I see a car and a delivery truck," the officer told his station chief, a captain. "No movement. Nothing else to be seen at the moment."

"Very well," the captain replied. "Take no action of any kind, and report any new developments to me at once. I will be there in a few minutes."

"Understood. *Ende.*"

The captain replaced the microphone. He was driving to the scene himself, alone in his Audi radio car. He'd met Ostermann once, at some official function in Vienna. Just a shake of the hand and a few cursory words, but he knew what the man looked like, and knew his reputation as a wealthy, civic-minded individual who was an especially faithful supporter of the opera . . . and the children's hospital, wasn't he? . . . Yes, that had been the reason for the reception at the city hall. Ostermann was a widower, had lost his first wife to ovarian cancer five years earlier. Now, it was said, he had a new interest in his life named Ursel von Prinze, a lovely dark-haired woman from an old family. That was the odd thing about Ostermann. He lived like a member of the nobility, but he'd come from humble roots. His father had been . . . an engineer, engine-driver actually, in the state railway, wasn't it? Yes, that was right. And so some of the old noble families had looked down on him, and to take care of that he'd bought social respectability with his charity work and his attendance at the opera. Despite the grandeur of his home, he lived fairly modestly. Little in the way of lavish entertaining. A quiet, modestly dignified man, and a very intelligent one, so they said of him. But now, his alarm company said, he had intruders in the house, Captain Willi Altmark told himself, taking the last turn and seeing the *schloss*. As often as he'd noticed it in passing, he had to remind himself now of the physical circumstances. A huge structure . . . perhaps four hundred meters of clear grass lawn between it and the nearest trees. Not good. Approaching the house covertly would be extremely difficult. He pulled his Audi close to the marked police car on the scene, and got out carrying a pair of binoculars.

"Captain," the first officer said by way of greeting.

"Have you seen anything?"

"No movement of any kind. Not even a curtain."

Altmark took a minute to sweep his binoculars over the building, then lifted the radio mike to tell all units en route to come quietly and slowly so as not to alert the criminals inside. Then he got a radio call from his superior, asking for his assessment of the situation.

"This may be a job for the military," Captain Altmark responded. "We know nothing at the moment. I can see an automobile and a truck. Nothing else. No gardeners out. Nothing. But I can only see two walls, and nothing behind the main house. I will get a perimeter set up as soon as additional units arrive."

"*Ja*. Make certain that no one can see us," the commissioner told the captain, quite unnecessarily.

"Yes, of course."

INSIDE, Ostermann had yet to rise from his chair. He took a moment to close his eyes, thanking God that Ursel was in London at the moment, having flown there in the private jet to do some shopping and meet with English friends. He'd hoped to join her there the following day, and now he wondered if he'd ever see his fiancée again. Twice he'd been approached by security consultants, an Austrian and a Brit. Both had lectured him on the implicit dangers of being so publicly rich, and told him how for a modest sum, less than £500,000 per year, he could greatly improve his personal security. The Britisher had explained that his people were all veterans of the SAS; the Austrian had employed Germans formerly of GSG-9. But he hadn't seen the need for employing gun-carrying commandos who would hover over him everywhere he went as though he were a chief of state, taking up space and just sitting there like—like bodyguards, Ostermann told himself. As a trader in stocks, commodities, and international currencies he'd had his share of missed opportunities, but this one . . .

"What do you want of me?"

"We want your personal access codes to the international trading network," Fürchtner told him. Hans was surprised to see the look of puzzlement on Ostermann's face.

"What do you mean?"

"The computer-access codes which tell you what is going on."

"But those are public already. Anyone can have them," Ostermann objected.

"Yes, certainly they are. That is why everyone has a house like this one." Petra managed an amused sneer.

"Herr Ostermann," Fürchtner said patiently. "We know there is a special network for people such as you, so that you can take advantage of special market conditions and profit by them. You think us fools?"

The fear that transformed the trader's face amused his two office guests. Yes, they knew what they weren't supposed to know, and they knew they could force him to give over the information. His thoughts were plain on his face.

Oh, my God, they think I have access to something that does not exist, and I will never be able to persuade them otherwise.

"We know how people like you operate," Petra assured him, immediately confirming his fear. "How you capitalists share information and manipulate your 'free' markets for your own greedy ends. Well, you will share that with us—or you will die, along with your lackeys." She waved her pistol at the outer office.

"I see." Ostermann's face was now as pale as his white Turnbull and Asser shirt. He looked out to the anteroom. He could see Gerhardt Dengler there, his hands on the top of his desk. Wasn't there an alarm system there? Ostermann couldn't remember now, so rapidly was his mind running through the data-avalanche that had so brutally interrupted his day.

THE first order of police business was to check the license-plate numbers of the vehicles parked close to the house. The automobile, they learned at once, was a rental. The truck tags had been stolen two days before. A detective team would go to the car-rental agency immediately to see what they might learn there. The next call was made to one of Herr Ostermann's business associates. The police needed to know how many domestic and clerical employees might be in the building along with the owner. That, Captain Altmark imagined, would take about an hour. He now had three additional police cars under his command. One of these looped around the property so that the two officers could park and approach from the rear on foot. Twenty minutes after arriving on the scene, he had a perimeter forming. The first thing he learned was that Ostermann owned a helicopter, sitting there behind the house. It was an American-made Sikorsky S-76B, capable of carrying a crew of two and a maximum of thirteen passengers—that information gave him the maximum number of hostages to be moved and criminals to move them. The helicopter landing pad was two hundred meters from the house. Altmark fixed on that. The criminals would almost certainly want to use the helicopter as their getaway vehicle. Unfortunately, the landing pad was a good three hundred meters from the treeline. This meant that some really good riflemen were needed, but his preset response team had them.

Soon after getting the information on the helicopter, one of his people turned up the flight crew, one at home, one at Schwechat International Airport doing some paperwork with the manufacturer's representative for an aircraft modification. Good, Willi Altmark thought, the helicopter wasn't going anywhere just yet. But by then the fact that Erwin Ostermann's house had been attacked had perked up to the senior levels of government, and then he received a very surprising radio call from the head of the *Staatspolizei.*

THEY barely made the flight—more precisely, the flight hadn't been delayed on their account. Chavez tightened his seat belt as the 737 pulled back from the jetway, and went over the preliminary briefing documents with Eddie Price. They'd just rolled off the tarmac when Price mated his portable computer with the aircraft's phone system. That brought up a diagram on his screen, with the caption "Schloss Ostermann."

"So, who is this guy?" Chavez asked.

"Coming in now, sir," Price replied. "A money-lender, it would appear, rather a wealthy one, friend of the prime minister of his country. I guess that explains matters so far as we are concerned."

"Yeah," Chavez agreed. *Two in a row for Team-2* was what he thought. A little over an hour's flight time to Vienna, he thought next, checking his watch. One such incident was happenstance, Chavez told himself, but terrorist incidents weren't supposed to happen so closely together, were they? Not that there was a rulebook out there, of course, and even if there were such a thing, these people would have violated it. Still . . . but there was no time for such thoughts. Instead, Chavez examined the information coming into Price's laptop and started wondering how he'd deal with this new situation. Farther aft, his team occupied a block of economy seats and spent their time reading paperback books, hardly talking at all about the upcoming job, since they knew nothing to talk about except where they were going.

"Bloody large perimeter for us to cover," Price observed, after a few minutes.

"Any information on the opposition?" Ding asked, then wondered how it was that he was adopting Brit-speak. *Opposition?* He should have said *bad guys.*

"None," Eddie replied. "No identification, no word on their numbers."

"Great," the leader of Team-2 observed, still staring sideways at the screen.

THE phones were trapped. Altmark had seen to that early on. Incoming calls were given busy signals, and outgoing calls would be recorded at the central telephone exchange—but there had been none, which suggested to Captain Altmark that the criminals were all inside, since they were not seeking external help. That could have meant they were using cellular phones, of course, and he didn't have the equipment to intercept those, though he did have similar traps on Ostermann's three known cellular accounts.

The *Staatspolizei* now had thirty officers on the scene and a tight perimeter fully formed and punctuated by a four-wheel armored vehicle, hidden in the trees. They'd stopped one delivery truck from coming in with some overnight express mail, but other vehicles had attempted to enter the property. For one so wealthy, Ostermann did indeed lead a quiet and unassuming life, the captain thought. He'd expected a constant parade of vehicles.

"HANS?"

"Yes, Petra?"

"The phones have not rung. We've been here for some time, but the phones have not rung."

"Most of my work is on computer," Ostermann said, having noted the same discrepancy himself. Had Gerhardt gotten the word out? If he had done so, was that good? He had no way of knowing. Ostermann had long joked about how cutthroat his profession was, how every step he took had danger, because others out there would try to rob him blind if they ever got the chance . . . but not one of them had ever threatened his life, nor had any ever pointed a loaded gun at him or a member of his staff. Ostermann used his remaining capacity for objectivity to realize that this was a new and dangerous aspect to the world that he'd never seriously considered, about which he knew very little, and against which he had nothing in the way of defenses. His only useful talent at the moment was his ability to read faces and the minds behind them, and though he'd never encountered anyone even vaguely close to the man and woman in his office now, he saw enough to be more afraid than he'd ever been before. The man, and even more the woman, were willing to kill him without any pangs of conscience whatsoever, no more emotion than he showed when picking up a million dollars of American T-bills. Didn't they know that his life had worth? Didn't they know that—

—no, Erwin Ostermann realized, they did not. They didn't know, and they didn't care. Worst of all, what they thought they did know wasn't true, and he would be hard-pressed indeed to persuade them otherwise.

Then, finally, a phone rang. The woman gestured for him to answer it.

"Hier ist Ostermann," he said on picking up the receiver. His male visitor did the same on another extension.

"Herr Ostermann, I am Captain Wilhelm Altmark of the *Staatspolizei.* You have guests there, I understand."

"Yes, I do, Captain," Ostermann replied.

"Could I speak with them, please?" Ostermann merely looked at Hans Fürchtner.

"You took your time, Altmark," Hans said. "Tell me, how did you find out?"

"I will not ask you about your secrets if you do not ask me about mine," the captain replied cooly. "I would like to know who you are and what you wish."

"I am Commander Wolfgang of the Red Workers' Faction."

"And what is it you want?"

"We want the release of several of our friends from various prisons, and transport to Schwechat International. We require an airliner with a range of more than five thousand kilometers and an international flight crew for a destination which we will make known when we board the aircraft. If we do not have these things by midnight, we will begin to kill some of our . . . our guests here in *Schloss Ostermann."*

"I see. Do you have a list of the prisoners whose release you require?"

Hans put one hand over the receiver and held the other out. "Petra, the list." She walked over and handed it to him. Neither seriously expected any cooperation on this issue, but it was part of the game, and the rules had to be followed. They'd decided on the way in that they'd have to kill one hostage certainly, more probably two, before they got the ride to the airport. The man, Gerhardt Dengler, would be killed first, Hans thought, then one of the women secretaries. Neither he nor Petra really wanted to kill any of the domestic help since they were genuine workers, not capitalist lackeys like the office staff. "Yes, here is the list, Captain Altmark . . ."

"OKAY," Price said, "we have a list of people we're expected to liberate for our friends." He turned the computer so that Chavez could see it.

"The usual suspects. Does this tell us anything, Eddie?"

Price shook his head. "Probably not. You can get these names from a newspaper."

"So, why do they do it?"

"Dr. Bellow will explain that they have to, to show solidarity with their compatriots, when in fact they are all sociopaths who don't care a rip for anyone but themselves." Price shrugged. "Cricket has rules. So does terrorism and—" Just then the captain of the airliner interrupted the revelation, and told everyone to put the seat backs up and tray tables away in preparation for landing.

"Showtime soon, Eddie."

"Indeed, Ding."

"So, this is just solidarity bullshit?" Ding asked, tapping the screen.

"Most likely, yes." With that, Price disconnected the phone line from his computer, saved his files, and shut the laptop down. Twelve rows aft, Tim Noonan did the same. All the Team-2 members started putting on their game faces as the British Airways 737 flared to land in Vienna. Someone had called ahead to someone else. The airliner taxied very rapidly indeed to its assigned jetway, and out his window Chavez could see a baggage truck with cops standing next to it waiting alongside the terminal.

IT was not an invisible event. A tower controller noted the arrival, having already noted a few minutes before that a Sabena flight scheduled in a slot ahead of the British aircraft had been given an unnecessary go-around order, and that a very senior police officer was in the tower, expressing interest in the British Airways flight. Then there was a second and very unnecessary baggage train with two police cars close by the A-4 jetway. What was this? he wondered. It required no great effort on his part to keep watch to learn more. He even had a pair of Zeiss binoculars.

▪ ▪ ▪

THE stewardess hadn't received instructions to get Team-2 off more quickly than anyone else, but she suspected there was something odd about them. They'd arrived without having been on her computerized manifest, and they were politer than the average business travelers. Their appearances were unremarkable, except all looked very fit, and all had arrived together in a single bunch, and headed to their seats in an unusually organized way. She had a job to do, however, as she opened the door into the jetway where, she saw, a uniformed policeman was waiting. He didn't smile or speak as she allowed the already-standing passengers to make their way off. Three from first class stopped just outside the aircraft, conferred with the policeman, then went out the door to the service stairs, which led directly to the tarmac. Being a serious fan of thriller and mystery novels, it was worth a look, she thought, to see who else went that way. The total was thirteen, and the number included all of the late-arriving passengers. She looked at their faces, most of which gave her a smile on the way out. Handsome faces, for the most part . . . more than that, manly ones, with expressions that radiated confidence, and something else, something conservative and guarded.

"Au revoir, madam," the last one said as he passed, with a very Gallic evaluative sweep of her figure and a charming smile.

"Christ, Louis," an American voice observed on the way out the side door. "You don't ever turn it off, do you?"

"Is it a crime to look at a pretty woman, George?" Loiselle asked, with a wink.

"Suppose not. Maybe we'll catch her on the flip-side," Sergeant Tomlinson conceded. She was pretty, but Tomlinson was married with four kids. Louis Loiselle never turned it off. Maybe it came along with being French, the American thought. At the bottom, the rest of the team was waiting. Noonan and Steve Lincoln were supervising the baggage transfer.

Three minutes later, Team-2 was in a pair of vans heading off the flight line with a police escort. This was noted by the tower controller, whose brother was a police reporter for a local paper. The cop who'd come to the tower departed without more than a *danke* to the controllers.

TWENTY minutes later, the vans stopped outside the main entrance to *Schloss Ostermann.* Chavez walked over to the senior officer.

"Hello, I am Major Chavez. This is Dr. Bellow, and Sergeant Major Price," he said, surprised to receive a salute from—

"Captain Wilhelm Altmark," the man said.

"What do we know?"

"We know there are two criminals inside, probably more, but the number is unknown. You know what their demands are?"

"Airplane to somewhere was the last I heard. Midnight deadline?"

"Correct, no changes in the past hour."

"Anything else. How will we get them to the airport?" Ding asked.

"Herr Ostermann has a private helicopter and pad about two hundred meters behind the house."

"Flight crew?"

"We have them over there." Altmark pointed. "Our friends have not yet asked for the flight, but that seems the most likely method of making the transfer."

"Who's been speaking with them?" Dr. Bellow asked from behind the shorter Chavez.

"I have," Altmark replied.

"Okay, we need to talk, Captain."

Chevez headed over to a van where he could change along with the rest of the team. For this night's mission—the sun was just setting—they wore not black but mottled green coveralls over their body armor. Weapons were issued and loaded, then selector switches went to the SAFE position. Ten minutes later, the team was outside and at the edge of the treeline, everyone with binoculars, checking out the building.

"I guess this here's the right side of the tracks," Homer Johnston observed. "Lotsa windows, Dieter."

"Ja," the German sniper agreed.

"Where you want us, boss?" Homer asked Chavez.

"Far side, both sides, crossfire on the chopper pad. Right now, people, and when you're set up, give me radio calls to check in. You know the drill."

"Everything we see, we call to you, *Herr Major,"* Weber confirmed. Both snipers got their locked rifle cases and headed off to where the local cops had their cars.

"Do we have a layout of the house?" Chavez asked Altmark.

"Layout?" the Austrian cop asked.

"Diagram, map, blueprints," Ding explained.

"Ach, yes, here." Altmark led them to his car. Blueprints were spread on the hood. "Here, as you see, forty-six rooms, not counting the basements."

"Christ," Chavez reacted at once. "More than one basement?"

"Three. Two under the west wing—wine cellar and cold-storage. East wing basement is unused. The doors down to it may be sealed. No basement under the center portion. The *schloss* was built in the late eighteenth century. Exterior walls and some interior ones are stone."

"Christ, it's a frickin' castle," Ding observed.

"That is what the word *schloss* means, *Herr Major,"* Altmark informed him.

"Doc?"

Bellow came over. "From what Captain Altmark tells me, they've been pretty businesslike to this point. No hysterical threats. They gave a deadline of midnight for movement to the airport, else they say they will start killing hostages. Their language is German, with a German accent, you said, Captain?"

Altmark nodded. *"Ja,* they are German, not Austrian. We have only one name, Herr Wolfgang—that is generally a Christian name, not a surname in our language, and we have no known criminal-terrorist by that name or pseudonym. Also, he said they are of the Red Workers' Faction, but we have no word on that organization either."

Neither did Rainbow. "So, we don't know very much?" Chavez asked Bellow.

"Not much at all, Ding. Okay," the psychiatrist went on, "what does that mean? It means they are planning to survive this one. It means they're serious businessmen in this game. If they threaten to do something, they will try to do it. They haven't killed anyone yet, and that also means they're pretty smart. No other demands made to this point. They will be coming, probably soon—"

"How do you know that?" Altmark asked. The absence of demands to this point had surprised him.

"When it gets dark, they'll be talking with us more. See how they haven't turned any lights on inside the building?"

"Yes, and what does that mean?"

"It means they think the darkness is their friend, and that means they will try to make use of it. Also, the midnight deadline. When it gets dark, we'll be closer to that."

"Full moon tonight," Price observed. "And not much cloud cover."

"Yeah," Ding noted in some discomfort when he looked up at the sky. "Captain, do you have searchlights we can use?"

"The fire department will have them," Altmark said.

"Could you please order them brought here?"

"Ja . . . Herr Doktor?"

"Yes?" Bellow said.

"They said that if they do not have those things done by midnight they will begin to kill hostages. Do you—"

"Yes, Captain, we have to take that threat very seriously. As I said, these folks are acting like serious people, well-trained and well-disciplined. We can make that work for us."

"How?" Altmark asked. Ding answered.

"We give them what they want, we let them think that they are in control . . . until it is time for us to take control. We feed their pride and their egos while we have to, and then, later, we stop doing it at a time that suits us."

OSTERMANN'S house staff was feeding the terrorists' bodies and their egos. Sandwiches had been made under the supervision of Fürchtner's team and brought around by deeply frightened staff members. Predictably, Ostermann's employees were not in a mood to eat, though their guests were.

Things had gone well to this point, Hans and Petra thought. They had their primary hostage under tight control, and his lackeys were now in the same room, with easy access to Ostermann's personal bathroom—hostages needed such access, and there was no sense in denying it to them. Otherwise, it stripped them of their dignity and made them desperate. That was inadvisable. Desperate people did foolish things, and what Hans and Petra needed at the moment was control over their every action.

Gerhardt Dengler sat in a visitor's chair directly across the desk from his employer. He knew he'd gotten the police to respond, and, like his boss, he was now wondering if that was a good or a bad thing. In another two years, he would have been ready to strike out on his own, probably with Ostermann's blessing. He'd learned much from his boss, the way a general's aide learns at the right hand of the senior officer. Though he'd been able to pursue his own destiny much more quickly and surely than a junior officer . . . what did he owe this man? What was required by this situation? Dengler was no more suited to this than Herr Ostermann was, but Dengler was younger, fitter . . .

One of the secretaries was weeping silently, the tears trickling down her cheeks from fear and from the rage of having her comfortable life upset so cruelly. What was wrong with these two that they thought they could invade the lives of ordinary people and threaten them with death? And what could she do about it? The answer to that was . . . nothing. She was skilled at routing calls, processing voluminous paperwork, keeping track of Herr Ostermann's money so ably that she was probably the best-paid secretary in the country—because Herr Ostermann was a generous boss, always with a kind word for his staff. He'd helped her and her husband—a stonemason—with their investments, to the point that they would soon be millionaires in their own right. She'd been with him long before his first wife had died of cancer, had watched him suffer through that, unable to help him do anything to ease the horrible pain, and then she'd rejoiced at his discovery of Ursel von Prinze, who'd allowed Herr Ostermann to smile again. . . .

Who were these people who stared at them as though they were objects, with guns in their hands like something from a movie . . . except that she and Gerhardt and the others were the bit players now. They couldn't go to the kitchen to fetch beer and pretzels. They could only live the drama to its end. And so she wept quietly at her powerlessness, to the contempt of Petra Dortmund.

HOMER Johnston was in his ghillie suit, a complex overall-type garment made of rags sewn into place on a gridded matrix, whose purpose was to make him appear to be a bush or a pile of leaves or compost, anything but a person with a rifle. The rifle was set up on its bipod, the hinged flaps on the front and back lenses of his telescopic sight flipped up. He'd picked a good place to the east of the helicopter pad that would allow him to cover the entire distance between the helicopter and the house. His laser rangefinder announced that he was 216 meters from a door on the back of the house and 147 meters from the front-left door of the helicopter. He was lying prone in a dry spot on the beautiful lawn, in the lengthening shadows close to the treeline, and the air brought to him the smell of horses, which reminded him of his childhood in the American northwest. Okay. He thumbed his radio microphone.

"Lead, Rifle Two-One."

"Rifle Two-One, Lead."

"In place and set up. I show no movement in the house at this time."

"Rifle Two-Two, in place and set up, I also see no movement," Sergeant Weber reported from his spot, two hundred fifty-six meters from Johnston. Johnston turned to see Dieter's location. His German counterpart had selected a good spot.

"Achtung," a voice called behind him. Johnston turned to see an Austrian cop approaching, not quite crawling on the grass. *"Hier,"* the man said, handing over some photos and withdrawing rapidly. Johnston looked at them. Good, shots of the hostages . . . but none of the bad guys. Well, at least he'd know whom *not* to shoot. With that, he backed off the rifle and lifted his green-coated military binoculars and began scanning the house slowly and regularly, left to right and back again. "Dieter?" he said over his direct radio link.

"Yes, Homer?"

"They get you the photos?"

"Yes, I have them."

"No lights inside . . ."

"Ja, our friends are being clever."

"I figure about half an hour until we have to go NVG."

"I agree, Homer."

Johnston grunted and turned to check the bag he'd carried in along with his rifle case and $10,000 rifle. Then he returned to scanning the building, patiently, like staking out a mountain deer trail for a big muley . . . a happy thought for the lifelong hunter . . . the taste of venison, especially cooked in the field over an open wood fire . . . some coffee from the blue, steel enamel pot . . . and the talking that came after a successful hunt . . . *Well, you can't eat what you shoot here, Homer,* the sergeant told himself, settling back into his patient routine. One hand reached into a pocket for some beef jerky to chew.

EDDIE Price lit his pipe on the far side of the dwelling. Not as big as Kensington Palace, but prettier, he thought. The thought disturbed him. It was something they'd talked about during his time in the SAS. What if terrorists—usually they thought of the Irish PIRA or INLA—attacked one of the Royal residences . . . or the Palace of Westminster. The SAS had walked through all of the buildings in question at one time or another, just to get a feel for the layout, the security systems, and the problems involved—especially after that lunatic had cracked his way into Buckingham Palace in the 1980s, walking into the Queen's own bedchamber. He still had chills about that!

The brief reverie faded. He had the *Schloss Ostermann* to worry about, Price remembered, scanning over the blueprints again.

"Bloody nightmare on the inside, Ding," Price finally said.

"That's the truth. All wood floors, probably creak, lots of places for the bad guys to hide and snipe at us. We'd need a chopper to do this right." But they didn't have a helicopter. That was something to talk with Clark about. Rainbow hadn't been fully thought through. Too fast on too many things. Not so much that they needed a helicopter as some good chopper crews trained in more than one type of aircraft, because when they deployed in the field, there was no telling what machines would be used by their host nation. Chavez turned: "Doc?"

Bellow came over. "Yes, Ding?"

"I'm starting to think about letting them out, walk to the helicopter behind the house, and taking them down that way rather than forcing our way in."

"A little early for that, isn't it?"

Chavez nodded. "Yeah, it is, but we don't want to lose a hostage, and come midnight, you said, we have to take that threat seriously."

"We can delay it some, maybe. My job to do that, over the phone."

"I understand, but if we make a move, I want it to be in the dark. That means tonight. I can't plan on having you talk them into surrender, unless you're thinking different? . . ."

"Possible, but unlikely," Bellow had to agree. He couldn't even speak confidently about delaying the threatened midnight kill.

"Next, we have to see if we can spike the building."

"I'm here," Noonan said. "Tall order, man."

"Can you do it?"

"I can probably get close unobserved, but there's over a hundred windows, and how the hell can I get to the ones on the second and third floors? Unless I do a dangle from a chopper and come down on the roof . . ." And that meant making sure that the local TV people, who'd show up as predictably as vultures over a dying cow, turned their cameras off and kept them off, which then ran the risk of alerting the terrorists when the TV reporters stopped showing the building of interest. And how could they fail to note that a helicopter had flown thirty feet over the roof of the building, and might there be a bad guy on the roof, already keeping watch?

"This is getting complicated," Chavez observed quietly.

"Dark and cold enough for the thermal viewers to start working," Noonan said helpfully.

"Yeah." Chavez picked up his radio mike. "Team, Lead, go thermal. Say again, break out the thermals." Then he turned. "What about cell phones?"

Noonan could do little more than shrug. There were now something like three hundred civilians gathered around, well back from the Ostermann property and controlled by local police, but most of them had a view of the house and the grounds, and if one of them had a cell phone and someone inside did as well, all that unknown person outside had to do was dial his buds on the inside to tell them what was going down. The miracles of modern communication worked both ways. There were over five hundred cellular frequencies, and the gear to cover them all was not part of Rainbow's regular kit. No terrorist or criminal operation had yet used that technique, to the best of their knowledge, but they couldn't all be dumb and stay dumb, could they? Chavez looked over at the *schloss* and thought again that they'd have to get the bad guys outside for this to work properly. Problem with that, he didn't know how many bad guys he'd have to deal with, and he had no way of finding out without spiking the building to gather additional information—which was a dubious undertaking for all the other reasons he'd just considered.

"Tim, make a note for when we get back about dealing with cellular phones and radios outside the objective. Captain Altmark!"

"Yes, Major Chavez?"

"The lights, are they here yet?"

"Just arrived, *ja,* we have three sets." Altmark pointed. Price and Chavez went over to look. They saw three trucks with attachments that looked for all the world like the lights one might see around a high-school football field. Meant to help fight a major fire, they could be erected and powered by the trucks that carried them. Chavez told Altmark where he wanted them and returned to the team's assembly point.

THE thermal viewers relied on difference in temperature to make an image. The evening was cooling down rapidly, and with it the stone walls of the house. Already the windows were glowing more brightly than the walls, because the house was heated, and the old-style full-length windows in the building's many doors were poorly insulated, despite the large drapes that hung just inside each one. Dieter Weber made the first spot.

"Lead, Rifle Two-Two, I have a thermal target first floor, fourth window from the west, looking around the curtains at the outside."

"Okay! That one's in the kitchen." It was the voice of Hank Patterson, who was hovering over the blueprints. "That's number one! Can you tell me anything else, Dieter?"

"Negative, just a shape," the German sniper replied. "No, wait . . . tall, probably a man."

"This is Pierce, I have one, first floor, east side, second window from east wall."

"Captain Altmark?"

"Ja?"

"Could you call Ostermann's office, please? We want to know if he's there." Because if he were, there would be one or two bad guys in with him.

"OSTERMANN office," a woman's voice answered.

"This is Captain Altmark. Who is this?"

"This is Commander Gertrude of the Red Workers' Faction."

"Excuse me, I was expecting to speak to Commander Wolfgang."

"Wait," Petra's voice told him.

"Hier ist Wolfgang."

"Hier ist Altmark. We have not heard from you in a long time."

"What news do you have for us?"

"No news, but we do have a request, Herr Commander."

"Yes, what is it?"

"As a sign of good faith," Altmark said, with Dr. Bellow listening in, a translator next to him. "We request that you release two of your hostages, from the domestic staff perhaps."

"*Wafür?* So they can help you identify us?"

"LEAD, Lincoln here, I have a target, northwest corner window, tall, probably male."

"That's three plus two," Chavez observed, as Patterson placed a yellow circle sticker on that part of the prints.

THE woman who'd answered the phone had remained on the line as well. "You have three hours until we send you a hostage, *todt,"* she emphasized. "You have any further requests? We require a pilot for Herr Ostermann's helicopter before midnight, and an airliner waiting at the airport. Otherwise, we will kill a hostage to show that we are quite serious, and then thereafter, at regular intervals. Do you understand?"

"Please, we respect your seriousness here," Altmark assured her. "We are looking for the flight crew now, and we have discussions underway with Austrian Airlines for the aircraft. These things take time, you know."

"You always say that, people like you. We have told you what *we* require. If you do not meet those requirements, then their blood is on your hands. *Ende,"* the voice said, and the line went dead.

CAPTAIN Altmark was both surprised and discomforted by the cold decisiveness on the other end of the phone and by the abrupt termination of the call. He looked up at Paul Bellow as he replaced the receiver. *"Herr Doktor?"*

"The woman is the dangerous one. They're both smart. They've definitely thought this one through, and they *will* kill a hostage to make their point, sure as hell."

■ ■ ■

"MAN-and-woman team," Price was saying over the phone. "German, ages . . . late thirties, early forties as a guess. Maybe older. Bloody serious," he added for Bill Tawney.

"Thanks, Eddie, stand by," came the reply. Price could hear the fingers tapping on the keyboard.

"Okay, lad, I have three possible teams for you. Uploading them now."

"Thank you, sir." Price opened his laptop again. "Ding?"

"Yeah?"

"Intelligence coming in."

"We have at least five terrs in there, boss," Patterson said, moving his finger around the prints. "Too quick for them to move around. Here, here, here, and two upstairs here. The placement makes sense. They probably have portable radios, too. The house is too big for them to communicate by shouting around at each other."

Noonan heard that and went off to his radio-intercept equipment. If their friends were using hand-held radios, then their frequency range was well known, determined by international treaty in fact, probably not the military sets the team used, and probably not encrypted. In seconds he had his computerized scanner set up and working off multiple antennas, which would allow him to triangulate on sources inside the house. These were coupled into his laptop computer, already overlaid with a diagram of the *schloss*. Three spear-carriers was about right, Noonan thought. Two was too few. Three was close to the right number, though the truck in front of the building could have easily held more. Two plus three, two plus four, two plus five? But they'd all be planning to leave, and the helicopter wasn't all that big. That made the total terrorist count at five to seven. A guess, and they couldn't go with a guess—well, they'd prefer not to—but it was a starting place. So many guesses. What if they were not using portable radios? What if they used cell phones? What if a lot of things, Noonan thought. You had to start somewhere, gather all the information you could, and then act on it. The problem with people like this was that they always decided the pace of the event. For all their stupidity and their criminal intent, which Noonan regarded as a weakness, they *did* control the pace, they decided when things happened. The team could alter it a little by cajolery—that was Dr. Bellow's part—but when you got down to it, well, the bad guys were the only ones willing to do murder, and that was a card that made a noise when it came down on the table. There were ten hostages inside, Ostermann, his three business assistants, and six people who looked after the house and grounds. Every one of them had a life and a family and the expectation to keep both. Team-2's job was to make sure that happened. But the bad guys still controlled too much, and this special agent of the Federal Bureau of Investigation didn't like that very much. Not for the first time, he wished he was one of the shooters, able, in due course, to go in and execute the take-down. But, good as he was at weapons and the physical side, he was better trained on the technical aspects of the mission. That was his area of personal expertise, and he served the mission best by sticking with his instruments. He didn't, however, have to like it.

"SO, what's the score, Ding?"

"Not all that good, Mr. C." Chavez turned to survey the building again. "Very difficult to approach the building because of the open ground, therefore difficult to spike and get tactical intelligence. We have two primary and probably three secondary subjects who seem professional and serious. I'm thinking in terms of letting them out to go to the helicopter and taking them down then. Snipers in place. But with the number of subjects, this might not be real pretty, John."

Clark looked at the display in his command center. He had continuous comm links with Team-2, including their computer displays. As before, Peter Covington was beside him to kibitz. "Might as well be a moated bloody castle," the British officer had observed earlier. He'd also noted the need for helicopter pilots as a permanent part of the team.

"One other thing," Chavez said. "Noonan says we need jamming gear for the cell phone freaks. We have a few hundred civilians around, and if one has a shoe phone, he can talk to our friends inside, tell them what we're doing. No way in hell we can prevent that without jamming gear. Write that one down, Mr. C."

"Noted, Domingo," Clark replied, looking over at David Peled, his chief technical officer.

"I can take care of that in a few days," Peled told his boss. Mossad had the right sort of equipment. Probably so did some American agencies. He'd find out in a hurry. Noonan, David told himself, was very good for a former policeman.

"Okay, Ding, you are released to execute at discretion. Good luck, my boy."

"GEE, thanks, dad" was the ironic reply. "Team-2, out." Chavez killed the radio and tossed the microphone back at the box. "Price!" he called.

"Yes, sir." The Sergeant Major materialized at his side.

"We have discretionary release," the leader told his XO.

"Marvelous, Major Chavez. What do you propose, sir?"

The situation had to be unfavorable, Ding told himself, if Price had reverted back to sirring him.

"Well, let's see what we got in the way of assets, Eddie."

KLAUS Rosenthal was Ostermann's head gardener, and at seventy-one the oldest member of the domestic staff. His wife was at home, he was sure, in her bed with a nurse in close attendance handling her medications, and worrying about him he was sure, and that worry could be dangerous to her. Hilda Rosenthal had a progressive heart condition that had invalidated her over the past three years. The state medical system had provided the necessary care for her, and Herr Ostermann had assisted as well, sending a friend of his, a full professor from Vienna's Algemeine Krankenhaus, to oversee the case, and a new drug-therapy treatment had actually improved Hilda's condition somewhat, but the fear she'd be feeling for him now certainly would not help, and that thought was driving Klaus mad. He was in the kitchen along with the rest of the domestic staff. He'd been inside getting a glass of water when they'd arrived—had he been outside he might well have escaped and raised the alarm and so helped to aid his employer, who'd been so considerate to all his staff, and Hilda! But luck had been against that when these swine had stormed into the kitchen with their weapons showing. Young ones, late twenties, the close one, whose name Rosenthal didn't know, was either a Berliner or from West Prussia, judging by his accent, and he'd recently been a skinhead, or so it appeared from the uniform-length stubble on his hatless head. A product of the DDR, the now-defunct East Germany. One of the new Nazis who'd grown out of that fallen communist nation. Rosenthal had met the old ones at Belzec concentration camp as a boy, and though he'd managed to survive that experience, the return of the terror of having one's life continue only at the whim of a madman with cruel piglike eyes . . . Rosenthal closed his eyes. He still had the nightmares that went along with the five-digit number tattooed on his forearm. Once a month he still awoke on sweaty sheets after reliving the former reality of watching people march into a building from which no one ever emerged alive . . . and always in the nightmare someone with a cruel young SS face beckons to him to follow them in there, too, because he needs a shower. *Oh, no,* he protests in the dream, *Hauptsturmführer Brandt needs me in the metalworking shop. Not today, Jude,* the young SS noncom says, with that ghastly smile, *Komm jetzt zu dem Braüserbad.* Every time he walks as bidden, for what else could one do, right to the door—and then every time he awakes, damp with perspiration, and sure that had he not awakened, he would not have awakened at all, just like all the people he'd watched march that way . . .

There are many kinds of fear, and Klaus Rosenthal had the worst of all. His was the certainty that he would die at the hands of one of *them,* the bad Germans, the ones who simply didn't recognize or care about the humanity of others, and there was no comfort in the certainty of it.

And that kind wasn't all gone, wasn't all dead yet. One was right in his field of view, looking back at him, his machine gun in his hands, looking at Rosenthal and the others in the kitchen like *Objekte,* mere objects. The other staff members, all Christians, had never experienced this, but Klaus Rosenthal had, and he knew what to expect—and knew that it was a certainty. His nightmare was real, risen from the past to fulfill his destiny, and then also kill Hilda, for her heart would not survive—and what could he do about it? Before, the first time, he'd been an orphaned boy apprenticed to a jeweler, where he'd learned to make fine metal items, which trade had saved his life—which trade he'd never followed afterward, so horrid were the memories associated with it. Instead he found the peace of working in the soil, making living things grow pretty and healthy. He had the gift; Ostermann had recognized it and told him that he had a job for life at this *schloss.* But that gift didn't matter to this Nazi with stubbly hair and a gun in his hands.

DING supervised the placement of the lights. Captain Altmark walked with him to each truck, then they both told the driver exactly where to go. When the light trucks were in place, and their light masts raised, Chavez returned to his team and sketched out the plan. It was after 11 now. It was amazing how fast time went when you needed more of it.

The helicopter crew was there, mostly sitting still, drinking coffee like good aviators, and wondering what the hell came next. It turned out that the copilot had a passing resemblance to Eddie Price, which Ding decided to make use of as a final backup part of his plan.

At 11:20, he ordered the lights switched on. The front and both sides of the *schloss* were bathed in yellow-white light, but not the back, which projected a triangular shadow all the way to the helicopter and beyond into the trees.

"Oso," Chavez said, "get over to Dieter and set up close to there."

"Roger, 'mano." First Sergeant Vega hoisted his M-60 onto his shoulder and made his way through the woods.

Louis Loiselle and George Tomlinson had the hardest part. They were dressed in their night greens. The coveralls over their black "ninja suits" looked like graph paper, light green background crosshatched in darker green lines, making blocks perhaps an eighth inch square. Some of the blocks were filled with the same dark green in random, squared-off patternless patterns. The idea dated back to World War II Luftwaffe night fighters whose designers had decided that the night was dark enough, and that black-painted fighter aircraft were easier to spot because they were darker than the night itself. These coveralls worked in principle and in exercises. Now they'd see if they worked in the real world. The blazing lights would help; aimed at and somewhat over the *schloss,* they'd serve to create an artificial well of darkness into which the green suits should disappear. They'd drilled it at Hereford often enough, but never with real lives at risk. That fact notwithstanding, Tomlinson and Loiselle moved out from different directions, keeping inside the triangular shadow all the way in. It took them twenty minutes of crawling.

"SO, Altmark," Hans Fürchtner said at 11:45, "are the arrangements set, or must we kill one of our hostages in a few minutes?"

"Please, do not do that, Herr Wolfgang. We have the helicopter crew on the way now, and we are working with the airline to get the aircraft released to us and ready for the flight. It is more difficult than you imagine to do these things."

"In fifteen minutes we shall see how difficult it is, Herr Altmark." And the line went dead.

Bellow didn't need a translator. The tone was enough. "He will do it," the psychiatrist told Altmark and Chavez. "The deadline is for real."

"Get the flight crew out," Ding ordered at once. Three minutes later, a marked police car approached the helicopter. Two men got out and entered the Sikorsky as the car drove away. Two minutes after that, the rotor started turning. Then Chavez keyed his command microphone.

"Team, this is Lead. Stand-to. I repeat, stand-to."

"EXCELLENT," Fürchtner said. He could barely see the turning rotor, but the blinking flying lights told the tale. "So, we begin. Herr Ostermann, stand up!"

Petra Dortmund made her way downstairs ahead of the important hostages. She frowned, wondering if she should be disappointed that they'd not killed this Dengler person to show their resolve. That time could come later when they started the serious interrogation aboard the airliner—and maybe Dengler knew all that Ostermann did. If so, killing him might be a tactical mistake. She activated her radio and called the rest of her people. They were assembling in the foyer as she came down the main staircase, along with the six hostages from the kitchen. No, she decided at the door, it would be better to kill a female hostage. That would have a greater impact on the police forces outside, all the more so if she were killed by another woman. . . .

"Are you ready?" Petra asked, receiving nods from the other four of her crew. "It will go as we planned," she told them. These people were disappointing ideologically, despite their having grown up and been educated in a proper socialist country—three of them even had military training, which had included political indoctrination. But they knew their jobs, and had carried them out to this point. She could ask for little more. The house staff was coming in from the kitchen area.

ONE of the cooks was having trouble walking, and that annoyed the stubble-headed swine, Rosenthal saw, as he stopped by the main food-preparation table. They were taking him, he knew, taking him to die, and as in his nightmare he was doing *nothing!* The realization came to him so suddenly as to cause a crippling wave of headachelike pain. His body twisted left, and he saw the table—and on it a small paring knife. His head snapped forward, saw the terrorists looking at Maria, the cook. In that moment, he made his decision, and snapped up the knife, tucking it up his right sleeve. Perhaps fate would give him a chance. If so, Klaus Rosenthal promised himself, this time he'd take it.

"TEAM-2, this is Lead," Chavez said over the radio links. "We should have them start to come out shortly. Everybody check in." He listened to two double clicks first of all, from Loiselle and Tomlinson close to the *schloss,* then the names.

"Rifle Two-One," Homer Johnston said. His night-vision system was now attached to his telescopic sight and trained rigidly on the building's main rear doors, as the rifleman commanded his breathing into a regular pattern.

"Rifle Two-Two," Weber called in a second later.

"Oso," Vega reported. He licked his lips as he brought his weapon up to his shoulder, his face covered with camouflage paint.

"Connolly."

"Lincoln."

"McTyler."

"Patterson."

"Pierce." They all reported from their spots on the grass.

"Price," the sergeant major reported from the left-side front seat of the helicopter.

"Okay, team, we are weapons-free. Normal rules of engagement in effect. Stay sharp, people," Chavez added unnecessarily. It was hard for the commander to stop talking in such a case. His position was eighty yards away from the helicopter, marginal range for his MP-10, with his NVGs aimed at the building.

"Door opening," Weber reported a fraction before Johnston.

"I have movement," Rifle Two-One confirmed.

"Captain Altmark, this is Chavez, kill the TV feed now," Ding ordered on his secondary radio.

"Ja, I understand," the police captain replied. He turned and shouted an order at the TV director. The cameras would stay on but would not broadcast, and the tapes from this point on were considered classified information. The signal going out on the airways now merely showed talking heads.

"Door open now," Johnston said from his sniper perch. "I see one hostage, looks like a male cook, and a subject, female, dark hair, holding a pistol." Sergeant Johnston commanded himself to relax, taking his finger off the double-set triggers of his rifle. He couldn't shoot now without a direct order from Ding, and that order would not come in such a situation. "Second hostage in view, it's Little Man," he said, meaning Dengler. Ostermann was Big Man, and the female secretaries were Blondie and Brownie, so named for their hair color. They didn't have photos for the domestic staff, hence no names for them. Known bad guys were "subjects."

They hesitated at the door, Johnston saw. Had to be a scary time for them, though how scary it was they would not and could not know. Too fucking bad, he thought, centering the crosshair reticle on her face from over two hundred yards away—which distance was the equivalent of ten feet for the rifleman. "Come on out, honey," he breathed. "We have something real special for you and your friends. Dieter?" he asked, keying his radio.

"On target, Homer," Rifle Two-Two replied. "We know this face, I think . . . I cannot recall the name. Leader, Rifle Two-Two—"

"Rifle Two, Lead."

"The female subject, we have seen her face recently. She is older now, but I know this face. Baader-Meinhof, Red Army Faction, one of those, I think, works with a man. Marxist, experienced terrorist, murderer . . . killed an American soldier, I think." None of which was particularly breaking news, but a known face was a known face.

Price broke in, thinking about the computer-morphing program they'd played with earlier in the week. "Petra Dortmund, perhaps?"

"Ja! That is the one! And her partner is Hans Fürchtner," Weber replied. *"Komm 'raus, Petra,"* he went on in his native language. *"Komm mir, Liebschen."*

SOMETHING was bothering her. It turned out to be difficult just to walk out of the *schloss* onto the open rear lawn, though she could plainly see the helicopter with its blinking lights and turning rotor. She took a step or started to, her foot not wanting to make the move out and downward onto the granite steps, her blue eyes screwed up, because the trees east and west of the *schloss* were lit so brightly by the lights on the far side of the house, with the shadow stretching out to the helicopter like a black finger, and maybe the thing that discomforted her was the deathlike image before her. Then she shook her head, disposing of the thought as some undignified superstition. She yanked at her two hostages and made her way down the six steps to the grass, then outward toward the waiting aircraft.

"YOU sure of the ID, Dieter?" Chavez asked.

"Ja, yes, I am, sir. Petra Dortmund."

Next to Chavez, Dr. Bellow queried the name on his laptop. "Age forty-four, ex-Baader-Meinhof, very ideological, and the word on her is that she's ruthless as hell. That's ten-year-old information. Looks like it hasn't changed very much. Partner was one Hans Fürchtner. They're supposed to be married, in love, whatever, and very compatible personalities. They're killers, Ding."

"For the moment, they are," Chavez responded, watching the three figures cross the grass.

"She has a grenade in one hand, looks like a frag," Homer Johnston said next. "Left hand, say again left."

"Confirmed," Weber chimed in. "I see the hand grenade. Pin is in. I repeat, pin is in."

"GREAT!" Eddie Price snarled over the radio. *Fürstenfeldbrück all bloody over again,* he thought, strapped into the helicopter, which would be holding the grenade and the fool who might pull the bloody pin. "This is Price. Just one grenade?"

"I only see the one," Johnston replied, "no bulges in her pockets or anything, Eddie. Pistol in her right hand, grenade in her left."

"I agree," Weber said.

"She's right-handed," Bellow told them over his radio circuit, after checking the known data on Petra Dortmund. "Subject Dortmund is right-handed."

Which explains why the pistol is there and the grenade in her left, Price told himself. It also meant that if she decided to throw the grenade properly, she'd have to switch hands. Some good news, he thought. Maybe it's been a long time since she played with one of the damned things. Maybe she was even afraid of things that went *bang,* his mind added hopefully. Some people just carried the damned things for visual effect. He could see her now, walking at an even pace toward the helicopter.

"Male subject in view—Fürchtner," Johnston said over the radio. "He has Big Man with him . . . and Brownie also, I think."

"Agree," Weber said, staring through his ten-power sight. "Subject Fürchtner, Big Man, and Brownie are in sight. Fürchtner appears to be armed with pistol only. Starting down the steps now. Another subject at the door, armed with submachine gun, two hostages with him."

"They're being smart," Chavez observed. "Coming in groups. Our pal started down when his babe was halfway . . . we'll see if the rest do that . . ." Okay, Ding thought. Four, maybe five, groups traversing the open ground. Clever bastards, but not clever enough . . . maybe.

As they approached the chopper, Price got out and opened both side doors for loading. He'd already stashed his pistol in the map pocket of the left-side copilot's door. He gave the pilot a look.

"Just act normally. The situation is under control."

"If you say so, Englishman," the pilot responded, with a rough, tense voice.

"The aircraft does not leave the ground under any circumstances. Do you understand?" They'd covered that before, but repetition of instructions was the way you survived in a situation like this.

"Yes. If they force me, I will roll it to your side and scream malfunction."

Bloody decent of you, Price thought. He was wearing a blue shirt with wings pinned on above the breast pocket and a name tag that announced his name as Tony. A wireless earpiece gave him the radio link to the rest of the team, along with a microphone chip inside his collar.

"Sixty meters away, not a very attractive woman, is she?" he asked his teammates.

"Brush your hair if you can hear me," Chavez told him from his position. A moment later, he saw Price's left hand go up nervously to push his hair back from his eyes. "Okay, Eddie. Stay cool, man."

"Armed subject at the door with three hostages," Weber called. "No, no, two armed subjects with three hostages. Hostage Blondie is with this one. Old man and middle-aged woman, all dressed as servants."

"At least one more bad guy," Ding breathed, and at least three more hostages to come. "Helicopter can't carry all of them . . ." What were they planning to do with the extras? he wondered. Kill them?

"I see two more armed subjects and three hostages inside the back door," Johnston reported.

"That's all the hostages," Noonan said. "Total of six subjects, then. How are they armed, Rifle One?"

"Submachine guns, look like Uzis or the Czech copy of it. They are leaning toward the door now."

"Okay, I got it," Chavez said, holding his own binoculars. "Riflemen, take aim on subject Dortmund."

"On target," Weber managed to say first. Johnston swiveled to take aim a fraction of a second later, and then he froze still.

The human eye is especially sensitive to movement at night. When Johnston moved clockwise to adjust the aim of his rifle, Petra Dortmund thought she might have seen something. It stopped her in her tracks, though she didn't know what it was that had stopped her. She stared right at Johnston, but the ghillie suit just looked like a clump of something, grass, leaves, or dirt, she couldn't tell in the semidarkness of green light reflecting off the pine trees. There was no man-shape to it, and the outline of the rifle was lost in the clutter well over a hundred meters away from her. Even so, she continued to look, without moving her gun hand, a look of curiosity on her face, not even visible alarm. Through Johnston's gunsight, the sergeant's open left eye could see the red strobe flashes from the helicopter's flying lights blinking on the ground around him while the right eye saw the crosshair reticle centered just above and between Petra Dortmund's eyes. His finger was on the trigger now, just barely enough to feel it there, about as much as one could do with so light a trigger pull. The moment lasted into several seconds, and his peripheral vision watched her gun hand most of all. If it moved too much, then . . .

But it didn't. She resumed walking to the helicopter, to Johnston's relief, not knowing that two sniper rifles followed her head every centimeter of the way. The next important part came when she got to the chopper. If she went around the right side, Johnston would lose her, leaving her to Weber's rifle alone. If she went left, then Dieter would lose her to his rifle alone. She seemed to be favoring . . . yes, Dortmund walked to the left side of the aircraft.

"Rifle Two-Two off target," Weber reported at once. "I have no shot at this time."

"On target, Rifle Two-One is on target," Johnston assured Chavez. *Hmm, let Little Man in first, honey,* he thought as loudly as he could.

Petra Dortmund did just that, pushing Dengler in the left-side door ahead of her, probably figuring to sit in the middle herself, so as to be less vulnerable to a shot from outside. A good theoretical call, Homer Johnston thought, but off the mark in this case. *Tough luck, bitch.*

The comfort of the familiar surroundings of the helicopter was lost on Gerhard Dengler at the moment. He strapped himself in under the aim of Petra's pistol, commanding himself to relax and be brave, as men did at such a time. Then he looked forward and felt hope. The pilot was the usual man, but the copilot was not. Whoever he was, he was fiddling with instruments as the flight crew did, but it wasn't him, though the shape of head and hair color were much the same, and both wore the white shirts with blue epaulets that private pilots tended to adopt as their uniforms. Their eyes met, and Dengler looked down and out of the aircraft, afraid that he'd give something away.

Good man, Eddie Price thought. His pistol was in the map pocket in the left-side door of the aircraft, well-hidden under a pile of flight charts, but easy to reach with his left hand. He'd get it, then turn quickly, bring it up and fire if it came to that. Hidden in his left ear, the radio receiver, which looked like a hearing aid if one saw it, kept him posted, though it was a little hard to hear over the engine and rotor sounds of the Sikorsky. Now Petra's pistol was aimed at himself, or the pilot, as she moved it back and forth.

"Riflemen, do you have your targets?" Chavez asked.

"Rifle Two-One, affirmative, target in sight."

"Rifle Two-Two, negative, I have something in the way. Recommend switch to subject Fürchtner."

"Okay, Rifle Two-Two, switch to Fürchtner. Rifle Two-One, Dortmund is all yours."

"Roger that, lead," Johnston confirmed. "Rifle Two-One has subject Dortmund all dialed in." The sergeant re-shot the range with his laser. One hundred forty-four meters. At this range, his bullet would drop less than an inch from the muzzle, and his "battle-sight" setting of two hundred fifty meters was a little high. He altered his crosshairs hold to just below the target's left eye. Physics would do the rest. His rifle had target-type double-set triggers. Pulling the rear trigger reduced the break-pull on the front one to a hard wish, and he was already making that wish. The helicopter would not be allowed to take off. Of more immediate concern, they couldn't allow the subjects to close the left-side door. His 7-mm match bullet would probably penetrate the polycarbonate window in the door, but the passage would deflect his round unpredictably, maybe causing a miss, perhaps causing the death or wounding of a hostage. He couldn't let that happen.

Chavez was well out of the action now, commanding instead of leading, something he'd practiced but didn't like very much. It was easier to be there with a gun in your hands than to stand back and tell people what to do by remote control. But he had no choice. Okay, he thought, we have Number One in the chopper and a gun on her. Number Two was in the open, two-thirds of the way to the chopper, and a gun on him. Two more bad guys were approaching the halfway point, with Mike Pierce and Steve Lincoln within forty meters, and the last two subjects still in the house, with Louis Loiselle and George Tomlinson in the bushes right and left of them. Unless the bad guys had set up overwatch in the house, one or more additional subjects to come out after the rest had made it to the chopper . . . very unlikely, Chavez decided, and in any case all the hostages were either in the open or soon would be—and rescuing them was the mission, not necessarily killing the bad guys, he reminded himself. It wasn't a game and it wasn't a sport, and his plan, already briefed to Team-2's members, was holding up. The key to it now was the final team of subjects.

ROSENTHAL saw the snipers. It was to be expected, though it had occurred to no one. He was the head gardener. The lawn was his, and the odd piles of material left and right of the helicopter were things that didn't belong, things that he would have known about. He'd seen the TV shows and movies. This was a terrorist incident, and the police would respond somehow. Men with guns would be out there, and there were two *things* on his lawn that hadn't been there in the morning. His eyes lingered on Weber's position, then fixed on it. There was his salvation or his death. There was no telling now, and that fact caused his stomach to contract into a tight, acid-laden ball.

"HERE they come," George Tomlinson announced, when he saw two legs step out of the house . . . women's legs, followed by a man's, then two more sets of women's . . . and then a man's. "One subject and two hostages out. Two more hostages to go . . ."

■ ■ ■

FÜRCHTNER was almost there, heading to the right side of the helicopter, to the comfort of Dieter Weber. But then he stopped, seeing inside the open right-side door to where Gerhardt Dengler was sitting, and decided to go to the other side.

"OKAY, Team, stand by," Chavez ordered, trying to keep all four groups juggled in the same control, sweeping his binoculars over the field. As soon as the last were in the open . . .

"YOU, get inside, facing back." Fürchtner pushed Brownie toward the aircraft.

"Off target, Rifle Two-Two is off the subject," Weber announced rather loudly over the radio circuit.

"Re-target on the next group," Chavez ordered.

"Done," Weber said. "I'm on the lead subject, group three."

"Rifle Two-One, report!"

"Rifle Two-One tight on Subject Dortmund," Homer Johnston replied at once.

"Ready here!" Loiselle reported next from the bushes at the back of the house. "We have the fourth group now."

Chavez took a deep breath. All the bad guys were now in the open, and now it was time:

"Okay, Lead to team, *execute, execute, execute!*"

LOISELLE and Tomlinson were already tensed to stand, and both fairly leaped to their feet invisibly, seven meters behind their targets, who were looking the wrong way and never had a clue what was going on behind them. Both soldiers lined up their tritium-lit sights on their targets. Both were pushing-dragging women, and both were taller than their hostages, which made things easy. Both MP-10 submachine guns were set on three-round burst, and both sergeants fired at the same instant. There was no immediate sound. Their weapons were fully suppressed by the design in which the barrel and silencer were integrated, and the range was too close to miss. Two separate heads were blown apart by multiple impacts of large hollow-point bullets, and both bodies dropped limp to the lush green grass almost as quickly as the cartridge cases ejected by the weapons that had killed them.

"This is George. Two subjects dead!" Tomlinson called over the radio, as he started running to the hostages who were still walking toward the helicopter.

HOMER Johnston was starting to cringe as a shape entered his field of view. It seemed to be a female body from the pale silk blouse, but his sight picture was not obscured yet, and with his crosshair reticle set just below Petra Dortmund's left eye, his right index finger pushed gently back on the set-trigger. The rifle roared, sending a meter-long muzzle flash into the still night air—

—she'd just seen two pale flashes in the direction of the house, but she didn't have time to react when the bullet struck the orbit just above her left eye. The bullet drove through the thickest part of her skull. It passed a few more centimeters and then the bullet fragmented into over a hundred tiny pieces, ripping her brain tissue to mush, which then exploded out the back of her skull in an expanding red-pink cloud that splashed over Gerhardt Dengler's face—

—Johnston worked the bolt, swiveling his rifle for another target; he'd seen the bullet dispatch the first.

EDDIE Price saw the flash, and his hands were already moving from the *execute* command heard half a second earlier. He pulled his pistol from the map pocket and dove out the helicopter's autolike door, aiming it one-handed at Hans Fürchtner's head, firing one round just below his left eye, which expanded and exploded out the top of his head. A second round followed, higher, and actually not a well-aimed shot, but Fürchtner was already dead, falling to the ground, his hand still holding Erwin Ostermann's upper arm, and pulling him down somewhat until the fingers came loose.

THAT left two. Steve Lincoln took careful aim from a kneeling position, then stopped as his target passed behind the head of an elderly man wearing a vest. "Shit," Lincoln managed to say.

Weber got the other one, whose head exploded like a melon from the impact of the rifle bullet.

Rosenthal saw the head burst apart like something in a horror movie, but the large stubbly head next to his was still there, eyes suddenly wide open, and a machine gun still in his hand—and nobody was shooting at this one, standing next to him. Then Stubble-Head's eyes met his, and there was fear/hate/shock there, and Rosenthal's stomach turned to sudden ice, all time stopped around him. The paring knife came out of his sleeve and into his hand, which he swung wildly, catching the back of Stubble-Head's left hand. Stubble-Head's eyes went wider as the elderly man jumped aside, and his one hand went slack on the forestock of his weapon.

That cleared the way for Steve Lincoln, who fired a second three-round burst, which arrived simultaneously with a second rifle bullet from Weber's semiautomatic sniper rifle, and this one's head seemed to disappear.

"CLEAR!" Price called. "Clear aircraft!"

"Clear house!" Tomlinson announced.

"Clear middle!" Lincoln said last of all.

AT the house, Loiselle and Tomlinson raced to their set of hostages and dragged them east, away from the house, lest there be a surviving terrorist inside to fire at them.

Mike Pierce did the same, with Steve Lincoln covering and assisting.

It was easier for Eddie Price, who first of all kicked the gun from Fürchtner's dead hand and made a quick survey of his target's wrecked head. Then he jumped into the helicopter to make sure that Johnston's first round had worked. He needed only to see the massive red splash on the rear bulkhead to know that Petra Dortmund was in whatever place terrorists went to. Then he carefully removed the hand grenade from her rigid left hand, checked to make sure the cotter pin was still in place, and pocketed it. Last of all, he took the pistol from her right hand, engaged the safety and tossed that.

"Mein Herr Gott!" the pilot gasped, looking back.

Gerhardt Dengler looked dead as well, his face fairly covered on its left side with a mask of dripping red, his open eyes looking like doorknobs. The sight shook Price for a moment, until he saw the eyes blink, but the mouth was wide open, and the man seemed not to be breathing. Price reached down to flip off the belt buckle, then let Johnston pull the man clear of the aircraft. Little Man made it one step before falling to his knees. Johnston poured his canteen over the man's face to rinse off the blood. Then he unloaded his rifle and set it on the ground.

"Nice work, Eddie," he told Price.

"And that was a bloody good shot, Homer."

Sergeant Johnston shrugged. "I was afraid the gal would get in the way. Another couple of seconds and I wouldn't've had shit. Anyway, Eddie, nice work coming out of the aircraft and doing him before I could get number two off."

"You had a shot on him?" Price asked, safing and holstering his pistol.

"Waste of time. I saw his brains come out from your first."

The cops were swarming in now, plus a covey of ambulances with blinking blue lights. Captain Altmark arrived at the helicopter, with Chavez at his side. Experienced cop that he was, the mess inside the Sikorsky made him back away in silence.

"It's never pretty," Homer Johnston observed. He'd already had his look. The rifle and bullet had performed as programmed. Beyond that, it was his fourth sniper kill, and if people wanted to break the law and hurt the innocent, it was their problem, not his. One more trophy he couldn't hang on the wall with the muley and elk heads he'd collected over the years.

Price walked toward the middle group, fishing in his pocket for his curved briar pipe, which he lit with a kitchen match, his never-changing ritual for a mission completed.

Mike Pierce was assisting the hostages, all sitting for the moment while Steve Lincoln stood over them, his MP-10 out and ready for another target. But then a gaggle of Austrian police exploded out the back door, telling him that there were no terrorists left inside the building. With that, he safed his weapon and slung it over his shoulder. Lincoln came up to the elderly gent.

"Well done, sir," he told Klaus Rosenthal.

"What?"

"Using the knife on his hand. Well done."

"Oh, yeah," Pierce said, looking down at the mess on the grass. There was a deep cut on the back of its left hand. "You did that, sir?"

"Ja" was all Rosenthal was able to say, and that took three breaths.

"Well, sir, good for you." Pierce reached down to shake his hand. It hadn't really mattered very much, but resistance by a hostage was rare enough, and it had clearly been a gutsy move by the old gent.

"Amerikaner?"

"Shhh." Sergeant Pierce held a finger up to his lips. "Please don't tell anyone, sir."

Price arrived then, puffing on his pipe. Between Weber's sniper rifle and someone's MP-10 burst, this subject's head was virtually gone. "Bloody hell," the sergeant major observed.

"Steve's bird," Pierce reported. "I didn't have a clear shot this time. Good one, Steve," he added.

"Thank you, Mike," Sergeant Lincoln replied, surveying the area. "Total of six?"

"Correct," Eddie answered, heading off toward the house. "Stand by here."

"Easy shots, both of 'em," Tomlinson said in his turn, surrounded by Austrian cops.

"Too tall to hide," Loiselle confirmed. He felt like having a smoke, though he'd quit two years before. His hostages were being led off now, leaving the two terrorists on the lush green grass, which their blood, he thought, would fertilize. Blood was good fertilizer, wasn't it? Such a fine house. A pity they'd not have the chance to examine it.

Twenty minutes later, Team-2 was back at the assembly point, changing out of their tactical clothes, packing their weapons and other gear for the ride back to the airport. The TV lights and cameras were running, but rather far away. The team was relaxing now, the stress bleeding off with the successful completion of their mission. Price puffed on his pipe outside the van, then tapped it out on the heel of his boot before boarding it.

CHAPTER 8

COVERAGE

THE TELEVISION COVERAGE WAS OUT BEFORE TEAM-2 flew into Heathrow. Fortunately, the video of the event was hampered by the *schloss*'s great size and the fact that the *Staatspolizei* kept the cameras well away from events, and on the wrong side of the building. About the only decent shot was of a team member lighting a pipe, followed by Captain Wilhelm Altmark's summary of events for the assembled reporters. A special and heretofore secret team of his country's federal police had dealt efficiently with the incident at Schloss Ostermann, he said, rescuing all of the hostages—no, unfortunately, no criminals had been arrested. All of this was taped for later use by Bill Tawney's staff off Austrian State Television, Sky News, and every other European news service that made use of the story. Though the British Sky News service had managed to get its own camera to Vienna, the only difference between its coverage and that of the locals was the angle. Even the various learned commentaries were essentially the same: specially trained and equipped police unit; probably with members of Austria's military; decisive action to resolve the incident with no injuries to the innocent victims; score one more, they didn't quite say, for the good guys. The bad guys' identities weren't put out with the initial reports. Tracking them down would be a police function, and the results would be fed to Tawney's intelligence section, along with the debriefs of the victims.

It had been a very long day for the Team-2 members, all of whom went home to sleep on arrival back at Hereford, with notification from Chavez that they'd dispense with morning PT the next day. There wasn't even time for a congratulatory set of beers in the local NCO Club—which in any case was closed by the time they got home.

On the flight home, Chavez noted to Dr. Bellow that despite the fitness of his people the fatigue factor was pretty high—more so than on their occasional night exercises. Bellow replied that stress was the ultimate fatigue generator, and that the team members were not immune to stress, no matter what their training or fitness. That evidently included himself, since after making the pronouncement, Bellow turned and slipped off to sleep, leaving Chavez to do the same after a glass of red Spanish wine.

IT was the lead news story in Austria, of course. Popov caught the first bit of it live in a *Gasthaus,* then more in his hotel room. He sipped orange schnapps while he applied his keen, professional eye to the screen. These antiterror groups all looked pretty much the same, but that was to be expected, since they all trained to do the same thing and worked out of the same international manual—first promulgated by the English with their Special Air Service commandos, then followed by the German GSG-9, and then the rest of Europe, followed by the Americans—down to the black clothing, which struck Popov as theatrical, but they all had to wear something, and black made more sense than white clothing, didn't it? Of more immediate interest, there in the room with him was the leather attaché case filled with D-mark banknotes, which he would take to Bern the following day for deposit in his account before flying back to New York. It was remarkable, he thought as he switched the TV off and pulled the bedclothes up, two simple jobs, and he now had just over one million American dollars in his numbered and anonymous account. Whatever his employers wanted him to accomplish for them, he was being well compensated for it, and they didn't seem overly concerned by the expense. So much the better that the money went to a good cause, the Russian thought.

"THANK God," George Winston noted. "Hell, I know that guy. Erwin's good people," the Secretary of the Treasury said on his way out of the White House, where the cabinet meeting had run very long.

"Who did the takedown?"

"Well—" That caught him short. He wasn't supposed to say, and wasn't supposed to know. "What did the news say?"

"Local cops, Vienna police SWAT team, I guess."

"Well, I suppose they learned up on how to do it," SecTreas opined, heading toward his car with his Secret Service detail.

"The *Austrians?* Who'd they learn it from?"

"Somebody who knows how, I guess," Winston replied, getting into the car.

"So, what's the big deal about it?" Carol Brightling asked the Secretary of the Interior. To her it looked like another case of boys and their toys.

"Nothing, really," the Secretary replied, her own protective detail guiding her to the door of her official car. "Just that what they showed on TV, it was a pretty good job of rescuing all those people. I've been to Austria a few times, and the cops didn't strike me as all that great. Maybe I'm wrong. But George acts like he knows more than he's telling."

"Oh, that's right, Jean, he's 'inner cabinet,' " Dr. Brightling observed. It was something those in the "outer cabinet" didn't like. Of course, Carol Brightling wasn't technically in the cabinet at all. She had a seat against the wall instead of around the table, there only in case the issues of the meeting required a scientific opinion, which they hadn't today. Good news and bad news. She got to listen in on everything, and she took her notes on all that happened in the ornate, stuffy room that overlooked the Rose Garden, while the President controlled the agenda and the pace—badly in today's case, she thought. Tax policy had taken over an hour, and they'd never gotten to use of national forests, which came under the Department of the Interior, which issue had been postponed to the next meeting, a week away.

She didn't have a protective detail, either, not even an office in the White House itself. Previous Presidential Science Advisors had been in the West Wing, but she'd been moved to the Old Executive Office Building. It was a larger and more comfortable office, with a window, which her basement office in the White House would not have had, but though the OEOB was considered part of the White House for administrative and security purposes, it didn't have quite the prestige, and prestige was what it was all about if you were part of the White House staff. Even under this President, who worked pretty hard to treat everyone the same and who wasn't into the status bullshit—there was no avoiding it at this level of government. And so, Carol Brightling clung to her right to have lunch in the White House Mess with the Big Boys and Big Girls of the Administration, and grumbled that to see the President except at his request, she had to go through the Chief of Staff and the appointments secretary to get a few minutes of His Valuable Time. As though she'd ever wasted it.

A Secret Service agent opened the door for her with a respectful nod and smile, and she walked into this surpassingly ugly building, then turned right to her office, which at least overlooked the White House. She handed her notes to her (male, of course) secretary on the way in for transcription, then sat down at her desk, finding there a new pile of papers to be read and acted upon.

She opened her desk drawer and got herself a starlight mint to suck on as she attacked the pile. Then on reflection she lifted her TV controller and turned her office television to CNN for a look at what was happening around the world. It was the top of the hour, and the lead story was the thing in Vienna.

God, what a house was her first thought. Like a king's palace, a huge waste of resources for one man, or even one large family, to use as a private residence. What was it Winston had said of the owner? Good people? Sure. All good people lived like wastrels, glomming up precious resources like that. Another goddamned plutocrat, stock trader, currency speculator, however he earned the money to buy a place like that—and then terrorists had invaded his privacy. Well, gee, she thought, I wonder why they picked him. No sense attacking a sheep farmer or truck driver. Terrorists went after the moneyed people, or the supposedly important ones, because going for ordinary folks had little in the way of a political point, and these were, after all, political acts. But they hadn't been as bright as they ought to have been. Whoever had picked them had . . . picked them to fail? Was *that* possible? She supposed that it was. It was a *political* act, after all, and such things could have all manner of real purposes. That brought a smile, as the reporter described the attack by the local police SWAT team—unfortunately not shown, because the local cops hadn't wanted cameras and reporters in the way—then the release of the hostages, shown in closeup to let people share the experience. They'd been so close to death, only to be released, saved by the local cops, who'd really only restored to them their programmed time of death, because everything died, sooner or later. That was Nature's plan, and you couldn't fight Nature . . . though you could help her along, couldn't you? The reporter went on to say that this had been the second terrorist incident in Europe over the last couple of months, both of them failures due to adroit police action. Carol remembered the attempted robbery in Bern, another botch . . . a creative one? She might have to find that out, though in this case a failure was as useful as—no, *more* useful than—a success, for the people who were planning things. That thought brought a smile. Yes. It was more useful than a success, wasn't it? And with that she looked down at a fax from Friends of the Earth, who had her direct number and frequently sent her what they thought was important information.

She leaned back in her comfortable high-backed chair to read it over twice. A good bunch of people with the right ideas, though few listened to them.

"Dr. Brightling?" Her secretary stuck his head in the door.

"Yes, Roy?"

"You still want me to show you those faxes—like the one you're reading, I mean?" Roy Gibbons asked.

"Oh, yes."

"But those people are card-carrying nuts."

"Not really. I like some of the things they do," Carol replied, tossing the fax in her trash can. She'd save their idea for some future date.

"Fair enough, doc." The head disappeared back into the outer office.

The next thing in her pile was pretty important, a report of procedures for shutting down nuclear power reactors, and the subsequent safety of the shut-down reactor systems: how long before environmental factors might attack and corrode the internal items, and what environmental damage could result from it. Yes, this was very important stuff, and fortunately the index appended to it showed data on individual reactors across the country. She popped another starlight mint into her mouth and leaned forward, setting the papers flat on the desktop so that she could stare straight down at them for reading purposes.

"THIS seems to work," Steve said quietly.

"How many strands fit inside?" Maggie asked.

"Anywhere from three to ten."

"And how large is the overall package?"

"Six microns. Would you believe it? The packaging is white in color, so it reflects light pretty well, especially UV radiation, and in a water-spray environment, it's just about invisible." The individual capsules couldn't be seen with the naked eye, and only barely with an optical microscope. Better still, their weight was such that they'd float in air about the same as dust particles, as readily breathable as secondhand smoke in a singles bar. Once in the body, the coating would dissolve, and allow release of the Shiva strands into the lungs or the upper GI, where they could go to work.

"Water soluble?" Maggie asked.

"Slowly, but faster if there's anything biologically active in the water, like the trace hydrochloric acid in saliva, for example. Wow, we could have really made money from the Iraqis with this one, kiddo—or anybody who wants to play bio-war in the real world."

Their company had invented the technology, working on an NIH grant designed to develop an easier way than needles to deliver vaccines. Needles required semiskilled use. The new technique used electrophoresis to wrap insignificantly tiny quantities of protective gel around even smaller amounts of airborne bioactive agents. That would allow people to ingest vaccines with a simple drink rather than the more commonly used method of inoculation.

If they ever fielded a working AIDS vaccine, this would be the method of choice for administering it in Africa, where countries lacked the infrastructure to do much of anything. Steve had just proven that the same technology could be used to deliver active virus with the same degree of safety and reliability. Or almost proven it.

"How do we proof-test it?" Maggie asked.

"Monkeys. How we fixed for monkeys in the lab?"

"Lots," she assured him. This would be an important step. They'd give it to a few monkeys, then see how well it spread through the laboratory population. They'd use rhesus monkeys. Their blood was so similar to humans'.

SUBJECT Four was the first, as expected. He was fifty-three years old and his liver function was so far off the scale as to qualify him for a high place on the transplant list at the University of Pittsburgh. His skin had a yellowish cast in the best of circumstances, but that didn't stop him from hitting the booze harder than any of their test subjects. His name, he said, was Chester something, Dr. John Killgore remembered. Chester's brain function was about the lowest in the group as well. He watched TV a lot, rarely talked to anyone, never even read comic books, which were popular with the rest, as were TV cartoons—watching the Cartoon Channel was among their most popular pastimes.

They were all in hog heaven, John Killgore had noted. All the booze and fast food and warmth that they could want, and most of them were even learning to use the showers. From time to time, a few would ask what the deal was here, but their inquiries were never pressed beyond the pro-forma answer they got from the doctors and security guards.

But with Chester, they had to take action now. Killgore entered the room and called his name. Subject Four rose from his bunk and came over, clearly feeling miserable.

"Not feeling good, Chester?" Killgore asked from behind his mask.

"Stomach, can't keep stuff down, feel crummy all over," Four replied.

"Well, come along with me and we'll see what we can do about that, okay?"

"You say so, doc," Chester replied, augmenting the agreement with a loud belch.

Outside the door, they put him in a wheelchair. It was only fifty yards to the clinical side of the installation. Two orderlies lifted Number Four into a bed, and restrained him into it with Velcro ties. Then one of them took a blood sample. Ten minutes later, Killgore tested it for Shiva antibodies, and the sample turned blue, as expected. Chester, Subject Number Four, had less than a week to live—not as much as the six to twelve months to which his alcoholism had already limited him, but not really all that much of a reduction, was it? Killgore went back inside to start an IV into his arm, and to calm Chester down, he hung a morphine drip that soon had him unconscious and even smiling slightly. Good. Number Four would soon die, but he would do so in relative peace. More than anything else, Dr. Killgore wanted to keep the process orderly.

He checked his watch when he got back to his office/viewing room. His hours were long ones. It was almost like being a real physician again. He hadn't practiced clinical medicine since his residency, but he read all the right journals and knew the techniques, and besides, his current crop of patient/victims wouldn't know the difference anyway. Tough luck, Chester, but it's a tough world out there, Steve thought, going back to his notes. Chester's early response to the virus had been a little unsettling—only half the time programmed—but it had been brought about by his grossly reduced liver function. It couldn't be helped. Some people would get hit sooner than others because of differing physical vulnerabilities. So the outbreak would start unevenly. It shouldn't matter in the eventual effects, though it would alert people sooner than he hoped it would. That would cause a run on the vaccines Steve Berg and his shop were developing. "A" would be widely distributed after the rush to manufacture it. "B" would be more closely held, assuming that he and his team could indeed get it ready for use. "A" would go out to everybody, while "B" would go only to those people who were supposed to survive, people who understood what it was all about, or who would accept their survival and get on with things with the rest of the crew.

Killgore shook his head. There was a lot of stuff left to be done, and as usual, not enough time to do it.

CLARK and Stanley went over the takedown immediately upon their arrival in the morning, along with Peter Covington, still sweaty from his morning workout with Team-1. Chavez and his people would just be waking up after their long day on the European mainland.

"It was a bloody awful tactical situation. And Chavez is right," Major Covington went on. "We need our own helicopter crews. Yesterday's mission cried out for that, but we didn't have what we needed. That's why he had to execute a poor plan and depend on luck to accomplish it."

"He could have asked their army for help," Stanley pointed out.

"Sir, we both know that one doesn't commit to an important tactical move with a helicopter crew one doesn't know and with whom one has not worked," Covington observed, in his best Sandhurst grammar. "We need to look at this issue immediately."

"True," Stanley agreed, looking over at Clark.

"Not part of the TO and E, but I see the point," Rainbow Six conceded. How the hell had they overlooked this requirement? He asked himself. "Okay, first let's figure all the chopper types we're likely to see, and then find out if we can get some drivers who're current in most of them."

"Ideally, I'd love to have a Night Stalker—but we'd have to take it with us everywhere we go, and that means—what? A C-5 or a C-17 transport aircraft assigned to us at all times?" Stanley observed.

Clark nodded. The Night Stalker version of the McDonnell-Douglas AH-6 Loach had been invented for Task Force 160, now redesignated the 160th Special Operations Aviation Regiment—SOAR—based at Fort Campbell, Kentucky. They were probably the wildest and craziest bunch of aviators in the world, who worked on the sly with brother aviators from selected other countries—Britain and Israel were the two most often allowed into the 160 compound at Campbell. In a real sense, getting the choppers and flight crews assigned to Rainbow would be the easy part. The hard part would be getting the fixed-wing transport needed to move the chopper to where they needed it. It'd be about as hard to hide as an elephant in a schoolyard. With Night Stalker they'd have all manner of surveillance gear, a special silent rotor—*and Santa on his fucking sleigh with eight tiny reindeer,* Clark's mind went on. It would never happen, despite all the drag he had in Washington and London.

"Okay, I'll call Washington for authorization to get some aviators on the team. Any problem getting some aircraft here for them to play with?"

"Shouldn't be," Stanley replied.

John checked his watch. He'd have to wait until 9:00 A.M. Washington time—2:00 P.M. in England—to make his pitch via the Director of the Central Intelligence Agency, which was the routing agency for Rainbow's American funding. He wondered how Ed Foley would react—more to the point, he needed Ed to be an enthusiastic advocate. Well, that ought not to be too hard. Ed knew field operations, after a fashion, and was loyal to the people at the sharp end. Better yet, Clark was asking after they'd had a major success, and that usually worked a lot better than a plea for help after a failure.

"Okay, we'll continue this with the team debrief." Clark stood and went to his office. Helen Montgomery had the usual pile of papers on his desk, somewhat higher than usual, as this one included the expected thank-you telegrams from the Austrians. The one from the Justice Minister was particularly flowery.

"Thank you, sir," John breathed, setting that one aside.

The amazing part of this job was all the admin stuff. As the commander of Rainbow, Clark had to keep track of when and how money came in and was spent, and he had to defend such things as the number of gun rounds his people fired every week. He did his best to slough much of this off on Alistair Stanley and Mrs. Montgomery, but a lot of it still landed on his desk. He had long experience as a government employee, and at CIA he'd had to report in endless detail on every field operation he'd ever run to keep the desk weenies happy. But this was well beyond that, and it accounted for *his* time on the firing range, as he found shooting a good means of stress relief, especially if he imagined the images of his bureaucratic tormentors in the center of the Q-targets he perforated with .45-caliber bullets. Justifying a budget was something new and foreign. If it wasn't important, why fund it at all, and if it was important, why quibble over a few thousand bucks' worth of bullets? It was the bureaucratic mentality, of course, all those people who sat at their desks and felt that the world would collapse around them if they didn't have all their papers initialed, signed, stamped, and properly filed, and if that inconvenienced others, too bad. So he, John Terrence Clark, CIA field officer for more than thirty years, a quiet legend in his agency, was stuck at his expensive desk, behind a closed door, working on paperwork that any self-respecting accountant would have rejected, on top of which he had to supervise and pass judgment on real stuff, which was both more interesting and far more to the point.

And it wasn't as though his budget was all that much to worry about. Less than fifty people, total, scarcely three million dollars in payroll expense, since everyone was paid the usual military rate, plus the fact that Rainbow picked up everyone's housing expense out of its multigovernment funding. One inequity was that the American soldiers were better paid than their European counterparts. That bothered John a little, but there was nothing he could do about it, and with housing costs picked up—the housing at Hereford wasn't lavish, but it was comfortable—nobody had any trouble living. The morale of the troops was excellent. He'd expected that. They were elite troopers, and that sort invariably had a good attitude, especially since they trained almost every day, and soldiers loved to train almost as much as they loved to do the things they trained for.

There would be a little discord. Chavez's Team-2 had drawn both field missions, as a result of which they'd swagger a little more, to the jealous annoyance of Peter Covington's Team-1, which was slightly ahead on the team/team competition of PT and shooting. Not even a cat's whisker of difference, but people like this, as competitive as any athletes could ever be, worked damned hard for that fifth of a percentage point, and it really came down to who'd had what for breakfast on the mornings of the competitive exercises, or maybe what they'd dreamed about during the night. Well, that degree of competition was healthy for the team as a whole. And decidedly unhealthy for those against whom his people deployed.

BILL Tawney was at his desk as well, going over the known information on the terrorists of the night before. The Austrians had begun their inquiries with the German Federal Police Office—the Bundes Kriminal Amt—even before the takedown. The identities of Hans Fürchtner and Petra Dortmund had been confirmed by fingerprints. The BKA investigators would jump onto the case hard that day. For starters, they'd trace the IDs of the people who'd rented the car that had been driven to the Ostermann home, and search for the house in Germany—probably Germany, Tawney reminded himself—that they'd lived in. The other four would probably be harder. Fingerprints had already been taken and were being compared on the computer scanning systems that everyone had now. Tawney agreed with the initial assessment of the Austrians that the four spear-carriers had probably been from the former East Germany, which seemed to be turning out all manner of political aberrants: converts from communism who were now discovering the joys of nazism, lingering true believers in the previous political-economic model, and just plain thugs who were a major annoyance to the regular German police forces.

But this had to be political. Fürchtner and Dortmund were—*had been,* Bill corrected himself—real, believing communists all their lives. They'd been raised in the former West Germany to middle-class families, the way a whole generation of terrorists had, striving all their active lives for socialist perfection or some such illusion. And so they had raided the home of a high-end capitalist . . . seeking what?

Tawney lifted a set of faxes from Vienna. Erwin Ostermann had told the police during his three-hour debrief that they'd sought his "special inside codes" to the international trading system. Were there such things? Probably not, Tawney judged—why not make sure? He lifted his phone and dialed the number of an old friend, Martin Cooper, a former "Six" man who now worked in Lloyd's ugly building in London's financial district.

"Cooper," a voice said.

"Martin, this is Bill Tawney. How are you this rainy morning?"

"Quite well, Bill, and you—what are you doing now?"

"Still taking the Queen's shilling, old man. New job, very hush-hush, I'm afraid."

"What can I do to help you, old man?"

"Rather a stupid question, actually. Are there any insider channels in the international trading system? Special codes and such things?"

"I bloody wish there were, Bill. Make our job here much easier," replied the former station chief for Mexico City and a few other minor posts for the British Secret Intelligence Service. "What exactly do you mean?"

"Not sure, but the subject just came up."

"Well, people at this level do have personal relationships and often trade information, but I take it you mean something rather more structured, an insider-network marketplace sort of thing?"

"Yes, that's the idea."

"If so, they've all kept it a secret from me and the people I work with, old man. International conspiracies?" Cooper snorted. "And this is a chatty mob, you know. Everyone's into everyone else's business."

"No such thing, then?"

"Not to my knowledge, Bill. It's the sort of thing the uninformed believe in, of course, but it doesn't exist, unless that's the mob who assassinated John Kennedy," Cooper added with a chuckle.

"Much what I'd thought, Martin, but I needed to tick that box. Thanks, my friend."

"Bill, you have any idea on who might have attacked that Ostermann chap in Vienna?"

"Not really. You know him?"

"My boss does. I've met him once. Seems a decent bloke, and bloody smart as well."

"Really all I know is what I saw on the telly this morning." It wasn't entirely a lie, and Martin would understand in any case, Tawney knew.

"Well, whoever did the rescue, my hat is off to them. Smells like SAS to me."

"Really? Well, that wouldn't be a surprise, would it?"

"Suppose not. Good hearing from you, Bill. How about dinner sometime?"

"Love to. I'll call you next time I'm in London."

"Excellent. Cheers."

Tawney replaced the phone. It seemed that Martin had landed on his feet after being let go from "Six," which had reduced its size with the diminution of the Cold War. Well, that was to be expected. *The sort of thing the uninformed believe in,* Tawney thought. Yes, that fit. Fürchtner and Dortmund were communists, and would not have trusted or believed in the open market. In their universe, people could only get wealthy by cheating, exploiting, and conspiring with others of the same ilk. And what did that mean? . . .

Why had they attacked the home of Erwin Ostermann? You couldn't rob such a man. He didn't keep his money in cash or gold bars. It was all electronic, theoretical money, really, that existed in computer memories and traveled across telephone wires, and that was difficult to steal, wasn't it?

No, what a man like Ostermann had was *information,* the ultimate source of power, ethereal though it was. Were Dortmund and Fürchtner willing to kill for that? It appeared so, but were the two dead terrorists the sort of people who could make use of such information? No, they couldn't have been, because then they would have known that the thing they'd sought didn't exist.

Somebody hired them, Tawney thought. Somebody had sent them out on their mission. But who?

And to what purpose? Which was even a better question, and one from which he could perhaps learn the answer to the first.

Back up, he told himself. If someone had hired them for a job, who could it have been? Clearly someone connected to the old terror network, someone who'd know where they were and whom they'd known and trusted to some degree, enough to risk their lives. But Fürchtner and Dortmund had been ideologically pure communists. Their acquaintances would be the same, and they would certainly not have trusted or taken orders from anyone of a different political shade. And how else could this notional person have known where and how to contact them, win their confidence, and send them off on a mission of death, chasing after something that didn't really exist? . . .

A superior officer? Tawney wondered, stretching his mind for more information than he really had. Someone of the same political bent or beliefs, able to order them, or at least to motivate them to do something dangerous.

He needed more information, and he'd use his SIS and police contacts to get every scrap he could from the Austrian/German investigation. For starters, he called Whitehall to make sure he got full translations of all the hostage interviews. Tawney had been an intelligence officer for a long time, and something had gotten his nose to twitch.

"DING, I didn't like your takedown plan," Clark said in the big conference room.

"I didn't either, Mr. C, but without a chopper, didn't have much choice, did I?" Chavez replied with an air of self-righteousness. "But that's not the thing that really scares me."

"What is?" John asked.

"Noonan brought this one up. Every time we go into a place, there are people around—the public, reporters, TV crews, all of that. What if one of them has a cell phone and calls the bad guys inside to tell them what's happening? Real simple, isn't it? We're fucked and so are some hostages."

"We should be able to deal with that," Tim Noonan told them. "It's the way a cell phone works. It broadcasts a signal to tell the local cell that it's there and it's on, so that the computer systems can route an incoming call to it. Okay, we can get instrumentation to read that, and maybe to block the signal path—maybe even clone the bad guys' phone, trap the incoming call and bag the bastards outside, maybe even flip 'em, right? But I need that software, and I need it now."

"David?" Clark turned to Dave Peled, their Israeli techno-genius.

"It can be done. I expect the technology exists already at NSA or elsewhere."

"What about Israel?" Noonan asked pointedly.

"Well . . . yes, we have such things."

"Get them," Clark ordered. "Want me to call Avi personally?"

"That would help."

"Okay, I need the name and specifications of the equipment. How hard to train the operators?"

"Not very," Peled conceded. "Tim can do it easily."

Thank you for that vote of confidence, Special Agent Noonan thought, without a smile.

"Back to the takedown," Clark commanded. "Ding, what were you thinking?"

Chavez leaned forward in his chair. He wasn't just defending himself; he was defending his team. "Mainly that I didn't want to lose a hostage, John. Doc told us we had to take those two seriously, and we had a hard deadline coming up. Okay, the mission as I understand it is *not* to lose a hostage. So, when they made it clear they wanted the chopper for transport, it was just a matter of giving it to them, with a little extra put in. Dieter and Homer did their jobs perfectly. So did Eddie and the rest of the shooters. The dangerous part was getting Louis and Geroge up to the house so they could take down the last bunch. They did a nice ninja job getting there unseen," Chavez went on, gesturing to Loiselle and Tomlinson. "That was the most dangerous part of the mission. We had them in a light-well and the camo stuff worked. If the bad guys had been using NVGs, that would have been a problem, but the additional illumination off the trees—from the lights the cops brought in, I mean—would have interfered with that. NVGs flare a lot if you throw light their way. It was a gamble," Ding admitted, "but it was a gamble that looked better than having a hostage whacked right in front of us while we were jerking off at the assembly point. That's the mission, Mr. C, and I was the commander on the scene. I made the call." He didn't add that his call had worked.

"I see. Well, good shooting from everybody, and Loiselle and Tomlinson did very well to get close undetected," Alistair Stanley said from his place, opposite Clark's. "Even so—"

"Even so, we need helicopters for a case like this one. How the hell did we overlook that requirement?" Chavez demanded.

"My fault, Domingo," Clark admitted. "I'm going to call in on that today."

"Just so we get it fixed, man." Ding stretched in his seat. "My troops got it done, John. Crummy setup, but we got it done. Next time, be better if things went a little smoother," he conceded. "But when the doc tells me that the bad guys will really kill somebody, that tells me I have to take decisive action, doesn't it?"

"Depending on the situation, yes," Stanley answered the question.

"Al, what does *that* mean?" Chavez asked sharply. "We need better mission guidelines. I need to have it spelled out. When can I allow a hostage to get killed? Does the age or sex of the hostage enter into the equation? What if somebody takes over a kindergarten or a hospital maternity ward? You can't expect us to disregard human factors like that. Okay, I understand that you can't plan for every possibility, and as the commanders on the scene, Peter and I have to exercise judgment, but my default position is to prevent the death of a hostage if I can do it. If that means taking risks—well, it's a probability measured against a certainty, isn't it? In a case like that, you take the risk, don't you?"

"Dr. Bellow," Clark asked, "how confident were you in your evaluation of the terrorists' state of mind?"

"Very. They were experienced. They'd thought through a lot of the mission, and in my opinion they were dead serious about killing hostages to show us their resolve," the psychiatrist replied.

"Then or now?"

"Both," Bellow said confidently. "These two were political sociopaths. Human life doesn't mean much to that sort of personality. Just poker chips to toss around the table."

"Okay, but what if they'd spotted Loiselle and Tomlinson coming in?"

"They would probably have killed a hostage and that would have frozen the situation for a few minutes."

"And my backup plan in that case was to rush the house from the east side and shoot our way in as quickly as possible," Chavez went on. "The better way is to zip-line down from some choppers and hit the place like a Kansas tornado. That's dangerous, too," he conceded. "But the people we're dealing with ain't the most reasonable folks in the world, are they?"

The senior team members didn't like this sort of discussion, since it reminded them that as good as the Rainbow troopers were, they weren't gods or supermen. They'd now had two incidents, both of them resolved without a civilian casualty. That made for mental complacency on the command side, further exacerbated by the fact that Team-2 had done a picture-perfect takedown under adverse tactical circumstances. They trained their men to be supermen, Olympic-perfect physical specimens, supremely trained in the use of firearms and explosives, and most of all, mentally prepared for the rapid destruction of human life.

The Team-2 members sitting around the table looked at Clark with neutral expressions, taking it all in with remarkable equanimity because they'd known last night that the plan was flawed and dangerous, but they'd brought it off anyway, and they were understandably proud of themselves for having done the difficult and saved their hostages. But Clark was questioning the capabilities of their team leader, and they didn't like that either. For the former SAS members among them, the reply to all this was simple, their old regimental motto: Who Dares, Wins. They'd dared and won. And the score for them was Christians ten, Lions nil, which wasn't a bad score at all. About the only unhappy member of the team was First Sergeant Julio Vega. "Oso" carried the machine gun, which had yet to come into play. The long-riflemen, Vega saw, were feeling pretty good about themselves, as were the light-weapons guys. But those were the breaks. He'd been there, a few meters from Weber, ready to cover if a bad guy had gotten lucky and managed to run away, firing his weapon. He'd have cut him in half with his M-60—his pistol work in the base range was one of the best. There was killing going on, and he wasn't getting to play. The religious part of Vega reproached the rest of him for thinking that way, which caused a few grumbles and chuckles when he was alone.

"So, where does that leave us?" Chavez asked. "What are our operational guidelines in the case where a hostage is likely to get killed by the bad guys?"

"The mission remains saving the hostages, where practicable," Clark replied, after a few seconds' thought.

"And the team leader on the scene decides what's practicable and what isn't?"

"Correct," Rainbow Six confirmed.

"So, we're right back where we started, John," Ding pointed out. "And that means that Peter and I get all the responsibility, and all the criticism if somebody else doesn't like what we've done." He paused. "I understand the responsibility that comes along with being in command in the field, but it would be nice to have something a little firmer to fall back on, y'know? Mistakes will happen out there sooner or later. We know it. We don't like it, but we know it. Anyway, I'm telling you here and now, John, I see the mission as the preservation of innocent life, and that's the side I'm going to come down on."

"I agree with Chavez," Peter Covington said. "That must be our default position."

"I never said it wasn't," Clark said, suddenly becoming angry. The problem was that there could well be situations in which it was not possible to save a life—but training for such a situation was somewhere between extremely difficult and damned near impossible, because all the terrorist incidents they'd have to deal with in the field would be as different as the terrorists and the sites they selected. So, he *had to* trust Chavez and Covington. Beyond that, he could set up training scenarios that forced them to think and act, in the hope that the practice would stand them in good stead in the field. It had been a lot easier as a field officer in the CIA, Clark thought. There he had always had the initiative, had almost always chosen the time and place of action to suit himself. Rainbow, however, was always *re*active, responding to the initiative of others. That simple fact was why he had to train his people so hard, so that their expertise could correct the tactical inequity. And that had worked twice. But would it continue to work?

So, for starters, John decided, from now on a more senior Rainbow member would always accompany the teams into the field to provide support, someone the team leaders could lean against. Of course, they wouldn't like the oversight right there at their shoulders, but that couldn't be helped. With that thought he dismissed the meeting, and called Al Stanley into his office, where he presented his idea.

"Fine with me, John. But who are the seniors who got out?"

"You and me, for starters."

"Very well. Makes sense—what with all the fitness and shooting training we subject ourselves to. Domingo and Peter might find it all a bit overpowering, however."

"They both know how to follow orders—and they'll come to us for advice when it's needed. Everybody does. I sure did, whenever the opportunity offered itself." Which hadn't been very damned often, though John remembered wishing for it often enough.

"I agree with your proposal, John," Stanley said. "Shall we write it up for the order book?"

Clark nodded. "Today."

CHAPTER 9

STALKERS

"I CAN DO THAT, JOHN," THE DIRECTOR OF CENTRAL Intelligence said. "It means talking to the Pentagon, however."

"Today if possible, Ed. We really need this. I was remiss in not considering the need earlier. Seriously remiss," Clark added humbly.

"It happens," DCI Foley observed. "Okay, let me make some calls and get back to you." He broke the connection and thought for a few seconds, then flipped through his rolodex, and found the number of CINC-SNAKE, as the post was laughingly called. Commander in Chief, Special Operations Command at MacDill Air Force Base outside Tampa, Florida, was the boss of all the "snake-eaters," the special-operations people from whom Rainbow had drawn its American personnel. General Sam Wilson was the man behind the desk, not a place he was especially comfortable. He'd started off as an enlisted man who'd opted for airborne and ranger training, then moved into Special Forces, which he'd left to get his college degree in history at North Carolina State University, then returned to the Army as a second lieutenant and worked his way up the ladder rapidly. A youthful fifty-three, he had four shiny stars on his shoulders now and was in charge of a unified multiservice command that included members from each of the armed services, all of whom knew how to cook snake over an open fire.

"Hi, Ed," the general said, on getting the call over his secure phone. "What's happening at Langley?" The special-operations community was very close with CIA, and often provided intelligence to it or the muscle to run a difficult operation in the field.

"I have a request from Rainbow," the DCI told him.

"Again? They've already raided my units, you know."

"They've put 'em to good use. That was their takedown in Austria yesterday."

"Looked good on TV," Sam Wilson admitted. "Will I get additional information?" By which he meant information on who the bad guys had been.

"The whole package when it's available, Sam," Foley promised.

"Okay, what does your boy need?"

"Aviators, helicopter crews."

"You know how long it takes to train those people, Ed? Jesus, they're expensive to maintain, too."

"I know that, Sam," the voice assured him from Langley. "The Brits have to put up, too. You know Clark. He wouldn't ask 'less he needed it."

Wilson had to admit that, yes, he knew John Clark, who'd once saved a wrecked mission and, in the process, a bunch of soldiers, a long time and several presidents ago. Ex-Navy SEAL, the Agency said of him, with a solid collection of medals and a lot of accomplishments. And this Rainbow group had two successful operations under its belt.

"Okay, Ed, how many?"

"One really good one for now."

It was the "for now" part that worried Wilson. But—"Okay, I'll be back to you later today."

"Thanks, Sam." One nice thing about Wilson, Foley knew, was that he didn't screw around on time issues. For him "right now" meant right the hell now.

CHESTER wasn't going to make it even as far as Killgore had thought. His liver function tests were heading downhill faster than anything he'd ever seen—or read about in the medical literature. The man's skin was yellow now, like a pale lemon, and slack over his flaccid musculature. Respiration was already a little worrisome, too, partly because of the large dose of morphine he was getting to keep him unconscious or at least stuporous. Both Killgore and Barbara Archer had wanted to treat him as aggressively as possible, to see if there were really a treatment modality that might work on Shiva, but the fact of the matter was that Chester's underlying medical conditions were so serious that no treatment regimen could overcome both those problems *and* the Shiva.

"Two days," Killgore said. "Maybe less."

"I'm afraid you're right," Dr. Archer agreed. She had all manner of ideas for handling this, from conventional—and almost certainly useless—antibiotics to Interleukin-2, which some thought might have clinical applications to such a case. Of course, modern medicine had yet to defeat any viral disease, but some thought that buttressing the body's immune system from one direction might have the effect of helping it in another, and there were a lot of powerful new synthetic antibiotics on the market now. Sooner of later, someone would find a magic bullet for viral diseases. But not yet: "Potassium?" she asked, after considering the prospects for the patient and the negligible value of treating him at all. Killgore shrugged agreement.

"I suppose. You can do it if you want." Killgore waved to the medication cabinet in the corner.

Dr. Archer walked over, tore a 40cc disposable syringe out of its paper and plastic container, then inserted the needle in a glass vial of potassium-and-water solution, and filled the needle by pulling back on the plunger. Then she returned to the bed and inserted the needle into the medication drip, pushing the plunger now to give the patient a hard bolus of the lethal chemical. It took a few seconds, longer than if she had done the injection straight into a major vein, but Archer didn't want to touch the patient any more than necessary, even with gloves. It didn't really matter that much. Chester's breathing within the clear plastic oxygen mask seemed to hesitate, then restart, then hesitate again, then become ragged and irregular for six or eight breaths. Then . . . it stopped. The chest settled into itself and didn't rise. His eyes had been semi-open, like those of a man in shallow sleep or shock, aimed in her direction but not really focused. Now they closed for the last time. Dr. Archer took her stethoscope and held it on the alcoholic's chest. There was no sound at all. Archer stood up, took off her stethoscope, and pocketed it.

So long, Chester, Killgore thought.

"Okay," she said matter-of-factly. "Any symptoms with the others?"

"None yet. Antibody tests are positive, however," Killgore replied. "Another week or so before we see frank symptoms, I expect."

"We need a set of healthy test subjects," Barbara Archer said. "These people are too—too sick to be proper benchmarks for Shiva."

"That means some risks."

"I know that," Archer assured him. "And you know we need better test subjects."

"Yes, but the risks are serious," Killgore observed.

"And I know *that,*" Archer replied.

"Okay, Barb, run it up the line. I won't object. You want to take care of Chester? I have to run over to see Steve."

"Fine." She walked to the wall, picked up the phone, and punched three digits onto the keypad to get the disposal people.

For his part, Killgore went into the changing area. He stopped in the decontamination chamber first of all, pushed the large square red button, and waited for the machinery to spray him down from all directions with the fog-solution of antiseptics that were known to be immediately and totally lethal to the Shiva virus. Then he went through the door into the changing room itself, where he removed the blue plastic suit, tossed it into the bin for further and more dramatic decontamination—it wasn't really needed, but the people in the lab felt better about it then—then dressed in surgical greens. On the way out, he put on a white lab coat. The next stop was Steve Berg's shop. Neither he nor Barb Archer had said it out loud yet, but everyone would feel better if they had a working vaccine for Shiva.

"Hey, John," Berg said, when his colleague came in.

" 'Morning, Steve," Killgore responded in greeting. "How're the vaccines coming?"

"Well, we have 'A' and 'B' working now." Berg gestured to the monkey cages on the other side of the glass. " 'A' batch has the yellow stickers. 'B' is the blue, and the control group is red."

Killgore looked. There were twenty of each, for a total of sixty rhesus monkeys. Cute little devils. "Too bad," he observed.

"I don't like it, either, but that's how it's done, my friend." Neither man owned a fur coat.

"When do you expect results?"

"Oh, five to seven days for the 'A' group. Nine to fourteen for the control group. And the 'B' group—well, we have hopes for them, of course. How's it going on your side of the house?"

"Lost one today."

"This fast?" Berg asked, finding it disturbing.

"His liver was off the chart to begin with. That's something we haven't considered fully enough. There will be people out there with an unusually high degree of vulnerability to our little friend."

"They could be canaries, man," Berg worried, thinking of the songbirds used to warn miners about bad air. "And we learned how to deal with that two years ago, remember?"

"I know." In a real sense, that was where the entire idea had come from. But they could do it better than the foreigners had. "What's the difference in time between humans and our little furry friends?"

"Well, I didn't aerosol any of these, remember. This is a vaccine test, not an infection test."

"Okay, I think you need to set up an aerosol control test. I hear you have an improved packing method."

"Maggie wants me to do that. Okay. We have plenty of monkeys. I can set it up in two days, a full-up test of the notional delivery system."

"With and without vaccines?"

"I can do that." Berg nodded. *You should have set it up already, idiot,* Killgore didn't say to his colleague. Berg was smart, but he couldn't see very far beyond the limits of his microscopes. Well, nobody was perfect, even here. "I don't go out of my way to kill things, John," Berg wanted to make clear to his physician colleague.

"I understand, Steve, but for every one we kill in proofing Shiva, we'll save a few hundred thousand in the wild, remember? And you take good care of them while they're here," he added. The test animals here lived an idyllic life, in comfortable cages, or even in large communal areas where the food was abundant and the water clear. The monkeys had a lot of room, with pseudo-trees to climb, air temperature like that of their native Africa, and no predators to threaten them. As in human prisons, the condemned got hearty meals to go along with their constitutional rights. But people like Steve Berg still didn't like it, important and indispensable as it was to the overall goal. Killgore wondered if his friend wept at night for the cute little brown-eyed creatures. Certainly Berg wasn't all that concerned with Chester—except that he might represent a canary, of course. That could indeed ruin anything, but that was also why Berg was developing "A" vaccine.

"Yeah," Berg admitted. "I still feel shitty about it, though."

"You should see my side of the house," Killgore observed.

"I suppose," Steve Berg responded diffidently.

THE overnight flight had come out of Raleigh-Durham International Airport in North Carolina, an hour's drive from Fort Bragg. The Boeing 757 touched down in an overcast drizzle to begin a taxi process almost as long as the flight itself, or so it often seemed to the passengers, as they finally came to the US Airways gate in Heathrow's Terminal 3.

Chavez and Clark had come up together to meet him. They were dressed in civilian clothes, and Domingo held a card with "MALLOY" printed on it. The fourth man off was dressed in Marine Class-As, complete to his Sam Browne belt, gold wings, and four and a half rows of ribbons on the olive-colored uniform blouse. His blue-gray eyes saw the card and came to it as he half-dragged his canvas bag with him.

"Nice to be met," Lieutenant Colonel Daniel Malloy observed. "Who are you guys?"

"John Clark."

"Domingo Chavez." Handshakes were exchanged. "Any more bags?" Ding asked.

"This is all I had time to pack. Lead on, people," Colonel Malloy replied.

"Need a hand with that?" Chavez asked a man about six inches taller and forty pounds heavier than himself.

"I got it," the Marine assured him. "Where we going?"

"Chopper is waiting for us. Car's this way." Clark headed through a side door, then down some steps to a waiting car. The driver took Malloy's bag and tossed it in the "boot" for the half-mile drive to a waiting British army Puma helicopter.

Malloy looked around. It was a crummy day to fly, the ceiling about fifteen hundred feet, and the drizzle getting a little harder, but he was not a white-knuckle flyer. They loaded into the back of the helicopter. He watched the flight crew run through the start-up procedure professionally, reading off their printed checklist, just as he did it. With the rotor turning, they got on the radio for clearance to lift off. That took several minutes. It was a busy time at Heathrow, with lots of international flights arriving to deliver business people to their work of the day. Finally, the Puma lifted off, climbed to altitude, and headed off in an undetermined direction to wherever the hell he was going. At that point, Malloy got on the intercom.

"Can anybody tell me what the hell this is all about?"

"What did they tell you?"

"Pack enough underwear for a week," Malloy replied, with a twinkle in his eye.

"There's a nice department store a few miles from the base."

"Hereford?"

"Good guess," Chavez responded. "Been there?"

"Lots of times. I recognized that crossroads down there from other flights. Okay, what's the story?"

"You're going to be working with us, probably," Clark told him.

"Who's 'us,' sir?"

"We're called Rainbow, and we don't exist."

"Vienna?" Malloy said through the intercom. The way they both blinked was answer enough. "Okay, that looked a little slick for cops. What's the makeup of the team?"

"NATO, mainly Americans and Brits, but others, too, plus an Israeli," John told him.

"And you set this up without any rotorheads?"

"Okay, goddamnit, I blew it, okay?" Clark observed. "I'm new at this command stuff."

"What's that on your forearm, Clark? Oh, what rank are you?"

John pulled back on his jacket, exposing the red seal tattoo. "I'm a simulated two-star. Ding here is a simulated major."

The marine examined the tattoo briefly. "I've heard of those, but never seen any. Third Special Operations Group, wasn't it? I knew a guy who worked with them."

"Who's that?"

"Dutch Voort, retired about five-six years ago as a full-bird."

"Dutch Voort! Shit, haven't heard that name in a while," Clark replied at once. "I got shot down with him once."

"You and a bunch of others. Great aviator, but his luck was kinda uneven."

"How's your luck, Colonel?" Chavez asked.

"Excellent, sonny, excellent," Malloy assured him. "And you can call me Bear."

It fit, both men decided of their visitor. He was Clark's height, six-one, and bulky, as though he pumped barbells for fun and drank his share of beer afterward. Chavez thought of his friend Julio Vega, another lover of free weights. Clark read over the medals. The DFC had two repeat clusters on it, as did the Silver Star. The shooting iron also proclaimed that Malloy was an expert marksman. Marines liked to shoot for entertainment and to prove that like all other Marines they were riflemen. In Malloy's case, a Distinguished Rifleman, which was as high as the awards went. But no Vietnam ribbons, Clark saw. Well, he would have been too young for that, which was another way for Clark to realize how old he'd grown. He also saw that Malloy was about the right age for a half-colonel, whereas someone with all those decorations should have made it younger. Had Malloy been passed over for full-bird colonel? One problem with special operations was that it often put one off the best career track. Special attention was often required to make sure such people got the promotions they merited—which wasn't a problem for enlisted men, but frequently a big one for commissioned officers.

"I started off in search-and-rescue, then I shipped over to Recon Marines, you know, get 'em in, get 'em out. You gotta have a nice touch. I guess I do."

"What are you current in?"

"H-60, Hueys, of course, and H-53s. I bet you don't have any of those, right?"

" 'Fraid not," Chavez said, immediately and obviously disappointed.

"Air Force 24th Special Operations Squadron at RAF Mildenhall has the MH-60K and MH-53. I am up to speed on both if you ever borrow them. They're part of 1st Special Operations Wing, and they're based both here and in Germany, last time I checked."

"No shit?" Clark asked.

"No shit, Simulated General, sir. I know the wing commander, Stanislas Dubrovnik, Stan the Man. Great helo driver. He's been around the block a few dozen times if you ever need a friend in a hurry."

"I'll keep that in mind. What else you know how to fly?"

"The Night Stalker, of course, but not many of them around. None based over here that I know of." The Puma turned then, circling, then flaring to settle into the Hereford pad. Malloy watched the pilot's stick work and decided he was competent, at least for straight-and-level stuff. "I'm not technically current on the MH-47 Chinook—we're only allowed to stay officially current on three types—technically I'm not current on Hueys either, but I was fucking born in a Huey, if you know what I mean, General. And I can handle the MH-47 if I have to."

"The name's John, Mr. Bear," Clark said, with a smile. He knew a pro when he saw one.

"I'm Ding. Once upon a time I was an 11-Bravo, but then the Agency kidnapped my ass. His fault," Chavez said. "John and I been working together a while."

"I suppose you can't tell me the good stuff, then. Kinda surprised I never met you guys before. I've delivered a few spooks here and there from time to time, if you know what I mean."

"Bring your package?" Clark asked, meaning his personnel file.

Malloy patted his bag. "Yes, sir, and very creative writing it is, if I do say so." The helicopter settled down. The crew chief jumped out to pull the sliding doors open. Malloy grabbed his bag, stepped down, and walked to the Rover parked just off the pad. There the driver, a corporal, took Mallory's bag and tossed it in the back. British hospitality, Malloy saw, hadn't changed very much. He returned the salute and got in the rear. The rain was picking up. English weather, the colonel thought, hadn't changed much either. Miserable place to fly helicopters, but not too bad if you wanted to get real close without being seen, and that wasn't too awful, was it? The Rover jeep took them to what looked like a headquarters building instead of his guest housing. Whoever they were, they were in a hurry.

"Nice office, John," he said, looking around on the inside. "I guess you really are a simulated two-star."

"I'm the boss," Clark admitted, "and that's enough. Sit down. Coffee?"

"Always," Malloy confirmed, taking a cup a moment later. "Thanks."

"How many hours?" Clark asked next.

"Total? Sixty-seven-forty-two last time I added it up. Thirty-one hundred of that is special operations. And, oh, about five hundred combat time."

"That much?"

"Grenada, Lebanon, Somalia, couple of other places— and the Gulf War. I fished four fast-mover drivers out and brought them back alive during that little fracas. One of them was a little exciting," Malloy allowed, "but I had some help overhead to smooth things out. You know, the job's pretty boring if you do it right."

"I'll have to buy you a pint, Bear," Clark said. "I've always been nice to the SAR guys."

"And I never turn down a free beer. The Brits in your team, ex-SAS?"

"Mainly. Worked with 'em before?"

"Exercises, here and over at Bragg. They are okay troops, right up there with Force Recon and my pals at Bragg." This was meant to be generous, Clark knew, though the local Brits might take slight umbrage at being compared to anyone. "Anyway, I suppose you need a delivery boy, right?"

"Something like that. Ding, let's run Mr. Bear through the last field operation."

"Roge-o, Mr. C." Chavez unrolled the big photo of the Schloss Ostermann on Clark's conference table and started his brief, as Stanley and Covington came in to join the conference.

"Yeah," Malloy said when the explanation ended. "You really did need somebody like me for that one, guys." He paused. "Best thing would be a long-rope deployment to put three or four on the roof . . . right about . . . here." He tapped the photo. "Nice flat roof to make it easy."

"That's about what I was thinking. Not as easy as a zip-line, but probably safer," Chavez agreed.

"Yeah, it's easy if you know what you're doing. Your boys will have to learn to land with soft feet, of course, but nice to have three or four people inside the castle when you need 'em. From how good the takedown went, I imagine your people know how to shoot and stuff."

"Fairly well," Covington allowed, in a neutral voice.

Clark was taking a quick riffle through Malloy's personnel file, while Chavez presented his successful mission. Married to Frances née Hutchins Malloy, he saw, two daughters, ten and eight. Wife was a civilian nurse working for the Navy. Well, that was easy to fix. Sandy could set that up at her hospital pretty easy. LTC Dan Malloy, USMC, was definitely a keeper.

For his part, Malloy was intrigued. Whoever these people were, they had serious horsepower. His orders to fly to England had come directly from the office of CINC-SNAKE himself, "Big Sam" Wilson, and the people he'd met so far looked fairly serious. The small one, Chavez, he thought, was one competent little fucker, the way he'd walked him through the Vienna job, and, from examining the overhead photo, his team must have been pretty good, too, especially the two who'd crept up to the house to take the last bunch of bad guys in the back. Invisibility was a pretty cool gig if you could bring it off, but a fucking disaster if you blew it. The good news, he reflected, was that the bad guys weren't all that good at their fieldcraft. Not trained like his Marines were. That deficiency almost canceled out their viciousness—but not quite. Like most people in uniform, Malloy despised terrorists as cowardly sub-human animals who merited only violent and immediate death.

Chavez next took him to his team's own building, where Malloy met his troops, shook hands, and evaluated what he saw there. Yeah, they were serious, as were Covington's Team-1 people in the next building over. Some people just had the look, the relaxed intensity that made them evaluate everyone they met, and decide at once if the person was a threat. It wasn't that they liked killing and maiming, just that it was their job, and that job spilled over into how they viewed the world. Malloy they evaluated as a potential friend, a man worthy of their trust and respect, and that warmed the Marine aviator. He'd be the guy whom they had to trust to get them where they needed to be, quickly, stealthily, and safely—and then get them out in the same way. The remaining tour of the training base was pure vanilla to one schooled in the business. The usual buildings, simulated airplane interiors, three real railroad passenger cars, and the other things they practiced to storm; the weapons range with the pop-up targets (he'd have to play there himself to prove that he was good enough to be here, Malloy knew, since every special-ops guy was and had to be a shooter, just as every Marine was a rifleman). By noon they were back in Clark's headquarters building.

"Well, Mr. Bear, what do you think?" Rainbow Six asked.

Malloy smiled as he sat down. "I think I'm seriously jet lagged. And I think you have a nice team here. So, you want me?"

Clark nodded. "I think we do, yes."

"Start tomorrow morning?"

"Flying what?"

"I called that Air Force bunch you told us about. They're going to lend us an MH-60 for you to play with."

"Neighborly of them." That meant to Malloy that he'd have to prove that he was a good driver. The prospect didn't trouble him greatly. "What about my family? Is this TAD or what?"

"No, it's a permanent duty station for you. They'll come over on the usual government package."

"Fair 'nuf. Will we be getting work here?"

"We've had two field operations so far, Bern and Vienna. There's no telling how busy we'll be with for-real operations, but you'll find the training regimen is pretty busy here."

"Suits me, John."

"You want to work with us?"

The question surprised Malloy. "This is a volunteer outfit?"

Clark nodded. "Every one of us."

"Well, how about that. Okay," Malloy said. "You can sign me up."

"MAY I ask a question?" Popov asked in New York.

"Sure," the boss said, suspecting what it would be.

"What is the purpose of all this?"

"You really do not need to know at this time" was the expected reply to the expected question.

Popov nodded his submission/agreement to the answer. "As you say, sir, but you are spending a goodly amount of money for no return that I can determine." Popov raised the money question deliberately, to see how his employer would react.

The reaction was genuine boredom: "The money is not important."

And though the response was not unexpected, it was nonetheless surprising to Popov. For all of his professional life in the Soviet KGB, he'd paid out money in niggardly amounts to people who'd risked their lives and their freedom for it, frequently expecting far more than they'd ever gotten, because often enough the material and information given *was* worth far more than they'd been paid for it. But this man had already paid out more than Popov had distributed in over fifteen years of field operations—for nothing, for two dismal failures. And yet, there was no disappointment on his face, Dmitriy Arkadeyevich saw. What the hell was this all about?

"What went wrong in this case?" the boss asked.

Popov shrugged. "They were willing, but they made the mistake of underestimating the skill of the police response. It was quite skillful indeed," he assured his employer. "More so than I expected, but not that great a surprise. Many police agencies across the world have highly trained counterterror groups."

"It was the Austrian police? . . ."

"So the news media said. I did not press my investigation further. Should I have done so?"

A shake of the head. "No, just idle curiosity on my part."

So, you don't care if these operations succeed or fail, Popov thought. *Then,* why *the hell do you fund them?* There was no logic to this. None at all. That would have been—*should* have been—troubling to Popov, yet it was not seriously so. He was becoming rich on these failures. He knew who was funding the operations, and had all the evidence—the cash—he needed to prove it. So, this man could not turn on him. If anything, he must fear his employee, mustn't he? Popov had contacts in the terrorist community and could as easily turn them against the man who procured the cash, couldn't he? It would be a natural fear for this man to hold, Dmitriy reflected.

Or was it? What, if anything, did this man fear? He was funding murder—well, attempted murder in the last case. He was a man of immense wealth and power, and such men feared losing those things more than they feared death. It kept coming down to the same thing, the former KGB officer told himself: What the hell was this all about? Why was he plotting the deaths of people, and asking Popov to—was he doing this to kill off the world's remaining terrorists? Did *that* make sense? Using Popov as a stalking horse, an *agent provocateur,* to draw them out and be dealt with by the various countries' highly trained counterterror teams? Dmitriy decided that he'd do a little research on his employer. It ought not to be too hard, and the New York Public Library was only two kilometers distant on Fifth Avenue.

"What sort of people were they?"

"Whom do you mean?" Popov asked.

"Dortmund and Fürchtner," the boss clarified.

"Fools. They still believed in Marxism-Leninism. Clever in their way, intelligent in the technical sense, but their political judgment was faulty. They were unable to change when their world changed. That is dangerous. They failed to evolve, and for that they died." It wasn't much of an epitaph, Popov knew. They'd grown up studying the works of Karl Marx and Friedrich Engels and all the rest—the same people whose words Popov had studied through his youth, but even as a boy Popov had known better, and his world travels as a KGB officer had merely reinforced his distrust for the words of those nineteenth century academicians. His first flight on an American-made airliner, chatting in a friendly way with the people next to him, had taught him so much. But Hans and Petra—well, they'd grown up within the capitalist system, sampled all of its wares and benefits, and nevertheless decided that theirs was a system bereft of something that they needed. Perhaps in a way they'd been as he had been, Dmitriy Arkadeyevich thought, just dissatisfied, wanting to be part of something better—but, no, he'd always wanted something better for himself, whereas they'd always wanted to bring others to Paradise, to lead and rule as good communists. And to reach that utopian vision, they'd been willing to walk through a sea of innocent blood. Fools. His employer, he saw, accepted his more abbreviated version of their lost lives and moved on.

"Stay in the city for a few days. I will call you when I need you."

"As you say, sir." Popov stood and left the office and caught the next elevator to street level. Once there, he decided to walk south to the library with the lions in front. The exercise might clear his head, and he still had a little thinking to do. "When I need you" could mean another mission, and soon.

"ERWIN? George. How are you, my friend?"

"It has been an eventful week," Ostermann admitted. His personal physician had him on tranquilizers, which, he thought, didn't work very well. His mind still remembered the fear. Better yet, Ursel had come home, arriving even before the rescue mission, and that night—he'd gotten to bed just after four in the morning, she'd come to bed with him, just to hold him, and in her arms he'd shaken and wept from the sheer terror that he'd been able to control right up to the moment that the man Fürchtner had died less than a meter to his left. There was blood and other tissue particles on his clothing. They'd had to be taken off for cleaning. Dengler had had the worst time of all, and wouldn't be at work for at least a week, the doctors said. For his part, Ostermann knew that he'd be calling that Britisher who'd come to him with the security proposal, especially after hearing the voices of his rescuers.

"Well, I can't tell you how pleased I am that you got through it okay, Erwin."

"Thank you, George," he said to the American Treasury Secretary. "Do you appreciate your bodyguards more today than last week?"

"You bet. I expect that business in that line of work will be picking up soon."

"An investment opportunity?" Ostermann asked with a forlorn chuckle.

"I didn't mean *that,*" Winston replied with an almost-laugh. It was good to laugh about it, wasn't it?

"George?"

"Yeah?"

"They were not Austrian, not what the television and newspapers said—and they told me not to reveal this, but you can know this. They were Americans and British."

"I know, Erwin, I know who they are, but that's all I can say."

"I owe them my life. How can I repay such a debt?"

"That's what they are paid to do, my friend. It's their job."

"*Vielieicht,* but it was *my* life they saved, and those of my employees. I have a personal debt to pay them. Is there any way I might do something for them?"

"I don't know," George Winston admitted.

"Could you find out? If you 'know about' them, could you find out? They have children, do they not? I can pay for their education, set up a fund of some sort, could I not?"

"Probably not, Erwin, but I can look into it," the SecTreas said, making a note on his desk. This would be a real pain in the ass for some security people, but there might well be a way, through some D.C. law firm, probably, to double-blind it. It pleased Winston that Erwin wanted to do this. *Noblesse oblige* was not entirely dead. "So, you sure you're okay, pal?"

"Thanks to them, yes, George, I am."

"Great. Thanks. Good to hear your voice, pal. See you next time I come over to Europe."

"Indeed, George. Have a good day."

"You, too. Bye." Winston switched buttons on his phone. Might as well check into this right away. "Mary, could you get me Ed Foley over at the CIA?"

CHAPTER 10

DIGGERS

POPOV HADN'T DONE THIS IN AGES, BUT HE REMEMBERED how. His employer had been written about more than many politicians—which was only just, Popov thought, as this man did far more important and interesting things for his country and the world—but these articles were mainly about business, which didn't help Popov much beyond a further appreciation of the man's wealth and influence. There was little about his personal life, except that he'd been divorced. A pity of sorts. His former wife seemed both attractive and intelligent, judging by the photos and the appended information on her. Maybe two such intelligent people had difficulty staying together. If so, that was too bad for the woman, the Russian thought. Maybe few American men liked having intellectual equals under their roof. It was altogether too intimidating for the weak ones—and only a weak man would be troubled by it, the Russian thought.

But there was nothing to connect the man with terrorists or terrorism. He'd never been attacked himself, not even a simple street crime, according to *The New York Times.* Such things did not always make the news, of course. Perhaps an incident that had never seen the light of day. But if it had been so major as to change the course of his life—it would had to have become known, wouldn't it?

Probably. Almost certainly, he thought. But *almost* was a troubling qualifier for a career intelligence officer. This was a man of business. A genius both in his scientific field and in running a major corporation. There, it seemed, was where his passions went. There were many photos of the man with women, rarely the same one twice, while attending various charity or social functions—

all nice women, to be sure, Popov noted, like fine trophies, to be used and mounted on the wall in the appropriate empty space, while he searched after another. So, what sort of man was he working for?

Popov had to admit that he really didn't know, which was more than troubling. His life was now in pawn to a man whose motivations he didn't understand. In not knowing, he could not evaluate the operational dangers that attached to himself as a result. Should the purpose be discerned by others, and his employer discovered and arrested, then he, Popov, was in danger of arrest on serious charges. Well, the former KGB officer thought, as he returned the last of the periodicals to the clerk, there was an easy solution to that. He'd always have a bag packed, and two false identities ready to be used. Then, at the first sign of trouble, he'd get to an international airport and be off to Europe as quickly as possible, there to disappear and make use of the cash he'd banked. He already had enough to ensure a comfortable life for a few years, perhaps longer if he could find a really good investment counselor. Disappearing off the face of the earth wasn't all that hard for one with proper training, he told himself, walking back out on Fifth Avenue. All you needed was fifteen or twenty minutes of warning. . . . Now how could he be sure to get that? . . .

THE German federal police were as efficient as ever, Bill Tawney saw. All six of the terrorists had been identified within forty-eight hours, and while detailed interviews of their friends, neighbors, and acquaintances were still underway, the police already knew quite a lot and had forwarded it to the Austrians, from there to the British Embassy in Vienna, and from there to Hereford. The package included a photo and blueprints of the home owned by Fürchtner and Dortmund. One of the couple, Tawney saw, had been a painter of moderate talent. The report said that they'd sold paintings at a local gallery, signed, of course, with a pseudonym. Perhaps they'd become more valuable now, the Six man thought idly, turning the page. They'd had a computer there, but the documents on it were not very useful. One of them, probably Fürchtner, the German investigators thought, had written long political diatribes, appended but not yet translated—Dr. Bellow would probably want to read them, Tawney thought. Other than that, there was little remarkable. Books, many of them political in character, most of them printed and purchased in the former DDR. A nice TV and stereo system, and plenty of records and CDs of classical music. A decent middle-class car, properly maintained, and insured through a local company, under their cover names, Siegfried and Hanna Kolb. They'd had no really close friends in their neighborhood, had kept largely to themselves, and every public aspect of their lives had been *in Ordnung,* thus arousing no comment of any kind. And yet, Tawney thought, they'd sat there like coiled springs . . . awaiting what?

What had turned them loose? The German police had no explanation for that. A neighbor reported that a car had visited their house a few weeks before—but who had come and to what purpose, no one knew. The tag number of the car had never been noted, nor the make, though the interview transcript said that it had been a German-made car, probably white or at least light in color. Tawney couldn't evaluate the importance of that. It might have been a buyer for a painting, an insurance agent—or the person who had brought them out of cover and back into their former lives as radical left-wing terrorists.

It was not the least bit unusual for this career intelligence officer to conclude that there was nothing he could conclude, on the basis of the information he had. He told his secretary to forward Fürchtner's writings to a translator for later analysis by both himself and Dr. Bellow, and that was about as far as he could go. Something had roused the two German terrorists from their professional sleep, but he didn't know what. The German federal police could conceivably stumble across the answer, but Tawney doubted it. Fürchtner and Dortmund had figured out how to live unobtrusively in a nation whose police were pretty good at finding people. Someone they'd known and trusted had come to them and persuaded them to set off on a mission. Whoever it had been had known how to contact them, which meant that there was some sort of terror network still in existence. The Germans had figured that out, and a notation on their preliminary report recommended further investigation through paid informants—which might or might not work. Tawney had devoted a few years of his life to cracking into the Irish terrorist groups, and he'd had a few minor successes, magnified at the time by their rarity. But there had long since been a Darwinian selection process in the terrorist world. The dumb ones died, and the smart ones survived, and after nearly thirty years of being chased by increasingly clever police agencies, the surviving terrorists were themselves very clever indeed—and the best of them had been trained at Moscow Centre itself by KGB officers . . . was that an investigative option? Tawney wondered. The new Russians had cooperated somewhat . . . but not very much in the area of terrorism, perhaps because of embarrassment over their former involvement with such people . . . or maybe because the records had been destroyed, which the Russians frequently claimed, and Tawney never quite believed. People like that destroyed nothing. The Soviets had developed the world's foremost bureaucracy, and bureaucrats simply *couldn't* destroy records. In any case, seeking cooperation from the Russians on such an item as this was too far above his level of authority, though he could write up a request, and it might even percolate a level or two up the chain before being quashed by some senior civil servant in the Foreign Office. He decided that he'd try it anyway. It gave him something to do, and it would at least tell the people at Century House, a few blocks across the Thames from the Palace of Westminster, that he was still alive and working.

Tawney slid all the papers, including his notes, back into the thick manila folder before turning to work on the foredoomed request. He could only conclude now that there still was a terror network, and that someone known to its members still had the keys to that nasty little kingdom. Well, maybe the Germans would learn more, and maybe the data would find its way to his desk. If it did, Tawney wondered, would John Clark and Alistair Stanley be able to arrange a strike of their own against them? No, more likely that was a job for the police of whatever nation or city was involved, and that would probably be enough. You didn't have to be all that clever to bag one. The French had proven that with Carlos, after all.

IL'YCH Ramirez Sanchez was not a happy man, but the cell in the Le Sante prison was not calculated to make him so. Once the most feared terrorist in the world, he'd killed men with his own hand, and done it as casually as zipping his fly. He'd once had every police and intelligence service in the world on his trail, and laughed at them all from the security of his safe houses in the former Eastern Europe. There, he'd read press speculation on who he really was and for whom he'd really worked, along with KGB documents on what the foreign services were doing to catch him . . . until Eastern Europe had fallen, and with it the nation-state support for his revolutionary acts. And so he'd ended up in Sudan, where he'd decided to take his situation a little more seriously. Some cosmetic surgery had been in order, and so he'd gone to a trusted physician for the surgery, submitted to the general anesthesia—

—and awakened aboard a French business jet, strapped down to a stretcher, with a Frenchman saying, *"Bonjour, Monsieur Chacal,"* with the beaming smile of a hunter who'd just captured the most dangerous of tigers with a loop of string. Tried, finally, for the murder of a cowardly informant and two French counterintelligence officers in 1975, he'd defended himself with panache, he thought, not that it mattered except to his own capacious ego. He'd proclaimed himself a "professional revolutionary" to a nation that had had its own revolution two hundred years before, and didn't feel the need for another.

But the worst part of it was being tried as a . . . criminal, as though his work hadn't had any political consequences. He'd tried hard to set that aside, but the prosecutor hadn't let go, his voice dripping with contempt in his summation—

actually worse than that, because he'd been so matter-of-fact in the presentation of his evidence, saving his contempt for later. Sanchez had kept his dignity intact throughout, but inwardly he'd felt the pain of a trapped animal, and had to call on his courage to keep his mien neutral at all times. And the ultimate result had hardly been a surprise.

The prison had already been a hundred years old on the day of his birth, and was built along the lines of a medieval dungeon. His small cell had but a single window, and he was not tall enough to see out the bottom of it. The guards, however, had a camera and watched him with it twenty-four hours a day, like a very special animal in a very special cage. He was as alone as a man could be, allowed no contact with other prisoners, and allowed out of his cage only once per day for an hour of "exercise" in a bleak prison yard. He could expect little more for the remainder of his life, Carlos knew, and his courage quailed at that. The worst thing was the boredom. He had books to read, but nowhere to walk beyond the few square meters of his cage—and worst of all, the whole world knew that the Jackal was caged forever and could therefore be forgotten.

Forgotten? The entire world had once feared his name. That was the most hurtful part of all.

He made a mental note to contact his lawyer. Those conversations were still privileged and private, and his lawyer knew a few names to call.

"STARTING up," Malloy said. Both turbo-shaft engines came to life, and presently the four-bladed rotor started turning.

"Crummy day," Lieutenant Harrison observed over the intercom.

"Been over here long?" Malloy asked.

"Just a few weeks, sir."

"Well, sonny, now you know why the Brits won the Battle of Britain. Nobody else can fly in this shit." The Marine looked around. Nothing else was up today. The ceiling was less than a thousand feet, and the rain was coming down pretty hard. Malloy checked the trouble-board again. All the aircraft systems were in the green.

"Roge-o, Colonel. Sir, how many hours in the Night Hawk?"

"Oh, about seven hundred. I like the Pave Low's capabilities a little better, but this one does like to fly. About time for us to see that, sonny." Malloy pulled up on the collective, and the Night Hawk lifted off, a little unevenly in the gusting thirty-knot winds. "Y'all okay back there?"

"Got my barf bag," Clark replied, to Ding's amusement. "You know a guy named Paul Johns?"

"Air Force colonel, down at Eglin? He retired about five years ago."

"That's the man. How good is he?" Clark asked, mainly to get a feel for Malloy.

"None better in a helo, 'specially a Pave Low. He just talked to the airplane, and it listened to him real nice. You know him, Harrison?"

"Only by reputation, sir," the copilot replied from the left seat.

"Little guy, good golfer, too. Does consulting now, and works on the side with Sikorsky. We see him up at Bragg periodically. Okay, baby, let's see what you got." Malloy reefed the chopper into a tight left turn. "Humph, nothing handles like a -60. Damn, I love these things. Okay, Clark, what's the mission here?"

"The range building, simulate a zip-line deployment."

"Covert or assault?"

"Assault," John told him.

"That's easy. Any particular spot?"

"Southeast corner, if you can."

"Okay, here we go." Malloy shoved the cyclic left and forward, dropping the helo like a fast elevator, darting for the range building like a falcon after a pheasant—and like a falcon, pulling up sharply at the right spot, transitioning into hover so quickly that the copilot in the left seat turned to look in amazement at how fast he'd brought it off. "How's that, Clark?"

"Not too bad," Rainbow Six allowed.

Next Malloy applied power to get the hell out of Dodge City—almost, but not quite, as though he hadn't stopped over the building at all. "I can improve that once I get used to your people, how fast they get out and stuff, but a long-line deployment is usually better, as you know."

"As long as you don't blow the depth perception and run us right into the friggin' wall," Chavez observed. That remark earned him a turned head and a pained expression.

"My boy, we do try to avoid that. Ain't nobody does the rocking chair maneuver better 'n me, people."

"It's hard to get right," Clark observed.

"Yes, it is," Malloy agreed, "but I know how to play the piano, too."

The man was not lacking in confidence, they saw. Even the lieutenant in the left seat thought he was a little overpowering, but he was taking it all in anyway, especially watching how Malloy used the collective to control power as well as lift. Twenty minutes later, they were back on the ground.

"And that's about how it's done, people," Malloy told them, when the rotor stopped turning. "Now, when do we start real training?"

"Tomorrow soon enough?" Clark asked.

"Works for me, General, sir. Next question, do we practice on the Night Hawk, or do I have to get used to flying something else?"

"We haven't worked that out yet," John admitted.

"Well, that does have a bearing on this stuff, y'know. Every chopper has a different feel, and that matters on how I do my deliveries," Malloy pointed out. "I'm at my best on one of those. I'm nearly as good with a Huey, but that one's noisy in close and hard to be covert with. Others, well, I have to get used to them. Takes a few hours of yankin' and bankin' before I feel completely comfortable." Not to mention learning where all the controls were, Malloy didn't add, since no two aircraft in the entire world had all the dials, gauges, and controls in the same places, something aviators had bitched about since the Wright Brothers. "If we deploy, I'm risking lives, mine and others, every time I lift off. I'd prefer to keep those risks to a minimum. I'm a cautious guy, y'know?"

"I'll work on that today," Clark promised.

"You do that." Malloy nodded, and walked off to the locker/ready room.

POPOV had himself a fine dinner in an Italian restaurant half a block from his apartment building, enjoyed the crisp weather in the city, and puffed on a Montecristo cigar after he got back to his flat. There was still work to do. He'd obtained videotapes of the news coverage of both of the terrorist incidents he'd instigated and wanted to study them. In both cases, the reporters spoke German—the Swiss kind, then Austrian—which he spoke like a native (of Germany). He sat in an easy chair with the remote control in his hand, occasionally rewinding to catch something odd of passing interest, studying the tapes closely, his trained mind memorizing every detail. The most interesting parts, of course, were those showing the assault teams who'd finally resolved both incidents with decisive action. The quality of the pictures was poor. Television simply didn't make for high-quality imagery, especially in bad lighting conditions and from two hundred meters away. With the first tape, that of the Bern case, there was no more than ninety seconds of pre-action pictures of the assault team—this part had not been broadcast during the attack, only afterward. The men moved professionally, in a way that somehow reminded the Russian of the ballet, so strangely delicate and stylized were the movements of the men in the black clothing, as they crept in from left and right . . . and then came the blindingly swift action punctuated by jerky camera movements when the explosives went off—that always made the cameramen jump. No sound of gunfire. So their firearms were silenced. It was done so that the victims could not learn from the sound where the shots had come from—but it had not really been a matter of importance in this case, since the terrorist/criminals had been dead before the information could have done them any good. But that was how it was done. This business was as programmed as any professional sport, with the rules of play enforced by deadly might. The mission over in seconds, the assault team came out, and the Bern city police went in to sort out the mess. The people in black acted unremarkably, he saw, like disciplined soldiers on a battlefield. No congratulatory handshakes or other demonstrations. No, they were too well-trained for that. No one even did so much as light a cigarette . . . ah, one did seem to light a pipe. What followed was the usual brainless commentary from the local news commentators, talking about this elite police unit and how it had saved all the lives of those inside, *undo so weiter,* Popov thought, rising to switch tapes.

The Vienna mission, he saw, had even poorer TV coverage, due to the physical conditions of the chap's house. Quite a nice one, actually. The Romanovs might have had such a fine country house. Here the police had ruthlessly controlled the TV coverage, which was perfectly sensible, Popov thought, but not overly helpful to him. The taped coverage showed the front of the country house with boring regularity, punctuated by the monotonous words of the TV reporter repeating the same things endlessly, telling his viewers that he was unable to speak very much with the police on the scene. The tape did show the movement of vehicles, and showed the arrival of what had to be the Austrian assault team. Interestingly, they appeared to be dressed in civilian clothing upon their arrival, and changed soon thereafter into their battle dress . . . it looked green for this team . . . no, he realized, green overgarments over black regular dress. Did that mean anything? The Austrians had two men with scope-sighted rifles who rapidly disappeared into cars, which must have taken them behind the *schloss.* The assault-team leader, not a very large man, much like the one Popov thought had headed the team in Bern, was seen from a great distance going over papers—the map/diagram/plans of the house and grounds, no doubt. Then, shortly before midnight, all of them had disappeared, leaving Popov to look at a tape of the dwelling illuminated by huge light standards, accompanied by more idiotic speculation by a singularly ill-informed TV journalist. . . . and then, just after midnight, came the distant *pop* of a rifle, followed by two more *pops,* silence, and then frantic activity by the uniformed police in the camera's field of view. Twenty of them raced into the front door carrying light machine guns. The reporter had then talked about a sudden burst of activity, which the thickest of viewers would have seen for themselves, followed by more nothing-at-all, and then the announcement that all the hostages were alive, and all the criminals dead. Another passage of time, and the green-and-black-clad assault team appeared again. As with Bern, there were no overt signs of self-congratulation. One of the assault team seemed to be puffing on a pipe, as he walked to the van that had brought them to the scene and stowed his weapons, while another of them conferred briefly with a civilian-clothed policeman, probably the Captain Altmark who'd had field command of the incident. The two must have known each other, their exchange of words was so brief before the paramilitary police team departed the scene, just as at Bern. Yes, both of the counterterror units trained from exactly the same book, Popov told himself again.

Later press coverage spoke of the skill of the special police unit. That had happened in Bern, too, but it was surprising in neither case, since reporters also spoke the same drivel, regardless of language or nationality. The words used in the statement by the police were almost identical. Well, someone had trained both teams, perhaps the same agency. Perhaps the German GSG-9 group, which, with British help, had ended the airplane incident at Mogadishu over twenty years before, had trained the forces of countries that shared their language. Certainly the thoroughness of the training and the coldness of demeanor of the assault teams struck Popov as very German. They'd acted like machines both before and after the attacks, arriving and leaving like ghosts, with nothing left behind but the bodies of the terrorists. Efficient people, the Germans, and the Germanic policemen whom they trained. Popov, a Russian by birth and culture, had little love for the nation that had once killed so many of his countrymen, but he could respect them and their work, and the people they killed were no loss to the world. Even when he'd helped to train them as an active-duty officer of the Soviet KGB, he'd not cared much for them, nor had anyone else in his agency. They were, if not exactly the useful fools Lenin had once spoken about, then trained attack dogs to be unleashed when needed, but never really trusted by those who semicontrolled them. And they'd never really been all that efficient. About the only thing they'd really accomplished was to force airports to install metal detectors, inconveniencing travelers all over the world. Certainly they'd made life hard on the Israelis, but what, really, did that country matter on the world stage? And even then, what had happened? If you forced countries to adapt to adverse circumstances, it happened swiftly. So, now, El Al, the Israeli airline, was the safest and most secure in the world, and policemen the world over were better briefed on whom to watch and to examine closely—and if everything else failed, then the policemen had special counterterror units like those who'd settled things in Bern and Vienna.

Trained by Germans to kill like Germans. Any other terrorists he sent out to do evil work would have to deal with such people. Too bad, Popov thought, turning his TV back to a cable channel while the last tape rewound. He hadn't learned much of anything from reviewing the tapes, but he was a trained intelligence officer, and therefore a thorough man. He poured himself an Absolut vodka to drink neat—he missed the superior Starka brand he would have had in Russia—and allowed his mind to churn over the information while he watched a movie on the TV screen.

"YES, General, I know," Clark said into the phone at 1:05 the next afternoon, damning time zones as he did so.

"That comes out of *my* budget, too," General Wilson pointed out. First, CINC-SNAKE thought, they ask for a man, then they ask for hardware, and *now,* they are asking for funding, too.

"I can try to help with that through Ed Foley, sir, but the fact of the matter is that we need the asset to train with. You did send us a pretty good man," Clark added, hoping to assuage Wilson's renowned temper.

It didn't help much. "Yes, I know he's good. That's why he was working for me in the first goddamned place."

This guy's getting ecumenical in his old age, John told himself. *Now he's praising a Marine*—rather unusual for an *Army* snake-eater and former commander of XVIII Airborne Corps.

"General—sir, you know we've had a couple of jobs already, and with all due modesty, my people handled them both pretty damned well. I have to fight for my people, don't I?"

And *that* calmed Wilson down. They were both commanders, they both had jobs to do, and people to command—and defend.

"Clark, I understand your position. I really do. But I can't train my people on assets that you've taken away."

"How about we call it time-sharing?" John offered, as a further olive branch.

"It still wears out a perfectly good Night Hawk."

"It also trains up the crews for you. At the end of this, you may just have a primo helicopter crew to bring down to Bragg to work with your people—and the training expense for your operation is just about nothing, sir." And that, he thought, was a pretty good play.

At MacDill Air Force Base, Wilson told himself that this was a losing proposition. Rainbow was a bulletproof operation, and everyone knew it. This Clark guy had sold it first of all to CIA, then to the President himself—and sure enough, they'd had two deployments, and both had worked out, though the second one had been pretty dicey. But Clark, clever as he was, and good commander that he seemed to be, hadn't learned how to run a unit in the modern military world, where half the time was spent managing money like some goddamned white-socked accountant, instead of leading from the front and training with the troops. That's what really rankled Sam Wilson, young for a four-star, a professional *soldier* who wanted to *soldier,* something that high command pretty well precluded, despite his fitness and desire. Most annoying of all, this Rainbow unit promised to steal a lot of his own business. The Special Operations Command had commitments all over the world, but the international nature of Rainbow meant that there was now somebody else in the same line of work, whose politically neutral nature was supposed to make their use a lot more palatable to countries that might need special services. Clark might just put him out of business in a real sense, and Wilson didn't like that at all.

But, really, he had no choice in the matter, did he?

"Okay, Clark, you can use the aircraft *so long as* the parent unit is able to part with it, and *so long as* its use by you does not interfere with training and readiness with that parent unit. Clear?"

"Yes, sir, that is clear," John Clark acknowledged.

"I need to come over to see your little circus," Wilson said next.

"I'd like that a lot, General."

"We'll see," Wilson grumbled, breaking the connection.

"Tough son of a bitch," John breathed.

"Quite," Stanley agreed. "We are poaching on his patch, after all."

"It's our patch now, Al."

"Yes, it is, but you mustn't expect him to like that fact."

"And he's younger and tougher than me?"

"A few years younger, and I personally would not wish to cross swords with the gentleman." Stanley smiled. "The war appears to be over, John, and you appear to have won."

Clark managed a smile and a chuckle. "Yeah, Al, but it's easier to go into the field and kill people."

"Quite."

"What's Peter's team doing?"

"Long-line practice."

"Let's go and watch," John said, glad to have an excuse to leave his desk.

"I want to get out of this place," he told his attorney.

"I understand that, my friend," the lawyer replied, with a look around the room. It was the law in France, as in America, that conversations between clients and attorneys were privileged, and could not be recorded or used in any way by the state, but neither man really trusted the French to abide by that law, especially since DGSE, the French intelligence service, had been so instrumental in bringing Il'ych to justice. The DGSE was not known for its willingness to abide by the rules of civilized international behavior, as people as diverse as international terrorists and Greenpeace had learned to their sorrow.

Well, there were other people talking in this room, and there were no obvious shotgun microphones here—and the two had not taken the seats offered by the prison guards, opting instead for one closer to the windows because, they'd said, they wanted the natural light. Of course, every booth could easily be wired.

"I must tell you that the circumstances of your conviction do not lend themselves to an easy appeal," the lawyer advised. This wasn't exactly news to his client.

"I am aware of that. I need you to make a telephone call."

"To whom?"

The Jackal gave him a name and a number. "Tell him that it is my wish to be released."

"I cannot be part of a criminal act."

"I am aware of that as well," Sanchez observed coldly. "Tell him also that the rewards will be great."

It was suspected, but not widely known for certain, that Il'ych Ramirez Sanchez had a goodly sum of money squirreled away as a result of his operations while a free man. This had come mainly as a result of his attack on the OPEC ministers in Austria almost twenty years earlier, which explained why he and his group had been so careful not to kill anyone really important, despite the political flap that would have caused—all the better for him to gain notice and acclaim at the time. Business was business, even for his sort of people. And *someone* had paid his own legal bills, the attorney thought.

"What else do you expect me to tell him?"

"That is all. If he has an immediate reply, you will convey it to me," the Jackal told him. There was still an intensity to his eyes, something cold and distant—but even so, right there looking deep into his interlocutor and telling him what must be.

For his part, the attorney asked himself again why he'd taken on this client. He had a long history of championing radical causes, from which notoriety he'd gained a wide and lucrative criminal practice. There was an attendant element of danger involved, of course. He'd recently handled three major drug cases, and lost all three, and those clients hadn't liked the idea of spending twenty or more years in prison and had expressed their displeasure to him recently. Might they arrange to have him killed? It had happened a few times in America and elsewhere. It was a more distant possibility here, the lawyer thought, though he'd made no promises to those clients except to do his best for them. It was the same with Carlos the Jackal. After his conviction, the lawyer had come into the case to look at the possibilities of an appeal, and made it, and lost—predictably. The French high courts held little clemency for a man who'd done murder on the soil of France, then essentially boasted of it. Now the man had changed his mind and decided petulantly that he didn't enjoy prison life. The lawyer knew that he'd pass along the message, as he had to, but did that make him part of a criminal act?

No, he decided. Telling an acquaintance of his client that the latter wanted out of prison—well, who would not wish to be liberated? And the message was equivocal, it held many possible meanings. Help on another appeal, revelation of new, exculpatory evidence, anything at all. And besides, whatever Sanchez asked him to do here was privileged information, wasn't it?

"I will pass along your message," he promised his client.

"Merci."

IT was a beautiful thing to watch, even in the dark. The MH-60K Night Hawk helicopter came in at about thirty miles per hour, almost two hundred feet over the ground, approaching the range building from the south, into the wind, traveling smoothly, not at all like a tactical deployment maneuver. But under the helicopter was a dark nylon rope, about one hundred fifty feet long, barely visible with the best of NVGs, and at the end of it were Peter Covington, Mike Chin, and another Team-1 member, dangling free below the black Sikorsky in their black ninja suits. The helicopter proceeded in so evenly and smoothly, as though on tracks, until the nose of the aircraft crossed the building's wall. Then the nose came up, and the aircraft flared, slowing rapidly. Below the aircraft, the people attached to the rope swept forward, as though on a child's swing, and then, at the limit of the arc, they swung backward. The backward swing froze them still in the air, their rearward velocity almost exactly matching the remaining forward motion of the helicopter, and then they were on the roof, almost as though they'd stepped off a stationary object. Instantly, Covington and his men unclipped their quick-release attachments and dropped down. The negligible speed difference between their feet and the stationary roof made for no noise at all. Scarcely had this been done when the helicopter nosed down, resuming its forward flight, and anyone on the ground would scarcely have known that the aircraft had done anything but fly at a steady pace over the building. And at night, it was nearly invisible, even with night-vision goggles.

"Bloody good," Al Stanley breathed. "Not a bloody sound."

"He is as good as he says," Clark observed.

As though hearing the remarks, Malloy brought the helicopter around, flashing a thumbs-up out the window to the men on the ground as he headed off to orbit the area for the remainder of the simulation. In a real situation, the orbit would be in case he was needed to do an emergency evacuation—and even more so, to get the people on the ground used to having a helicopter overhead, to make his presence as much a part of the landscape as the trees, so he'd disappear into the normal background of the night, no more remarkable than the song of nightingales despite the danger inherent from his presence. It surprised everyone in the business that you could get away with this, but it was just an application of human nature to the world of special operations. If a tank had driven into the parking lot, after a day or two it would be just another car. Covington's trio of shooters circulated about the roof for a few minutes, then disappeared down ladders into the interior and emerged a few seconds later from the front door.

"Okay, Bear, this is Six, exercise concluded. Back to the bird farm, Colonel, over."

"Roger, Six, Bear is RTB. Out" was the terse reply, and the Night Hawk broke off from the orbit and headed down to the helo pad.

"What do you think?" Stanley asked Major Covington.

"Bloody good. Like stepping off the train to the platform. Malloy knows what he's about. Master Chief?"

"Put him on the payroll, sir," Master Chief Chin confirmed. "That's a guy we can work with."

"THE aircraft is nicely set up," Malloy said twenty minutes later, in the club. He was wearing his green Nomex flight suit, with a yellow scarf around his neck, like a good aviator, though it struck Clark as odd.

"What's with the necktie?"

"Oh, this? It's the A-10 scarf. One of the guys I rescued in Kuwait gave it to me. I figure it's lucky, and I've always kinda liked the Warthog as an airplane. So, I wear it on missions."

"How hard is it to do that transition maneuver?" Covington asked.

"Your timing has to be pretty good, and you have to read the wind. You know what helps me prepare for it?"

"Tell me," Clark said.

"Piano playing." Malloy sipped at his pint of bitter and grinned. "Don't ask me why, but I always fly better after I've played some. Maybe something to do with getting the fingers loose. Anyway, that chopper they lent us is set up just right. Control cables have the right tension, throttles are just so. That Air Force ground crew—well, I have to meet 'em and buy 'em all a round. They really know how to prepare a chopper. Good team of mechanics."

"They are that," First Lieutenant Harrison agreed. He belonged to 1st Special Operations Wing, and technically, therefore, he was responsible for the helicopter, though now he was very pleased to have so fine a teacher as Malloy.

"That's half the battle of flying helos, getting the bird dialed in just so," Malloy went on. "That one, you can just sweet talk to her, and she listens real nice."

"Like a good rifle," Chin observed.

"Roger that, Master Chief," Malloy said, saluting with his beer. "So, what can you guys tell me about your first two missions?"

"Christians 10, Lions 1," Stanley replied.

"Who'd you lose?"

"That was the Bern job. The hostage was killed before we were on the scene."

"Eager beavers?"

"Something like that." Clark nodded. "They weren't real swift, crossing the line like that. I sorta thought they were just bank robbers, but later investigation turned up the terrorist connection. Of course, maybe they just wanted some cash. Dr. Bellow never really decided what they were all about."

"Any way you look at it, they're just hoods, murderers, whatever you want to call 'em." Malloy said. "I helped train the FBI chopper pilots, spent a few weeks at Quantico with the Hostage Rescue Team. They kinda indoctrinated me on the psychological side. It can be pretty interesting. This Dr. Bellow, is it Paul Bellow, the guy who wrote the three books?"

"Same guy."

"He's pretty smart."

"That's the idea, Colonel Malloy," Stanley said, waving for another round.

"But the thing is, you know, there's only one thing you really need to know about them," Malloy said, reverting back to identity as a colonel of the United States Marine Corps.

"How to whack them," Master Chief Chin agreed.

THE Turtle Inn Bar and Lounge was something of a fixture on Columbus Avenue, between Sixty-eighth and Sixty-ninth, well known and well patronized by locals and tourists. The music was loud, but not too loud, and the area was lighted, but not very well. The booze was a little more expensive than the norm, but the added price was for the atmosphere, which, the owner would have said, was priceless.

"So." The man sipped at his rum and coke. "You live around here?"

"Just moving in," she answered, sipping her own drink. "Looking for a job."

"What d'ya do?"

"Legal secretary."

A laugh. "Lots of room for that here. We got more lawyers 'n we got taxi drivers. Where'd you say you were from?"

"Des Moines, Iowa. Ever been there?"

"No, local boy," the man replied, lying. He'd been born in Los Angeles thirty years before. "I'm an accountant with Peat Marwick." That was a lie, too.

But a singles bar was a place for lies, as everyone knew. The woman was twenty-three or so, just out of secretarial school, brown hair and eyes, and needed to lose about fifteen pounds, though she was attractive enough if you liked them short. The three drinks she'd already consumed to show that she was a burgeoning Big Apple sophisticate had her pretty mellow.

"Been here before?" he asked.

"No, first time, what about you?"

"Last few months, nice place to meet people." Another lie, but they came easily in a place like this.

"Music's a little loud," she said.

"Well, other places it's a lot worse. You live close?"

"Three blocks north. Got a little studio apartment, subleasing it. Rent control in the building. My stuff gets here in another week."

"So, you're not really moved in yet?"

"Right."

"Well, welcome to New York . . . ?"

"Anne Pretloe."

"Kirk Maclean." They shook hands, and he held hers a little longer than necessary so that she'd get a feel for his skin, a necessary precondition to casual affection, which he needed to generate. In another few minutes, they were dancing, which mainly meant bumping into people in the dark. He was turning on the charm, and she was smiling up at his six-foot height. Under other circumstances, this could have developed into something, Kirk thought. But not tonight.

The bar closed after two in the morning, and he walked her out. She was quite drunk now from a total of seven drinks barely diluted by bar peanuts and pretzel nuggets. He'd carefully nursed his three, and eaten a lot of peanuts. "So," he asked out on the sidewalk, "let me drive you, okay?"

"It's only three blocks."

"Annie, it's late, and this is New York; okay? You need to learn where you can go and where you can't. Come on," he concluded, pulling her hand and leading her around the corner. His BMW was parked halfway to Broadway. He gallantly held the door open, shut it behind her, then walked around to get in himself.

"You must do okay," Anne Pretloe noted, surveying the car.

"Yeah, well, lots of people like to dodge taxes, y'know?" He started the car and moved out onto the cross street, actually in the wrong direction, though she was a little too much in her cups to appreciate that. He turned left on Broadway and spotted the blue van, parked in a quiet spot. Half a block away, he flashed his lights, whereupon he slowed the car, and pushed the button to lower both the driver-side and passenger windows.

"Hey," he said, "I know this guy."

"Huh?" Pretloe replied, somewhat confused about where they were and where they were going. It was too late for her to do much in any case.

"Yo, Kirk," the man in coveralls said, leaning down to the open passenger window.

"Hey, buddy," Maclean replied, giving a thumbs-up.

The man in coveralls leaned in and produced a small aerosol can from his sleeve. Then he depressed the red plastic button and gave Anne Pretloe a blast of ether right in the face. Her eyes popped open for a second of shock and surprise. She turned to look at Kirk for a long lingering second or so, and then her body went slack.

"Be careful with the drugs, man, she's got a lot of booze in her."

"No problem." The man banged the side of the truck and another man appeared. This one looked up and down the street for a police car, then helped open the passenger door, lifted Anne Pretloe, and carried her limp form through the rear door of the van, where she joined another young woman picked up by another company employee earlier that night. With that, Maclean drove off, letting the night air blow the stink of the ether out of the car as he headed right, onto the West Side Highway and north to the George Washington Bridge. Okay, that made two he'd bagged, and the others should have gotten a total of six more by now. Another three, and they could end this most dangerous part of the operation.

CHAPTER 11

INFRASTRUCTURE

THE LAWYER MADE THE CALL, AND UNSURPRISINGLY found that it developed into a luncheon in a restaurant where a man of forty or so asked a few simple questions, then left before the dessert cart was wheeled up to the table. That ended his involvement with whatever would happen. He paid the check with cash and walked back to his office haunted by the question—what had he done, what might he have started? The answer for both, he told himself forcefully, was that he didn't know. It was the intellectual equivalent of a shower after a sweaty day's work, and though ultimately not as satisfying, he was a lawyer, and accustomed to the vicissitudes of life.

His interlocutor left the restaurant and caught the Métro, changing trains three times before settling on the one that ran near his home, close to a park known for the prostitutes who stood about, peddling their multivalued wares for passersby in automobiles. If there were anywhere an indictment of the capitalist system, it was here, he thought, though the tradition went further back than the onset of the current economic system. The women had all the gaiety of serial killers, as they stood there in their abbreviated clothing made to be removed as rapidly as possible, so as to save time. He turned away, and headed to his flat, where, with luck, others would be waiting for him. And luck, it turned out, was with him. One of his guests had even made coffee.

"**THIS** is where it has to stop," Carol Brightling said, even though she knew it wouldn't.

"Sure, doc," her guest said, sipping OEOB coffee. "But how the hell do you sell it to *him?*"

The map was spread on her coffee table: East of Alaska's Prudhoe Bay was a piece of tundra, over a thousand square miles of it, and geologists for British Petroleum and Atlantic Richfield—the two companies that had largely exploited the Alaskan North Slope, built the pipeline, and therefore helped cause the *Exxon Valdez* disaster—had made their public pronouncement. This oilfield, called AARM, was at least double the size of the North Slope. The report, still semiclassified in the industrial sense, had come to the White House a week earlier, with confirming data from the United States Geological Survey, a federal agency tasked to the same sort of work, along with the opinion of the geologists that the field extended farther east, across the Canadian border—and exactly how far it extended they could only guess, because the Canadians had not yet begun *their* survey. The conclusion of the executive summary posited the possibility that the entire field could rival the one in Saudi Arabia, although it was far harder to transport oil from it—*except for the fact,* the report went on, that the Trans-Alaska pipeline had already been built, and the new fields would only need a few hundred miles of extension on the existing pipeline, which, the summary concluded arrogantly, had produced a negligible environmental impact.

"Except for that damned tanker incident," Dr. Brightling observed into her morning coffee. Which had killed thousands of innocent wild birds and hundreds of sea otters, and had sullied several hundred square miles of pristine seacoast.

"This will be a catastrophe if Congress lets it go forward. My God, Carol, the caribou, the birds, all the predators. There are polar bears there, and browns, and barren-ground grizzly, and this environment is as delicate as a newborn infant. We *can't* allow the oil companies to go in there!"

"I *know,* Kevin," the President's Science Advisor responded, with an emphatic nod—

"The damage might *never* be repaired. The permafrost—there's *nothing* more delicate on the face of the planet," the president of the Sierra Club said, with further, repetitive emphasis. "We owe it to ourselves, we owe it to our children—we owe it to the *planet.* This bill has to be *killed!* I don't care what it takes, this bill must *die!* You *must* convince the President to withdraw any *semblance* of support for it. We cannot allow this environmental *rape* to take place."

"Kevin, we have to be smart about how we do this. The President sees this as a balance-of-payments issue. Domestic oil doesn't force us to spend our money buying oil from other countries. Worse, he believes the oil companies when they say they drill and transport the oil without doing great environmental damage, and that they can fix what damage they do *accidentally.*"

"That's horseshit, and you know it, Carol." Kevin Mayflower spat out his contempt for the oil companies. Their goddamned pipeline is a bleeding scar on the face of Alaska, an ugly, jagged steel line crossing the most beautiful land on the face of the earth, an affront to Nature Herself—and what for? So that people could drive motor vehicles, which further polluted the planet merely because lazy people didn't want to walk to work or ride bicycles or horses. (Mayflower didn't reflect on the fact that he'd flown to Washington to deliver his plea instead of riding one of his Appaloosa horses across the country, and that his rented car had been parked on West Executive Drive.) Everything the oil companies touched, they ruined, he thought. They made it dirty. They sullied the very earth itself, removing what they thought of as a precious resource here, there, and everywhere, whether it was oil or coal, gashing the earth, or poking holes into it, sometimes spilling their liquid treasure because they didn't know and didn't care about the sanctity of the planet, which belonged to everyone, and which needed proper stewardship. The stewardship, of course, required proper guidance, and that was the job of the Sierra Club and similar groups, to tell the people how important the earth was, and how they *must* respect and treat it. The good news was that the President's Science Advisor *did* understand, and that she *did* work in the White House Compound, and *did* have access to the President.

"Carol, I want you to walk across the street, go into the Oval Office, and *tell* him what has to be done."

"Kevin, it's not that easy."

"Why the hell not? He's not that much of a *dunce,* is he?"

"He occasionally has a different point of view, and the oil companies are being very clever about this. Look at their proposal," she said, tapping the report on the table. "They promise to indemnify the entire operation, to put up a *billion-dollar* bond in case something goes wrong—for God's sake, Kevin, they even offer to let the Sierra Club be on the council to oversee their environmental protection programs!"

"And be outnumbered there by their own cronies! Be damned if they'll co-opt us that way!" Mayflower snarled. "I won't let anyone from my office be a part of this rape, and *that's* final!"

"And if you say that out loud, the oil companies will call you an extremist, and marginalize the whole environmental movement—and you can't afford to let that happen, Kevin!"

"The *hell* I can't. You have to stand and fight for something, Carol. *Here* is where we stand and fight. We let those polluting bastards drill oil in Prudhoe Bay, but that's *it!*"

"What will the rest of your board say about this?" Dr. Brightling asked.

"They'll goddamned well say what I goddamned *tell* them to say!"

"No, Kevin, they won't." Carol leaned back and rubbed her eyes. She'd read the entire report the previous night, and the sad truth was that the oil companies had gotten pretty damned smart about dealing with environmental issues. It was plain business sense. The *Exxon Valdez* had cost them a *ton* of money, in addition to the bad public relations. Three pages had been devoted to the changes in tanker safety procedures. Now, ships leaving the huge oil terminal at Valdez, Alaska, were escorted by tugs all the way to the open sea. A total of twenty pollution-control vessels were on constant standby, with a further number in reserve. The navigation systems on every tanker had been upgraded to beyond what nuclear submarines carried; the navigation officers were compelled to test their skills on simulators every six months. It was all hugely expensive, but far less so than another serious spill. A series of commercials proclaimed all of these facts on television—worst of all, the high-end intellectual cable/satellite channels, History, Learning, Discovery, and A&E, for whom the oil companies were also sponsoring new shows on wildlife in the Arctic, never touched upon what the companies did, but there were plenty of pictures of caribou and other animals traversing under the elevated portions of the pipeline. They were getting their message out very skillfully indeed, even to members of the Sierra Club's board, Brightling thought.

What they didn't say, and what both she and Mayflower knew, was that once the oil was safely out of the ground, safely transported through the monster pipeline, safely conveyed over the sea by the newly double-hulled supertankers, *then* it just became more air pollution, out the tailpipes of cars and trucks and the smokestacks of electric-power stations. So it really was all a joke, and that joke included Kevin's bitching about hurting the permafrost. At most, what would be seriously damaged? Ten or twenty acres, probably, and the oil companies would make more commercials about how they cleaned *that* up, as though the polluting end-use of the oil was not an issue at all!

Because to the ignorant Joe Sixpack, sitting there in front of his TV, watching football games, it *wasn't* an issue, was it? There were a hundred or so million motor vehicles in the United States, and a larger number across the world, and they *all* polluted the air, and *that* was the real issue. How did one stop that from poisoning the planet?

Well, there were ways, weren't there? she reflected.

"Kevin, I'll do my best," she promised. "I will advise the President not to support this bill."

The bill was S-1768, submitted and sponsored by both Alaskan senators, whom the oil companies had bought long before, which would authorize the

Department of the Interior to auction off the drilling rights into the AAMP arca. Thc moncy involved would be huge, both for the federal government and for the state of Alaska. Even the Native American tribes up there would look the other way. The money they got from the oil would buy them lots of snowmobiles with which to chase and shoot the caribou, and motorboats to fish and kill the odd whale, which was part of their racial and cultural heritage. Snowmobiles weren't needed in the modern age of plastic-wrapped USDA Choice Iowa beef, but the Native Americans clung to the end-result of their traditions, if not the traditional methods. It was a depressing truth that even these people had set aside their history and their very gods in homage to a new age of mechanistic worship to oil and its products. Both the Alaskan senators would bring down tribal elders to testify in favor of S-1768, and they would be listened to, since who more than Native Americans knew what it was like to live in harmony with nature? Only today they did it with Ski-Do snowmobiles, Johnson outboard motors, and Winchester hunting rifles. . . . She sighed at the madness of it all.

"Will he listen?" Mayflower asked, getting back to business. Even environmentalists had to live in the real world of politics.

"Honest answer? Probably not," Carol Brightling admitted quietly.

"You know," Kevin observed in a low voice. "There are times when I understand John Wilkes Booth."

"Kevin, I didn't hear that, and you didn't say it. Not here. Not in this building."

"Damn it, Carol, you know how I feel. And you know I'm right. How the hell are we supposed to protect the planet if the idiots who run the world don't give a *fuck* about the world we live on?"

"What are you going to say? That *Homo sapiens* is a parasitic species that hurts the earth and the ecosystem? That we don't belong here?"

"A lot of us don't, and that's a fact."

"Maybe so, but what do you do about it?"

"I don't know," Mayflower had to admit.

Some of us know, Carol Brightling thought, looking up into his sad eyes. *But are you ready for that one, Kevin?* She thought he was, but recruitment was always a troublesome step, even for true believers like Kevin Mayflower. . . .

CONSTRUCTION was about ninety percent complete. There were twenty whole sections around the site, twenty one-square-mile blocks of land, mainly flat, a slight roll to it, with a four-lane paved road leading north to Interstate

70, which was still covered with trucks heading in and out. The last two miles of the highway were set up without a median strip, the rebarred concrete paving a full thirty inches deep, as though it had been built to land airplanes on, the construction superintendent had observed, big ones, even. The road led into an equally sturdy and massively wide parking lot. He didn't care enough about it, though, to mention it at his country club in Salina.

The buildings were fairly pedestrian, except for their environmental-control systems, which were so state-of-the-art that the Navy could have used them on nuclear submarines. It was all part of the company's leading-edge posture on its systems, the chairman had told him on his last visit. They had a tradition of doing everything ahead of everyone else, and besides, the nature of their work required careful attention to every little squiggly detail. You didn't make vaccines in the open. But even the worker housing and offices had the same systems, the super thought, and that was odd, to say the least. Every building had a basement—it was a sensible thing to build here in tornado country, but few ever bothered with it, partly out of sloth, and partly from the fact that the ground was not all that easy to dig here, the famous Kansas hardpan whose top was scratched to grow wheat. That was the other interesting part. They'd continue to farm most of the area. The winter wheat was already in, and two miles away was the farm-operations center, down its own over-wide two-lane road, outfitted with the newest and best farm equipment he'd ever seen, even in an area where growing wheat was essentially an art form.

Three hundred million dollars, total, was going into this project. The buildings were huge—you could convert them to living space for five or six thousand people, the super thought. The office building had classrooms for continuing education. The site had its own powerplant, along with a huge fuel-tank farm, whose tanks were semiburied in deference to local weather conditions, and connected by their own pipeline to a filling point just off I-70 at Kanopolis. Despite the local lake, there were no fewer than ten twelve-inch artesian wells drilled well down into—and *past*—the Cherokee Aquifer that local farmers used to water their fields. Hell, that was enough water to supply a small city. But the company was footing the bill, and he was getting his usual percentage of the total job cost to bring it in on time, with a substantial bonus for coming in early, which he was determined to earn. It had been twenty-five months to this point, with two more to go. And he'd make it, the super thought, and he'd get that bonus, after which he'd take the family to Disney World for two weeks of Mickey and golf on the wonderful courses there, which he needed in order to get his game back in shape after two years of seven-day weeks.

But the bonus meant he wouldn't need to work again for a couple of years. He specialized in large jobs. He'd done two skyscrapers in New York, an oil refinery in Delaware, an amusement park in Ohio, and two huge housing projects elsewhere, earning a reputation for bringing things in early and under budget—not a bad rep for someone in his business. He parked his Jeep Cherokee, and checked notes for the things remaining this afternoon. Yeah, the window-seal tests in Building One. He used his cell phone to call ahead, and headed off, across the landing strip, as he called it, where the access roads came together. He remembered his time as an engineer in the Air Force. Two miles long, and almost a yard thick, yeah, you could land a 747 on this road if you wanted. Well, the company had a fleet of its own Gulfstream business jets, and why not land them here instead of the dinky little airfield at Ellsworth? And if they ever bought a jumbo, he chuckled, they could do that here, too. Three minutes later, he was parked just outside of One. This building *was* complete, three weeks early, and the last thing to be done was the environmental checks. Fine. He walked in through the revolving door—an unusually heavy, robust one, which was immediately locked upon his entry.

"Okay, we ready, Gil?"

"We are now, Mr. Hollister."

"Run her up, then," Charlie Hollister ordered.

Gil Trains was the supervisor of all the environmental systems at the project. Ex-Navy, and something of a control freak, he punched the wall-mounted controls himself. There was no noise associated with the pressurization—the systems were too far away for that—but the effect was almost immediate. On the walk over to Gil, Hollister felt it in his ears, like driving down a mountain road, your ears *click*ed, and you had to work your jaw around to equalize the pressure, which was announced by another *click*.

"How's it holding?"

"So far, so good," Trains replied. "Zero-point-seven-five PSI overpressure, holding steady." His eyes were on the gauges mounted in this control station. "You know what this is like, Charlie?"

"Nope," the superintendent admitted.

"Testing watertight integrity on a submarine. Same method, we overpressure a compartment."

"Really? It's all reminded me of stuff I did in Europe at fighter bases."

"What's that?" Gil asked.

"Overpressurizing pilots' quarters to keep gas out."

"Oh yeah? Well, I guess it works both ways. Pressure is holding nicely."

Damned well ought to, Hollister thought, *with all the hell we went through to make sure every fucking window was sealed with vinyl gaskets.* Not that there were all that many windows. That had struck him as pretty odd. The views here were pretty nice. Why shut them out?

The building was spec'd for a full 1.3 pounds of overpressure. They'd told him it was tornado protection, and that sorta-kinda made sense, along with the increased efficiency of the HVAC systems that came along with the seals. But it could also make for sick-building syndrome. Buildings with overly good environmental isolation kept flu germs in, and helped colds spread like a goddamned prairie fire. Well, that had to be part of the idea, too. The company worked on drugs and vaccines and stuff, and that meant that this place was like a germ-warfare factory, didn't it? So, it made sense to keep stuff in—and keep stuff out, right? Ten minutes later they were sure. Instruments all over the building confirmed that the overpressurization systems worked—on the first trial. The guys who'd done the windows and doors had earned all that extra pay for getting it right.

"Looks pretty good. Gil, I have to run over to the uplink center." The complex also had a lavish collection of satellite-communications systems.

"Use the air lock." Trains pointed.

"See you later," the super said on his way out.

"Sure thing, Charlie."

IT wasn't pleasant. They now had eleven people, healthy ones, eight women and three men—segregated by gender, of course—and eleven was actually one more than they'd planned, but after kidnapping them you couldn't very well give them back. Their clothing had been taken away—in some cases it had been removed while they'd been unconscious—and replaced with tops and bottoms that were rather like prison garb, if made of somewhat better material. No undergarments were permitted—imprisoned women had actually used bras to hang themselves on occasion, and that couldn't be allowed here. Slippers for shoes, and the food was heavily laced with Valium, which helped to calm people down somewhat, but not completely. It wouldn't have been very smart to drug them that much, since the depression of all their bodily systems might skew the test, and they couldn't allow that either.

"What is all this?" the woman demanded of Dr. Archer.

"It's a medical test," Barbara replied, filling out the form. "You volunteered for it, remember? We're paying you for this, and after it's over you can go back home."

"When did I do that?"

"Last week," Dr. Archer told her.

"I don't remember."

"Well, you did. We have your signature on the consent form. And we're taking good care of you, aren't we?"

"I feel dopey all the time."

"That's normal," Dr. Archer assured her. "It's nothing to worry about."

She—Subject F4—was a legal secretary. Three of the women subjects were that, which was mildly troubling to Dr. Archer. What if the lawyers they worked for called the police? Letters of resignation had been sent, with the signatures expertly forged, and plausible explanations for the supposed event included in the text of the letters. Maybe it would hold up. In any case, the kidnappings had been expertly done, and nobody here would talk to anybody about it, would they?

Subject F4 was nude, and sitting in a comfortable cloth-covered chair. Fairly attractive, though she needed to lose about ten pounds, Archer thought. The physical examination had revealed nothing unusual. Blood pressure was normal. Blood chemistry showed slightly elevated cholesterol, but nothing to worry about. She appeared to be a normal, healthy, twenty-six-year-old female. The interview for her medical history was similarly unremarkable. She was not a virgin, of course, having had twelve lovers over the nine years of her sexual activity. One abortion carried out at age twenty by her gynecologist, after which she'd practiced safe sex. She had a current love interest, but he was out of town for a few weeks on business, and she suspected that he had another woman in his life anyway.

"Okay, that about does it, Mary." Archer stood and smiled. "Thank you for your cooperation."

"Can I get dressed now?"

"First there's something we want you to do. Please walk through the green door. There's a fogging system in there. You'll find it feels nice and cool. Your clothes will be on the other side. You can get dressed there."

"Okay." Subject F4 rose and did as she was told. Inside the sealed room was—nothing, really. She stood there in drugged puzzlement for a few seconds, noting that it was hot in there, over ninety degrees, but then invisible spray ports in the wall sent out a mist . . . fog, something like that, which cooled her down instantly and comfortably for about ten seconds. Then the fog stopped, and the far door clicked open. As promised, there was a dressing room there, and she donned her green jamms, then walked out into the corridor, where a security guard waved her to the door at the far end—he never got closer than ten feet—back to the dormitory, where lunch was waiting. Meals were pretty good here, and after meals she always felt like a nap.

■ ■ ■

"FEELING bad, Pete?" Dr. Killgore asked in a different part of the building.

"Must be the flu or something. I feel beat-up all over, and I can't keep anything down." Even the booze, he didn't say, though that was especially disconcerting for the alcoholic. Booze was the one thing he could always keep down.

"Okay, let's give it a look, then." Killgore stood, donning a mask and putting on latex gloves for his examination. "Gotta take a blood sample, okay?"

"Sure, doc."

Killgore did that very carefully indeed, giving him the usual stick inside the elbow, and filling four five-cc test tubes. Next he checked Pete's eyes, mouth, and did the normal prodding, which drew a reaction over the subject's liver—

"Ouch! That hurts, doc."

"Oh? Doesn't feel very different from before, Pete. How's it hurt?" he asked, feeling the liver, which, as in most alcoholics, felt like a soft brick.

"Like you just stabbed me with a knife, doc. Real sore there."

"Sorry, Pete. How about here?" the physician asked, probing lower with both hands.

"Not as sharp, but it hurts a little. Somethin' I ate, maybe?"

"Could be. I wouldn't worry too much about it," Killgore replied. Okay, this one was symptomatic, a few days earlier than expected, but small irregularities were to be expected. Pete was one of the healthier subjects, but alcoholics were never really what one could call healthy. So, Pete would be Number 2. *Bad luck, Pete,* Killgore thought. "Let me give you something to take the edge off."

The doctor turned and pulled open a drawer on the wall cabinet. Five milligrams, he thought, filling the plastic syringe to the right line, then turning and sticking the vein on the back of the hand.

"Oooh!" Pete said a few seconds later. "Oooh . . . that feels okay. Lot better, doc. Thanks." The rheumy eyes went wide, then relaxed.

Heroin was a superb analgesic, and best of all, it gave its recipient a dazzling rush in the first few seconds, then reduced him to a comfortable stupor for the next few hours. So, Pete would feel just fine for a while. Killgore helped him stand, then sent him back. Next he took the blood samples off for testing. In thirty minutes, he was sure. The antibody tests still showed positive, and microscopic examination showed what the antibodies were fighting against . . . and losing to.

Only two years earlier, people had tried to infect America with the natural version of this bug, this "shepherd's crook," some called it. It had been somewhat modified in the genetic-engineering lab with the addition of cancer DNA to make this negative-strand RNA virus more robust, but that was really like putting a raincoat on the bug. The best news of all was that the genetic engineering had more than tripled the latency period. Once thought to be four to ten days, now it was almost a month. Maggie really knew her stuff, and she'd even picked the right name for it. Shiva was one nasty little son of a bitch. It had killed Chester—well, the potassium had done that, but Chester had been doomed—and it was now starting to kill Pete. There would be no merciful help for this one. Pete would be allowed to live until the disease took his life. His physical condition was close enough to normal that they'd work to see what good supportive care could do to fight off the effects of the Ebola-Shiva. Probably nothing, but they had to establish that. Nine remaining primary test subjects, and then eleven more on the other side of the building—they would be the real test. They were all healthy, or so the company thought. They'd be testing both the method of primary transmission and the viability of Shiva as a plague agent, plus the utility of the vaccines Steve Berg had isolated the previous week.

That concluded Killgore's work for the day. He made his way outside. The evening air was chilly and clean and pure—well, as pure as it could be in this part of the world. There were a hundred million cars in the country, all spewing their complex hydrocarbons into the atmosphere. Killgore wondered if he'd be able to tell the difference in two or three years, when all that stopped. In the glow of the building lights, he saw the flapping of bats. Cool, he thought, one rarely saw bats. They must be chasing insects, and he wished his ears could hear the ultrasonic sounds they projected like radar to locate the bugs and intercept them.

There would be birds up there, too. Owls especially, magnificent raptors of the night, flying with soft, quiet feathers, finding their way into barns, where they'd catch mice, eat and digest them, and then regurgitate the bones of their prey in compact little capsules. Killgore felt far more kinship for the wild predators than he did for the prey animals. But that was to be expected, wasn't it? He *did* have kinship with the predators, those wild, magnificent things that killed without conscience, because Mother Nature had no conscience at all. It gave life with one hand, and took it back with the other. The ageless process of life, that had made the earth what it was. Men had tried so hard and so long to change it, but other men now would change it back, quickly and dramatically, and he'd be there to see it. He wouldn't see all the scars fade from the land, and that was too bad, but, he judged, he'd live long enough to see the important things change. Pollution would stop almost completely. The animals would no longer be fettered and poisoned. The sky would clear, and the land would soon be covered with life, as Nature intended, with him and his colleagues to see the magnificence of the transformation. And if the price was high, then the prize it earned was worth it. The earth belonged to those who appreciated and understood her. He was even using one of Nature's methods to take possession—albeit with a little human help. If humans could use their science and arts to harm the world, then other humans could use them to fix it. Chester and Pete would not have understood, but then, they'd never understood much of anything, had they?

"THERE will be thousands of Frenchmen there," Juan said. "And half of them will be children. If we wish to liberate our colleagues, the impact must be a strong one. This should be strong enough."

"Where will we go afterwards?" René asked.

"The Bekaa Valley is still available, and from there, wherever we wish. I have good contacts in Syria, still, and there are always options."

"It's a four-hour flight, and there is always an American aircraft carrier in the Mediterranean."

"They will not attack an aircraft filled with children," Esteban pointed out. "They might even give us an escort," he added with a smile.

"It is only twelve kilometers to the airport," Andre reminded them, "a fine multilane highway."

"So, then, we must plan the mission in every detail. Esteban, you will get yourself a job there. You, too, Andre. We must pick our places, then select the time and the day."

"We'll need more men. At least ten more."

"That is a problem. Where can we get ten reliable men?" Juan asked.

"*Sicarios* can be hired. We need only promise them the right amount of money," Esteban pointed out.

"They must be faithful men," René told them forcefully.

"They will be faithful enough," the Basque told them. "I know where to go for them."

They were all bearded. It was the easiest disguise to adopt, and though the national police in their countries had pictures of them, the pictures were all of young, shaven men. A passerby might have thought them to be artists, the way they looked, and the way they all leaned inward on the table to speak with intense whispers. They were all dressed moderately well, though not expensively so. Perhaps they were arguing over some political issue, the waiter thought from his station ten meters away, or some confidential business matter. He couldn't know that he was right on both counts. A few minutes later, he watched them shake hands and depart in different directions, having left cash to pay the bill, and, the waiter discovered, a niggardly tip. Artists, he thought. They were notoriously cheap bastards.

"BUT this is an environmental disaster waiting to happen!" Carol Brightling insisted.

"Carol," the chief of staff replied. "It's about our balance of payments. It will save America something like fifty billion dollars, and we need that. On the environmental side, I know what your concerns are, but the president of Atlantic Richfield has promised me personally that this will be a clean operation. They've learned a lot in the past twenty years, on the engineering side and the public relations side, about cleaning up their act, haven't they?"

"Have you ever been there?" the President's science advisor asked.

"Nope." He shook his head. "I've flown over Alaska, but that's it."

"You would think differently if you'd ever seen the place, trust me."

"They strip-mine coal in Ohio. I've seen that. And I've seen them cover it back up and plant grass and trees. Hell, one of those strip mines—in two years they're going to have the PGA championship on the golf course that they built there! It's *cleaned up,* Carol. They know how now, and they know it makes good sense to do it, economically *and* politically. So, no, Carol, the President will *not* withdraw his support for this drilling project. It makes economic sense for the country." *And who really cares a rat's ass for land that only a few hundred people have ever seen?* he didn't add.

"I have to talk to him personally about it," the science advisor insisted.

"No." The chief of staff shook his head emphatically. "That's not going to happen. Not on this issue. All you'd accomplish is to undercut your position, and that isn't smart, Carol."

"But I *promised!*"

"Promised whom?"

"The Sierra Club."

"Carol, the Sierra Club isn't part of this administration. And we get their letters. I've read them. They're turning into an extremist organization on issues like this. Anybody can say 'do nothing,' and that's about all they're saying since this Mayflower guy took it over."

"Kevin is a good man and a very smart one."

"You couldn't prove that by me, Carol," the chief of staff snorted. "He's a Luddite."

"Goddamnit, Arnie, not everyone who disagrees with you is an extremist, okay?"

"That one is. The Sierra Club's going to self-destruct if they keep him on top of the masthead. Anyway." The chief of staff checked his schedule. "I have work to do. Your position on this issue, Dr. Brightling, is to support the Administration. That means *you* personally *support* the drilling bill for AAMP. There is only one position in this building, and that position is what the President says it is. That's the price you pay for working as an advisor to the President, Carol. You get to influence policy, but once that policy is promulgated, you support it, whether you believe it or not. You will say publicly that you think that drilling that oil is a good thing for America and for the environment. Do you understand that?"

"No, Arnie, I won't!" Brightling insisted.

"Carol, you will. And you will do it convincingly, in such a way as to make the more moderate environmental groups see the logic of the situation. If, that is, you like working here."

"Are you threatening me?"

"No, Carol, I am not threatening you. I am explaining to you how the rules work here. Because you have to play by the rules, just like I do, and just like everyone else does. If you work here you must be loyal to the President. If you are not loyal, then you cannot work here. You knew those rules when you came onboard, and you knew you had to live by them. Okay, now it's time for a gut check. Carol, will you live by the rules or won't you?"

Her face was red under the makeup. She hadn't learned to conceal her anger, the chief of staff saw, and that was too bad. You couldn't afford to get angry over minor bullshit items, not at this level of government. And this was a minor bullshit item. When you found something as valuable as several billion barrels of oil in a place that belonged to you, you drilled into the ground to get it out. It was as simple as that—and it was simpler still if the oil companies promised not to hurt anything as a result. It would remain that simple as long as the voters drove automobiles. "Well, Carol?" he asked.

"Yes, Arnie, I know the rules, and I will live by the rules," she confirmed at last.

"Good. I want you to prepare a statement this afternoon for release next week. I want to see it today. The usual stuff, the science of it, the safety of the engineering measures, that sort of thing. Thanks for coming over, Carol," he said in dismissal.

Dr. Brightling stood and moved to the door. She hesitated there, wanting to turn and tell Arnie what he could do with his statement . . . but she kept moving into the corridor in the West Wing, turned north, and went down the stairs for the street level. Two Secret Service agents noted the look on her face and wondered what had rained on her parade that morning—or maybe had turned a hail-storm loose on it. She walked across the street with an unusually stiff gait, then up the steps into the OEOB. In her office, she turned on her Gateway computer and called up her word-processing program, wanting to put her fist through the glass screen rather than type on the keyboard.

To be ordered around by that *man!* Who didn't know *anything* about science, and didn't *care* about environmental policy. All Arnie cared about was politics, and politics was the most artificial damned thing in the world!

But then, finally, she calmed down, took a deep breath, and began drafting her defense of something that, after all, would never happen, would it?

No, she told herself. It would never happen.

CHAPTER 12

WILD CARDS

THE THEME PARK HAD LEARNED WELL FROM ITS more famous model. It had taken care to hire away a dozen senior executives, their lavish salary increases paid for by the park's Persian Gulf financial backers, who had already exceeded their fiscal expectations and looked forward to recouping their total investment in less than six years instead of the programmed eight and a half.

Those investments had been considerable, since they determined not merely to emulate the American corporation, but to exceed it in every respect. The castle in *their* park was made of stone, not mere fiberglass. The main street was actually three thoroughfares, each adapted to three separate national themes. The circular railroad was of standard gauge and used two real steam locomotives, and there was talk of extending the line to the international airport, which the Spanish authorities had been so kind as to modernize in order to support the theme park—as well they might: the park provided twenty-eight thousand full-time and ten thousand more part-time or seasonal jobs. The ride attractions were spectacular, most of them custom designed and built in Switzerland, and some of them adventurous enough to make a fighter pilot go pale. In addition, it had a Science World section, with a moonwalk attraction that had impressed NASA, an underwater walk-through mega-aquarium, and pavilions from every major industry in Europe—the one from Airbus Industrie was particularly impressive, allowing children (and adults) to pilot simulated versions of its aircraft.

There were characters in costumes—gnomes, trolls, and all manner of mythical creatures from European history, plus Roman legionnaires to fight barbarians—and the usual marketing areas where guests could buy replicas of everything the park had to offer.

One of the smartest things the investors had done was to build their theme park in Spain rather than France. The climate here, while hotter, was also sunny and dry most of the year, which made for full-year-round operations. Guests flew in from all over Europe, or took the trains, or came down on bus tours to stay at the large, comfortable hotels, which were designed for three different levels of expense and grandeur, from one that might have been decorated by César Ritz down to several with more basic amenities. Guests at all of them shared the same physical environment, warm and dry, and could take time off to bathe in the many pools surrounded by white-sand beaches, or to play on one of the two existing golf courses—three more were under construction, and one of them would soon be part of the European Professional Tour. There was also a busy casino, something no other theme park had tried. All in all, Worldpark, as it was called, had been an instant and sensational success, and it rarely had fewer than ten thousand guests, and frequently more than fifty thousand.

A thoroughly modern facility, it was controlled by six regional and one master command center, and every attraction, ride, and food outlet was monitored by computers and TV cameras.

Mike Dennis was the operations director. He'd been hired away from Orlando, and while he missed the friendly managerial atmosphere there, the building and then running of Worldpark had been the challenge he'd waited for all his life. A man with three kids, *this* was his baby, Dennis told himself, looking out the battlements of the tower. His office and command center was in the castle keep, the tall tower in the twelfth-century fortress they'd built. Maybe the Duke of Aquitaine had enjoyed a place like this, but he'd used only swords and spears, not computers and helicopters, and as wealthy as his grace had been back in the twelfth century, he hadn't handled money in this quantity—Worldpark took in ten *million* dollars in cash alone on a good day, and far more than that from plastic. Every day a cash truck with a heavy police escort left the park for the nearest bank.

Like its model in Florida, Worldpark was a multistory structure. Under the main concourses was a subterranean city where the support services operated, and the cast members changed into costumes and ate their lunches, and where he was able to get people and things from place to place quickly and unseen by the guests in the sunlight. Running it was the equivalent of being mayor of a not-so-small city—harder, actually, since he had to make sure that everything worked all the time, and that the cost of operations was always less than the city's income. That he did his job well, actually about 2.1 percent better than his own pre-opening projections, meant that he had a sizable salary, and that he'd earned the $1,000,000 bonus that had been delivered to him only five weeks earlier. Now, if only his kids could get used to the local schools. . . .

EVEN as an object of hatred, it was breathtaking. It *was* a city, Andre saw, the construction of which had cost billions. He'd lived through the indoctrination process in the local "Worldpark University," learned the absurd ethos of the place, learned to smile at everything and everybody. He'd been assigned, fortuitously, to the security department, the notional Worldpark *Policia,* which means that he wore a light blue shirt and dark blue trousers with a vertical blue stripe, carried a whistle and a portable radio, and spent most of his time telling people where the restrooms were, because Worldpark needed a police force about as much as a ship needed wheels. He'd gotten this job because he was fluent in three languages, French, Spanish, and English, and thus could be helpful to the majority of the visitors—"guests"—to this new Spanish city, all of whom needed to urinate from time to time, and most of whom, evidently, lacked the wit to notice the hundreds of signs (graphic rather than lettered) that told them where to go when the need became overwhelming.

Esteban, Andre saw, was in his usual place, selling his helium-filled balloons. Bread and circuses, they both thought. The vast sums expended to build this place—and for what purpose? To give the children of the poor and working classes a brief few hours of laughter before they returned to their dreary homes? To seduce their parents into spending their money for mere amusement? Really, the purpose of the place was to enrich further the Arab investors who'd been persuaded to spend so much of their oil money here, building this fantasy city. Breathtaking, perhaps, but still an object of contempt, this icon of the unreal, this opiate for the masses of workers who had not the sense to see it for what it was. Well, that was the task of the revolutionary elite.

Andre walked about, seemingly in an aimless way, but actually in accordance with plans, both his and the park's. He was being paid to look around and make arrangements while he smiled and told parents where their little darlings could relieve themselves.

"THIS will do it," Noonan said, walking into the morning meeting.

"What's 'this'?" Clark asked.

Noonan held up a computer floppy disk. "It's just a hundred lines of code, not counting the installation stuff. The cells—the phone cells, I mean—all use the same computer program to operate. When we get to a place, I just insert this in their drives and upload the software. Unless you dial in the right prefix to make a call—7-7-7, to be exact—the cell will respond that the number you're calling is busy. So, we can block any cellular calls into our subjects from some helpful soul outside and also prevent them from getting out."

"How many spare copies do you have?" Stanley asked.

"Thirty," Noonan answered. "We can get the local cops to install them. I have instructions printed up in six languages." *Not bad, eh?* Noonan wanted to say. He'd gone through a contact at the National Security Agency at Fort Meade, Maryland, to get it. Pretty good for just over a week's effort. "It's called Cellcop, and it'll work anywhere in the world."

"Good one, Tim." Clark made a note. "Okay, how are the teams?"

"Sam Houston's down with a sprained knee," Peter Covington told Clark. "Hurt it coming down a zip-line. He can still deploy, but he won't be running for a few days."

"Team-2's fully mission-capable, John," Chavez announced. "George Tomlinson is a little slowed down with his Achilles tendon, but no big deal."

Clark grunted and nodded, making a further note. Training was so hard here that the occasional injury was inevitable—and John well remembered the aphorism that drills were supposed to be bloodless combat, and combat supposed to be bloody drills. It was fundamentally a good thing that his troops worked as hard in practice as they did in the real thing—it said a lot for their morale, and just as much for their professionalism, that they took every aspect of life in Rainbow that seriously. Since Sam Houston was a long-rifleman, he really was about seventy percent mission-capable, and George Tomlinson, strained tendon and all, was still doing his morning runs, gutting it out as an elite trooper should.

"Intel?" John turned to Bill Tawney.

"Nothing special to report," the Secret Intelligence Service officer replied. "We know that there are terrorists still alive, and the various police forces are still doing their investigations to dig them out, but it's not an easy job, and nothing promising appears to be underway, but . . ." But one couldn't predict a break in a case. Everyone around the table knew that. This very evening someone of the class of Carlos himself could be pulled over for running a stop sign and be recognized by some rookie cop and snapped up, but you couldn't plan for random events. There were still over a hundred known terrorists living somewhere in Europe probably, just like Ernst Model and Hans Fürchtner, but they'd learned a not-very-hard lesson about keeping a low profile, adopting a simple disguise, and keeping out of trouble. They had to make some greater or lesser mistake to be noticed, and the ones who made dumb mistakes were long since dead or imprisoned.

"How about cooperation with the local police agencies?" Alistair Stanley asked.

"We keep speaking with them, and the Bern and Vienna missions have been very good press for us. Wherever something happens, we can expect to be summoned swiftly."

"Mobility?" John asked next.

"That's me, I guess," Lieutenant Colonel Malloy responded. "It's working out well with the 1st Special Operations Wing. They're letting me keep the Night Hawk for the time being, and I've got enough time on the British Puma that I'm current in it. If we have to go, I'm ready to go. I can get MC-130 tanker support if I need it for a long deployment, but as a practical matter I can be just about anywhere in Europe in eight hours in my Sikorsky, with or without tanker support. Operational side, I'm comfortable with things. The troops here are as good as any I've seen, and we work well together. The only thing that worries me is the lack of a medical team."

"We've thought about that. Dr. Bellow is our doc, and you're up to speed on trauma, right, doc?" Clark asked.

"Fairly well, but I'm not as good as a real trauma surgeon. Also, when we deploy, we can get local paramedics to help out from police and fire services on the scene."

"We did it better at Fort Bragg," Malloy observed. "I know all our shooters are trained in emergency-response care, but a properly trained medical corpsman is a nice thing to have around. Doctor Bellow's only got two hands," the pilot noted. "And he can only be in one place at a time."

"When we deploy," Stanley said, "we do a routine call-up to the nearest local casualty hospital. So far we've had good cooperation."

"Okay, guys, but I'm the one who has to transport the wounded. I've been doing it for a long time, and I think we could do it a little better. I recommend a drill for that. We should practice it regularly."

That wasn't a bad idea, Clark thought. "Duly noted, Malloy. Al, let's do that in the next few days."

"Agreed," Stanley responded with a nod.

"The hard part is simulating injuries," Dr. Bellow told them. "There's just no substitute for the real thing, but we can't put our people in the emergency room. It's too time-wasteful, and they won't see the right kind of injuries there."

"We've had this problem for years," Peter Covington said. "You can teach the procedures, but practical experience is too difficult to come by—"

"Yeah, unless we move the outfit to Detroit," Chavez quipped. "Look, guys, we all know the right first-aid stuff, and Doctor Bellow *is* a doc. There's only so much we have time to train for, and the primary mission is paramount, isn't it? We get there and do the job, and that minimizes the number of wounds, doesn't it?" Except to the bad guys, he didn't add, and nobody really cared about them, and you couldn't treat three 10-mm bullets in the head, even at Walter Reed. "I like the idea of training to evac wounded. Fine, we can do that, and practice first-aid stuff, but can we realistically go farther than that? I don't see how."

"Comments?" Clark asked. He didn't see much past that, either.

"Chavez is correct . . . but you're never fully prepared or fully trained," Malloy pointed out. "No matter how much you work, the bad guys always find a way to dump something new on you. Anyway, in Delta we deploy with a full medical-response team, trained corpsmen—experts, used to trauma care. Maybe we can't afford to do that here, but that's how we did it at Fort Bragg."

"We'll just have to depend on local support for that," Clark said, closing the issue. "This place can't afford to grow that much. I don't have the funding."

And that's the magic word in this business, Malloy didn't have to add. The meeting broke up a few minutes later, and with it the working day ended. Dan Malloy had grown accustomed to the local tradition of closing out a day at the club, where the beer was good and the company cordial. Ten minutes later, he was hoisting a jar with Chavez. This little greaser, he thought, really had his shit together.

"That call you made in Vienna was pretty good, Ding."

"Thanks, Dan." Chavez took a sip. "Didn't have much of a choice, though. Sometimes you just gotta do what you gotta do."

"Yep, that's a fact," the Marine agreed.

"You think we're thin on the medical side . . . so do I, but so far that hasn't been a problem."

"So far you've been lucky, my boy."

"Yeah, I know. We haven't been up against any crazy ones yet."

"They're out there, the real sociopathic personalities, the ones who don't care a rat's ass about anything at all. Well, truth is, I haven't seen any of them either except on TV. I keep coming back to the Ma'alot thing, in Israel twenty-plus years ago. Those fuckers wasted little kids just to show how tough they were—and remember what happened a while back with the President's little girl. She was damned lucky that FBI guy was there. I wouldn't mind buying that guy a beer."

"Good shooting," Chavez agreed. "Better yet, good timing. I read up on how he handled it—talking to them and all, being patient, waiting to make his move, then taking it when he got it."

"He lectured at Bragg, but I was traveling that day. Saw the tape. The boys said he can shoot a pistol as well as anybody on the team—but better yet, he was smart."

"Smart counts," Chavez agree, finishing his beer. "I gotta go fix dinner."

"Say again?"

"My wife's a doc, gets home in an hour or so, and it's my turn to do dinner."

A raised eyebrow: "Nice to see you're properly trained, Chavez."

"I am secure in my masculinity," Domingo assured the aviator and headed for the door.

ANDRE worked late that night. Worldpark stayed open until 2300 hours, and the shops remained open longer than that, because even so huge a place as Worldpark couldn't waste the chance to earn a few extra copper coins from the masses for the cheap, worthless souvenirs they sold, to be clutched in the greedy hands of little children, often nearly asleep in the arms of their weary parents. He watched the process impassively, the way so many people waited until the very last ride on the mechanical contrivances, and only then, with the chains in place and after the good-bye waves of the ride operators, did they finally turn and shuffle their way to the gates, taking every opportunity to stop and enter the shops, where the clerks smiled tiredly and were as helpful as they'd been taught to be at the Worldpark University. And then when, finally, all had left, the shops were closed, and the registers emptied, and under the eyes of Andre and his fellow security staff, the cash was taken off to the counting room. It wasn't, strictly speaking, part of his current job, but he tagged along anyway, following the three clerks from the Matador shop, out onto the main street, then into an alleyway, through some blank wooden doors, and down the steps to the underground, the concrete corridors that bustled with electric carts and employees during the day, now empty except for employees heading to dressing rooms to change into their street clothes. The counting room was in the very center, almost under the castle itself. There the cash was handed over, each bag labeled for its point of origin. The coins were dumped into a bin, where they were separated by nationality and denomination and counted, wrapped, and labeled for transport to the bank. The paper currency, already bundled by currency and denomination was . . . weighed. The first time he'd seen it, it had amazed him, but delicate scales actually weighed it—there, one point zero-six-one-five kilos of hundred-mark German notes. Two point six-three-seven-zero kilos of five-pound British ones. The corresponding amount was flashed on the electronic screen, and the notes were whisked off for wrapping. Here the security officers carried weapons, Astra pistols, because the total amount of the currency for the day was—the master tally display said £11,567,309.35 . . . all used cash, the very best sort, in all denominations. It all fit into six large canvas bags that were placed on a four-wheeled cart for transport out the back of the underground into an armored car with a police escort for transport to the central branch of the local bank, still open this time of day for a deposit of this magnitude. Eleven million British pounds in cash—this place took in billions per year in *cash,* Andre thought tiredly.

"Excuse me," he said to his security supervisor. "Have I broken any rules by coming here?"

A chuckle: "No, everyone comes down sooner or later to see. That's why the windows are here."

"Is it not dangerous?"

"I think not. The windows are thick, as you see, and security inside the counting room is very strict."

"Mon dieu, all that money—what if someone should try to steal it?"

"The truck is armored, and it has a police escort, two cars, four men each, all heavily armed." And those would be only the obvious watchers, Andre thought. There would be others, not so close, and not so obvious, but equally well armed. "We were initially concerned that the Basque terrorists might try to steal the money—this much cash could finance their operations for years—but the threat has not developed, and besides, you know what becomes of all this cash?"

"Why not fly the money to the bank on a helicopter?" Andre asked.

The security supervisor yawned. "Too expensive."

"So, what becomes of the cash?"

"Much of it comes right back to us, of course."

"Oh." Andre thought for a moment. "Yes, it must, mustn't it?"

Worldpark was largely a cash business, because so many people still preferred to pay for things that way, despite the advent of credit cards, which the park was just as pleased to use, and despite the ability of guests to charge everything to their hotel-room accounts—instructions for which were printed on every plastic card-key in the language of the individual guest.

"I wager we use the same five-pound British note fifteen times before it's too worn and has to be sent to London for destruction and replacement."

"I see," Andre said with a nod. "So, we deposit, and then we withdraw from our own account just to make change for our guests. How much cash do we keep on hand, then?"

"For change purposes?" A shrug. "Oh, two or three million at minimum—British pounds, that is. To keep track of it all, we have those computers." He pointed.

"Amazing place," Andre observed, actually meaning it. He nodded at his supervisor and headed off to punch his time card and change. It had been a good day. His wanderings had confirmed his previous observations of the park. He now knew how to plan the mission, and how to accomplish it. Next he had to bring in his colleagues and show them the plan, after which came the execution. Forty minutes later, he was in his flat, drinking some Burgundy and thinking everything through. He'd been the plans and operations officer for Action Directe for over a decade—he'd planned and executed a total of eleven murders. This mission, however, would be by far the grandest of all, perhaps the culmination of his career, and he had to think it all through. Affixed to the wall of his flat was a map of Worldpark, and his eyes wandered over it, back and forth. Way-in, way-out. Possible routes of access by the police. Ways to counter them. Where to place his own security personnel. Where to take the hostages. Where to keep them. How to get everyone out. Andre kept going over it, again and again, looking for weaknesses, looking for mistakes. The Spanish national police, the Guardia Civil, would respond to this mission. They were to be taken with respect, despite their comical hats. They'd been fighting the Basques for a generation, and they'd learned. They doubtless had an arrangement with Worldpark already, because this was too obvious a target for terr—for progressive elements, Andre corrected himself. Police were not to be taken lightly. They'd almost killed or arrested him twice in France, but both of those occasions were because he'd made obvious mistakes, and he'd learned from both of them. No, not this time. He'd keep them at bay this time by his choice of hostages, and by showing his willingness to use them to his political ends, and as tough as the Guardia Civil might be, they would quail before that demonstration of resolve, because tough as they were, they were vulnerable to bourgeois sentimentality, just as all like them were. It was the purity of his purpose that gave him the edge, and he'd hold on to that, and he *would* achieve his objective, or many would die, and neither the government of Spain nor France could stand up to that. The plan was nearly ready. He lifted his phone and made an international call.

■ ■ ■

PETE came back early in the evening. His face was pale now, and he was even more listless, but also uncomfortable, judging from the pained way in which he moved.

"How you feeling?" Dr. Killgore asked cheerily.

"Stomach is real bad, doc, right here," Pete said, pointing with his finger.

"Still bothering you, eh? Well, okay, why don't you lie down here and we'll check you out," the physician said, donning mask and gloves. The physical examination was cursory, but unnecessary for all that. Pete, like Chester before him, was dying, though he didn't know it yet. The heroin had done a good job of suppressing his discomfort, removing the pain and replacing it with chemical nirvana. Killgore carefully took another blood sample for later microscopy.

"Well, partner, I think we just have to wait this one out. But let me give you a shot to ease the pain, okay?"

"Sure thing, doc. The last one worked pretty good."

Killgore filled another plastic syringe and injected the heroin into the same vein as before. He watched Pete's brown eyes go wide with the initial rush, then droop as the pain went away, to be replaced with a lethargy so deep that he could almost have done major surgery on the spot without getting a rise from the poor bastard.

"How are the rest of the guys, Pete?"

"Okay, but Charlie is bitching about his stomach, something he ate, I guess."

"Oh, yeah? Maybe I'll see him, too," Killgore thought. *So, number three will be in here tomorrow, probably.* The timing was just about right. After Chester's earlier-than-expected symptoms, the rest of the group was right on the predicted timeline. Good.

MORE telephone calls were made, and by early morning, people rented cars with false IDs, drove in pairs or singly south from France to Spain, and were waved through the cursory border checkpoints, usually with a friendly smile. Various travel agents made the necessary reservations at park hotels, all mid-level, and linked to the park by monorail or train, the stations right in the shop-filled hotel lobbies, so that the guests wouldn't get lost.

The highways to the park were wide and comfortable to drive on, and the signs easy to follow even for those who didn't speak Spanish. About the only hazards were the huge tourist buses, which moved along at over 150 kilometers per hour, like land-bound ocean liners, their windows full of people, many of them children who waved down at the drivers of the passenger cars. The drivers waved back with smiles of their own, and allowed the buses to plow on, exceeding the speed limit as though it were their right to do so, which the car drivers didn't want to risk. They had plenty of time. They'd planned their mission that way.

TOMLINSON reached down to his left leg and grimaced. Chavez dropped back from the morning run to make sure he was okay.

"Still hurts?"

"Like a son of a bitch," Sergeant Tomlinson confirmed.

"So go easier on it, you dumb bastard. The Achilles is a bad thing to hurt."

"Just found that one out, Ding." Tomlinson slowed down to a walk, still favoring the left leg after running over two miles on it. His breathing was far heavier than usual, but pain was always a bad thing for the endurance.

"See Doc Bellow?"

"Yeah, but ain't nothing he can do 'cept let it heal, he says."

"So, let it heal. That's an order, George. No more running until it stops hurting so much. 'Kay?"

"Yes, sir," Sergeant Tomlinson agreed. "I can still deploy if you need me."

"I know that, George. See you in the shooting house."

"Right." Tomlinson watched his leader speed up to rejoin the rest of Team-2. It hurt his pride that he wasn't keeping up. He'd never allowed any sort of injury to slow him down—in Delta Force he'd kept up with the training despite two broken ribs, hadn't even told the medics about it for fear of being thought a pussy by the rest of his team. But while you could conceal and gut out bad ribs, a stretched tendon was something you couldn't run on—the pain was just so bad that the leg stopped working right, and it was hard to stand up straight. Damn, the soldier thought, can't let the rest of the team down. He'd never been second-best in anything in his life, back to Little League baseball, where he'd played shortstop. But today instead of running the rest of the way, he walked, trying to maintain a military one-hundred-twenty steps per minutes, and even *that* hurt, but not enough to make him stop. Team-1 was out running also, and they went past him, even Sam Houston with his bad knee, limping as he ran past with a wave. The pride in this unit was really something. Tomlinson had been a special-ops trooper for six years, a former Green Beret drafted into Delta, now almost a college graduate with a major in psychology—that was the field special-ops people tended to adopt for some reason or other—and was trying to figure out how to complete his studies in

England, where the universities worked differently, and where it was a little unusual for enlisted soldiers to have parchment degrees. But in Delta they often sat around and talked about the terrorists they were supposed to deal with, what made them tick, because in understanding that came the ability to predict their actions and weaknesses—the easier to kill them, which was the job, after all. Strangely, he'd never done a takedown in the field before coming here, and stranger still, the experience hadn't been at all different from training. You played as you practiced, the sergeant thought, just like they'd told him every step of the way since basic training at Fort Knox eleven years before. Damn, his lower leg was still on fire, but less so than it had been in the run. Well, the doc had told him at least a week, more likely two, before he'd be fully mission-capable again, all because he'd hit a curb the wrong way, not looking, like a damned fool. At least Houston had an excuse for his knee. Zip-lining could be dangerous, and everybody slipped once in a while—in his case landing on a rock, which must have hurt like a bastard. . . . But Sam wasn't a quitter either, Tomlinson told himself, hobbling forward toward the shooting house.

"Okay, this is a live-fire exercise," Chavez told Team-2. "The scenario is five bad guys, eight hostages. The bad guys are armed with handguns and SMGs. Two of the hostages are kids, two girls, ages seven and nine. Other hostages are all females, mothers. The bad guys hit a day-care center, and it's time to do the takedown. Noonan has predicted the location of the bad guys like this." Chavez pointed to the blackboard. "Tim, how good's your data?"

"Seventy percent, no better than that. They're moving around some. But the hostages are all here in this corner." His pointer tapped the blackboard.

"Okay. Paddy, you got the explosives. Pair off as normal. Louis and George go in first, covering the left side. Eddie and I go in right behind with the center. Scotty and Oso in last, covering the right. Questions?"

There were none. The team members examined the blackboard diagram. The room was straightforward, or as much as it could be.

"Then let's do it," Ding told them. The team filed out, wearing their ninja suits.

"Your leg, George, how is it?" Loiselle asked Tomlinson.

"We'll just have to see, I guess. But my hands are okay," the sergeant said, holding his MP-10 up.

"Bien." Loiselle nodded. The two were semipermanently paired together, and worked well as a mini-team, almost to the point that one of them could read the other's mind in the field, and both had the gift for moving unseen. That was difficult to teach—instinctive hunters just knew it somehow, and the good ones practiced it incessantly.

Two minutes later, they were on the outside of the shooting house. Connolly set the Primacord around the door. This aspect of training kept the base carpenters pretty busy, Chavez thought. It took only thirty seconds before Connolly backed off, waving his hand, thumb up, to indicate he'd connected the wires to the detonator box.

"Team-2, this is Lead," they all heard over their radio earpieces. "Stand-to and stand by. Paddy, three . . . two . . . one . . . *MARK!*"

Clark, as usual, jumped when the *ka-BOOM!* sounded. A former demolitions expert himself, he knew that Connolly was his superior, with an almost magical touch for the stuff, but he knew also that no demo expert in the world ever used too little on a job. The door flew across the room and slammed into the far wall, fast enough to cause injury to anyone it hit, though probably not fatally. John covered his ears with his hands and shut his eyes because next through was a flash-bang that attacked his ears and eyes like an exploding sun. He had the timing down perfectly, as he opened back up to see the shooters come in.

Tomlinson ignored the protests from his leg, and followed Loiselle in with his weapon up. That's when the first surprise hit the shooters; this exercise was to be a tricky one. No hostages and no bad guys on the left. Both men went to the far wall, turning right to cover that side.

Chavez and Price were already in, scanning their area of responsibility, and also seeing nothing. Then Vega and McTyler had the same experience on the right side of the room. The mission was not going as briefed, as sometimes happened.

Chavez saw there were no bad guys or hostages in view, and that there was but one door, open, into another room. "Paddy, flash-bangs, now!" he ordered over his radio, while Clark watched from the corner wearing his white observer's shirt and body armor. Connolly had come through behind Vega and McTyler, two flash-bangs in his hands. One, then another, sailed through the door, and again the building shook. Chavez and Price took the lead this time. Alistair Stanley was in there in his white don't-shoot-at-me garb while Clark stayed in the front room. The latter heard the suppressed chatter of the weapons, followed by shouts of "Clear!" "Clear!" "Clear!"

On entering the shooting room, John saw all the targets perforated in the heads, as before. Ding and Eddie were with the hostages, covering them with their armored bodies, weapons trained on the cardboard targets, which in real life would be on the floor and bleeding explosively from their shattered skulls.

"Excellent," Stanley pronounced. "Good improvisation. You, Tomlinson, you were slow, but your shooting was bloody perfect. You, too, Vega."

"Okay, people, let's head over to the office to see the instant replay," John told them, heading outside and still shaking his head to clear his ears from the insult of the flash-bangs. He'd have to get ear protectors and goggles if he did much more of this, lest his hearing be permanently damaged—even though he felt it his duty to experience the real thing to be able to appreciate how everything worked. He grabbed Stanley on the walk over.

"Fast enough, Al?"

"Yes." Stanley nodded. "The flash-bangs give us, oh, three to five seconds of incapacitation, and another fifteen or so of subnormal performance. Chavez adapted well. The hostages would all have survived, probably. John, our lads are right on the crest of the wave. They cannot get any better. Tomlinson, bad leg and all, didn't lose more than half a step, if that much, and our little Frenchman moves like a bloody mongoose. Even Vega, big as he is, isn't the least bit oafish. John, these lads are as good as any team I've ever seen."

"I agree, but—"

"But still so much is in the hands of our adversaries. Yes, I know, but God help the bastards when we come for them."

C H A P T E R 13

AMUSEMENT

POPOV WAS STILL TRYING TO LEARN MORE ABOUT his employer, but finding nothing to enlighten himself. The combination of the New York Public Library and the Internet had turned up reams of information, but nothing that gave the slightest clue as to why he'd employed the former KGB officer to dig up terrorists and turn them loose upon the world. It was as likely that a child would conspire a murder plot against a loving parent. It wasn't the morality of the event that troubled him. Morality had little place in intelligence operations. As a trainee at the KGB academy outside Moscow, the subject had never come up, except insofar as he and his classmates had always been given to understand that the State Was *Never* Wrong. "You will occasionally be ordered to do things you may find personally upsetting," Colonel Romanov had said once. "Such things will be done, because the reasons, unknown to you or not, will always be proper ones. You *do* have the right to question something for tactical reasons—as the officer in the field, *how* you do the mission will generally be your affair. But to refuse an assignment is not acceptable." And that had been that. Neither Popov nor his classmates had even made notes on the issue. It was understood that orders were orders. And so, once he accepted employment, Popov had done the jobs assigned . . .

. . . but as a servant of the Soviet Union he'd always known the overall mission, which was to get vital information to his country, because his country needed the information either for itself or to assist others whose actions would be of real benefit to his country. Even dealing with Il'ych Ramirez Sanchez, Popov had thought at the time, had served some special interest. He knew better now, of course. Terrorists were like wild dogs or rabid wolves that one tossed into someone's back garden just to create a stir, and, yes, perhaps that had been strategically useful—or had been thought so by his masters, in the service of a state now dead and gone. But, no, the missions had not really been useful, had they? And as good as KGB had once been—he still thought them the best espionage agency the world had ever seen—it had ultimately been a failure. The Party for which the Committee for State Security had been the Sword and Shield was no more. The sword had not slain the Party's enemies, and the Shield had not protected against the West's various weapons. And so, had his superiors really known what they'd needed to do?

Probably not, Popov admitted to himself, and because of that, perhaps *every* mission he'd been assigned had been to some greater or lesser degree a fool's errand. The realization would have been a bitter one, except that his training and experience were paying off now with a lavish salary, not to mention the two suitcases of cash he'd managed to steal—but for doing *what?* Getting terrorists killed off by European police forces? He could just as easily, if not so profitably, have fingered them to the police and allowed them to be arrested, tried, and imprisoned like the criminal scum they were, which would actually have been far more satisfying. A tiger in a cage, pacing back and forth behind his bars and waiting for his daily five kilos of chilled horsemeat, was far more entertaining than one stuffed in a museum, and just as helpless. He was some sort of Judas goat, Dmitriy Arkadeyevich thought, but if so, serving what sort of abattoir?

The money was good. Several more missions like the first two and he could take his money, his false identity papers, and vanish from the face of the earth. He could lie on some beach, drinking tasty beverages and watching pretty girls in skimpy bathing suits or—what? Popov didn't know exactly what sort of retirement he could stomach, but he was certain he could find something. Maybe use his talents to trade in stocks and bonds like a real capitalist, and thus spend his time enriching himself further. Perhaps that, he mused, sipping his morning coffee and staring out the window, looking south toward Wall Street. But he wasn't quite ready for that life yet, and until he was, the fact that he didn't know the nature of his missions' purpose was troublesome. In not knowing, he couldn't evaluate all the dangers to himself. But for all his skill, experience, and professional training, he hadn't a clue as to why his employer wanted him to let the tigers from their cages, out in the open where the hunters were waiting. What a pity, Popov thought, that he couldn't just ask. The answer might even be amusing.

■ ■ ■

CHECK-IN at the hotel was handled with mechanical precision. The reception desk was huge, and crowded with computers that raced electronically to get the guests checked in, the quicker to get them spending money in the park itself. Juan took his card-key and nodded his thanks at the pretty female clerk, then hoisted his bags and headed off to his room, grateful that there were no metal detectors here. The walk was a short one, and the elevators unusually large, to accommodate people in wheelchairs, he imagined. Five minutes later, he was in his room, unpacking. He'd just about finished when a knock came at the door.

"Bonjour." It was René. The Frenchman came in and sat on the bed, stretching as he did so. "Are you ready, my friend?" he asked in Spanish.

"Sí," the Basque replied. He didn't look especially Spanish. His hair was on the red side of strawberry blond, his features handsome, and his beard neatly trimmed. Never arrested by the Spanish police, he was bright, careful, but thoroughly dedicated, with two car-bombings and a separate murder to his credit. This, René knew, would be Juan's boldest mission, but he looked ready enough, tense, a little edgy perhaps, but coiled like a spring and prepared to play his role. René, too, had done this sort of thing before, most often murders right on crowded streets; he'd walk right up to his target, fire a suppressed pistol, and just walk on normally, which was the best way to do it, since you were almost never identified—people never saw the pistol, and rarely noticed a person walking normally down the Champs-Élysées. And so, you just changed your clothes and switched on the television to see the press coverage of your work. Action Directe had been largely, but not quite completely, broken up by the French police. The captured men had kept faith with their at-large comrades, hadn't fingered or betrayed them, despite all the pressure and the promises of their uniformed countrymen—and perhaps some of them would be released as a result of this mission, though the main objective was to release their comrade Carlos. It would not be easy to get him out of Le Sante, René thought, rising to look out the window at the train station used by people going to the park, but—he saw the children there, waiting for their ride in—there were some things that no government, however brutal, could overlook.

Two buildings away, Jean-Paul was looking out at the same scene and contemplating much the same thoughts. He'd never married and had rarely even enjoyed a proper love affair. He knew now, at forty-three, that this had created a hole in his life and his character, an abnormality that he'd tried to fill with political ideology, with his beliefs in principles and his vision of a radiant socialist future for his country and for Europe and ultimately for the whole world.

But a niggling part of his character told him that his dreams were mere illusions, and that reality was before him, three floors down and a hundred meters west, in the distant faces of children waiting to board the steam train to the park, and—but, no, such thoughts were aberrations. Jean-Paul and his friends *knew* the rightness of their cause and their beliefs. They'd discussed them at the greatest length over the years and concluded that their path was the right one. They'd shared their frustration that so few understood—but someday they *would* understand, someday they *would* see the path of justice that socialism offered the entire world, *would* understand that the road to the radiant future had to be paved by the revolutionary elite who understood the meaning and force of history . . . and they wouldn't make the mistakes the Russians had made, those backward peasants in that over-large, foolish nation. And so he was able to look down on the assembled people, as they tightened up at the platform while the steam whistle announced the coming of the train, and see . . . things. Even the children were not people, really, but political statements to be made by others, people like himself who understood how the world actually worked, or how it should work. Would work, he promised himself. Someday.

MIKE Dennis always took his lunch outside, a habit he'd formed in Florida. One thing he liked about Worldpark was that you could have a drink here, in his case a nice red Spanish wine, which he sipped from a plastic cup as he watched how people circulated, and looked for goofs of one kind or another. He found no obvious ones. The walkways had been laid out after careful and thorough planning, using computer simulations.

The rides here were the things that drew people most of all, and so the walkways had been planned to lead people to the more spectacular of them. The big expensive ones *were* pretty spectacular. His own kids loved to ride them, especially the Dive Bomber, a top-hanging coaster that looked fit to make a fighter pilot lose his lunch, next to which was the Time Machine, a virtual-reality ride that accommodated ninety-six guests per seven-minute cycle—any longer and some patrons could get violently ill, tests had shown. Out of that and it was time for some ice cream or a drink, and there were concessions planted right there to answer the cravings. Farther away was Pepe's, an excellent sit-down restaurant specializing in Catalonian cuisine—you didn't put restaurants too close to the rides. Such attractions were not complementary, since watching the Dive Bomber didn't exactly heighten the appetite, and for adults, neither did riding it. There was a science and an art to setting up and operating theme parks like this one, and Mike Dennis was one of the handful of people in the world who knew how it was done, which explained his enormous salary and the quiet smile that went with his sips of wine, as he watched *his* guests enjoy the place. If this was work, then it was the best job in the world. Even the astronauts who rode the space shuttle didn't have this sort of satisfaction. He got to play with his toy every day. They were lucky to fly twice in a year.

His lunch completed, Dennis rose and walked back toward his office on Strada España, the Spanish Main Street, the central spoke on the partial wheel. It was another fine day at Worldpark, the weather clear, the temperature twenty-one Celsius, the air dry and pure. The rain in Spain did not, in his experience, stay mainly in the plain. The local climate was much like California's, which, he reflected, went just fine with the Spanish language of the majority of his employees. On the way, he passed one of the park security people. *Andre,* the name tag said, and the language tag on the other shirt pocket said he spoke Spanish, French, and English. Good, Dennis thought. They didn't have enough people like that.

THE meeting place was prearranged. The Dive Bomber ride used as its symbol the German Ju-87 Stuka, complete to the Iron Cross insignia on the wings and fuselage, though the swastika on the tail had been thoughtfully deleted. It ought to have greatly offended Spanish sensibilities, Andre thought. Did no one remember Guernica, that first serious expression of Nazi *Schreklichkeit,* when thousands of Spanish citizens had been massacred? Was historical appreciation that shallow here? Evidently it was. The children and adults in line frequently reached out to touch the half-scale model of the Nazi aircraft that had dived on both soldiers and civilians with its "Trumpet of Jericho" siren. The siren was replicated as part of the ride itself, though on the hundred-fifty-meter first hill, the screams of the riders as often as not drowned it out, followed by the compressed-air explosion and fountain of water at the bottom when the cars pulled out through simulated flak bursts for the climbing loop into the second hill after dropping a bomb on a simulated ship. Was he the only person in Europe who found the symbology here horrid and bestial?

Evidently so. People raced off the ride to rejoin the line to ride it again, except for those who bumbled off to recover their equilibrium, sometimes sweating, and twice, he'd seen, to vomit. A cleanup man with a mop and bucket stood by for that—not the choicest job in Worldpark. The medical-aid post was a few meters farther away, for those who needed it. Andre shook his head. It served the bastards right to feel ill after choosing to ride that hated symbol of fascism.

Jean-Paul, René, and Juan appeared almost together close to the entrance of the Time Machine, all sipping soft drinks. They and the five others were marked by the hats they'd bought at the entrance kiosk. Andre nodded to them, rubbing his nose as planned. René came over to him.

"Where is the men's room?" he asked in English.

"Follow the signs," Andre pointed. "I get off at eighteen hours. Dinner as planned?"

"Yes."

"All are ready?"

"Entirely ready, my friend."

"Then I will see you at dinner." Andre nodded and walked off, continuing his patrol as he was paid to do, while his comrades walked about, some taking the time to enjoy the rides, he imagined. The park would be even busier tomorrow, he'd been told at the morning briefing session. Another nine-thousand-plus would be checking into the hotels tonight or tomorrow morning in preparation for the bank-holiday weekend in this part of Europe, for Good Friday. The park was set up for mobs of people, and his fellow security personnel had told him all manner of amusing stories about the things that happened here. Four months earlier, a woman had delivered twins in the medical post twenty minutes after riding the Dive Bomber, much to her husband's surprise and the delight of Dr. Weiler—the children had been awarded lifetime passes to Worldpark on the spot, which had made the local TV news, part of the park's genius for public relations. Maybe she'd named the boy Troll, Andre snorted, as he spotted one ahead. The Trolls were short-leg/massive-head costumes worn by petite females, he'd learned on coming to work. You could tell by the skinny legs that fitted in to the huge feet-shoes they wore. There was even a water supply in the costume to make the monstrous lips drool . . . and over there was a Roman legionnaire dueling comically with a Germanic barbarian. One of them would alternately run from the other, usually to the applause of the people sitting down to watch the spectacle. He turned to walk over to the German *Straße,* and was greeted by the oom-pah music of a marching band—why didn't they play the *Horst Wessel Lied?* Andre wondered. It would have gone well with the damned green Stuka. Why not dress the band in SS black, maybe have compulsory shower baths for some of the guests—wasn't *that* part of European history, too? *Damn this place!* Andre thought. The symbology was designed to incur the rage of anyone with the most rudimentary political awareness. But, no, the masses had no memory, no more than they had any understanding of political and economic history. He was glad they'd chosen this place to make their political statement. Maybe *this* would get the idiots to think, just a little bit, perhaps, about the shape of the world. The mis-shape, Andre corrected himself, allowing himself a very un-Worldpark frown at the sunny day and smiling crowds.

There, he told himself. *That* was the spot. The children loved it. There was a crowd of them there even now, dragging, pulling the hands of their parents, dressed in their shorts and sneakers, many wearing hats, with helium-filled balloons tied to their little wrists. And there was a special one, a little girl in a wheelchair, wearing the Special Wish button that told every ride attendant to allow her on without the need to stand in line. A sick one, Dutch from the style of her parents' dress, Andre thought, probably dying from cancer, sent here by some charity or other modeled on the American Make-A-Wish Foundation, which paid for the parents to bring their dying whelp here for one first and last chance to see the Trolls and other cartoon characters, their rights licensed to Worldpark for sale and other exploitation. How brightly their sick little eyes shone here, Andre saw, on their quick road to the grave, and how solicitous the staff was to them, as though *that* mattered to anyone, this bourgeois sentimentality upon which the entire park was founded. Well. They'd see about all that, wouldn't they? If there were ever a place to make a political statement, to bring the attention of all Europe and all the world to what really mattered, this was it.

DING finished his first pint of beer. He'd have only one more. It was a rule that no one had written down and that no one had actually enforced, but by common agreement nobody on the teams had more than two at a time while the teams were on-call, as they almost always were—and besides, two pints of Brit beer were quite a lot, really. Anyway, all the members of Team-2 were home having dinner with their families. Rainbow was an unusual outfit in that sense. *Every* soldier was married, with a wife and at least one kid. The marriages even appeared to be stable. John didn't know if that was a mark of special-operations troopers, but these two-legged tigers who worked for him were pussycats at home, and the dichotomy was both amazing and amusing to him.

Sandy served the main course, a fine roast beef. John rose to get the carving knife so that he could do his duty. Patsy looked at the huge hunk of dead steer and thought briefly about mad-cow disease, but decided that her mother had cooked the meat thoroughly. Besides, she liked good roast beef, cholesterol and all, and her mom was the world's champ at making gravy.

"How's it going at the hospital?" Sandy asked her physician daughter.

"OB is pretty routine. We haven't had a single hard one in the last couple of weeks. I've kinda hoped for a placenta previa, maybe even a placenta abrupta to see if we have the drill down, but—"

"Don't wish for those, Patsy. I've seen them happen in the ER. *Total* panic, and the OB better have his act together, or things can go to hell in a New York minute. Dead mother *and* a dead child."

"Ever see that happen, Mom?"

"No, but I've seen it come close to that twice in Williamsburg. Remember Dr. O'Connor?"

"Tall, skinny guy, right?"

"Yeah." Sandy nodded. "Thank God he was on duty for the second one. The resident came unglued, but Jimmy came in and took over. I was sure we'd lose that one."

"Well, if you know what you're doing—"

"If you know what you're doing, it's still tense. Routine is fine with me. I've done ER duty too long," Sandy Clark went on. "I love a quiet night when I can get caught up on my reading."

"Voice of experience," John Clark observed, serving the meat.

"Makes sense to me," Domingo Chavez agreed, stroking his wife's arm. "How's the little guy?"

"Kicking up a storm right now," Patsy replied, moving her husband's hand to her belly. It never failed, she saw. The way his eyes changed when he felt it. Always a warm, passionate boy, Ding just about melted when he felt the movement in her womb.

"Baby," he said quietly.

"Yeah." She smiled.

"Well, no nasty surprises when the time comes, okay?" Chavez said next. "I want everything to go routinely. This is exciting enough. Don't want to faint or anything."

"Right!" Patsy laughed. *"You? Faint? My commando?"*

"You never know, honey," her father observed, taking his seat. "I've seen tough guys fold before."

"Not this one, Mr. C," Domingo noted with a raised eyebrow.

"More like a fireman," Sandy said from her seat. "The way you guys just hang around 'til something happens."

"That's true," Domingo agreed. "And if the fire never starts, it's okay with us."

"You really mean that?" Patsy asked.

"Yes, honey," her husband told her. "Going out isn't fun. We've been lucky so far. We haven't lost a hostage."

"But that'll change," Rainbow Six told his subordinate.

"Not if I have anything to say about it, John."

"Ding," Patsy said, looking up from her food. "Have you—I mean . . . I mean, have you actually—"

The look answered the question, though the words were "Let's not talk about that."

"We don't carve notches in our guns, Pats," John told his daughter. "Bad form, you see."

"Noonan came over today," Chavez went on. "Says he's got a new toy to look at."

"What's it cost?" John asked first of all.

"Not much, he says, not much at all. Delta just started looking at it."

"What's it do?"

"It finds people."

"Huh? Is this classified?"

"Commercial product, and, no, it's not classified at all. But it finds people."

"How?"

"Tracks the human heart up to five hundred meters away."

"What?" Patsy asked. "How's it do that?"

"Not sure, but Noonan says the guys at Fort Bragg are going nuts—I mean, *real* enthusiastic about it. It's called 'Lifeguard' or something like that. Anyway, he asked the headquarters snake people to send us a demo team."

"We'll see," John said, buttering his roll. "Great bread, Sandy."

"It's that little bakery on Millstone Road. Isn't the bread wonderful over here?"

"And everybody knocks Brit food," John agreed. "The idiots. Just what I was raised with."

"All this red meat," Patsy worried aloud.

"My cholesterol is under one-seventy, honey," Ding reminded her. "Lower than yours. I guess it's all that good exercise."

"Wait until you get older," John groused. He was nudging two hundred for the first time in his life, exercise and all.

"No hurry here." Ding chuckled. "Sandy, you are still one of the best cooks around."

"Thanks, Ding."

"Just so our brains don't rot from eating this English cow." A Spanish grin. "Well, this is safer than zip-lining out of the Night Hawk. George and Sam are still hurtin'. Maybe we ought to try different gloves."

"Same ones the SAS uses. I checked."

"Yeah, I know. I talked it over with Eddie, day 'fore yesterday. He says we have to expect training accidents, and Homer says that Delta loses a guy a year, dead, in training accidents."

"What?" Alarm from Patsy.

"And Noonan says the FBI lost a guy once, zipping down from a Huey. Hand just slipped. Oops." Team-2 Lead shrugged.

"Only security against that is more training," John agreed.

"Well, my guys are right at the proper edge. Now I have to figure a way to keep them right there without breaking it."

"That's the hard part, Domingo."

"I s'pose." Chavez finished his plate.

"What do you mean, the edge?" Patsy asked.

"Honey, I mean Team-2 is lean and mean. We always were, but I don't see us getting any better than we are now. Same with Peter's bunch. Except for the two injuries, there isn't room for any improvement I can see—'specially with Malloy on the team now. Damn, he knows how to drive a chopper."

"Ready to kill people? . . ." Patsy asked dubiously. It was hard for her to be a physician, dedicated to saving life, and yet be married to a man whose purpose often seemed to be the taking of it—and Ding *had* killed someone, else he wouldn't have suggested that she not think about it. How could he do that, and still turn to mush when he felt the baby inside her? It was a lot for her to understand, much as she loved her diminutive husband with the olive skin and flashing white smile.

"No, honey, ready to rescue people," he corrected her. "That's the job."

"BUT how sure can we be that they will let them out?" Esteban asked.

"What choice will they have?" Jean-Paul replied. He poured the carafe of wine into the empty glasses.

"I agree," Andre said. "What choice will they have? We can disgrace them before the world. And they are cowards, are they not, with their bourgeois sentimentality? They have no strength, not as we do."

"Others have made the mistake of believing that," Esteban said, not so much playing devil's advocate as voicing worries that they all had to have, to one extent or another. And Esteban had always been a worrier.

"There has never been a situation like this. The Guardia Civil is effective, but not trained for a situation like this one. Policemen," Andre snorted. "That is all. I do not think they will arrest any of us, will they?" That remark earned him a few smirks. It was true. They *were* mere policemen, accustomed to dealing with petty thieves, not dedicated political soldiers, men with the proper arms and training and dedication. "Did you change your mind?"

Esteban bristled. "Of course not, comrade. I simply counsel objectivity when we evaluate the mission. A soldier of the revolution must not allow himself to be carried away by mere enthusiasm." Which was a good cover for his fears, the others thought. They all had them, the proof of which was their denial of that fact.

"We'll get Il'ych out," René announced. "Unless Paris is willing to bury a hundred children. That they will not do. And some children will get to fly to Lebanon and back as a result. On that we are agreed, are we not?" He looked around the table and saw all nine heads nod. *"Bien.* Only the children need foul their underpants for this, my friends. Not us." That turned the nods into smiles, and two discreet laughs, as the waiters circulated around the restaurant. René waved for some more wine. The selection was good here, better than he could expect in an Islamic country for the next few years, as he dodged DGSE's field intelligence officers, hopefully with more success than Carlos had enjoyed. Well, their identities would never be known. Carlos had taught the world of terrorism an important lesson. It did *not* pay to advertise. He scratched his beard. It itched, but in that itching was his personal safety for the next few years. "So, Andre, who comes tomorrow?"

"Thompson CSF is sending six hundred employees and their families here, a company outing for one of their departments. It could not be better," the security guard told them. Thompson was a major French arms manufacturer. Some of the workers, and therefore their children, would be known and important to the French government. French, and politically important—no, it could not get much better than that. "They will be moving about as a group. I have their itinerary. They come to the castle at noon for lunch and a show. That is our moment, my friends." Plus one other little addition Andre had decided on earlier in the day. They were always around somewhere, especially at the shows.

"D'accord?" René asked the people around the table, and again he got his nods. Their eyes were stronger now. Doubts would be set aside. The mission lay before them. The decision to undertake it was far behind. The waiter arrived with two new carafes, and the wine was poured around. The ten men savored their drinks, knowing they might be the last for a very long time, and in the alcohol they found their resolve.

■ ■ ■

"DON'T you just love it?" Chavez asked. "Only Hollywood. They hold their weapons like they're knives or something, and then they hit a squirrel in the left nut at twenty yards. Damn, I wish *I* could do that!"

"Practice, Domingo," John suggested with a chuckle. On the TV screen, the bad guy flew about four yards backward, as though he'd been hit with an anti-tank rocket instead of a mere 9-mm pistol round. "I wonder where you buy those."

"We can't afford them, O great accounting expert!"

John almost spilled his remaining beer at that one. The movie ended a few minutes later. The hero got the girl. The bad guys were all dead. The hero left his parent agency in disgust at their corruption and stupidity and walked off into the sunset, content at his unemployment. Yeah, Clark thought, that was Hollywood. With that comfortable thought, the evening broke up. Ding and Patsy went home to sleep, while John and Sandy did the same.

IT was all a big movie set, Andre told himself, walking into the park an hour before it opened to the guests already piling up at the main gate. How very American, despite all the effort that had gone into building the place as a European park. The whole idea behind it, of course, was American, that fool Walt Disney with his talking mice and children's tales that had stolen so much money from the masses. Religion was no longer the opiate of the people. No, today it was escapism, to depart from the dull day-to-day reality they all lived and all hated, but which they couldn't see for what it was, the bourgeois fools. Who led them here? Their children with their shrill little demands to see the Trolls and the other characters from Japanese cartoons, or to ride the hated Nazi Stuka. Even Russians, those who'd gotten enough money out of their shattered economy to throw it away here, even *Russians* rode the Stuka! Andre shook his head in amazement. Perhaps the children didn't have the education or memory to appreciate the obscenity, but surely their *parents* did! But they came here anyway.

"Andre?"

The park policeman turned to see Mike Dennis, the chief executive officer of Worldpark, looking at him.

"Yes, Monsieur Dennis?"

"The name's Mike, remember?" The executive tapped his plastic name tag. And, yes, it was a park rule that everyone called everyone else by his Christian name—something else doubtless learned from the Americans.

"Yes, Mike, excuse me."

"You okay, Andre? You looked a little upset about something."

"I did? No . . . *Mike,* no, I am fine. Just a long night for me."

"Okay." Dennis patted him on the shoulder. "Busy day planned. How long you been with us?"

"Two weeks."

"Like it here?"

"It is a unique place to work."

"That's the idea, Andre. Have a good one."

"Yes, Mike." He watched the American boss walk quickly away, toward the castle and his office. *Damned Americans,* they expected everyone to be happy all the time, else something must be wrong, and if something went wrong, it had to be fixed. Well, Andre told himself, something *was* wrong, and it *would* be fixed this very day. But Mike wouldn't like that very much, would he?

One kilometer away, Jean-Paul transferred his weapons from his suitcase to his backpack. He'd ordered room service to bring breakfast in, a big American breakfast, he'd decided, since it might have to stand him in good stead for most of this day, and probably part of another. Elsewhere in this hotel and other hotels in the same complex, the others would be doing the same. His Uzi submachine gun had a total of ten loaded magazines, with six more spares for his 9-mm pistol, and three fragmentation hand grenades in addition to his radio. It made for a heavy backpack, but he wouldn't be carrying it all day. Jean-Paul checked his watch and took one final look at his room. All the toiletries were recently bought. He'd wiped all of them with a damp cloth to make sure he left no fingerprints behind, then the table and desktops, and finally his breakfast dishes and silverware. He didn't know if the French police might have his prints on file somewhere, but if so, he didn't want to give them another set, and if not, why make it easy for them to start a file? He wore long khaki trousers and a short-sleeve shirt, plus the stupid white hat he'd bought the previous day. It would mark him as just one more guest in this absurd place, totally harmless. With all that done, he picked up his backpack and walked out the door, taking a final pause to wipe the doorknob both inside and outside before walking to the elevator bank. He pressed the DOWN button with a knuckle instead of a fingertip, and in a few seconds was on his way out the hotel door and walking casually to the train station, where his room key-card was his passport to the Worldpark Transportation System. He took off the backpack to sit down and found himself joined in the compartment by a German, also carrying a backpack, with his wife and two children. The backpack bumped loudly when the man set it on the seat next to him.

"My Minicam," the man explained, in English, oddly enough.

"I, also. Heavy things to carry about, aren't they?"

"Ah, yes, but this way we will have much to remember from our day in the park."

"Yes, you will," Jean-Paul said in reply. The whistle blew, and the train lurched forward. The Frenchman checked his pocket for his park ticket. He actually had three more days of paid entry into the theme park. Not that he'd need it. In fact, nobody in the area would.

"WHAT the hell?" John mumbled, reading the fax on the top of his pile. "Scholarship fund?" And who had violated security? George Winston, Secretary of the Treasury? What the hell? "Alice?" he called.

"Yes, Mr. Clark," Mrs. Foorgate said on coming into his office. "I rather thought that would cause a stir. It seems that Mr. Ostermann feels it necessary to reward the team for rescuing him."

"What's the law on this?" John asked next.

"I haven't a clue, sir."

"How do we find out?"

"A solicitor, I imagine."

"Do we have a lawyer on retainer?"

"Not to my knowledge. And you will probably need one, a Briton and an American as well."

"Super," Rainbow Six observed. "Could you ask Alistair to come in?"

"Yes, sir."

CHAPTER 14

SWORD OF THE LEGION

THE COMPANY OUTING FOR THOMPSON CSF HAD been planned for some months. The three hundred children had been working overtime to get a week ahead in their schoolwork, and the event had business implications as well. Thompson was installing computerized control systems in the park—it was part of the company's transition from being mainly a military-products producer to a more generalized electronics-engineering firm—and here their military experience helped. The new control systems, with which Worldpark management could monitor activities throughout the establishment, were a linear development of data-transfer systems developed for NATO ground forces. They were multilingual, user-friendly gadgets that transmitted their data through ether-space rather than over copper land-lines, which saved a few million francs, and Thompson had brought the systems in on time and on budget, which was a skill that they, like many defense contractors all over the globe, were struggling to learn.

In recognition of the successful fulfillment of the contract to a high-profile commercial customer, senior Thompson management had cooperated with Worldpark to arrange this company picnic. Everyone in the group, children included, wore red T-shirts with the company logo on the front, and for the moment they were mainly together, moving toward the center of the park in a group escorted by six of the park Trolls, who were dancing their way to the castle with their absurdly large bare-feet shoes and hairy head-bodies. The group was further escorted by legionnaires, two wolfskin-wearing *signifers* bearing cohort standards, and the one lion-skinned *aquilifer,* carrying the gold eagle, the hallowed emblem of the VI *Legio Victrix,* now quartered at Worldpark,

Spain, as its antecedent had been under the Emperor Tiberius in 20 A.D. The park employees tasked to be part of the resident legion had developed their own esprit, and took to their marching with a will, their Spanish-made *spatha* swords scabbarded awkwardly, but accurately, high up on their right sides, and their shields carried in their left hands. They moved in a group as proudly as their notional *Victrix* or "victorious" legion had once done twenty centuries before—their predecessors once the first and only line of defense for the Roman colony that this part of Spain had been.

About the only thing the group didn't have was a coterie of people leading them with flags, which was mainly a Japanese affectation, anyway. After the first day's ceremonies, the Thompson people would wander off on their own, and enjoy their four days here as normal tourists.

Mike Dennis watched the procession on his office TV monitors while he gathered his notes. The Roman soldiers were a signature item for his theme park, and, for some reason or other, had proven to be wildly popular, enough so that he'd recently increased their number from fifty to over a hundred and established a trio of centurions to command them. You could spot them by the sideways plumes on their helmets instead of the fore-and-aft on the helms of the ordinary legionnaires. The guys in the outfit had taken to real sword practice, and it was rumored that some of the swords actually had edges, which Dennis hadn't bothered to verify and which he'd have to put a stop to if he did. But anything that was good for employee morale was good for the park, and it was his practice to let his people run their departments with minimal interference from his command center in the castle. He used his computer mouse to zoom in on the approaching mob. They were about twenty minutes early, and that was . . . oh, yeah, it was Francisco de la Cruz leading the parade. Francisco was a retired sergeant in the Spanish army's paratroops, and the guy just grooved to leading parades and such, didn't he? Tough-looking old bastard, over fifty, with burly arms and so heavy a beard—Worldpark allowed mustaches but not beards for its employees—that he had to shave twice a day. The little kids found him intimidating, but Francisco had a way of scooping them up like a bearish grandfather and putting them instantly at ease—the kids especially liked playing with his red horsehair plume. Dennis made a mental note to have lunch with Francisco sometime soon. He ran his little department well, and deserved some attention from topside.

Dennis pulled the manila folder from his action tray. He had to give a welcoming speech to the Thompson guests, to be followed by music from one of the park's roving bands and a parade of the Trolls, then dinner in the castle restaurant. He checked his watch and rose, heading for the corridor that led to a disguised passage with a "secret" door into the castle courtyard. The architects for this place had been handed a blank check, and they'd utilized the Gulf oil money well, though the castle wasn't totally authentic. It had fire escapes, sprinklers, and structural steel, not just blocks piled up and mortared together.

"Mike?" a voice called. The park manager turned.

"Yeah, Pete?"

"Telephone, it's the chairman calling."

The executive turned and hustled back to his office, still clutching his prepared speech.

Francisco—Pancho to his friends—de la Cruz was not a tall man, only five-seven, but wide across the chest, and his pillarlike legs made the ground shake when he marched, stiff-legged, as an historian had told him was the custom of the legions. His iron helmet was heavy, and he could feel the flopping of the plume atop it. His left arm held the large and heavy *scutum,* the shield of the legionnaire that reached almost from neck to ankles, made of glue-laminated wood, but with a heavy iron boss in the center in the image of the Medusa, and metal edges. The Romans, he'd long since learned, had been tough soldiers to march into battle with this heavy gear—almost sixty pounds of it at full load with food and mess kit, about what he'd marched with as a soldier in the field. The park had duplicated all of it, though the quality of the metal was surely better than that which had been produced in the blacksmith shops of the Roman empire. Six young boys had formed up on him, emulating his heavy-footed march. De la Cruz liked that. His own sons were now in the Spanish army, following in their father's footsteps, just as these French boys were now doing. For de la Cruz the world was in its proper shape.

ONLY a few meters away, it was getting that way as well for Jean-Paul, René, and Esteban, the last of them with a cloud of balloons affixed to his wrist, selling one even now. The others were all wearing their white Worldpark hats, all getting into position around the crowd. None of the terrorists were wearing the red Thompson shirts, though doing so would not have been all that difficult. Instead, they wore black Worldpark shirts to go with the hats, and all but Esteban and Andre were also wearing backpacks, like so many other visitors to Worldpark.

The Trolls had everyone in place a few minutes early, they all saw. The adults were joking among themselves, and the children pointing and laughing, their faces illuminated with joy that would soon change to something else, some racing around the taller adults, playing games of hide-and-seek within the crowd . . . and two were in wheelchairs—no, Esteban saw, they were not part of the Thompson group. They wore their special-access buttons, but not the red shirts.

Andre saw those guests, too. One was the little dying Dutch girl from the previous day and one other . . . English by the look of his father, pushing the wheelchair up to the castle and through the crowd. Yes, they'd want both of those. So much the better that these two weren't French, wasn't it?

Dennis had sat down at his desk. The call required detailed information that he'd had to call up on his computer. Yes, quarterly park revenues were 4.1 percent over projections. . . . Yes, the slow season had turned out to be somewhat less slow than they'd expected. Unusually favorable weather, Dennis explained, was the explanation, and one couldn't count on that, but things were going smoothly, except for some computer problems on two of the rides. Yes, they had some software engineers in the back-lot area working on that right now. . . . Yes, that was warranty coverage from the manufacturer, and the manufacturer's representatives were being entirely cooperative—well, they should, as they were bidding on two more mega-rides whose designs would make the entire world take a breathless step back, Dennis told the chairman, who hadn't seen the proposals yet, and would on his next trip to Spain in three weeks. They'd be doing TV shows about conception and design on these two, Dennis promised the chairman, especially for the American cable-channel market, and wouldn't it be something if they increased their draw of American patrons—stealing guests from the Disney empire, which had invented the theme park. The Saudi chairman, who'd initially invested in Worldpark because his children loved to ride things that he had trouble even looking at, was enthusiastic about the proposed new attractions, enough so that he didn't ask about them, willing to be surprised by Dennis when the time came.

"What the hell?" Dennis said over the phone, looking up when he heard it.

Everyone jumped at the noise, the shattering staccato of Jean-Paul's submachine gun, firing a long burst up into the air. In the castle courtyard, people turned and cringed instinctively at the same time, as they first saw the one bearded man aiming upward and swinging his weapon, which ejected a brief shower of brass cases into the air. Being untrained civilians, they did little for the first few seconds but look in shock, without even time to show real fear yet—

—and when they turned to see the shooter in their midst—those around him drawing instinctively away instead of trying to grab him—and the others withdrawing their weapons from their backpacks, at first just bringing them out without firing—waiting a beat or so—

Francisco de la Cruz was standing behind one of the others, and saw the weapon coming out even before the first one fired. His brain recognized the unfriendly yet familiar shape of an Israeli Uzi nine-millimeter submachine gun, and his eyes locked on it, reporting direction and distance, and that this was something that didn't belong in his park. The shock of the moment lasted only that long, and then his twenty-plus years of uniformed service flashed into his consciousness, and two meters behind that bearded criminal, he started moving.

Claude's eyes caught the movement, and he turned to see—what was this? A man wearing Roman armor and the strangest of headgear was moving toward him. He turned to face the threat and—

—Centurion de la Cruz acted on some sort of soldierly instinct that had transformed itself in time and place from the era to which his uniform belonged to where he was this noon. His right hand pulled the *spatha* from its scabbard high up on his right side, and the shield came up, its center iron boss aimed at the muzzle of the Uzi as the sword came straight in the air. He'd had this sword custom-made by a distant cousin in Toledo. It was formed of laminated carbon steel, just as the sword of El Cid had once been, and it had an edge fit to shave with, and he was suddenly a soldier again, and for the first time in his career, he had an armed enemy before him and a weapon in his hand, and the distance was less than two meters now, and gun or not, he was going to—

—Claude fired off a quick burst, just as he had learned so many times, into the center of mass of his advancing target, but that happened to be the three-centimeter-thick iron boss of the *scutum,* and the bullets deflected off it, fragmenting as they did so—

—de la Cruz felt the impact of the fragments peppering his left arm, but the stings of insects would have felt worse as he closed, and his right sword-arm came left, then right, slashing in a way the *spatha* was not designed for, but the razor's edge in the last twenty centimeters near the point did the rest, catching the *cabron*'s upper arm and laying it open just below the end of the short sleeve, and for the first time in his life, Centurion Francisco de la Cruz drew blood in anger—

—Claude felt the pain. His right arm moved, and his finger depressed the trigger, and the long burst hit the oncoming shield low and right of the boss. Three bullets hit de la Cruz's left leg, all below the knee, through the metal greaves, one of them breaking the tibia, causing the centurion to scream in pain as he went down, his second, lethal slash of the sword missing the man's throat by a whisker. His brain commanded his legs to act, but he had only one working leg at the moment, and the other failed him utterly, causing the former paratrooper to fall to the left and forward—

Mike Dennis ran to the window instead of using the TV monitors. Others were watching those, and the take from the various cameras was being recorded automatically in a bank of VCRs elsewhere in the park. His eyes saw, and though his brain didn't believe, it was there, and impossible as it was, it had to be real. A number of people with guns were surrounding the sea of red shirts, and they herded them now, like sheepdogs, inward and toward the castle courtyard. Dennis turned:

"Security lockdown, security lockdown *now!*" he called to the man on the master control board, and with a mouse click the castle's doors were all dead-bolted.

"Call the police!" Dennis ordered next. That was also pre-programmed. An alarm system fired off a signal to the nearest police barracks. It was the robbery-alert signal, but that would be sufficient for the moment. Dennis next lifted a desk phone and punched in the police number from the sticker on his phone. The one emergency contingency they'd planned for was a robbery of their cash room, and since that would necessarily be a major crime committed by a number of armed criminals, the park's internal response to the signal was also pre-programmed. All park rides would be stopped at once, all attractions closed, and shortly people would be instructed to return to their hotel rooms, or to the parking lot, because the park was closing due to an unexpected emergency . . . The noise of the machine guns would have carried a long way, Dennis thought, and the park guests would understand the urgency of the moment.

THIS was the amusing part, Andre thought. He donned a spare white hat from one of his comrades and took the gun that Jean-Paul had packed for him. A few meters away, Esteban cut the balloons loose from his hand, and they soared into the air as he, too, took up his weapon.

The children were not as overtly frightened as their parents were, perhaps thinking that this also was one of the magic things to be expected at the park, though the noise hurt their little ears and had made them jump. But fear is contagious, and the children quickly saw that emotion in their parents' eyes, and one by one they held tight to hands and legs, looking about at the adults who were moving quickly now, around the red-shirted crowd, holding things that looked like . . . guns, the boys recognized the shape from their own toys, which these clearly were not.

René was in command. He moved toward the castle entrance, clear of the nine others who were holding the crowd in place. Looking around, he could see others outside the perimeter of his group, looking in, many crouching down now, hiding, taking what cover there was. Many of them were taking pictures, some with television cameras, and some of those would be zooming in to catch his face, but there was nothing he could do about that.

"Two!" he called. "Select our guests!"

"Two" was Jean-Paul. He approached a knot of people roughly, and first of all grabbed the arm of a four-year-old French girl.

"No!" her mother screamed. Jean-Paul pointed his weapon at her, and she cringed but stood her ground, holding both shoulders of the child.

"Very well," "Two" told her, lowering his aim. "I will shoot her, then." In less than a second, the muzzle of his Uzi was against the little girl's light-brown hair. That made the mother scream all the louder, but she pulled her hands back from her child.

"Walk over there," Jean-Paul told the child firmly, pointing to Juan. The little girl did so, looking back with an open mouth at her stunned mother, while the armed man selected more children.

Andre was doing the same on the other side of the crowd. He went first of all to the little Dutch child. Anna, her special-access name-tag read. Without a word, he pushed Anna's father away from the wheelchair and shoved it off toward the castle.

"My child is ill," the father protested in English.

"Yes, I can see that," Andre replied in the same language, moving off to select another sick child. What fine hostages these two would make.

"You bloody swine!" this one's mother snarled at him. For her trouble she was clubbed by the extended stock of Andre's Uzi, which broke her nose and bathed her face in blood.

"Mummy!" a little boy screamed, as Andre one-handed his chair up the ramp to the castle. The child turned in his chair to see his mother collapse. A park employee, a street-sweeper, knelt down to assist her, but all she did was scream louder for her son: *"Tommy!"*

To her screams were soon added those of forty sets of parents, all of them wearing the red T-shirts of the Thompson company. The small crowd withdrew into the castle, leaving the rest to stand there, stunned, for several seconds before they moved off, slowly and jerkily, down to Strada España.

"Shit, they're coming here," Mike Dennis saw, still talking on the phone to the captain commanding the local Guardia Civil barracks.

"Get clear," the captain told him immediately. "If there is a way for you to leave the area, make use of it now! We need you and your people to assist us. Leave now!"

"But, goddamnit, these people are my responsibility."

"Yes, they are, and you can take that responsibility outside. *Now!*" the captain ordered him. *"Leave!"*

Dennis replaced the phone, turning then to look at the fifteen-person duty staff in the command center. "People, everybody, follow me. We're heading for the backup command center. Right now," he emphasized.

The castle, real as it appeared, wasn't real. It had been built with the modern conveniences of elevators and fire stairwells. The former were probably compromised, Dennis thought, but one of the latter descended straight down to the underground. He walked to that fire door and opened it, waving for his employees to head that way. This they did, most with enthusiasm for escaping this suddenly dangerous place. The last tossed him keys on the way through, and when Dennis left, he locked this door behind him, then raced down the four levels of square-spiral stairs. Another minute and he was in the underground, which was crowded with employees and guests hustled out of harm's way by Trolls, Legionnaires, and other uniformed park personnel. A gaggle of park-security people were there, but none of them were armed with anything more dangerous than a radio. There *were* guns in the counting room, but they were under lock, and only a few of the Worldpark employees were trained and authorized to use them, and Dennis didn't want shots to be fired here. Besides, he had other things to do. The alternate Worldpark command post was actually outside the park grounds, just at the end of the underground. He ran there, following his other command personnel north toward the exit that led to the employees' parking lot. That required about five minutes, and Dennis darted in the door to see that the alternate command post was double-manned now. His own alternate desk was vacant, and the phone already linked to the Guardia Civil.

"Are you safe?" the captain asked.

"For now, I guess," Dennis responded. He keyed up his castle office on his monitor.

"THIS way," Andre told them. The door was locked, however. He backed off and fired his pistol at the doorknob, which bent from the impact, but remained locked, movies to the contrary. Then René tried his Uzi, which wrecked that portion of the door and allowed him to pull it open. Andre led them upstairs, then kicked in the door to the command center—empty. He swore foully at that discovery.

"I see them!" Dennis said into the phone. "One man—two—six men with guns—Jesus, they have kids with them!" One of them walked up to a surveillance camera, pointed his pistol, and the picture vanished.

"How many men with guns?" the captain asked.

"At least six, maybe ten, maybe more. They have taken children hostage. You get that? They've got kids with them."

"I understand, Señor Dennis. I must leave you now and coordinate a response. Please stand by."

"Yeah." Dennis worked other camera controls to see what was happening in his park. "Shit," he swore with a rage that was now replacing shock. Then he called his chairman to make his report, wondering what the hell he would say when the Saudi prince asked what the hell was going on—a terrorist assault on an *amusement park?*

IN his office, Captain Dario Gassman called Madrid to make his first report of the incident. He had a crisis plan for his barracks, and that was being implemented now by his policemen. Ten cars and sixteen men were now racing down the divided highway from various directions and various patrol areas, merely knowing that Plan W had been implemented. Their first mission was to establish a perimeter, with orders to let no one in or out—the last part of which would soon prove to be utterly impossible. In Madrid other things were happening while Captain Gassman walked to his car for the drive to Worldpark. It was a thirty-minute drive for him, even with lights and siren, and the drive gave him the chance to think in relative peace, despite the noise from under the hood. He had sixteen men there or on the way, but if there were ten armed criminals at Worldpark, that would not be enough, not even enough to establish an inner and outer perimeter. How many more men would he need? Would he have to call up the national response team formed a few years ago by the Guardia Civil? Probably yes. What sort of criminals would hit Worldpark at this time of day? The best time for a robbery was at closing time, even though that was what he and his men had anticipated and trained for—because *that* was the time all the money was ready, bundled and wrapped in canvas bags for transfer to the bank, and guarded by park personnel and sometimes his own . . . that was the time of highest vulnerability. But no, whoever this was, they had chosen the middle of the day, and they'd taken hostages—children, Gassman reminded himself. So, were they robbers or something else? What sort of criminals were they? What if they were terrorists . . . they had taken hostages . . . children . . . Basque terrorists? Damn, what then?

■ ■ ■

BUT things were already leaving Gassman's hands. The senior Thompson executive was on his cell phone, talking with his corporate headquarters, a call quickly bucked up to his own chairman, caught in a sidewalk café having a pleasant lunch that the call aborted instantly. This executive called the Defense Minister, and that got things rolling very rapidly indeed. The report from the Thompson manager on the scene had been concise and unequivocal. The Defense Minister called him directly and had his secretary take all the notes they needed. These were typed up and faxed to both the Prime Minister and the Foreign Minister, and the latter called his Spanish counterpart with an urgent request for confirmation. It was already a political exercise, and in the Defense Ministry another phone call was made.

"YES, this is John Clark," Rainbow Six said into the phone. "Yes, sir. Where is that exactly . . . I see . . . how many? Okay. Please send us whatever additional information you receive. . . . No, sir, we cannot move until the host government makes the request. Thank you, Minister." Clark changed buttons on his phone. "Al, get in here. We have some more business coming in." Next he made the same request of Bill Tawney, Bellow, Chavez, and Covington.

THE Thompson executive still in Worldpark assembled his people at a food stand and polled them. A former tank officer in the French army, he worked hard and quickly to bring order from chaos. Those employees who still had their children, he set aside. Those who did not, he counted, and determined that thirty-three children were missing, along with one or maybe two children in wheelchairs. The parents were predictably frantic, but he got and kept them under control, then called his chairman again to amplify his initial report on the situation. After that he got some paper on which to compile a list of names and ages, keeping his own emotions under control as best he could and thanking God that his own children were too old to have made this trip. With that done, he took his people away from the castle, found a park employee and asked where he might find phones and fax machines. They were all escorted through a wooden swinging door, into a well-disguised service building and down into the underground, then walked to the alternate park command post, where they met Mike Dennis, still holding the folder with his welcoming speech for the Thompson group and trying to make some sense of things.

■ ■ ■

GASSMAN arrived just then, in time to see the fax machine transmitting a list of the known hostages to Paris. Not a minute later, the French Defense Minister called. It turned out that he knew the senior Thompson executive, Colonel Robert Gamelin, who'd headed the development team for the LeClerc battle tank's second-generation fire-control system a few years before.

"How many?"

"Thirty-three from our group, perhaps a few more, but the terrorists seem to have selected our children quite deliberately, Monsieur Minister. This is a job for the Legion," Colonel Gamelin said forcefully, meaning the Foreign Legion's special-operations team.

"I will see, Colonel." The connection broke.

"I am Captain Gassman," the guy in the strange hat said to Gamelin.

"BLOODY hell, I took the family there last year," Peter Covington said. "You could use up a whole fucking battalion retaking the place. It's a bloody nightmare, lots of buildings, lots of space, multilevel. I think it even has an underground service area."

"Maps, diagrams?" Clark asked Mrs. Foorgate.

"I'll see," his secretary replied, leaving the conference room.

"What do we know?" Chavez asked.

"Not much, but the French are pretty worked up, and they're requesting that the Spanish let us in and—"

"This just arrived," Alice Foorgate said, handing over a fax and leaving again.

"List of hostages—Jesus, they're all kids, ages four to eleven . . . thirty-three of them . . . holy shit," Clark breathed, looking it over, then handing it to Alistair Stanley.

"Both teams, if we deploy," the Scotsman said immediately.

"Yeah." Clark nodded. "Looks that way." Then the phone beeped.

"Phone call for Mr. Tawney," a female voice announced on the speaker.

"This is Tawney," the intel chief said on picking up the receiver. "Yes, Roger . . . yes, we know, we got a call from—oh, I see. Very well. Let me get some things done here, Roger. Thank you." Tawney hung up. "The Spanish government have requested through the British embassy in Madrid that we deploy at once."

"Okay, people," John said, standing. "Saddle up. Christ, that was a fast call."

Chavez and Covington ran from the room to head for their respective team buildings. Then Clark's phone rang again. "Yeah?" He listened for several minutes. "Okay, that works for me. Thank you, sir."

"What was that, John?"

"MOD just requested an MC-130 from the First Special Ops Wing. They're chopping it to us, along with Malloy's helo. Evidently, there's a military airfield about twenty clicks from where we're going, and Whitehall is trying to get us cleared into it." And better yet, he didn't have to add, the Hercules transport could lift them right out of Hereford. "How fast can we get moving?"

"Less than an hour," Stanley replied after a second's consideration.

"Good, 'cuz that Herky Bird will be here in forty minutes or less. The crew's heading out to it right now."

"Listen up people," Chavez was saying half a klick away as he walked into the team's bay. "We got a job. Boots and saddles, people. Shag it."

They started moving at once for the equipment lockers before Sergeant Patterson raised the obvious objection: "Ding, Team-1's the go-team. What gives?"

"Looks like they need us both for this ride, Hank. Everybody goes today."

"Fair 'nuff." Patterson headed off to his locker.

Their gear was already packed, always set up that way as a matter of routine. The mil-spec plastic containers were wheeled to the door even before the truck arrived to load them up.

COLONEL Gamelin got the word before Captain Gassman did. The French Defense Minister called him directly to announce that a special-operations team was flying down at the request of the Spanish government, and would be there in three hours or less. He relayed this information to his people, somewhat to the chagrin of the Spanish police official, who then called his own minister in Madrid to inform him of what was happening, and it turned out that the minister was just getting the word from his own Foreign Ministry. Additional police were on the way, and their orders were to take no action beyond the establishment of a perimeter. Gassman's reaction to being whipsawed was predictable disorientation, but he had his orders. Now with thirty of his cops on the scene or on the way, he ordered a third of them to move inward, slowly and carefully, toward the castle on the surface, while two more did the same in the underground, with their weapons holstered or on safe, and with orders not to fire under any circumstances, an instruction more easily given than followed.

■ ■ ■

THINGS had come well to this point, René thought, and the park command center was better than anything he'd hoped for. He was learning to use the computer system to select TV cameras that seemed to cover the entire grounds, from the parking lots to the waiting areas for the various rides. The pictures were in black and white, and once a venue was selected he could zoom and pan the camera to find anything he wished. There were twenty monitors set on the walls of the office, each of them linked by a computer terminal to at least five cameras. Nobody would get close to the castle without his knowledge. Excellent.

In the secretaries' room just through the door, Andre had the children sitting on the floor in one tight little knot, except for the two in their wheelchairs, whom he'd placed against the wall. The children were uniformly wide-eyed and frightened-looking, as well they might be, and at the moment they were quiet, which suited him. He'd slung his submachine gun over his shoulder. It wasn't needed at the moment, was it?

"You will stay still," he told them in French, then backed to the door into the command center. "One," he called.

"Yes, Nine," René answered.

"Things are under control here. Time to make a call?"

"Yes," One agreed. He took his seat and picked up a phone, then examined the buttons, and finding a likely one, he pressed it.

"Yes?"

"Who is this?"

"I am Mike Dennis. I am managing director of the park."

"Bien, I am One, and I am now in command of your Worldpark."

"Okay, Mr. One. What do you want?"

"You have the police here?"

"Yes, they are here now."

"Good. I will speak with their commander then."

"Captain?" Dennis waved. Gassman took the three steps to his desk.

"I am Captain Dario Gassman of the Guardia Civil."

"I am One. I am in command. You know that I have taken over thirty hostages, yes?"

"Sí, I am aware of this," the captain replied, keeping his voice as calm as circumstances allowed. He'd read books and had training on talking with hostage-holding terrorists, and now wished that he'd had a lot more of it. "Do you have a request for me?"

"I do not make requests. I will give you orders to be carried out at once, and have you relay orders to others. Do you understand?" René asked in English.

"Sí, comprendo."

"All of our hostages are French. You will establish a line of communication with the French embassy in Madrid. My orders are for them. Please keep in mind that none of our hostages are citizens of your country. This affair is between us and the French. Do you understand that?"

"Señor One, the safety of those children is my responsibility. This is Spanish soil."

"Be that as it may," One replied, "you will open a telephone link to the French embassy at once. Let me know when it is done."

"I must first of all relay your request to my superiors. I will get back to you when I have my instructions from them."

"Quickly," René told him, before hanging up.

IT was noisy in the back. The four Allison engines screamed, as they accelerated the MC-130 down the runway, then the aircraft rotated abruptly, jumping into the sky for its flight to Spain. Clark and Stanley were in the communications compartment forward, listening as best they could with their heavily insulated headphones to information coming to them, disjointed and fragmentary as usual. The voice promised maps and plans when they got there, but there was no additional information on the number or identity of the terrorists—they were working on that, the voice told them. Just then, a fax arrived from Paris via the American 1st Spec-Operations Wing headquarters, which had secure communications equipment currently linked to Hereford. It was just another list of the hostages, and this time Clark took the time to read the names, and part of his mind tried to conjure up faces to go with them, knowing he'd be wrong in every case, but doing it even so. Thirty-three children sitting in an amusement-park castle surrounded by men with guns, number at least six, maybe ten, maybe more; they were still trying to develop that information. Shit, John thought. He knew that some things couldn't be hurried, but nothing in this business ever went fast enough, even when you were doing it all yourself.

Aft the men slipped off their seat belts and started suiting up in their black Nomex, saying little to one another while the two team leaders went forward to find out what they could. Back ten minutes later to dress themselves, Chavez and Covington tilted their heads in the typical what-the-hell expression that their troopers recognized as news that was something other than good. The team leaders told their men what little they knew, and the expressions were transferred to the shooters, along with neutral thoughts. Kids as hostages.

Over thirty of them probably, and maybe more, held by an unknown number of terrorists, nationality and motivation still unknown. As a practical matter, they knew nothing about how they'd be used, except that they were going somewhere to do something, which they'd find out about once they got there. The men settled back into their seats, re-buckled their belts, and said little. Most closed their eyes and affected trying to sleep, but mainly they didn't sleep, merely sat with eyes closed, seeking and sometimes finding an hour's peace amid the screeching noise of the turboprop engines.

"I require your fax machine number," One said to the French ambassador, speaking in his native language instead of English.

"Very well" was the reply, followed by the number.

"We are sending you a list of political prisoners whose release we require. They will be released immediately and flown here on an Air France airliner. Then my people, our guests, and I will board the aircraft and fly with them to a destination that I will give to the pilot of our aircraft after we board it. I advise you to accede to our demands rapidly. We have little patience, and if our demands are not met, we will be forced to kill some of our hostages."

"I will forward your request to Paris," the ambassador said.

"Good, and be sure to tell them that we are not in a patient mood."

"Oui, I will do that as well," the diplomat promised. The line went dead and he looked at his immediate staff, the deputy chief of mission, his military attaché, and the DGSE station chief. The ambassador was a businessman who had been awarded this embassy as a political favor, since the proximity of Paris and Madrid did not require a seasoned member of the diplomatic service for the post. "Well?"

"We will look at the list," the DGSE man answered. A second later, the fax machine chirped, and a few seconds after that, the curled paper emerged. The intelligence officer took it, scanned it, and handed it over. "Not good," he announced for the others in the room.

"The Jackal?" the DCM said. "They will never—"

" 'Never' is a long time, my friend," the spook told the diplomat. "I hope these commandos know their business."

"What do you know about them?"

"Nothing, not a single thing."

"HOW long?" Esteban asked René.

"They will take time," One replied. "Some will be real, and some will be creative on their part. Remember that their strategy is to lengthen the process as much as possible, to tire us, to wear us down, to weaken our resolve. Against that we have the ability to force the issue by killing a hostage. That is not a step to be taken lightly. We have selected our hostages for their psychological impact, and we will need to consider their use carefully. But above all, we must control the pace of events. For now, we will let them take their time while we consolidate our position." René walked to the corner to see how Claude was doing. There was a nasty gash on his upper arm from that fool of a Roman soldier, the only thing that had gone wrong. He was sitting on the floor, holding a bandage over it, but the wound was still bleeding. Claude would need stitches to close it properly. It was bad luck, but not that serious, except to Claude, who was still in considerable pain from the wound.

HECTOR Weiler was the park physician, a general surgeon trained at the University of Barcelona who spent most of his time putting Band-Aids on skinned knees and elbows, though there was a photo on his wall of the twins he'd delivered once upon a time after a pregnant woman had been foolish enough to ride the Dive Bomber—there was now a very emphatic sign at the entrance warning against that. For all that, he was a skilled young doctor who'd done his share of work in his medical school's emergency room, and so this wasn't his first gunshot victim. Francisco was a lucky man. At least six shots had been fired at him, and though the first three had merely resulted in fragment-peppering on his left arm, one of the second bursts had hurt his leg badly. A broken tibia would take a long time to heal for a man of his years, but at least it was broken fairly high up. A break lower down could take six months to heal, if ever.

"I could have killed him," the centurion groused through the anesthesia. "I could have taken his head off, but I missed!"

"Not with the first one," Weiler observed, seeing the red crust on the sword that now lay atop his *scutum* in the corner of the treatment room.

"Tell me about him," Captain Gassman ordered.

"Forties, early forties," de la Cruz said. "My height plus ten or twelve centimeters, lightly built. Brown hair, brown beard, some speckles of gray in it. Dark eyes. Uzi machine gun. White hat," the former sergeant reported, biting off his words. The anesthesia he'd been given was not enough for all the pain, but he had to tell what he knew, and accepted the discomfort as the physician worked to get the leg set. "There were others. I saw four others, maybe more."

"We think ten or so," Gassman said. "Did he say anything?"

De la Cruz shook his head. "Nothing I heard."

"Who are they?" the surgeon asked, not looking up from his work.

"We think they are French, but we are not sure," the captain of the Guardia Civil answered.

IT was hardest of all for Colonel Malloy. Crossing the English Channel, he headed south-southwest at a steady cruising speed of 150 knots. He'd stop at a French military airfield outside Bordeaux for refueling, since he lacked the external fuel tanks used for ferrying the Night Hawk long distances. Like nearly all helicopters, the Night Hawk didn't have an autopilot, forcing Malloy and Lieutenant Harrison to hand-fly the aircraft all the way. It made for stiffness since the helicopter wasn't the most comfortable aircraft in the world to sit in, but both were used to it and used to grumbling about it as they switched off the controls every twenty minutes or so. Three hours to get where they were going. In the back was their crew chief, Sergeant Jack Nance, now just sitting and looking out the plastic windows as they crossed over the French coast, cruising at two thousand feet over a fishing port filled with boats.

"This got laid on in a hurry," Harrison remarked over the intercom.

"Yeah, well, I guess Rainbow lives on a short fuse."

"You know anything about what's happening?"

"Not a clue, son." The helmeted head shook left and right briefly. "You know, I haven't been to Spain since I deployed on *Tarawa* back in . . . 1985, I think. I remember a great restaurant in Cádiz, though . . . wonder if it's still there. . . ." And with that the crew lapsed back into silence, the chopper nose down and pulling south under its four-bladed rotor while Malloy checked the digital navigation display every few seconds.

"DIMINISHING returns," Clark observed, checking the latest fax. There was nothing new on it, just data already sent being rearranged by some helpful intelligence officer somewhere. He left Alistair Stanley to handle that, and walked aft.

There they were, the Rainbow team, almost all of them looking as if asleep, but probably just chimped down, as he'd done with 3rd SOG more than a generation before, just pretending to sleep, eyes closed and powering their minds and bodies down, because it made no sense to think about things you didn't know jack shit about, and tension sapped the strength even when your muscles were idle. So, your defense against it was to make your body turn off.

These men were smart and professional enough to know that the stress would come in its own good time, and there was no point in welcoming it too soon. In that moment John Clark, long before a Chief SEAL, U.S. Navy, was struck with the honor he held, commanding such men as these. The thought had surprising impact, just standing there and watching them do nothing, because that's what the best people did at a time like this one, because they understood what the mission was, because they knew how to handle that mission, every step of the way. Now they were heading out on a job about which they'd been told nothing, but it had to be something serious because never had teams -1 and -2 *both* gone out. And yet they treated it like another routine training mission. They didn't make men better than these, and his two leaders, Chavez and Covington, had trained them to a razor's edge of perfection.

And somewhere ahead were terrorists holding children hostage. Well, the job wouldn't be an easy one, and it was far too soon for him to speculate on how it would play out, but John knew anyway that it was better to be here on this noisy Herky Bird than it would be in that theme park still a half an hour ahead, for soon his men would open their eyes and shuffle out, bringing their boxed combat gear with them. Looking at them, John Clark saw Death before his eyes, and Death, here and now, was his to command.

Tim Noonan was sitting in the right-side forward corner of the cargo area, playing with his computer, with David Peled at his side. Clark went over to them and asked what they were doing.

"This hasn't made the newswire services yet," Noonan told him. "I wonder why."

"That'll change in a hurry," Clark predicted.

"Ten minutes, less," the Israeli said. "Who's meeting us?"

"Spanish army and their national police, I just heard. We've been authorized to land . . . twenty-five minutes," he told them, checking his watch.

"There, Agence France-Press just started a flash," Noonan said, reading it over for possible new information. "Thirty or so French kids taken hostage by unknown terrorists—nothing else except where they are. This isn't going to be fun, John," the former FBI agent observed. "Thirty-plus hostages in a crowded environment. When I was with Hostage Rescue, we sweated this sort of scenario. Ten bad guys?" he asked.

"That's about what they think, but it isn't confirmed yet."

"Shitty chemistry on this one, boss." Noonan shook his head in worry. He was dressed like the shooters, in black Nomex and body armor, with his holstered Beretta on his right hip, because he still preferred to think of himself as a shooter rather than a tech-weenie, and his shooting, practiced at Hereford with the team members, was right on the line . . . and children were in danger, Clark reflected, and child-in-danger was perhaps the strongest of all human drives, further reinforced by Noonan's time in the Bureau, which regarded child crimes as the lowest of the low. David Peled took a more distant view, sitting there in civilian clothing and staring at the computer screen like an accountant examining a business spreadsheet.

"John!" Stanley called, heading aft with a new fax. "Here's what they're asking for."

"Anybody we know?"

"Il'ych Ramirez Sanchez is at the top of the list."

"Carlos?" Peled looked up. "Someone really wants that *schmuck?*"

"Everybody's got friends." Dr. Bellow sat down and took the fax, scanning it before handing it over to Clark.

"Okay, doc, what do we know?"

"We're dealing with ideological ones again, just like Vienna, but they have a definite fixed objective, and these 'political' prisoners . . . I know these two, from Action Directe, the rest are just names to me—"

"I got it," Noonan said, calling up his roster of known terrorists and inputting the names off the fax. "Okay, six Action Directe, eight Basques, one PFLP currently held in France. Not a long list."

"But a definite one," Bellow observed. "They know what they want, and if they have children as hostages, they really want them out. The selection of hostages is designed to put additional political pressure on the French government." That wasn't exactly a surprising opinion, and the psychiatrist knew it. "Question is, will the French government deal at all?"

"They have, in the past, bargained quietly, off the stage," Peled told them. "Our friends may know this."

"Kids," Clark breathed.

"The nightmare scenario," Noonan said with a nod. "But who has the stones to whack a kid?"

"We'll have to talk with them to see," Bellow responded. He checked his watch and grunted. "Next time, a faster airplane."

"Be cool, doc," Clark told him, knowing that Paul Bellow would have the toughest job from the moment they landed and got to the objective. He had to read their minds, evaluate the terrorists' resolve, and hardest of all, predict their actions, and he, like the rest of the Rainbow team, didn't know anything of consequence yet. Like the rest of the team, he was like a sprinter in the starting blocks, poised to go, but having to wait for the gun to fire. But unlike the others, he was not a shooter. He could not hope for the emotional release they would have if they went into action, for which he quietly envied the soldiers. *Children,* Paul Bellow thought. He had to figure a way to reason with people he didn't know, in order to protect the lives of children. How much rope would the French and Spanish governments let him have? He knew that he'd need some rope to play with, though how much depended on the mental state of the terrorists. They'd deliberately chosen children, and French children at that, to maximize the pressure on the government in Paris . . . and that had been a considered act . . . which forced him to think that they'd be willing to kill a child despite all the taboos associated with such an act in any normal human mind. Paul Bellow had written and lectured the world over on people like this, but somewhere deep inside his own mind he wondered if he truly understood the mentality of the terrorist, so divorced was it from his own supremely rational outlook on reality. He could simulate their thinking, perhaps, but did he truly understand it? That was not a question he wanted to pose to himself right now, with plugs stuffed in his ears to protect his hearing and his equilibrium from the punishing noise of the MC-130's engines. And so he, too, sat back and closed his eyes and commanded his mind into a neutral setting, seeking a respite from the stress sure to come in less than an hour.

Clark saw what Bellow did, and understood it for what it was, but that option didn't exist for Rainbow Six, for his was the ultimate responsibility of command, and what he saw before his eyes were the faces he'd made up to go with the names on the fax sheet he held in his hand. Which ones would live? Which would not? That responsibility rested on shoulders not half so strong as they appeared.

Kids.

"THEY have not gotten back to me yet," Captain Gassman said into the telephone, having initiated the call himself.

"I have not yet given you a deadline," One replied. "I would like to think that Paris values our goodwill. If that is not the case, then they will soon learn to respect our resolve. Make that clear to them," René concluded, setting the phone down and breaking the contact.

And so much for calling them to establish a dialogue, Gassman said to himself. That was one of the things he was supposed to do, his training classes and all the books had told him. Establish some sort of dialogue and rapport with the criminals, even a degree of trust that he could then exploit to his benefit, get some of the hostages released in return for food or other considerations, erode their resolve, with the ultimate aim of resolving the crime without loss of innocent life—or criminal life for that matter. A real win for him meant bringing them all before the bar of justice, where a robed judge would pronounce them guilty and sentence them to a lengthy term as guests of the Spanish government, there to rot like the trash they were. . . . But the first step was to get them talking back and forth with him, something that this One person didn't feel the need to do. This man felt comfortably in command of the situation . . . as well he might, the police captain told himself. With children sitting in front of his guns. Then another phone rang.

"They have landed, and are unloading now."

"How long?"

"Thirty minutes."

"HALF an hour," Colonel Tomas Nuncio told Clark, as the car started rolling. Nuncio had come by helicopter from Madrid. Behind him, three trucks of the Spanish army were loading up the equipment off the plane and would soon start down the same road with his people aboard.

"What do we know?"

"Thirty-five hostages. Thirty-three of them are French children—"

"I've seen the list. Who are the other two?"

Nuncio looked down in distaste. "They seem to be sick children in the park as part of a special program, the ones sent here—you started it in America, how do you say . . ."

"Make-A-Wish?" John asked.

"Yes, that is it. A girl from Holland and a boy from England, both in wheelchairs, both reportedly quite ill. Not French like the others. I find that strange. All the rest are children of workers for Thompson, the defense equipment company. The leader of that group called on his own to his corporate headquarters, and from there the news went high up in the French government, explaining the rapid response. I have orders to offer you all the assistance my people can provide."

"Thank you, Colonel Nuncio. How many people do you have on the scene now?"

"Thirty-eight, with more coming. We have an inner perimeter established and traffic control."

"Reporters, what about them?"

"We are stopping them at the main gate to the park. I will not give these swine a chance to speak to the public," Colonel Nuncio promised. He'd already lived up to what John expected of the Guardia Civil. The hat was something out of another century, but the cop's blue eyes were ready for the next one, cold and hard as he drove his radio car out onto the interstate-type highway.

A sign said that Worldpark was but fifteen kilometers away, and the car was moving very fast now.

JULIO Vega tossed the last Team-2 box aboard the five-ton truck and pulled himself aboard. His teammates were all there in the back, with Ding Chavez taking the right-front seat of the truck next to the driver, as commanders tended to do. Eyes were all open now and heads perked up, checking out the surrounding terrain even though it had no relevance to the mission. Even commandos could act like tourists.

"COLONEL, what sort of surveillance systems are we up against?"

"What do you mean?" Nuncio asked in reply.

"The park, does it have TV cameras spread around? If it does," Clark said, "I want us to avoid them."

"I will call ahead to see."

"WELL?" Mike Dennis asked his chief technician.

"The back way in, no cameras there until they approach the employee parking lot. I can turn that one off from here."

"Do it." Dennis got on Captain Gassman's radio to give directions for the approaching vehicles. He checked his watch as he did so. The first shots had been fired three and a half hours before. It only felt like a lifetime. Giving the directions, he walked to the office coffee urn, found it empty, and cursed as a result.

COLONEL Nuncio took the last exit before the one that went into the park, instead breaking off onto a two-lane blacktop road and slowing down. Presently they encountered a police car whose occupant, standing alongside it, waved them through. Two minutes more, and they were parked outside what appeared to be a tunnel with a steel door sitting partially open. Nuncio popped open his door, and Clark did the same, then walked quickly into the entrance.

"Your Spanish is very literate, Señor Clark. But I cannot place your accent."

"Indianapolis," John replied. It would probably be the last light moment of the day. "How are the bad guys talking to you?"

"What language, you mean? English so far."

And *that* was the first good break of the day. For all his expertise, Dr. Bellow's language skills were not good, and he would take point as soon as his car arrived, in about five minutes.

The park's alternate command center was a mere twenty meters inside the tunnel. The door was guarded by yet another Civil Guard, who opened it and saluted Colonel Nuncio.

"Colonel." It was another cop, John saw.

"Señor Clark, this is Captain Gassman." Handshakes were exchanged.

"Howdy. I am John Clark. My team is a few minutes out. Can you please update me on what's happening?"

Gassman waved him to the conference table in the middle of the room whose walls were lined with TV cameras and other electronic gear whose nature was not immediately apparent. A large map/diagram of the park was laid out.

"The criminals are all here," Gassman said, tapping the castle in the middle of the park. "We believe there to be ten of them, and thirty-five hostages, all children. I have spoken with them several times. My contact is a man, probably a Frenchman, calling himself One. The conversations have come to nothing, but we have a copy of their demands—a dozen convicted terrorists, mainly in French custody, but some in Spanish prisons as well."

Clark nodded. He had all this already, but the diagram of the park was new. He was first of all examining sightlines, what could be seen and what could not. "What about where they are, blueprints, I mean."

"Here," a park engineer said, sliding the castle blueprints on the table. "Windows here, here, here, and here. Stairs and elevators as marked." Clark referenced them against the map. "They have stair access to the roof, and that's forty meters above street level. They have good line of sight everywhere, down all the streets."

"If I want to keep an eye on things, what's the best place?"

"That's easy. The Dive Bomber ride, top of the first hill. You're damned near a hundred fifty meters high there."

"That's nearly five hundred feet," Clark said, with some measure of incredulity.

"Biggest 'coaster in the world, sir," the engineer confirmed. "People come from all over to ride this one. The ride sits in a slight depression, about ten meters, but the rest of it's pretty damned tall. If you want to perch somebody, that's the spot."

"Good. Can you get from here to there unseen?"

"The underground, but there're TV cameras in it—" He traced his hand over the map. "Here, here, here, and another one there. Better to walk on the surface, but dodging all the cameras won't be easy."

"Can you turn them off?"

"We can override the primary command center from here, yes—hell, if necessary, I can send people out to pull the wires."

"But if we do that, it might annoy our friends in the castle," John noted. "Okay, we need to think that one through before we do anything. For the moment," Clark told Nuncio and Gassman, "I want to keep them in the dark on who's here and what we're doing. We don't give them anything for free, okay?"

Both cops nodded agreement, and John saw in their eyes a desperate sort of respect. Proud and professional as they were, they had to feel some relief at having him and his team on the scene to take charge of the situation, and also to take over the responsibility for it. They could get credit for supporting a successful rescue operation, and they could also stand back and say that whatever went wrong wasn't their fault. The bureaucratic mind was part and parcel of every government employee in the known world.

"Hey, John."

Clark turned. It was Chavez, with Covington right behind him. Both team leaders strode in, wearing their black assault gear now, and looking to the others in the room like angels of death. They came to the conference table and started looking at the diagrams.

"Domingo, this is Colonel Nuncio and Captain Gassman."

"Good day," Ding said in his Los Angeles Spanish, shaking hands. Covington did the same, speaking his own language.

"Sniper perch here?" Ding asked at once, tapping the Dive Bomber. "I saw the thing from the parking lot. Some ride. Can I get Homer there unobserved?"

"We're working on that right now."

Noonan came in next, his backpack full of electronics gear. "Okay, this looks pretty good for our purposes," he observed, checking all the TV screens out.

"Our friends have a duplicate facility here."

"Oops," Noonan said. "Okay, first, I want to shut down the cell phone nodes."

"What?" Nuncio asked. Why?"

"In case our friends have a pal outside with a cell phone to tell them what we're doing, sir," Clark answered.

"Ah. Can I help?"

Noonan handled the answer. "Have your people go to each node and have the technicians insert these disks into their computers. There are printed instructions with each."

"Filipe!" Nuncio turned and snapped his fingers. A moment later his man had the disks and orders, leaving the room with them.

"How deep underground are we?" Noonan asked next.

"No more than five meters."

"Rebarred concrete overhead?"

"Correct," the park engineer said.

"Okay, John, our portable radios should work fine." Then teams -1 and -2 entered the command center. They crowded around the conference table.

"Bad guys and hostages here," John told them.

"How many?" Eddie Price asked.

"Thirty-five hostages, all kids, two of them in wheelchairs. Those are the two who are not French."

"Who's been talking to them?" This was Dr. Bellow.

"I have," Captain Gassman answered. Bellow grabbed him and walked him to the corner for a quiet chat.

"First of all, overwatch," Chavez said. "We need to get Homer to the top of that ride . . . unseen . . . How do we do that?"

"There's people moving around on the TV screens," Johnston said, turning to look. "Who are they?"

"Park people," Mike Dennis said. "We have them moving around to make sure all our guests are out." It was the routine shutdown procedure, albeit many hours off in time.

"Get me some coveralls . . . but I still have to pack my rifle. You have mechanics here?"

"Only about a thousand," the park manager replied.

"Okay, then that's what I am, toolbox and all. You have the rides running?"

"No, they're all shut down."

"The more things moving, the more they have to watch," Sergeant Johnston told his boss.

"I like it," Chavez agreed, looking up at Clark.

"So do I. Mr. Dennis, turn them all on, if you would, please."

"They have to be started up individually. We can turn them off from here by killing the power, but we can't turn them on from this position."

"Then get your people out to do it. Sergeant Johnston will go with your man to the 'coaster. Homer, set up there. Your mission is to gather information and get it to us. Take the rifle and get zeroed."

"How high will I be?"

"About one hundred forty meters above the ground."

The sniper reached in his pocket for a calculator and switched it on to make sure it worked. "Fair enough. Where do I change?"

"This way." The engineer led him out the door and across the hall to an employee dressing room.

"A perch on the other side?" Covington asked.

"Here's a good one," Dennis answered. "The virtual reality building. Not anywhere near as high, but direct line of sight to the castle."

"I'll put Houston there," Covington said. "His leg's still bothering him."

"Okay, two sniper-observers plus the TV cameras give us pretty good visual coverage of the castle," Clark said.

"I need to take a leader's recon to figure the rest out," Chavez said. "I need a diagram with the camera positions marked on it. So does Peter."

"When's Malloy get here?" Covington asked.

"Another hour or so. He'll have to gas up when he lands. After that, endurance on the chopper is about four hours, figure thirty minutes' cycle time when he touches down."

"How far can the cameras see, Mr. Dennis?"

"They cover the parking lot this way pretty good, but not the other side. They could do better with people on top of the castle."

"What do we know about their equipment?"

"Just the guns. We have that on tape."

"I want to see those," Noonan put in. "Right now, if possible."

Things started moving then. Chavez and Covington got their park maps—they used the same ones sold to park guests, with the camera positions hand-marked with black sticky-dots stolen from a secretary. An electric cart—actually a golf cart—met them out in the corridor and whisked them outside, then back into the park on a surface road. Covington navigated from the map, avoiding camera positions as they made their way along the back-lot areas of Worldpark.

Noonan ran the three videotapes that showed the terrorists own takedown operation. "Ten of 'em, all right, all male, most of them are bearded, all wearing white hats when they executed their attack. Two look like park employees. We have any information on them?"

"Working on it," Dennis replied.

"You fingerprint them?" Noonan asked, getting a negative head-shake as an answer. "How about photographs?"

"Yes, we all have photo-ID passes to get in." Dennis held up his.

"That's something. Let's get that off to the French police PDQ."

"Mark!" Dennis waved to his personnel boss.

"We should have gotten uniforms," Covington said topside.

"Yeah, haste makes waste, doesn't it, Peter?" Chavez was peering around a corner, smelling the food from the concession stand. It made him a little hungry. "Getting in there's going to be fun, man."

"Quite," Covington agreed.

The castle certainly looked real enough, over fifty meters square and about the same in height. Mainly it was empty space, the blueprints had told them, but there were both a staircase and elevator to the flat roof, and sooner or later the bad guys would put someone there, if they had half a brain amongst them. Well, that was the job for the snipers. Homer Johnston and Sam Houston would have fairly easy direct shots, four hundred meters from one side and a mere one-sixty or so from the other.

"How big do those windows look to you?"

"Big enough, Ding."

"Yeah, I think so, too." And already a plan was coming together in the two minds. "I hope Malloy is well rested."

Sergeant Homer Johnston, now wearing park coveralls over his ninja suit, popped out of the ground fifty meters from the Dive Bomber. The ride was even more intimidating this close. He walked toward it, escorted by a park employee who was also a ride operator for this attraction.

"I can take you to the top and stop the car there."

"Great." It sure looked like a long way to climb, even though there were regular steps heading up. They walked under the canopied entrance, past the crowd-control bars, and Johnston sat in the lead seat on the right side, his gun case on the seat next to his. "Go," he told the operator. The ride up the first hill was slow—deliberately so, designed that way to scare the bejeebers out of the riders, and that gave Johnston another insight into the mind of a terrorist, he thought with a wry smile. The gang of ten three-seat cars stopped just at the crest. Johnston wriggled out, taking his gun case with him. This he set in an equipment bay, opening it to extract a rubber mat, and a ghillie blanket to drape over himself. Last came his rifle and binoculars. He took his time, setting the mat down—the decking here was perforated steel, and lying there would soon become uncomfortable. He deployed the blanket atop his prone frame. It was essentially a light fishing net covered with green plastic leaves, whose purpose was to break up his outline. Then he set up his rifle on its bipod, and took out his green-plastic-coated binoculars. His personal radio microphone dangled in front of his lips.

"Rifle Two-One to command."

"This is Six," Clark responded.

"Rifle Two-One in place, Six. I have a good perch here. I can see the whole roof of the castle and the doors to the elevator and stairwell. Good line of sight to the back, too. Not a bad spot, sir."

"Good. Keep us posted."

"Roger that, boss. Out." Sergeant Johnston propped himself up on his elbows and watched the area through his 7×50 binoculars. The sun was warm. He'd have to get used to that. Johnston thought for a moment and reached for his canteen. Just then the car he'd ridden up wheeled forward and then dropped from sight. He heard the steel overhead wheels roll along the metal tubing and wondered what it was like to ride the damned thing. Probably right up there with skydiving, something he knew how to do, but didn't much care for, airborne-ranger training or not. There was something nice about having your fucking feet on the fucking ground, and you couldn't shoot a rifle while falling through the air at a hundred-thirty knots, could you? He directed his binoculars at a window . . . they were flat on the bottom but curved into a point at the top, like in a real castle, and made of clear glass segments held together with leaded strips. Maybe hard to shoot through, he thought, though getting a shot at this angle would not be easy . . . no, if he got a shot, he'd have to take it on someone outside. That would be easy. He got behind the rifle scope and punched the laser-rangefinder button, selecting the middle of the courtyard as his point of aim. Then he punched a few numbers into his calculator to allow for the vertical drop, came up with an adjusted range setting, and turned the elevation knob on the scope the right number of clicks. The direct line of sight was three hundred eighty-nine meters. Nice and close if he had to take a shot.

"YES, Minister," Dr. Bellow said. He was sitting in a comfortable chair—Mike Dennis's—and staring at the wall. There was now a pair of photographs for him to stare at—they were unknowns, because Tim Noonan didn't have them in his computer, and neither the French nor the Spanish police had turned either into a name with a history attached. Both had apartments a few miles away, and both were being thoroughly tossed now, and phone records checked as well, to see where they'd called.

"They want this Jackal fellow out, do they?" the French Minister of Justice asked.

"Along with some others, but he would seem to be their primary objective, yes."

"My government will *not* negotiate with these creatures!" the Minister insisted.

"Yes, sir, I understand that. Giving over the prisoners is generally not an option, but every situation is different, and I need to know what leeway, if any, you will give me as a negotiating position. That could include taking this Sanchez guy out of prison and bringing him here as . . . well, as bait for the criminals we have surrounded here."

"Do you recommend that?" the Minister asked.

"I am not sure yet. I haven't spoken with them, and until I do I cannot get a feel for what they're all about. For the moment, I must assume that we are dealing with serious, dedicated people who are willing to kill hostages."

"Children?"

"Yes, Minister, we must consider that a real threat," the doctor told him. That generated a silence that lasted for a full ten seconds by the wall clock Bellow was staring at.

"I must consider this. I will call you later."

"Thank you, sir." Bellow hung up the phone and looked up at Clark.

"So?"

"So, they don't know what to do. Neither do I yet. Look, John, we're up against a number of unknowns here. We do not know much about the terrorists. No religious motivation, they're not Islamic fundamentalists. So I can't use religion or God or ethics against them. If they're ideological Marxists, they're going to be ruthless bastards. So far they haven't been really communicative. If I can't talk to them, I got bupkis."

"Okay, so, what's our play?"

"Put 'em in the dark for starters."

Clark turned: "Mr. Dennis?"

"Yes?"

"Can we cut the electricity to the castle?"

"Yes," the park engineer answered for his boss.

"Do it, doc?" John asked Bellow, getting a nod. "Okay, pull the plug now."

"Fair enough." The engineer sat at a computer terminal and worked the mouse to select the power-control program. In a few seconds, he isolated the castle and clicked the button to turn their electricity off.

"Let's see how long this takes," Bellow said quietly.

It took five seconds. Dennis's phone rang.

"Yes?" the park manager said into the speakerphone.

"Why did you do that?"

"What do you mean?"

"You know what I mean. The lights went off."

Dr. Bellow leaned over the speaker. "I am Dr. Bellow. Who am I talking to?"

"I am One. I am in control of Worldpark. Who are you?"

"My name is Paul Bellow, and I have been asked to speak with you."

"Ah, you are the negotiator, then. Excellent. Turn the lights back on immediately."

"Before we do that," Bellow said calmly, "I would like to know who you are. You have my name. I do not have yours."

"I told you that. I am One. You will call me Mr. One," the voice replied evenly, devoid of excitement or anger.

"Okay, Mr. One, if you insist, you can call me Paul."

"Turn the electricity back on, Paul."

"In return for which you will do what, Mr. One?"

"In return for which I will abstain from killing a child—for the moment," the voice added coldly.

"You do not sound like a barbarian, Mr. One, and the taking of a child's life is a barbaric act—and also one calculated to make your position more difficult, not less so."

"Paul, I have told you what I require. Do it immediately." And then the line went dead.

"Oh, shit," Bellow breathed. "He knows the playbook."

"Bad?"

Bellow nodded. "Bad. He knows what we're going to try to do, on my side, I mean."

"ANDRE," René called from his desk. "Select a child."

He'd already done that, and pointed to the little Dutch girl, Anna, in her wheelchair, wearing her special-access button. René nodded his approval. So, the other side had a physician talking to him. The name Paul Bellow meant nothing to him, but the man would be a Spanish psychiatrist, probably one experienced or at least trained in negotiations. His job would be to weaken their resolve, ultimately to get them to surrender and so condemn themselves to life in prison. Well, he'd have to see about that. René checked his watch and decided to wait ten minutes.

MALLOY eased back on the cyclic control, flaring his helicopter for landing where the fuel truck was parked. There were five soldiers there, one of them waving orange-plastic wands. In another few seconds, the Night Hawk touched down. Malloy killed the engines, and watched the rotor slow as Sergeant Nance opened the side door and hopped out.

"Time for some crew rest?" Lieutenant Harrison asked over the intercom.

"Right," Malloy snorted, opening his door to climb down. He walked to what looked like an officer standing a few yards away, answering his salute when he got there to shake hands. Malloy had an urgent request to make.

"THE trick will be to get close enough," Covington said.

"Yeah." Chavez nodded. They'd circulated carefully to the other side of the castle now. They could hear the Dive Bomber ride running behind them. There was a good forty meters of open ground all around the castle, doubtless planned by the main architect of the park to give the structure primacy of place. It did that, but it didn't give Ding and Peter much to work with. Both men took their time, examining everything from the little man-made streams to the bridges over them. They could see the windows into the command center where the terrorists were, and the line of sight was just too damned good, even before they considered the task of racing up the interior stairs—and those were probably covered by men with guns.

"They don't make it easy for us, do they?" Covington observed.

"Well, that's not their job, is it?"

"How's the recon going?" Clark asked over the encrypted radio circuit.

"Pretty well done, Mr. C," Chavez replied. "Malloy in yet?"

"Just landed."

"Good, 'cuz we're gonna need him if we gotta go in."

"Two groups, up and down," Covington added. "But we need something to tell us about that room."

THE Spanish officer, an army major, nodded instant agreement and waved to some people in the helicopter hangar. They trotted over, got their orders, and trotted back. With that done, Malloy headed to the hangar, too. He needed a men's room. Sergeant Nance, he saw, was heading back with two thermos jugs. Good man, the Marine thought, he knew how important coffee was at a time like this.

"THAT camera is dead. They shot it out," Dennis said. "We have a tape of him doing it."

"Show me," Noonan commanded.

The layout of the room was not unlike this one, Tim Noonan saw in the fifty seconds of tape they had. The children had been herded to the corner opposite the camera. Maybe they'd even stay there. It was not much, but it was something. "Anything else? Audio systems in the room, a microphone or something?"

"No," Dennis replied. "We have phones for that."

"Yeah." The FBI agent nodded resignedly. "I have to figure a way to spike it, then." Just then the phone rang.

"Yes, this is Paul," Bellow said instantly.

"Hello, Paul, this is One. The lights remain out. I told you to restore power. It has not been done. I tell you again, do it immediately."

"Working on that, but the police here are fumbling around some."

"And there is no one from the park there to assist you? I am not a fool, Paul. I say it one last time, turn the electricity back on immediately."

"Mr. One, we're working on it. Please be a little patient with us, okay?" Bellow's face was sweating now. It started quite suddenly, and though he knew why, he hoped that he was wrong.

"ANDRE," René said, doing so mistakenly before he killed the phone line.

The former park security guard walked over to the corner. "Hello, Anna. I think it is time for you to go back to your mother."

"Oh?" the child asked. She had china-blue eyes and light brown hair, nearly blond in fact, though her skin had the pale, delicate look of parchment. It was very sad. Andre walked behind the chair, taking the handles in his hands and wheeling her to the door. "Let's go outside, *mon petit chou,*" he said as they went through the door.

The elevator outside had a default setting. Even without electricity it could go down on battery power. Andre pushed the chair inside, flipped off the red emergency-stop switch, and pressed the 1 button. The doors closed slowly, and the elevator went down. A minute later, the doors opened again. The castle had a wide walk-through corridor that allowed people to transit from one part of Worldpark to another, and a mosaic that covered the arching walls. There was also a pleasant westerly breeze, and the Frenchman wheeled Anna right into it.

"WHAT'S this?" Noonan asked, looking at one of the video monitors. "John, we got somebody coming out."

"Command, this is Rifle Two-One, I see a guy pushing a wheelchair with a kid in it, coming out the west side of the castle." Johnston set his binoculars down and got on his rifle, centering the crosshairs on the man's temple, his finger lightly trouching the set-trigger. "Rifle Two-One is on target, on the guy, on target now."

"Weapons tight" was the reply from Clark. "I repeat, weapons are tight. Acknowledge."

"Roger, Six, weapons tight." Sergeant Johnston took his finger out of the trigger guard. What was happening here?

"Bugger," Covington said. They were only forty meters away. He and Chavez had an easy direct line of sight. The little girl looked ill in addition to being scared; she was slumped to her left in the chair, trying to look up and back at the man pushing her. He was about forty, they both thought, a mustache but no beard, average-normal in height, weight, and build, with dark eyes that displayed nothing. The park was so quiet now, so empty of people, that they could hear the scrape of the rubber tires on the stone courtyard.

"Where is Momma?" Anna asked in English she'd learned in school.

"You will see her in a moment," Nine promised. He wheeled her around the curving entrance to the castle. It circled around a statue, took a gentle upward and clockwise turn, then led down to the courtyard. He stopped the chair in the middle of the path. It was about five meters wide, and evenly paved.

Andre looked around. There had to be policemen out here, but he saw nothing moving at all, except for the cars on the Dive Bomber, which he didn't have to look at to see. The familiar noise was enough. It really was too bad. Nine reached into his belt, took out his pistol, and—

"—GUN, he's got a pistol out!" Homer Johnston reported urgently. "Oh, fuck, he's gonna—"

—THE gun fired into Anna's back, driving straight through her heart. A gout of blood appeared on the flat child chest, and her head dropped forward. The man pushed the wheelchair just then, and it rolled down the curving path, caroming off the stone wall and making it all the way into the flat courtyard, where it finally stopped.

Covington drew his Beretta and started to bring it up. It would not have been an easy shot, but he had nine rounds in his pistol, and that was enough, but—

"Weapons tight!" the radio earpiece thundered. "Weapons tight! Do not fire," Clark ordered them.

"Fuck!" Chavez rasped next to Peter Covington.

"Yes," the Englishman agreed. "Quite." He holstered his pistol, watching the man turn and walk back into the shelter of the stone castle.

"I'm on target, Rifle Two-One is on target!" Johnston's voice told them all.

"Do *not* fire. This is Six, weapons are tight, goddamnit!"

"FUCK!" Clark snarled in the command center. He slammed his fist on the table. "Fuck!" Then the phone rang.

"Yes?" Bellow said, sitting next to the Rainbow commander.

"You had your warning. Turn the electricity back on, or we will kill another," One said.

CHAPTER 15

WHITE HATS

"THERE WAS NOTHING WE COULD HAVE DONE, John. Not a thing," Bellow said, giving voice to words that the others didn't have the courage to say.

"Now what?" Clark asked.

"Now I guess we turn the electricity back on."

As they watched the TV monitors, three men raced to the child. Two wore the *tricornio* of the Guardia Civil. The third was Dr. Hector Weiler.

CHAVEZ and Covington watched the same thing from a closer perspective. Weiler wore a white lab coat, the global uniform for physicians, and his race to reach the child ended abruptly as he touched the warm but still body. The slump of his shoulders told the tale, even from fifty meters away. The bullet had gone straight through her heart. The doctor said something to the cops, and one of them wheeled the chair down and out of the courtyard, turning to go past the two Rainbow members.

"Hold it, doc," Chavez called, walking over to look. In this moment Ding remembered that his own wife held a new life in her belly, even now probably moving and kicking while Patsy was sitting in their living room, watching TV or reading a book. The little girl's face was at peace now, as though asleep, and he could not hold his hand back from touching her soft hair. "What's the story, doc?"

"She was quite ill, probably terminal. I will have a file on her back at my office. When these children come here, I get a summary of their condition should an emergency arise." The physician bit his lip and looked up. "She was probably dying, but not yet dead, not yet completely without hope." Weiler was the son of a Spanish mother and a German father who'd emigrated to Spain after the Second World War. He'd studied hard to become a physician and surgeon, and this act, this murder of a child, was the negation of all that. Someone had decided to make all his training and study worthless. He'd never known rage, quiet and sad though it was, but now he did. "Will you kill them?"

Chavez looked up. There were no tears in his eyes. Perhaps they'd come later, Domingo Chavez thought, his hand still on the child's head. Her hair wasn't very long, and he didn't know that it had grown back after her last chemotherapy protocol. He did know that she was supposed to be alive, and that in watching her death, he had failed to do that which he'd dedicated his life to doing. *"Sí,"* he told the doctor. "We will kill them. Peter?" He waved at his colleague, and together they accompanied the others to the doctor's office. They walked over slowly. There was no reason to go fast now.

"THAT'LL do," Malloy thought, surveying the still-wet paint on the side of the Night Hawk. POLICIA, the lettering said. "Ready, Harrison?"

"Yes, sir. Sergeant Nance, time to move."

"Yessir." The crew chief hopped in, buckled his safety belt, and watched the pilot go through the startup sequence. "All clear aft," he said over the intercom, after leaning out to check. "Tail rotor is clear, Colonel."

"Then I guess it's time to fly." Malloy applied power and lifted the Night Hawk into the sky. Then he keyed his tactical radio. "Rainbow, this is the Bear, over."

"Bear, this is Rainbow Six, reading you five by five, over."

"Bear's in the air, sir, be there in seven minutes."

"Roger, please orbit the area until we tell you otherwise."

"Roger that, sir. I'll notify when we commence the orbit. Out." There was no particular hurry. Malloy dipped the nose and headed into the gathering darkness. The sun was almost down now, and the park lights in the distance were all coming on.

"WHO is this?" Chavez asked.

"Francisco de la Cruz," the man replied. His leg was bandaged, and he looked to be in pain.

"Ah, yes, we saw you on the videotape," Covington said. He saw the sword and shield in the corner and turned to nod his respect at the seated man. Peter lifted the *spatha* and hefted it briefly. At close range it would be formidable as hell, not the equal of his MP-10, but probably a very satisfying weapon for all that.

"A child? They kill a child?" de la Cruz asked.

Dr. Weiler was at his file cabinet. "Anna Groot, age ten and a half," he said, reading over the documents that had preceded the little one. "Metastatic osteosarcoma, terminally ill. . . . Six weeks left, her doctor says here. Osteo, that is a bad one." Against the wall, the two Spanish cops lifted the body from the chair and laid it tenderly on the examining table, then covered it with a sheet. One looked close to tears, blocked only by the cold rage that made his hands tremble.

"John must feel pretty shitty about now," Chavez said.

"He had to do it, Ding. It wasn't the right time to take action—"

"I know that, Peter! But how the fuck do we tell *her* that?" A pause. "Doc, you have any coffee around here?"

"There." Weiler pointed.

Chavez walked to the urn and poured some into a Styrofoam cup. "Up and down, sandwich 'em?"

Covington nodded. "Yes, I think so."

Chavez emptied the cup and tossed it into a wastebasket. "Okay, let's get set up." They left the office without another word and made their way in the shadows back to the underground, thence to the alternate command center.

"Rifle Two-One, anything happening?" Clark was asking when they walked in.

"Negative, Six, nothing except shadows on the windows. They haven't put a guy on the roof yet. That's a little strange."

"They're pretty confident in their TV coverage," Noonan thought. He had the blueprints of the castle in front of him. "Okay, we are assuming that our friends are all in here . . . but there's a dozen other rooms on three levels."

"This is Bear," a voice said over the speaker Noonan had set up. "I am orbiting now. What do I need to know, over?"

"Bear, this is Six," Clark replied. "The subjects are all in the castle. There's a command-and-control center on the second floor. Best guess, everybody's there right now. Also, be advised the subjects have killed a hostage—a little girl," John added.

In the helicopter, Malloy's head didn't move at the news. "Roger, okay, Six, we will orbit and observe. Be advised we have all our deployment gear aboard, over."

"Roger that. Out." Clark took his hand off the transmit button.

The men were quiet, but their looks were intense, Chavez saw. Too professional for an overt display—nobody was playing with a personal weapon, or anything as Hollywood as that—yet their faces were like stone, only their eyes moving back and forth over the diagrams or flickering back and forth to the TV monitors. It must have been very hard on Homer Johnston, Ding thought. He'd been on the fucker when he shot the kid. Homer had kids, and he could have transported the subject into the next dimension as easily as blinking his eyes. . . . But no, that would not have been smart, and they were paid to be smart. The men hadn't been ready for even an improvised assault, and anything that smacked of improvisation would only get more children killed. And that wasn't the mission, either. Then a phone rang. Bellow got it, hitting the speaker button.

"Yes?" the doctor said.

"We regret the incident with the child, but she was soon to die anyway. Now, when will our friends be released?"

"Paris hasn't gotten back to us yet," Bellow replied.

"Then, I regret to say, there will be another incident shortly."

"Look, Mr. One, I cannot force Paris to do anything. We are talking, negotiating with government officials, and they take time to reach decisions. Governments never move fast, do they?"

"Then I will help them. Tell Paris that unless the aircraft bringing our friends is ready for us to board it in one hour, we will kill a hostage, and then another every hour until our demands are met," the voice said, entirely without emotional emphasis.

"That is unreasonable. Listen to me: even if they brought all of them out of their prisons *now,* it would take at least two hours to get them here. Your wishes cannot make an airplane fly faster, can they?"

That generated a thoughtful pause. "Yes, that is true. Very well, we will commence the shooting of hostages in three hours from now . . . no, I will start the countdown on the hour. That gives you an additional twelve minutes. I will be generous. Do you understand?"

"Yes, you say that you will kill another child at twenty-two hundred hours, and another one every hour after that."

"Correct. Make sure that Paris understands." And the line went dead.

"Well?" Clark asked.

"John, you don't need me here for this. It's pretty damned clear that they'll do it. They killed the first one to show us who's the boss. They plan to succeed, and they don't care what it takes for them to do so. The concession he just made may be the last one we're going to get."

■ ■ ■

"WHAT is that?" Esteban asked. He walked to the window to see. "Helicopter!"

"Oh?" René went there also. The windows were so small that he had to move the Basque aside. "Yes, I see the police have them. Large one," he added with a shrug. "This is not a surprise." But—"José, get up to the roof with a radio, and keep us informed."

One of the other Basques nodded and headed for the fire stairwell. The elevator would have worked fine, but he didn't want to be inconvenienced by another power shutoff.

"COMMAND, Rifle Two-One," Johnston called a minute later.

"Rifle Two-One, this is Six."

"I got a guy on the castle roof, one man, armed with what looks like a Uzi, and he's got a brick, too. Just one, nobody else is joining up at this time."

"Roger that, Rifle Two-One."

"This isn't the guy who whacked the kid," the sergeant added.

"Okay, good, thank you."

"Rifle Three has him, too . . . just walked over to my side. He's circulating around . . . yeah, looking over the edge, looking down."

"John?" It was Major Covington.

"Yes, Peter?"

"We're not showing them enough."

"What do you mean?"

"Give them something to look at. Policemen, an inner perimeter. If they don't see something, they're going to wonder what's going on that they cannot see."

"Good idea," Noonan said.

Clark liked it. "Colonel?"

"Yes," Nuncio replied. He leaned over the table. "I propose two men, here, two more here . . . here . . . here."

"Yes, sir, please make that happen right away."

"RENÉ," Andre called from in front of a TV screen. He pointed. "Look."

There were two Guardia cops moving slowly and trying to be covert as they approached up Strada España to a place fifty meters from the castle. René nodded and picked up his radio. "Three!"

"Yes, One."

"Police approaching the castle. Keep an eye on them."

"I will do that, One," Esteban promised.

"OKAY, they're using radios," Noonan said, checking his scanner. "Citizen-band walkie-talkies, regular commercial ones, set on channel sixteen. Pure vanilla."

"No names, just numbers?" Chavez asked.

"So far. Our point of contact calls himself One, and this guy is Three. Okay, does that tell us anything?"

"Radio games," Dr. Bellow said. "Right out of the playbook. They're trying to keep their identities secret from us, but that's also in the playbook." The two photo-ID pictures had long since been sent to France for identification, but both the police and intelligence agencies had come up dry.

"Okay, will the French deal?"

A shake of the head. "I don't think so. The minister, when I told him about the Dutch girl, he just grunted and said Carlos stays in the jug no matter what—and he expects us to resolve the situation successfully, and if we can't, his country has a team of his own to send down."

"So, we've gotta have a plan in place and ready to go—by twenty-two hundred."

"Unless you want to see them kill another hostage, yes," Bellow said. "They're denying me my ability to guide their behavior. They know how the game is played."

"Professionals?"

Bellow shrugged. "Might as well be. They know what I'm going to try, and if they know it ahead of time, then they know how to maneuver clear."

"No way to mitigate their behavior?" Clark asked, wanting it clear.

"I can try, but probably not. The ideological ones, the ones who have a clear idea of what they want—well, they're hard to reason with. They have no ethical base to play with, no morality in the usual sense, nothing I can use against them. No conscience."

"Yeah, we saw that, I guess. Okay." John stood up straight and turned to look at his two team leaders. "You got two hours to plan it, and one more to set it up. We go at twenty-two hundred hours."

"We need to know more about what's happening inside," Covington told Clark.

"Noonan, what can you do?"

The FBI agent looked down at the blueprints, then over at the TV monitors. "I need to change," he said, heading over to his equipment case and pulling out the green-on-green night gear. The best news he'd seen so far was that the castle windows made for two blind spots. Better yet, they could control the lights that bled energy into both of them. He walked over to the park engineer next. "Can you switch off these lights along here?"

"Sure. When?"

"When the guy on the roof is looking the other way. And I need somebody to back me up," Noonan added.

"I can do that," First Sergeant Vega said, stepping forward.

THE children were whining. It had started two hours earlier and only gotten worse. They wanted food—something adults would probably not have asked for, since adults would be far too frightened to eat, but children were different somehow. They also needed to use the restroom quite a bit, and fortunately there were two bathrooms adjacent to the control room, and René's people didn't stop them from going—the restrooms had no windows or phones or anything to make escape or communication possible, and it wasn't worth the aggravation to have the children soiling their pants. The children didn't talk directly to any of his people, but the whining was real and growing. Well-behaved kids, else it would be worse, René told himself, with an ironic smile. He looked at the wall clock.

"Three, this is One."

"Yes, One," came the reply.

"What do you see?"

"Eight policemen, four pairs, watching us, but doing nothing but watching."

"Good." And he set the radio down.

"LOG that," Noonan said. He'd checked the wall clock. It was about fifteen minutes since the last radio conversation. He was in his night costume now, the two-shade greens they'd used in Vienna. His Beretta .45 automatic, with suppressor, was in a special, large shoulder holster over his body armor, and he had a backpack slung over one shoulder. "Vega, ready to take a little walk?"

"You betcha," Oso replied, glad at last to be doing *something* on a deployment. As much as he liked being responsible for the team's heavy machine gun, he'd never gotten to use it, and, he thought, probably never would. The biggest man on the team, his hobby was pumping iron, and he had a chest about the dimensions of a half-keg of beer. Vega followed Noonan out the door, then outside.

"Ladder?" the first sergeant asked.

"Tool and paint shop fifty yards from where we're going. I asked. They have what we need."

"Fair 'nuff," Oso replied.

It was a fast walk, dodging through a few open areas visible to the fixed cameras, and the shop they headed for had no sign on it at all. Noonan slipped the ground-bolted door and walked in. None of the doors, remarkably enough, were locked. Vega pulled a thirty-foot extension ladder off its wall brackets. "This ought to do."

"Yeah." They went outside. Movement would now be trickier. "Noonan to command."

"Six here."

"Start doing the cameras, John."

In the command center, Clark pointed to the park engineer. There was danger here, but not much, they hoped. The castle command center, like this one, had only eight TV monitors, which were hard-wired into over forty cameras. You could have the computer simply flip through them in an automatic sequence, or select cameras for special use. With a mouse-click, one camera was disabled. If the terrorists were using the automatic sequence, as seemed likely, they probably would not notice that one camera's take was missing during the flip-through. They had to get through the visual coverage of two of them, and the park engineer was ready to flip them off and on as needed. The moment a hand appeared in camera twenty-three's field of view, the engineer flipped it off.

"Okay, twenty-three is off, Noonan."

"We're moving," Noonan said. The first walk took them twenty meters, and they stopped behind a concession stand. "Okay, we're at the popcorn building."

The engineer flipped twenty-three back on, and then turned off twenty-one.

"Twenty-one is off," Clark reported next. "Rifle Two-One, where's the guy on the roof?"

"West side, just lit up a smoke, not looking down over the edge anymore. Staying still at the moment," Sergeant Johnston reported.

"Noonan, you are clear to move."

"Moving now," the FBI agent replied. He and Vega double-timed it across the stone slabs, their rubber-soled boots keeping their steps quiet. At the side of the castle was a dirt strip about two meters wide, and some large boxwoods. Carefully, Noonan and Vega angled the ladder up, setting it behind a bush. Vega pulled the rope to extend the top portion, stopping it just under the window. Then he got between the ladder and the building, grabbed the treads and held them tight, pulling the ladder against the rough stone blocks.

"Watch your ass, Tim," Oso whispered.

"Always." Noonan went up quickly for the first ten feet, then slowed to a vertical crawl. *Patience,* Tim told himself. *Plenty of time to do this.* It was the sort of lie that men tell themselves.

"OKAY," Clark heard. "He's going up the ladder now. The roof guy is still on the opposite side, fat, dumb, and happy."

"Bear, this is Six, over," John said, getting another idea.

"Bear copies, Six."

"Play around a little on the west side, just to draw some attention, over."

"Roger that."

MALLOY stopped his endless circling, leveled out, and then eased toward the castle. The Night Hawk was a relatively quiet aircraft for a helicopter, but the guy on the roof turned to watch closely, the colonel saw through his night-vision goggles. He stopped his approach at about two hundred meters. He wanted to get their attention, not to spook them. The roof sentry's cigarette blazed brightly in the goggles. It moved to his lips, then away, then back, staying there.

"Say hello, sweetie," Malloy said over the intercom. "Jesus, if I was in a Night Stalker, I could spray your ass into the next time zone."

"You fly the Stalker? What's it like?"

"If she could cook, I'd fucking marry her. Sweetest chopper ever made," Malloy said, holding hover. "Six, Bear, I have the bastard's attention."

"NOONAN, Six, we've frozen the roof sentry for you. He's on the opposite side from you."

Good, Noonan didn't say. He took off his Kevlar helmet and edged his face to the window. It was made of irregular segments held in place by lead strips, just like in the castles of old. The glass wasn't as good as float-plate, but it was transparent. *Okay.* He reached into his backpack and pulled a fiber-optic cable with the same cobra-head arrangement he'd used in Bern.

"Noonan to Command, you getting this?"

"That's affirmative." It was the voice of David Peled. The picture he saw was distorted, but you quickly got used to that. It showed four adults, but more important, it showed a crowd of children sitting on the floor in the corner, close to two doors with labels—the toilets, Peled realized. That worked. That worked pretty well. "Looks good, Timothy. Looks very good."

"Okay." Noonan glued the tiny instrument in place and headed down the ladder. His heart was racing faster than it ever did on the morning three-mile run. At the bottom, he and Vega both hugged the wall.

THE cigarette flew off the roof, and the sentry got tired of looking at the chopper, Johnston saw.

"Our friend's moving east on the castle roof. Noonan, he's coming your way."

MALLOY thought of maneuvering to draw the attention back, but that was too dangerous a play. He turned the helicopter sideways and continued his circling, but closer in, his eyes locked on the castle roof. There wasn't much else he could do except to draw his service pistol and fire, but at this range it would be hard enough to hit the castle. And killing people wasn't his job, unfortunately, Malloy told himself. There were times when he found the idea rather appealing.

"THE helicopter annoys me," the voice on the phone said.

"Pity," Dr. Bellow replied, wondering what response it would get. "But police do what police do."

"News from Paris?"

"Regrettably not yet, but we hope to hear something soon. There is still time." Bellow's voice adopted a quiet intensity that he hoped would be taken for desperation.

"Time and tide wait for no man," One said, and hung up.

"What's that mean?" John asked.

"It means he's playing by the rules. He hasn't objected to the cops he can see on the TV, either. He knows the things he has to put up with." Bellow sipped his coffee. "He's very confident. He figures he's in a safe place, and he's holding the cards, and if he has to kill a few more kids, that's okay, because it'll get him what he wants."

"Killing children." Clark shook his head. "I didn't think—hell, I'm supposed to know better, right?"

"It's a very strong taboo, maybe the strongest," Dr. Bellow agreed. "The way they killed that little girl, though . . . there was no hesitation, just like shooting a paper target. Ideological," the psychiatrist went on. "They've subordinated everything to their belief system. That makes them rational, but only within that system. Our friend Mr. One has chosen his objective, and he'll stick to it."

THE remote TV system, the park engineer saw, was really something. The objective lens now affixed to the castle window was less than two millimeters across at its widest point, and even if noticed, would be mistaken for a drop of paint or some flaw in the window glass. The quality of the image wasn't very good, but it showed where people were, and the more you looked at it, the more you understood what initially appeared to be a black-and-white photograph of clutter. He could count six adults now, and with a seventh atop the castle, that left only three unaccounted for—and were all the children in view? It was harder with them. All their shirts were the same color, and the red translated into a very neutral gray on the black-and-white picture. There was the one in a wheelchair, but the rest blended together in the out-of-focus image. The commandos, he could see, were worried about that.

"HE'S heading back west again," Johnston reported. "Okay, he's at the west side now."

"Let's go," Noonan told Vega.

"The ladder?" They'd taken it down and laid it behind the bushes on its side.

"Leave it." Noonan ran off in a crouch, reaching the concession structure in a few seconds. "Noonan to Command, time to do the cameras again."

"It's off," the engineer told Clark.

"Camera twenty-one is down. Get moving, Tim."

Noonan popped Vega on the shoulder and ran another thirty meters. "Okay, take down twenty-three."

"Done," the park engineer said.

"Move," Clark commanded.

Fifteen seconds later, they were in a safe position. Noonan leaned against a building wall and took a long breath. "Thanks, Julio."

"Any time, man," Vega replied. "Just so the camera gadget works."

"It will," the FBI agent promised, and with that they headed back to the underground command post.

"Blow the windows? Can we do that, Paddy?" Chavez was asking when they got there.

Connolly was wishing for a cigarette. He'd quit years before—it was too hard on the daily runs to indulge—but at times like this it seemed to help the concentration. "Six windows . . . three or four minutes each . . . no, I think not, sir. I can give you two—if we have the time."

"How sturdy are the windows?" Clark asked "Dennis?"

"Metal frames set into the stone," the park manager said with a shrug.

"Wait." The engineer turned a page on the castle blueprints, then two more, and then a finger traced down the written portion on the right side. "Here's the specs . . . they're held in by grouting only. You should be able to kick them in, I think."

The "I think" part was not as reassuring as Ding would have preferred, but how strong could a window frame be with a two-hundred-pound man swinging into it with two boots leading the way?

"What about flash-bangs, Paddy?"

"We can do that," Connolly answered. "It will not do the frames any good at all, sir."

"Okay." Chavez leaned over the plans. "You'll have time to blow two windows—this one and this one." He tapped the prints. "We'll use flash-bangs on the other four and swing in a second later. Eddie here, me here, Louis here. George, how's the leg?"

"Marginal," Sergeant Tomlinson replied with painful honesty. He'd have to kick through a window, swing in, drop to a concrete floor, then come up shooting . . . and the lives of children were at stake. No, he couldn't risk it, could he? "Better somebody else, Ding."

"Oso, think you can do it?" Chavez asked.

"Oh, yeah," Vega replied, trying not to smile. "You bet, Ding."

"Okay, Scotty here, and Mike take these two. What's the exact distance from the roof?"

That was on the blueprints. "Sixteen meters exactly from the level of the roof. Add another seventy centimeters to allow for the battlements."

"The ropes can do that easily," Eddie Price decided. The plan was coming together. He and Ding would have as their primary mission getting between the kids and the bad guys, shooting as they went. Vega, Loiselle, McTyler, and Pierce would be primarily tasked to killing the subjects in the castle's command room, but that would be finally decided only when they entered the room. Covington's Team-1 would race up the stairs from the underground, to intercept any subjects who ran out, and to back up Team-2 if something went wrong on their assault.

Sergeant Major Price and Chavez looked over the blueprints again, measuring distances to be covered and the time in which to do it. It looked possible, even probable, that they could carry it off. Ding looked up at the others. "Comments?"

Noonan turned to look at the picture from the fiber-optic gear he'd installed. "They seem to be mainly at the control panels. Two guys keeping an eye on the children, but they're not worried about them—makes sense, they're just kids, not adults able to start real resistance . . . but . . . it only takes one of these bastards to turn and hose them, man."

"Yeah," Ding nodded. There was no denying or avoiding that fact. "Well, we have to shoot fast, people. Any way to string them out?"

Bellow thought about that. "If I tell them the plane's on the way . . . that's a risk. If they think we're lying to them, well, they could start taking it out on the hostages, but the upside is, if they think it's about time to head for the airport, probably Mr. One will send a couple of his troops down to the underground—that's the most likely way for them to leave the area, I think. Then, if we can play some more with the surveillance cameras, and get a guy in close—"

"Yeah, pop them right away," Clark said. "Peter?"

"Get us within twenty meters and it's a piece of cake. Plus, we kill the lights right before we hit. Disorient the bastards," Covington added.

"There's emergency lights in the stairwells," Mike Dennis said. "They click on when the power goes down—shit, there's two in the command center, too."

"Where?" Chavez asked.

"The left—I mean the northeast corner and the southwest one. The regular kind, two lights, like car headlights, they run off a battery."

"Okay, no NVGs when we go in, I guess, but we'll still kill the lights right before we hit, just to distract them. Anything else? Peter?" Ding asked.

Major Covington nodded. "It ought to work."

Clark observed and listened, forced to let his principal subordinates do all the planning and talking, leaving him only able to comment if they made a mistake, and they hadn't done that. Most of all, he wanted to lift an MP-10 and go in with the shooters, but he couldn't do that, and inwardly he swore at the fact. Commanding just wasn't as satisfying as leading.

"We need medics standing by in case the bad guys get lucky," John said to Colonel Nuncio.

"We have paramedics outside the park now—"

"Dr. Weiler is pretty good," Mike Dennis said. "He's had trauma training. We insisted on that in case we have something bad happen here."

"Okay, we'll have him stand-to when the time comes. Dr. Bellow, tell Mr. One that the French have caved, and their friends will be here. . . . What do you think?"

"Ten-twenty or so. If they agree to that, it's a concession, but the kind that will calm them down—should, anyway."

"Make the call, doc," John Clark ordered.

"YES?" René said.

"Sanchez is being released from Le Sante prison in about twenty minutes. Six of the others, too, but there's a problem on the last three. I'm not sure what that is. They'll be taken to De Gaulle International Airport and flown here on an Air France Airbus 340. We think they'll be here by twenty-two-forty. Is that acceptable? How will we get you and the hostages to them for the flight out?" Bellow asked.

"A bus, I think. You will bring the bus right to the castle. We will take ten or so of the children with us, and leave the rest here as a show of good faith on our part. Tell the police that we know how to move the children without giving them a chance to do something foolish, and any treachery will have severe consequences."

"We do not want any more children harmed," Bellow assured him.

"If you do as you are told, that will not be necessary, but understand," René went on firmly, "if you do anything foolish, then the courtyard will run red with blood. Do you understand that?"

"Yes, One, I understand," the voice replied.

René set the phone down and stood. "My friends, Il'ych is coming. The French have granted our demands."

"HE looks like a happy camper," Noonan said, eyes locked on the black-and-white picture. The one who had to be Mr. One was standing now, walking toward another of the subjects, and they appeared to shake hands on the fuzzy picture.

"They're not going to lie down and take a nap," Bellow warned. "If anything, they're going to be more alert now."

"Yeah, I know," Chavez assured him. *But if we do our job right, it doesn't matter how alert they are.*

■ ■ ■

MALLOY headed back to the airfield for refueling, which took half an hour. While there he heard what was going to happen in another hour. In the back of the Night Hawk, Sergeant Nance set up the ropes, set to fifty feet length exactly, and hooked them into eyebolts on the chopper's floor. Like the pilots, Nance, too, had a pistol holstered on his left side. He never expected to use it, and was only a mediocre shot, but it made him feel like part of the team, and that was important to him. He supervised the refueling, capped the tank, and told Colonel Malloy the bird was ready.

Malloy pulled up on the collective, brought the Night Hawk into the air, then pushed the cyclic forward to return to Worldpark. From this point on, their flight routine would be changing. On arriving over the park, the Night Hawk didn't circle. Instead it flew directly over the castle every few minutes, then drew off into the distance, his anticollision strobe lights flashing as he moved around the park grounds, seemingly at random, bored with the orbiting he'd done before.

"OKAY, people, let's move," Chavez told his team. Those directly involved in the rescue operation headed out into the underground corridor, then out to where the Spanish army truck stood. They boarded it, and it drove off, looping around into the massive parking lot.

Dieter Weber selected a sniper perch opposite Sergeant Johnston's position, on top of the flat roof of a theater building where kids viewed cartoons, only a hundred twenty meters from the castle's east side. Once there, he unrolled his foam mat, set up his rifle on the bipod, and started training his ten-power scope over the castle's windows.

"Rifle Two-Two in position," he reported to Clark.

"Very well, report as necessary, Al?" Clark said, looking up.

Stanley looked grim. "A sodding lot of guns, and a lot of children."

"Yeah, I know. Anything else we could try?"

Stanley shook his head. "It's a good plan. If we try outside, we give them too much maneuvering space, and they will feel safer in this castle building. No, Peter and Ding have a good plan, but there's no such bloody thing as a perfect one."

"Yeah," John said. "I want to be there, too. This command stuff sucks the big one."

Alistair Stanley grunted. "Quite."

▪ ▪ ▪

THE parking lot lights all went off at once. The truck, also with lights out, stopped next to a light standard. Chavez and his team jumped out. Ten seconds later, the Night Hawk came in, touching down with the rotor still turning fast. The side doors opened, and the shooters clambered aboard and sat down on the floor. Sergeant Nance closed one door, then the other.

"All aboard, Colonel."

Without a word, Malloy pulled the collective and climbed back into the sky, mindful of the light standards, which could have wrecked the whole mission. It took only four seconds to clear them, and he banked the aircraft to head back toward the park.

"A/C lights off," Malloy told Lieutenant Harrison.

"Lights off," the copilot confirmed.

"We ready?" Ding asked his men in the back.

"Goddamn right, we are," Mike Pierce said back. *Fucking murderers,* he didn't add. But every man on the bird was thinking that. Weapons were slung tight across their chests, and they had their zip-lining gloves on. Three of the men were pulling them tight on their hands, a show of some tension on their part that went along with the grim faces.

"WHERE is the aircraft?" One asked.

"About an hour and ten minutes out," Dr. Bellow replied. "When do you want your bus?"

"Exactly forty minutes before the aircraft lands. It will then be refueled while we board it."

"Where are you going?" Bellow asked next.

"We will tell the pilot when we get aboard."

"Okay, we have the bus coming now. It will be here in about fifteen minutes. Where do you want it to come?"

"Right to the castle, past the Dive Bomber ride."

"Okay, I will tell them to do that," Bellow promised.

"Merci." The phone went dead again.

"Smart," Noonan observed. "They'll have two surveillance cameras on the bus all the way in, so we can't use it to screen a rescue team. And they probably plan to use the mountaineer technique to get the hostages aboard." *Tough shit,* he didn't add.

"Bear, this is Six," Clark called on the radio.

"Bear copies, Six, over."

"We execute in five minutes."

"Roger that, we party in five."

MALLOY turned in his seat. Chavez had heard the call and nodded, holding up one hand, fingers spread.

"Rainbow, this is Six. Stand-to, repeat stand-to. We commence the operation in five minutes."

IN the underground, Peter Covington led three of his men east toward the castle stairwells, while the park engineer selectively killed off the surveillance cameras. His explosives man set a small charge on the fire door at the bottom and nodded at his boss.

"Team-1 is ready."

"Rifle Two-One is ready and on target," Johnston said.

"Rifle Two-Two is ready, but no target at this time," Weber told Clark.

"Three, this is One," the scanner crackled in the command room.

"Yes, One," the man atop the castle replied.

"Anything happening?"

"No, One, the police are staying where they are. And the helicopter is flying around somewhere, but not doing anything."

"The bus should be here in fifteen minutes. Stay alert."

"I will," Three promised.

"Okay," Noonan said. "That's a time-stamp. Mr. One calls Mr. Three about every fifteen minutes. Never more than eighteen, never less than twelve. So—"

"Yeah." Clark nodded. "Move it up?"

"Why not," Stanley said.

"Rainbow, this is Six. Move in and execute. Say again, *execute now!*"

ABOARD the Night Hawk, Sergeant Nance moved left and right, sliding the side doors open. He gave a thumbs up to the shooters that they returned, each man hooking up his zip-line rope to D-rings on their belts. All of them turned inward, getting up on the balls of their feet so that their backsides were now dangling outside the helicopter.

"Sergeant Nance, I will flash you when we're in place."

"Roger, sir," the crew chief replied, crouching in the now-empty middle of the passenger area, his arms reaching to the men on both sides.

"ANDRE, go down and look at the courtyard," René ordered. His man moved at once, holding his Uzi in both hands.

"SOMEBODY just left the room," Noonan said.

"Rainbow, this is Six, one subject has left the command center."

EIGHT, Chavez thought. *Eight subjects to take down.* The other two would go to the long-riflemen.

THE last two hundred meters were the hard ones, Malloy thought. His hands tingled on the cyclic control stick, and as many times as he'd done this, this one was not a rehearsal. *Okay* . . . He dropped his nose, heading toward the castle, and without the anticollision lights, the aircraft would only be a shadow, slightly darker than the night—better yet, the four-bladed rotor made a sound that was nondirectional. Someone could hear it, but locating the source was difficult, and he needed that to last only a few more seconds.

"RIFLE Two-One, stand by."

"Rifle Two-One is on target, Six," Johnston reported. His breathing regularized, and his elbows moved slightly, so that only bone, not muscle, was in contact with the mat under him. The mere passage of blood through his arteries could throw his aim off. His crosshairs were locked just forward of the sentry's ear. "On target," he repeated.

"Fire," the earpiece told him.

Say good night, Gracie, a small voice in his mind whispered. His finger pushed back gently on the set trigger, which snapped cleanly, and a gout of white flame exploded from the muzzle of the rifle. The flash obscured the sight picture for a brief moment, then cleared in time for him to see the bullet impact. There was a slight puff of gray-looking vapor from the far side of the head, and the body dropped straight down like a puppet with cut strings. No one inside would hear the shot, not through thick windows and stone walls from over three hundred meters away.

"Rifle Two-One. Target is down. Target is down. Center head," Johnston reported.

"THAT'S a kill," Lieutenant Harrison breathed over the intercom. From the helicopter's perspective, the destruction of the sentry's head looked quite spectacular. It was the first death he'd ever seen, and it struck him as something in a movie, not something real. The target hadn't been a living being to him, and now it would never be.

"Yep," Malloy agreed, easing back on the cyclic. "Sergeant Nance—*now!*"

In the back, Nance pushed outward. The helicopter was still slowing, nose up now, as Malloy performed the rocking-chair maneuver to perfection.

Chavez pushed off with his feet, and went down the zip-line. It took less than two seconds of not-quite free-fall before he applied tension to the line to slow his descent, and his black, rubber-soled boots came down lightly on the flat roof. He immediately loosed his rope, and turned to watch his people do the same. Eddie Price ran over to the sentry's body, kicked the head over with his boot, and turned, making a thumbs-up for his boss.

"Six, this is Team-2 Lead. On the roof. The sentry is dead," he said into his microphone. "Proceeding now." With that, Chavez turned to his people, waving his arms to the roof's periphery. The Night Hawk was gone into the darkness, having hardly appeared to have stopped at all.

The castle roof was surrounded by the battlements associated with such places, vertical rectangles of stone behind which archers could shelter while loosing their arrows at attackers. Each man had one such shelter assigned, and they counted them off with their fingers, so that every man went to the right one. For this night, the men looped their rappelling ropes around them, then stepped into the gaps. When all of them were set up, they held up their hands. Chavez did the same, then dropped his as he kicked off the roof and slid down the rope to a point a meter to the right of a window, using his feet to stand off the wall. Paddy Connolly came down on the other side, reached to apply his Primacord around the edges, and inserted a radio-detonator on one edge. Then Paddy moved to his left, swinging on the rope as though it were a jungle vine to do the same to one other. Other team members took flash-bang grenades and held them in their hands.

"Two-Lead to Six—lights!"

In the command center, the engineer again isolated the power to the castle and shut it off.

Outside the windows, Team-2 saw the windows go dark, and then a second or two later the wall-mounted emergency lights came on, just like miniature auto headlights, not enough to light the room up properly. The TV monitors they were watching went dark as well.

"Merde," René said, sitting and reaching for a phone. If they wanted to play more games, then he could—he thought he saw some movement outside the window and looked more closely—

"Team-2, this is lead. Five seconds . . . five . . . four . . . three—" At "three," the men holding the flash-bangs pulled the pins and set them right next to the windows, then turned aside. "— . . . two . . . one . . . *fire!*"

Sergeant Connolly pressed his button, and two windows were sundered from the wall by explosives. A fraction of a second later, three more windows were blown in by a wall of noise and blazing light. They flew across the room in a shower of glass and lead fragments, missing the children in the corner by three meters.

Next to Chavez, Sergeant Major Price tossed in another flash-bang, which exploded the moment it touched the floor. Then Chavez pushed outward from the wall, swinging into the room through the window, his MP-10 up and in both hands. He hit the floor badly, falling backward, unable to control his balance, then felt Price's feet land on his left arm. Chavez rolled and jolted to his feet, then moved to the kids. They were screaming with alarm, covering their faces and ears from the abuse of the flash-bangs. But he couldn't worry about them just yet.

Price landed better, moved right as well, but turned to scan the room. There. It was a bearded one, holding an Uzi. Price extended his MP-10 to the limit of the sling and fired a three-round burst right into his face from three meters away. The force of the bullet impacts belied the suppressed noise of the shots.

Oso Vega had kicked his window loose on leg-power alone, and landed right on top of a subject, rather to the surprise of both, but Vega was ready for surprises, and the terrorist was not. Oso's left hand slammed out, seemingly of its own accord, and hit him in the face with enough force to split it open into a bloody mess that a burst of three 10-mm rounds only made worse.

René was sitting at his desk, the phone in his hand, and his pistol on the tabletop before him. He was reaching for it when Pierce fired into the side of his head from six feet away.

In the far corner, Chavez and Price skidded to a stop, their bodies between the terrorists and the hostages. Ding came to one knee, his weapon up while his eyes scanned for targets, as he listened to the suppressed chatter of his men's weapons. The semidarkness of the room was alive now with moving shadows. Loiselle found himself behind a subject, close enough to touch him with the muzzle of his submachine gun. This he did. It made the shot an easy one, but sprayed blood and brains all over the room.

One in the corner got his Uzi up, and his finger went down on the trigger, spraying in the direction of the children. Chavez and Price both engaged him, then McTyler as well, and the terrorist went down in a crumpled mass.

Another had opened a door and raced through it, splattered by bullet fragments from a shooter whose aim was off and hit the door. This one ran down, away from the shooting, turning one corner, then another—and tried to stop when he saw a black shape on the steps.

It was Peter Covington, leading his team up. Covington had heard the noise of his steps and taken aim, then fired when the surprised-looking face entered his sights. Then he resumed his race topside, with four men behind him.

That left three in the room. Two hid behind desks, one holding his Uzi up and firing blindly. Mike Pierce jumped over the desk, twisting in midair as he did so, and shot him three times in the side and back. Then Pierce landed, turned back and fired another burst into the back of his head. The other one under a desk was shot in the back by Paddy Connolly. The one who was left stood, blazing away wildly with his weapon, only to be taken down by no fewer than four team members.

Just then the door opened, and Covington came in. Vega was circulating about, kicking the weapons away from every body, and after five seconds shouted: *"Clear!"*

"Clear!" Pierce agreed.

ANDRE was outside, in the open and all alone. He turned to look up at the castle.

"Dieter!" Homer Johnston called.

"Yes!"

"Can you take his weapon out?"

The German somehow read the American's mind. The answer was an exquisitely aimed shot that struck Andre's submachine gun just above the trigger guard. The impact of the .300 Winchester Magnum bullet blasted through the rough, stamped metal and broke the gun nearly in half. From his perch four hundred meters away, Johnston took careful aim, and fired his second round of the engagement. It would forever be regarded as a very bad shot. Half a second later, the 7-mm bullet struck the subject six inches below the sternum.

For Andre, it seemed like a murderously hard punch. Already the match bullet had fragmented, ripping his liver and spleen as it continued its passage, exiting his body above the left kidney. Then, following the shock of the initial impact, came a wave of pain. An instant later, his screech ripped across the 100 acres of Worldpark.

"CHECK this out," Chavez said in the command center. His body armor had two holes in the torso. They wouldn't have been fatal, but they would have hurt. "Thank God for DuPont, eh?"

"Miller Time!" Vega said with a broad grin.

"Command, this is Chavez. Mission accomplished. The kids—uh oh, we got one kid hurt here, looks like a scratch on the arm, the rest of 'em are all okay. Subjects all down for the count, Mr. C. You can turn the lights back on."

As Ding watched, Oso Vega leaned down and picked up a little girl. "Hello, *querida.* Let's find your *mamacita,* eh?"

"Rainbow!" Mike Pierce exulted. "Tell 'em there's a new sheriff in town, people!"

"Bloody right, Mike!" Eddie Price reached into his pocket and pulled out his pipe and a pouch of good Cavendish tobacco.

There were things to be done. Vega, Pierce, and Loiselle collected the weapons, safed them, and stacked them on a desk. McTyler and Connolly checked out the restrooms and other adjacent doors for additional terrorists, finding none. Scotty waved to the door.

"Okay, let's get the kids out," Ding told his people. "Peter, lead us out!"

Covington had his team open the fire door and man the stairway, one man on each landing. Vega took the lead, holding the five-year-old with his left arm while his right continued to hold his MP-10. A minute later, they were outside.

Chavez stayed behind, looking at the wall with Eddie Price. There were seven holes in the corner where the kids had been, but all the rounds were high, into the drywall paneling. "Lucky," Chavez said.

"Somewhat," Sergeant Major Price agreed. "That's the one we both engaged, Ding. He was just firing, not aiming—and maybe at us, not them, I think."

"Good job, Eddie."

"Indeed," Price agreed. With that they both walked outside, leaving the bodies behind for the police to collect.

▪ ▪ ▪

"COMMAND, this is Bear, what's happening, over."

"Mission accomplished, no friendlies hurt. Well done, Bear," Clark told him.

"Roger and thank you, sir. Bear is RTB. Out. I need to take a piss," the Marine told his copilot, as he horsed the Night Hawk west for the airfield.

HOMER Johnston fairly ran down the steps of the Dive Bomber ride, carrying his rifle and nearly tripping three times on the way down. Then he ran the few hundred meters to the castle. There was a doctor there, wearing a white coat and looking down at the man Johnston had shot.

"How is he?" the sergeant asked when he got there. It was pretty clear. The man's hands were holding his belly, and were covered with blood that looked strangely black in the courtyard lighting.

"He will not survive," Dr. Weiler said. Maybe if they were in a hospital operating room right now, he'd have a slim chance, but he was bleeding out through the lacerated spleen, and his liver was probably destroyed as well. . . . And so, no, absent a liver transplant, he had no chance at all, and all Weiler could do was give him morphine for the pain. He reached into his bag for a syringe.

"That's the one shot the little girl," Johnston told the doctor. "I guess my aim was a little off," he went on, looking down into the open eyes and the grimacing face that let loose another moaning scream. If he'd been a deer or an elk, Johnston would have finished him off with a pistol round in the head or neck, but you weren't supposed to do that with human targets. *Die slow, you fuck,* he didn't say aloud. It disappointed Johnston that the doctor gave him a pain injection, but physicians were sworn to their duty, as he was to his.

"Pretty low," Chavez said, coming up to the last living terrorist.

"Guess I slapped the trigger a little hard," the rifleman responded.

Chavez looked straight in his eyes. "Yeah, right. Get your gear."

"In a minute." The target's eyes went soft when the drug entered his bloodstream, but the hands still grabbed at the wound, and there was a puddle of blood spreading from under his back. Finally, the eyes looked up at Johnston one last time.

"Good night, Gracie," the rifleman said quietly. Ten seconds later, he was able to turn away and head back to the Dive Bomber to retrieve the rest of his gear.

There were a lot of soiled underpants in the medical office, and a lot of kids still wide-eyed in shock, having lived through a nightmare that all would relive for years to come. The Rainbow troopers fussed over them. One bandaged the only wound, a scratch really, on a young boy.

Centurion de la Cruz was still there, having refused evacuation. The troops in black stripped off their body armor and set it against the wall, and he saw on their uniform jackets the jump wings of paratroopers, American, British, and German, along with the satisfied look of soldiers who'd gotten the job done.

"Who are you?" he asked in Spanish.

"I'm sorry, I can't say," Chavez replied. "But I saw what you did on the videotape. You did well, Sergeant."

"So did you, ah? . . ."

"Chavez. Domingo Chavez."

"American?"

"Sí."

"The children, were any hurt?"

"Just the one over there."

"And the—criminals?"

"They will break no more laws, *amigo.* None at all," Team-2 Lead told him quietly.

"Bueno." De la Cruz reached up to take his hand. "It was hard?"

"It is always hard, but we train for the hard things, and my men are—"

"They have the look," de la Cruz agreed.

"So do you." Chavez turned. "Hey, guys, here's the one who took 'em on with a sword."

"Oh, yeah?" Mike Pierce came over. "I finished that one off for you. Ballsy move, man." Pierce took his hand and shook it. The rest of the troopers did the same.

"I must—I must—" De la Cruz stood and hobbled out the door. He came back in five minutes later, following John Clark, and holding—

"What the hell is that?" Chavez asked.

"The eagle of the legion, VI *Legio Victrix,"* the centurion told them, holding it in one hand. "The victorious legion. *Señor* Dennis, *con permiso?"*

"Yes, Francisco," the park manager said with a serious nod.

"With the respect of my legion, *Señor* Chavez. Keep this in a place of honor."

Ding took it. The damned thing must have weighed twenty pounds, plated as it was with gold. It would be a fit trophy for the club at Hereford. "We will do that, my friend," he promised the former sergeant, with a look at John Clark.

The stress was bleeding off now, to be followed as usual by elation and fatigue. The troopers looked at the kids they'd saved, still quiet and cowed by the night, but soon to be reunited with their parents. They heard the sound of a bus outside. Steve Lincoln opened the door, and watched the grown-ups leap out of it. He waved them through the door, and the shouts of joy filled the room.

"Time to leave," John said. He, too, walked over to shake hands with de la Cruz as the troops filed out.

Out in the open, Eddie Price had his own drill to complete. His pipe now filled, he took a kitchen match from his pocket and struck it on the stone wall of the medical office, lighting the curved briar pipe for a long, victorious puff as parents pushed in, and others pushed out, holding their children, many weeping at their deliverance.

Colonel Gamelin was standing by the bus and came over. "You are the Legion?" he asked.

Louis Loiselle handled the answer. "In a way, monsieur," he said in French. He looked up to see a surveillance camera pointed directly at the door, probably to record the event, the parents filing out with their kids, many pausing to shake hands with the Rainbow troopers. Then Clark led them off, back to the castle, and into the underground. On the way the Guardia Civil cops saluted, the gestures returned by the special-ops troopers.

CHAPTER 16

DISCOVERY

THE SUCCESSFUL CONCLUSION OF THE WORLDPARK operation turned out to be a problem for some, and one of them was Colonel Tomas Nuncio, the senior officer of the Guardia Civil on the scene. Assumed by the local media to be the officer in command of the operation, he was immediately besieged with requests for details of the operation, along with videotapes for the TV reporters. So successful had he been in isolating the theme park from press coverage that his superiors in Madrid themselves had little idea what had taken place, and this also weighed on his decision. So the colonel decided to release Worldpark's own video coverage, deeming this to be the most innocuous footage possible, as it showed very little. The most dramatic part had been the descent of the shooting team from the helicopter to the castle roof, and then from the roof of the castle to the control-room windows, and that, Nuncio decided, was pure vanilla, lasting a mere four minutes, the time required for Paddy Connolly to place his line charges on the window frames and move aside to detonate them. Nothing of the shooting inside the room had been taped, because the terrorists had themselves wrecked the surveillance camera inside the facility. The elimination of the castle-roof sentry had been taped, but was not released due to the gruesome nature of his head wound, and the same was true of the killing of the last of them, the one named Andre who had killed the little Dutch girl—which scene had also been recorded, but was withheld for the same reason. The rest was all let go. The distance of the cameras from the actual scene of action prevented the recognition, or even the sight of the faces of the rescue team, merely their jaunty steps outside, many of them carrying the rescued children—that, he decided, could harm or offend no one, least of all the special-operations team from England, who now had one of the *tricornio* hats from his force to go along with the eagle of Worldpark's notional VI Legion as a souvenir of their successful mission.

And so, the black-and-white video was released to CNN, Sky News, and other interested news agencies for broadcast around the world, to give substance to the commentary of various reporters who'd assembled at Worldpark's main gate, there to comment at great and erroneous length about the expertise of the Guardia Civil's special-action team dispatched from Madrid to resolve this hateful episode at one of the world's great theme parks.

It was eight o'clock in the evening when Dmitriy Arkadeyevich Popov saw it in his New York apartment, as he smoked a cigar and sipped a vodka neat while his VCR taped it for later detailed examination. The assault phase, he saw, was both expert and expected in all details. The flashes of light from the explosives used were dramatic and singularly useless for showing him anything, and the parade of the rescuers as predictable as the dawn, their springy steps, their slung weapons, and their arms full of small children. Well, such men would naturally feel elation at the successful conclusion of such a mission, and the trailing footage showed them walking off to a building, where there must have been a physician to take care of the one child who'd sustained a minor injury during the operation, as the reporters said. Then, later, the troops had come outside, and one of them had swiped an arm against the stone wall of the building, lighting a match, which he used . . .

. . . to light a pipe . . .

To light a pipe, Popov saw. He was surprised at his own reaction to that. He blinked hard, leaning forward in his seat. The camera didn't zoom in, but the soldier/policeman in question was clearly smoking a curved pipe, puffing the smoke out every few seconds as he spoke with his comrades . . . doing nothing dramatic, just talking unrecorded words calmly, as such men did after a successful mission, doubtless discussing who had done what, what had gone according to plan and what had not. It might as easily have been in a club or bar, for trained men always spoke the same way in those circumstances, whether they were soldiers or doctors or football players, after the stress of the job was concluded, and the lessons-learned phase began. It was the usual mark of professionals, Popov knew. Then the picture changed, back to the face of some American reporter who blathered on until the break for the next commercial, to be followed, the anchorman said, by some political development or other in Washington. With that, Popov rewound the tape, ejected it, and then reached for a different tape. He inserted it into the VCR, then fast-forwarded to the end of the incident in Bern, through the takedown phase and into the aftermath where . . . yes, a man had lit a pipe. He'd remembered that from watching from across the street, hadn't he?

Then he got the tape of the press coverage from the Vienna incident, and . . . yes, at the end a man had lit a pipe. In every case it was a man of about one hundred eighty centimeters in height, making much the same gesture with the match, holding the pipe in exactly the same way, gesturing to another with it in exactly the same manner, the way men did with pipes . . .

". . . ahh, *nichevo,*" the intelligence officer said to himself in the expensive high-rise apartment. He spent another half an hour, cueing and rerunning the tapes. The clothing was the same in every case. The man the same size, the same gestures and body language, the same weapons slung the same way, the same *everything,* the former KGB officer saw. And that meant the same man . . . in three separate countries.

But this man was not Swiss, not Austrian, and not Spanish. Next Popov backed off his deductive thoughts, searching for other facts he could discern from the visual information he had there. There were other people visible in all the tapes. The pipe smoker was often attended by another man, shorter than he, to whom the pipe smoker appeared to speak with some degree of friendly deference. There was another around, a large, muscular one who in two of the tapes carried a heavy machine gun, but in the third, carrying a child, did not. So, he had two and maybe a third man on the tapes who had appeared in Bern, Vienna, and Spain. In every case, the reporters had credited the rescue to local police, but no, that wasn't the truth, was it? So, who were these people who arrived with the speed and decisiveness of a thunderbolt—in *three* different countries . . . twice to conclude operations that he had initiated, and once to settle one begun by others—and who they had been, he didn't know nor especially care. The reporters said that they'd demanded the release of his old friend, the Jackal. What fools. The French would as soon toss Napoleon's corpse from Les Invalides as give up that murderer. Il'ych Ramirez Sanchez, named with Lenin's own patronymic by his communist father. Popov shook that thought off. He'd just discovered something of great importance. Somewhere in Europe was a special-operations team that crossed international borders as easily as a businessman flying in an airliner, that had freedom to operate in different countries, that displaced and did the work of local police . . . and did it well, expertly . . . and this operation would not hurt them, would it? Their prestige and international acceptability would only grow from the rescue of the children at Worldpark . . .

"Nichevo," he whispered to himself again. He'd learned something of great importance this night, and to celebrate he poured himself another vodka.

Now he had to follow it up. How? He'd think that one over, sleeping on the thought, trusting his trained brain to come up with something.

THEY were nearly home already. The MC-130 had picked them up and flown the now relaxed team back to Hereford, their weapons re-packed in the plastic carrying cases, their demeanor not the least bit tense. Some of the men were cutting up. Others were explaining what they'd done to team members who'd not had the chance to participate directly. Mike Pierce, Clark saw, was especially animated in his conversation with his neighbor. He was now the Rainbow kill-leader. Homer Johnston was chatting with Weber—they'd come to some sort of deal, something agreed between them. Weber had taken a beautiful but out-of-policy shot to disable the terrorist's Uzi, allowing Johnston to—of course, John told himself, he didn't just want to kill the bastard who'd murdered the little girl. He'd wanted to *hurt* the little prick, to send him off to hell with a special, personal message. He'd have to talk to Sergeant Johnston about that. It was outside of Rainbow policy. It was unprofessional. Just killing the bastards was enough. You could always trust God to handle the special treatment. But—well, John told himself he could understand that, couldn't he? There had once been that little bastard called Billy to whom he'd given a very special interrogation in a recompression chamber, and though he remembered it with a measure of pain and shame, at the time he'd felt it justified . . . and he'd gotten the information he'd needed at the time, hadn't he? Even so, he'd have to talk with Homer, advise him never to do such a thing again. And Homer would listen, John knew. He'd exorcised the demons once, and once, usually, was enough. It must have been hard for him to sit at his rifle, watching the murder of a child, the power to avenge her instantly right there in his skilled hands, and yet do nothing. *Could* you *have done that, John?* Clark asked himself, not really knowing what the answer was in his current, exhausted state. He felt the wheels thump down on the Hereford runway, and the props roar into reverse pitch to slow the aircraft.

Well, John thought, his idea, his concept for Rainbow was working out rather well, wasn't it? Three deployments, three clean missions. Two hostages killed, one before his team deployed to Bern, the other just barely after their arrival in the park, neither one the result of negligence or mistake on the part of his men. Their mission performance had been as nearly perfect as anything he'd ever seen. Even his fellow animals of 3rd SOG in Vietnam hadn't been this good, and *that* was something he'd *never* expected to say or even think. The thought came suddenly, and just as unexpectedly came the near-need for tears, that he might have the honor to command such warriors as these, to send them out and bring them back as they were now, smiling as they stood, hoisting their gear on their shoulders and walking to the open rear cargo door on the Herky Bird, behind which waited their trucks. His men.

"The bar is open!" Clark called to them, when he stood.

"A little late, John," Alistair observed.

"If the door's locked, we'll have Paddy blow it," Clark insisted, with a vicious grin.

Stanley considered that and nodded. "Quite so, the lads have earned a pint or two each." Besides which, he knew how to pick locks.

They walked into the club still wearing their ninja suits, and found the barman waiting. There were a few others in the club as well, mainly SAS troopers sipping at their last-call pints. Several of them applauded when the Rainbow team came in, which warmed the room. John walked to the bar, leading his men and ordering beer for all.

"I do love this stuff," Mike Pierce said a minute later, taking his Guinness and sipping through the thin layer of foam.

"Two, Mike?" Clark asked.

"Yeah." He nodded. "The one at the desk, he was on the phone. Tap-tap," Pierce said, touching two fingers to the side of his head. "Then another one, shooting from behind a desk. I jumped over and gave him three on the fly. Landed, rolled, and three more in the back of the head. So long, Charlie. Then one more, got a piece of him, along with Ding and Eddie. Ain't supposed to like this part of the job. I know that—but, Jesus, it felt good to take those fuckers down. Killin' kids, man. Not good. Well, they ain't gonna be doing anymore of that, sir. Not with the new sheriff in town."

"Well, nice going, Mr. Marshal," John replied, with a raised-glass salute. There'd be no nightmares about this one, Clark thought, sipping his own dark beer. He looked around. In the corner, Weber and Johnston were talking, the latter with his hand on the former's shoulder, doubtless thanking him for the fine shot to disable the murderer's Uzi. Clark walked over and stood next to the two sergeants.

"I know, boss," Homer said, without being told anything. "Never again, but goddamn, it felt good."

"Like you said, never again, Homer."

"Yes, sir. Slapped the trigger a little hard," Johnston said, to cover his ass in an official sense.

"Bullshit," Rainbow Six observed. "I'll accept it—just this once. And you, Dieter, nice shot, but—"

"Nie wieder. Herr General. I know, sir." The German nodded his submission

to the moment. "Homer, *Junge,* the look on his face when you hit him. *Ach,* that was something to see, my friend. Good for the one on the castle roof, too."

"Easy shot," Johnston said dismissively. "He was standing still. Zap. Easier 'n throwing darts, pal."

Clark patted both on the shoulder and wandered over to Chavez and Price.

"Did you have to land on my arm?" Ding complained lightly.

"So, next time, come through the window straight, not at an angle."

"Right." Chavez took a long sip of the Guinness.

"How'd it go?" John asked them.

"Aside from being hit twice, not bad," Chavez replied. "I have to get a new vest, though." Once hit, the vests were considered to be ruined for further use. This one would go back to the manufacturer for study to see how it had performed. "Which one was that, you think, Eddie?"

"The last one, I think, the one who just stood and sprayed at the children."

"Well, that was the plan, for us to stop those rounds, and that one went down hard. You, me, Mike, and Oso, I think, took him apart." Whatever cop had recovered that body would need a blotter and a freezer bag to collect the spilled brains.

"That we did," Price agreed as Julio came over.

"Hey, that was okay, guys!" First Sergeant Vega told them, pleased to have finally participated in a field operation.

"Since when do we punch our targets?" Chavez asked.

Vega looked a little embarrassed. "Instinct, he was so close. You know, probably could have taken him alive, but—well, nobody ever told me to do that, y'know?"

"That's cool, Oso. That wasn't part of the mission, not with a room full of kids."

Vega nodded. "What I figured, and the shot was pretty automatic, too, just playin' like we practice, man. Anyway, that one went down real good, *jefe.*"

"Any problem on the window?" Price wanted to know.

Vega shook his head. "Nah, gave it a good kick, and it moved just fine. Bumped a shoulder coming through the frame, but no problems there. I was pretty pumped. But you know, you shoulda had me cover the kids. I'm bigger, I woulda stopped more bullets."

Chavez didn't say that he'd worried about Vega's agility—wrongly, as it had turned out. An important lesson learned. Bulky as Oso was, he moved lightly on his feet, far more so than Ding had expected. The bear could dance pretty well, though at 225 pounds, he was a little large for a tutu.

"Fine operation," Bill Tawney said, joining the group.

"Anything develop?"

"We have a possible identification on one of them, the chap who killed the child. The French ran the photo through some police informants, and they think it might be an Andre Herr, Parisian by birth, thought to be a stringer for Action Directe once upon a time, but nothing definite. More information is on the way, they say. The whole set of photos and fingerprints from Spain is on its way to Paris now for follow-up investigation. Not all of the photos will be very useful, I am told."

"Yeah, well, a burst of hollowpoints will rearrange a guy's face, man," Chavez observed with a chuckle. "Not a hell of a lot we can do about that."

"So, who initiated the operation?" Clark asked.

Tawney shrugged. "Not a clue at this point. That's for the French police to investigate."

"Would be nice to know. We've had three incidents since we got here. Isn't that a lot?" Chavez asked, suddenly very serious.

"It is," the intelligence officer agreed. "It would not have been ten or fifteen years ago, but things had quieted down recently." Another shrug. "Could be mere coincidence, or perhaps copycatting, but—"

"Copycat? I shouldn't think so, sir," Eddie Price observed. "We've given bloody little encouragement to any terr' who has ambitions, and today's operation ought to have a further calming effect on those people."

"That makes sense to me," Ding agreed. "Like Mike Pierce said, there's a new sheriff in town, and the word on the street ought to be 'don't fuck with him' even if people think we're just local cops with an attitude. Take it a step further, Mr. C."

"Go public?" Clark shook his head. "That's never been part of the plan, Domingo."

"Well, if the mission's to take the bastards down in the field, that's one thing. If the mission is to make these bastards think twice about raising hell—to stop terrorist incidents from happening at all—then it's another thing entirely. The idea of a new sheriff in town might just take the starch out of their backs and put them back to washing cars, or whatever the hell they do when they're not being bad. Deterrence, we call it, when nation-states do it. Will it work on a terrorist mentality? Something to talk with Doc Bellow about, John," Chavez concluded.

And again Chavez had surprised him, Clark realized. Three straight successes, all of them covered on the TV news, might well have an effect on the surviving terrorists in Europe or elsewhere with lingering ambitions, mightn't it? And that *was* something to talk to Paul Bellow about. But it was much too soon for anyone on the team to be that optimistic . . . probably, John told himself with a thoughtful sip. The party was just beginning to break up. It had been a very long day for the Rainbow troopers, and one by one they set their glasses down on the bar, which ought to have closed some time before, and headed for the door for the walk to their homes. Another day and another mission had ended. Yet another day had already begun, and in only a few hours, they'd be awakened to run and exercise and begin another day of routine training.

"WERE you planning to leave us?" the jailer asked Inmate Sanchez in a voice dripping with irony.

"What do you mean?" Carlos responded.

"Some colleagues of yours misbehaved yesterday," the prison guard responded, tossing a copy of *Le Figaro* through the door. "They will not do so again."

The photo on the front page was taken off the Worldpark video, the quality miserably poor, but clear enough to show a soldier dressed in black carrying a child, and the first paragraph of the story told the tale. Carlos scanned it, sitting on his prison bed to read the piece in detail, then felt a depth of black despair that he'd not thought possible. Someone had heard his plea, he realized, and it had come to nothing. Life in this stone cage beckoned as he looked up to the sun coming in the single window. Life. It would be a long one, probably a healthy one, and certainly a bleak one. His hands crumpled the paper when he'd finished the article. Damn the Spanish police. Damn the world.

"YES, I saw it on the news last night," he said into the phone as he shaved.

"I need to see you. I have something to show you, sir," Popov's voice said, just after seven in the morning.

The man thought about that. Popov was a clever bastard who'd done his jobs without much in the way of questions . . . and there was little in the way of a paper trail, certainly nothing his lawyers couldn't handle if it came to that, and it wouldn't. There were ways of dealing with Popov, too, if it came to that.

"Okay, be there at eight-fifteen."

"Yes, sir," the Russian said, hanging up.

PETE was in real agony now, Killgore saw. It was time to move him. This he ordered at once, and two orderlies came in dressed in upgraded protective gear to load the wino onto a gurney for transport to the clinical side. Killgore followed them and his patient. The clinical side was essentially a duplication of the room in which the street bums had lounged and drunk their booze, waiting unknowingly for the onset of symptoms. He now had them all, to the point that booze and moderate doses of morphine no longer handled the pain. The orderlies loaded Pete onto a bed, next to which was an electronically operated "Christmas tree" medication dispenser. Killgore handled the stick, and got the IV plugged into Pete's major vein. Then he keyed the electronic box, and seconds later, the patient relaxed with a large bolus of medication. The eyes went sleepy and the body relaxed while the Shiva continued to eat him alive from the inside out. Another IV would be set up to feed him with nutrients to keep his body going, along with various drugs to see if any of them had an unexpectedly beneficial effect on the Shiva. They had a whole roomful of such drugs, ranging from antibiotics—which were expected to be useless against this viral infection—to Interleukin-2 and a newly developed -3a, which, some thought, might help, plus tailored Shiva antibodies taken from experimental animals. None were expected to work, but all had to be tested to make sure they didn't, lest there be a surprise out there when the epidemic spread. Vaccine-B was expected to work, and that was being tested now with the new control group of people kidnapped from Manhattan bars, along with the notional Vaccine-A, whose purpose was rather different from -B. The nanocapsules developed on the other side of the house would come in very handy indeed.

AS was being demonstrated even as he had the thought, looking down at Pete's dying body. Subject F4, Mary Bannister, felt sick to her stomach, just a mild queasiness at this point, but didn't think much of it. That sort of thing happened, and she didn't feel all that bad, some antacids would probably help, and those she got from her medicine cabinet, which was pretty well stocked with over-the-counter medications. Other than that, she felt pretty mellow, as she smiled at herself in the mirror and liked what she saw, a youngish, attractive woman wearing pink silk jammies. With that thought, she walked out of her room, her hair glossy and a spring in her step. Chip was in the sitting room, reading a magazine slowly on the couch, and she made straight for him and sat down beside him.

"Hi, Chip." She smiled.

"Hi, Mary." He smiled back, reaching to touch her hand.

"I upped the Valium in her breakfast," Barbara Archer said in the control room, zooming the camera in. "Along with the other one." The other one was an inhibition reducer.

"You look nice today," Chip told her, his words imperfectly captured by the hidden shotgun microphone.

"Thank you." Another smile.

"She looks pretty dreamy."

"She ought to be," Barbara observed coldly. "There's enough in her to make a nun shuck her habit and get it on."

"What about him?"

"Oh, yeah—didn't give him any steroids." Dr. Archer had a little chuckle at that.

In proof of which, Chip leaned over to kiss Mary on the lips. They were alone in the sitting room.

"How's her blood work look, Barb?"

"Loaded with antibodies, and starting to get some small bricks. She ought to be symptomatic in another few days."

"Eat, drink, and be merry, people, for next week, you die," the other physician told the TV screen.

"Too bad," Dr. Archer agreed. She showed the emotion one might display on seeing a dead dog at the side of the road.

"Nice figure," the man said, as the pajama tops came off. "I haven't seen an X-rated movie in a long time, Barb." A videotape was running, of course. The experimental protocol was set in stone. Everything had to be recorded so that the staff could monitor the entire test program. *Nice tits,* he thought, about the same time Chip did, right before he caressed them on the screen.

"She was fairly inhibited when she got here. The tranquilizers really work, depressing them that way." Another clinical observation. Things progressed rapidly from that point on. Both doctors sipped their coffee as they watched. Tranquilizers or not, the baser human instincts charged forward, and within five minutes Chip and Mary were humping madly away, with the usual sound effects, though the picture, blessedly, wasn't all that clear. A few minutes later, they were lying side by side on the thick shag rug, kissing tiredly and contentedly, his hand stroking her breasts, his eyes closed, his breathing deep and regular as he rolled onto his back.

"Well, Barb, if nothing else, we have a pretty good weekend getaway for couples here," the man observed with a sly grin. "How long do you figure on his blood work?"

"Three or four days until he starts showing antibodies, probably." Chip hadn't been exposed in the shower as Mary had.

"What about the vaccine testers?"

"Five with -A. We have three left as uncontaminated controls for -B testing."

"Oh? Who are we letting live?"

"M2, M3, and F9," Dr. Archer replied. "They seem to have proper attitudes. One's a member of the Sierra Club, would you believe? The others like it outdoors, and they should be okay with what we're doing."

"Political criteria for scientific tests—what *are* we coming to?" the man asked with another chuckle.

"Well, if they're going to live, they might as well be people we can get along with," Archer observed.

"True." A nod. "How confident are you with -B?"

"Very. I expect it to be about ninety-seven percent effective, perhaps a little better," she added conservatively.

"But not a hundred?"

"No, Shiva's a little too nasty for that," Archer told him. "The animal testing is a little crude, I admit, but the results follow the computer model almost exactly, well within the testing-error criteria. Steve's been pretty good on that side."

"Berg's pretty smart," the other doctor agreed. Then he shifted in his chair. "You know, Barb, what we're doing here isn't exactly—"

"I know that," she assured him. "But we all knew that coming in."

"True." He nodded submission, annoyed at himself for the second thoughts. Well, his family would survive, and they all shared his love of the world and its many sorts of inhabitants. Still, these two people on the TV, they were *humans,* just like himself, and he'd just peeped in on them like some sort of pervert. Oh, yeah, they'd only done it because both were loaded with drugs fed to them through their food or in pill form, but they were both sentenced to death and—

"Relax, will you?" Archer said, looking at his face and reading his mind. "At least they're getting a little love, aren't they? That's a hell of a lot more than the rest of the world'll get—"

"I won't have to watch *them.*" Being a voyeur wasn't his idea of fun, and he'd told himself often enough that he wouldn't have to watch what he'd be helping to start.

"No, but we'll know about it. It'll be on the TV news, won't it? But then it *will* be too late, and if *they* find out, their last conscious act will be to come after us. That's the part that has me worried."

"The Project enclave in Kansas is pretty damned secure, Barb," the man assured her. "The one in Brazil's even more so." Which was where he'd be going eventually. The rain forest had always fascinated him.

"Could be better," Barbara Archer thought.

"The world isn't a laboratory, doctor, remember?" Wasn't *that* what the whole Shiva project was about, for Christ's sake? Christ? he wondered. Well, another idea that had to be set aside. He wasn't cynical enough to invoke the name of God into what they were doing. Nature, perhaps, which wasn't *quite* the same thing, he thought.

"GOOD morning, Dmitriy," he said, coming into his office early.

"Good morning, sir," the intelligence officer said, rising to his feet as his employer entered the anteroom. It was a European custom, harkening back to royalty, and one that had somehow conveyed itself to the Marxist state that had nurtured and trained the Russian now living in New York.

"What do you have for me?" the boss asked, unlocking his office door and going in.

"Something very interesting," Popov said. "How important it is I am not certain. You can better judge that than I can."

"Okay, let's see it." He sat down and turned in his swivel chair to flip on his office coffee machine.

Popov went to the far wall, and slid back the panel that covered the electronics equipment in the woodwork. He retrieved the remote control and keyed up the large-screen TV and VCR. Then he inserted a videocassette.

"This is the news coverage of Bern," he told his employer. The tape only ran for thirty seconds before he stopped it, ejected the cassette, and inserted another. "Vienna," he said then, hitting the PLAY button. Another segment, which ran less than a minute. This he also ejected. "Last night at the park in Spain." This one he also played. This segment lasted just over a minute before he stopped it.

"Yes?" the man said, when it was all over.

"What did you see, sir?"

"Some guys smoking—the same guy, you're saying?"

"Correct. In all three incidents, the same man, or so it would appear."

"Go on," his employer told Popov.

"The same special-operations group responded to and terminated all three incidents. That is very interesting."

"Why?"

Popov took a patient breath. This man may have been a genius in some areas, but in others he was a babe in the woods. "Sir, the same team responded to incidents in *three* separate countries, with *three* separate national police forces, and in all *three* cases, this special team took over from those *three* separate national police agencies and dealt with the situation. In other words, there is now some special internationally credited team of special-operations troops—I would expect them to be military rather than policemen—currently operating in Europe. Such a group has never been admitted to in the open press. It is, therefore, a 'black' group, highly secret. I can speculate that it is a NATO team of some sort, but that is only speculation. Now," Popov went on, "I have some questions for you."

"Okay." The boss nodded.

"Did you know of this team? Did you know they existed?"

A shake of the head. "No." Then he turned to pour a cup of coffee.

"Is it possible for you to find out some things about them?"

A shrug. "Maybe. Why is it important?"

"That depends on another question—why are you paying me to incite terrorists to do things?" Popov asked.

"You do not have a need to know that, Dmitriy."

"Yes, sir, I do have such a need. One cannot stage operations against sophisticated opposition without having some idea of the overall objective. It simply cannot be done, sir. Moreover, you have applied significant assets to these operations. There must be a point. I need to know what it is." The unspoken part, which got through the words, was that he wanted to know, and in due course, he might well figure it out, whether he was told or not.

It also occurred to his employer that his existence was somewhat in pawn to this Russian ex-spook. He could deny everything the man might say in an open public forum, and he even had the ability to make the man disappear, an option less attractive than it appeared outside of a movie script, since Popov might well have told others, or even left a written record.

The bank accounts from which Popov had drawn the funds he'd distributed were thoroughly laundered, of course, but there *was* a trail of sorts that a very clever and thorough investigator *might* be able to trace back closely enough to him to cause some minor concern. The problem with electronic banking was that there was always a trail of electrons, and bank records were both time-stamped and amount-specific, enough to make some connection appear to exist. That could be an embarrassment of large or small order. Worse, it wasn't something he could easily afford, but a hindrance to the larger mission now under way in places as diverse as New York, Kansas, and Brazil. And Australia, of course, which was the whole point of what he was doing.

"Dmitriy, will you let me think about that?"

"Yes, sir. Of course. I merely say that if you want me to do my job effectively, I need to know more. Surely you have other people in your confidence.

Show these tapes to those people and see if they think the information is significant." Popov stood. "Call me when you need me, sir."

"Thanks for the information." He waited for the door to close, then dialed a number from memory. The phone rang four times before it was answered:

"Hi," a voice said in the earpiece. "You've reached the home of Bill Henriksen. Sorry, I can't make it to the phone right now. Why don't you try my office."

"Damn," the executive said. Then he had an idea, and picked up the remote for his TV. CBS, no, NBC, no . . .

"But to kill a sick child," the host said on ABC's *Good Morning, America.*

"Charlie, a long time ago, a guy named Lenin said that the purpose of terrorism was to terrorize. That's who they are, and that's what they do. It's still a dangerous world out there, maybe even more so today that there are no nation-states who, though they used to support terrorists, actually imposed some restraints on their behavior. Those restraints are gone now," Henriksen said. "This group reportedly wanted their old friend Carlos the Jackal released from prison. Well, it didn't work, but it's worth noting that they cared enough to try a classic terrorist mission, to secure the release of one of their own. Fortunately, the mission failed, thanks to the Spanish police."

"How would you evaluate the police performance?"

"Pretty good. They all train out of the same playbook, of course, and the best of them cross-train at Fort Bragg or at Hereford in England, and other places, Germany and Israel, for example."

"But one hostage was murdered."

"Charlie, you can't stop them all," the expert said sadly. "You can be ten feet away with a loaded weapon in your hands, and sometimes you can't take action, because to do so would only get more hostages killed. I'm as sickened by that murder as you are, my friend, but these people won't be doing any more of that."

"Well, thanks for coming in. Bill Henriksen, president of Global Security and a consultant to ABC on terrorism. It's forty-six minutes after the hour." Cut to commercial.

In his desk he had Bill's beeper number. This he called, keying in his private line. Four minutes later, the phone rang.

"Yeah, John, what is it?" There was street noise on the cellular phone. Henriksen must have been outside the ABC studio, just off Central Park West, probably walking to his car.

"Bill, I need to see you in my office ASAP. Can you come right down?"

"Sure. Give me twenty minutes."

Henriksen had a clicker to get into the building's garage, and access to one of the reserved spaces. He walked into the office eighteen minutes after the call.

"What gives?"

"Caught you on TV this morning."

"They always call me in on this stuff," Henriksen said. "Great job taking the bastards down, least from what the TV footage showed. I'll get the rest of it."

"Oh?"

"Yeah, I have the right contacts. The video they released was edited down quite a bit. My people'll get all the tapes from the Spanish—it isn't classified in any way—for analysis."

"Watch this," John told him, flipping his office TV to the VCR and running the released tape of Worldpark. Then he had to rise and switch to the cassette of Vienna. Thirty seconds of that and then Bern. "So, what do you think?"

"The same team on all three?" Henriksen wondered aloud. "Sure does look like it—but who the hell are they?"

"You know who Popov is, right?"

Bill nodded. "Yeah, the KGB guy you found. Is he the guy who twigged to this?"

"Yep." A nod. "Less than an hour ago, he was in here to show me these tapes. It worries him. Does it worry you?"

The former FBI agent grimaced. "Not sure. I'd want to know more about them first."

"Can you find out?"

This time he shrugged. "I can talk to some contacts, rattle a few bushes. Thing is, if there is a really black special-ops team out there, I should have known about it already. I mean, I've got the contacts throughout the business. What about you?"

"I can probably try a few things, quietly. Probably mask it as plain curiosity."

"Okay, I can check around. What else did Popov say to you?"

"He wants to know why I'm having him do the things."

"That's the problem with spooks. They like to know things. I mean, he's thinking, what if he starts a mission and one of the subjects gets taken alive. Very often they sing like fucking canaries once they're in custody, John. If one fingers him, he could be in the shitter. Unlikely, I admit, but possible, and spooks are trained to be cautious."

"What if we have to take him out?"

Another grimace. "You want to be careful doing that, in case he's left a package with a friend somewhere. No telling if he has, but I'd have to assume he's done it. Like I said, they're trained to be cautious. This operation is not without its dangers, John. We knew that going in. How close are we to having the technical—"

"Very close. The test program is moving along nicely. Another month or so and we'll know all we need to know."

"Well, all I have to do is get the contract for Sydney. I'm flying down tomorrow. These incidents won't hurt."

"Who will you be working with?"

"The Aussies have their own SAS. It's supposed to be small—pretty well-trained, but short on the newest hardware. That's the hook I plan to use. I got what they need, at cost," Henriksen emphasized. "Run that tape again, the one of the Spanish job," he said.

John rose from his desk, inserted the tape, and rewound it back to the beginning of the released TV coverage. It showed the assault team zip-lining down from the helicopter.

"Shit, I missed that!" the expert admitted.

"What?"

"We need to have the tape enhanced, but that doesn't look like a police chopper. It's a Sikorsky H-60."

"So?"

"So, the -60 has never been certified for civilian use. See how it's got POLICE painted on the side? That's a civilian application. It isn't a police chopper, John. It's military . . . and if this is a refueling probe," he said, pointing, "then it's a special-ops bird. *That* means U.S. Air Force, man. That also tells us where these people are based—"

"Where?"

"England. The Air Force has a special-ops wing based in Europe, part in Germany, part in England . . . MH-60K, I think the designation of the chopper is, made for combat search-and-rescue and getting people into special places to do special things. Hey, your friend Popov is right. There *is* a special bunch of people handling these things, and they've got American support at least, maybe a lot more. Thing is, who the hell are they?"

"It's important?"

"Potentially, yes. What if the Aussies call them in to help out on the job I'm trying to get, John? That could screw up the whole thing."

"You rattle your bushes. I'll rattle mine."

"Right."

CHAPTER 17

BUSHES

PETE NOW HAD SIX FRIENDS IN THE TREATMENT center. Only two of the subjects felt well enough now to remain in the open bay with the TV cartoons and the whiskey, and Killgore figured they'd be in here by the end of the week, so full was their blood with Shiva antibodies. It was odd how the disease attacked different people in such different ways, but everyone had a different immune system. That was why some people got cancer, and others did not despite smoking and other methods of self-abuse.

Aside from that, it was going easier than he'd expected. He supposed it was due to the high doses of morphine that had all of them pretty well zonked out. It was a relatively new discovery in medicine that there really wasn't a maximum safe dosage of painkillers. If the patient still felt pain, you could give more until it went away. Dose levels that would cause respiratory arrest in healthy people were perfectly safe for those in great pain, and that made his job far easier. Every drug-dispensing machine had a button the subjects could hit if they needed it, and so they were medicating themselves into peaceful oblivion, which also made things safer for the staffs, who didn't have to do all that many sticks. They hung nutrients on the trees, checked to make sure the IVs were secure, and avoided touching the subjects as much as possible. Later today, they'd all get injected with Vaccine-B, which was supposed to safeguard them against Shiva with a high degree of reliability—Steve Berg said 98 to 99 percent. They all knew that wasn't the same as 100 percent, though, and so the protective measures would be continued.

Agreeably, there was little sympathy for the subjects. Picking winos off the street had been a good call. The next set of test subjects would appear more sympathetic, but everyone in this side of the building had been fully briefed. Much of what they did might be distasteful, but it would still be done.

"YOU know, sometimes I think the Earth First people are right," Kevin Mayflower said in the Palm restaurant.

"Oh? How so?" Carol Brightling asked.

The president of the Sierra Club looked into his wine. "We destroy everything we touch. The shores, the tidal wetlands, the forests—look at what 'civilization' has done to them all. Oh, sure, we preserve some areas—and that's what? A hot three percent, maybe? Big fucking deal. We're poisoning everything, including ourselves. The ozone problem is really getting worse, according to the new NASA study."

"Yeah, but did you hear about the proposed fix?" the President's science advisor asked.

"Fix? How?"

She grimaced. "Well, you get a bunch of jumbo jets, fill them up with ozone, fly them out of Australia, and release ozone at high altitude to patch it up. I have that proposal on my desk right now."

"And?"

"And it's like doing abortions at half-time in a football game, with instant replay and color commentary. No way it can possibly work. We have to let the planet heal herself—but we won't, of course."

"Any more good news?"

"Oh, yeah, the CO_2 issue. There's a guy up at Harvard who says if we dump iron filings into the Indian Ocean, we can encourage the growth of phytoplankton, and that will fix the CO_2 problem almost overnight. The math looks pretty good. All these geniuses who say they can fix the planet, like she needs fixing—instead of leaving her the hell alone."

"And the President says what?" Mayflower asked.

"He says for me to tell him if it'll work or not, and if it looks like it's going to work, then test it to make sure, then try it for real. He hasn't got a clue, and he doesn't listen." She didn't add that she had to follow his orders whether she liked them or not.

"Well, maybe our friends at Earth First are right, Carol. Maybe we are a parasitic species on the face of the earth, and maybe we're going to destroy the whole damned planet before we're done."

"Rachel Carson come to life, eh?" she asked.

"Look, you know the science as well as I do—maybe better. We're doing things like—like the Alvarez Event that took the dinosaurs out, except we're doing it willfully. It took how long for the planet to recover from that?"

"Alvarez? The planet *didn't* recover, Kevin," Carol Brightling pointed out. "It jump-started mammals—*us,* remember? The preexisting ecological order never returned. Something new happened, and that took a couple of million years just to stabilize." Must have been something to see, she told herself. To watch something like that in progress, what a scientific and personal blessing it must have been, but there'd probably been nobody back then to appreciate it. Unlike today.

"Well, in a few more years we'll get to see the first part of it, won't we? How many more species will we kill off this year, and if the ozone situation keeps getting worse—my God, Carol, why don't people get it? Don't they *see* what's happening? Don't they *care?"*

"Kevin, no, they don't see, and, no, they don't care. Look around." The restaurant was filled with important people wearing important-looking clothes, doubtless discussing important things over their important dinners, none of which had a thing to do with the planetary crisis that hung quite literally over all their heads. If the ozone layer really evaporated, as it might, well, they'd start using sunblock just to walk the streets, and maybe that would protect them enough . . . but what of the natural species, the birds, the lizards, all the creatures on the planet who had no such option? The studies suggested that their eyes would be seared by the unblocked ultraviolet radiation, which would kill them off, and so the entire global ecosystem would rapidly come apart. "Do you think any of these people know about it—or give a damn if they do?"

"I suppose not." He sipped down some more of his white wine. "Well, we keep plugging away, don't we?"

"It's funny," she went on. "Not too long ago we fought wars, which kept the population down enough that we couldn't damage the planet all that much—but now peace is breaking out all over, and we're advancing our industrial capacity, and so, peace is destroying us a lot more efficiently than war ever did. Ironic, isn't it?"

"And modern medicine. The anopheles mosquito was pretty good at keeping the numbers down—you know that Washington was once a malarial swamp, diplomats deemed it a hazardous-duty post! So then we invented DDT. Good for controlling mosquitoes, but tough on the peregrine falcon. We never get it right. Never," Mayflower concluded.

"What if? . . ." she asked wistfully.

"What if what, Carol?"

"What if nature came up with something to knock the human population back?"

"The Gaea Hypothesis?" That made him smile. The idea was that the earth was itself a thinking, self-correcting organism that found ways to regulate the numerous living species that populated the planet. "Even if that's valid—and I hope it is, really—I'm afraid that we humans move too fast for Gaea to deal with us and our work. No, Carol, we've created a suicide pact, and we're going to take down everything else with us, and a hundred years from now, when the human population worldwide is down to a million or so people, they'll know what went wrong and read the books and look at the videotapes of the paradise we once had, and they'll curse our names—and maybe, if they're lucky, they'll learn from it when they crawl back up from the slime. Maybe. I doubt it. Even if they try to learn, they'll worry more about building nuclear-power reactors so they can use their electric toothbrushes. Rachel was right. There will be a Silent Spring someday, but then it'll be too late." He picked at his salad, wondering what chemicals were in the lettuce and tomatoes. Some, he was sure. This time of year, the lettuce came up from Mexico, where farmers did all sorts of things to their crops, and maybe the kitchen help had washed it off, but maybe not, and so here he was, eating an expensive lunch and poisoning himself as surely as he was watching the whole planet being poisoned. His quietly despairing look told the tale.

He was ready to be recruited, Carol Brightling thought. It was time. And he'd bring some good people with him, and they'd have room for them in Kansas and Brazil. Half an hour later, she took her leave, and headed back to the White House for the weekly cabinet meeting.

"HEY, Bill," Gus said from his office in the Hoover Building. "What's happening?"

"Catch the TV this morning?" Henriksen asked.

"You mean the thing in Spain?" Werner asked.

"Yep."

"Sure did. I saw you on the tube, too."

"My genius act." He chuckled. "Well, it's good for business, you know?"

"Yeah, I suppose it is. Anyway, what about it?"

"That wasn't the Spanish cops, Gus. I know how they train. Not their style, man. So, who was it, Delta, SAS, HRT?"

Gus Werner's eyes narrowed. Now Assistant Director of the FBI, he'd once been the special agent in charge of the FBI's elite Hostage Rescue Team. Promoted out, he'd been Special Agent in Charge of the Atlanta field division, and now was the AD in charge of the new Terrorism Division. Bill Henriksen had once worked for him, then left the Bureau to start his own consulting company, but once FBI always FBI, and so now, Bill was fishing for information.

"I really can't talk much about that one, buddy."

"Oh?"

"Oh? Yes. Can't discuss," Werner said tersely.

"Classification issues?"

"Something like that," Werner allowed.

A chuckle: "Well, that tells me something, eh?"

"No, Bill, it doesn't tell you anything at all. Hey, man, I can't break the rules, you know."

"You always were a straight shooter," Henriksen agreed. "Well, whoever they are, glad they're on our side. The takedown looked pretty good on TV."

"That it did." Werner had the complete set of tapes, transmitted via encrypted satellite channel from the U.S. Embassy in Madrid to the National Security Agency, and from there to FBI headquarters. He'd seen the whole thing, and expected to have more data that afternoon.

"Tell them one thing, though, if you get a chance."

"What's that, Bill?" was the noncommittal response.

"If they want to look like the local cops, they ought not use a USAF helicopter. I'm not stupid, Gus. The reporters might not catch it, but it was pretty obvious to somebody with half a brain, wasn't it?"

Oops, Werner thought. He'd actually allowed that one to slip through his mental cracks, but Bill had never been a dummy, and he wondered how the news media had failed to notice it.

"Oh?"

"Don't give me that, Gus. It was a Sikorsky Model 60 chopper. We used to play with them when we went down to Fort Bragg to play, remember? We liked it better than the Hueys they issued us, but it ain't civilian-certified, and so they wouldn't let you buy one," he reminded his former boss.

"I'll pass that one along," Werner promised. "Anybody else catch on to that?"

"Not that I know of, and I didn't say anything about it on ABC this morning, did I?"

"No, you didn't. Thanks."

"So, can you tell me anything about these folks?"

"Sorry, man, but no. It's codeword stuff, and truth is," Werner lied, "I don't know all that much myself." *Bullshit,* he almost heard over the phone line. It was weak. If there were a special counterterror group, and if America had a piece of it, sure as hell the top FBI expert in the field would have to know something about it. Henriksen would know that without being told. But, damn it, rules were rules, and there was no way a private contractor would be let into the classification compartment called Rainbow, and Bill knew what the rules were, too.

"Yeah, Gus, sure," came the mocking reply. "Anyway, they're pretty good, but Spanish isn't their primary language, and they have access to American aircraft. Tell them they ought to be a little more careful."

"I'll do that," Werner promised, making a note.

"Black project," Henriksen told himself, after hanging up. "I wonder where the funding comes from? . . ." Whoever those people were, they had FBI connections, in addition to DOD. What else could he figure? How about where they were based? . . . To do that . . . yes, it was possible, wasn't it? All he needed was a start time for the three incidents, then figure when it was the cowboys showed up, and from that he could make a pretty good guess as to their point of origin. Airliners traveled at about five hundred knots, and that made the travel distance . . .

. . . *has to be England,* Henriksen decided. It was the only location that made sense. The Brits had all the infrastructure in place, and security at Hereford was pretty good—he'd been there and trained with the SAS while part of the FBI's Hostage Rescue Team, working for Gus. Okay, he'd confirm it from written records on the Bern and Vienna incidents. His staff covered all counterterror operations as a normal part of doing business . . . and he could call contacts in Switzerland and Austria to find out a few things. That ought not to be hard. He checked his watch. Better to call right away, since they were six hours ahead. He flipped through his rolodex and placed a call on his private line.

Black project, eh? he asked himself. He'd see about that.

THE cabinet meeting ended early. The President's congressional agenda was moving along nicely, which made things easy for everyone. They'd taken just two votes—actually, mere polls of the cabinet members, since the President had the only real vote, as he'd made clear a few times, Carol reminded herself. The meeting broke up, and people headed out of the building.

"Hi, George," Dr. Brightling greeted the Secretary of the Treasury.

"Hey, Carol, the trees hugging back yet?" he asked with a smile.

"Always," she laughed in reply to this ignorant plutocrat. "Catch the TV this morning?"

"What about?"

"The thing in Spain—"

"Oh, yeah, Worldpark. What about it?"

"Who were those masked men?"

"Carol, if you have to ask, then you're not cleared into it."

"I don't want their phone number, George," she replied, allowing him to hold open the door for her. "And I *am* cleared for just about everything, remember?"

SecTreas had to admit that this was true. The President's Science Advisor was cleared into all manner of classified programs, including weapons, nuclear and otherwise, and she oversaw the crown jewel secrets of communications security as a routine part of her duties. She really was entitled to know about this if she asked. He just wished she hadn't asked. Too many people knew about Rainbow as it was. He sighed.

"We set it up a few months ago. It's black, okay? Special operations group, multinational, works out of someplace in England, mainly Americans and Brits, but others, too. The idea came from an Agency guy the Boss likes—and so far they seem to be batting a thousand, don't they?"

"Well, rescuing those kids was something special. I hope they get a pat on the head for it."

A chuckle. "Depend on it. The Boss sent off his own message this morning."

"What's it called?"

"Sure you want to know?" George asked.

"What's in a name?"

"True." SecTreas nodded. "It's called Rainbow. Because of the multinational nature."

"Well, whoever they are, they scored some points last night. You know, I really ought to get briefed in on stuff like this. I *can* help, you know," she pointed out.

"So, tell the Boss you want in."

"I'm kinda on his shit list now, remember?"

"Yeah, so dial back on your environmental stuff, will you? Hell, we all like green grass and tweety birds. But we can't have Tweety Bird telling us how to run the country, can we?"

"George, these really are important scientific issues I have to deal with," Carol Brightling pointed out.

"You say so, doc. But if you dial the rhetoric back some, maybe people will listen a little better. Just a helpful hint," the Secretary of the Treasury suggested, as he opened his car door for the two-block ride back to his department.

"Thanks, George, I'll think about it," she promised. He waved at her as his driver pulled off.

"Rainbow," Brightling said to herself as she walked across West Executive Drive. Was it worth taking it a step further? The funny part about dealing with classification issues was that if you were inside, then you were inside. . . . Reaching her office, she inserted the plastic key into her STU-4 secure telephone and dialed up CIA on the Director's private line.

"Yeah?" a male voice answered.

"Ed, this is Carol Brightling."

"Hi. How'd the cabinet meeting go?"

"Smooth, like always. I have a question for you."

"What's that, Carol?" the DCI asked.

"It's about Rainbow. That was some operation they ran in Spain last night."

"Are you in on that?" Ed asked.

"How else would I know the name, Ed? I know one of your people set it up. Can't remember the name, the guy the President likes so much."

"Yeah, John Clark. He was my training officer once, long time ago. Solid citizen. He's been there and done that even more than Mary Pat and I have. Anyway, what's your interest?"

"The new tactical-radio encryption systems NSA is playing with. Do they have it yet?"

"I don't know," the DCI admitted. "Are they ready for prime time yet?"

"Should be in another month. E-Systems will be the manufacturer, and I thought they ought to be fast-tracked into Rainbow. I mean, they're out there at the sharp end. They ought to get it first."

On the other end of the line, the Director of Central Intelligence reminded himself that he should pay more attention to the work done at the National Security Agency. He'd allowed himself to forget, moreover, that Brightling had the "black card" clearance that admitted her into that Holy of Holies at Fort Meade.

"Not a bad idea. Who do I talk to about that?"

"Admiral McConnell, I suppose. It's his agency. Anyway, just a friendly suggestion. If this Rainbow team is so hot, they ought to have the best toys."

"Okay, I'll look into it. Thanks, Carol."

"Anytime, Ed, and maybe get me fully briefed into the program someday, eh?"

"Yeah, I can do that. I can send a guy down to get you the information you need."

"Okay, whenever it's convenient. See you."

"Bye, Carol." The secure line was broken. Carol smiled at the phone. Ed would never question her about the issue, would he? She'd known the name, said nice things about the team, and offered to help, just like a loyal bureaucrat should. And she even had the name of the team leader now. John Clark. Ed's own training officer, once upon a time. It was so easy to get the information you needed if you spoke the right language. Well, that's why she'd gone after this job, frustrations and all.

ONE of his people did the math and estimated the travel times, and the answer came up England, just as he'd suspected. The triangle of time for both Bern and Vienna both apexed at London, or somewhere close to it. That made sense, Henriksen told himself. British Airways went everywhere, and it had always had a cordial relationship with the British government. So, whoever it was, the group had to be based . . . Hereford, almost certainly there. It was probably multinational . . . that would make it more politically acceptable to other countries. So, it would be American and British, maybe other nationalities as well, with access to American hardware like that Sikorsky helicopter. Gus Werner knew about it—might it have some FBI people in the team? Probably, Henriksen thought. The Hostage Rescue Team was essentially a police organization, but since its mission was counterterrorism, it practiced and played with other such organizations around the world, even though those were mainly military. The mission was pretty much the same, and therefore the people on the mission were fairly interchangeable—and the FBI HRT members were as good as anyone else in the world. So probably, someone from HRT, perhaps even someone he knew, was on the team. It would have been useful to find out who, but for now, that was too much of a stretch.

The important thing at the moment was that this national counterterror outfit was a potential danger. What if they deployed to Melbourne? Would that hurt anything? It surely wouldn't help, especially if there was an FBI agent on the team. He'd spent fifteen years in the Bureau, and Henriksen was under no illusions about those men and women. They had eyes that could see and brains that could think, and they looked into everything. And so, his strategy to raise the world's consciousness of the terrorist threat, and so help himself get the Melbourne job, might have gone an unplanned step further. Damn. But the Law of Unintended Consequences could hit anyone, couldn't it? That's why he was in the loop, because it was his job to deal with the unintended things. And so here he was, still in the intelligence-gathering mode. He needed to learn more. The really bad news was that he had to fly off to Australia in less than a day, and would himself be unable to do any more gathering. Well. He'd have dinner tonight with his boss to pass along what he knew, and maybe that ex-KGB guy on the payroll could take it a little further. Damned sure he'd performed pretty well to this point. A pipe smoker. It never ceased to amaze Henriksen how such little things could break open a case. You just had to keep your head up and eyes open.

"THE Interleukin isn't doing anything," John Killgore said, looking away from the monitor. The screen of the electron microscope was clear. The Shiva strands were reproducing merrily away, devouring healthy tissue in the process.

"So?" Dr. Archer asked.

"So, that's the only treatment option I was worried about. -3a is an exciting new development, but Shiva just laughs at it and moves on. This is one scary little mother of a bug, Barb."

"And the subjects?"

"I was just in there. Pete's a goner, so are the rest. The Shiva's eating them up. They all have major internal bleeds, and nothing is stopping the tissue breakdown. I've tried everything in the book. These poor bastards wouldn't be getting better treatment at Hopkins, Harvard, or the Mayo Clinic, and they're all going to die. Now," he allowed, "there will be some whose immune systems can deal with it, but that's going to be pretty damned rare."

"How rare?" she asked the epidemiologist.

"Less than one in a thousand, probably, maybe one in ten thousand. Even the pneumonic variant of plague doesn't kill everybody," he reminded her. That was about the most lethal disease on the planet, and allowed only one in ten thousand to survive. Some people, she knew, had immune systems that killed everything that didn't belong. Those were the ones who lived to a hundred years of age or so. It had nothing to do with smoking, not smoking, having a drink in the morning, or any of the other rubbish they published in the papers as the secret of living forever. It was all in the genes. Some were better than others. It was that simple.

"Well, that's not really something to worry about, is it?"

"World population is between five and six billion now. That's a little more than five times ten to the ninth people, subtract four orders from that and you have something on the order of five times ten to the fifth survivors. Figure a few hundred thousand who might not like us very much."

"Spread all over the world," Barbara told him. "Not organized, needing leadership and scientific knowledge to help them survive. How will they even connect? The only eight hundred people surviving in New York? And what about the diseases that come with all those deaths? The best immune system in the world can't protect you against them."

"True," Killgore conceded. Then he smiled. "We're even improving the breed, aren't we?"

Dr. Archer saw the humor of that. "Yes, John, we are. So, Vaccine-B is ready?"

He nodded. "Yes, I had my injection a few hours ago. Ready for yours?"

"And -A?"

"In the freezer, ready for mass production as soon as people need it. We'll be able turn it out in thousand-liter lots per week when we have to. Enough to cover the planet," he told her. "Steve Berg and I worked that out yesterday."

"Can anybody else—"

"No way. Not even Merck can move that fast—and even if they did, they'd have to use our formula, wouldn't they?"

That was the ultimate hook. If the plan to spread Shiva around the globe didn't work as well as hoped, then the entire world would be given Vaccine-A, which Antigen Laboratories, a division of The Horizon Corp., just happened to be working on as part of its corporate effort to help the Third World, where all the hemorrhagic fevers lived. A fortunate accident, albeit one already known in the medical literature. Both John Killgore and Steve Berg had published papers on these diseases, which had been made quite high-profile by the big scare America and the world had gone through not so long before. So, the medical world knew that Horizon/Antigen was working in this area, and wouldn't be surprised to learn that there was a vaccine in the works. They'd even test the vaccines in laboratories and find that, sure enough, the liquid had all manner of antibodies. But they'd be the wrong antibodies, and the live-virus vaccine would be a death sentence to anyone who had it enter his system. The time from injection to onset of frank symptoms was programmed at four to six weeks, and, again, the only survivors would be those lucky souls from the deepest end of the gene pool. One hundred such people out of a million would survive. Maybe less. Ebola-Shiva was one nasty little bastard of a bug, three years in the making, and how odd, Killgore thought, that it had been *that* easy to construct. Well, that was science for you. Gene manipulation was a new field, and those things were unpredictable. The sad part, maybe, was that the same people in the same lab were charging along a new and unexpected path—human longevity—and reportedly making real progress. Well, so much the better. An extended life to appreciate the new world that Shiva would bring about.

And the breakthroughs wouldn't stop. Many on the select list to receive

Vaccine-B were scientists. Some of them wouldn't like the news, when they were told, but they'd have little choice, and being scientists, they'd soon get back to their work.

Not everyone in the Project approved. Some of the radical ones actually said that bringing physicians along was contrary to the nature of the mission—because medicine didn't allow nature to take her course. Sure, Killgore snorted to himself. Fine, they'd let those idiots have their babies in farm fields after a morning's plowing or hunter-gathering, and soon enough those ideologues would breed themselves out. He planned to study and enjoy nature, but he'd do so wearing shoes and a jacket to keep the chill out. He planned to remain an educated man, not revert to the naked ape. His mind wandered.... There'd be a division of labor, of course. Farmers to grow the food and tend the cattle they'd eat—or hunters to shoot the buffalo, whose meat was healthier, lower in cholesterol. The buffalo should come back pretty fast, he thought. Wheat would continue to grow wild in the Great Plains, and they'd grow fat and healthy, especially since their predators had been so ruthlessly hunted down that they'd be slower to catch up. Domestic cattle would thrive also, but they'd ultimately be edged out by the buffalo, a much hardier breed better suited to free life. Killgore wanted to see that, see the vast herds that had once covered the West. He wanted to see Africa, too.

That meant that the Project needed airplanes and pilots. Horizon already had its own collection of G-V business jets, capable of spanning most of the world, and so they'd also need small teams of people to manage and maintain a few airports—Zambia, for instance. He wanted to see Africa wild and free. That would take perhaps ten years to come about, Killgore estimated, and it wasn't all that big a deal. AIDS was killing off that continent at a nasty pace, and Shiva would only make it go faster, and so the Dark Continent would again be free of man, and he'd be able to go there and observe nature in all her glory . . . and maybe shoot a lion to make a rug for his home in Kansas? Some of the people in the Project would raise pure fucking hell over that, but what was one lion more or less? The Project would be saving hundreds of thousands of them, perhaps millions, free to roam and hunt in their prides. What a beautiful New World it would be, once you eliminated the parasitic species that was working so hard to destroy it.

A beeper went off. He turned to look at the control panel. "It's Ernie, M5—looks like cardiac arrest," he said.

"What are you going to do?" Barbara Archer asked.

Killgore stood. "Make sure he's dead." He bent down to select a camera for the big monitor on his desk. "Here, you can watch."

Two minutes later, he appeared on the screen. An orderly was already there, but did little more than watch. She saw Killgore check the man's pulse, then check his eyes. Despite having the -B vaccine, Killgore used gloves and a mask. Well, that made sense. Then he stood back up and switched off the monitoring equipment. The orderly detached the IV lines and covered the body with a sheet. Killgore pointed to the door, and soon the orderly wheeled the gurney out, heading off for the incinerator. Killgore took the time to look at other subjects, and even appeared to speak with one before leaving the screen for good.

"I figured that," he said, returning to the control room without his protective gear. "Ernie's heart wasn't all that good, and Shiva went right after it. Wendell's going to be next, M2. Maybe tomorrow morning. Liver function's off the chart, and he's bleeding out big-time in the upper GI."

"What about the control group?"

"Mary, F4, two more days she's going to be in frank symptoms."

"So the delivery system works?" Archer asked.

"Like a charm." Killgore nodded, getting some coffee before he sat back down. "It's all going to work, Barb, and the computer projections look better than our requirement parameters. Six months from initiation, the world is going to be a very different place," he promised her.

"I still worry about those six months, John. If anybody figures out what's happened—their last conscious act will be to try and kill us all."

"That's why we have guns, Barb."

"IT'S called 'Rainbow,' " he told them, having gotten the best information of the day. "It's based in England. It was set up by a CIA guy named John Clark, and he's evidently the boss of the outfit."

"That makes sense," said Henriksen. "Multinational, right?"

"I think so," John Brightling confirmed.

"Yes," Dmitriy Popov said, picking at his Caesar salad. "That is all sensible, some sort of NATO unit, I imagine, based at Hereford?"

"Correct," said Henriksen. "By the way, nice job figuring out who they were."

Popov shrugged. "It was simple, really. I ought to have made the guess sooner. My question now, what do you want me to do about it?"

"I think we need to learn more," Henriksen said, with a glance at his boss. "A lot more."

"How do you do that?" Brightling asked.

"It is not difficult," Popov assured him. "Once you know where to look—

that is most of the battle. Once you know that, you merely go there and look. And I already have one name, do I not?"

"You want to take it?" John asked the Russian.

"Certainly." *If you pay me to do so.* "There are dangers, but—"

"What kind of dangers?"

"I once worked in England. There is the possibility that they have a photograph of me, under a different name, but I do not think that likely."

"Can you fake the accent?" Henriksen asked.

"Most certainly, old boy," Popov replied with a grin. "You were FBI once?"

A nod. "Yep."

"Then you know how it is done. A week, I think."

"Okay," Brightling said. "Fly over tomorrow."

"Travel documents?" Henriksen asked.

"I have several sets, all current, and all perfect," the intelligence officer assured him.

It was nice to have a pro on the payroll, Henriksen thought to himself. "Well, I have an early flight, and I haven't packed yet, guys. See you next week when I get back."

"Easy on the jet lag, Bill," John advised.

The former FBI agent laughed. "You got a drug that works on that?"

C H A P T E R 1 8

LOOKS

POPOV BOARDED THE MORNING CONCORDE FLIGHT. He'd never flown the Concorde before, and found the interior of the aircraft cramped, though the leg room was all right. He settled into seat 4-C. Meanwhile, at another terminal, Bill Henriksen was in a first-class seat in an American DC-10 for his trip to Los Angeles.

William Henriksen, Dmitriy Arkadeyevich Popov thought. Formerly of the FBI's Hostage Rescue Team, and an expert on counterterrorism, president of an international security-consulting company now headed off to Australia to seek a consulting contract for the next Olympics. . . . How did *that* factor into what Popov had been doing for John Brightling's Horizon Corporation? What, exactly, was he doing—more properly, what idea was he serving? What task? He was certainly being paid top dollar—he hadn't even raised the money issue over dinner, because he was sure he'd get whatever he asked for. He was thinking in terms of $250,000 for this job alone, even though it held few dangers, aside from driving an automobile in British traffic. $250,000? Maybe more, Popov told himself. After all, this mission seemed pretty important to them.

How did an expert on the mission side of terrorism and an expert on counterterrorism factor into the same plan? Why had they so rapidly seized on his discovery that there was a new international counterterror organization? It was important to them—but *why?* What the hell were they up to? He shook his head. He was so smart, yet he didn't have a clue. And he wanted to know, now more than ever.

Again, it was the not-knowing that worried him. Worried? Yes, he was worried now. The KGB had never encouraged curiosity, but even they knew that you had to tell intelligent people something, and so with mission orders had usually come some kind of explanation—and at the least he'd always known that he was serving the interests of his country. Whatever information he'd gathered, whatever foreign national he'd recruited, it had all been aimed at making his nation more secure, more knowledgeable, more strong. That the entire effort had failed was not his fault. The KGB had never failed the State. It had been the State that had failed the KGB. He'd been part of the world's finest intelligence service, and he remained proud of its abilities and his own.

But he didn't know what he was doing now. He was supposed to gather information, and it was quite easy for him, but he still didn't know why. The things he'd learned at dinner the night before had merely opened another door into another mystery. It seemed so like some Hollywood movie of conspiracy or some detective book whose ending he could not yet discern. He'd take the money and do the job, but for the first time he was uneasy, and the feeling was not a pleasant one, as the aircraft raced down the runway and took off into the rising sun for London Heathrow.

"ANY progress, Bill?"

Tawney leaned back in his chair. "Not much. The Spanish have identified two of the terrorists as Basque separatists, and the French think they have a line on another of their citizens at the park, but that's all. I suppose we could ask Carlos for some information, but it's rather doubtful that he'd cooperate—and who's to say that he even knew the buggers in the first place?"

"True." Clark took a seat. "You know, Ding's right. One of these incidents was probably to be expected, but three all in the brief time we've been here seems like a lot. Is it possible that somebody is setting them loose somehow, Bill?"

"I suppose it's possible, but who would do it—and *why* would he do it?" Tawney asked.

"Back up. Stay with the 'who' part first. Who has the ability?"

"Someone who had access to them back in the seventies and eighties—that means someone well inside the movement or someone who controlled them, 'influenced' them, from the outside. That would mean a KGB type. Notionally this chap would be known to them, would have means to contact them, and thus the ability to activate them."

"All three groups have been heavily ideological. . . ."

"That's why the contact would have to be former—or maybe active?—KGB. He'd have to be someone they trust—more than that, a person with the kind of authority they would recognize and respect." Tawney sipped at his tea. "That has to mean an intelligence officer, perhaps a fairly senior one with whom they'd worked back in the old days, someone who interfaced with them for their training and support in the old East Bloc."

"German, Czech, Russian?"

"Russian," Tawney said. "Remember that KGB let the other Bloc countries support them only under their close direction—the standoff nature of the arrangement was always paper-thin, John. It was meant more for their own comfort than for anyone else's. 'Progressive elements,' and all that rubbish. They were usually trained outside of Moscow, and then quartered in safe houses in Eastern Europe, mainly East Germany. We got a good deal of material from the old East German Stasi when the DDR collapsed. I have some colleagues at Century House going back over the information right now. That will take time. It was, unfortunately, never computerized or even properly cross-referenced. Funding problems," Tawney explained.

"Why not go straight to KGB? Hell, I've met Golovko."

Tawney didn't know that. "You're kidding."

"How do you think Ding and I got into Iran so quick with a Russian cover? You think CIA can pull off an operation that fast? I wish, Bill. No, Golovko set it up, and Ding and I were in his office before we flew down."

"Well, then, if you can, why not give it a try?"

"I'd have to get authorization from Langley."

"Will Sergey actually cooperate?"

"Not sure," John admitted. "Even money at best. But before I do such a thing, I'd need a good idea of exactly what I want. It can't be a fishing expedition. It has to be well directed."

"I can see what we might have on the name of an intelligence officer who worked with them. . . . Problem is, it won't be a real name, will it?"

Clark nodded. "Probably not. You know, we have to try harder to get one of these people alive. Kinda hard to interrogate a corpse."

"That opportunity hasn't presented itself yet," Tawney pointed out.

"Maybe," Clark thought. And even if you got one alive, who was to say that he'd know what was needed? But you had to start somewhere.

"Bern was a bank robbery. Vienna was an attempted kidnapping, and from what Herr Ostermann said, the subjects were after something that doesn't exist—private, insider computer codes into the international trading system. The most recent incident was something right out of the seventies."

"Okay, two out of three were about money," Clark agreed. "But the terrorists in both those cases were supposed to be ideological, right?"

"Correct."

"Why the interest in money? In the first one, okay, maybe it was a straight robbery. But the second one was more sophisticated—well, both sophisticated and dumb, 'cuz they were after something that doesn't exist, but as ideological operators they would not have known that. Bill, *somebody* told them to go after it. They didn't start that one by themselves, did they?"

"I agree, your supposition is likely," the spook said. "Very likely, perhaps."

"So, in that case we have two ideological operators, technically fairly competent, but going after something that doesn't really exist. The combination of operational cleverness and objective stupidity just seems to cry out to us, doesn't it?"

"But what of Worldpark?"

Clark shrugged. "Maybe Carlos knows something they need. Maybe he has a stash somewhere that they want, or information, or contact numbers, maybe even cash—there's no telling, is there?"

"And I think it unlikely that he can be persuaded to cooperate with us."

Clark grunted. "Damned skippy."

"What I can do is talk with the chaps at 'Five,' too. Perhaps this Russian shadow fellow worked with the PIRA. Let me do some nosing around, John."

"Okay, Bill, and I'll talk things over with Langley." Clark stood, wandered out of the room, and headed back to his own, still groping for the idea he needed before he could do something useful.

IT didn't start well, and Popov nearly laughed about it. On reaching his rental car he opened the left-side door instead of the right side. But he figured it out in as few seconds as it took him to load his luggage into the trunk—boot—and get in the driver's side. From that point he opened the mapbook he'd purchased in the terminal and made his way away from Heathrow's Terminal Four onto the motorway that would lead him to Hereford.

"SO, how does this thing work, Tim?"

Noonan moved his hand away, but the pointer stayed right on Chavez. "Damn, this is slick. It's supposed to track the electromagnetic field generated by the human heart. It's a unique low-frequency signal . . . doesn't even get confused by gorillas and animals. . . ."

The gadget looked like a ray-gun pistol from a '30s science-fiction movie, with a slim antenna wire out the front and a pistol grip underneath. It swung on a frictionless bearing, drawn to the signal it received. Noonan moved away from Chavez and Covington, and headed for the wall. There was a secretary sitting right . . . there. The gadget locked on her. As he walked, it stayed pointed at her, through the blank wall.

"It's like a bloody divining rod," Peter observed, no small amount of wonder in his voice. "Like finding water. . . ."

"Does look that way, doesn't it? Damn, no wonder the Army wants this baby. Forget about being ambushed. This thing's supposed to find people underground, behind trees, in the rain—whenever they're there, this thing'll pick them up."

Chavez thought about that. He thought especially about his operation in Colombia so many years before, walking point in the weeds, looking and listening for people who might have worried his ten-man team. Now this thing replaced all the skills he'd learned in the 7th Light. As a defensive tool, it could put the ninjas out of business. As an offensive tool, it could tell you where the bad guys were long before you could see or hear them, and allow you to get close enough to . . .

"What's it for—what's the manufacturer say, I mean?"

"Search and rescue—firemen in a burning building, avalanche victims, lots of things, Ding. As a counter-intruder tool, this puppy's going to be hard to beat. They've been playing with it at Fort Bragg for a couple of weeks. The Delta Guys have fallen in love with it. Still a little hard to use, and it can't tell range yet, but all they have to do is modify the antenna for greater gain, then link two of the detectors with GPS, and triangulate. . . . The ultimate range this thing can achieve hasn't been determined yet. They say this one can lock onto a person at five hundred meters."

"Bloody hell," Covington observed. But the instrument still looked like some sort of an expensive small-boy's toy.

"What good will it be for us? It can't tell a hostage from a terrorist," Chavez pointed out.

"Ding, you never know, do you? Damned sure it can tell you where the bad guys are *not,*" Noonan pointed out. He'd be playing with this thing all day, getting a feel for how to use it effectively. He hadn't felt like a kid with a new toy in quite a while, but this gadget was so new and so unexpected that it should have arrived under a decorated pine tree.

THE Brown Stallion was the name of the pub right next door to his motel. It was only half a kilometer from the main gate at Hereford, and seemed like a good place to start, and better yet to have a beer. Popov ordered a pint of Guinness and sipped at it, surveying the room. A television was on, carrying a soccer match—live or taped, he couldn't tell at the moment—between Manchester United and Rangers from up in Scotland, and that attracted the attention of the pub's patrons, and the barman, as it turned out. Popov watched as well, sipping at his pint and listening to the chitchat around the room. He was trained to be patient, and knew from experience that patience was usually rewarded in the business of intelligence, all the more so in this culture, where people came to their regular pub every night to chat with their friends, and Popov had unusually good hearing.

The football game ended in a 1–1 tie around the time Popov ordered a second pint.

"Tie, bloody tie," one man observed at the bar seat next to Popov's.

"That's sport for you, Tommy. At least the chaps down the road never tie, and never bloody lose."

"How are the Yanks fitting in, Frank?"

"Good bunch, that lot, very polite. I had to fix the sink for one of the houses today. The wife is very nice indeed, tried to give me a tip. Amazing people, the Americans. Think they have to give you money for everything." The plumber finished off his pint of lager and called for another.

"You work on the base?" Popov asked.

"Yes, have for twelve years, plumbing and such."

"Good lot of men, the SAS. I like how they sort the IRA buggers out," the Russian offered, in his best British blue-collar accent.

"That they do," the plumber agreed.

"So, some Americans are based there now, eh?"

"Yes, about ten of them, and their families." He laughed. "One of the wives nearly killed me in her car last week, driving on the wrong side of the bloody road. You do have to be careful around them, especially in your car."

"I may know one of them, chap name of Clark, I think," Popov offered as a somewhat dangerous ploy.

"Oh? He's the boss. Wife's a nurse in the local hospital. Haven't met him, but they say he's a very serious chappie—must be to command that lot. Scariest people I've ever met, not the sort you'd like to find in a dark alley—very polite of course, but you only have to look at them to know. Always out running and such, keeping fit, practicing with their weapons, looking dangerous as bloody lions."

"Were they involved in the show down in Spain last week?"

"Well, they don't tell us any of that, see, but"—the man smiled—"I saw a Hercules fly out of the airstrip the very day it happened, and they were back in their club late that night, Andy told me, looking very chuffed with themselves, he said. Good lads, dealing with those bastards."

"Oh, yes. What sort of swine would kill a sick child? *Bahst'ds,"* Popov went on.

"Yes, indeed. Wish I could have seen them. Carpenter I work with, George Wilton, sees them practice their shooting from time to time. George says they're like something from a film, magical stuff, he says."

"Were you a soldier?"

"Long time ago, Queen's Regiment, made corporal. That's how I got this job." He sipped at his beer while the TV screen changed over to cricket, a game for which Popov had no understanding at all. "You?"

Popov shook his head. "No, never. Thought about it, but decided not to."

"Not a bad life, really, for a few years anyway," the plumber said, reaching for the bar peanuts.

Popov drained his glass and paid the bill. It had been a pretty good night for him, and he didn't want to press his luck. So, the wife of John Clark was a nurse at the local hospital, eh? He'd have to check that out.

"YEAH, Patsy, I did," Ding told his wife, reading the morning paper a few hours late. Press coverage on the Worldpark job was still on page one, though below the fold this time. Fortunately, nobody in the media had a clue yet about Rainbow, he saw. The reporters had bought the story about the well-trained special-action group of the Spanish Civil Guard.

"Ding, I—well, you know, I—"

"Yeah, baby, I know. You're a doc, and your job is saving lives. So's mine, remember? They had thirty-some kids in there, and they murdered one . . . I didn't tell you. I was less than a hundred feet away when they did it. I saw that little girl die, Pats. Worst damned thing I ever saw, and I couldn't do a damned thing about it," he said darkly. He'd have dreams about that for a few more weeks, Chavez knew.

"Oh?" She turned her head. "Why?"

"'Cuz we didn't—I mean we couldn't, because there was still a bunch of others inside with guns on them, and we'd just got there, and we weren't ready to hit the bastards yet, and they wanted to show us how serious and dedicated they were—and that's how people like that show their resolve, I suppose. They kill a hostage so we'll know how tough they are." Ding set his paper down, thinking about it. He'd been brought up with a particular code of honor even before the United States Army had taught him the Code of Arms: you never, *ever* hurt an innocent person. To do so forever placed you beyond the pale, irredeemably cursed among men as a murderer, unworthy to wear a uniform or accept a salute. But these terrorists seemed to revel in it. What the hell was wrong with them? He'd read all of Paul Bellow's books, but somehow the message had not gotten through. Bright as he was, his mind could not make that intellectual leap. Well, maybe all you really needed to know about these people was how to put steel on target. That always worked, didn't it?

"What's with them?"

"Hell, baby, I don't know. Dr. Bellow says they believe in their ideas so much that they can step away from their humanity, but I—I just don't get it. I can't see myself doing that. Okay, sure, I've dropped the hammer on people, but never for kicks, and never for abstract ideas. There has to be a good reason for it, something that my society says is important, or because somebody broke the law that we're all supposed to follow. It's not nice, and it's not fun, but it is important, and that's why we do it. Your father's the same way."

"You really like Daddy," Patsy Chavez, M.D., observed.

"He's a good man. He's done a lot for me, and we've had some interesting times in the field. He's smart, smarter than the people at CIA ever knew—well, maybe Mary Pat knew. She really gets it, though she's something of a cowgirl."

"Who? Mary who?"

"Mary Patricia Foley. She's DO, head of the field spooks at the Agency. Great gal, in her mid-forties now, really knows her stuff. Good boss, looks out for us worker bees."

"Are you still in the CIA, Ding?" Patsy Clark Chavez asked.

"Technically yes." Her husband nodded. "Not sure how the administrative chain works, but as long as the checks keep coming"—he smiled—"I'm not going to worry about it. So, how's life at the hospital?"

"Well, Mom's doing fine. She's charge nurse for her shift in the ER now, and I'm rotating to ER, too, next week."

"Deliver enough babies?" Ding asked.

"Just one more this year, Domingo," Patsy replied, patting her belly. "Have to start the classes soon, assuming you're going to be there."

"Honey, I *will* be there," he assured her. "You ain't having my kid without my help."

"Daddy was never there. I don't think it was allowed back then. Prepared childbirth wasn't fashionable yet."

"Who wants to read magazines at a time like that?" Chavez shook his head. "Well, I guess times change, eh? Baby, I *will* be there, unless some terrorist jerk gets us called out of town, and then he better watch his ass, 'cuz this boy's going to be seriously pissed if that happens."

"I know I can depend on you." She sat down next to him, and as usual he took her hand and kissed it. "Boy or girl?"

"Didn't get the sonogram, remember? If it's a boy—"

"He'll be a spook, like his father and grandfather," Ding observed with a twinkle. "We'll start him on languages real early."

"What if he wants to be something else?"

"He won't," Domingo Chavez assured her. "He'll see what fine men his antecedents are, and want to emulate them. It's a Latino thing, babe"—he kissed her with a smile—"following in the honorable footsteps of your father." He couldn't say that he hadn't done so himself. His father had died at too early an age for his son to be properly imprinted. Just as well. Domingo's father, Esteban Chavez, had driven a delivery truck. Too dull, Domingo thought.

"What about the Irish? I thought it was their 'thing,' too."

"Pretty much." Chavez grinned. "That's why there are so many paddies in the FBI."

"REMEMBER Bill Henriksen?" Augustus Werner asked Dan Murray.

"Used to work for you on HRT, bit of a nut, wasn't he?"

"Well, he was heavily into the environmental stuff, hugging trees and all that crap, but he knew the job at Quantico. He laid a good one on me for Rainbow."

"Oh?" The FBI Director looked up and instantly focused at the use of the codeword.

"In Spain they were using an Air Force chopper. The media hasn't caught on to it, but it's there on the videotapes if anyone cares to notice. Bill said it wasn't real bright. He's got a point."

"Maybe," the FBI Director allowed. "But as a practical matter—"

"I know, Dan, there are the practical considerations, but it *is* a real problem."

"Yeah, well, Clark's thinking about maybe going a little public on Rainbow. One of his people brought it up, he tells me. If you want to deter terrorism, you might want to let the word get out there's a new sheriff in town, he said. Anyway, he hasn't made any decision for an official recommendation to the Agency, but evidently he's kicking the idea around."

"Interesting," Gus Werner said. "I can see the point, especially after three successful operations. Hey, if I were one of those idiots, I'd think twice before having the Wrath of God descend on me. But they don't think like normal people, do they?"

"Not exactly, but deterrence is deterrence, and John has me thinking about it now. We could leak the data at several levels, let the word out that there's a secret multinational counterterror team now operating." Murray paused. "Not take them black to white, but maybe black to gray."

"What will the Agency say?" Werner asked.

"Probably no, with an exclamation point behind it," the Director admitted. "But like I said, John has me thinking about it a little."

"I can see his point, Dan. If the world knows about it, maybe people will think twice, but then people will start to ask questions, and reporters show up, and pretty soon you have people's faces on the front page of *USA Today,* along with articles about how they screwed up on a job, written by somebody who can't even put a clip in a gun the right way."

"They can put a D-Notice on stories in England," Murray reminded him. "At least they won't make the local papers."

"Fine, so then they come out in the *Washington Post,* and *nobody* reads that, right?" Werner snorted. And he well knew the problems that the FBI's HRT had gotten into with Waco and Ruby Ridge after his tenure as commander of the unit. The media had screwed up the reporting of events in both cases—as usual, he thought, but that was the media for you. "How many people are into Rainbow?"

"About a hundred . . . pretty big number for a black outfit. I mean, their security hasn't been broken yet that we know of, but—"

"But as Bill Henriksen said, anybody who knows the difference 'tween a Huey and a Black Hawk knows that there was something odd about the Worldpark job. Hard to keep secrets, isn't it?"

"Sure as hell, Gus. Anyway, give the idea some thought, will you?"

"Will do. Anything else?"

"Yeah, also from Clark—does anybody think three terrorist incidents since Rainbow set up is a big number? Might somebody be activating cells of bad guys and turning them loose? If so, who, and if so, what for?"

"Christ, Dan, we get our European intelligence from *them,* remember? Who's the guy they have working the spook side?"

"Bill Tawney's his chief analyst. 'Six' guy, pretty good as a matter of fact—I know him from when I was the legal attaché in London a few years ago. He doesn't know, either. They're wondering if some old KGB guy or something like that might be traveling around, telling the sleeping vampires to wake up and suck some blood."

Werner considered that for about half a second or so before speaking. "If so, he hasn't been a raving success. The operations have some of the earmarks of professionalism, but not enough of it to matter. Hell, Dan, you know the drill. If the bad guys are in the same place for more than an hour, we descend on them and take them out the instant they screw up. Professional terrorists or not, they are *not* well-trained people, they don't have anything like our resources, and they surrender the initiative to us sooner or later.

All we need to know is where they are, remember? After that, the thunderbolt is in our hands."

"Yeah, and you have zapped a few, Gus. And that's why we need better intelligence, to zap them before they show up on the radarscope of their own accord."

"Well, one thing I can't do is their intel for them. They're closer to the sources than we are," Werner said, "and I bet they don't send us everything they have anyway."

"They can't. Too much of it to fax back and forth."

"Okay, yes, three hard incidents looks like a lot, but we can't tell if it's just coincidence or part of a plan unless we have people to ask. Like a live terrorist. Clark's boys haven't taken anyone alive yet, have they?"

"Nope," Murray agreed. "That's not part of their mission statement."

"So tell them that if they want hard intel, they have to have somebody with a live brain and a mouth after the shooting stops." But Werner knew that that wasn't easy under the best of circumstances. Just as taking tigers alive was far harder than taking them dead, it was difficult to capture someone possessing a loaded submachine gun and the will to use it. Even the HRT shooters, who were trained to bring them in alive in order to toss them in front of a Federal District Court judge for proper sentencing and caging at Marion, Illinois, hadn't done well in that area. And Rainbow was made up of soldiers for whom the niceties of law were somewhat foreign. The Hague Convention established rules for war that were looser than anything found in the United States Constitution. You couldn't kill prisoners, but you had to capture them alive before they *were* prisoners, and that was something armies generally didn't emphasize.

"Does our friend Mr. Clark require any more guidance from us?" Werner asked.

"Hey, he's on our side, remember?"

"He's a good guy, yes. Hell, Dan, I met with him while they were setting Rainbow up, and I let him have one of our best troops in Timmy Noonan, *and* I'll grant you he's done a great job—three of them so far. But he's *not* one of us, Dan. He doesn't think like a cop, but if he wants better intel, that's what he has to do. Tell him that, will ya?"

"I will, Gus," Murray promised. Then they moved on to other things.

"SO what are we supposed to do?" Stanley asked. "Shoot the bloody guns out of their hands? That only happens in the cinema, John."

"Weber did exactly that, remember?"

"Yes, and that was against policy, and we damned well can't encourage it," Alistair replied.

"Come on, Al, if we want better intelligence information, we have to capture some alive, don't we?"

"Fine, *if possible,* which it rarely will be, John. Bloody rarely."

"I know," Rainbow Six conceded. "But can we at least get the boys to think about it?"

"It's possible, but to make that sort of decision on the fly is difficult at best."

"We need the intel, Al," Clark persisted.

"True, but not at the cost of death or injury to one of our men."

"All things in life are a compromise of some sort," Rainbow Six observed. "Would you like to have some hard intelligence information on these people?"

"Of course, but—"

" 'But,' my ass. If we need it, let's figure a way to get it," Clark persisted.

"We're not police constables, John. That is *not* part of our mission."

"Then we're going to change the mission. If it becomes *possible* to take a subject alive, then we'll give it a try. You can always shoot 'em in the head if it's not. The guy Homer took with that gut shot. We *could* have taken him alive, Al. He wasn't a direct threat to anyone. Okay, he deserved it, and he was standing out in the open with a weapon, and our training said *kill,* and sure enough, Johnston took the shot, and decided to make a statement of his own because he wanted to—but it would have been just as easy to take out his kneecap, in which case we'd have somebody to talk to now, and maybe he would have sung like most of them do, and *then* maybe we'd know something we'd sure as hell *like* to know now, wouldn't we?"

"Quite so, John," Stanley conceded. Arguing with Clark wasn't easy. He'd come to Rainbow with the reputation of a CIA knuckle-dragger, but that's not what he was at all, the Brit reminded himself.

"We just don't know enough, and I don't like not knowing enough about the environment. I think Ding's right. Somebody's setting these bastards loose. If we can figure out a little about that, then maybe we can locate the guy and have the local cops put the bag on him wherever he is, and then maybe we can have a friendly little chat and maybe the ultimate result will be fewer incidents to go out and take risks on." The ultimate goal of Rainbow was an odd one, after all: to train for missions that rarely—if ever—came, to be the fire department in a town with no fires.

"Very well, John. We should talk with Peter and Domingo about it first of all, I think."

"Tomorrow morning, then." Clark stood from his desk. "How about a beer at the club?"

■ ■ ■

"DMITRIY Arkadeyevich, I haven't seen you in quite some time," the man said.

"Four years," Popov confirmed. They were in London, at a pub three blocks from the Russian Embassy. He'd taken the train here just on the off chance that one of his former colleagues might show up, and so one had, Ivan Petrovich Kirilenko. Ivan Petrovich had been a rising star, a few years younger than Popov, a skilled field officer who'd made full colonel at the age of thirty-eight. Now, he was probably—

"You are the *rezident* for Station London now?"

"I am not allowed to say such things, Dmitriy." Kirilenko smiled and nodded even so. He'd come very far and very fast in a downsized agency of the Russian government, and was doubtless still actively pursuing political and other intelligence, or rather, had a goodly staff of people to do it for him. Russia was worried about NATO expansion; the alliance once so threatening to the Soviet Union was now advancing eastward toward his country's borders, and some in Moscow worried, as they were paid to worry, that this could be the precursor to an attack on the Motherland. Kirilenko knew this was rubbish, as did Popov, but even so he was paid to make sure of it, and the new *rezident* was doing his job as instructed. "So, what are *you* doing now?"

"I am not permitted to say." Which was the obvious reply. It could mean anything, but in the context of their former organization, it meant that Popov was still a player of some sort. What sort, Kirilenko didn't know, though he'd heard that Dmitriy Arkadeyevich had been RIF'd from the organization. That had been a surprise to him. Popov still enjoyed an excellent service reputation as a field spook. "I am living between worlds now, Vanya. I work for a commercial business, but I perform other duties as well," he allowed. The truth was so often a useful tool, in the service of lies.

"You did not appear here by accident," Kirilenko pointed out.

"True. I hoped to see a colleague here." The pub was too close to the Embassy on Palace Green, Kensington, for serious work, but it was a comfortable place, for casual meets, and besides, Kirilenko believed his status as *rezident* to be entirely secret. Showing up in a place like this enhanced that. No real spook, everybody knew, would take the chance. "I need some help with something."

"What might that be?" the intelligence officer asked, over a sip of bitter.

"A report on a CIA officer who is probably known to us."

"The name?"

"John Clark."

"Why?"

"He is now, I believe, the leader of a black operation based here in England. I would like to offer the information I have on the man in return for whatever information you might have. I can perhaps add a few things to that dossier. I believe my information will be of interest," Popov concluded mildly. In context, it was a large promise.

"John Clark," Kirilenko repeated. "I will see what I can do for you. You have my number?"

Popov slipped a piece of paper on the bar unseen. "Here is my number. No. Do you have a card?"

"Certainly." The Russian pocketed the scrap of paper and pulled out his wallet and handed the card over. I. P. Kirilenko, it said, Third Secretary, Russian Embassy, London. 0181-567-9008, with -9009 as the fax number. Popov pocketed the card. "Well, I must get back. Good to see you, Dmitriy." The *rezident* set his glass down and walked out onto the street.

"GET the picture?" one "Five" man said to the other on the way out the door, about forty seconds behind their surveillance target.

"Well, not good enough for the National Portrait Gallery, but . . ." The problem with covert cameras was that the lenses were too small to make a really good photo. They were usually good enough for identification purposes, however, and he'd gotten eleven exposures, which, combined with computer-enhancement, should be entirely adequate. Kirilenko, they knew, thought his cover to be adequate. He didn't and couldn't know that "Five," once called MI-5, and now officially called the Security Service, had its own source inside the Russian Embassy. The Great Game was still ongoing in London and elsewhere, new world order or not. They hadn't caught Kirilenko in a compromising act yet, but he was the *rezident,* after all, and therefore not given to such action. But you tracked such people anyway, because you knew who they were, and sooner or later, you got something on them, or from them. Like the chap he'd just had a beer with. Not a regular for this pub—they knew who they were. No name. Just some photos that would be compared with the library of photos at "Five's" new headquarters building, Thames House, right on the river near Lambeth Bridge.

Popov stepped outside, turned left, and walked past Kensington Palace to catch a cab to the train station. Now, if only Kirilenko could get him something of use. He should be able to. He'd offered something juicy in return.

CHAPTER 19

SEARCHING

THREE OF THE WINOS DIED THAT DAY, ALL FROM IN-ternal bleeds in the upper GI. Killgore went down to check them. Two had died in the same hour, the third five hours later, and the morphine had helped them expire either unconscious or in a painless, merciful stupor. That left five out of the original ten, and none of them would see the end of the week. Shiva was every bit as deadly as they'd hoped, and, it would seem, just as communicable as Maggie had promised. Finally, the delivery system worked. That was proven by Mary Bannister, Subject F4, who'd just moved into the treatment center with the onset of frank symptoms. So, the Shiva Project was fully successful to this point. Everything was nominal to the test parameters and the experimental predictions.

"How bad is the pain?" he asked his doomed patient.

"Cramping, pretty bad," she replied. "Like flu, plus something else."

"Well, you do have a moderate fever. Any idea where you may have caught it? I mean, there *is* a new strain of flu out of Hong Kong, and looks like you have it."

"Maybe at work . . . before I came here. Can't remember. I'm going to be okay, right?" The concern had fought its way through the Valium-impregnated food she got every day.

"I think so." Killgore smiled around his surgical mask. "This one can be dangerous, but only to infants and the elderly, and you're not either one of those, are you?"

"I guess not." She smiled, too, at the reassurance from the physician, which was always comforting.

"Okay, what we're going to do is get an IV started to keep you properly hydrated. And we'll work on the discomfort a little with a little morphine drip, okay?"

"You're the doctor," Subject F4 replied.

"Okay, hold your arm still. I have to make a stick, and it will hurt a little bit . . . there," he said, on doing it. "How was that?"

"Not too bad."

"Okay." Killgore punched in the activation number on the Christmas tree. The morphine drip started instantly. About ten seconds later, it got into the patient's bloodstream.

"Ohhhh, oh yes," she said, eyes closed when the initial rush of the drug hit her system. Killgore had never experienced it himself, but he imagined it to be almost a sexual feeling, the way the narcotic soothed her entire body. The tension in her musculature all went away at once. You could see the body relax. Her mouth changed most of all, from tension to the slackness of sleep. It was too bad, really. F4 wasn't exactly beautiful, but she was pretty in her way, and judging from what he'd watched on the control-room TV monitor, she was a sexual treat for her partners, even though that had been caused by the tranquilizers. But, good lay or not, she would be dead in five to seven days, despite the best efforts he and his people would render. On the tree was a small drip-bottle of Interleukin-3a, recently developed by SmithKline's excellent collection of research scientists for cancer treatment—it had also shown some promise in countering viruses, which was unique in the world of medicine. Somehow it encouraged the body's immune system, though through a mechanism that was not yet understood. It would be the most likely treatment for Shiva victims once the disease became widespread, and he had to confirm that it wouldn't work. That had been the case with the winos, but they also needed to test it in fundamentally healthy patients, male and female, just to make sure. Too bad for her, he thought, since she had a face and a name to go along with her number. It would also be too bad for millions—actually billions—of others. But it would be easier with them. He might see their faces on TV, but TV wasn't real, was it? Just dots on a phosphor screen.

The idea was simple enough. A rat was a pig was a dog, was a boy—woman in this case. All had an equal right to life. They'd done extensive testing of Shiva on monkeys, for whom it had proved universally lethal, and he'd watched all those tests, and shared the pain of the subsentient animals who felt pain as real as what F4 felt, though in the case of the monkeys morphine hadn't been possible, and he'd *hated* that—hated inflicting pain on innocent creatures with whom he could not talk and to whom he could not explain things. And though it was justifiable in the big-picture sense—they would be saving millions, billions of animals from the depredations of humans—to see an animal suffer was a lot for him and his colleagues to bear, for they all empathized with all creatures great and small, and more for the small, the innocent, and the helpless than for the larger two-legged creatures who cared not a whim about them. As F4 probably did not, though they'd never asked. Why confuse the issue, after all? He looked down again. F4 was already stuporous from the narcotic he'd administered. At least she, unlike the experimental monkeys, was not in pain. That was merciful of them, wasn't it?

"WHAT black operation is that?" the desk officer asked over the secure phone link.

"I have no idea, but he is a serious man, remember? A colonel of the *Innostrannoye Upravleniye,* you will recall, Division Four, Directorate S."

"Ah, yes, I know him. He spent much time at Fensterwalde and Karlovy Vary. He was RIF'd along with all those people. What is he doing now?"

"I do not know, but he offers us information on this Clark in return for some of our data. I recommend that we make the trade, Vasily Borissovich."

"Clark is a name known to us. He has met personally with Sergey Nikolay'ch," the desk officer told the *rezident.* "He's a senior field officer, principally a paramilitary type, but also an instructor at the CIA Academy in Virginia. He is known to be close to Mary Patricia Foleyeva and her husband. It is also said that he has the ear of the American President. Yes, I think we would be interested in his current activities."

The phone they spoke over was the Russian version of the American STU-3, the technology having been stolen about three years before by a team working for Directorate T of the First Chief Directorate. The internal microchips, which had been slavishly copied, scrambled the incoming and outgoing signals with a 128-bit encryption system whose key changed every hour, and changed further with the individual users whose personal codes were part of the insertable plastic keys they used. The STU system had defied the Russians' best efforts to crack it, even with exact knowledge of the internal workings of the system hardware, and they assumed that the Americans had the same problems—after all, for centuries Russia had produced the world's best mathematicians, and the best of them hadn't even come up with a theoretical model for cracking the scrambling system.

But the Americans had, with the revolutionary application of quantum theory to communications security, a decryption system so complex that only a handful of the "Directorate Z" people at the National Security Agency actually understood it. But they didn't have to. They had the world's most powerful supercomputers to do the real work. These were located in the basement of the sprawling NSA headquarters building, a dungeonlike area whose roof was held up with naked steel I-beams because it had been excavated for just this purpose. The star machine there was one made by a company gone bankrupt, the Super-Connector from Thinking Machines, Inc., of Cambridge, Massachusetts. The machine, custom-built for NSA, had sat largely unused for six years, because nobody had come up with a way to program it efficiently, but the advent of quantum theory had changed that, too, and the monster machine was now cranking merrily away while its operators wondered who they could find to make the next generation of this complex machine.

All manner of signals came into Fort Meade, from all over the world, and one such source included GCHQ, Britain's General Communications Headquarters at Cheltenham, NSA's sister service in England. The British knew what phones were whose in the Russian Embassy—they hadn't changed the numbers, even with the demise of the USSR—and this one was on the desk of the *rezident.* The sound quality wasn't good enough for a voice-print, since the Russian version of the STU system digitized signals less efficiently than the American version, but once the encryption was defeated, the words were easily recognizable. The decrypted signal was cross-loaded to yet another computer, which translated the Russian conversation to English with a fair degree of reliability. Since the signal was from the London *rezident* to Moscow, it was placed on the top of the electronic pile, and cracked, translated, and printed less than an hour after it had been made. That done, it was transmitted to Cheltenham immediately, and at Fort Meade routed to a signals officer whose job it was to send intercepts to the people interested in the content. In this case, it was routed straight to the Director of Central Intelligence and, because it evidently discussed the identity of a field spook, to the Deputy Director (Operations), since all the field spooks worked for her. The former was a busier person than the latter, but that didn't matter, since the latter was married to the former.

"Ed?" his wife's voice said.

"Yeah, honey?" Foley replied.

"Somebody's trying to ID John Clark over in U.K."

Ed Foley's eyes went fully open at that news. "Really? Who?"

"The station chief in London talked with his desk officer in Moscow, and we intercepted it. The message ought to be in your IN pile, Eddie."

"Okay." Foley lifted the pile and leafed through it. "Got it. Hmmm," he said over the phone. "The guy who wants the information, Dmitriy Arkadeyevich Popov, former Colonel in—a terrorism guy, eh? I thought they were all RIF'd . . . Okay, they were, at least he was."

"Yeah, Eddie, a terrorism guy is interested in Rainbow Six. Isn't that interesting?"

"I'd say so. Get this out to John?"

"Bet your sweet little tushie," the DO replied at once.

"Anything on Popov?"

"I ran the name through the computer. Zip," his wife responded. "I'm starting a new file on the name. Maybe the Brits have something."

"Want me to call Basil about it?" the DCI asked.

"Let's see what we develop first. Get the fax off to John right away, though."

"It'll go out soon as I get the cover note done," Mary Pat Foley promised.

"Hockey game tonight." The Washington Capitals were closing in on the playoffs, and tonight was a grudge match with the Flyers.

"I haven't forgotten. Later, honey-bunny."

"BILL," John said over the office phone forty minutes later. "You want to come into my office?"

"On the way, John." He walked through the door in about two minutes. "What's the news?"

"Check this out, pal." Clark handed over the four pages of transcript.

"Bloody hell," the intelligence officer said, as soon as he got to page two. "Popov, Dmitriy Arkadeyevich. Doesn't ring a bell—oh, I see, they don't know the name at Langley either. Well, one cannot know them all. Call Century House about it?"

"I think we cross-index our files with yours, but it can't hurt. It would appear that Ding was right on this one. How much you want to bet that this is our guy? Who's your best friend in the Security Service?"

"Cyril Holt," Tawney said at once. "Deputy Director. I've known Cyril back to Rugby. He was a year behind me there. Outstanding chap." He didn't have to explain to Clark that old school ties were still a major part of British culture.

"Want to get him into this?"

"Bloody right, John."

"Okay, let's make the call. If we decide to go public, I want us to make the decision, not the fucking Russians."

"They know your name, then?"

"More than that. I've met Chairman Golovko. He's the guy who got Ding and me into Tehran last year. I've run a couple of cooperative operations with 'em, Bill. They know everything down to my dick size."

Tawney didn't react. He was learning how Americans talked, and it was often very entertaining. "You know, John, we ought not to get too excited about this information."

"Bill, you've been in the field as much as I have, maybe a little more. If this doesn't make your nose twitch, get something to clean your sinuses out, will you?" Clark paused for a second. "We got somebody who knows me by name, and is hinting that he can tell the Russians what I'm doing now. He's gotta know, man. He picked the London *rezident* to tell, not the one in Caracas. A terrorism guy, maybe a guy who knows names and numbers, and we've had three incidents since we got here, and we've agreed that's a lot for so short a time, and now this guy comes up on the scope, asking about me. Bill, I think it's time to get a *little* excited, okay?"

"Quite so, John. I'll get Cyril on the phone." Tawney left the room.

"Fuck," John breathed, when the door closed. That was the problem with black operations. Sooner or later, some bastard flipped the light switch, and it was generally somebody you didn't even want in the room. How the hell has this one leaked? His face darkened as he looked down at his desk, acquiring an expression that those who knew it considered very dangerous indeed.

"SHIT," Director Murray said at his desk in FBI Headquarters.

"Yeah, Dan, that about covers it," Ed Foley agreed from his seventh-floor office in Langley. "How the hell did this leak?"

"Beats the hell out of me, man. You have anything on this Popov that I don't know about?"

"I can check with Intelligence and Terrorism divisions, but we cross-deck everything to you. What about the Brits?"

"If I know John, he's already on the phone to 'Five' and 'Six.' His intel guy is Bill Tawney, and Bill's top-drawer in any outfit. Know him?"

"Rings a vague bell, but I can't put a face on it. What's Basil think of him?"

"Says he's one of his best analysts, and was a primo field-spook until a few years ago. He's got a good nose," the DCI told Murray.

"How big a threat is this?"

"Can't tell yet. The Russians know John pretty well from Tokyo and Tehran. Golovko knows him personally—called me about the Tehran job to compliment him on the job he and Chavez pulled off. I gather they hit it off, but this is business, not personal, y'know?"

"I hear you, Don Corleone. Okay, what do you want me to do?"

"Well, there's a leak somewhere. I haven't got a clue yet where it might be. The only talk I've heard about Rainbow has been people with codeword clearance. They're supposed to know about keeping their mouths shut."

"Right." Murray snorted. The only people able to leak stuff like this were the people you trusted, people who'd passed a serious background check done by special agents of the FBI. Only a trusted and checked-out person could really betray his country, and unfortunately the FBI hadn't yet learned to look inside a person's brain and heart. And what if it had been an inadvertent leak? You could interview the person who'd done it, and even he or she couldn't reply that it had happened. Security and counterespionage were two of the hardest tasks in the known universe. Thank God, he thought, for the cryppies at NSA, as always the most trusted and productive of his country's intelligence services.

"BILL, we have a two-man team on Kirilenko almost continuously. They just photographed him having a pint with a chap at his usual pub last night," Cyril Holt told his "Six" colleague.

"That may well be our man," Tawney said.

"Quite possible. I need to see your intercepts. Want me to drive out?"

"Yes, as quickly as you can."

"Fine. Give me two hours, old man. I still have a few things on my desk to attend to."

"Excellent."

The good news was that they knew this phone was secure in two different ways. The STU-4 encryption system could be beaten, but only by technology that only the Americans had—or so they thought. Better still, the phone lines used were computer-generated. One advantage to the fact that the British telephone system was essentially owned by the government was that the computers controlling the switching systems could randomize the routings and deny anyone the chance to tap into a call, unless there was a hard-wire connection at the point of origin or reception. For that bit of security, they relied on technicians who checked the lines on a monthly basis—unless one of them was working for someone else as well, Tawney reminded himself. You couldn't prevent everything, and while maintaining telephone silence could deny information to a potential enemy, it also had the effect of stopping the transfer of information within the government—thus causing that institution to grind to an immediate, smoking halt.

■ ■ ■

"GO ahead, say it," Clark told Chavez.

"Easy, Mr. C, not like I predicted the outcome of the next World Series. It was pretty obvious stuff."

"Maybe so, Domingo, but you still said it first."

Chavez nodded. "Problem is, what the hell do we do about it? John, if he knows your name, he either already knows or can easily find out your location—and that means us. Hell, all he needs is a pal in the phone company, and he starts staking us out. Probably has a photo of you, or a description. Then he gets a tag number and starts following you around."

"We should be so lucky. I know about countersurveillance, and I have a ohoc phone everywhere I go. I'd *love* for somebody to try that on me. I'd have you and some of your boys come out to the country, do a pick-and-roll, bag the fucker, and then we could have a friendly little chat with him." That generated a thin smile. John Clark knew how to extract information from people, though his techniques for doing so didn't exactly fit guidelines given to the average police departments.

"I suppose, John. But for now there's not a damned thing we can do 'cept to keep our eyes open and wait for someone else to generate some information for us."

"I've never been a target like this before. I don't like it."

"I hear you, man, but we live in an imperfect world. What's Bill Tawney say?"

"He has a 'Five' guy coming out later today."

"Well, they're the pros from Dover on this. Let 'em do their thing," Ding advised. He knew it was good advice—indeed, the only possible advice—and knew that John knew that, and he also knew that John would hate it. His boss liked doing things himself, not waiting for others to do things for him. If Mr. C had a weakness, that was it. He could be patient while working, but not while waiting for things to happen beyond his purview. Well, nobody was perfect.

"Yeah, I know" was the reply. "How are your troops?"

"Riding the crest of the wave, man, right in the curl and looking down the pipeline. I have never seen morale this good, John. The Worldpark job just lit everybody up. I think we can conquer the whole world if the bad guys line up properly."

"The eagle looks pretty good in the club, doesn't it?"

"Bet your sweet ass, Mr. C. Ain't no nightmares from this one . . . well, except for the little girl. That wasn't fun to watch, even if she was dying anyway, you know? But we got the bastards, and Mr. Carlos is still in his cage. I don't figure anybody else is going to try to spring his sorry ass."

"And he knows it, the French tell me."

Chavez stood. "Good. I gotta get back. Keep me in the loop on this, okay?"

"Sure will, Domingo," Rainbow Six promised.

"SO what sort of work do you do?" the plumber asked.

"I sell plumbing supplies," Popov said. "Wrenches and so forth, wholesale to distributors and retailers."

"Indeed. Anything useful?"

"Rigid pipe wrenches, the American brand. They're the best in the world, and they have a lifetime guarantee. If one breaks, we replace it free, even twenty years from now. Various other things as well, but Rigid wrenches are my best product."

"Really? I've heard about them, but I've never used them."

"The adjustment mechanism is a little steadier than the English Stilson spanner. Other than that, the only real advantage is the replacement policy. You know, I've been selling these things for . . . what? Fourteen years, I think. I've had one break from all the thousands I've sold."

"Hmph. I broke a wrench last year," the plumber said.

"Anything unusual about work on the base?"

"Not really. Plumbing is plumbing. Some of the things I work on are rather old—the water coolers, for example. Getting parts for the bloody things can be troublesome, and they can't make the decision to get new ones. Bloody government bureaucrats. They must spend thousands a week for bullets for their bloody machine guns, but purchase some new water coolers that people will use every day? Not bloody likely!" The man had a good laugh and sipped at his lager.

"What sort of people are they?"

"The SAS team? Good blokes, very polite chaps. They make no trouble for me and my mates at all."

"What about the Americans?" Popov asked. "I've never really known any, but you hear stories about how they do things their own way and—"

"Not in my experience. Well, I mean, only lately have we had any at the base, but the two or three I've worked for are just like our chaps—and remember I told you, they try to tip us! Bloody Yanks! But friendly chaps. Most of them have kids, and the children are lovely. Learning to play proper football now, some of them. So, what are you doing around here?"

"Meeting with the local ironmongers, trying to get them to carry my brands of tools, and also the local distributor."

"Lee and Dopkin?" The plumber shook his head. "Both are old buggers, they won't change very much. You'll do better with the little shops than with them, I'm afraid."

"Well, how about your shop? Can I sell *you* some of my tools?"

"I don't have much of a budget—but, well, I'll look at your wrenches."

"When can I come in?"

"Security, mate, is rather tight here. I doubt they'll allow me to drive you onto the base . . . but, well, I could bring you in with me—say, tomorrow afternoon?"

"I'd like that. When?"

"Tomorrow afternoon? I could pick you up here."

"Yes," Popov said. "I'd like that."

"Excellent. We can have a ploughman's lunch here and then I'll take you in myself."

"I'll be here at noon," Popov promised. "With my tools."

CYRIL Holt was over fifty, and had the tired look of a senior British civil servant. Well dressed in a finely tailored suit and an expensive tie—clothing over there, Clark knew, was excellent, but not exactly cheap—he shook hands all around and took his seat in John's office.

"So," Holt said. "I gather we have a problem here."

"You've read the intercept?"

"Yes." Holt nodded. "Good work by your NSA chaps." He didn't have to add that it was good work by his chaps as well, identifying the line used by the *rezident.*

"Tell me about Kirilenko," Clark said.

"Competent chap. He has a staff of eleven field officers, and perhaps a few other off-the-books helpers to do pickups and such. Those are all 'legals' with diplomatic cover. He has illegals as well who report to him, of course. We know two of them, both covered as businessmen who do real business in addition to espionage. We've been building up this book for some time. In any case, Vanya is a competent, capable chap. He's covered as the embassy's third secretary, does his diplomatic duties like a genuine diplomat, and is well liked by the people with whom he comes into contact. Bright, witty, good chap to have a pint with. Drinks beer more than vodka, oddly enough. He seems to like it in London. Married, two children, no bad habits that have come to our attention. His wife doesn't work at all, but we haven't seen anything covert on her part. Just a housewife, so far as we can discern. Also well liked in the diplomatic community." Holt passed across photographs of both. "Now," he went on, "just yesterday our friend was having a friendly pint in his favorite pub. It's a few blocks from the embassy in Kensington, close to the palace—the embassy dates back to the Czars, just like the one you have in Washington—and this pub is rather upscale. Here's the enhanced photo of the chap he had his beer with." Another photo was passed across.

The face, Clark and Tawney saw, was grossly ordinary. The man had brown hair and eyes, regular features, and was about as distinctive as a steel garbage can in an alley. In the photo, he was dressed in jacket and tie. The expression on his face was unremarkable. They might have been discussing football, the weather, or how to kill someone they both didn't like—there was no telling.

"I don't suppose he has a regular seat?" Tawney asked.

"No, usually sits at the bar, but sometimes in a booth, and rarely in the same seat twice in a row. We've thought about placing a bug," Holt told them, "but it's technically difficult, it would let the publican know we're up to something, and it's very doubtful that we'd get anything useful from it. His English is superb, by the way. The publican seems to think he's a Briton from the North Country."

"Does he know you're following him?" Tawney asked, before Clark could.

Holt shook his head. "Hard to say, but we do not think so. The surveillance teams switch off, and they're some of my best people. They go to this pub regularly, even when he's not there, in case he has a chap of his own there to do countersurveillance. The buildings in the area allow us to track him fairly easily by camera. We've seen a few possible brush-passes, but you both know the drill on that. We all bump into people on a crowded sidewalk, don't we? They're not all brush-passes. That's why we teach our field officers to do it. Especially when the streets are crowded, you can have a dozen cameras on your subject and not see it being done."

Clark and Tawney both nodded at that. The brush-pass had probably been around as long as spies had. You walked down a street and at most you pretended to bump into someone. In the process, his hand delivered something into yours, or dropped it in your pocket, and with minimal practice it was virtually invisible even to people watching for it. To be successful, only one of the parties had to wear something distinctive, and that could be a carnation in your buttonhole, the color of a necktie or the way one carried a newspaper, or sunglasses, or any number of other markers known only to the participants in the mini-operation. It was the simplest of examples of fieldcraft, the easiest to use, and for that reason the curse of counterespionage agencies.

But if he did a pass to this Popov guy, they had a photograph of the bastard. Maybe had it, he reminded himself. There was no guarantee that the guy he'd drunk with yesterday was the right fellow. Maybe Kirilenko was swift enough that he'd go to a pub and strike up a conversation with some other patron just to piss the "Five" people off and give them another randomly selected person to check out. Doing that required personnel and time, neither of which the Security Service had in infinite quantities. Espionage and counterespionage remained the best damned game in town, and even the players themselves never really knew what the score was.

"So, you'll increase your coverage of Kirilenko?" Bill Tawney asked.

"Yes." Holt nodded. "But do remember we're up against a highly skilled player. There are no guarantees."

"I know that, Mr. Holt. I've been in the field, and the Second Chief Directorate never got their hands on me," Clark told the visitor from the Security Service. "So anything at all on Popov?"

He shook his head. "That name is not in our files. It's possible, I suppose, that we have him under another name. Perhaps he's been in contact with our PIRA friends—that actually seems likely, if he's a terrorism specialist. There were many such contacts. We've got informers inside the PIRA, and I'm thinking about showing the photograph to some of them. But that's something we have to do carefully. Some of our informers are doubles. Our Irish friends have their own counterespionage operations, remember?"

"I've never worked directly against them," John said next. "How good are they?"

"Bloody good," Holt assured him, catching a nod also from Bill Tawney. "They're highly dedicated, and superbly organized, but now the organization's fragmenting somewhat. Obviously, some of them do not want peace to break out. Our good friend Gerry Adams is by profession a publican, and if the Troubles come to an end, and he fails to get himself elected to high public office, as he clearly hopes, then his fallback job is rather lower in prestige than the position he now holds—but the majority of them seem willing to terminate their operations, declare victory, and give peace a chance. That has helped our informer-recruiting somewhat, but there are elements of the PIRA who are more militant today than they were ten years ago. It's a cause for concern," Holt told them.

"Same story in the Bekaa Valley," Clark agreed. What did you do when Satan came to Jesus? Some would never want to stop fighting sin, and if that meant creating some sin themselves, well, that was just the cost of doing business, wasn't it? "They just don't want to let go."

"That is a problem. And I need not tell you that one of the main targets of those chaps is right here. The SAS is not exactly beloved of the PIRA."

That wasn't news either. The British Special Air Service commandos had gone into the field often enough to "sort out" IRA members who had made the two serious mistakes of breaking the law and being known. John thought it a mistake to use soldiers to perform what was essentially a police function—but then he had to admit that Rainbow was tasked to that exact mission, in a manner of speaking. But the SAS had done things that in some contexts could be called premeditated murder. Britain, much as it resembled America in so many ways, was a different country with different laws and very different rules in some areas. So security at Hereford was tight, because someday ten or so bad guys might appear with AK-47s and an attitude, and his people, like many of the resident SAS troops, had families, and terrorists didn't always respect the rights of noncombatants, did they? Not hardly.

THE decision had come with unusual speed from Number 2 Dzerzhinsky Square, and a courier was now on his way. Kirilenko was surprised to get the coded message. The courier was flying Aeroflot to Heathrow with a diplomatic bag, which was inviolable so long as the courier kept it in his possession—countries had been known to steal them for their contents, which were often uncoded, but couriers knew about that, and played by a strict set of rules—if they had to visit the can, so did the bag. And so with their diplomatic passports they breezed through control points and went off to the waiting cars that were always there, carrying the usually canvas bags often full of valuable secrets past the eyes of people who would trade their daughters' virtue for one look.

So it happened here. The courier arrived on the evening flight from Moscow's Sheremetyevo International, was waved through customs, and hopped into the waiting car driven by an embassy employee. From there it was a mere forty minutes through rush-hour traffic to Kensington, and from there to Kirilenko's office. The manila envelope was sealed with wax to ensure that it hadn't been tampered with. The *rezident* thanked the courier for this and two other packages and went to work. It was late enough that he'd have to pass on his usual pint of bitter tonight. It was an annoyance to him. He honestly enjoyed the atmosphere of his favorite pub. There was nothing like it in Moscow, or any of the other countries he'd served in. So now, in his hands was the complete dossier on Clark, John T., senior CIA field officer. It ran to twenty single-spaced pages, plus three photographs. He took the time to read the package over. It was impressive. According to this, in his first and only meeting with Chairman Golovko, he'd admitted to smuggling the wife and daughter of former KGB Chairman Gerasimov right out of the country . . . using a *submarine* to do it? So, the story he'd read in the Western media was true? It was like something from Hollywood. Then later he'd operated in Romania around the time of Nicolae Ceauçescu's downfall, then in cooperation with Station Tokyo he'd rescued the Japanese prime minister, and again with Russian assistance participated in the elimination of Mamoud Haji Daryaei? "Believed to have the ear of the American president," the analysis page pronounced—and well he should! Kirilenko thought. Sergey Nikolay'ch Golovko himself had added his thoughts to the file. A highly competent field officer, an independent thinker, known to take his own initiative on operations, and believed never to have put a foot wrong . . . training officer at the CIA Academy in Yorktown, Virginia, believed to have trained both Edward and Mary Patricia Foley, respectively the Director of Central Intelligence and the Deputy Director for Operations. This was one formidable officer, Kirilenko thought. He'd impressed Golovko himself, and few enough Russians accomplished that.

So, now, he was in England somewhere, doing something covert, and his parent agency wanted to know about it, because you tried very hard to keep track of such people. The *rezident* took the paper scrap from his wallet. It looked like a cellular phone number. He had several of those in his desk drawers, all cloned from existing accounts, because it kept his signals people busy, cost the embassy no money, and was very secure. Tapping into a known cellular account was difficult, but absent the electronic codes, it was just one more signal in a city awash in them.

Dmitriy Arkadeyevich had the same thing. In every city in the world were people who cloned phones and sold them illegally on the street. London was no exception.

"Yes?" a distant voice said.

"Dmitriy, this is Vanya."

"Yes?"

"I have the package you requested. I will require payment in the terms we agreed upon."

"It will be done," Popov promised. "Where can we make the exchange?"

That was easy. Kirilenko proposed the time, place, and method.

"Agreed." And the connection broke after a mere seventy seconds. Perhaps Popov had been RIF'd, but he still knew about communications discipline.

CHAPTER 20

CONTACTS

SHE KNEW SHE WAS SICK. SHE WASN'T SURE HOW much, but Mary Bannister knew that she didn't feel well. And through the drugs, part of her worried that it might be serious. She'd never been in a hospital, except once to the local emergency room for a sprained ankle that her father worried might be broken, but now she was in a hospital-type bed with an IV tree next to her, and a clear plastic line that ran down into the inside of her right arm, and just the sight of it frightened her, despite the drugs going into her system. She wondered what they were giving her. Dr. Killgore had said fluids to keep her hydrated and some other stuff, hadn't he? She shook her head, trying to get the cobwebs loose enough to remember. Well, why not find out? She swung her legs to the right and stood, badly and shakily, then bent down to look at the items hanging on the tree. She had trouble making her eyes focus, and bent closer, only to find that the markings on the tag-tapes were coded in a way she didn't understand. Subject F4 stood back up and tried to frown in frustration but didn't quite make it. She looked around the treatment room. Another bed was on the far side of what appeared to be a brick partition about five feet high, but it was unoccupied. There was a TV, off at the moment, hanging on the far wall. The floor was tile, and cold on her bare feet. The door was wood, and had a latch rather than a knob—it was a standard hospital door, but she didn't know that. No phone anywhere. Didn't hospitals have phones in the room? Was she *in* a hospital? It looked and seemed like one, but she knew that her brain was working more slowly than usual, though she didn't know how she knew. It was as if she'd had too much to drink. Besides feeling ill, she felt vulnerable not in total command of herself. It was time to do *some-*

thing, though exactly what she wasn't sure. She stood there for a brief time to consider it, then took the tree in her right hand and started walking for the door. Fortunately, the electronic control unit on the tree was battery-powered and not plugged into the wall. It rolled easily on the rubber wheels.

The door, it turned out, was unlocked. She pulled it open, stuck her head out, and looked around the door frame into the corridor. Empty. She walked out, still dragging the IV tree behind her. She saw no nurses' station at either end, but did not find that remarkable. Subject F4 headed to her right, pushing the IV tree ahead of her now, looking for—something, she wasn't sure what. She managed a frown and tried other doors, but while they opened, they revealed only darkened rooms, most of them smelling of disinfectant until she got to the very end. This door was labeled T-9, and behind it she found something different. No beds here, but a desk with a computer whose monitor screen was on, meaning that the computer was powered up. She walked in and leaned over the desk. It was an IBM-compatible, and she knew how to work those. It even had a modem, she saw. Well, then, she could do—what?

It took another couple of minutes to decide. She could get a message off to her father, couldn't she?

FIFTY feet and one floor away, Ben Farmer got himself a mug of coffee and sat back down into his swivel chair after a quick trip to the men's room. He picked up the copy of *Bio-Watch* he'd been reading. It was three in the morning, and all was quiet on his end of the building.

> DADDY, I'M NOT SURE WHERE I AM. THEY SAY I SIGNED A FORM ALLOW THEM TO SIGN ME IN FOR SOME MEDICAL TESTS, SOME NEW DRUG OR SOMETHING BUT I FEEL PRETTY CRUMMY NOW, AND IM NOT SUREW WHY. THEY HAVE BE HOOKEDUP TO A MEDICAION THING THATS PLUGGED INTOMY ARM, FEEL PRETTY CRUMMY AND I—

Farmer finished the article on global warming, and then checked the TV display. The computer flipped through the operating cameras, showing all the sickies in their beds—

—except one. Huh? he thought, waiting for the cameras to flip back, having missed the code number for the one with the empty bed. It took about a minute. Oh, shit, T-4 was missing. That was the girl, wasn't it? Subject F4, Mary something. Oh, shit, where had she gone to? He activated the direct controls and checked the corridor. Nobody there, either. Nobody had tried to go through the doors into the rest of the complex. They were both locked and alarmed. Where the hell were the docs? The one on duty now was a woman, Lani something, the other staff all disliked her 'cause she was an arrogant, obnoxious bitch. Evidently, Killgore didn't like her either, 'cause she always had the night duty. Palachek, that was her last name. Farmer wondered vaguely what nationality that was as he lifted the microphone for the PA system.

"Dr. Palacheck, Dr. Palachek, please call security," he said over the speaker system. It took about three minutes before his phone rang.

"This is Dr. Palachek. What is it?"

"Subject F4 has taken a walk. I can't spot her on the surveillance cameras."

"On the way. Call Dr. Killgore."

"Yes, doctor." Farmer called that number from memory.

"Yeah?" came the familiar voice.

"Sir, it's Ben Farmer. F4 has disappeared from her room. We're looking for her now."

"Okay, call me back when you find her." And the phone went dead. Killgore wasn't all that excited. You might be able to walk around for a while, but you couldn't leave the building without someone seeing you.

IT was still rush hour in London. Ivan Petrovich Kirilenko had an apartment close to the embassy, which allowed him to walk to work. The sidewalks were crowded with rapidly moving people on their way to their own jobs—the Brits are a polite people, but Londoners tend to race along—and he got to the agreed-upon corner at exactly 8:20 A.M. He carried his copy of the *Daily Telegraph,* a conservative morning newspaper, in his left hand as he stopped at the corner, waiting for the light to change.

The switch was expertly done. No words were exchanged, just a double bump on the elbow to tell him to slacken his grip, to allow one *Telegraph* to be changed for another. It was done below the waist, hidden from the casual view of those around him, and low enough to be hidden by the crowd from cameras that might be looking down from the rooftops around the busy corner. It was all the *rezident* could do not to smile. The exercise of fieldcraft was always a pleasure for him. Despite his currently high rank, he enjoyed the day-to-day business of espionage, just to prove to himself that he could still do it as well as the youngsters working under him. A few seconds later, the light changed, and a man in a tan coat angled away from him, walking briskly forward with his morning paper. It was two more blocks to the embassy. He walked through the iron gate, into the building, past security, and up to his second-floor office. There, his coat hung on the hook on the back of his door, he sat down and opened the paper on his desk.

So, Dmitriy Arkadeyevich had kept his word. There were two sheets of unlined white paper liberally covered with handwritten commentary. CIA Field Officer John Clark was now in Hereford, England, and was now the commander of a new multinational counterterrorist group known as "Rainbow," composed of ten to twenty men selected from English, American, and perhaps some other nationalities. It was a black operation, known only to a handful of highly placed people. His wife was a nurse working at the local public hospital. His team was well regarded by the local civilians who worked on the SAS base. Rainbow had been on three missions, Bern, Vienna, and Worldpark, where, in every case, it had dealt with the terrorists—Kirilenko noted that Popov had avoided use of the previous term of art, "progressive elements"—efficiently, quickly, and under the cover of local police agencies. The Rainbow team had access to American hardware, which had been used in Spain, as was clear from television coverage of the event, which he recommended that the embassy get hold of. Through the Defense Attaché would probably be best, Popov noted.

On the whole a useful, concise, and informative report, the *rezident* thought, and a fair trade for what he'd exchanged on the street corner.

"WELL, see anything this morning?" Cyril Holt asked the head of the surveillance group.

"No," the other "Five" man replied. "He was carrying the usual paper in the usual hand, but the pavement was crowded. There could have been a switch, but if there was, we didn't see it. And we are dealing with a professional, sir," the chief of the surveillance section reminded the Deputy Director of the Security Service.

POPOV, his brown wide-brimmed hat in his lap, was sitting in the train on the way back to Hereford, seemingly reading the newspaper, but in fact leafing through the photocopies of the single-spaced pages relayed from Moscow. Kirilenko was as good as his word, Dmitriy Arkadeyevich saw with pleasure. As a good *rezident* should be. And so, now, here he was, sitting alone in the first-class carriage of the inter-city train out of Paddington Station, learning more about this John Clark chap, and impressed with what he saw. His former agency in Moscow had paid quite a bit of attention to him. There were three photographs, one of them quite good that appeared to have been shot in the office of the RVS chairman himself in Moscow. They'd even taken the time to learn about his family. Two daughters, one still in college in America, and one a physician now married to one Domingo Chavez—*another* CIA field officer! Popov saw, in his middle thirties. Domingo Estebanovich, who'd also met Golovko, and was evidently partnered with the older officer. Both were paramilitary officers . . . might this Chavez be in England, too? A physician, so that was easily checked. Clark and his diminutive partner were officially described as formidable and experienced field-intelligence officers, both spoke Russian in a manner described as literate and cultured—graduates of the U.S. military's language school at Monterey, California, no doubt. Chavez, the report went on, had an undergraduate and a master's degree in International Relations from George Mason University outside of Washington, doubtless paid for by CIA. So, neither he nor Clark was merely a strong back. Both were educated as well. And the younger one was married to a physician.

Their known and confirmed field operations—*nichevo!* Popov thought. Two really impressive ones done with Russian assistance, *plus* the exfiltration of Gerasimov's wife and daughter ten years before, along with several others suspected but not confirmed . . . "Formidable" was the right word for both of them. Himself a field-intelligence officer for over twenty years, he knew what to be impressed with. Clark had to be a star at Langley, and Chavez was evidently his protégé, following in the wide, deep footsteps of his . . . father-in-law . . . Wasn't *that* interesting?

THEY found her at three-forty, still typing away on the computer, slowly and badly. Ben Farmer opened the door and saw, first, the IV tree, then the back on the hospital gown.

"Well, hello," the security guard said, not unkindly. "Taking a little walk, eh?"

"I wanted to tell daddy where I was," Mary Bannister replied.

"Oh, really. By e-mail?"

"That's right," she answered pleasantly.

"Well, how about we get you back to your room now, okay?"

"I guess," she agreed tiredly. Farmer helped her to her feet and walked her out into the corridor, gently, his hand around her waist. It was a short walk, and he opened the door into Treatment 4, got her in bed, and pulled the blanket up. He dimmed the lights before leaving, then found Dr. Palachek walking the halls.

"We may have a problem, doc."

Lani Palachek didn't like being called "doc," but didn't make an issue of it now. "What's the problem?"

"I found her on the computer in T-9. She says she e-mailed her father."

"What?" That popped the doc's eyes open, Farmer saw.

"That's what she said."

Oh, shit! the doctor thought. "What does she know?"

"Probably not much. None of them know where they are." And even looking out the windows wouldn't help. The scenery showed only wooded hills, not even a parking lot whose auto license plates might give a clue. That part of the operation had been carefully thought through.

"Any way to recover the letter she sent?"

"If we get her password and the server she logged into, maybe," Farmer replied. He was fully checked out on computers. Just about everyone in the company was. "I can try that when we wake her up—say, in about four hours?"

"Any way to un-send it?"

Farmer shook his head. "I doubt it. Not many of them work that way. We don't have AOL software on the systems, just Eudora, and if you execute the IMMEDIATE-SEND command, it's all-the-way gone, doc. That goes right into the Net, and once it's there—oh, well."

"Killgore is going to freak."

"Yes, ma'am," the former Marine said. "Maybe we need to codeword access to the 'puters." He didn't add that he'd been off the monitors for a while, and that it was all his fault. Well, he hadn't been briefed on this contingency, and why the hell didn't they lock the rooms they wanted to keep people out of? Or just locked the subjects in their rooms? The winos from the first group of test subjects had spoiled them. None of those street bums had had the ability to use a computer, nor the desire to do much of anything, and it hadn't occurred to anyone that the current group of experimental animals might. Oops. Well, he'd seen bigger mistakes than that happen before. The good news, however, was that there was no way they could know where they were, nor anything about the name of the company that owned the facility. Without those things, what could F4 have told anyone? Nothing of value, Farmer was sure. But she was right about one thing, Farmer knew. Dr. John Killgore was going to be seriously pissed.

THE ENGLISH ploughman's lunch was a national institution. Bread, cheese, lettuce, baby tom*ah*toes, chutney, and some meat—turkey in this case—along with a beer, of course. Popov had found it to be agreeable on his first trip to Britain. He'd taken the time to remove his tie and change into more casual clothes, in order to appear a working-class type.

"Well, hello," the plumber said as he sat down. His name was Edward Miles. A tall, powerfully built man with tattoos on his arm—a British affectation, especially for men in uniform, Popov knew. "Started ahead of me, I see."

"How did the morning go?"

"The usual. Fixed a water-heater in one of the houses, for a French chap, in fact, part of the new team. His wife is a smasher," Miles reported. "Only saw a picture of him. A sergeant in the French army, it would seem."

"Really?" Popov took a bite of his open-face sandwich.

"Yes, have to go back this afternoon to finish up. Then I have a water-cooler to fix in the headquarters building. Bloody things, must be fifty years old. I may have to make the part I need to repair the damned thing. Impossible to get them. The maker went out of business a dog's age ago." Miles started on his own lunch, expertly dividing the various ingredients and then piling them on the freshly made bread.

"Government institutions are all the same," Popov told him.

"That's a fact!" Miles agreed. "And my helper called in sick. Sick my *ahss,*" the plumber said. "No rest for the bloody wicked."

"Well, perhaps my tools can help," Popov offered. They continued talking about sports until lunch was finished, then both stood and walked to Miles's truck, a small blue van with government tags. The Russian tossed his collection of tools in the back. The plumber started it up, pulled onto the road, and headed for the main gate of the Hereford base. The security guard waved them through without a close look.

"See, you just need to know the right bloke to get in here." Miles laughed at his conquest of base security, which, the sign said, was on BLACK status, the lowest alert state. "I suppose the IRA chaps have calmed down quite a bit, and it would never have been a good idea to come here, not against these chaps, like tweaking a lion's nose—bad job, that," he went on.

"I suppose that's so. All I know about the SAS is what I see on the telly. They certainly look like a dangerous lot."

"That's the bloody truth," Miles confirmed. "All you need do is to look at them, the way they walk and such. They know they're lions. And this new lot, they're exactly the same, maybe even better, some folks say. They've had three jobs, or so I understand, and they've all been on the telly. They sorted that mob out at Worldpark for fair, didn't they?"

The base engineer's building was so typical of its type that the ones in the former Soviet Union could hardly have been different. The paint was peeling, and the parking area lumpy and fragmented. The double doors into the back had locks on them, of the type a child could have picked with a hairpin, Popov thought, but, then, the most dangerous weapon in there would have been a screwdriver. Miles parked his truck and waved for Popov to follow him. Inside was also as expected: a cheap desk for the plumber to do his paperwork on, a well-worn swivel chair whose stuffing was visible through the cracked vinyl on the seat, and a pegboard hung with tools, few of which could have been younger than five years, judging by the chipped paint on the forged steel.

"Do they let you purchase new tools?" Popov asked, just to stay in character.

"I have to make a request, with justification, to the chief of the physical-plant department. He's usually a decent bloke about it, and I don't ask for things I don't need." Miles pulled a Post-it note from his desk. "They want that water-cooler fixed today. Why can't they just drink Coca-Cola?" he wondered aloud. "Well, want to come along?"

"Why not?" Popov stood and followed him out the door. Five minutes later, he regretted it. An armed soldier was outside the entrance to headquarters—and then he realized that this *was* the headquarters for Rainbow. Inside would be Clark, Ivan Timofeyevich, himself.

Miles parked the truck, got out, walked to the rear door, and opened it, pulling out his toolbox.

"I'll need a small pipe wrench," he told Popov, who opened the canvas sack he'd brought, and extracted a brand-new twelve-inch Rigid wrench.

"Will this do?"

"Perfect." Miles waved him along. "Good afternoon, Corp," he said to the soldier, who nodded politely in reply, but said nothing.

For his part, Popov was more than surprised. In Russia the security would have been much tighter. But this was England, and the plumber was doubtless known to the guard. With that, he was inside, trying not to look around too obviously, and exercising all of his self-control not to appear nervous. Miles immediately set to work, unscrewing the front, setting the cover aside, and peering back into the guts of the water-cooler. He held his hand out for the small wrench, which Popov handed to him.

"Nice feel for the adjustment . . . but it's brand-new, so that's to be expected . . ." He tightened on a pipe and gave the wrench a twist. "Come on, now . . . there." He pulled the pipe out and inspected it by holding it up to a light. "Ah, well, *that* I can fix. Bloody miracle," he added. He slid back on his knees and looked in his toolbox. "The pipe is merely clogged up. Look, must be thirty years of sediment in there." He handed it over.

Popov made a show of looking through the pipe, but saw nothing at all, the metal tube was so packed with—sediment, he guessed from what Miles had said. Then the plumber took it back and inserted a small screwdriver, jammed it like the ramrod of a musket to clear it out, then switched ends to do the same from the other direction.

"So, we're going to get clean water for our coffee?" a voice asked.

"I expect so, sir," Miles replied.

Popov looked up and managed to keep his heart beating. It was Clark, Ivan Timofeyevich, as the KGB file had identified him. Tall, middle fifties, smiling down at the two workmen, dressed in suit and tie, which somehow looked uncomfortable on him. He nodded politely at the man, and looked back down to his tools while thinking as loudly as he could, *Go away!*

"There, that should do it," Miles said, reaching to put the pipe back inside, then taking the wrench from Popov to screw it into place. In another moment he stood and turned the plastic handle. The water that came out was dirty. "We just need to keep this open for five minutes or so, sir, to allow the pipe to flush itself out."

"Fair enough. Thanks," the American said, then walked off.

"A pleasure, sir," Miles said to the disappearing back. "That was the boss, Mr. Clark."

"Really? Polite enough."

"Yes, decent bloke." Miles stood and flipped the plastic level. The water coming out of the spigot was clouded at first, but after a few minutes it appeared totally clear. "Well, that's one job done. It's a nice wrench," Miles said, handing it back. "What do they cost?"

"This one—it's yours."

"Well, thank you, my friend." Miles smiled on his way out the door and past the corporal of the British Army's military police.

Next they rode around the base. Popov asked where Clark lived, and Miles obliged by taking a left turn and heading off to the senior officers' quarters.

"Not a bad house, is it?"

"It looks comfortable enough." It was made of brown brick, with what appeared to be a slate roof, and about a hundred square meters, and a garden in the back.

"I put the plumbing in that one myself," Miles told him, "back when it was renovated. Ah, that must be the missus."

A woman came out dressed in a nurse's uniform, walked to the car, and got in. Popov looked and recorded the image.

"They have a daughter who's a doctor at the same hospital the mum works at," Miles told him. "Bun in the oven for that one. I think she's married to one of the soldiers. Looks just like her mum, tall, blond, and pretty—smasher, really."

"Where do they live?"

"Oh, over that way, I think," Miles replied, waving vaguely to the west. "Officer housing, like this one, but smaller."

"SO, what can you offer us?" the police superintendent asked.

Bill Henriksen liked the Australians. They came right to the point. They were sitting in Canberra, Australia's capital, with the country's most senior cop and some people in military uniforms.

"Well, first of all, you know my background." He'd already made sure that his FBI experience and the reputation of his company were well known. "You know that I work with the FBI, and sometimes even with Delta at Fort Bragg. Therefore I have contacts, good ones, and perhaps in some ways better than your own," he said, risking a small boast.

"Our own SAS are excellent," the chief told him.

"I know it," Bill responded, with a nod and a smile. "We worked together several times when I was in the Hostage Rescue Team, in Perth twice, Quantico and Fort Bragg once each, back when Brigadier Philip Stocker was the boss. What's he do now, by the way?"

"Retired three years ago," the chief answered.

"Well, Phil knows me. Good man, one of the best I ever met," Henriksen pronounced. "Anyway, what do I bring to the party? I work with all the hardware suppliers. I can connect you with H&K for the new MP-10 that our guys like—it was developed for an FBI requirement, because we decided the nine millimeter wasn't powerful enough. However, the new Smith & Wesson ten-millimeter cartridge is—it's a whole new world for the H&K weapon. But anyone can get guns for you. I also do business with E-Systems, Collins, Fredericks-Anders, Micro-Systems, Halliday, Inc., and all the other electronics companies. I know what's happening in communications and surveillance equipment. Your SAS is weak in that area, according to my contacts. I can help fix that, and I can get you good prices for the equipment you need. In addition, my people can help train you up on the new equipment. I have a team of former Delta and HRT people. Mostly NCOs, including the regimental sergeant major from the Special Operations Training Center at Bragg, Dick Voss. He's the best in the world, and he works for me now."

"I've met him," the Aussie SAS major noted. "Yes, he's very good indeed."

"So, what can I do for you?" Henriksen asked. "Well, you've all seen the upsurge of terrorist activity in Europe, and that's a threat you need to take seriously for the Olympics. Your SAS people don't need any advice from me or anyone else on tactics, but what my company can do is to get you state-of-the-art electronics gear for surveillance and communication. I know all the people who custom-make the gear our guys use, and that's stuff your people want to have. I know that—they have to want it. Well, I can help you get exactly what you need, and train your troops up on it. There's no other company in the world with our expertise."

The reply was silence. Henriksen could read their minds, however. The terrorism they'd watched on TV, just like everyone else had, had perked up their ears. It must have. People in this line of work worried for a living, always searched for threats, real and imagined. The Olympic games were a catch of immense prestige for their nation, and also the most prestigious terrorist target on the planet, which the German police had learned the hard way at Munich in 1972. In many ways the Palestinian attack had been the kick-off of the world terrorist game, and as a result the Israeli team was *always* a little better looked-after than any other national collection of athletes, and invariably had some of their own military's commandos tucked in with the wrestlers, generally with the knowledge of the host nation's security people. *Nobody* wanted Munich to happen again.

The recent terrorism incidents in Europe had lit up awareness across the world, but nowhere more seriously than in Australia, a nation with great sensitivity to crime—not long ago, a madman had shot to death a number of innocent people, including children, which had resulted in the outlawing of guns throughout the country by the parliamentarians in this very city.

"What do you know about the European incidents?" the Aussie SAS officer asked.

Henriksen affected a sensitive look. "Much of what I know is, well, off-the-record, if you know what I mean."

"We all have security clearances," the cop told him.

"Okay, but you see, the problem is, I am *not* cleared into this stuff, exactly, and—oh, what the hell. The team doing the takedowns is called 'Rainbow.' It's a black operation composed mainly of Americans and Brits, but some other NATO nationalities tossed in, too. They're based in U.K., at Hereford. Their commander is an American CIA type, guy name of John Clark. He's a serious dude, guys, and so's his outfit. Their three known operations went down smooth as a baby's ass. They have access to American equipment—helicopters and such—and they evidently have diplomatic agreements in place to operate all over Europe, when the countries with problems invite them in. Has your government talked to anyone about them?"

"We're aware of it," the chief cop replied. "What you said is correct in all details. In honesty, I didn't know the name of the commander. Anything else you can tell us about him?"

"I've never met the man. Only know him by reputation. He's a very senior field officer, close to the DCI, and I gather that our President knows him personally as well. So, you would expect him to have a very good intelligence staff and, well, his operational people have shown what they can do, haven't they?"

"Bloody right," the major observed. "The Worldpark job was as good a bit of sorting out as I have ever seen, even better than the Iranian Embassy job in London, way back when."

"You could have handled it about the same way," Henriksen observed generously, and meaning it. The Australian Special Air Service was based on the British model, and while it didn't seem to get much work, the times he'd exercised with them during his FBI career had left him in little doubt as to their abilities. "Which squadron, Major?"

"First Saber," the young officer replied.

"I remember Major Bob Fremont and—"

"He's our colonel now," the major informed him.

"Really? I have to keep better track. That's one kick-ass officer. He and Gus Werner got along very well." Henriksen paused. "Anyway, that's what I bring to the party, guys. My people and I all speak the language. We have all the contacts we need on the operational side and the industrial side. We have access to all the newest hardware. And we can be down here to assist your people in three or four days from the moment you say 'come.' "

There were no additional questions. The top cop seemed properly impressed, and the SAS major even more so.

"Thanks very much indeed for coming," the policeman said, standing. It was hard not to like the Aussies, and their country was still largely in a pristine state. A forbidding desert, most of it, into which camels had been admitted, the only place outside Arabia where they'd done well. He'd read somewhere that Jefferson Davis, of all people, had tried to get them to breed in the American Southwest, but it hadn't worked out, probably because the initial population had been too small to survive. He couldn't decide if that was bad luck or not. The animals weren't native to either country, and interfering with nature's plan was usually a bad thing to do. On the other hand, horses and burros weren't native, either, and he liked the idea of wild horses, so long as they were properly controlled by predators.

No, he reminded himself, Australia wasn't really pristine, was it? Dingoes, the wild dogs of the Outback, had also been introduced, and they'd killed off or crowded out the marsupial animals that belonged there. The thought made him vaguely sad. There were relatively few people here, but even that small number had still managed to upset the ecostructure. Maybe that was a sign that man simply couldn't be trusted anywhere, he thought, even a few of them in a whole continental landmass. And so, the Project was needed here as well.

It was a pity he didn't have more time. He wanted to see the Great Barrier Reef. An avid skin diver, he'd never made it down here with flippers and wet suit to see that most magnificent exemplar of natural beauty. Well, maybe someday, in a few years, it would be easier, Bill thought, as he looked across the table at his hosts. He couldn't think of them as fellow human beings, could he? They were competitors, rivals for the ownership of the planet, but unlike himself they were poor stewards. Not all of them, perhaps. Maybe some loved nature as much as he did, but, unfortunately, there wasn't time to identify them, and so they had to be lumped together as enemies, and for that, they'd have to pay the price. A pity.

SKIP Bannister had been worried for some time. He hadn't wanted his daughter to go off to New York in the first place. It was a long way from Gary, Indiana. Sure, the papers said that crime was down in that dreadful city on the Hudson, but it was still too damned big and too damned anonymous for real people to live in—especially single girls. For him, Mary would always be his little girl, remembered forever as a pink, wet, noisy package in his arms, delivered by a mother who'd died six years later, a daughter who'd grown up needing doll houses to be built, a series of bicycles to be assembled, clothes to be bought, an education provided for, and then, finally, to his great discomfort, the little bird had finally grown her feathers and flown from the nest—for New York City, a hateful, crowded place full of hateful, obnoxious people. But he'd kept his peace on that, as he'd done when Mary had dated boys he hadn't been all that crazy about, because Mary had been as strong-willed as all girls her age tended to be. Off to make her fortune, meet Mr. Right, or something like that.

But then she'd disappeared, and Skip Bannister had had no idea what to do. It had started when she hadn't called for five straight days. So, he'd called her New York number and let the phone ring for several minutes. Maybe she'd been out on a date or perhaps working late. He would have tried her work number, but she'd never gotten around to giving it to him. He'd indulged her all through her life—maybe a mistake, he thought now, or maybe not—as single fathers tended to do.

But now she was gone. He'd kept calling that number at all hours of day and night, but the phone had just kept ringing, and after a week of it he'd gotten worried. Another few days and he'd gotten worried enough to call the police to make a missing-person's report. That had been a very disagreeable event. The officer he'd finally gotten had asked all manner of questions about his daughter's previous conduct, and explained patiently after twenty minutes that, you know, young women did this sort of thing all the time, and they almost always turned up safe somewhere, hey, you know, it's just part of growing up, proving to themselves that they're their own persons. And so, somewhere in New York was a paper file or a computer entry on one Bannister, Mary Eileen, female, missing, whom the NYPD didn't even regard as important enough for them to send an officer to her apartment on the Upper West Side to check things out. Skip Bannister had done that himself, driving in only to find a "super" who asked him if he was going to take his daughter's stuff out, because he hadn't seen her in weeks, and the rent would soon be due . . .

At that point Skip—James Thomas—Bannister had panicked and gone to the local police precinct station to make a report in person and demand further action, and learned that he'd come to the wrong place, but, yes, they could take down a missing-person's report there, too. And there, from a fiftyish police detective, he'd heard exactly the same thing he'd listened to over the phone. Look, it's only been a few weeks. No dead female of your daughter's description has turned up—so, she's probably alive and healthy somewhere, and ninety-nine out of a hundred of these cases turn out to be a girl who just wanted to spread her wings some and fly on her own, y'know?

Not his Mary, James T. "Skip" Bannister had replied to a calm and unlistening policeman. Sir, they all say that, and in ninety-nine out of a hundred cases—no, you know, it's actually higher than that—that's how it turns out, and I'm sorry but we don't have the manpower to investigate all of these cases. Sorry, but that's just how this sort of thing works. So, why not just go home and wait for the phone to ring?

That he'd done, and driven all the way back to Gary in a rage that grew out of his panic, arriving, finally, to find six messages on his answering machine, and he'd run through them quickly, hoping to—but not finding one from his missing daughter.

Like most Americans, James Thomas Bannister owned a personal computer, and while he'd bought it on a whim and not really used it all that much, this day, like every other, he turned it on and logged onto the Net to check his e-mail. And finally, this morning, he saw a letter in the IN box from his daughter. He moved his mouse, clicking on the letter, which sprang into life on his RGB monitor and—

—now he was truly panicked.

She didn't know where she was? Medical experiments? Most frightening of all, the letter was disjointed and poorly written. Mary had always gotten good marks in school. Her handwriting was always neat and easy to read. Her letters had been like reading stories in the morning paper, loving, of course, and clear, concise, easy to read. This could have been written by a three-year-old, Skip Bannister thought. Not even typed neatly, and his daughter knew how to type well—she'd gotten an "A" in that class.

What to do now? His little girl was missing. . . . And now his gut told him that his daughter was in danger. His stomach compressed into a knot just below his sternum. His heart speeded up. His face broke out in beads of sweat. He closed his eyes, thinking as hard as he could. Then he picked up his phone book. On the first page were the emergency numbers, from which he selected one and dialed it.

"FBI," the female voice said. "How can I help you?"

CHAPTER 21

STAGES

THE LAST OF THE WINOS HAD OUTLASTED ALL PRE-dictions, but it had only prolonged the inevitable. This one was named Henry, a black man of forty-six years who only appeared to be twenty years older. A veteran, he'd told everyone who'd listen, and a man with a considerable thirst, which had not, miraculously, done a great deal of liver damage. And his immune system had done a valiant job of fighting off Shiva. He was probably from the deep part of the gene pool, Dr. Killgore thought, for what little good it had done him. It would have been useful to take a history from him, to find out how long his parents had lived, but he was too far gone by the time they'd realized it. But now, the printout of his blood work said, he was surely doomed. His liver had finally succumbed to the Shiva strands, and his blood chemistry was off the chart in every category that mattered. In a way, it was too bad. The doctor still living in Killgore somehow wanted patients to survive. Maybe it was sportsmanship, he thought, heading down to the patient's room.

"How are we doing, Henry?" the doctor asked.

"Shitty, doc, just shitty. Feels like my belly is coming apart inside out."

"You can feel it?" Killgore asked. That was a surprise. He was getting nearly twelve milligrams of morphine a day now—a lethal dose for a healthy man, but the really sick ones could somehow take a lot more of the drug.

"Some," Henry replied, grimacing.

"Well, let me fix that for you, okay?" The physician extracted a 50cc needle from his pocket, along with a vial of Dilaudid. Two to four milligrams was a strong dose for a normal person. He decided to go to forty, just to be sure.

Henry had suffered enough. He filled the syringe, flicked the plastic body with a fingernail to take care of the little air bubble, then inserted it in the IV line, and pushed the plunger down quickly.

"Ah," Henry had time to say as the dazzling rush hit him. And just that fast, his face went still, eyes wide open, pupils dilated in the last pleasure he would ever know. Ten seconds later, Killgore touched the right carotid artery. There was nothing happening there, and Henry's breathing had stopped at once. Just to be completely sure, Killgore took his stethoscope from his pocket and touched it to Henry's chest. Sure enough, the heart had stopped.

"Nice fight, partner," the doctor told the body. Then he unhooked the IV line, switched off the electronic drug monitor system, and tossed the sheet over the face. So, that was the end of the winos. Most of them had checked out early, except for Henry. The bastard was a fighter to the end, defying all predictions. Killgore wondered if they might have tried one of the vaccines on him—"B" would almost certainly have saved him, but then they'd just have a healthy wino on their hands, and the Project wasn't aimed at saving that sort of person. What use was he to anyone, really? Except maybe a liquor-store owner. Killgore left the room, waving to an orderly as he did so. In fifteen minutes, Henry would be ashes floating in the air, his chemicals useful to some grass and trees as fertilizer when they fell back to earth, which was about as much a contribution as a person like that could hope to make.

Then it was time to see Mary, F4, in her room.

"How are you doing?" he asked.

"Fine," she replied sleepily. Whatever discomfort she ought to be feeling was well submerged in the morphine drip.

"You took a little walk last night?" Killgore asked, checking her pulse. It was 92, strong and regular still. Well, she wasn't really into serious symptoms yet, though she'd never last as long as Henry had.

"Wanted to tell daddy that I was okay," she explained.

"Think he's worried?"

"I haven't talked to him since I got here, and, I thought . . ." She dozed off.

"Yeah, sure, you thought," Dr. Killgore said to the unconscious form, "and we'll make sure that doesn't happen again." He changed the programming on the IV monitor, increasing the morphine drip by 50 percent. That should keep her in the bed.

Ten minutes later he was outside, walking north to where . . . there it was, and he saw Ben Farmer's pickup truck parked in the usual place. The inside of the building smelled of birds, as well it might, though it looked more like a horse barn. Every door was barred too closely for an arm to reach in—or for a bird to get out. He walked down the row of doors until he found Farmer in with one of his favorites.

"Working overtime?" Killgore asked.

"A little," the security man agreed. "Come on, Festus," he said next. The barn owl flapped its wings angrily then lifted off for the six-foot trip to Farmer's gloved arm. "I think you're all fixed, my friend."

"Doesn't look very friendly," the physician observed.

"Owls are hard to work with sometimes, and Festus has a mean side," the former Marine told him, walking the owl back to its perch and leaving him there. Then he slipped out of the door. "Not the smartest raptors, owls. Hard as hell to train. Not even going to try with him."

"Just release him?"

"Yeah. End of the week, I think." Farmer nodded. "It's been two months, but his wing's all healed now. I 'spect he's ready to go back out and find hisself a barn full o' mice to eat."

"Was that the one hit by the car?"

"No, that's Niccolo, the great horned owl. No, Festus, I think he probably flew into a power line. Wasn't looking the right way, I guess. Both his eyes seem to work just fine. But birds screw up, too, just like people. Anyway, I fixed his broke wing—did a good job of it, if I do say so myself." Farmer allowed himself a satisfied smile. "But ol' Festus ain't very grateful about it."

"Ben, you ought to be a doctor, you're so good at this. Were you a medic in the Marines?"

"Just a grunt. Marines get their medics from the Navy, doc." Farmer took off his thick leather gauntlet and flexed his fingers before putting it back on. "You here about Mary?"

"What happened?"

"Truth? I was off taking a leak, sat back down reading my magazine, and when I looked up, she wasn't there. I figure she was loose for, oh, ten minutes before I put the call out. I screwed up, doc, and that's a fact," he admitted.

"No real harm done, I think."

"Yeah, well, how about me moving that computer to a room with a lock on the door, eh?" He walked to the end of the room, opened another door. "Hey, Baron," the man said next. A moment later, the Harris hawk jumped onto the offered leather arm. "Yeah, that's my buddy. You're ready to go back outside, too, ain't you? Find yourself some juicy rabbits, maybe?"

There was a real nobility to these birds, Killgore thought. Their eyes were sharp and clear, their motions powerful and redolent of purpose, and while that purpose might seem cruel to their prey, that was Nature at work, wasn't it?

These raptors kept the balance in place, winnowing out the slow, the crippled, and the stupid—but more than that, the birds of prey were just plain noble in the way they soared upward and looked down on the world that lay beneath them and decided who would live and who would die. Much as he and his fellow team members were doing, Killgore thought, though human eyes lacked the hardness he saw here. He had to smile at Baron, who was soon to be released into the wild, soon to soar on the thermals above Kansas. . . .

"Will I be able to do this when we're out in the Project?" Farmer asked, setting Baron back on his wooden perch.

"What do you mean, Ben?"

"Well, doc, some people say that I won't be able to keep birds once we're out there, 'cuz it interferes, like. Hell, I take good care of my birds—you know, captive raptors live two, three times as long as the ones in the wild, and, yeah, I know that upsets things a little bit, but, damn it—"

"Ben, it's not big enough to worry about. I understand you and the hawks, okay? I like 'em, too."

"Nature's own smart bomb, doc. I love to watch 'em work. And when they get hurt, I know how to fix 'em."

"You're very good at that. All your birds look healthy."

"Oughta be. I feed 'em good. I live-trap mice for 'em. They like their meals warm, y'know?" He walked back to his work table, took his gauntlet off, and hung it on the hook. "Anyway, that's my work for the morning."

"Okay, get on home, Ben. I'll see that the computer room is secured. Let's not have any more subjects taking any walks."

"Yes, sir. How's Henry doing?" Farmer asked, fishing in his pocket for his car keys.

"Henry checked out."

"I didn't figure he had much time left. So, no more of the winos, eh?" He saw the shake of Killgore's head. "Well, too bad for him. Tough bastard, wasn't he?"

"Sure was, Ben, but that's the way it goes."

"Sure 'nuff, doc. Shame we can't just lay the body out for the buzzards. They have to eat, too, but it is kinda gross to watch how they do it." He opened the door. "See you tonight, doc."

Killgore followed him out, killing the lights. No, they couldn't deny Ben Farmer the right to keep his birds. Falconry was the real sport of kings, and from it you could learn so much about birds, how they hunted, how they lived. They'd fit into Nature's Great Plan. The problem was that the Project had some really radical people in it, like the ones who objected to having physicians, because they interfered with Nature—curing *people* of disease was interference, allowed them to multiply too fast and upset the balance again. Yeah, sure. Maybe in a hundred years, more like two hundred, they might have Kansas fully repopulated—but not all of them would remain in Kansas, would they? No, they'd spread out to study the mountains, the wetlands, the rain forests, the African savanna, and then they'd return to Kansas to report what they'd learned, to show their videotapes of Nature in action. Killgore looked forward to that. Like most Project members he devoured the Discovery Channel on his cable system. There was so *much* to learn, so *much* to understand, because he, like many, wanted to get the whole thing, to understand Nature in Her entirety. That was a tall order, of course, maybe an unrealistic one, but if he didn't make it, then his children would. Or their children, who'd be raised and educated to appreciate Nature in all her glory. They'd travel about, field scientists all. He wondered what the ones who went to the dead cities would think. . . . It'd probably be a good idea to make them go, so that they'd understand how many mistakes man had made and learn not to repeat them. Maybe he'd lead some of those field trips himself. New York would be the big one, the really impressive don't-do-this lesson. It would take a thousand years, maybe more, before the buildings collapsed from rusting structural steel and lack of maintenance. . . . The stone parts would never go away, but relatively soon, maybe ten years or so, deer would return to Central Park.

The vultures would do just fine for some time. Lots of bodies to eat . . . or maybe not. At first the corpses would be buried in the normal civilized way, but in a few weeks those systems would be overwhelmed, and then people would die, probably in their own beds and then—rats, of course. The coming year would be a banner one for rats. The only thing was: Rats depended on people to thrive. They lived on garbage and the output of civilization, a fairly specialized parasite, and this coming year they'd have a gut-filling worldwide feast and then—what? What would happen to the rat population? Dogs and cats would live off them, probably, gradually reaching a balance of some sort, but without millions of people to produce garbage for the rats to eat, their numbers would decline over the next five or ten years. That would be an interesting study for one of the field teams. How quickly would the rat population trend down, and how far down might it go?

Too many of the people in the Project concerned themselves with the great animals. Everyone loved wolves and cougars, noble beautiful animals so harshly slaughtered by men because of their depredation of domestic animals. And they'd do just fine once the trapping and poisoning stopped. But what of the lesser predators? What about the rats? Nobody seemed to care about them, but they were part of the system, too. You couldn't apply aesthetics to the study of Nature, could you? If you did, then how could you justify killing Mary Bannister, Subject F4? She was an attractive, bright, pleasant woman, after all, not very like Chester, or Pete, or Henry, not offensive to behold as they had been . . . but like them, a person who didn't understand Nature, didn't appreciate her beauty, didn't see her place in the great system of life, and was therefore unworthy to participate. Too bad for her. Too bad for all the test subjects, but the planet was dying, and had to be saved, and there was only one way to do it, because too many others had no more understanding of the system than the lower animals who were an unknowing part of the system itself. Only man could hope to understand the great balance. Only man had the responsibility to sustain that balance, and if that meant the reduction of his own species, well, everything had its price. The greatest and finest irony of all was that it required a huge sacrifice, and that the sacrifice came from man's own scientific advances. Without the instrumentalities that threatened to kill the planet, the ability to save it would not have existed. Well, of such irony was reality made, the epidemiologist told himself.

The Project would save Nature Herself, and the Project was made of relatively few people, less than a thousand, plus those who had been selected to survive and continue the effort, the unknowing ones whose lives would not be forfeit to the crimes committed in their names. Most would never understand the cause for their survival—that they were the wife or child or close relative of a Project member, or had skills that the Project needed: airplane pilots, mechanics, farmers, communication specialists, and the like. Someday they might figure it out—that was inevitable, of course. Some people talked, and others listened. When the listeners figured it out, they would probably be horrified, but then it would be far too late for them to do anything about it. There was a wonderful inevitability to it all. Oh, there would be some things he'd miss. The theater, the good restaurants in New York, for example, but surely there would be some good cooks in the Project—certainly there would be wonderful raw materials for them to work with. The Project's installation in Kansas would grow all the grain they needed, and there would be cattle as well, until the buffalo spread out.

The Project would support itself by hunting for much of its meat. Needless to say, some members objected to that—they objected to killing anything, but cooler and wiser heads had prevailed on that issue. Man was both a predator *and* a toolmaker, and so guns were okay, too. A far more merciful way to kill game, and man had to eat, too. And so, in a few years men would saddle up their horses and ride out to shoot a few buffalo, butcher them, and bring back the healthy low-fat meat. And deer, and pronghorn antelope, and elk.

Cereals and vegetables would be grown by the farmers. They'd all eat well, and live in harmony with Nature—guns weren't all that great an advancement on bows and arrows, were they?—and they'd be able to study the natural world in relative peace.

It was a beautiful future to look forward to, though the initial four to eight months would be pretty dreadful. The stuff that'd be on TV, and the radio, and the newspapers—while they lasted—would be horrible, but again, everything had a price. Humanity as the dominant force on the planet had to die, to be replaced by Nature herself, with just enough of the right people to observe and appreciate what she was and what she did.

"DR. Chavez, please," Popov told the operator at the hospital.

"Wait, please," the female voice replied. It took seventy seconds.

"Dr. Chavez," another female voice said.

"Oh, sorry, I have the wrong number," Popov said, and cradled the phone. Excellent, both Clark's wife and daughter worked at the hospital, just as he'd been told. That confirmed that this Domingo Chavez was over in Hereford as well. So, he knew both the chief of this Rainbow group, and one of its senior staff members. Chavez probably was one of those. Maybe the chief of intelligence for the group? No, Popov thought, he was too junior for that. That would be a Brit, a senior man from MI-6, someone known to the continental services. Chavez was evidently a paramilitary officer, just as his mentor was. That meant that Chavez was probably a soldier type, maybe a field leader? A supposition on his part, but a likely one. A young officer, physically fit by reports. Too junior for much of anything else. Yes, that made sense.

Popov had stolen a base map from Miles, and had marked the location of Clark's home on it. From that he could easily deduce the route his wife took to the local hospital, and figuring out her hours would not be terribly difficult. It had been a good week for the intelligence officer, and now it was time to leave. He packed his clothes and walked to his rented car, then drove to the lobby to check out. At London-Heathrow, a ticket was waiting for the 747 flight back to New York's JFK International. He had some time, so he rested in the British Airways first-class lounge, always a comfortable place, with the wine—even champagne—bottles set out in the open. He indulged himself, then sat on one of the comfortable couches and picked up a complimentary newspaper, but instead of reading, he started going over the things he'd learned and wondering what use his employer would wish to make of it. There was no telling at the moment, but Popov's instincts made him think about telephone numbers he had in Ireland.

■ ■ ■

"YES, this is Henriksen," he said into the hotel phone.

"This is Bob Aukland," the voice said. He was the senior cop at the meeting, Bill remembered. "I have good news for you."

"Oh? What might that be, sir?"

"The name's Bob, old man. We spoke with the Minister, and he agrees that we should award Global Security the consulting contract for the Olympics."

"Thank you, sir."

"So, could you come down in the morning to work out the details with me?"

"Okay, good. When can I go out to the facility?"

"I'll fly you down myself tomorrow afternoon."

"Excellent, Bob. Thank you for listening to me. What about your SAS people?"

"They'll be at the stadium as well."

"Great. I look forward to working with them," Henriksen told them.

"They want to see that new communications equipment you told them about."

"E-Systems has just started manufacturing it for our Delta people. Six ounces per unit, real-time 128-bit encryption, X-band frequency, side-band, burst-transmission. Damned near impossible to intercept, and highly reliable."

"FOR what do we deserve this honor, Ed?" Clark asked.

"You have a fairy godmother at the White House. The first thirty sets go to you. Ought to be there in two days," the DCI told Rainbow Six.

"Who at the White House?"

"Carol Brightling, Presidential Science Advisor. She's into the cryppie gear, and after the Worldpark job she called me to suggest you get these new radios."

"She's not cleared into us, Ed," Clark remembered. "At least, I don't remember her name on the list."

"Well, somebody must have told her something, John. When she called, she knew the codeword, and she *is* cleared into damned near everything, remember. Nuclear weapons, and all the commo stuff."

"The President doesn't like her, or so I hear. . . ."

"Yeah, she's a radical tree-hugger, I know. But she's pretty smart, too, and getting you this gear was a good call on her part. I talked to Sam Wilson down at Snake Headquarters, and his people have signed off on it with enthusiasm. Jam-proof, encrypted, digital clarity, and light as a feather." As well it ought to be, at seven thousand dollars per set, but that included the R&D costs, Foley reminded himself. He wondered if it might be something his field officers could use for covert operations.

"Okay, two days, you said?"

"Yep. Regular trash-haul out of Dover to RAF Mildenhall, and a truck from there, I guess. Oh, one other thing."

"What's that?"

"Tell Noonan that his letter about that people-finder gadget has generated results. The company's sending a new unit for him to play with—four of them, as a matter of fact. Improved antenna and GPS locator, too. What is that thing, anyway?"

"I've only seen it once. It seems to track people from their heartbeats."

"Oh, how's it do that?" Foley asked.

"Damned if I know, Ed, but I've seen it track people through blank walls. Noonan's going nuts over it. He said it needed improvements, though."

"Well, DKL—that's the company—must have listened. Four new sets are in the same shipment with a request for your evaluation of the upgrade."

"Okay, I'll pass that along to Tim."

"Any further word on the terrorists you got in Spain?"

"We're faxing it over later today. They've ID'd six of them now. Mainly suspected Basques, the Spanish figured out. The French have largely struck out, just two probables—well, one of them's fairly certain. And still no clue on who might be sending these people out of the dugout after us."

"Russian," Foley said. "A KGB RIF, I bet."

"I won't disagree with that, seeing how that guy showed up in London—we think—but the 'Five' guys haven't turned up anything else."

"Who's working the case at 'Five'?"

"Holt, Cyril Holt," Clark answered.

"Oh, okay, I know Cyril. Good man. You can believe what he tells you."

"That's nice, but right now I believe it when he says he doesn't have jack-shit. I've been toying with the idea of calling Sergey Nikolay'ch myself and asking for a little help."

"I don't think so, John. That'll have to go through me, remember? I like Sergey, too, but not on this one. Too open-ended."

"That leaves us dead in the water, Ed. I do not like the fact that there's some Russkie around who knows my name and my current job."

Foley had to nod at that. No field officer liked the idea of being known to anyone at all, and Clark had ample reason to worry about it, with his family sharing his current duty station. He'd never taken Sandy into the field to use them as cover on a job, as some field officers had done in their careers. No officer had ever lost a spouse that way, but a few had been roughed up, and it was now contrary to CIA policy. More than that, John had lived his entire professional life as an unperson, a ghost seen by few, recognized by none, and known only to those on his own side. He would no more wish to change that than to change his sex, but his anonymity had been changed, and it upset him. Well, the Russians knew him and knew about him, and that had been his own doing in Japan and Iran; he must have known then that his actions would have consequences.

"John, they know you. Hell, Golovko knows you personally, and it figures they'd be interested in you, right?"

"I know, Ed, but—damn it!"

"John, I understand, but you're high-profile now, and there's no evading that fact. So, just sit tight, do your job, and let us rattle some bushes to find out what's happening, okay?"

"I guess, Ed" was the resigned reply.

"If I turn anything, I'll be on the phone to you immediately."

"Aye aye, sir," Clark replied, using the naval term that had been part of his life a long time ago. Now he reserved it for things he really didn't like.

THE Assistant Special Agent in Charge of the Gary, Indiana, FBI field office was a serious black man named Chuck Ussery. Forty-four, a recent arrival in this office, he'd been in the Bureau for seventeen years, and before that a police officer in Chicago. Skip Bannister's call had rapidly been routed to his desk, and inside five minutes he'd told the man to drive to the office at once. Twenty-five minutes later, the man came in. Five-eleven, stocky, fifty-five or so, and profoundly frightened, the agent saw. First of all he got the man sat down and offered him coffee, which was refused. Then came the questions, routine at first. Then the questions got a lot more directed.

"Mr. Bannister, do you have the e-mail you told me about?"

James Bannister pulled the sheet of paper from his pocket and handed it across.

Three paragraphs, Ussery saw, disjointed and ungrammatical. Confused. His first impression was . . .

"Mr. Bannister, do you have any reason to suspect that your daughter has ever used drugs of any kind?"

"Not my Mary!" was the immediate reply. "No way. Okay, she likes to drink beer and wine, but no drugs, not my little girl, not ever!"

Ussery held up his hands. "Please, I understand how you feel. I've worked kidnappings before and—"

"You think she's been kidnapped?" Skip Bannister asked, now faced with the confirmation of his greatest fear. That was far worse than the suggestion that his daughter was a doper.

"Based on this letter, yes, I think it's a possibility, and we will treat this case as a kidnapping investigation." Ussery lifted his phone. "Send Pat O'Connor in, will you?" he told his secretary.

Supervisory Special Agent Patrick D. O'Connor was one of the Gary office's squad supervisors. Thirty-eight, red-haired, fair-skinned, and very fit, O'Connor headed the office kidnapping squad. "Yeah, Chuck?" he said coming in.

"This is Mr. James Bannister. He has a missing daughter, age twenty one, disappeared in New York about a month ago. Yesterday he got this on his e-mail." Ussery handed it over.

O'Connor scanned it and nodded. "Okay, Chuck."

"Pat, it's your case. Run with it."

"You bet, Chuck. Mr. Bannister, would you come with me, please?"

"Pat runs these cases for us," Ussery explained. "He will take charge of it, and report to me on a daily basis. Mr. Bannister, the FBI treats kidnappings as major felonies. This will be a top-priority case until we clear it. Ten men, Pat?"

"For starters, yes, more in New York. Sir," he said to their guest, "we all have kids. We know how you feel. If there's a way to locate your daughter for you, we'll find it. Now I need to ask you a bunch of questions so that we can get started, okay?"

"Yeah." The man stood and followed O'Connor out into the office bay. He'd be there for the next three hours, telling everything he knew about his daughter and her life in New York to this and other agents. First of all he handed over a recent photograph, a good one as it turned out. O'Connor looked at it. He'd keep it for the case file. O'Connor and his squad hadn't worked a kidnapping in several years. It was a crime the FBI had essentially extinguished in the United States—kidnapping for money, in any case. There was just no percentage in it. The FBI *always* solved them, came down on the perps like the Wrath of God. Today's kidnappings were generally of children, and, parental kidnappings aside, were almost always by sexual deviants who most often used them for personal gratification, and often as not killed them thereafter. If anything, that merely increased the FBI's institutional rage. The Bannister Case, as it was already being called, would have the highest priority in manpower and resources in every office it might touch. Pending cases against organized crime families would be set aside for this one. That was just part of the FBI's institutional ethos.

FOUR hours after Skip Bannister's arrival in the Gary office, two agents from the New York field division in the Jacob Javits Building downtown knocked on the door of the superintendent of Mary Bannister's dingy apartment building. The super gave them the key and told them where the apartment was. The two agents entered and commenced their search, looking first of all for notes, photographs, correspondence, anything that might help. They'd been there an hour when a NYPD detective showed up, summoned by the FBI office to assist. There were 30,000 policemen in the city, and for a kidnapping, they could all be called upon to assist in the investigation and canvassing.

"Got a picture?" the detective asked.

"Here." The lead agent handed over the one faxed from Gary.

"You know, I got a call a few weeks ago from somebody in Des Moines, girl's name was . . . Pretloe, I think. Yeah, Anne Pretloe, mid-twenties, legal secretary. Lived a few blocks from here. Just up and disappeared. Didn't show up for work—just vanished. Roughly the same age and sex, guys," the detective pointed out. "Connection, maybe?"

"Been checking Jane Does?" the junior agent asked. He didn't have to go further. Their instant thought was the obvious one: Was there a serial killer operating in New York City? That sort of criminal nearly always went after women between eighteen and thirty years of age, as selective a predator as there was anywhere in nature.

"Yeah, but nothing that fit the Pretloe girl's description, or this one for that matter." He handed the photo back. "This case is a head-scratcher. Find anything?"

"Not yet," the senior agent replied. "Diary, but nothing useful in it. No photos of men. Just clothes, cosmetics, normal stuff for a girl this age."

"Prints?"

A nod. "That's next. We have our guy on the way now." But they all knew that this was a thin reed, after the apartment had been vacant for a month. The oils that made fingerprints evaporated over time, though there was some hope here, in a climate-controlled and sealed apartment.

"This one's not going to be easy," the NYPD detective observed next.

"They never are," the senior FBI agent replied.

"What if there's more than two?" the other FBI agent asked.

"Lots of people turn up missing in this town," the detective said. "But I'll run a computer check."

SUBJECT F5 was a hot little number, Killgore saw. And she liked Chip, too. That wasn't very good news for Chip Smitton, who hadn't been exposed to Shiva by injection, vaccine testing, or the fogging system. No, he'd been exposed by sexual contact only, and now his blood was showing antibodies, too. So, that means of transmission worked also, and better yet, it worked female-to-male, not just male-to-female. Shiva was everything they'd hoped it would be.

It was distasteful to watch people making love. Not the least bit arousing for him, playing voyeur. Anne Pretloe, F5, was within two days of symptoms, judging by her bloodwork, eating, drinking, and being very merry right before his eyes on the black-and-white monitor. Well, the tranquilizers had lowered every subject's resistance to loose behavior, and there was no telling what she was like in real life, though she certainly knew the techniques well enough.

Strangely, Killgore had never paid attention to this sort of thing in animal tests. Rats, he imagined, came into season, and when they did, the boy rats and girl rats must have gotten it on, but somehow he'd never noticed. He respected rats as a life-form, but didn't find their sexual congress the least bit interesting, whereas here, he had to admit to himself, he *did* find his eyes returning to the screen every few seconds. Well, Pretloe, Subject F5, was the cutest of the bunch, and if he'd found her in a singles bar, he might have offered her a drink and said hello and . . . let things develop. But she was doomed, too, as doomed as white, bred-for-the-purpose lab rats. Those cute little pink-eyed creatures were used all over the world because they were genetically identical, and so test results in one country would match the test results generated anywhere else in the world. They probably didn't have the wherewithal to survive in the wild, and that was too bad. But their white color would work against them—cats and dogs would spot them far more easily, and that was not a good thing in the wild, was it? And they were an artificial species anyway, not part of Nature's plan, but a work of Man, and therefore unworthy of continuance. A pity they were cute, but that was a subjective, not objective, observation, and Killgore had long since learned to differentiate between the two. After all, Pretloe, F5, was cute, too, and his pity for her was a lingering atavistic attitude on his part, unworthy of a Project member. But that got him thinking as he watched Chip Smitton screw Anne Pretloe. This was the kind of thing Hitler might have done with Jews, saved a small number of them as human lab rats, maybe as crash-test dummies for auto-safety tests. . . . So, did that make *him* a Nazi? Killgore thought. They were using F5 and M7 as such . . . but, no, they didn't discriminate on race or creed, or gender, did they? There were no politics involved, really—well, maybe, depending on how one defined the term, not in the way *he* defined the term. This was science, after all. The whole Project was *about* science and love of Nature. Project members included all races and categories of people, though not much in the way of religions, unless you considered love of Nature to be a religion . . . which in a way it was, the doctor told himself. Yes, surely it was.

What they were doing on his TV screen was natural, or nearly so—as it *had* been largely instigated by mood depressants—but the mechanics certainly were. So were their instincts, he to spread his seed as far as possible, and she to receive his seed—and *his own,* Killgore's mind went on, to be a predator, and through his depredations to decide which members of that species would live and which would not.

These two would not live, attractive as both were . . . like the lab rats with their cute white hair and cute pink eyes and twitching white whiskers. Well, none of them would be around much longer, would they? It was aesthetically troubling, but a valid choice in view of the future that they all beheld.

CHAPTER 22

COUNTERMEASURES

"SO, NOTHING ELSE FROM OUR RUSSIAN FRIEND?" Bill Tawney asked.

"Nothing," Cyril Holt confirmed. "Tapes of Kirilenko show that he walks to work the same way every day and at exactly the same time, when the streets are crowded, stops in his pub for a pint four nights out of five, and bumps into all manner of people. But all it takes is a minor attempt at disguise and a little knowledge of trade-craft to outfox us, unless we really tighten our coverage, and there's too great a chance that Ivan Petrovich would notice it and simply upgrade his own efforts to remain covert. It's a chance we'd prefer not to take."

"Quite so," Tawney had to agree, despite his disappointment. "Nothing from other sources?"

"Other sources" meant whomever the Security Service might have working for them inside the Russian Embassy. There almost had to be someone there, but Holt would not discuss it over a telephone line, encrypted or not, because if there was one thing you had to protect in this business, it was the identity of your sources. Not protecting them could get them killed.

"No, Bill, nothing. Vanya hasn't spoken over his phone line to Moscow on this subject. Nor has he used his secure fax line. Whatever discussions developed from this incident, well, we do not have even a confirmed face, just that chap in the pub, and that might well have been nothing. Three months ago, I had one of my chaps strike up a conversation with him at the pub, and they talked about football—he's a serious fan, and he knows the game quite well, and never even revealed his nationality. His accent is bloody perfect. So that chap in the photo might well be nothing at all, just another coincidence. Kirilenko is a professional, Bill. He doesn't make many mistakes. Whatever information came out of this was doubtless written up and couriered off."

"So we probably have a KGB RIF prowling around London still, probably with whatever information Moscow has on our Mr. Clark, and doing what, we do not know."

"Correct, Bill," Holt agreed. "I can't say that I like it either, but there you are."

"What have you turned up on KGB-PIRA contacts?"

"We have a few things. One photo of someone else from a meeting in Dublin eight years ago, and oral reports of other contacts, with physical description. Some might be the chap in the photo, but the written descriptions fit about a third of male humanity, and we're leery of showing the photos around quite yet." Tawney didn't need to be told why. It was well within the realm of possibility that some of Holt's informants were indeed double-agents, and showing them the photos of the man in the pub might well do nothing more than alert the target of the investigation to the fact that someone knew who he was. That would cause *him* to become more cautious, perhaps change his appearance, and the net result would be to make things worse instead of better. This *was* the most complex of games, Tawney reminded himself. And what if the whole thing was nothing more than curiosity on the part of the Russians, merely keeping track of a known intelligence officer on the other side? Hell, *everyone* did that. It was just a normal part of doing business.

The bottom line was that they knew what they didn't know—no, Tawney thought. They didn't even know that much. They knew *that* they didn't know something, but they didn't even know what it was that they wanted to find out. What was the significance of this blip of information that had appeared on the scope?

"WHAT'S this for?" Henriksen asked innocently.

"A fog-cooling system. We got it from your chaps," Aukland said.

"Huh? I don't understand," the American replied.

"One of our engineers saw it in—Arizona, I think. It sprays a very fine water mist. The tiny droplets absorb heat energy and evaporate into the atmosphere, has the same effect as air-conditioning, but with a negligible energy expenditure."

"Ahh," Bill Henriksen said, doing his best to act surprised. "How widely distributed is the system?"

"Just the tunnels and concourses. The architect wanted to put it all over the stadium, but people objected, said it would interfere with cameras and such," Aukland answered, "too much like a real fog."

"Okay, I think I need to look at that."

"Why?"

"Well, sir, it's a hell of a good way to deliver a chemical agent, isn't it?" The question took the police official seriously aback.

"Well . . . yes, I suppose it would be."

"Good. I have a guy in the company, former officer in the U.S. Army Chemical Corps, expert on this sort of thing, degree from MIT. I'll have him check it out ASAP."

"Yes, that is a good idea, Bill. Thank you," Aukland said, kicking himself for not thinking of that on his own. Well, he was hiring expertise, wasn't he? And this Yank certainly seemed to be an expert.

"Does it get that hot here?"

"Oh, yes, quite. We expect temperatures in the nineties—Fahrenheit, that is. We're supposed to think in Celsius nowadays, but I never did learn that."

"Yeah, me neither," Henriksen noted.

"Anyway, the architect said that this was an inexpensive way to cool the spectators down, and quite reasonable to install. It feeds off the fire-sprinkler system. Doesn't even use much water for what it does. It's been installed for over a year. We test it periodically. American company, can't recall the name at the moment."

Cool-Spray of Phoenix, Arizona, Henriksen thought. He had the plans for the system in the file cabinet in his office. It would play a crucial role in the Project's plans, and had been seen as a godsend from the first moment. Here was the place. Soon would come the time.

"Heard anything more from the Brits?"

"We have an inquiry in, but no reply yet," Aukland answered. "It is a very hush-hush project, evidently."

Henriksen nodded. "Politics, always gets in the way." And with luck it would stay that way.

"Quite," Aukland agreed, with a nod.

DETECTIVE Lieutenant Mario d'Allessandro punched up his computer and accessed the NYPD central-records file. Sure enough, Mary Bannister was in there, as was Anne Pretloe. Then he set up a search routine, picking gender WOMEN, age eighteen to thirty for starters, and picking the RUN icon with his mouse. The system generated forty-six names, all of which he saved to a file he created for the purpose. The system didn't have photos built in. He'd have to access the paper files for those. He de-selected ten names from Queens and Richmond boroughs for the moment, saving for the moment only Manhattan missing girls. That came down to twenty-one. Next he de-selected African-American women, because if they were dealing with a serial killer, such criminals usually selected clones as victims—the most famous of them, Theodore Bundy, had almost exclusively picked women who parted their hair down the middle, for instance. Bannister and Pretloe were white, single, reasonably attractive, ages twenty-one and twenty-four, and dark-haired. So, eighteen to thirty should be a good straddle, he thought, and he further de-selected the names that didn't fit that model.

Next he opened the department's Jane Doe file, to look up the recovered bodies of murder victims who had not yet been identified. He already knew all of these cases from his regular work. Two fit the search parameters, but neither was Bannister or Pretloe. So this was, for the moment, a dry hole. That was both good and bad news. The two missing women were not definitely dead, and that was the good news. But their bodies could have been cleverly disposed of—the Jersey marshes were nearby, and that area had been a prime dumping site for bodies since the turn of the century.

Next he printed up his list of missing women. He'd want to examine all the paper files, including the photos, with the two FBI agents. Both Pretloe and Bannister had brown hair of roughly the same length, and maybe that was enough of a commonality for a serial killer—but, no, Bannister was still alive, or so the e-mail letter suggested . . . unless the serial killer was the kind of sick person who wanted to taunt the families of his victims. D'Allessandro had never come across one of those before, but serial killers were seriously sick bastards, and you could never really predict the things they might do for personal amusement. If one of those fucks were loose in New York, then it wasn't just the FBI who'd want his ass. Good thing the state of New York finally had a death-penalty statute . . .

"YES, I've seen him," Popov told his boss.

"Really?" John Brightling asked. "How close?"

"About as close as we are, sir," the Russian replied. "It was not intentional, but it happened. He's a large, powerful man. His wife is a nurse at the local community hospital, and his daughter is a medical doctor, married to one of the other team members, working at the same hospital. She is Dr. Patricia

Chavez. Her husband is Domingo Chavez, also a CIA field officer, now assigned to this Rainbow group, probably as a commando leader. Both Clark and Chavez are CIA field officers. Clark was involved in the rescue of the former KGB chairman's wife and daughter from Soviet territory some years ago—you'll recall the story made the press recently. Well, Clark was the officer who got them out. He was also involved in the conflict with Japan, and the death of Mahmoud Haji Daryaei in Iran. He and Chavez are highly experienced and very capable intelligence officers. It would be very dangerous to underestimate either of them," Popov concluded.

"Okay, what does that tell us?"

"It tells us that Rainbow is what it appears to be, a multinational counter-terror group whose activities spread all across Europe. Spain is a NATO member, but Austria and Switzerland are not, you will recall. Could they expand their operations to other countries? Certainly, yes. They are a very serious threat to any terrorist operation. It is not," Popov went on, "an organization I would like to have in the field against me. Their expertise in actual 'combat' operations we have seen on television. Behind that will be excellent technical and intelligence support as well. The one cannot exist without the other."

"Okay. So we know about them. Is it possible that they know about us?" Dr. Brightling asked.

"Possible, but unlikely," Popov thought. "If that were the case, then you would have agents of your FBI in here to arrest you—and me—for criminal conspiracy. I am not being tracked or followed—well, I do not think that I am. I know what to look for, and I have seen nothing of the sort, but, I must also admit, it is possible that a very careful and expert effort could probably follow me without my noticing it. That is difficult—I have been trained in counter-surveillance—but theoretically possible."

That shook his employer somewhat, Popov saw. He'd just made an admission that he was not perfect. His former supervisors in KGB would have known it beforehand and accepted it as a normal risk of the intelligence trade . . . but those people never had to worry about being arrested and losing their billions of dollars of personal worth.

"What are the risks?"

"If you mean what methods can be used against you? . . ." He got a nod. "That means that your telephones could be tapped, and—"

"My phones are encrypted. The system is supposed to be break-proof. My consultants on that tell me—"

Popov cut him off with a raised hand. "Sir, do you really think that your government allows the manufacture of encryption systems that it cannot itself break?" he asked, as though explaining something to a child. "The National Security Agency at Fort Meade has some of the brightest mathematicians in the world, and the world's most powerful computers, and if you ever wonder how hard they work, you need only look at the parking lots."

"Huh? What do you mean?"

"If the parking lots are filled at seven in the evening, that means they are hard at work on something. Everyone has a car in your country, and parking lots are generally too large to be enclosed and protected from even casual view. It's an easy way for an intelligence officer to see how active one of your government agencies is." And if you were *really* interested, you found out a few names and addresses, so as to know the car types and tag numbers. The KGB had tracked the head of NSA's "Z" group—the people tasked both to crack and to create encryption systems and codes—that way for over a decade, and the reborn RVS was doubtless doing the same. Popov shook his head. "No, I would not trust a commercially available encoding system. I have my doubts about the systems used by the Russian government. Your people are very clever at cracking cipher systems. They've been so for over sixty years, well before World War Two, and they are allied with the British, who also have a tradition of excellence in that area of expertise. Has no one told you this?" Popov asked in surprise.

"Well . . . no, I've been told that this system I have here could not be broken because it is a 128-bit—"

"Ah, yes, the STU-3 standard. That system has been around in your government for about twenty years. Your people have changed to STU-4. Do you think they made that change merely because they wanted to spend money, Dr. Brightling? Or might there have been another reason? When I was in the field for KGB, I only used one-time pads. That is an encryption system only used one time, composed of random transpositions. It cannot be broken, but it is tedious to use. To send a single message that way could take hours. Unfortunately, it's very difficult to use for verbal communications. Your government has a system called TAP-DANCE, which is similar in concept, but we never managed to copy it."

"So, you mean people could be listening in on every phone call I make?"

Popov nodded. "Of course. Why do you suppose all of our substantive conversations have been made face-to-face?" Now he was really shaken, Dmitriy Arkadeyevich saw. The genius *was* a babe-in-the-woods. "Now, perhaps, is the time for you to tell me why I have undertaken these missions for you?"

▪ ▪ ▪

"YES, Minister . . . excellent . . . thank you," Bob Aukland said into his cellular phone. He thumbed the END button and put the phone back in his pocket, then turned to Bill Henriksen. "Good news. We'll have that Rainbow group down to consult on our security as well."

"Oh?" Bill observed. "Well, I guess it can't hurt all that much."

"Nose a little out of joint?" the cop asked.

"Not really," Henriksen lied. "I probably know a few of them, and they know me."

"And your fee will remain the same, Bill," the Aussie said. They headed off to his car, and from there they'd drive to a pub for a few pints before he drove the American off to the airport.

Oh, shit, the American thought. Once more the Law of Unintended Consequences had risen up to bite him in the ass. His mind went briefly into overdrive, but then persuaded itself that it didn't really matter all that much as long as he did his job right. It might even help, he told himself, almost believing it.

HE couldn't tell Popov, Brightling knew. He trusted him in many ways—hell, what Popov knew could put him in federal prison, even on death row—but to tell him what this was really all about? No, he couldn't risk that. He didn't know Popov's views on the Environment and Nature. So he couldn't predict the Russian's reaction to the project. Popov was dangerous to him in many ways, like a falcon trained to the fist, but still a free agent, willing to kill a quail or a rabbit, perhaps, but never entirely his, always able to fly off and reclaim his previous free life . . . and if he was free to do that, he was also free to give information to others. Not for the first time, Brightling thought about having Bill Henriksen take care of this potential problem. He'd know how. Surely, the former FBI agent knew how to investigate a murder, and thus how to befuddle the investigators as well, and this little problem would go away.

Assets, Brightling thought next. What other things could he do to make his position and his Project more secure? If this Rainbow was a problem, would it be possible to strike at it directly? To destroy it at best, or at worst, distract it, force it to focus in another direction?

"I have to think that one through first, Dmitriy," he said finally.

Popov nodded soberly, wondering what thoughts had gone through his employer's mind in the fifteen seconds he'd taken to consider the question. Now it was his turn to be concerned. He'd just informed John Brightling of the operational dangers involved in using him, Popov, to set up the terrorist incidents, and especially of the flaws in his communications security. The latter, especially, had frightened the man. Perhaps he ought to have warned him earlier, but somehow the subject had never arisen, and Dmitriy Arkadeyevich now realized that it had been a serious error on his part. Well, perhaps not that great an error. Operational security was not all that bad. Only two people knew what was happening . . . well, probably that Henriksen fellow as well. But Bill Henriksen was former FBI, and if he were an informer, then they'd all be in jail now. The FBI would have all the evidence it needed for a major felony investigation and trial, and would not allow things to proceed any further unless there were some vast criminal conspiracy yet to be uncovered—

—but how much larger would it have to be than conspiracy to commit murder? Moreover, they would have to know what the conspiracy was, else they would have no reason to hold off on their arrests. No, security here was good. And though the American government had the technical ability to decode Brightling's supposedly secure phone lines, even to tap them required a court order, and evidence was needed for that, and that evidence would itself be sufficient to put several people in death-row cages. Including me, Popov reminded himself.

What was going on here? the Russian demanded. He'd just thought it through enough to realize something. Whatever his employer was doing, it was *larger* than mass murder. What the *hell* could *that* be? Most worrisome of all, Popov had undertaken the missions in the hope—a realized hope, to be sure—of making a good deal of money off the job. He now had over a million dollars in his Bern bank account. Enough for him to return to Mother Russia and live very well indeed . . . but not enough for what he really wanted. So strange to discover that a "million," that magic word to describe a magic number, was something that, once you had it . . . wasn't magical at all. It was just a number from which you had to subtract to buy the things you wanted. A million American dollars wasn't enough to buy the home he wanted, the car he wanted, the food he wanted, and then have enough left over to sustain the lifestyle he craved for the remainder of his life—except, probably, in Russia, where he did not, unfortunately, wish to live. To visit, yes; to stay, no. And so Dmitriy was trapped, too.

Trapped into what, he didn't know. And so here he was, sitting across the desk from someone who, like himself, was also busily trying to think things through, but neither of them knew where to go just yet. One of them knew what was happening and the other did not—but the other one knew how to *make* things happen, and his employer did not. It was an interesting and somewhat elegant impasse.

And so they just sat there for a minute or so, each regarding the other, and if not *not* knowing what to say, then unwilling to take the risk of saying what they needed to. Finally, Brightling broke the silence.

"I really need to think this situation through. Give me a day or so to do that?"

"Certainly." Popov stood, shook hands, and walked out of the office. A player for most of his adult life in that most interesting and fascinating of games, he realized now that he was in a new game, with new parameters. He'd taken possession of a vast sum of money—but an amount that his employer had regarded as trivial. He was involved in an operation whose import was larger than that of mass murder. That was not entirely new to him, Popov realized on reflection. He'd once served a nation called by its ultimately victorious enemy the Evil Empire, and *that* cold war had been greater in size than mass murder. But Brightling was not a nation-state, and however huge his resources might be, they were minuscule in comparison with those of any advanced country. The great question remained—what the hell was this man trying to achieve? And why did he need the services of Dmitriy Arkadeyevich Popov to achieve it?

HENRIKSEN caught the Qantas flight for Los Angeles. He had the better part of a day ahead of him in his first-class seat, a good deal of time to consider what he knew.

The plan for the Olympics was essentially in the bag. The fogging system was in place, which was just plain perfect for the Project's purposes. He'd have one of his men check out the system, and thereby get himself in place for the delivery part on the last day. It was that simple. He had the consulting contract needed to make it all happen. But now this Rainbow bunch would be down there as well. How intrusive might they be? Damn, there was just no telling on that one. Worst case, it was possible that something small could toss a wrench into the works. It so often happened that way. He knew that from his time in the FBI. A random police patrol, a man on foot or in a radio-car could wander by and cause a well-planned robbery to stop. Or in the investigation phase, the unexpectedly sharp memory of a random passerby, or a casual remark made by a subject to a friend, could come to the right investigator and blow a case wide open. Boom, that simple—it had happened a million times. And the breaks always went to the other side, didn't they?

And so, from his perspective, he knew he had to eliminate the chance for such random events. He'd been so close to it. The operational concept had been brilliant—it had mainly been his from the beginning; John Brightling had merely funded it. Getting the terrorists to operate in Europe had raised the international consciousness about the threat, and *that* had allowed him and his company to get the contract to oversee the security for the Olympics. But then this damned Rainbow team had appeared, and handled three major incidents—and what asshole had instigated the third one? he demanded of himself—so well that now the Australians had asked *them* to come down for a look. And if they came down, they'd stay and keep looking, and if *that* happened, they might be there for the games, and if they wondered about chemical weapons, then they might spot the perfect delivery system for them and—

A lot of ifs, Henriksen told himself. A lot of ifs. A lot of things had to go wrong for the Project to be thwarted. There was comfort in that thought. Maybe he could meet with the Rainbow people and direct them away from the threat. After all, he had a chemical weapons expert on the payroll, and they probably did not, and that gave him the edge, didn't it? With a little cleverness, his man could do his job right in front of them and not even be seen to have done it. That's what planning was for, wasn't it?

Relax, he told himself, as the stewardess came around with drinks, and he had another glass of wine. *Relax*. But, no, he couldn't do that. He had too much experience as an investigator to accept the mere chance of random interference without consideration of the possible consequences. If his man were stopped, even by accident, then it was also possible that the entire Project could be uncovered. And *that* would mean more than failure. It would mean lifelong imprisonment at best, which was not something he was prepared to accept. No, he was committed to the Project for more than one reason. It was his task to save the world first of all—and second, he wanted to be around to enjoy what he'd had a hand in saving.

And so, risks of any type and any magnitude were unacceptable. He had to come up with a way to eliminate them. The key to that was the Russian, Popov. He wondered what that spook had discovered on his trip to England. With the right information, he could devise a plan to deal with that Rainbow bunch directly. Wouldn't that be interesting? He settled back into his seat and chose a movie to semiwatch, to disguise what he was doing. Yes, he decided ten minutes later, with the right people and the right assets, it could work.

POPOV was eating dinner alone in a disreputable-looking restaurant at the southern end of Manhattan. The food was reportedly good, but the place looked as though rats cleaned up the floor at night. But the vodka here was superb, and as usual, a few drinks helped him think abstractly.

What did he know about John Brightling? Well, the man was a scientific genius and also very impressive in his business skills. He'd been married some years ago to another bright person, now the presidential science advisor, but the marriage had ended badly, and now his employer flitted from bed to bed, one of the most eligible bachelors in America—and with the financial statement to prove it—with his photo frequently in the society pages, which must have been the cause of some discomfort to his former wife.

He had good connections in the community of people admitted into classified matters. This Rainbow group was evidently "black," but he'd gotten its name and the name of its commander in a day. Just one day, Popov reminded himself. That was beyond impressive. It was startling. How the hell had he accomplished that?

And he was into an operation whose implications were more serious than mass murder. That was where his mind came to a befuddled halt once again. It was like walking down a busy street and then coming up against a blank wall. What could a businessman be doing that was more serious than *that?* More serious than the risk of losing his freedom, even the death penalty? If it were greater than mass murder, then did the plan contemplate even larger murder? But to serve *what* end? To start a war, perhaps, but he was not a chief of state, and could not, therefore, start a war. Was Brightling a spy, feeding vital national-security-class information to a foreign government—but in return for *what?* How could anyone, government or not, bribe a billionaire? No, money was out. What did that leave?

There was a classic acronym for the reasons for making treason against your native land: MICE. Money, Ideology, Conscience, and Ego. Money was out. Brightling had too much of that. Ideology was always the best motivation for a traitor/spy—people would risk their lives far more readily for their closely held beliefs than for filthy lucre—but what ideology did this man have? Popov didn't know. Next came Conscience. But Conscience against *what?* What wrong was he trying to right? There could hardly be one, could there? That left Ego. Well, Brightling had a capacious ego, but ego assumed the motive of revenge against some more powerful person or institution that had wronged him. Who could possibly have hurt billionaire John Brightling, so much that his material success was not a sufficient salve against the wound? Popov waved to the waiter for another vodka. He'd be taking a cab home tonight.

No, Money was out. So was Ego. That left Ideology and Conscience. What beliefs or what wrong could motivate a man to do murder on a large scale? In the former case, Brightling was not a religious fanatic. In the latter, he had no overt dissatisfaction with his country. And so while Money and Ego could readily be dismissed, Ideology and Conscience were almost as unlikely, and Popov did not dismiss them only because—why? he asked himself. Because he only had four possible motivations, unless Brightling was a total madman, and he wasn't that, was he?

No, Popov told himself. His employer was not mentally unbalanced. He was thoughtful in his every action, and though his perspective, especially on the issue of money, was very different from his own—well, he had so much that such a difference in outlook was understandable; it was just a matter of perspective, and to him a million dollars was like pocket change to Dmitriy Arkadeyevich. Could he then be some sort of madman who . . . like a chief of state, a new Saddam Hussein or Adolf Hitler or Josef Vissarionovich Stalin—but, no, he was not a chief of state, had no aspirations for such a thing, and only those men could entertain that form of madness.

In his career in the KGB, Popov had dealt with all manner of curiosities. He'd played the game against world-class adversaries and never once been caught, never once failed in an assignment. As a result, he considered himself a clever sort. That made the current impasse all the more frustrating. He had over a million dollars in a Bern bank. He had the prospect of more in due course. He'd set up two terrorist missions that had accomplished their goal—had they? His employer evidently thought so, despite the abject tactical failure of both. But he knew even less now, Dmitriy Arkadeyevich told himself. The more he delved into it, the less he knew. And the less he knew, the unhappier he became. He'd asked his employer more than once the reason for his activities, but Brightling wasn't telling. It had to be something vast . . . but what the devil was it?

THEY practiced the breathing exercises. Ding found it amusing, but he was also persuaded that it was necessary. Tall and rangy though Patsy was, she was not the athlete he'd become to lead Team-2, and so she had to practice how to breathe to make the baby come more easily, and practice did make perfect. And so they sat on the floor of their house, both with their legs spread, huffing and puffing as though to destroy the home of a mythical pig, and it was all he could do not to laugh.

"Deep, cleansing breath," Domingo said, after timing the notional contraction. Then he reached for her hand and bent forward to kiss it. "How we doing, Pats?"

"I'm ready, Ding. I just want it to happen and be over."

"Worried?"

"Well," Patsy Clark Chavez, M.D., replied, "I know it's going to hurt some, and I'd just as soon have it behind me, y'know?"

"Yeah." Ding nodded. The anticipation of unpleasant things was usually worse than their realization, at least on the physical side. He knew that from experience, but she didn't yet. Maybe that was why second deliveries were almost always easier than the first. You knew what to expect, knew that though it was uncomfortable you'd make it through, and have a baby at the end of it. That was the key to the whole thing for Domingo. To be a *father!* To have a child, to begin the greatest of all adventures, raising a new life, doing the best you could, making some mistakes, but learning from all of them, and ultimately presenting to society a new, responsible citizen to carry on. That, he was sure, was what it meant to be a man. Oh, sure, carrying a gun and doing his job was important, too, since he was now a guardian of society, a righter of wrongs, a protector of the innocent, one of the forces of order from which came civilization itself, but this was his chance to be personally involved in what civilization really was, the raising of kids in the right way, educating and guiding them to do the Right Thing, even at three in the morning and half asleep. Maybe the kid would be a spook/soldier like him, or maybe even better, a physician like Pats, an important and good part of society, serving others. Those things could only happen if he and Pats did the job right, and that responsibility was the greatest that any person could undertake. Domingo looked forward to it, lusted to hold his child in his arms, to kiss and cuddle, to change diapers and clean bottoms. He'd already assembled the crib, decorated the walls of the nursery with pink and blue bunnies, and bought toys to distract the little beast, and though all of these things seemed incongruous with his regular life, both he and the men of Rainbow knew different, for all of them had children as well, and for them the covenant was exactly the same. Eddie Price had a boy of fourteen years, somewhat rebellious and decidedly headstrong—probably just as his father had once been—but also bright enough to question everything to seek his own answers, which he would find in due course, just as his father had done. The kid had "soldier" written all over him, Ding thought . . . but with luck he'd go to school first and become an officer, as Price should have done, and would have done in America. Here the system was different, though, and so he'd become a superb command sergeant major, Ding's most trusted subordinate, always ready to offer his thoughts, and then execute his orders perfectly. Yes, there was much to look forward to, Ding told himself, still holding Patsy's hand in his own.

"Scared?"

"Not scared, a little nervous," Patsy admitted.

"Honey, if it were all that hard, how come there's so many people in the world?"

"Spoken like a man," Dr. Patricia Chavez noted. "It's easy for you to say. You don't have to do it."

"I'll be there to help," her husband promised.

"You better be!"

CHAPTER 23

OVERWATCH

HENRIKSEN ARRIVED AT JFK INTERNATIONAL WITH his body feeling as though it had been shredded, spindled, and mutilated before being tossed into a wastepaper basket, but that was to be expected. He'd flown literally halfway around the globe in about a day, and his internal body-clock was confused and angry and punishing. For the next week or so, he'd find himself awake and asleep at random times, but that was all right. The right pills and a few drinks would help him rest when rest was needed. An employee was waiting for him at the end of the jetway, took his carry-on without a word, and led off to the baggage-claim area, where, blessedly, his two-suiter was the fifth bag on the carousel, which allowed them to scoot out of the terminal and onto the highway to New York City.

"How was the trip?"

"We got the contract," Henriksen told his man, who was not part of the Project.

"Good," the man said, not knowing how good it was, and how bad it would be for himself.

Henriksen buckled his seat belt and leaned back to catch a few winks on the way in, ending further conversation.

"**SO**, what do we got?" the FBI agent asked.

"Nothing so far," d'Allessandro replied. "I have one other possible missing girl, same area for her apartment, similar looks, age, and so forth, disappeared around the same time as your Miss Bannister. Name is Anne Pretloe, legal secretary, just vanished off the face of the earth."

"Jane Does?" the other federal officer asked.

"Nothing that matches. Guys, we have to face the possibility that we have a serial killer loose in the area—"

"But why did this e-mail message come out?"

"How does it match with other e-mails Miss Bannister sent to her dad?" the NYPD detective asked.

"Not very well," the senior FBI agent admitted. "The one he initially brought into the Gary office looks as though—well, it smells to me like drugs, y'know?"

"Agreed," d'Allessandro said. "You have others?"

"Here." The agent handed over six printouts faxed to the New York office. The detective scanned them. They were all perfectly grammatical, and organized, with no misspelling on any of them.

"What if she didn't send it? What if somebody else did?"

"The serial killer?" the junior FBI agent asked. Then he thought about it, and his face mirrored what he thought. "He'd have to be a real sick one, Mario."

"Yeah, well, serial killers aren't Eagle Scouts, are they?"

"Tormenting the families? Have we ever had one like that?" the senior man wondered.

"Not that I know of, Tom, but, like the man said . . ."

"Shit," observed the senior agent, Tom Sullivan.

"Call Behavioral Sciences in on this one?" the junior agent, Frank Chatham, asked.

Sullivan nodded. "Yeah, let's do that. I'll call Pat O'Connor about it. Next step here, I think we get some flyers printed up with the photo of Mary Bannister and start passing them out on the West Side. Mario, can you get us some cooperation from your people?"

"No problem," d'Allessandro replied. "If this is what it looks like, I want the fuck before he starts going for some sort of record. Not in my town, guys," the detective concluded.

"GOING to try the Interleukin again?" Barbara Archer asked.

"Yeah." Killgore nodded. "-3a is supposed to enhance the immune system, but they're not sure how. I'm not either, but if it has any effect, we need to know about it."

"What about lung complications?" One of the problems with Interleukin was that it attacked lung tissue, also for unknown reasons, and could be dangerous to smokers and others with respiratory problems.

Another nod. "Yeah, I know, just like -2, but F4 isn't a smoker, and I want to make sure that -3a doesn't do anything to compromise Shiva. We can't take that chance, Barb."

"Agreed," Dr. Archer observed. Like Killgore, she didn't think that this new version of Interleukin was the least bit helpful, but that had to be confirmed. "What about Interferon?"

"The French have been trying that on hemorrhagic fever for the last five years, but no results at all. We can hang that, too, but it's going to be a dry hole, Barb."

"Let's try it on F4 anyway," she suggested.

"Fair enough." Killgore made a notation on the chart and left the room. A minute later he appeared on the TV monitor.

"Hi, Mary, how are we feeling this morning? Any better?"

"No." She shook her head. "Stomach still hurts pretty bad."

"Oh, really? Let's see what we can do about that." This case was proceeding rapidly. Killgore wondered if she had a genetic abnormality in her upper GI, maybe some vulnerability to peptic ulcer disease? . . . If so, then the Shiva was going to rip her apart in a hurry. He increased the morphine dosage rate on the machine next to her bed. "Okay, now we're going to give you a couple of new medications. These ought to fix you up in two or three days, okay?"

"Are these the ones I signed up for?" F4 asked weakly.

"Yes, that's right," Killgore replied, hanging the Interferon and Interleukin-3a on the medication tree. "These ought to make you feel a lot better," he promised with a smile. It was so odd, talking to his lab rats. Well, as he'd told himself many times, a rat was a pig was a dog was a . . . girl, in this case. There wasn't really all that much of a difference, was there? *No,* he told himself this afternoon. Her body relaxed with the increased morphine dose, and her eyes became unfocused. Well, that *was* one difference, wasn't it? They didn't give rats sedatives or narcotics to ease their pain. It wasn't that they didn't want to, just that there was no practical way to ease their discomfort. It had never pleased him to see those cute pink eyes change from bright to dull, reflecting the pain. Well, in this case, at least, the dullness mirrored a respite from the pain.

THE information was very interesting, Henriksen thought, and this Russian was pretty good at developing it. He would have made a good agent for the Foreign Counterintelligence Division . . . but then, that's just what he had been, in a way, only working for the other side, of course. And with the information, he recalled his idea, from the Qantas flight.

"Dmitriy," Bill asked, "do you have contacts in Ireland?"

Popov nodded. "Yes, several of them."

Henriksen looked over at Dr. Brightling for approval and got a nod. "How would they like to get even with the SAS?"

"That has been discussed many times, but it is not practical. It is like sending a bank robber into a guarded bank—no, that is not right. It is like sending a robber into the government agency which prints the money. There are too many defensive assets to make the mission practical."

"But they actually wouldn't be going to Hereford, would they? What if we could draw them out into the open, and then stage our own little surprise for them? . . ." Henriksen explained on.

It was a very interesting idea, Popov thought. But: "It is still a very dangerous mission."

"Very well. What is the current condition of the IRA?"

Popov leaned back in his chair. "They are badly split. There are now several factions. Some want peace. Some want the disorders to continue. The reasons are both ideological and personal to the faction members. Ideological insofar as they truly believe in their political objective of overturning both the British rule in Northern Ireland and the Republican government in Dublin, and establishing a 'progressive socialist' government. As an objective, it's far too ambitious for a practical world, yet they believe in it and hold to it. They are committed Marxists—actually more Maoist than Marxist, but that is not important to us at the moment."

"And the personal side?" Brightling asked.

"When one is a revolutionary, it is not merely a matter of belief, but also a matter of perception by the public. To many people a revolutionary is a romantic character, a person who believes in a vision of the future and is willing to risk his life for it. From that comes his social status. Those who know such people often respect them. Therefore, to lose that status injures the former revolutionary. He must now work for a living, drive a truck or whatever he is capable of—"

"Like what happened to you when the KGB RIF'd you, in other words," Henriksen offered.

Popov had to nod at that. "In a way, yes. As a field officer of State Security, I had status and importance enjoyed by few others in the Soviet Union, and losing that was more significant to me than the loss of my modest salary. It will be the same for these Irish Marxists. And so they have two reasons for wanting the disorders to continue: their political ideological beliefs, and their need for personal recognition as something more than ordinary worker-citizens."

"Do you know such people?" Henriksen asked pointedly.

"Yes, I can probably identify some. I met many in the Bekaa Valley in Lebanon, where they trained with other 'progressive elements.' And I have traveled to Ireland on occasion to deliver messages and money to support their activities. Those operations tied up large segments of the British Army, you see, and were, therefore, worthy of Soviet support as a distraction to a large NATO enemy." Popov ended his discourse, looking at the other two men in the room. "What would you have them do?"

"It's not so much a question of what as of how," Bill told the Russian. "You know, when I was in the Bureau, we used to say that the IRA was composed of the best terrorists in the world, dedicated, smart, and utterly vicious."

"I would agree with that assessment. They were superbly organized, ideologically sound, and willing to undertake nearly anything if it had a real political impact."

"How would they view this mission?"

"What mission is that?" Dmitriy asked, and then Bill explained his basic mission concept. The Russian listened politely and thoughtfully before responding: "That would appeal to them, but the scope and the dangers are very large."

"What would they require to cooperate?"

"Money and other support, weapons, explosives, the things they need to carry on their operations. The current faction-fighting has probably had the effect of disrupting their logistical organization. That's doubtless how the peace faction is trying to control the continued-violence faction, simply by restricting their access to weapons. Without that, they cannot take physical action, and cannot therefore enhance their own prestige. So, if you offer them the wherewithal to conduct operations, they will listen seriously to your plan."

"Money?"

"Money allows one to purchase things. The factions with which we would deal have probably been cut off from regular funding sources."

"Which are?" Brightling asked.

"Drinking clubs, and what you call the 'protection racket,' yes?"

"That's right," Henriksen confirmed with a nod. "That's how they get their money, and that source is probably well controlled by the peace factions."

"So, then, how much do you think, Dmitriy?" John Brightling asked.

"Several million dollars, I should say, at the least, that is."

"You'll have to be very careful laundering it," Bill warned their boss. "I can help."

"Call it five million? . . ."

"That should be enough," Popov said, after a moment's reflection, "plus the psychological attraction of bearding the lion so close to his own den. But I can offer no promises. These people make their own decisions, for their own reasons."

"How quickly could you arrange the meeting?"

"Two days, perhaps three, after I arrive in Ireland," Popov answered.

"Get your tickets," Brightling told him decisively.

"ONE of them did some talking before he deployed," Tawney said. "His name was René. Before he set off to Spain, he chatted with a girlfriend. She had an attack of conscience and came in on her own. The French interviewed her yesterday."

"And?" Clark asked.

"And the purpose of the mission was to free Carlos, but he said nothing to her about their being assigned the mission by anyone. In fact he said little, though the interview did develop the name of another participant in the mission, or so our French colleagues think. They're running that name down now. The woman in question—well, he and she had been friends, lovers, for some time, and evidently he confided in her. She came to the police on her own because of the dead Dutch child. The Paris papers have made a big show of that, and it evidently troubled her conscience. She told the police that she tried to talk him out of the job—not sure that I believe that—and that he told her that he'd think about it. Evidently he didn't follow through on that, but the French are now wondering if someone might have opted out. They're sweeping up the usual suspects for a chat. Perhaps they'll turn up something," Tawney concluded hopefully.

"That's all?" Clark asked.

"It's quite a lot, really," Peter Covington observed. "It's rather more than we had yesterday, and it allows our French friends to pursue additional leads."

"Maybe," Chavez allowed. "But *why* did they go out? Who's turning these bastards loose?"

"Anything from the other two incidents?" Clark asked.

"Not a bloody peep," Tawney replied. "The Germans have rattled every bush. Cars were seen going in and out of the Fürchtner/Dortmund house, but she was an artist, and they might well have been buyers of her paintings. In any case, no vehicle descriptions, much less license-plate numbers. That is dead, unless someone else walks into a police station and makes a statement."

"Known associates?" Covington asked.

"All interviewed by the BKA, with no results. Hans and Petra were never known for talking. The same was true of Model and Guttenach." Tawney waved his hands in frustration.

"It's out there, John," Chavez said. "I can feel it."

"I agree," Covington said with a nod. "But the trick's getting our hands on it."

Clark frowned mightily, but he knew the drill, too, from his time in the field. You wanted information to develop, but merely wanting it never made it happen. Things like that just came to you when they decided to come. It was that simple, and that maddening, especially when you knew it was there and you knew that you needed it. With one small bit of information, Rainbow could turn some national police force loose and sweep up the person or persons they wanted and grill them over a slow fire until they got what they needed. The French or the Germans would be best—neither of them had the legal restrictions that the Americans and Brits had placed on their police forces. But that wasn't a good way to think, and the FBI usually got people to spill their guts, even though they treated all criminals with white kid gloves. Even terrorists, once caught, usually told what they knew—well, not the Irish, John remembered. Some of those bastards wouldn't say "boo," not even their own names. Well, there were ways of handling that level of recalcitrance. It was just a matter of speaking to them outside of police view, putting the fear of God, and of pain, into them. That usually worked—had *always* worked in John Clark's experience. But first you needed somebody to talk to. That was the hard part.

As a field officer of the CIA he'd often enough been in distant, uncomfortable places on a mission, then had the mission aborted—or just as bad, postponed—because some vital bit of information had been missing or lost. He'd seen three men and one woman die for that reason, in four different places, all of them behind the Iron Curtain. Four people, all of whose faces he'd known, lost, judicially murdered by their parent countries. Their struggle against tyranny had ultimately been successful, but they hadn't lived to see it or enjoy the fruits of their courage, and it was part of Clark's conscience that he remembered every single one of them—and because of that he'd grown to hate the people who'd had the information he'd needed but had not been able to get out in time. So it was now. Ding was right. *Somebody* was calling these animals out of their lairs, and he wanted that somebody. Finding him or her would give them all manner of names and telephone numbers and addresses for the European police agencies to sweep up into one big bag, and so end much of the terrorism that still hung over Europe like a cloud. And *that* would be a hell of a lot better than sending his troopers out into the field with loaded guns.

POPOV packed his bags. He was getting quite expert at this, the Russian told himself, and had learned to pack his shirts without their coming out of the bag wrinkled, which he'd never learned as a KGB officer. Well, the shirts were more expensive now, and he'd learned to take better care of them. The suitcases, however, reflected his previous occupation, and included some special pockets and compartments in which he could keep his "alternate" travel documents. These he kept with him at all times now. Should the whole project collapse of its own weight, he wanted to be able to disappear without a trace, and his three unused sets of documents should help in that. In the final extreme, he could access his Bern bank account and disappear back into Russia, though he had other plans for his future—

—but he worried that greed might be clouding his judgment. Five million dollars. If he could bank that to himself, then he'd have the resources he needed to live in comfort forever, in virtually any place of his choosing, especially if he invested it wisely. But how could he defraud the IRA out of the money detailed to them? Well, that might easily come to him. Then his eyes closed and he asked himself about greed. Was it indeed clouding his operational judgment? Was he taking an unnecessary chance, led along by his wish to have this huge amount of money? It was hard to be objective about one's own motivations. And it was hard to be a free man now, not just one of thousands of field officers in the Committee for State Security, having to justify every single dollar, pound, or ruble he spent to the accountants at Number 2 Dzerzhinsky Square, the most humorless people in a singularly humorless agency.

Greed, Popov thought, worrying about it. He had to set that whole issue aside. He had to go forward as the professional he'd always been, careful and circumspect at every turn, lest he be caught by enemy counterintelligence services or even by the people with whom he would be meeting. The Provisional Wing of the Irish Republican Army was as ruthless as any terrorist organization in the world. Though its members could be jolly fellows over a drink—in their drinking they so closely resembled Russians—they killed their enemies, inside and outside their organization, with as little compunction as medical testers with their laboratory rats. Yet they could also be loyal to a fault. In that they were predictable, and that was good for Popov. And he knew how to deal with them. He'd done so often enough in the past, both in Ireland and the

Bekaa Valley. He just couldn't let them discern his desire to bank the money earmarked to them, could he?

The packing done, Popov took his bags to the elevator, then down to the street level, where the apartment house's doorman flagged him a cab for La Guardia, where he'd board the shuttle for Boston's Logan International, and there to catch the Aer Lingus flight to Dublin. If nothing else, his work for Brightling had gotten him a lot of frequent-flyer miles, though with too many different airlines to be of real help. But they always flew him first-class, which KGB had never done, Dmitriy Arkadeyevich thought with a suppressed smile in the back seat of the cab. All he had to do, he reminded himself, was deal honestly with the PIRA. If the opportunity came to steal their money, then he'd take it. But he already knew one thing: they'd jump at the proposed operation. It was too good to pass up, and if nothing else, the PIRA had *élan*.

SPECIAL Agent Patrick O'Connor looked over the information faxed from New York. The trouble with kidnapping investigations was time. No investigation ever ran quickly enough, but it was worse with kidnappings, because you knew that somewhere was a real person whose life depended upon your ability to get the information and act upon it before the kidnapper decided to end his nasty little game, kill the current hostage, and go grab another. Grab another? Yes, probably, because there had been no ransom demand, and that meant that whoever had snatched Mary Bannister off the street wasn't willing to sell her back. No, he'd be using her as a toy, almost certainly for sexual gratification, until he tired of her, and then, probably, he'd kill her. And so, O'Connor thought himself to be in a race, albeit on a track he couldn't see, and running against a stopwatch hidden in the hand of another. He had a list of Ms. Bannister's local friends and associates, and he had his men and women out talking to them, hoping to turn up a name or a phone number that would lead them on to the next step in the investigation . . . but probably not, he thought. No, this case was all happening in New York. This young woman had gone there to seek her fortune in the bright city lights, like so many others. And many of them did find what they were seeking, which was why they went, but this one, from the outskirts of Gary, Indiana, had gone there without knowing what it was like in a big city, and lacked the self-protective skills one needed in a city of eight million . . .

. . . and she was probably already dead, O'Connor admitted quietly to himself, killed by whatever monster had snatched her off the street. There was not a damned thing he could do about it except to identify, arrest, and convict the creep, which would save others, but wouldn't be worth a damn to the victim whose name titled the case file on his desk. Well, that was one of the problems of being a cop. You couldn't save them all. But you did try to avenge them all, and that was something, the agent told himself, as he rose to get his coat for the drive home.

CHAVEZ sipped his Guinness and looked around the club. The Eagle of the Legion had been hung on the wall opposite the bar, and people already went over to touch the wooden staff in respect. Three of his Team-2 people were at a table, drinking their brews and chatting about something or other with two of Peter Covington's troops. The TV was on—snooker championships? Chavez wondered. That was a national event? Which changed into news and weather.

More El Niño stuff, Ding saw with a snort. Once it had just been called *weather,* but then some damned oceanographer had discovered that the warm/cold water mix off the coast of South America changed every few years, and that when it happened the world's climate changed a little bit here and there, and the media had latched onto it, delighted, so it seemed, to have another label to put on things they lacked the education to understand. Now they said that the current rendition of the "El Niño Effect" was unusually hot weather in Australia.

"Mr. C, you're old enough to remember. What did they say before this crap?"

"They called it unusually hot, cold, or seasonable weather, tried to tell you if it was going to be hot, cold, sunny, or rainy the next day, and then they told you about the baseball scores." With rather less accuracy on the weather side, Clark didn't say. "How's Patsy doing?"

"Another couple of weeks, John. She's holding up pretty well, but she bitches about how big her belly's gotten to be." He checked his watch. "Ought to be home in another thirty minutes. Same shift with Sandy."

"Sleeping okay?" John went on.

"Yeah, a little restless when the little *hombre* rolls around, but she's getting all she needs. Be cool, John. I'm taking good care of her. Looking forward to being a grandpa?"

Clark sipped at his third pint of the evening. "One more milestone on the road to death, I suppose." Then he chuckled. "Yeah, Domingo, I am looking forward to it." *I'll spoil the shit out of this little bastard, and then just hand him back when he cries.* "Ready to be a pop?"

"I think I can handle it, John. How hard can it be? You did it."

Clark ignored the implicit challenge. "We're going to be sending a team down to Australia in a few weeks."

"What for?" Chavez asked.

"The Aussies are a little worried about the Olympics, and we look pretty sexy 'cause of all the missions we've had. So, they want some of us to come on down and look over things with their SAS."

"Their guys any good?"

Clark nodded. "So I am told, but never hurts to get an outside opinion, does it?"

"Who's going down?"

"I haven't decided yet. They already have a consulting company, Global Security, Ltd., run by a former FBI guy. Noonan knows him. Hamilton, something like that."

"Have they ever had a terrorist incident down there?" Domingo asked next.

"Nothing major that I can remember, but, well, you don't remember Munich in 1972, do you?"

Chavez shook his head. "Just what I've read about it. The German cops really screwed the pooch on that mission."

"Yeah, I guess. Nobody ever told them that they'd have to face people like that. Well, now we all know, right? That's how GSG-9 got started, and they're pretty good."

"Like the *Titanic,* eh? Ships have enough lifeboats because she didn't?"

John nodded agreement. "That's how it works. It takes a hard lesson to make people learn, son." John set his empty glass down.

"Okay, but how come the bad guys never learn?" Chavez asked, finishing off his second of the evening. "We've delivered some tough lessons, haven't we? But you think we can fold up the tents? Not hardly, Mr. C. They're still out there, John, and they're not retiring, are they? They ain't learned shit."

"Well, I'd sure as hell learn from it. Maybe they're just dumber than we are. Ask Bellow about it," Clark suggested.

"I think I will."

POPOV was fading off to sleep. The ocean below the Aer Lingus 747 was dark now, and his mind was well forward of the aircraft, trying to remember faces and voices from the past, wondering if perhaps his contact had turned informer to the British Security Service, and would doom him to identification and possible arrest. Probably not. They'd seemed very dedicated to their cause—but you could never be sure. People turned traitor for all manner of reasons. Popov knew that well. He'd helped more than his share of people do just that, changing their loyalties, betraying their countries, often for small amounts of cash. How much the easier to turn against an atheist foreigner who'd given them equivocal support? What if his contacts had come to see the futility of their cause? Ireland would not turn into a Marxist country, for all their wishes. The list of such nations was very thin now, though across the world academics still clung to the words and ideas of Marx and Engels and even Lenin. Fools. There were even those who said that Communism had been tried in the wrong country—that Russia had been far too backward to make those wonderful ideas work.

That was enough to bring an ironic smile and a shake of the head. He'd once been part of the organization called the Sword and Shield of the Party. He'd been through the Academy, had sat through all the political classes, learned the answers to the inevitable examination questions and been clever enough to write down exactly what his instructors wanted to hear, thus ensuring high marks and the respect of his mentors—few of whom had believed in that drivel any more than he had, but none of whom had found within themselves the courage to speak their real thoughts. It was amazing how long the lies had lasted, and truly Popov could remember his surprise when the red flag had been pulled down from its pole atop the Kremlin's Spasskaya Gate. Nothing, it seemed, lived longer than a perverse idea.

CHAPTER 24

CUSTOMS

ONE OF THE DIFFERENCES BETWEEN EUROPE AND America was that the former's countries truly welcomed foreigners, while America, for all her hospitality, made entering the country remarkably inconvenient. Certainly the Irish erected no barriers, Popov saw, as his passport was stamped and he collected his luggage for an "inspection" so cursory that the inspector probably hadn't noticed if the person carrying it was male or female. With that, Dmitriy Arkadeyevich walked outside and flagged a cab for his hotel. His reservation gave him a one-bedroom suite overlooking a major thoroughfare, and he immediately undressed to catch a few more hours of sleep before making his first call. His last thought before closing his eyes on this sunny morning was that he hoped the contact number hadn't been changed, or compromised. If the latter, then he'd have to do some explaining to the local police, but he had a cover story, if necessary. While it wasn't perfect, it would be good enough to protect a person who'd committed no crimes in the Republic of Ireland.

"AIRBORNE, Airborne, have you heard?" Vega sang, as they began the final mile. "We're gonna jump from the big-ass bird!"

It surprised Chavez that as bulky as First Sergeant Julio Vega was, he never seemed to suffer from it on the runs. He was a good thirty pounds heavier than any other Team-2 member. Any bigger across the chest and he'd have to get his fatigue shirts custom-made, but despite the ample body, his legs and wind hadn't failed him yet. And so, today, he was taking his turn leading the morning run. . . . In another four minutes they could see the stop line, which they all welcomed, though none of them would admit it.

"Quick time—*march!*" Vega called, as he crossed the yellow line, and everyone slowed to the usual one-hundred-twenty steps per minute. "Left, left, your left your right your left!" Another half minute and: "Detail . . . *halt!*" And everyone stopped. There was a cough or two from those who'd had a pint or two too many the night before, but nothing more than that.

Chavez walked to the command position in front of the two lines of troopers. "Fall out," he ordered, allowing Team-2 to walk to their building for a shower, having stretched and exercised all their muscles for the day. Later today they'd have another run through the shooting house for a live-fire exercise. It would be boring in content, since they'd already tried just about every possible permutation of hostages and bad guys. Their shooting was just about perfect. Their physical condition *was* perfect, and their morale was so high that they seemed bored. They were so confident in their abilities, they'd demonstrated them so convincingly in the field, firing real bullets into real targets. Even his time with the 7th Light Infantry Division had not given him such confidence in his people. They'd gotten to the point that the British SAS troopers, who had a long, proud history of their own, and who'd initially looked upon the Rainbow teams with a great degree of skepticism, now welcomed them into the club and even admitted they had things to learn from them. And *that* was quite a stretch, since the SAS had been the acknowledged world masters at special operations.

A few minutes later, showered and dressed, Chavez came out to the squad bay, where his people were at their individual desks, going over intelligence information from Bill Tawney and his crew, and checking out photos, many of them massaged by the computer systems to allow for the years since they'd originally been taken. The systems seemed to get better on a daily basis as the software evolved. A picture taken from an angle was now manipulated by the computer into a straight-on portrait shot, and his men studied them as they might examine photos of their own children, along with whatever information they had of who was suspected to be where, with what known or suspected associates, and so forth. It seemed a waste of time to Chavez, but you couldn't run and shoot all day, and knowing the faces wasn't a total waste of time. They *had* identified Fürchtner and Dortmund that way on their Vienna deployment, hadn't they?

Sergeant Major Price was going over budget stuff, which he'd toss onto Ding's desk for later examination, so that his boss could justify expenditures, and then maybe request some new training funds for some new idea or other. Tim Noonan was working away with his new electronic toys, and Clark was always, so it seemed, fighting money battles with CIA and other American agencies. That struck Chavez as a total waste of effort. Rainbow had been pretty bulletproof from the very beginning—Presidential sponsorship never hurt—and their missions hadn't exactly diminished the credibility from which their funding derived. In another two hours, they'd go to the range for their daily expenditure of one hundred rounds of pistol and SMG ammunition, followed by the live-five exercise . . . another routine day. For "routine," Ding often substituted "boring," but that couldn't be helped, and it was a hell of a lot less boring than it had been on field missions for CIA, most of which time had been spent sitting down waiting for a meet and/or filling out forms to describe the field operation for the Langley bureaucrats who demanded full documentation of everything that happened in the field because—because that was one of the rules. Rules at best enforced by people who'd been out there and done that a generation before and thought they still knew all about it, and at worst by people who didn't have a clue, and were all the more demanding for that very reason. But the government, which tossed away billions of dollars every day, could often be so niggardly over a thousand or so, and nothing Chavez could do would ever change that.

COLONEL Malloy now had his own office in the headquarters building, since it had been decided that he was a Rainbow division commander. A staff-grade officer in the United States Marine Corps, he was accustomed to such nonsense, and he thought about hanging a dartboard on the wall for amusement when he wasn't working. Work for him was driving his chopper—which, he reminded himself, he didn't really have, since the one assigned to him was, at the moment, down for maintenance. Some widget was being replaced with a new and improved widget that would enhance his ability to do something of which he was not yet fully informed, but which, he was sure, would be important, especially to the civilian contractor, which had conceived of, designed, and manufactured the new and improved widget.

It could have been worse. His wife and kids liked it here, and Malloy liked it, as well. His was a skill position rather than a dangerous one. There was little hazard in being a helicopter pilot in a special-operations outfit. The only thing that worried him was hitting power lines, since Rainbow mainly deployed to operations in built-up areas, and in the past twenty years more helicopters had been lost to electrical power lines than to all known antiaircraft weapons around the world. His MH-60K didn't have cable cutters, and he'd written a scathing memo on that fact to the commander of the 24th Special

Operations Squadron, who had replied contritely with six photocopies of memos he'd dispatched to his parent-unit commander on the same issue. He'd explained further on that some expert in the Pentagon was considering the modification to the existing aircraft—which, Malloy thought, was the subject of a consulting contract worth probably $300,000 or so to some Beltway Bandit whose conclusion would be, *Yes, that's a good idea,* couched in about four hundred pages of stultifying bureaucratic prose, which nobody would ever read but which would be enshrined in some archive or other for all time. The modification would cost all of three thousand dollars in parts and labor—the labor part would be the time of a sergeant who worked full-time for the Air Force anyway, whether actually working or sitting in his squad bay reading *Playboy*—but the rules were, unfortunately, the rules. And who knew, maybe in a year the Night Hawks would have the cable cutters.

Malloy grimaced and wished for his darts. He didn't need to see the intelligence information. The faces of known or suspected terrorists were of no use to him. He never got close enough to see them. That was the job of the shooters, and division commander or not he was merely their chauffeur. Well, it could have been worse. At least he was able to wear his "bag," or flight suit, at his desk, almost as though this were a proper organization of aviators. He got to fly four days or so out of seven, and that wasn't bad, and after this assignment, his detailer had hinted, he might go on to command of VMH-1, and maybe fly the President around. It would be dull, but career-enhancing. It surely hadn't hurt his old friend, Colonel Hank Goodman, who had just appeared on the star list, a fairly rare achievement for a rotor-head, since naval aviation, which was mainly helicopter drivers, was run, and run ruthlessly, by fast-movers in their jet-powered fixed-wing fighter bombers. Well, they all had prettier scarves. To amuse himself before lunch, Malloy pulled out his manual for the MH-60K and started to memorize additional information on engine performance, the kind of thing usually done by an engineering officer or maybe his crew chief, Sergeant Jack Nance.

THE initial meeting took place in a public park. Popov had checked the telephone book and called the number for one Patrick X. Murphy just before noon.

"Hello, this is Joseph Andrews. I'm trying to find Mr. Yates," he'd said.

That statement was followed by silence, as the man on the other end of the phone had searched his memory for the codephrase. It was an old one, but after ten seconds or so, he'd fished it out.

"Ah, yes, Mr. Andrews. We haven't heard from you in some time."

"I just arrived in Dublin this morning, and I'm looking forward to seeing him. How quickly can we get together?"

"How about one this afternoon?" And then had come the instructions.

So, here he was now, wearing his raincoat and wide-brimmed fedora hat, carrying a copy of the *Irish Times* in his right hand, and sitting on a particular bench close to an oak tree. He used the downtime to read the paper and catch up on what was happening in the world—it wasn't very different from what he'd seen on CNN the previous day in New York ... international news had gotten so dull since the demise of the Soviet Union, and he wondered how the editors of major newspapers had learned to deal with it. Well, people in Rwanda and Burundi were still slaughtering one another with obscene gusto, and the Irish were wondering aloud if soldiers from their army might be sent down as peacekeepers. Wasn't that odd? Popov thought. They'd proven singularly unable to keep the peace at home, so why, then, send them elsewhere to do it?

"Joe!" a happy voice said out of his field of vision. He looked up to see a fortyish man with a beaming smile.

"Patrick!" Popov responded, standing, going over to shake hands. "It's been a long time." Very long, as he'd never met this particular chap before, though they exchanged greetings like old friends. With that, they walked off to O'Connell Street, where a car was waiting. Popov and his new friend got in the back, and the driver took off at once, not speeding, but checking his rearview mirror carefully as he took several random turns. "Patrick" in the back looked up for helicopters. Well, Dmitriy thought, these PIRA soldiers hadn't lived to their current ages by being careless. For his part, Popov just sat back and relaxed. He might have closed his eyes, but that would have been overly patronizing to his hosts. Instead, he just stared forward. It was not his first time in Dublin, but except for a few obvious landmarks, he remembered little of the city. His current companions would not have believed that, since intelligence officers were supposed to have trained, photographic memories—which was true, but only to a point. It took forty minutes of weaving through the city until they came to a commercial building and looped around into an alley. There the car stopped, and they got out to enter a door in a blank brick wall.

"Iosef Andreyevich," a voice said calmly in the darkness. Then a face appeared.

"Sean, it has been a long time." Popov stepped forward, extending his hand.

"Eleven years and six months, to be exact," Sean Grady agreed, taking the hand and shaking it warmly.

"Your trade-craft remains excellent." Popov smiled. "I have no idea where we are."

"Well, one must be careful, Iosef." Grady waved. "Come this way, if you would."

Grady directed him to a small room with a table and a few chairs. There was tea brewing. The Irish hadn't lost their sense of hospitality, Dmitriy Arkadeyevich saw, removing his coat and dumping it on an armchair. Then he sat down.

"What can we do for you?" Grady asked. He was nearing fifty, Popov saw, but the eyes retained their youth and their dedicated look, narrow, overtly without passion, but intense as ever.

"Before we get to that, how are things going for you, Sean?"

"They could be better," Grady admitted. "Some of our former colleagues in Ulster have committed themselves to surrendering to the British Crown. Unfortunately, there are many who share those leanings, but we are working to persuade others to a more realistic point of view."

"Thank you," Popov said to the one who gave him a cup of tea. He took a sip before speaking. "Sean, you know, from the first time we met in Lebanon, I have respected your commitment to your ideals. I am surprised that so many others have wavered."

"It's been a long war, Iosef, and I suppose that not everyone can maintain his dedication. And more is the pity, my friend." Again his voice was singularly devoid of emotion. His face wasn't so much cruel as blank. He would have made a superb field intelligence officer, the Russian thought. He gave away nothing, not even the satisfaction he occasionally felt when he accomplished a mission. He'd probably showed as little passion when he'd tortured and murdered two British SAS commandos who'd made the mistake of letting down their guard just once. Such things had not happened often, but Sean Grady had achieved that most difficult of goals twice—at the cost, truth be told, of a bloody vendetta between the British Army's most elite unit and Grady's own cell of the PIRA. The SAS had killed no fewer than eight of his closest associates, and on one other occasion some seven years before they'd missed Grady only because his car had broken down on the way to a meeting—a meeting crashed by the SAS, who had killed three senior PIRA officials there. Sean Grady was a marked man, and Popov was certain that the British Security Service had spent hundreds of thousands of pounds in their attempt to track him down and target him for another commando raid. This, like intelligence operations, was a very dangerous game for all the players, but most of all for the revolutionaries themselves. And now his own leadership was selling out, or so Grady must have thought. This man would never make peace with the British. He believed too firmly in his vision of the world, warped though it was. Iosef

Vissarionovich Stalin had possessed a face like this one, and the same single-mindedness of purpose, and the same total inability to compromise on strategic issues.

"There is a new counter-terror team operating in England now," Dmitriy told him.

"Oh?" Grady hadn't known that, and the revelation surprised him.

"Yes. It is called Rainbow. It is a joint effort of the British and Americans, and it was they who handled the jobs at Worldpark, Vienna, and Bern. They have not yet been committed to this particular mission, but that is only, I think, a matter of time."

"What do you know about this new group?"

"Quite a lot." Popov handed over his written summary.

"Hereford," Grady observed. "We've been there to look, but it is not a place one can easily attack."

"Yes, I know that, Sean, but there are additional vulnerabilities, and with proper planning, we think it possible to strike a hard blow on this Rainbow group. You see, both the wife and daughter of the group commander, this American, John Clark, work at the nearby community hospital. They would be the bait for the mission—"

"Bait?" Grady asked.

"Yes, Sean." And then Popov went on to describe the mission concept. Grady, as ever, didn't react, but two of his people did, shifting in their chairs and trading looks while waiting for their commander to speak. This he finally did, rather formally.

"Colonel Serov, you propose that we undertake a major risk."

Dmitriy nodded. "Yes, that is true, and it is for you to decide if the risk is worth the rewards." Popov didn't have to remind the IRA chieftain that he'd helped them in the past—in a minor way to be sure, but these were not people to forget assistance—but neither did he have to point out that this mission, if successful, would not only catapult Grady to the forefront of IRA commanders, but also, perhaps, poison the peace process between the British government and the "official" faction of the PIRA. To be the man who humbled the SAS and other special-operations teams on their own turf would win him such prestige as no Irish revolutionary had enjoyed since 1920. That was always the weakness of such people, Popov knew. Their dedication to ideology made them hostage to their egos, to their vision, not only of their political objectives, but of themselves.

"Iosef Andreyevich, unfortunately, we do not have the resources to consider such a mission as this."

"I understand that. What resources do you require, Sean?"

"More than you can offer." From his own experience, and from speaking with others in the community of world terrorists, Grady knew how tight the KGB was with its cash. But that only set him up for the next surprise.

"Five million American dollars, in a numbered and codeword-controlled Swiss account," Popov said evenly, and this time he saw emotion on Grady's face. The eyes blinked. The mouth opened slightly, as though to voice an objection, but then he restored his self-control.

"Six," Grady said, just to take control of the agenda.

That suited Popov just fine. "Very well, then, I suppose I can offer as much as six million. How quickly will you need it?"

"How quickly can you deliver it?"

"A week, I think. How long for you to plan the operation?"

Grady thought for a few seconds. "Two weeks." He already knew much of the area around Hereford. That he had not been able to conduct an attack in earlier days hadn't prevented him from thinking—dreaming—about it, and gathering the needed intelligence. He had also tried to gather information on SAS operations, but had found that the SAS didn't talk very much, even afterward, except within their own community. A few covert photographs had been generated, but they hadn't proven very useful in the field. No, what they'd needed and hadn't had in previous years was a combination of people willing to undertake a huge risk and the resources to obtain the items the mission would require.

"One other thing," Grady said.

"Yes?"

"How good are your contacts with drug dealers?" Grady asked.

Popov allowed himself to be shocked, though he didn't react visibly. Grady wanted drugs to sell? That was a huge change in the PIRA's ethos. In earlier years, the Provos had made a point of killing or kneecapping drug dealers as a means of showing that they were worthy of community support. So, this had changed, too?

"I have some indirect contacts, I suppose. What would you require?"

"Cocaine, a large quantity of it, preferably pure."

"To sell here?"

"Yes. Money is money, Iosef," Grady pointed out. "And we need a continuing income to maintain operations."

"I make no promises, but I will see what I can do."

"Very well. Let me know about the money. When it is available to us, I will let you know if the mission can be carried out, and when we might be able to do it."

"Weapons?"

"That is not a concern," Grady assured him.

"I need a telephone number to call."

Grady nodded, took a pad from the table, and wrote it out for him. It was clearly a cellular phone. The Russian pocketed the note. "That should be good for another few weeks. Is that sufficient to your needs?"

"Yes, it is." Popov stood. There was nothing else to be said. Popov was led out of the building and back to his car. The meeting had gone well, Dmitriy told himself on the drive back to his hotel.

"SEAN, this is a suicide mission!" Roddy Sands warned back in the warehouse.

"Not if we control the situation, Roddy," Grady replied. "And we can do that if we have the proper resources. We'll have to be careful, and very quick, but we can do it." *And when we do,* Grady didn't have to go on, *then the entire movement will see who really represents the people of Ireland.* "We'll need fifteen men or so. We can get the right fifteen men, Roddy." Then Grady stood and walked out the other door in the room and got his own car for the drive to his safe house. There he had work to do, the sort of work he always did alone.

HENRIKSEN was assembling his team. He figured ten men total, all experienced, and all briefed in on the Project. Foremost among them would be Lieutenant Colonel Wilson Gearing, formerly of the United States Army Chemical Corps. A genuine expert on chemical weapons, he would be the deliveryman. The rest would consult with the local security forces, and tell them things they already knew, establishing and enforcing the international rule that an Expert Was Somebody From Out Of Town. The Australian SAS would listen politely to everything his people said, and maybe even learn a thing or two, especially when his people brought down the new radio gear from E-Systems and Dick Voss trained the Aussies up on them. The new radios for special-operations troops and SWAT cops were a thing of beauty. After that, they'd merely strut around with special ID to get them through all the security checkpoints, and even onto the track-and-field grounds of the huge stadium. They'd be able to watch the Olympics close up, which would be an interesting fringe benny for his people, some of whom, he was sure, were real sports fans who would enjoy seeing the last Olympics.

He selected his best people, and then had the corporation's travel agent set up the flights and accommodations—the latter through the Australian police, which had reserved a block of hotel suites close to the stadium for their own use throughout the Olympic games. Henriksen wondered if there would be media attention for his company. Ordinarily, he would have insisted on it, just as advertising, but not this time, he decided. There wasn't much point in advertising his company anymore, was there?

SO, this project was done. Hollister looked over the buildings, the roads, parking lots, and the ersatz airplane runway whose construction he'd supervised here in the Kansas plains. The final stuff had been the usual confusion of niggling little details, but all the subcontractors had responded well to his browbeating, especially since their contracts all had incentive clauses as well.

The company car pulled up to his four-by-four and stopped, and then Hollister was surprised. The guy who got out was the big boss, John Brightling himself. He'd never met the chairman of the corporation, though he knew the name, and had seen the face on TV once or twice. He must have flown in this very morning on one of his corporate jets, and the construction superintendent was somewhat disappointed that he hadn't used the approach road, which could have easily accommodated the Gulfstream.

"Mr. Hollister, I presume?"

"Yes, sir." He took the extended hand and shook it. "It's all done, as of today, sir."

"You beat your promise by two and a half weeks," Brightling observed.

"Well, the weather helped us out some. I can't take credit for that."

Brightling laughed. "I would."

"The toughest part was the environmental systems. That's the most demanding set of specifications I've ever seen. What's the big deal, Dr. Brightling?"

"Well, some of the things we work with demand full isolation—Level Four, we call it in the business. Hot Lab stuff, and we have to treat it very carefully, as you might imagine. Federal rules on that we have to follow."

"But the whole building?" Hollister asked. It had been like building a ship or an aircraft. Rarely was any large structure designed to be completely airtight. But this one was, which had forced them to do air-pressure tests when each module had been completed, and driven his window contractors slightly crazy.

"Well, we just wanted it done our way."

"Your building, doc," Hollister allowed. That one specification had added five million dollars of labor costs to the project, all of it to the window contractor, whose workers had hated the detail work, though not the extra pay to do it. The old Boeing plant down the road at Wichita had hardly been called upon to do such finely finished work. "You picked a pretty setting for it, though."

"Didn't we, though?" All around, the land was covered with a swaying green carpet of wheat, just about a quarter way into its growing cycle. There were some farm machines visible, fertilizing and weeding the crop. Maybe not as pretty as a golf course, but a lot more practical. The complex even had its own large institutional bakery to bake its own bread, maybe from the wheat grown right here on the campus? Hollister wondered. Why hadn't he thought about that one before? The farms that had been bought along with the land even included a feed-lot for fattening up cattle, and other land used for truck-farm vegetables. This whole complex could be self-sustaining if somebody ever wanted it to be. Well, maybe they just wanted it to fit in with the area. This part of Kansas was all farms, and though the steel-and-glass buildings of the project didn't exactly look like barns and equipment sheds, their surroundings somehow muted their invasiveness. And besides, you could hardly see them from the interstate highway to the north, and only from a few public roads closer than that, and the gatehouses for limiting access were stout buildings, almost like pillboxes—to protect against tornadoes, the specifications had said, and sure enough no tornado could hurt them—hell, even some loony farmer with a .50-caliber machine gun couldn't hurt those security huts.

"So, you've earned your bonus. The money will be in your account by the close of business tomorrow," Dr. John Brightling promised.

"Suits me, sir." Hollister fished in his pocket and pulled out the master key, the one that would open any door in the complex. It was a little ceremony he always performed when he finished a project. He handed it over. "Well, sir, it's your building complex now."

Brightling looked at the electronic key and smiled. This was the last major hurdle for the Project. This would be the home of nearly all of his people. A similar but much smaller structure in Brazil had been finished two months earlier, but that one barely accommodated a hundred people. This one could house three thousand—somewhat crowded, but comfortably even so—for some months, and that was about right. After the first couple of months, he could sustain his medical research efforts here with his best people—most of them *not* briefed in on the Project, but worthy of life even so—because that work was heading in some unexpectedly promising directions. So promising that he wondered how long he himself might live here. Fifty years? A hundred? A thousand, perhaps? Who could say now?

Olympus, he'd call it, Brightling decided on the spot. The home of the gods, for that was exactly what he expected it to be. From here they could watch the world, study it, enjoy it, *appreciate* it. He would use the call-sign OLYMPUS-1 on his portable radio. From here he'd be able to fly all over the world with picked companions, to observe and learn how the ecology was supposed to work. For twenty years or so, they'd be able to use communications satellites—no telling how long they'd last, and after that they'd be stuck with long-wire radio systems. That was an inconvenience for the future, but launching his own replacement satellites was just too difficult in terms of manpower and resources, and besides, satellite launchers polluted like nothing else humankind had ever invented.

Brightling wondered how long his people would choose to live here. Some would scatter quickly, probably drive all over America, setting up their own enclaves, reporting back by satellite at first. Others would go to Africa—that seemed likely to be the most popular destination. Still others to Brazil and the rain forest study area. Perhaps some of the primitive tribes down there would be spared the Shiva exposure, and his people would study them as well and how Primitive Man lived in a pristine physical environment, living in full harmony with Nature. They'd study them as they were, a unique species worthy of protection—and too backward to be a danger to the environment. Might some African tribes survive as well? His people didn't think so. The African countries allowed their primitives to interface too readily with city folk, and the cities would be the focal centers of death for every nation on earth—especially when Vaccine-A was distributed. Thousands of liters of it would be produced, flown all over the world, and then distributed, ostensibly to preserve life, but really to take it ... slowly, of course.

Progress was going well. Back at his corporate headquarters the fictional documentation for -A was already fully formulated. It had been supposedly tested on over a thousand monkeys who were then exposed to Shiva, and only two of them had become symptomatic, and only one of those had died over the nineteen-month trial that existed only on paper and computer memories. They hadn't yet approached the FDA for human trials, because that wasn't necessary—but when Shiva started appearing all over the world, Horizon Corporation would announce that it had been working quietly on hemorrhagic fever vaccines ever since the Iranian attack on America, and faced with a global emergency and a fully documented treatment modality, the FDA would have no choice but to approve human use, and so officially bless the Project's goal of global human extermination. Not so much the elimination, John Brightling thought more precisely, as the culling back of the most dangerous species on the planet, which would allow Nature to restore Herself, with just enough human stewards to watch and study and appreciate the process. In a thousand or so years, there might be a million or so humans, but that was a small number in the great scheme of things, and the people would be properly educated to understand and respect nature instead of destroying her. The goal of the Project wasn't to end the world. It was to build a new one, a new world in the shape that Nature Herself intended. On that he would put his own name for all eternity. John Brightling, the man who saved the planet.

Brightling looked at the key in his hand, then got back into his car. The driver took him to the main entrance, and there he used the key, surprised and miffed to see that the door was unlocked. Well, there were still people going in and out. He took the elevator to his office-apartment atop the main building. That door, he saw, *was* locked as it was supposed to be, and he opened it with a kind of one-person ceremony, and walked into the seat of Olympus's chief god. No, that wasn't right. Insofar as there was a god, it was Nature. From his office windows, he could see out over the plains of Kansas, the swaying young wheat . . . it was so beautiful. Almost enough to bring tears to his eyes. Nature. She could be cruel to individuals, but individuals didn't matter. Despite all the warnings, humankind hadn't learned that.

Well, learn it they would, the way Nature taught all Her lessons. The hard way.

PAT O'Connor made his daily report to the ASAC in the evening. Coatless, he slid into the chair opposite Ussery's desk with his folder in hand. It was already fairly thick.

"Bannister case," Chuck Ussery said. "Anything shaking loose yet, Pat?"

"Nothing," the supervisory special agent replied. "We've interviewed fourteen friends in the Gary area. None of them had any idea what Mary was doing in New York. Only six of them even knew she was there, and she never discussed jobs or boyfriends, if any, with them. So, nothing at all has happened here."

"New York?" the ASAC asked next.

"Two agents on the case there, Tom Sullivan and Frank Chatham. They've established contact with a NYPD detective lieutenant named d'Allessandro. Forensics has been through her apartment—nothing. Latent prints are all hers, not even a maid. Neighbors in the building knew her by sight, but no real friendships established, and therefore no known associates. The New York idea is to print up some flyers and pass them out via the NYPD. The local detective is worried there might be a serial killer loose. He has another missing female, same age, roughly the same appearance and area of residence, fell off the world about the same time."

"Behavioral Sciences?" Ussery asked at once.

O'Connor nodded. "They've looked over the facts we have to date. They wonder if the e-mail was sent by the victim or maybe by a serial killer who wants to fuck over the family. Style differences on the message that Mr. Bannister brought in—well, we both saw that it appeared to have been written by a different person, or someone on drugs, but she was evidently not a drug user. And we can't trace the e-mail back anywhere. It went into an anonymous-remailer system. That sort of thing is designed to protect the originator of electronic mail, I guess so people can swap porno over the Net. I talked with Eddie Morales in Baltimore. He's the technical wizard in Innocent Images"—that was an ongoing FBI project to track down, arrest, and imprison those who swapped kiddie porn over their computers—"and Bert said they're playing with some technical fixes. They have a hacker on the payroll who thinks he can come up with a way to crack through the anonymity feature, but he's not there yet, and the local U.S. Attorney isn't sure it's legal anyway."

"Shit." Ussery thought of that legal opinion. Kiddie porn was one of the Bureau's pet hates, and Innocent Images had turned into a high-priority nationwide investigation, run from the Baltimore Field Division.

O'Connor nodded. "That's exactly what Bert said, Chuck."

"So, nothing happening yet?"

"Nothing worthwhile. We have a few more of Mary's friends to interview—five are set up for tomorrow, but if anything breaks loose, my bet's on New York. Somebody must have known her. Somebody must have dated her. But not here, Chuck. She left Gary and didn't look back."

Ussery frowned, but there was no fault to be found with O'Connor's investigative procedures, and there was a total of twelve agents working the Bannister case. Such cases ran and broke at their own speed. If James Bannister called, as he did every day, he'd just have to tell him that the Bureau was still working on it, then ask him for any additional friends he might have forgotten to list for the Gary team of agents.

CHAPTER 25

SUNRISE

"YOU DIDN'T STAY VERY LONG, SIR," THE IMMIGRAtion inspector observed, looking at Popov's passport.

"A quick business meeting," the Russian said, in his best American accent. "I'll be back again soon." He smiled at the functionary.

"Well, do hurry back, sir." Another stamp on the well-worn passport, and Popov headed into the first-class lounge.

Grady would do it. He was sure of that. The challenge was too great for one of his ego to walk away, and the same was true of the reward. Six million dollars was more than the IRA had ever seen in one lump sum, even when Libya's Muammar Qaddafi had bankrolled them in the early 1980s. The funding of terrorist organizations was always a practical problem. The Russians had historically given them some arms, but more valuably to the IRA, places to train, and operational intelligence against the British security services, but never very much money. The Soviet Union had never possessed a very large quantity of foreign exchange, and mainly used it to purchase technology with military applications. Besides, it had turned out, the elderly married couple they'd used as couriers to the West, delivering cash to Soviet agents in America and Canada, had been under FBI control almost the entire time! Popov had to shake his head. Excellent as the KGB had been, the FBI was just as good. It had a long-standing institutional brilliance at false-flag operations, which, in the case of the couriers, had compromised a large number of sensitive operations run by the "Active Measures" people in KGB's Service A. The Americans had had the good sense not to burn the operations, but rather use them as expanding resources in order to gain a systematic picture of what KGB was doing—targets and objectives—and so learn what the Russians *hadn't* already penetrated.

He shook his head again, as he walked off to the gate. And he was still in the dark, wasn't he? The questions continued to swarm: Exactly *what* was he doing? *What* did Brightling want? *Why* attack this Rainbow group?

CHAVEZ decided to set his MP-10 submachine gun aside today and concentrate instead on his Beretta .45. He hadn't missed a shot with the Heckler & Koch weapon in weeks—in this context, a "miss" meant not hitting within an inch of the ideal bullet placement, between and slightly above the eyes on the silhouette target. The H&K's diopter sights were so perfectly designed that if you could see the target through the sights, you hit the target. It was that simple.

But pistols were not that simple, and he needed the practice. He drew the weapon from the green Gore-Tex holster and brought it up fast, his left hand joining the right on the grip as his right foot took half a step back, and he turned his body, adopting the Weaver stance that he'd been taught years before at The Farm in the Virginia Tidewater. His eyes looked down, off the target, acquiring the pistol's sights as it came up to eye level, and when it did, his right index finger pulled back evenly on the trigger—

—not quite evenly enough. The shot would have shattered the target's jaw, and maybe severed a major blood vessel, but it would not have been instantly fatal. The second shot, delivered about half a second later, would have been. Ding grunted, annoyed with himself. He dropped the hammer with the safety-decock lever and reholstered the pistol. *Again.* He looked down, away from the target, then looked up. There he was, a terrorist with his weapon to the head of a child. Like lightning, the Beretta came up again, the sights matched up and Chavez pulled back his finger. Better. That one would have gone through the bastard's left eye, and the second round, again half a second later, made the first between-the-eyes hole into a cute little figure-eight.

"Excellent double-tap, Mr. Chavez."

Ding turned to see Dave Woods, the range master.

"Yeah, my first was wide and low," Ding admitted. That it would have blown half the bastard's face right off was not good enough.

"Less wrist, more finger," Woods advised. "And let me see your grip again." Ding did that. "Ah, yes, I see." His hands adjusted Chavez's left hand somewhat. "More like that, sir."

Shit, Ding thought. Was it that simple? By moving two fingers less than a quarter of an inch, the pistol slipped into a position as though the grip had been custom-shaped for his hands. He tried it a few times, then reholstered again and executed his version of a quick-draw. This time, the first round was dead between the eyes of the target seven meters away, and the second right beside it.

"Excellent," Woods said.

"How long you been teaching, Sergeant Major?"

"Quite some time, sir. Nine years here at Hereford."

"How come you never joined up with SAS?"

"Bad knee. Hurt it back in 1986, jumping down off a Warrior. I can't run more than two miles without its stiffening up on me, you see." The red mustache was waxed into two rather magnificent points, and the gray eyes sparkled. This son of a bitch could have taught shooting to Doc Holliday, Chavez knew at that moment. "Do carry on, sir." The range master walked off.

"Well, shit," Chavez breathed to himself. He executed four more quick-draws. *More finger, less wrist, lower the left hand a skosh on the grip . . . bingo . . .* In three more minutes there was a two-inch hole right in the middle of the instant-incapacitation part of the target. He'd have to remember this little lesson, Ding told himself.

Tim Noonan was in the next lane over, using his own Beretta, shooting slower than Chavez, and not quite as tight in his groups, but *all* of his rounds would have driven through the bottom of the brain, and right into the stem, where instant kills happened, because that was where the spinal cord entered the brain. Finally, both ran out of ammunition. Chavez took off his ear-protectors and tapped Noonan on the shoulder.

"A little slow today," the technical expert observed, with a frown.

"Yeah, well, you dropped the fucker. You were HRT, right?"

"Yeah, but not really a shooter. I did the tech side for them, too. Well, okay, I shot with them regularly, but not quite good enough for the varsity. Never got as fast as I wanted to be. Maybe I have slow nerves." Noonan grinned as he field-stripped his pistol for cleaning.

"So how's that people-finder working out?"

"The damned thing is fucking magic, Ding. Give me another week and I'll have the new one figured out. There's a parabolic attachment for the antenna, looks like something out of *Star Trek,* I guess, but goddamn, does it find people." He wiped the parts off and sprayed Break-Free on them for cleaning and lubrication. "That Woods guy's a pretty good coach, isn't he?"

"Yeah, well, he just fixed a little problem for me," Ding said, taking the spray can to start cleaning his own service automatic.

"The head guy at the FBI Academy when I was there did wonders for me, too. Just how your hands match up on the butt, I guess. And a steady finger." Noonan ran a patch through the barrel, eyeballed it, and reassembled his pistol. "You know, the best part about being over here is, we're about the only people who get to carry guns."

"I understand civilians can't own handguns over here, eh?"

"Yeah, they changed the law a few years ago. I'm sure it'll help reduce crime," Noonan observed. "They started their gun-control laws back in the '20s, to control the IRA. Worked like a charm, didn't it?" The FBI agent laughed. "Oh, well, they never wrote down a Constitution like we did."

"You carry all the time?"

"Hell, yes!" Noonan looked up. "Hey, Ding, I'm a cop, y'dig? I feel naked without a friend on my belt. Even when I was working Lab Division in Headquarters, reserved parking space and all, man, I *never* walked around D.C. without a weapon."

"Ever have to use it?"

Tim shook his head. "No, not many agents do, but it's part of the mystique, you know?" He looked back at his target. "Some skills you just like to have, man."

"Yeah, same for the rest of us." It was a fillip of British law that the Rainbow members *were* authorized to carry weapons everywhere they went, on the argument that as counterterror people they were always on duty. It was a right Chavez hadn't exercised very much, but Noonan had a point. As Chavez watched, he slapped a full magazine into the reassembled and cleaned handgun, dropped the lever to close the slide, then after safing the weapon, ejected the magazine to slide one more round into it. The gun went back into his hip holster, along with two more full magazines in covered pockets on the outside. Well, it was part of being a cop, wasn't it?

"Later, Tim."

"See you around, Ding."

MANY people can't do it, but some people simply remember faces. It's a particularly useful skill for bartenders, because people will come back to establishments where the guy at the bar remembers your favorite drink. This was true at New York's Turtle Inn Bar and Lounge, on Columbus Avenue. The foot patrolman came in just after the bar opened at noon and called, "Hey, Bob."

"Hi, Jeff, coffee?"

"Yeah," the young cop said, watching the bartender get some Starbuck's from the urn. Unusually for a bar, this place served good coffee, since that was the yuppie thing in this part of town. One sugar and some cream, and he passed the cup over.

Jeff had been on this beat for just under two years, long enough that he knew most of the business owners, and most of them knew him and his habits. He was an honest cop, but never one to turn down free food or drink, especially good donuts, the American cop's favorite food.

"So, what's shakin'?" Bob asked.

"Looking for a missin' girl," Jeff replied. "Know this face?" He handed the printed flyer over.

"Yeah, Annie something, likes Kendall Jackson Reserve Chardonnay. Used to be a regular. Haven't seen her in a while, though."

"How about this one?" The second flyer went across the bar. Bob looked at it for a second or two.

"Mary . . . Mary Bannister. I remember that, 'cuz it's like the thing on a set of steps, like you know? Haven't seen her in a while, either."

The patrolman could hardly believe his luck. "What do you know about them?"

"Wait a minute, you said they're missing, like kidnapped or something?"

"That's right, man." Jeff sipped his coffee. "FBI is on this one." He tapped the Bannister photo. "The other one we turned."

"Well, I'll be damned. Don't know much about them. Used to see 'em both here couple days a week, they dance and stuff, you know, like single girls do, trolling for guys."

"Okay, tell you what, some people will be in here to talk to you about 'em. Think about it, will ya?" The cop had to consider the possibility that Bob was the one who'd made them disappear, but there were chances you had to take in an investigation, and that likelihood was pretty damned slim. Like many New York waiters and bartenders, this guy was an aspiring actor, which probably explained his memory.

"Yeah, sure, Jeff. Damn, kidnapped, eh? Don't hear very much about that stuff anymore. Shit," he concluded.

"Eight million stories in the Naked City, man. Later," the patrolman said, heading for the door. He felt as though he'd done a major portion of his day's work, and as soon as he got outside, he used his epaulet-mounted radio microphone to call the newly developed information into his precinct house.

▪ ▪ ▪

GRADY'S face was known in the U.K., but not the red beard and glasses, which, he hoped, would obscure his visage enough to reduce the chance of being spotted by an alert police constable. In any case, the police presence wasn't as heavy here as in London. The gate into the base at Hereford was just as he'd remembered it, and from there it wasn't a long drive to the community hospital, where he examined the roads, shoulders, and parking areas and found them to his liking, as he shot six rolls of film with his Nikon. The plan that started building in his mind was simple, as all good plans were. The roads seemed to work in his favor, as did the open ground. As always, surprise would be his primary weapon. He'd need that, since the operation was so close to the U.K.'s best and most dangerous military organization, but the distances told him the time factor. Probably forty minutes on the outside, thirty on the inside to make the plan work. Fifteen men, but he could get fifteen good men. The other resources money could purchase, Grady thought, as he sat in the hospital parking lot. Yes, this could and would work. The only question was daylight or nighttime. The latter was the usual answer, but he'd learned the hard way that counterterror teams loved the night, because their night-vision equipment made the time of day indistinguishable in a tactical sense—and people like Grady were not trained to operate as well in the dark. It had given the police an enormous advantage recently at Vienna, Bern, and Worldpark. So, why *not* try it in broad daylight? he wondered. It was something to discuss with his friends, Grady concluded, as he restarted the car and headed back toward Gatwick.

"YEAH, I've been thinking about it since Jeff showed me the pictures," the bartender said. His name was Bob Johnson. He was now dressed for the evening, in a white tuxedo shirt, black cummerbund, and bowtie.

"You know this woman?"

"Yeah." He nodded positively. "Mary Bannister. The other one is Anne Pretloe. They used to be regulars here. Seemed nice enough. They danced and flirted with the men. This place gets pretty busy at night, 'specially on weekends. They used to come in around eight or so, then leave at eleven or eleven-thirty."

"Alone?"

"When they left? Most of the time, but not always. Annie had a guy she liked. His name's Hank, don't know the last name. White, brown hair, brown eyes, about my size, growing a gut, but not really overweight. I think he's a lawyer. He'll probably be in tonight. He's pretty regular here. Then there was another guy . . . maybe the last time I saw her here . . . what the hell's his name . . . ?" Johnson looked down at the bar. "Kurt, Kirk, something like that. Now that I think of it, I saw Mary dancing with him, too, once or twice. White guy, tall, good-lookin', haven't seen him in a while, liked whiskey sours made with Jim Beam, good tipper." A bartender always remembered good and bad tippers. "He was a hunter."

"Huh?" Agent Sullivan asked.

"Huntin' for babes, man. That's why guys come to a place like this, you know?"

This guy was a godsend, Sullivan and Chatham thought. "But you haven't seen him in a while?"

"The guy Kurt? No, couple of weeks at least, maybe more."

"Any chance that you could help us put a picture together?"

"You mean the artists' sketch thing, like in the papers?" Johnson asked them.

"That's right," Chatham confirmed.

"I suppose I can try. Some of the gals who come in here might know him, too. I think Marissa knew him. She's a regular, in here nearly every night, shows up around seven, seven-thirty."

"I guess we're going to be here awhile," Sullivan thought aloud, checking his watch.

IT was midnight at RAF Mildenhall. Malloy lifted the Night Hawk off the ramp and set off west for Hereford. The controls felt just as tight and crisp as ever, and the new widget worked. It turned out to be a fuel-gauge widget, digitized to tell him with numbers rather than a needle how much fuel he had. The switch also toggled back and forth between gallons (U.S., not Imperial) and pounds. Not a bad idea, he thought. The night was relatively clear, which was unusual for this part of the world, but there was no moon, and he had opted to use his night-vision goggles. These turned darkness into greenish twilight, and though they reduced his visual acuity from 20/20 down to about 20/40, that was still a major improvement on being totally blind in the dark. He kept the aircraft at three hundred feet, to avoid power lines, which scared the hell out of him, as they did all experienced helicopter pilots. There were no troops in the back, only Sergeant Nance, who still wore his pistol in order to feel more warriorlike—side arms were authorized for special-operations troops, even those who had little likelihood of ever using them. Malloy kept his Beretta M9 in his flight bag rather than a shoulder holster, which he found melodramatic, especially for a Marine.

"Chopper down there at the hospital pad," Lieutenant Harrison said, seeing it as they angled past for the base. "Turnin' and blinkin'."

"Got it," Malloy confirmed. They'd pass well clear even if the guy lifted off right now. "Nothing else at our level," he added, checking aloft for the blinking lights of airliners heading in and out of Heathrow and Luton. You never stopped scanning if you wanted to live. If he got command of VHM-1 at Anacostia Naval Air Station in D.C., the traffic at Reagan National Airport meant that he'd be flying routinely through very crowded air space, and though he respected commercial airline pilots, he trusted them less than he trusted his own abilities—which, he knew, was exactly how they viewed him and everybody in green flight suits. To be a pilot for a living, you had to think of yourself as the very best, though in Malloy's case he knew this to be true. And this kid Harrison showed some real promise, if he stayed in uniform instead of ending up a traffic reporter in West Bumfuck, Wherever. Finally, the landing pad at Hereford came into view, and Malloy headed for it. Five minutes and he'd be on the ground, cooling the turboshaft engines down, and twenty minutes after that, in his bed.

"YES, he will do it," Popov said. They were in a corner booth, and the background music made it a secure place to talk. "He has not confirmed it, but he will."

"Who is he?" Henriksen asked.

"Sean Grady. Do you know the name?"

"PIRA . . . worked in Londonderry mainly, didn't he?"

"For the most part, yes. He captured three SAS people and . . . disposed of them. Two separate incidents. The SAS then targeted him on three separate missions. Once they came very close to getting him, and they eliminated ten or so of his closest associates. He then cleaned out some suspected informers in his unit. He's quite ruthless," Popov assured his associates.

"That's true," Henriksen assured Brightling. "I remember reading what he did to the SAS guys he caught. Wasn't very pretty. Grady's a nasty little fucker. Does he have enough people to make this attempt?"

"I think yes," Dmitriy Arkadeyevich replied. "And he held us up for money. I offered five, and he demanded six, plus drugs."

"Drugs?" Henriksen was surprised.

"Wait, I thought the IRA didn't approve of drug trafficking," Brightling objected.

"We live in a practical world. The IRA worked for years to eliminate drug dealers throughout Ireland—mainly kneecappings, to make the action very public. That was a psychological and political move on his part. Perhaps now he entertains the idea as a continuing source of income for his operations," Dmitriy explained. The morality of the issue didn't seem very important to anyone at the table.

"Yeah, well, I suppose we can entertain that request," Brightling said, with a small measure of distaste. "Kneecappings? What does that mean?"

"You take a pistol," Bill explained, "and place it behind the knee, then you fire forward. It blows the kneecap to smithereens. Painful, and permanently crippling. It's how they used to deal with informers and other people they didn't like. The Protestant terrorists preferred a Black and Decker drill for the same purpose. It puts the word out on the street that you are not to be messed with," Henriksen concluded.

"Ouch," the physician in Brightling commented.

"That's why they're called terrorists," Henriksen pointed out. "These days, they just kill them. Grady has a reputation for ruthlessness, doesn't he?"

"Yes, he does," Popov confirmed. "There's no doubt that he will undertake this mission. He likes the concept and your suggestion for how it should be set up, Bill. There is also his ego, which is large." Popov took a sip of his wine. "He wants to take the lead in the IRA politically, and that will mean doing something dramatic."

"That's the Irish for you—the land of sad loves and happy wars."

"Will he succeed?" Brightling asked.

"The concept is a clever one. But remember that to him success means elimination of the primary targets, the two women, and then a few of the reaction team of soldiers. After that, he will doubtless flee the area and try to return to Ireland and safety. Just surviving an operation of this type is successful enough for his political purposes. To fight a full military action would be madness for him, and Grady is not a madman," Dmitriy told them, not really sure he believed it. Weren't all revolutionaries mad? It was difficult to understand people who let visions take control of their lives. Those who'd succeeded, Lenin, Mao, and Gandhi in this century, were the ones who'd used their visions effectively, of course—but even then, which of the three had really succeeded? The Soviet Union had fallen, the People's Republic of China would eventually succumb to the same political-economic realities that had doomed the USSR, and India was still an economic disaster that somehow managed to hover in stagnation. By that model, Ireland was more surely doomed by the possible success of the IRA than it was by its economic marriage to Britain. At least Cuba had the tropical sun to keep it warm. To survive, with no natural resources to speak of, Ireland needed a close economic tie to someone, and the closest was the U.K. But that was off the dinner topic.

"So, you expect him to try a hit-and-run," Bill asked.

Dmitriy nodded. "Nothing else makes tactical sense. He hopes to live long enough to utilize the money we've offered him. Assuming you will approve the increase he requires."

"What's another million or so?" Henriksen asked, with a suppressed grin.

So both of them regarded such a large sum as trivial, Popov saw, and again he was struck in the face with the fact that they were planning something monstrous—but what?

"How do they want it? Cash?" Brightling asked.

"No, I told them it would be deposited in a numbered Swiss account. I can arrange that."

"I have enough already laundered," Bill told his employer. "We could set that up tomorrow if you want."

"And that means I fly to Switzerland again," Dmitriy observed sourly.

"Getting tired of flying?"

"I have traveled a great deal, Dr. Brightling." Popov sighed openly. He was jet lagged, and it showed for once.

"John."

"John." Popov nodded, seeing some actual affection in his boss for the first time, somewhat to his surprise.

"I understand, Dmitriy," Henriksen said. "The Australia trip was a pain in the ass for me."

"What was it like to grow up in Russia?" Brightling asked.

"Harder than America. There was more violence in the schools. No serious crime," Popov explained. "But lots of fights between the boys, for example. Dominance fights, as boys will. The authorities usually looked the other way."

"Where did you grow up?"

"Moscow. My father was also an officer in State Security. I was educated in Moscow State University."

"What major?"

"Language and economics." The former had proven very useful. The latter had been totally valueless, since the Marxist idea of economics had not exactly proven to be an effective one.

"Ever get out of the city? You know, like Boy Scouts do here, that sort of stuff?"

Popov smiled, wondering where this was going, and why they were asking it. But he played along. "One of my happiest memories of childhood. I was in the Young Pioneers. We traveled out to a state farm and worked there for a month, helping with the harvest, living with nature, as you Americans say." And then, at age fourteen, he'd met his first love, Yelena Ivanovna. He wondered where she was now. He succumbed to a brief attack of nostalgia, as he remembered her feel in the darkness, his first conquest . . .

Brightling noted the distant smile and took it for what he wanted it to be. "You liked that, eh?"

Clearly they didn't want to hear that story. "Oh, yes. I have often wondered what it was like to live out there in a place like that, the sun on your back all the time, working in the soil. My father and I used to walk into the woods, hunting for mushrooms—that was a common pastime for Soviet citizens in the sixties, walking in the woods." Unlike most Russians, they'd driven there in his father's official car, but as a boy he'd liked the woods as a place of adventure and romanticism, as all boys do, and enjoyed the time with his father as well.

"Any game in the woods there?" Bill Henriksen asked.

"One would see birds, of course, many kinds, and occasionally elk—you call them moose here, I think—but rarely. State hunters were always killing them. Wolves are their main target. They hunt them from helicopters. We Russians do not like wolves as you do here in America. Too many folk tales of rabid ones killing people, you see. Mostly lies, I expect."

Brightling nodded. "Same thing here. Wolves are just big wild dogs, you can train them as pets if you want. Some people do that."

"Wolves are cool," Bill added. He'd often thought about making one a pet, but you needed a lot of land for that. Maybe when the Project was fulfilled.

What the hell was *this* all about? Dmitriy wondered, still playing along. "I always wanted to see a bear, but there are none of them left in the Moscow area. I saw them only at the zoo. I loved bears," he added, lying. They'd always frightened the hell out of him. You heard scores of bear stories as a child in Russia, few of them friendly, though not as antinature as the wolf stories. Large dogs? Wolves *killed* people in the steppes. The farmers and peasants hated the damned things and welcomed the state hunters with their helicopters and machine guns, the better to hunt them down and slaughter them.

"Well, John and I are Nature Lovers," Bill explained, waving to the waiter for another bottle of wine. "Always have been. All the way back to Boy Scouts—like your Young Pioneers, I suppose."

"The state was not kind to nature in the Soviet Union. Much worse than the problems you've had here in America. Americans have come to Russia to survey the damage and suggest ways to fix the problems of pollution and such."

Especially in the Caspian Sea, where pollution had killed off most of the sturgeon, and with it the fish eggs known as caviar, which had for so long been a prime means of earning foreign currency for the USSR.

"Yes, that was criminal," Brightling agreed soberly. "But it's a global problem. People don't respect nature the way they should," Brightling went on for several minutes, delivering what had to be a brief canned lecture, to which Dmitriy listened politely.

"That is a great political movement in America, is it not?"

"Not as powerful as many would like," Bill observed. "But it's important to some of us."

"Such a movement would be useful in Russia. It is a pity that so much has been destroyed for no purpose," Popov responded, meaning some of it. The state should conserve resources for proper exploitation, not simply destroy them because the local political hacks didn't know how to use them properly. But then the USSR had been so horridly inefficient in everything it did—well, except espionage, Popov corrected himself. America had done well, he thought. The cities were far cleaner than their Russian counterparts, even here in New York, and you only needed to drive an hour from any city to see green grass and tidy productive farms. But the greater question was: why had a conversation that had begun with the discussion of a terrorist incident drifted into this? Had he done anything to invite it? No, his employer had abruptly steered it in this direction. It had not been an accident. That meant they were sounding him out—but on what? This nature drivel? He sipped at his wine and stared at his dinner companions. "You know, I've never really had a chance to see America. I would like very much to see the national parks. What is the one with the geysers? Gold stone? Something like that?"

"Yellowstone, it's in Wyoming. Maybe the prettiest place in America," Henriksen told the Russian.

"Nope, Yosemite," Brightling countered. "In California. That's the prettiest valley in the whole world. Overrun with goddamned tourists now, of course, but that'll change."

"Same story at Yellowstone, John, and, yeah, that'll change, too. Someday," Bill Henriksen concluded.

They seemed pretty positive about the things that would change. But the American state parks were run by the federal government for all citizens, weren't they? They had to be, because they were tax-supported. No limited access for the elite here. Equality for all—something he'd been taught in Soviet schools, except here they actually lived it. One more reason, Dmitriy thought, why one country had fallen, and the other had grown stronger.

"What do you mean 'that'll change'?" Popov asked.

"Oh, the idea is to lessen the impact of people on the areas. It's a good idea, but some other things have to happen first," Brightling replied.

"Yeah, John, just one or two," Henriksen agreed, with a chuckle. Then he decided that this feeling-out process had gone far enough. "Anyway, Dmitriy, how will we know when Grady wants to go forward?"

"I will call him. He left me a mobile-phone number which I can use at certain times of the day."

"Trustful soul."

"For me, yes. We have been friends since the 1980s, back when he was in the Bekaa Valley. And besides, the phone is mobile, probably bought with a false credit card by someone else entirely. These things are very useful to intelligence officers. They are difficult to track unless you have very sophisticated equipment. America has them, and so does England, but other nations, no, not very many of them."

"Well, call him as soon as you think proper. We want this one to run, don't we, John?"

"Yes," Dr. Brightling said definitively. "Bill, set up the money for the transfer tomorrow. Dmitriy, go ahead and set up the bank account."

"Yes, John," Popov replied, as the dessert cart approached the table.

GRADY, they saw, was excited about this mission. It was approaching two in the Dublin morning. The photos had been developed by a friend of the movement, and six of them blown up. The large ones were pinned to the wall. The small ones lay in appropriate places on a map unfolded on the worktable.

"They will approach from here, right up this road. Only one place for them to park their vehicles, isn't there?"

"Agreed," Rodney Sands said, checking angles.

"Okay, Roddy, then we do this . . ." Grady outlined the plan.

"How do we communicate?"

"Cellular phones. Every group will have one, and we'll select speed-dial settings so that we can trade information rapidly and efficiently."

"Weapons?" Danny McCorley asked.

"We have plenty of those, lad. They will respond with five men, perhaps as many as ten, but no more than that. They've never deployed more than ten or eleven men to a mission, even in Spain. We've counted them on the TV tapes, haven't we? Fifteen of us, ten of them, and surprise works for us in both phases."

The Barry twins, Peter and Sam, looked skeptical at first, but if the mission was run quickly . . . if it ran according to the schedule . . . yes, it was possible.

"What about the women?" Timothy O'Neil asked.

"What about them?" Grady asked. "They are our primary targets."

"A pregnant woman, Sean . . . it will not look good politically."

"They are Americans, and their husbands are our enemies, and they are bait for getting them close. We will not kill them at once, and if circumstances permit, they might well be left alive to mourn their loss, lad," Grady added, just to assuage the conscience of the younger man. Timmy wasn't a coward, but he did have some lingering bourgeois sentimentality.

O'Neil nodded submission. Grady wasn't a man to cross, and was in any case their leader. "I lead the group into the hospital, then?"

Grady nodded. "Yes. Roddy and I will remain outside with the covering group."

"Very well, Sean," Timmy agreed, committing himself to the mission now and forever.

CHAPTER 26

CONCLUSIONS

ONE PROBLEM WITH AN INVESTIGATION LIKE THIS was that you risked alerting the subject, but that couldn't always be helped. Agents Sullivan and Chatham circulated around the bar until nearly midnight, finding two women who knew Mary Bannister, and one who knew Anne Pretloe. In the case of the former, they got the name of a man with whom Bannister had been seen dancing—a bar regular who hadn't shown up that night, but whose address they'd get rapidly enough from his telephone number, which was known, it seemed, to quite a few of the women here. By midnight they were ready to leave, somewhat annoyed to have spent so much time in a lively bar drinking nothing more potent than Coca-Cola, but with a few new leads to run down. It was so far a typical case. Special Agent Sullivan thought of it like walking through a supermarket looking for dinner, picking over the shelves randomly, selecting things to eat, never knowing how the selections would turn out in the kitchen.

" **'MORNING,** baby," Ding said, before he rolled out of bed, as always starting his day off with a kiss.

"Hi, Ding." Patsy tried to roll over, but it was difficult, almost as much as sleeping on her back, unable to move with her belly full of child. It couldn't come soon enough, Patricia Clark Chavez thought, despite the discomfort the delivery was sure to inflict upon her. She felt his hand slide over the stretched skin of what had once been a flat, trim abdomen.

"How's the little guy?"

"Waking up, feels like," she answered with a distant smile, wondering what he or she would look like. Ding was convinced it had to be a boy. It seemed he would accept no other possibility. Must be a Latino thing, she figured. A physician, she knew different. Whatever it was, however, it would almost certainly be healthy. The little thing inside her had been active since she'd felt the first "bloop," as she called it, at three months. "There he goes," she reported, when he/she turned over inside the sea of amniotic fluid.

Domingo Chavez felt it on the palm of his hand, smiled, and leaned down to kiss his wife again before heading to the bathroom. "Love ya, Pats," he said on the way. As usual, the world was in its proper shape. On the way to the bathroom, he sneaked a look at the nursery, with the colored critters on the wall, and the crib all ready for use. Soon, he told himself. Just about any time, the OB had said, adding that first babies were usually late, however. Fifteen minutes later, he was in his morning sweats and on his way out the door, some coffee in him but nothing else, since he didn't like to eat breakfast before exercising. His car took the short drive to the Team-2 building, where everyone else was arriving.

"Hey, Eddie," Chavez said to Price in greeting.

"Good morning, Major," the sergeant major called in return. Five minutes later, the team was out on the grass, all dressed in their morning workout gear. This morning Sergeant Mike Pierce, still the team's kill leader, led the routine. The stretching and strength exercises took fifteen minutes, and then came the morning run.

"Airborne rangers jump from planes," Pierce called, and then the remainder of the team chorused:

"They ain't got no goddamned brains!"

The traditional chant made perfectly good sense to Chavez, who'd been through Ranger School at Fort Benning, but not Jump School. It made far better sense, he thought, to come to battle in a helicopter rather than as skeet for the bastards on the ground to shoot at, a perfect target, unable to shoot back. The very idea frightened him. But he was the only member of Team-2 who'd never jumped, and that made him a "fucking leg," or straight-legged infantryman, not one of the anointed people with the silver ice cream cone badge. Strange that he'd never heard any of his people josh him about it, he thought, passing the first mile post on the track. Pierce was a gifted runner, and was setting a fast pace, maybe trying to get somebody to fall out. But no one would do that, and everyone knew it. At home, Ding thought, Patsy was getting herself ready for work in the hospital emergency room. She was leaning toward specialization in ER medicine at the moment, which meant getting a general surgery certification. Funny that she hadn't selected her area of medical specialty yet. She certainly had the brains to do nearly anything, and her smallish hands would be perfect for surgery. She often practiced dexterity by playing with a deck of cards, and over the past few months she'd become expert at dealing seconds. She'd showed him what she was doing and how, but even then, watching closely, he couldn't see her do it, which had amazed and annoyed her husband. Her motor-control nerves must be incredible, Domingo thought proudly, pounding into the third mile of the run. This was when you began to feel it, because in mile three your legs were thinking that they'd gone pretty far already, and maybe slowing down would be nice. At least that was true for Ding. Two members of the team ran marathons, and as far as he'd been able to tell, those two, Loiselle and Weber, respectively the smallest and largest members of the team, *never* got tired. The German especially, graduate of the Bundeswehr mountain warfare school, and holder of the Bergermeister badge, was about the toughest son of a bitch he'd ever met—and Chavez thought of himself as a tough little son of a bitch. Loiselle was just like a little damned rabbit, moving along with grace and invisible power.

Ten more minutes, Chavez thought, his legs starting to complain to him, but not allowing any of it to show, his face set in a calm, determined mien, almost bored as his feet pounded on the cinders of the track. Team-1 was running, too, opposite them on the track, and fortunately neither team raced the other. They did record their times for the run, but direct competition would have forced all of the Rainbow troopers into a destructive regimen that would only produce injuries—and enough of those happened from routine training, though Team-2 was fully mission-capable at the moment, with all injuries healed.

"Detail . . . quick-time, march!" Pierce finally called, as they completed the morning jaunt. Another fifty meters and they halted.

"Well, people, good morning. I hope you all enjoyed waking up for another day of safeguarding the world from the bad guys," Pierce told them, sweat on his smiling face. "Major Chavez," he said next, walking back to his usual place in the ranks.

"Okay, gentlemen, that was a good workout. Thank you, Sergeant Pierce, for leading the run this morning. Showers and breakfast, troops. Fall out." With that command the two ranks of five each disintegrated, the men heading off to their building to shower off the sweat. A few of them worked legs or arms a little for some exercise-induced cricks. The endorphins had kicked in, the body's own reward for exertion, creating the "runner's high," as some called it, which would mellow in a few minutes to the wonderful sense of well-being that they'd enjoy for the rest of the morning. Already they were chatting back and forth about various things, professional and not.

An English breakfast was much the same as an American one: bacon, eggs, toast, coffee—English breakfast tea for some—fuel for the coming day. Some of the troopers ate light, and some ate heavy, in accordance with their personal metabolic rates. By this time, all were in their day uniforms, ready to head off to their desks. Tim Noonan would be giving a lecture today on communications security. The new radios from E-Systems hardly needed the introduction, but Noonan wanted them to know everything about them, including how the encryption systems worked. Now the team members could talk back and forth, and anyone trying to listen in would hear only the hiss of static. The same had been true before, but the new portable radios, with their headsets and reed-thin microphones that hung out in front of their faces, were a great technical improvement, Noonan had told Chavez. Then Bill Tawney would brief them on any new developments in the intelligence and investigations on their three field deployments. After that came the before-lunch trip to the range for marksmanship practice, but today no live-fire/live-target exercise. Instead they'd practice long-rope deployments from Malloy's helicopter.

It promised to be a full, if routine, day for Rainbow. Chavez almost added "boring" to the description, but he knew that John worked hard to vary the routine, and, besides, you practiced the fundamentals, because they were, well, fundamental to getting the job done, the things you held on to when the tactical situation went to shit and you didn't have the time to think about what to do. By this time, every Team-2 member knew how every other member thought, and so, on exercises where the actual scenario was different from the tactical intelligence they'd been given going in, somehow the team members just adapted, sometimes without words, every trooper knowing what his partner and the others in the team would do, as if they'd communicated by telepathy. That was the reward for the intensive, intellectually boring training. Team-2, and Peter Covington's Team-1, had evolved into living, thinking organisms whose parts just acted properly—and seemed to do so automatically. When Chavez thought about it, he found it remarkable, but on training exercises, it seemed as natural as breathing. Like Mike Pierce leaping over the desk in Worldpark. That hadn't been part of the training regimen, but he'd done it, and done it perfectly, and the only thing wrong was that his first burst hadn't taken his subject in the head, but instead had stitched down his back—causing wounds that would have been rapidly fatal—then followed it with a second burst that had blown the bastard's head apart. Boom. Zap. Splatter. And the other team members had trusted Pierce to cover his sector, and then, after cleansing it of opposition, to assist with others. Like the fingers of his hand, Chavez thought, able to form into a deadly fist, but also able to do separate tasks, because each finger had a brain. And they were all his men. That was the best part of all.

GETTING the weapons was the easiest part. It struck outsiders as comical—Irishmen with guns were like squirrels with nuts, always stashing them, and sometimes forgetting where the hell they'd been stashed. For a generation, people had shipped arms to the IRA, and the IRA had cached them, mainly burying them for the coming time when the entire Irish nation would rise up under Provo leadership and engage the English invaders, driving them forever from the sacred soil of Ireland . . . or something like that, Grady thought. He'd personally buried over three thousand weapons, most of them Russian-made AKMS assault rifles, like this stash in a farm field in County Tipperary. He'd buried this shipment forty meters west of a large oak tree, over the hill from the farm house. They were two meters—six feet—down, deep enough that the farmer's tractor wouldn't hurt or accidentally unearth them, and shallow enough that getting them took only an hour's spadework. There were a hundred of them, delivered in 1984 by a helpful soul he'd first met in Lebanon, along with pre-loaded plastic magazines, twenty per rifle. It was all in a series of boxes, the weapons and the ammunition wrapped in greased paper, the way the Russians did it, to protect them against moisture. Most of the wrappings were still intact, Grady saw, as he selected carefully. He removed twenty weapons, tearing open each one's paper to check for rust or corrosion, working the bolts back and forth, and in every case finding that the packing grease was intact, the same as when the weapons had left the factory at Kazan. The AKMS was the updated version of the AK-47, and these were the folding-stock version, which were much easier to conceal than the full-size military shoulder weapon. More to the point, this was the weapon his people had trained on in Lebanon. It was easy to use, reliable, and concealable. Those characteristics made it perfect for the purpose intended. The fifteen he took, along with three hundred thirty-round magazines, were loaded into the back of the truck, and then it was time to refill the hole. After three hours, the truck was on its way to yet another farm, this one on the seacoast of County Cork, where there lived a farmer with whom Sean Grady had an arrangement.

SULLIVAN and Chatham were in the office before seven in the morning, beating the traffic and finding decent parking places for once. The first order of business was to use a computerized crisscross directory to track down the names and addresses from the phone numbers. That was quick. Next up was to meet with the three men who were reported to have known Mary Bannister and Anne Pretloe and interview them. It was possible that one of them was a serial killer or kidnapper. If the first, he would probably be a very clever and circumspect criminal. A serial killer was a hunter of human beings. The smart ones acted strangely like soldiers, first scouting out their victims, discerning their habits and weaknesses, and then moving in to use them as entertaining toys until the fun faded, and it was time to kill them. The homicide aspects of a serial killer's activities were not, strictly speaking, in the purview of the FBI, but the kidnapping was, if the killer had moved his victims across state lines, and since there was a state line only a few hundred yards from Manhattan, that was enough to allow the agents to look into it. They'd have to ask their questions carefully, and remember that a serial killer almost always had an elegant disguise, the better to win the trust of his victims. He'd be kind, maybe handsome, friendly, and totally nonthreatening—until it was too late, and at that point his victim was doomed. He was, both agents knew, the most dangerous of criminals.

SUBJECT F4 was progressing rapidly. Neither the Interferon nor the Interleukin-3a had touched her Shiva strands, which were replicating with gusto, and in her case attacking her liver with ferocious speed. The same was true of her pancreas, which was disintegrating, causing a serious internal bleed. Strange, Dr. Killgore thought. The Shiva had taken its time to assert itself, but then once it had started affecting the test subject's body, it had gone to town, eating away like a glutton at a feast. Mary Bannister, he decided, had about five days left.

M7, Chip Smitton, was little better off. His immune system was doing its best, but Shiva was just too malignant for him, working more slowly than in F4, but just as inexorably.

F5, Anne Pretloe, was from the deep end of the gene pool. He'd bothered to take full medical histories of all the current crop of test subjects. Bannister had a family history of cancer—breast cancer had claimed her mother and grandmother, and he saw that Shiva was working rapidly in her. Might there be a correlation between vulnerability to cancer and infectious disease? Could that indicate that cancer was fundamentally a disease of the immune system, as many physician-scientists suspected? It was the stuff of a paper for the *New England Journal of Medicine,* might get himself some additional standing in his community—but he didn't have the time, and anyway, by the time he published, there'd be few to read it. Well, it would be something to talk about in Kansas, because they'd still be practicing medicine there, and still working on the Immortality Project. Most of Horizon's best medical researchers were not really part of the Project, but they couldn't kill *them,* could they? And so, like many others, they'd find themselves beneficiaries of the Project's largesse. They would be allowing far more people than necessary to live—oh, sure, they needed the genetic diversity, and why not pick smart people who'd eventually understand why the Project had done what it had? And even if they didn't, what choice would they have but to live? All of them were earmarked for the -B vaccine Steve Berg had developed along with the lethal -A variant. In any case, his speculation had scientific value, even though it was singularly useless for the test subjects who now filled every available room in the treatment area. Killgore gathered his notes and started rounds, beginning with F4, Mary Bannister.

Only the heavy morphine dose made life tolerable for her. The dosage might have killed a healthy person, and would have been enough to delight the most hardened IV-drug user.

"How are we feeling this morning?" the doctor asked brightly.

"Tired . . . weak . . . crummy," Mary Bannister replied.

"How's the pain, Mary?"

"It's there, but not so bad . . . mainly my stomach." Her face was deathly pale from the internal bleeding, and the petechiae were sufficiently prominent on her face that she couldn't be allowed to use a mirror, lest the sight panic her. They wanted all the subjects to die comfortably. It would be far less trouble for everyone that way—a kindness not shown to other test subjects, Killgore thought. It wasn't fair, but it was practical. The lower animals they tested didn't have the capacity to make trouble, and there were no useful data on how to medicate them against pain. Maybe he'd develop some in Kansas. That would be a worthy use of his abilities, he thought, as he made another upward adjustment in F4's morphine drip . . . just enough to . . . yes, make her stuporous. He could show her the mercy he would have liked to have shown rhesus monkeys. Would they do animal experimentation in Kansas? There would be practical difficulties. Getting the animals to the labs would be very difficult in the absence of international air-freight service, and then there was the aesthetic issue. Many of the project members would not approve, and they had a point. But, damn it, it was *hard* to develop drugs and treatment modalities without *some* animal testing. Yes, Killgore thought, leaving one treatment room for another, it was tough on the conscience, but scientific progress had a price, and they *were* saving literally millions of animals, weren't they?

They'd needed thousands of animals to develop Shiva, and nobody had really objected to that. Another subject for discussion at the staff conference, he decided, entering M7's room.

"How are we feeling, Chip?" he asked.

THEY collectively thanked Providence for the lack of Garda in this part of County Cork. There was little crime, after all, and therefore little reason for them. The Irish national police were as efficient as their British colleagues, and their intelligence section unfortunately cooperated with the "Five" people in London, but neither service had managed to find Sean Grady—at least not after he'd identified and eliminated the informers in his cell. Both of them had vanished from the face of the earth and fed the salmon, or whatever fish liked the taste of informer flesh. Grady remembered the looks on their faces as they protested their innocence right up until the moment they'd been thrown into the sea, fifteen miles offshore, with iron weights on their legs. Protested their innocence? Then why had the SAS never troubled his cell again after three serious attempts to eliminate them all? Innocence be damned.

They had half-filled a delightful provincial pub called The Foggy Dew, named after a favored rebel song, after several hours of weapons practice on the isolated coastal farm, which was too far from civilization for people to hear the distinctive chatter of automatic-weapons fire. It had required a few magazines each for his men to reassert their expertise with the AKMS assault rifles, but shoulder weapons were easily mastered, and that one more easily than most. Now they talked about nonbusiness matters, just a bunch of friends having a few pints. Most watched the football game on the wall-hung telly. Grady did the same, but with his brain in neutral, letting it slide over the next mission, examining and reexamining the scene in his mind, thinking about how quickly the British or this new Rainbow group might arrive. The direction of their approach was obvious. He had that all planned for, and the more he went over his operational concept, the better he seemed to like it. He might well lose some people, but that was the cost of doing business for the revolutionary, and looking around the pub at his people, he knew that they accepted the risks just as readily as he did.

He checked his watch, subtracted five hours, and reached into his pocket to turn on his cell phone. He did this three times per day, never leaving it on for more than ten minutes at a time, as a security measure. He had to be careful. Only that knowledge—and some luck, he admitted to himself—had allowed him to carry on the war this long. Two minutes later, it rang. Grady rose from his seat and walked outside to take the call.

"Hello."

"Sean, this is Joe."

"Hello, Joe," Grady said pleasantly. "How are things in Switzerland?"

"Actually, I'm in New York at the moment. I just wanted to tell you that the business thing we talked about, the financing, it's done," Popov told him.

"Excellent. What of the other matter, Joe?"

"I'll be bringing that myself. I'll be over in two days. I'm flying into Shannon on my business jet. I should get in about six-thirty in the morning."

"I shall be there to see you," Grady promised.

"Okay, my friend. I will see you then."

"Good-bye, Joe."

"Bye, Sean." And the line went dead. Grady thumbed off the power and replaced the phone in his pocket. If anyone had overheard it—not likely, since he could see all the way to the horizon, and there were no parked trucks in evidence . . . and, besides, if anyone knew where he was, they would have come after him and his men with a platoon of soldiers and/or police—all they would have heard was a business chat, brief, cryptic, and to the point. He went back inside.

"Who was it, Sean?" Roddy Sands asked.

"That was Joe," Grady replied. "He's done what we asked. So, I suppose we get to move forward as well."

"Indeed." Roddy hoisted his pint glass in salute.

THE Security Service, once called MI (Military Intelligence) 5, had lived for more than a generation with two high-profile missions. One was to keep track of Soviet penetration agents within the British government—a regrettably busy mission, since the KGB and its antecedents had more than once penetrated British security. At one point, they'd almost gotten their agent-in-place Kim Philby in charge of "Five," thus nearly giving the Soviets control of the British counterintelligence service, a miscue that still sent a collective shiver throughout "Five." The second mission was the penetration of the Irish Republican Army and other Irish terrorist groups, the better to identify their leaders and eliminate them, for this war was fought by the old rules. Sometimes, police were called in to make arrests, and other times, SAS commandos were deployed to handle things more directly. The differences in technique had resulted from the inability of Her Majesty's Government to decide if the "Irish Problem" was a matter of crime or national security—the result of that indecision had been the lengthening of "The Troubles" by at least a decade, in the view of the American FBI.

But the employees of "Five" didn't have the ability to make policy. That was done by elected officials, who often as not failed to listen to the trained experts who'd spent their lives handling such matters. Without the ability to make or affect policy, they soldiered on, assembling and maintaining voluminous records of known and suspected IRA operatives for eventual action by other government agencies.

This was done mainly by recruiting informers. Informing on one's comrades was another old Irish tradition, and one that the British had long exploited for their own ends. They speculated on its origins. Part of it, they all thought, was religion. The IRA regarded itself as the protector of *Catholic* Irishmen, and with that identification came a price: the rules and ethics of Catholicism often spilled over into the hearts and minds of people who killed in the name of their religious affiliation. One of the things that spilled over was guilt. On the one hand, guilt was an inevitable result of their revolutionary activity, and on the other hand, it was the one thing they could not afford to entertain in their own consciences.

"Five" had a thick file on Sean Grady, as they did for many others. Grady's was special, though, since they'd once had a particularly well-placed informer in his unit who had, unfortunately, disappeared, doubtless murdered by him. They knew that Grady had given up kneecapping early on and chosen murder as a more permanent way of dealing with security leaks, and one that never left bodies about for the police to find. "Five" had twenty-three informants currently working in various PIRA units. Four were women of looser morality than was usual in Ireland. The other nineteen were men who'd been recruited one way or another—though three of them didn't know that they were sharing secrets with British agents. The Security Service did its collective best to protect them, and more than a few had been taken to England after their usefulness had been exhausted, then flown to Canada, usually, for a new, safer life. But in the main "Five" treated them as assets to be milked for as long as possible, because the majority of them were people who'd killed or assisted others in killing, and that made them both criminals and traitors, whose consciences had been just a little too late to encourage much in the way of sympathy from the case officers who "worked" them.

Grady, the current file said, had fallen off the face of the earth. It was possible, some supposed, that he'd been killed by a rival, but probably not, as that bit of news would have percolated through the PIRA leadership. Grady was respected even by his factional enemies in the Movement as a True Believer in the Cause and an effective operator who had killed more than his fair share of cops and soldiers in Londonderry. And the Security Service still wanted him for the three SAS troopers he'd somehow captured, tortured, and killed. Those bodies had been recovered, and the collective rage in SAS hadn't gone away, for the 22nd Special Air Service Regiment never forgave and never forgot such things. Killing, perhaps, but never torture.

Cyril Holt, Deputy Director of the Security Service, was doing his quarterly review of the major case files, and stopped when he got to Grady's. He'd disappeared from the scope entirely. If he'd died, Holt would have heard about it. It was also possible that he'd given up the fight, seen that his parent organization was finally ready to negotiate some sort of peace, and decided to play along by terminating his operations. But Holt and his people didn't believe that either. The psychological profile that had been drawn up by the chief of psychiatry at Guy's Hospital in London said that he'd be one of the last to set the gun down and look for a peaceful occupation.

The third possibility was that he was still lurking out there, maybe in Ulster, maybe in the Republic . . . more probably the latter, because "Five" had most of its informants in the North. Holt looked at the photos of Grady and his collection of twenty or so PIRA "soldiers," for whom there were also files. None of the pictures were very good despite the computer enhancement. He had to assume he was still active, leading his militant PIRA faction somehow, planning operations that might or might not come off, but meanwhile keeping a low profile with the cover identities he had to have generated. All he could do was keep a watch on them. Holt made a brief notation, closed the file, placed it on his OUT pile and selected another. By the following day, the notations would be placed into the "Five" computer, which was slowly supplanting the paper files, but which Holt didn't like to use. He preferred files he could hold in his hands.

"THAT quickly?" Popov asked.

"Why not?" Brightling responded.

"As you say, sir. And the cocaine?" he added distastefully.

"The suitcase is packed. Ten pounds in medically pure compounding condition from our own stores. The bag will be on the plane."

Popov didn't like the idea of transporting drugs at all. It wasn't a case of sudden morality, but simply concern about customs officials and luggage-sniffing dogs. Brightling saw the worry on his face, and smiled.

"Relax, Dmitriy. If there is any problem, you're transporting the stuff to our subsidiary in Dublin. You'll have documents to that effect. Just try to make sure you don't need to use them. It could be embarrassing."

"As you say." Popov allowed himself to be relieved. He'd be flying a chartered Gulfstream V private business jet this time, because bringing the drugs through a real airport on a real international flight was just a little too dangerous. European countries tended to give casual treatment to arriving Americans, whose main objective was to spend their dollars, not cause trouble, but everyone had dogs now, because every country in the world worried about narcotics.

"Tonight?"

Brightling nodded and checked his watch. "The plane'll be at Teterboro Airport. Be there at six."

Popov left and caught a cab back to his apartment. Packing wasn't difficult but thinking was. Brightling was violating the most rudimentary security considerations here. Chartering a private business jet linked his corporation with Popov for the first time, as did the protective documentation attached to the cocaine. There was no effort to cut Popov loose from his employer. Perhaps that meant that Brightling didn't trust his employee's loyalty, didn't trust that if arrested he would keep his mouth shut . . . but, no, Dmitriy Arkadeyevich thought. If he wasn't trusted, then the mission would not be undertaken. Popov had always been the link between Brightling and the terrorists.

So, the Russian thought, *he* does *trust me.* But he was also violating security . . . and that could only mean that in Brightling's mind security didn't matter. Why—*how* could it not matter? Perhaps Brightling planned to have him eliminated? That was a possibility, but he didn't think so. Brightling was ruthless, but not sufficiently clever—rather, too clever. He would have to consider the possibility that Popov had left a written record somewhere, that his death would trigger the unveiling of his own part in mass murder. So he could discount that, the Russian thought.

Then what?

The former intelligence officer looked in the mirror at a face that still didn't know what it needed to know. From the beginning, he'd been seduced by money. He'd turned into a hired agent of sorts, motivated by personal gain—the "M" of MICE—but was working for someone for whom money had no importance. Even CIA, rich as it had always been, measured the money it gave out to its agents. The American intelligence service paid a hundred times better than its Russian counterpart, but even *that* had to be justified, because CIA had accountants who ruled the field officers as the Czar's courtiers and bureaucrats had once ruled over the smallest village. Popov knew from his research that Horizon Corporation had a huge amount of money, but one did not become wealthy from profligacy. In a capitalist society, one became wealthy by cleverness, perhaps ruthlessness, but not by stupidity, and throwing money about as a government agency did was stupid.

So, what is it? Dmitriy wondered, moving away from the mirror and packing his bag.

Whatever he's planning, whatever his reason for these terrorist incidents—is close at hand?

That did make a little sense. You concealed as long as you had to, but when you no longer had to, then you didn't waste the effort. It was an amateur's move, though. An amateur, even a gifted one like Brightling, didn't know, hadn't learned from bitter institutional experience that you *never* broke tradecraft, even *after* an operation had been successfully concluded, because even then your enemy might find things out that he could use against you in your next one . . .

. . . *unless there is not to be a next one?* Dmitriy thought, as he selected his underwear. *Is this the last operation to be run? No,* he corrected himself, *is this the last operation which* I *need to run?*

He ran through it again. The operations had grown in magnitude, until now he was transporting *cocaine* to make a terrorist happy, *after* transferring *six million* dollars! To make the drug smuggling easier, he would have documentation to justify the drug shipment from one branch of a major corporation to another, tying himself and the drugs to Brightling's company. Perhaps his false ID would hold up if the police showed interest in him—well, they would almost certainly hold up, unless the Garda had a direct line into MI-5, which was not likely, and neither was it likely that the British Security Service had his cover name, or even a photo, good or bad—and besides, he'd changed his haircut ages ago.

No, Popov decided as he finished packing, the only thing that made sense was that this was the last operation. Brightling would be closing things down. To Popov that meant that this was his last chance to cash in. And so he found himself hoping that Grady and his band of murderers would come to as shabby an end as all the others in Bern and Vienna—and even Spain, though he'd had no part in that one. He had the number and control code for the new Swiss account, and in that was enough money to support him for the rest of his life. All he needed to happen was for the Rainbow team to kill them off, and then he could disappear forever. With that hopeful thought in his mind, Popov went outside and flagged a cab to take him to Teterboro Airport.

He'd think about it all the way across the Atlantic.

CHAPTER 27

TRANSFER AGENTS

"IT REALLY IS A WASTE OF TIME," BARBARA ARCHER said at her seat in the conference room. "F4 is dead, just her heart's still beating. We've tried everything. Nothing stops Shiva. Not a damned thing."

"Except the -B vaccine antibodies," Killgore noted.

"Except them," Archer agreed. "But nothing else works, does it?"

There was agreement around the table. They had literally tried every treatment modality known to medicine, including things merely speculated upon at CDC, USAMRIID, and the Pasteur Institute in Paris. They'd even tried every antibiotic in the arsenal from penicillin to Keflex, and two new synthetics under experimentation by Merck and Horizon. The use of the antibiotics had merely been t-crossing and i-dotting, since not one of them helped viral infections, but in desperate times people tried desperate measures, and perhaps something new and unexpected might have happened—

—but not with Shiva. This new and improved version of Ebola hemorrhagic fever, genetically engineered to be hardier than the naturally produced version that still haunted the Congo River Valley, was as close to 100 percent fatal and 100 percent resistant to treatment as anything known to medical science, and absent a landmark breakthrough in infectious-disease treatment, nothing would help those exposed to it. Many would suffer exposure from the initial release, and the rest would get it from the -A vaccine Steve Berg had developed, and through both modalities, Shiva would sweep across the world like a slow-developing storm. Inside of six months, the people left alive would fall into three categories. First, those who hadn't been exposed in any way. There would be few of them, since every nation on earth would gobble up supplies of the -A vaccine and inject their citizens with it, because the first Shiva victims would horrify any human with access to a television. The second group would be those rarest of people whose immune systems were sufficient to protect them from Shiva. The lab had yet to discover any such individuals, but some would inevitably be out there—happily, most of those would probably die from the collapse of social services in the cities and towns of the world, mainly from starvation or from the panicked lawlessness sure to accompany the plague or from the ordinary bacterial diseases that accompanied large numbers of unburied dead.

The third group would be the few thousand people in Kansas. Project Lifeboat, as they thought of it. That group would be composed of active Project members—just a few hundred of them—and their families, and other selected scientists protected by Berg's -B vaccine. The Kansas facility was large, isolated, and protected by large quantities of weapons, should any unwelcome visitors approach.

Six months, they thought. Twenty-seven weeks. That's what the computer projections told them. Some areas would go faster than others. The models suggested that Africa would go last of all, because they'd be the last to get the -A vaccine distributed, and because of the poor infrastructure for delivering vital services. Europe would go down first, with its socialized medical-care systems and pliant citizens sure to show up for their shots when summoned, then America, then, in due course, the rest of the world.

"The whole world, just like that," Killgore observed, looking out the windows at the New York/New Jersey border area, with its rolling hills and green deciduous trees. The great farms on the plains that ran from Canada to Texas would go fallow, though some would grow wild wheat for centuries to come. The bison would expand rapidly from their enclaves in Yellowstone and private game farms, and with them the wolves and barren-ground grizzly bear, and the birds, and the coyotes and the prairie dogs. Nature would restore Her balance very quickly, the computer models told them; in less than five years, the entire earth would be transformed.

"Yes, John," Barb Archer agreed. "But we're not there yet. What do we do with the test subjects?"

Killgore knew what she'd be suggesting. Archer hated clinical medicine. "F4 first?"

"It's a waste of air to keep her breathing, and we all know it. They're all in pain, and we're not learning anything except that Shiva is lethal—and we already knew that. Plus, we're going to be moving out west in a few weeks, and why keep them alive that long? We're not moving them out with us, are we?"

"Well, no," another physician admitted.

"Okay, I am tired of wasting my time as a clinician for dead people. I move that we do what we have to do, and be done with it."

"Second," agreed another scientist at the table.

"In favor?" Killgore asked, counting the hands. "Opposed." Only two of those. "The ayes have it. Okay. Barbara and I will take care of it—today, Barb?"

"Why wait, John?" Archer inquired tiredly.

"KIRK Maclean?" Agent Sullivan asked.

"That's right," the man said from behind the door.

"FBI." Sullivan held up his ID. "Can we talk to you?"

"About what?" The usual alarm, the agents saw.

"Do we have to stand in the hall to talk?" Sullivan asked reasonably.

"Oh, okay, sure, come in." Maclean stepped back and opened the door to let them in, then led them into his living room. The TV was on, some cable movie, the agents saw. Kung fu and guns mostly, it appeared.

"I'm Tom Sullivan, and this is Frank Chatham. We're looking into the disappearance of two women," the senior agent said, after sitting down. "We're hoping that you might be able to help us."

"Sure—you mean, like they were kidnapped or something?" the man asked.

"That is a possibility. Their names are Anne Pretloe and Mary Bannister. Some people have told us that you might have known one or both of them," Chatham said next.

They watched Maclean close his eyes, then look off to the window for a few seconds. "From the Turtle Inn, maybe?"

"Is that where you met them?"

"Hey, guys, I meet a lot of girls, y'know? That's a good place for it, with the music and all. Got pictures?"

"Here." Chatham handed them across.

"Okay, yeah, I remember Annie—never learned her last name," he explained. "Legal secretary, isn't she?"

"That's correct," Sullivan confirmed. "How well did you know her?"

"We danced some, talked some, had a few drinks, but I never dated her."

"Ever leave the bar with her, take a walk, anything like that?"

"I think I walked her home once. Her apartment was just a few blocks away, right? . . . Yeah," he remembered after a few seconds. "Half a block off

Columbus Avenue. I walked her home—but, hey, I didn't go inside—I mean we never—I mean, I didn't, well—you know, I never did have sex with her." He appeared embarrassed.

"Do you know if she had any other friends?" Chatham asked, taking interview notes.

"Yeah, there was a guy she was tight with, Jim something. Accountant, I think. I don't know how tight they were, but when the two of them were at the bar, they'd usually have drinks together. The other one, I remember the face, but not the name. Maybe we talked some, but I don't remember much. Hey, you know, it's a singles bar, and you meet lotsa people, and sometimes you connect, but mainly you don't."

"Phone numbers?"

"Not from those two. I have two from other gals I met there. Want 'em?" Maclean asked.

"Did they know Mary Bannister or Anne Pretloe?" Sullivan asked.

"Maybe. The women connect better than the men do, y'know, little cliques, like, checking us out—like the guys do, but they're better organized, like, y'know?"

There were more questions, about half an hour's worth, some repeated a few times, which Maclean didn't seem to mind, as some did. Finally they asked if they could look around the apartment. They had no legal right to do this, but oddly, even criminals often allowed it, and more than one of them had been caught because they'd had evidence out in plain view. In this case the agents would be looking for periodicals with photographs of deviant sex practices or even personal photographs of such behavior. But when Maclean led them about, the only photos they saw were of animals and periodicals about nature and conservation—some of them from groups the FBI deemed to be extremist—and all manner of outdoors gear.

"Hiker?" Chatham asked.

"Love it in the backcountry," Maclean confirmed. "What I need is a gal who likes it, too, but you don't find many of those in this town."

"Guess not." Sullivan handed over his card. "If you think of anything, please call me right away. My home number's on the back. Thanks for your help."

"Not sure I helped very much," the man observed.

"Every little bit, as they say. See you," Sullivan said, shaking his hand.

Maclean closed the door behind them and let out a long breath. How the *fuck* had they gotten his name and address? The questions were everything he would have expected, and he'd thought about the answers often enough—but a long time ago, he told himself. Why now? Were the cops dumb, or slow, or what?

"WHOLE lot of nothing," Chatham said, as they got to their car.

"Well, maybe the women he gave us can tell us something."

"I doubt it. I talked to the second one last night at the bar."

"Go back to her. Ask her what she thinks of Maclean," Sullivan suggested.

"Okay, Tom. That I can do. You get any vibes off the guy? I didn't," Chatham said.

Sullivan shook his head. "No, but I haven't learned to read minds yet."

Chatham nodded. "Right."

IT was time, and there was no point in delaying it. Barbara Archer unlocked the medication cabinet with her keys and took out ten ampoules of potassium-saline solution. These went into her pockets. Outside F4's treatment room, she filled a 50cc syringe, then opened the door.

"Hello." Mainly a groan from the patient, who was lying in bed and watching the wall-mounted TV listlessly.

"Hello, Mary. How are we feeling?" Archer suddenly wondered why it was that physicians asked how *we* were feeling. An odd linguistic nuance, she told herself, learned in medical school, probably, maybe to establish solidarity with the patient—which hardly existed in this case. One of her first summer jobs in college had been working at a dog pound. The animals had been given seven days, and if nobody claimed them, they were euthanized—*murdered,* as she thought of it, mainly with heavy doses of phenobarbital. The injection always went into the left foreleg, she remembered, and the dogs just went to sleep in five seconds or so. She'd always cried afterward—it had always been done on Tuesday, right before lunch, she recalled, and she'd never eaten lunch afterward, sometimes not even supper if she'd been forced to terminate a particularly cute dog. They'd lined them up on stainless-steel treatment tables, and another employee had held them still to make the murders easier. She'd always talk soothingly to the dogs, to lessen their fear and so give them an easier death. Archer bit her lip, feeling rather like Adolf Eichmann must have—well, should have, anyway.

"Pretty rotten," Mary Bannister replied finally.

"Well, this will help," Archer promised, pulling the syringe out and thumbing off the plastic safety cover from the needle. She took the three steps to the left side of the bed, reached for F4's arm, and held it still, then pushed the needle into the vein inside the elbow. Then she looked into F4's eyes and slid the plunger in.

Mary's eyes went wide. The potassium solution seared the veins as it moved through them. Her right hand flew to the upper left arm, and then, a second later, to her upper chest, as the burning sensation moved rapidly to her heart. The potassium stopped the heart at once. The EKG machine next to the bed had shown fairly normal sinus rhythm, but now the moving line jumped once and went totally flat, setting off the alarm beeper. Somehow Mary's eyes remained open, for the brain has enough oxygen for up to a minute's activity even after the heart stops delivering blood. There was shock there. F4 couldn't speak, couldn't object, because her breathing had stopped along with her heart, but she looked straight into Archer's eyes . . . rather as the dog had done, the doctor thought, though the dog's eyes had never seemed to accuse her as these two did. Archer returned the look, no emotion at all in her face, unlike her time at the pound. Then, in less than a minute, F4's eyes closed, and then she was dead. One down. Nine more to go, before Dr. Archer could go to her car and drive home. She hoped her VCR had worked properly. She'd wanted to tape the Discovery Channel's show on the wolves in Yellowstone, but figuring the damned machine out sometimes drove her crazy.

Thirty minutes later, the bodies were wrapped in plastic and wheeled to the incinerator. It was a special model designed for medical applications, the destruction of disposable biological material such as fetuses or amputated limbs. Fueled by natural gas, it reached an extremely high temperature, even destroying tooth fillings, and converted all to an ash so fine that prevailing winds lifted it into the stratosphere, and then carried it out to sea. The treatment rooms would be scrubbed down so that there would be no lingering Shiva presence, and for the first time in months the facility would have no virus strands actively looking for hosts to feed upon and kill. The Project members would be pleased by that, Archer thought on her drive home. Shiva was a useful tool for their objective, but sufficiently creepy that they'd all be glad when it was gone.

POPOV managed five hours of sleep on the trip across and was awakened when the flight attendant shook his shoulder twenty minutes out of Shannon. The former seaplane facility where Pan American's Boeing-made clippers had landed before flying on to Southampton—and where the airline had invented Irish coffee to help the passengers wake up—was on the West Coast of Ireland, surrounded by farms and green wetlands that seemed to glisten in the light of dawn. Popov washed up in the lavatory, and retook his seat for the arrival. The touchdown was smooth, and the roll-out brief as the aircraft approached the general aviation terminal, where a few other business jets sat, similar to the G-V that Horizon Corporation had chartered for him. Barely had it stopped when a dingy official car approached the aircraft, and a man in uniform got out to jump up the stairs. The pilot waved the man to the back.

"Welcome to Shannon, sir," the immigration official said. "May I see your passport, please?"

"Here." Popov handed it across.

The bureaucrat thumbed through it. "Ah, you've been here recently. The purpose of your trip, sir?"

"Business. Pharmaceuticals," the Russian added, in case the immigration official wanted to open his bags.

"Mm-hmm," the man responded, without a shred of interest. He stamped the passport and handed it back. "Anything to declare?"

"Not really."

"Very well. Have a pleasant time, sir." The smile was as mechanical as his movement forward, then he left to go down the steps to his car.

Popov didn't so much sigh in relief as grumble at his tension, which had clearly been wasted. Who would charter such an aircraft for $100,000 to smuggle drugs, after all? Something else to learn about capitalism, Dmitriy Arkadeyevich told himself. If you had enough money to travel like a prince, then you *couldn't* be outside the law. Amazing, he thought. He put on his overcoat and walked out of the aircraft, where a black Jaguar was waiting, his bags already loaded into the boot.

"Mr. Serov?" the driver asked, holding the door open. There was enough noise out here that he didn't have to worry about being overheard.

"That's right. Off to see Sean?"

"Yes, sir."

Popov nodded and got into the back. A minute later, they were heading off the airport grounds. The country roads were like those in England, narrower than those in America—and he was still driving on the wrong side of the road. How strange, Popov thought. If the Irish didn't like the English, then why did they emulate their driving patterns?

The ride took half an hour, and ended in a farmhouse well off the main roads. Two cars were there and a van, with one man standing outside to keep watch. Popov recognized him. It was Roddy Sands, the cautious one of this unit.

Dmitriy got out and looked at him, without shaking hands. He took the black drug-filled suitcase from the boot and walked in.

"Good morning, Iosef," Grady said in greeting. "How was your flight?"

"Comfortable." Popov handed the bag over. "This is what you requested, Sean."

The tone of voice was clear in its meaning. Grady looked his guest in the eye, a little embarrassment on his face. "I don't like it, either, but one must have money to support operations, and this is a means of getting it." The ten pounds of cocaine had a variable value. It had cost Horizon Corporation a mere $25,000, having bought it on the market that was open to drug companies. Diluted, on the street, it would be worth five hundred times that. Such was another aspect of capitalism, Popov thought, dismissing it now that the transfer had been made. Then he handed over a slip of paper.

"That is the account number and activation code for the secure account in Switzerland. You can only make withdrawals on Monday and Wednesday as an added security measure. The account has in it six million dollars of United States currency. The amount in the account can be checked at any time," Popov told him.

"A pleasure to do business with you, as always, Joe," Sean said, allowing himself a rare smile. He'd never had so much as a tenth of that much money under his control, for all his twenty-plus years as a professional revolutionary. Well, Dmitriy Arkadeyevich thought, they weren't businessmen, were they?

"When will you move?"

"Very soon. We've checked out the objective, and our plan is a thing of beauty, my friend. We will sting them, Iosef Andreyevich," Grady promised. "We will hurt them badly."

"I will need to know when, exactly. There are things I must do as well," Popov told him.

That stopped him, Dmitriy saw. The issue here was operational security. An outsider wanted to know things that only insiders should have knowledge of. Two sets of eyes stared at each other for a few seconds. But the Irishman relented. Once he verified that the money was in place, then his trust in the Russian was confirmed—and delivery of the ten pounds of white powder was proof of the fact in and of itself—assuming that he wasn't arrested by the Garda later this day. But Popov wasn't that sort, was he?

"The day after tomorrow. The operation will commence at one in the afternoon, exactly."

"So soon?"

Grady was pleased that the Russian had underestimated him. "Why delay? We have everything we need, now that the money is in place."

"As you say, Sean. Do you require anything else of me?"

"No."

"Then I will be off, with your permission."

This time they shook hands. "Daniel will drive you—to Dublin?"

"Correct, the airport there."

"Tell him, and he will take you."

"Thank you, Sean—and good luck. Perhaps we will meet afterwards," Dmitriy added.

"I would like that."

Popov gave him a last look—sure that it would be the last, despite what he'd just said. Grady's eyes were animated now, thinking about a revolutionary demonstration that would be the capstone of his career. There was a cruelty there that Popov had not noted before. Like Fürchtner and Dortmund, this was a predatory animal rather than a human being, and, as much experience as he'd had with such people, Popov found himself troubled by it. He was supposed to be skilled at reading minds, but in this one he saw only emptiness, only the absence of human feelings, replaced by ideology that led him—where? Did Grady know? Probably not. He thought himself on the path to some Radiant Future—the term most favored by the Communist Party of the Soviet Union—but the light that beckoned him was far more distant than he realized, and its bright glow hid the holes in the road immediately before him. And truly, Popov thought on, were he ever to achieve that which he wanted, then he'd be a disaster as a ruler of men, like those he resembled—Stalin, Mao, and the rest—so divorced from the common man's outlook as to be an alien, for whom life and death were mere tools to achieve his vision, not something of humanity at all. Of all the things Karl Marx had given the world, surely that outlook was the worst. Sean Grady had replaced his humanity and emotions with a geometrically precise model of what the world should be—and he was too wedded to that vision to take note of the fact that it had failed wherever it had been tried. His pursuit was one after a chimera, a creature not real, never quite within reach, but drawing him onward to his own destruction—and as many others as he might kill first. And his eyes sparkled now in his enthusiasm for the chase. His ideological soundness denied him the ability to see the world as it really was—as even the Russians had come to see, finally, after seventy years of following the same chimera. Sparkling eyes serving a blind master, how strange, the Russian thought, turning to leave.

"OKAY, Peter, you have the duty," Chavez told his Team-1 counterpart. As of now Team-1 was the go-team, and Team-2 was on standby/standdown, and back into the more intensive training regimen.

"As you say, Ding," Covington replied. "But nothing seems to be happening anywhere."

The intelligence that had been passed on to them from the various national agencies was actually rather encouraging. Informants who'd chatted with known or suspected terrorists—mostly the latter, since the more active ones would have been arrested—reported back that the Worldpark incident had chilled the atmosphere considerably, especially since the French had finally published the names and photos of the known terrorists who'd been killed in Spain, and one of them, it had turned out, had been a revered and respected former member of Action Directe, with six known murders to his credit and something of a reputation as an expert operator. His public destruction had rumbled through the community, along with greatly increased respect for the Spanish police, which was basking institutionally in the glow of Rainbow's deeds, to the great discomfort of Basque terrorists, who, Spanish sources reported, were also somewhat chastened by the loss of some of their most respected members.

If this was true, Bill Tawney's summary document suggested, then Rainbow was indeed having the effect that had been hoped for when it had been formed. Maybe this meant that they wouldn't have to move into the field and kill people as frequently to prove their mettle.

But there was still nothing to suggest why there had been three such incidents so close in time, or who, if anyone, might have instigated them. The British Secret Intelligence Service's analysis section called it random, pointing out that Switzerland, Germany, and Spain were different countries, and that it was unlikely that anyone had contacts in the underground groups in all three of them. Two of them, perhaps, but not all three. It also suggested that contacts be made with former East Bloc intelligence services, to check out what was happening with certain retired members. It might even be worth buying their information for the going price, which was rather high now that the former intelligence officers had to make a real living in the real world—but not as high as the cost of an incident in which people got hurt. Tawney had highlighted that when he passed it on to John Clark, and the latter had discussed it with Langley again, only to be rebuffed again, which had Rainbow Six grumbling all week about the REMFs at CIA headquarters. Tawney thought about suggesting it to the London headquarters of "Six" on his own hook, but without the positive endorsement of CIA, it would have been wasted effort.

On the other hand, Rainbow *did* seem to be working. Even Clark admitted that, unhappy though he continued to be, he was a "suit" working behind a desk and sending younger men off to do the exciting stuff. For much of his career as an intelligence officer, John had grumbled at oversight from above.

Now that he was doing it, he thought that maybe he understood it a little better. Being in command might be rewarding, but it could never be much fun for someone who'd been out in the weeds, dodging the fire and involved in the things that happened out at the sharp end. The idea that he knew how it was done and could therefore tell people how to do it was as unpopular a stance for him to take as it had been . . . for him to accept, as recently as five years earlier. Life was a trap, Clark told himself, and the only way out of the trap wasn't much fun either. So, he donned his suitcoat every morning and grumbled at the effect age had on his life, just like every other man of his age did across the planet. Where had his youth gone? How had he lost it?

POPOV arrived at Dublin Airport before lunch. There he purchased a ticket to Gatwick for the hour's flight back to England. He found himself missing the G-V business jet. A very convenient way to travel, liberating from the bustle of the airports. It rode every bit as well as a jumbo jet—but he'd never have enough money to permit him to indulge himself that much, and so he struck the thought from his mind. He'd have to settle for mere first-class travel, the Russian grumbled to himself, sipping some wine as the 737 climbed to cruising altitude. Now, again, he had some thinking to do, and he'd found that the solitary time in the first-class cabin of an aircraft helped.

Did he want Grady to succeed? More to the point, did his employer want Grady to succeed? It hadn't seemed so for Bern and Vienna, but was this a different matter? Maybe Henriksen thought so. He'd given Popov that impression in their discussions. Was there a difference? If so, what was it?

Henriksen was former FBI. Perhaps that explained it. Like Popov, he wouldn't court failure in anything. Or did he really want this Rainbow group damaged to the point that it couldn't—couldn't what? Interfere with some operation?

Again the brick wall, and again Popov struck his head against it. He'd started two terrorist operations, and the only purpose for them he could discern was to raise the international consciousness about terrorism. Henriksen had an international consulting company in that area, and Henriksen wanted the consciousness raised so that he could win contracts—but on the surface it seemed an expensive and inefficient way of doing it, Popov reflected. Certainly the money to be gained from the contracts won would be less than the money Popov had already expended—or pocketed. And again he reminded himself that the money had come from John Brightling and his Horizon Corporation—perhaps from Brightling himself—*not* Henriksen's Global Security, Inc. So, the two companies were related in their objectives, but not in their financial support.

Therefore, Popov thought, sipping his French Chablis, the operation is entirely Brightling's doing, with Henriksen as a support service, providing expertise and advice—

—*but,* one objective was to get Henriksen the consulting contract for the Sydney Olympics, to start in only a few weeks. That had been very important to *both* Brightling *and* Henriksen. Therefore, Henriksen was doing something of great importance to Brightling, doubtless in support of the latter's goal, whatever the hell that was.

But what did Brightling and his company do? Horizon Corporation and all of its numerous international subsidiaries were in the business of medical research. The company manufactured medicines, and spent a huge amount of money every year to invent new ones. It was a world leader in the field of medical research. It had Nobel Prize winners working in its labs, and, his Internet research had determined, it was working in some very exciting areas of potential medical advancement. Popov shook his head again. What did genetic engineering and pharmaceutical manufacturing have to do with terrorism?

The lightbulb that went off over the Irish Sea reminded him that only a relatively few months before, America had been attacked with biological warfare. It had killed about five thousand people, and incurred the lethal wrath of the United States and her President. The dossier he'd been given said that the chief of this Rainbow group, Clark, and his son-in-law, Chavez, had played a quiet but very dramatic role in concluding that bloody little war.

Bio-war, Popov thought. It had given the entire world a reason to shudder. In the event it had proven to be an ineffective weapon of statecraft—especially since America had reacted with her customary speed and furious effectiveness on the battlefields of Saudi Arabia. As a result, no nation-state today dared even to contemplate an attack on America. Its armed forces strode the world like a frontier sheriff in a Western movie, respected and, more to the point, feared for their lethal capabilities.

Popov finished his wine, and fingered the empty glass in his hand as he looked down at the approaching green coastline of England. Bio-war. It had made the whole world shiver in fear and disgust. Horizon Corporation was deeply into cutting-edge research in medical science. So, surely, Brightling's business could well be involved with biological-warfare research—but to what possible end? Besides, it was a mere *corporation,* not a nation-state. It had no foreign policy. It had nothing to gain from warlike activities. Corporations didn't make war, except, perhaps, on other corporations. They might try to steal trade secrets, but actually shed blood? Of course not. Again, Popov told himself, he had merely found a blank hard wall to smash his head against.

"OKAY," Sergeant Major Dick Voss told them. "First of all, the sound quality of these digital radios is so good that you can recognize voices just like a regular conversation in a living room. Second, the radios are coded so that if you have two different teams operating in the field, one team comes in the left ear, and the other team comes in the right ear. That's to keep the commander from getting too confused," he explained, to the amusement of the Australian NCOs. "This gives you more positive control of your operations, and it keeps everybody informed on what's going on. The more you people know, the more effective you will be in the field. You can adjust volume on this dial here—" He showed them the knob on the microphone root.

"What's the range?" a senior Aussie NCO asked.

"Up to ten miles, or fifteen thousand meters, a little longer if you have line of sight. After that, it breaks up some. The batteries are rechargeable, and every set comes with two spares. The batteries will hold their charge for about six months in the spare holders you have, but we recommend recharging them every week. No big deal, the charger comes with every set, and it has a universal plug set. It'll fit into a wall socket here, or anyplace else in the world. You just play with the little fucker until you get the right plug pattern here—" He demonstrated. Most of the people in the room looked at theirs for a few seconds. "Okay, people, let's put them on and try them out. Power-on/off switch is here. . . ."

"FIFTEEN kilometers, eh?" Malloy asked.

"Right," Noonan said. "This way you can listen to what we're doing on the ground, instead of waiting to be told. It fits inside your aircraft headset and shouldn't interfere much with what you need to get over your intercom. This little switch can be attached, and the control button goes down your sleeve into your hand, so you can flip it on or off. It also has a listen-only mode. That's the third position here."

"Slick," Sergeant Nance observed. "Be nice to know what's happening on the ground."

"Damned right. If you ground-pounders need an evac, I'll be halfway in before you make the call. I like it," Colonel Malloy noted. "I guess we'll keep it, Tim."

"It's still experimental. E-Systems says there may be a few bugs in it, but nobody's found them yet. The encryption system is state-of-the-art 128-bit continuous, synchronized off the master set, but hierarchicalized so that if a set goes down, another automatically takes that function over. The boys and girls at Fort Meade can probably crack it, but only twelve hours after you use it."

"Any problem with being inside an aircraft—interference with any of the onboard systems?" Lieutenant Harrison asked.

"Not that we know of. It's been tested on Night Hawks and Stalkers at Fort Bragg, no problems discovered."

"Let's check that one out," Malloy said at once. He'd learned not to trust electronics—and besides, it was a perfectly good excuse to take their Night Hawk off the ground. "Sergeant Nance, head out to the bird."

"You bet, Colonel." The sergeant stood and moved toward the door.

"Tim, you stay here. We'll try it inside and outside, and get a range check, too."

Thirty minutes later, the Night Hawk was circling around Hereford.

"How's this, Noonan?"

"Loud and clear, Bear."

"Okay, good, we're about, oh, eleven clicks out, and you are coming through like Rush Limbaugh across the street. These digital radios work nice, don't they?"

"Yep." Noonan got in his car, and confirmed that the metal cage around him had no effect on performance. It turned out that the radios continued to work at over eighteen kilometers, or eleven miles, which wasn't bad, they thought, for something with a battery the size of two quarters and an antenna half again the length of a toothpick. "This'll make your long-rope deployments go smoother, Bear."

"How so, Noonan?"

"Well, the guys on the end of the rope'll be able to tell you when you're a little high or low."

"Noonan," came the irate reply, "what do you think depth perception is for?"

"Roger that, Bear," the FBI agent laughed.

CHAPTER 28

BROAD DAYLIGHT

THE MONEY MADE IT FAR EASIER. INSTEAD OF STEALing trucks, they could buy them with cashier's checks drawn from an account set up by a person with false identification papers, who'd also been wearing a disguise at the time. The trucks were large Swedish-made Volvo commercial vehicles, straight or nonarticulated trucks with canvas covers over the load area that proclaimed the names of nonexistent businesses.

The trucks came across the Irish Sea to Liverpool on commercial ferries, their interiors laden with cardboard cartons for refrigerators, and passed through British customs with no trouble, and from there it was just a matter of driving within the legal limit on the motorways. The trucks traveled in close formation through the West Country, and arrived near Hereford just before dusk. There, at a prearranged point, they all parked. The drivers dismounted at the local equivalent of a truck stop and headed for a pub.

Sean Grady and Roddy Sands had flown in the same day. They'd passed through customs/immigration control at Gatwick with false papers that had stood the test of time on numerous previous occasions, and again proved to their satisfaction that British immigration officers were blind as well as deaf and dumb. Both of them rented cars with false credit cards and drove west to Hereford, also along preplanned routes, and arrived at the same pub soon before the arriving trucks.

"Any problems?" Grady asked the Barry twins.

"None," Sam replied, accompanied by a nod from Peter. As always, the members of his unit made a show of sangfroid, despite the pre-mission jitters they all had to have. Soon everyone was there, and two groups, one of seven and one of eight, sat in booths, sipping their Guinness and chatting quietly, their presence not a matter of interest to pub regulars.

"THEY work pretty good," Malloy told Noonan, over a pint in the club. "E-Systems, eh?"

"Pretty good outfit. We used a lot of their hardware at HRT."

The Marine nodded. "Yeah, same thing in Special Operations Command. But I still prefer things with control wires and cables."

"Well, yeah, Colonel, sir, but kinda hard to do two paper cups and string out of a chopper, ain't it?"

"I ain't that backward, Tim." But it was good enough for a grin. "And I ain't never needed help doing a long-wire deployment."

"You are pretty good at it." Noonan sipped at his beer. "How long you been flying choppers?"

"Twenty years—twenty-one come next October. You know, it's the last real flying left. The new fast-movers, hell, computers take a vote on whether they like what you're doing 'fore they decide to do it for you. I play with computers, games and e-mail and such, but damned if I'll *ever* let them fly for me." It was an empty boast, or nearly so, Noonan thought. Sooner or later, that form of progress would come to rotary-wing aircraft, too, and the drivers would bitch, but then they'd accept it as they had to, and move on, and probably be safer and more effective as a result. "Waiting for a letter from my detailer right now," the colonel added.

"Oh? What for?"

"I'm in the running for CO of VMH-1."

"Flying the President around?"

Malloy nodded. "Hank Goodman's got the job now, but he made star and so they're moving him up to something else. And somebody, I guess, heard that I'm pretty good with a stick."

"Not too shabby," Noonan said.

"Boring, though, straight and level all the time, no fun stuff," the Marine allowed, with a show of false distaste. Flying in VMH-1 was an honor for a captain, and command of it was the Corps' way of showing confidence in his abilities. "I ought to know in another two weeks. Be nice to see some Redskins games in person again."

"What's up for tomorrow?"

"Right before lunch, practice low-level insertion, paperwork in the afternoon. I have to do a ton of it for the Air Force. Well, they own the damned aircraft, and they are nice about maintaining it and giving me a good flight crew. I bet airliner pilots don't have to do this, though." Those lucky bastards just had to fly, though their brand of flying was about as exciting as a paint-drying race, or maybe a grass-growing marathon.

CHAVEZ hadn't yet gotten used to British humor, and as a result the series television on the local stations mainly bored him. He did have cable service, however, and that included The History Channel, which had become his favorite, if not Patsy's.

"Just one, Ding," she told him. Now that she was close to delivery time, she wanted her husband sober at all times, and that meant only one beer per night.

"Yes, honey." It was so easy for women to push men around, Domingo thought, looking at the nearly empty glass and feeling like another. It was great to sip beer in the club and discuss business matters in a comfortable, informal setting, and generally bond with his people—but right now he was going no farther than fifty feet from his wife, except when he had to, and she had his beeper number when they were apart. The baby had dropped, whatever that meant—well, he knew it meant that delivery was imminent, but not what "dropped" signified. And now it meant that he could only have one beer per night, though he could be stone sober with three . . . maybe even four. . . .

They sat in side-by-side easy chairs. Ding was trying both to watch TV and read intelligence documents. It was something he seemed able to do, to the amazed annoyance of his wife, who was reading a medical journal and making some marginal notes on the glossy paper.

IT wasn't terribly different at the Clark home, though here a movie cassette was tucked into the VCR and was playing away.

"Anything new at the office?" Sandy asked.

At the office, John thought. She hadn't said that when he'd come back from out in the field. No, then it had been "Are you okay?" Always asked with a tinge of concern, because, though he'd never—well, almost never—told her about the things he did in the field, Sandy knew that it was a little different from sitting at a desk. So, this was just one more confirmation that he was a REMF. *Thanks, honey,* he thought. "No, not really," he said. "How about the hospital?"

"A car accident right after lunch. Nothing major."

"How's Patsy doing?"

"She'll be a pretty good doc when she learns to relax a little more. But, well,

I've been doing ER for twenty-some years, right? She knows more than I do in the theoretical area, but she needs to learn the practical side a little better. But, you know, she's coming along pretty well."

"Ever think you might have been a doc?" her husband asked.

"I suppose I could have, but—wasn't the right time back then, was it?"

"How about the baby?"

That made Sandy smile. "Just like I was, impatient. You get to that point and you just want it to happen and be done with it."

"Any worries?"

"No, Dr. Reynolds is pretty good, and Patsy is doing just fine. I'm just not sure I'm ready to be a grandma yet," Sandy added with a laugh.

"I know what you mean, babe. Any time, eh?"

"The baby dropped yesterday. That means he's pretty ready."

" 'He'?" John asked.

"That's what everybody seems to think, but we'll find out when it pops out."

John grumbled. Domingo had insisted that it *had to be* a son, handsome as his father was—and bilingual, *jefe,* he'd always added with that sly Latino grin. Well, he could have gotten worse as a son-in-law. Ding was smart, about the fastest learner he'd ever stumbled across, having risen from young staff sergeant 11-Bravo light-infantryman, U.S. Army, to a respected field intelligence officer in CIA, with a master's degree from George Mason University . . . and now he occasionally mused about going another two years for his Ph.D. Maybe from Oxford, Ding had speculated earlier in the week, if he could arrange the off-time to make it possible. Wouldn't that be a kick in the ass—an East L.A. Chicano with a hood from Oxford University! He might end up DCI someday, and *then* he would really be intolerable. John chuckled, sipped his Guinness, and returned his attention to the television.

POPOV told himself that he had to watch. He was in London again, checked into a medium-class hotel made from a bunch of row houses strung together and renovated. This one he had to see. It would be a first for a terrorist operation. They had a real plan, albeit suggested by Bill Henriksen, but Grady had jumped on the idea, and it certainly seemed a tactically sound concept, as long as they knew when to end it and run away. In any case, Dmitriy wanted to see it happen, the better to know if he could then call the bank and recode the money into his own account and then . . . disappear from the face of the earth whenever he wished. It hadn't occurred to Grady that there were at least *two* people who could access the funds transferred. Perhaps Sean was a trusting soul, Popov thought, odd as that proposition sounded. He'd accepted the contact from his former KGB friend readily, and though he'd posed two major tests, the money and the cocaine, once they'd been delivered he'd stood right up to take the action promised. That was remarkable, now that Popov allowed himself to think about it. But he'd take his rented Jaguar saloon car to go and watch. It ought not to be overly hard, he thought, nor overly dangerous if he did it right. With that thought he tossed off his last Stolichnaya of the night and flipped off the light.

THEY woke up at the same time that morning. Domingo and Patricia in one home, and John and Sandra in another, opened their eyes at 5:30 when their alarms went off, and both couples adjusted their routine to the schedule of the day. The women had to be at the local hospital at 6:45 for the beginning of their 7:00 A.M. to 3:00 P.M. day shift in the emergency room, and so in both homes, the womenfolk got the bathroom first, while the men padded into the kitchen to feed the coffee machine and flip it on, then collect the morning papers from the front step, and turn the radios on to the BBC for the morning news. Twenty minutes later, the bathrooms and newspapers were exchanged, and fifteen minutes after that, the two couples sat down in the kitchen for breakfasts—though in Domingo's case, just a second cup of coffee, as he customarily breakfasted with his people after morning PT. In the Clark home, Sandy was experimenting with fried tomatoes, a local delicacy that she was trying to learn, but which her husband utterly rejected on principle as an American citizen. By 6:20, it was time for the women to dress in their respective uniforms, and for the men to do the same, and soon thereafter all left their homes to begin their different daily activities.

CLARK didn't work out with the teams. He was, he'd finally admitted to himself, too old to sustain the full grind, but he showed up at roughly the same place and did roughly the same daily exercise. It wasn't very different from his time as a SEAL, though without the lengthy swim—there was a pool here, but it wasn't large enough to suit him. Instead, he ran for three miles. The teams did five, though . . . and, he admitted shamefully to himself, at a faster pace. For a man of his years, John Clark knew himself to be in superb physical shape, but keeping himself there got harder every day, and the next major milestone on his personal road to death had the number sixty on it. It seemed so very odd that he was no longer the young piss-and-vinegar guy he'd been when he'd married Sandy. It seemed as if someone had robbed him of something, but if it had happened, he'd never noticed it. It was just that one day he'd looked around and found himself different from what he'd thought himself to be. Not an agreeable surprise at all, he told himself, finishing his three miles, sweating over sore legs and needing his second shower of the day.

On the walk to headquarters, he saw Alistair Stanley setting out for his own morning exercise routine. Al was younger than he by five years and probably still had the illusion of youth. They'd become good friends. Stanley had the instincts, especially for intelligence information, and was an effective field operator in his oddly laid-back British way. Like a spiderhole, John thought, Stanley didn't appear to be much of anything until you looked at his eyes, and even then you had to know what to look for. Good-looking, rakish sort, blond hair still and a toothy smile, but like John he'd killed in the field, and like John he didn't have nightmares about it. In truth he had better instincts as a commander than Clark did, the latter admitted to himself—but only to himself. Both men were still as competitive as they'd been in their twenties, and neither gave praise away for free.

Finished with his shower, Clark walked to his office, sat down at his desk, and went over the morning paperwork, cursing it quietly for the time it required, and all the thought that had to go into such wasteful items as budgeting. Right in his desk drawer was his Beretta .45, proof that he wasn't just one more civil servant, but today he wouldn't have time to walk over to the range to practice the martial skills that had made him the commander of Rainbow—a position that ironically denied him the ability to prove he belonged. Mrs. Foorgate arrived just after eight, looked into her boss's office, and saw the frown she always saw when he was doing administrative work, as opposed to going over intelligence information or operational matters, which at least he appeared to find interesting. She came in to start his coffee machine, got the usual morning greeting-grunt, then returned to her desk, and checked the secure fax machine for anything that might have to go to the boss at once. There was nothing. Another day had started at Hereford.

GRADY and his people were awake as well. They went through their breakfast routine of tea and eggs and bacon and toast, for the typical Irish breakfast was little different from the English. In fact, the countries were little different in any of their fundamental habits, a fact Grady and his people did not reflect upon. Both were polite societies, and extremely hospitable to visitors. Citizens in both countries smiled at one another, worked fairly hard at their jobs, largely watched the same TV, read the same sports pages, and played mainly the same sports, which in both countries were true national passions—and drank similar quantities of similar beers in pubs that could have easily been in one nation as another, down to the painted signs and names that identified them.

But they attended different churches, and had different accents—seemingly so similar to outsiders—that sounded totally different to each of them. An ear for such things remained an important part of daily life, but global television was changing that slowly. A visitor from fifty years earlier would have noted the many Americanisms that had crept into the common language, but the process had been so gradual that those living through it took little note of the fact. It was a situation common to countries with revolutionary movements. The differences were small to outside observers, but all the more magnified to those who advocated change, to the point that Grady and his people saw English similarities merely as camouflage that made their operations convenient, not as commonalties that might have drawn their nations closer. People with whom they might have shared a pint and a discussion of a particularly good football match were as alien to them as men from Mars, and therefore easy to kill. They were things, not "mates," and as crazy as that might have appeared to an objective third party, it was sufficiently inculcated into them that they took no more note of it than they did of the air on this clear, blue morning, as they moved to their trucks and cars, preparing for the day's mission.

AT 10:30 A.M. Chavez and his team moved to the indoor range for marksmanship practice. Dave Woods was there, and had set the boxes of ammunition in the proper places for the Team-2 members. As before, Chavez decided to work on his pistol rather than the easier-to-use MP-10, which anyone with two functioning eyes and one working trigger finger could shoot well. As a result, he turned in the 10mm ammunition and swapped it for two boxes of .45ACP, U.S.-made Federal "Hydra-Shok" premium ammo, with a huge hollowpoint in which one could nearly mix a drink, or so it seemed when you looked into them.

Lieutenant Colonel Malloy and his flight crew, Lieutenant Harrison and Sergeant Nance, walked in just as Team-2 started. They were armed with the standard American-military-issue Beretta M9, and fired full-metal-jacket 9-mm rounds as required by the Hague Convention—America had never signed the international treaty detailing what was proper and what was not on the battlefield, but America lived by the rules anyway. The special-operations people of Rainbow used different, more effective ammo, on the principle that they were not *on* a battlefield, but were, rather, engaging *criminals* who did not merit the solicitude accorded better-organized and -uniformed enemies. Anyone who thought about the issue found it slightly mad, but they knew that there was no hard-and-fast rule requiring the world to make sense, and shot the rounds they were issued. In the case of the Rainbow troopers, it was no less than a hundred rounds per day. Malloy and his crew got to shoot perhaps fifty rounds per week, but they weren't supposed to be shooters, and their presence here was merely a matter of courtesy. As it happened, Malloy was an excellent shot, though he fired his pistol one-handed in the manner once taught by the U.S. military. Harrison and Nance used the more modern Weaver stance, both hands on the weapons. Malloy also missed the .45 of his youth, but the American armed services had gone to the smaller-diameter round to make the NATO countries happy, even though it made much smaller holes in the people whom you were supposed to shoot.

THE girl was named Fiona. She was just about to turn five years old and had fallen off a swing at her day-care center. The wood chips there had scratched her skin, but it was also feared that she might have broken the radius in her left forearm. Sandy Clark held the arm while the child cried. Very slowly and carefully, she manipulated it, and the intensity of the child's tears didn't change. This wasn't broken . . . well, possibly a very minor green-stick fracture, but probably not even that.

"Let's get an x-ray," Patsy said, handing over a grape sucker to the kid. It worked as well in England as it did in America. The tears stopped as she used her good right arm and teeth to rip off the plastic, then stuck the thing into her cute little mouth. Sandy used wetted gauze to clean off the arm. No need for stitches, just a few nasty scrapes that she'd paint with antiseptic and cover with two large Band-Aids.

This ER wasn't as busy as its American counterparts. For one thing, it was in the country, and there was less opportunity for a major injury—they'd had a farmer the previous week who'd come close to ripping his arm off with a farm implement, but Sandy and Patsy had been off-duty then. There were fewer severe auto accidents than in a comparable American area, because the Brits, despite their narrow roads and looser speed limits, seemed to drive more safely than Americans, a fact that had both of the American medics scratching their heads. All in all, duty here was fairly civilized. The hospital was overstaffed by American standards, and that made everyone's workload on the easy side of reasonable, somewhat to the surprise of both Americans. Ten minutes later, Patsy looked over the x-ray and saw that the bones of Fiona's forearm were just fine. Thirty minutes after that, she was on her way back to day care, where it was time for lunch. Patsy sat down at her desk and went back to reading the latest issue of *The Lancet,* while her mother returned to her stand-up desk and chatted with a colleague. Both perversely wished for more work to do, though that meant pain for someone they didn't know. Sandy Clark remarked to her English friend that she hadn't seen a gunshot wound in her whole time in England. In her Williamsburg, Virginia, hospital they'd been almost a daily occurrence, a fact that somewhat horrified her colleagues but was just part of the landscape for an American ER nurse.

HEREFORD wasn't exactly a sleepy community, but the vehicular traffic didn't make it a bustling metropolis either. Grady was in his rented car, following the trucks to the objective, and going more slowly than usual, here in the far-left lane, because he'd anticipated thicker traffic and therefore a longer trip in terms of time. He could have moved off at a faster clip, and therefore started the mission earlier, but he was a methodical sort, and once his plan was drafted, he tended to stick to it almost slavishly. That way, everyone knew what had to happen and when, which made operational sense. For the unexpected, every team member carried a cellular phone with speed-dial settings for every other member. Sean figured they were almost as good as the tactical radios the soldiers carried.

There was the hospital. It sat at the bottom of a shallow slope. The parking lot didn't seem to be very crowded. Maybe there weren't many patients in their beds, or maybe the visitors were off having lunch before coming back to see their loved ones.

DMITRIY pulled his rental car over to the side of the through-road and stopped. He was half a kilometer or so from the hospital, and from the top of this hill, he could see two sides, the front and the side entrance for the hospital's emergency room. He switched the motor off after lowering the power windows and waited to see what would happen next. On the back seat he had an inexpensive set of 7×35 binoculars purchased at an airport shop, and he decided to get them out. Next to him on the seat was his cellular phone, should he need it. He saw three heavy trucks pull up and stop close to the hospital in positions far nearer than his, but, like his spot, able to cover the front and the emergency side entrance.

It was then that Popov had a random thought. Why not call that Clark fellow at Hereford and warn him of what was to happen? *He,* Popov, didn't want these people to survive the afternoon, did he? If they didn't, then he'd have that five-million-plus American dollars, and *then* he could disappear from the face of the earth. The islands of the Caribbean appealed to him; he'd gone over some travel brochures. They'd have some British amenities—honest police, pubs, cordial people—plus a quiet, unhurried life, yet were close enough to America that he could travel there to manage his funds in whatever investment scheme he opted for . . .

But . . . no. There was the off chance that Grady would get away from this one, and he didn't want to risk being hunted by that intense and vicious Irishman. No, it was better that he let this play out without his interference, and so he sat in the car, binoculars in his lap, listening to classical music on one of the regular BBC radio stations.

GRADY got out of his Jaguar. He opened the boot, withdrew his parcel, and pocketed the keys. Timothy O'Neil dismounted his vehicle—he'd chosen a small van—and stood still, waiting for the other five men to join him. This they did after a few minutes. Timmy lifted his cell phone and thumbed the number-one speed-dial setting. A hundred yards away, Grady's phone started chirping.

"Yes?"

"We are ready here, Sean."

"Go on, then. We're ready here as well. Good luck, lad."

"Very well, we are moving in now."

O'Neil was wearing the brown coveralls of a package deliveryman. He walked toward the hospital's side entrance carrying a large cardboard box, followed by four other men in civilian clothes carrying boxes similar in size, but not in color.

POPOV looked into his rearview mirror in annoyance. A police car was pulling over to the side of the road, and a few seconds later, a constable got out and walked to his car.

"Having a problem, sir?" the cop asked.

"Oh, no, not really—that is, I called the rental company, and they're sending someone out, you see."

"What went wrong?" the policeman asked.

"Not sure. The motor started running badly, and I thought it a good idea to pull over and shut it off. Anyway," the Russian repeated, "I called into the company, and they're sending someone to sort it out."

"Ah, very good, then." The police constable stretched, and it seemed as though he'd pulled over as much to get some fresh air as to render assistance to a stranded motorist. The timing, Popov thought, could have been better.

"CAN I help you?" the desk clerk said.

"I have a delivery for Dr. Chavez, and Nurse"—he looked down at the slip of paper on the box, which seemed to him a clever bit of acting—"Clark. Are they in this afternoon?" Timmy O'Neil asked.

"I'll fetch them," the clerk said helpfully, heading back into the work area.

The IRA soldier's hand slid along the inside of the lid, ready to flip the box open. He turned and nodded to the other four, who waited politely in line behind him. O'Neil thumbed his nose, and one of them—his name was Jimmy Carr—walked back outside. There was a police car there, a Range Rover, white with an orange stripe down the side. The policeman inside was eating a sandwich, taking lunch at a convenient place, in what American cops sometimes called "cooping," just killing time when nothing was going on. He saw the man standing outside the casualty-receive entrance holding what looked like a flower box. Several others had just gone inside holding similar boxes, but this was a hospital, and people gave flowers to those inside of them . . . Even so . . . the man with the large white box was staring at his police automobile, as people often did. The cop looked back at him, mainly in curiosity, though his cop instincts were beginning to light up.

"I'M Dr. Chavez," Patsy said. She was almost as tall as he was, O'Neil saw, and very pregnant beneath her starched white lab coat. "You have something for me?"

"Yes, doctor, I do." Then another woman approached, and the resemblance was striking from the first moment he saw the two of them. They had to be mother and daughter . . . and that meant that it was time.

O'Neil flipped the top off the box and instantly extracted the AKMS rifle. He was looking down at it and missed the wide-eyed shock on the faces of the two women in front of him. His right hand withdrew one of the magazines and slapped it home into the weapon. Then he changed hands and let his right hand take hold of the pistol grip while his left slapped the bolt back into the battery position. The entire exercise hadn't lasted two seconds.

Patsy and Sandy froze, as people usually did when suddenly confronted with weapons. Their eyes were wide and faces shocked. To their left, someone screamed. Behind this deliveryman, three others now held identical weapons, and faced outward, aiming at the others in the reception area, and a routine day in the Emergency Room changed to something very different.

OUTSIDE, Carr popped open his box, smiling as he aimed it at the police car only twenty feet away.

The engine was running, and the cop's first instinct was to get clear and report in. His left hand slipped the selector into reverse, and his foot slammed down on the accelerator, causing the car to jolt backward.

Carr's response was automatic. The weapon up, bolt back, he aimed and pulled the trigger, firing fifteen rounds into the automobile's windscreen. The result was immediate. The Rover had been moving backward in a fairly straight line, but the moment the bullets started hitting, it swerved right, and ended up against the brick wall of the hospital. There it stopped, the pressure off the accelerator now. Carr sprinted over and looked inside to see that there was one less police constable in the world, and that, to him, was no great loss.

"WHAT'S that?" It was the helpful roadside cop rather than Popov who asked the rhetorical question. It was rhetorical because automatic-weapons fire is not something to be mistaken for anything else. His head turned, and he saw the police car—an identical twin to his own—scream backward, then stop, and then a man walked up to it, looked, and walked away. "Bloody hell!"

Dmitriy Arkadeyevich sat still, now watching the cop who'd come to his unneeded assistance. The man ran back to his vehicle, reached inside and pulled out a radio microphone. Popov couldn't hear what was said, but, then, he didn't need to.

"WE'VE got them, Sean," O'Neil's voice told him. Grady acknowledged the information, thumbed the END button and speed-dialed Peter Barry's cell phone.

"Yes?"

"Timothy has them. The situation appears to be under control."

"Okay." And this call ended. Then Sean speed-dialed yet another number. "Hello, this is Patrick Casey. We have seized the Hereford community hospital. We are currently holding as hostages Dr. Sanchez and Nurse Clark, plus numerous others. We will release our hostages if our demands are met. If they are not met, then it will be necessary for us to kill hostages until such time as you see the error of your ways. We require the release of all political prisoners held in Albany and Parkhurst prisons on the Isle of Wight. When they are released and seen to be released on the television, we will leave this area. Do you understand?"

"Yes, I understand," the desk sergeant replied. He didn't, but he had a tape of this call, and he'd forward the information to someone who would understand.

CARR took the casualty-receiving entrance; the Barry twins, Peter and Sam, walked through the inside of the building to the main entrance. Here things were somewhat chaotic. Carr's initial fusillade hadn't been heard clearly here, and most of the people had turned their heads to the rough direction of the noise, and on seeing nothing, had turned back to attend to their business. The hospital's security guard, a man of fifty-five who was wearing something that looked like a police uniform, was heading for the door into the hospital proper when he saw the twins coming toward him with weapons in hand. The retired policeman managed to say, "What's all this?"—the usual words of a British constable—before a jerk of one rifle muzzle convinced him to raise his hands and shut up. Sam grabbed his collar and shoved him back into the main lobby. There, people saw the weapons. Some screamed. A few made for the doors, and all of them got outside without being fired upon, since the Barry twins had enough to do already.

THE police constable's radio call from the side of the road generated a greater response than Grady's phone call, especially with the report that a constable had been shot and probably killed in his car. The first reaction of the local superintendent was to summon all of his mobile units to the general area of the hospital. Only about half of them had firearms, and those were mainly Smith & Wesson revolvers—not nearly enough to deal with the reported use of machine guns. The death of the constable was established when an officer who had been parked near the hospital failed to report in, despite numerous calls over the police radio.

Every police station in the world has preset responses for various emergencies. This one had a folder labeled "Terrorism," and the superintendent pulled it out, even though he had the contents memorized, just to make sure he didn't forget anything. The top emergency number went to a desk in the Home Office, and he reported what little he knew to the senior civil servant there, adding that he was working to get more information and would report back.

The Home Office headquarters building, close to Buckingham Palace, housed the bureaucrats who had oversight over nearly every aspect of life in the British Isles. That included law enforcement, and in that building, too, was a procedures folder, which was pulled from its slot. In this one was a new page and a new number.

"FOUR-two-double-three," Alice Foorgate said, on picking up the phone. This was the line used exclusively for important voice traffic.

"Mr. Clark, please."

"Yes. Wait, please."

"Mr. Clark, a call on double-three," she said into the intercom.

"This is John Clark," Rainbox Six said, lifting the receiver.

"This is Frederick Callaway at the Home Office. We have a possible emergency situation," the civil servant said.

"Okay, where is it?"

"Just up the road from you, I'm afraid, the Hereford hospital. The voice which called in identified itself as Patrick Casey. That is a codename that the PIRA use to designate their operations."

"Hereford Hospital?" John asked, his hand suddenly cold on the phone.

"That is correct."

"Hold for a second. I want to get one of my people on this line." John put his hand over the receiver. "Alice! Get Alistair on this one right now!"

"Yes, John?"

"Mr. Callaway, this is Alistair Stanley, my second-in-command. Please repeat what you just told me."

He did so, then added, "The voice identified two hostages by name, a Nurse Clark, and a Dr. Chavez."

"Oh, shit," John breathed.

"I'll get Peter's team moving, John," Stanley said.

"Right. Anything else, Mr. Callaway?"

"That is all we have now. The local police superintendent is attempting to gather more information at this time."

"Okay, thank you. You can reach me at this number if you need me." Clark replaced the receiver in its cradle. "Fuck," he said quietly.

His mind was racing. Whoever had scouted out Rainbow had done so for a reason, and those two names had not been an accident. This was a direct challenge to him and his people—and they were using his wife and daughter as a weapon. His next thought was that he would have to pass command over to Al Stanley, and the next—that his wife and daughter were in mortal danger . . . and he was helpless.

"CHRIST," Major Peter Covington muttered over his phone. "Yes, sir. Let me get moving here." He stood and walked into his squad bay. "Attention, we have some business. Everyone get ready to move immediately."

Team-1's members stood and headed to their lockers. It didn't seem like a drill, but they handled it as though it were. Master Chief Mike Chin was the first to be suited up. He came to see his boss, who was just putting on his body armor.

"What gives, skipper?"

"PIRA, local hospital, holding Clark's and Ding's wives as hostages."

"What's that?" Chin asked, blinking his eyes hard.

"You heard me, Mike."

"Oh, shit. Okay." Chin went back into the squad bay. "Saddle up, people, this ain't no fuckin' drill."

Malloy had just sprinted to his Night Hawk. Sergeant Nance was already there, pulling red-flagged safety pins from their plug points and holding them up for the pilot to confirm the count.

"Looking good, let's start 'er up, Lieutenant."

"Turning one," Harrison confirmed, as Sergeant Nance reboarded the aircraft and strapped on his move-around safety belt, then shifted to the left-side door to check the tail of the Night Hawk.

"Tail rotor is clear, Colonel."

Malloy acknowledged that information as he watched his engine instruments spooling up. Then he keyed his radio again. "Command, this is Bear, we are turnin' and burnin'. What do you want us to do, over?"

"Bear, this is Five," Stanley's voice came back, to Malloy's surprise. "Lift off and orbit the local hospital. That is the site of the current incident."

"Say again, Five, over."

"Bear, we have subjects holding the local hospital. They are holding Mrs. Clark and Mrs. Chavez as hostages. They've identified both of them by name. Your orders are to lift off and orbit the hospital."

"Roger, copy that. Bear is lifting off now." His left hand pulled the collective, climbing the Sikorsky into the sky.

"Did I hear that right, Colonel?" Harrison asked.

"You must have. Fuck," the Marine observed. Somebody was grabbing the tiger by the balls, Malloy thought. He looked down to see a pair of trucks speeding off the base, heading in the same direction as he. That would be Covington and Team-1, he thought. With a little more reflection, he took the Night Hawk to four thousand feet, called the local air-traffic-control center to tell them what he was doing, and got a transponder code so that they could track him properly.

There were four police vehicles there now, blocking the access to the hospital parking lots but doing nothing else, Popov saw through his binoculars. The constables inside were just looking, all standing outside their cars, two of them holding revolvers but not pointing them at anything but the ground.

IN one truck, Covington relayed the information he had. In the other, Chin did it. The troopers were as shocked as they had ever allowed themselves to be, having considered themselves and their families to be *ipso facto* immune to this sort of thing because nobody had *ever* been foolish enough to try something like this. You might walk up to a lion cage and prod him with a stick, but not when there weren't any bars between you and him. And you never ever messed with the lion's cubs, did you? Not if you wanted to be alive at sundown. This was family for all of them. Attacking the wife of the Rainbow commander was a slap in all their faces, an act of incomprehensible arrogance—and Chavez's wife was pregnant. She represented two innocent lives, both of them belonging to one of the people with whom they exercised every morning and with whom they had the occasional pint in the evening, a fellow soldier, one of their team. They all flipped on their radios and sat back, holding their individual weapons, allowing their thoughts to wander, but not very far.

"AL, I have to let you run this operation," John said, standing by his desk and preparing to leave. Dr. Bellow was in the room, along with Bill Tawney.

"I understand, John. You know how good Peter and his team are."

A long breath. "Yeah." There wasn't much of anything else to say right then.

Stanley turned to the others. "Bill?"

"They used the right codename. 'Patrick Casey' is not known to the press. It's a name they use to let us know that their operation is real—usually used with bomb threats and such. Paul?"

"Identifying your wife and daughter is a direct challenge to us. They're telling us that they know about Rainbow, that they know who we are, and, of course, who *you* are, John. They're announcing their expertise and their willingness to go all the way." The psychiatrist shook his head. "But if they're really PIRA, that means they're Catholic. I can work on that. Let's get me out there and establish contact, shall we?"

TIM Noonan was already in his personal car, his tactical gear in the back. At least this was easy for him. There were two cell-phone nodes in the Hereford area, and he'd been to both of them while experimenting with his lock-out software. He drove to the farther of the two first. It was a fairly typical setup, the usual candelabra tower standing in a fenced enclosure with a truck-type trailer—called a caravan over here, he remembered. A car was parked just outside. Noonan pulled alongside and hopped out without bothering to lock it up. Ten seconds later, he pulled open the door to the caravan.

"What's this?" the technician inside asked.

"I'm from Hereford. We're taking this cell off-line right now."

"Says who?"

"Says me!" Noonan turned so that the guy could see the holstered pistol on his hip. "Call your boss. He knows who I am and what I do." And with no further talk, Noonan walked to the master-power panel and flipped the breaker, killing transmissions from the tower. Then he sat in front of the computer control system and inserted the floppy disk he'd carried in his shirt pocket. Two mouse clicks and forty seconds later the system was modified. Only a number with a 777 prefix would be accepted now.

The technician didn't have a clue, but did have the good sense not to dispute the matter with a man carrying a gun.

"Anybody at the other one—on the other side of town?" Noonan asked.

"No, that would be me if there's a problem—but there isn't."

"Keys." Noonan held his hand out.

"I can't do that. I mean, I do not have authorization to—"

"Call your boss right now," the FBI agent suggested, handing him the land-line receiver.

COVINGTON jumped out of the truck near where some commercial trucks were parked. The police had established a perimeter to keep the curious at bay. He trotted over to what appeared to be the senior cop at the site.

▪ ▪ ▪

"THERE they are," Sean Grady said over his phone to Timmy O'Neil. "Sure, and they responded quickly. Ever so formidable they look," he added. "How are things inside?"

"Too many people for us to control properly, Sean. I have the twins in the main lobby, Jimmy here with me, and Daniel is patrolling upstairs."

"What of your hostages?"

"The women, you mean? They're sitting on the floor. The young one is very pregnant, Sean. She could have it today, looks like."

"Try to avoid that, lad," Grady advised, with a smile. Things were going according to his plan, and the clock was running. The bloody soldiers had even parked their trucks within twenty meters of his own. It could scarcely have been better.

HOUSTON'S first name wasn't really Sam—his mother had named him Mortimer, after a favored uncle—but the current moniker had been laid on him during boot camp at Fort Jackson, South Carolina, eleven years before, and he hadn't objected. His sniper rifle was still in its boxy carrying case to safeguard it from shock, and he was looking around for a good perch. Where he was standing wasn't bad, the sergeant thought. He was ready for whatever the day offered. His rifle was a virtual twin to that used by his friend Homer Johnston, and his marksmanship was just as good, too—a little better, he'd quickly tell anyone who asked. The same was true of Rifle One-Two, Sergeant First Class Fred Franklin, formerly an instructor at the Army's marksmanship training unit at Fort Benning and a deadly shot out to a mile with his huge MacMillan .50 bolt-action rifle.

"What d'ya think, Sam?"

"I like it here, Freddy. How about you go to that knoll past the helo pad?"

"Looks good to me. Later." Franklin hoisted the case onto his shoulder and headed off that way.

"THOSE people scare me," Roddy Sands admitted over the phone.

"I know, but one of them is close enough to take out at once, Roddy. You take that job, lad."

"I will, Sean," Sands agreed from inside the cargo area of the big Volvo truck.

■ ■ ■

NOONAN, now with the keys to the other site, was back in his car and heading that way. The drive would take twenty minutes—no, more, he realized. Traffic was backing up on this "A"-class road, and though he had a gun on his hip, and even police identification, his car didn't have a siren and gumball machine—an oversight he himself had never considered, to his sudden and immediate rage. How the fuck had they forgotten that? He *was* a cop, wasn't he? He pulled to the shoulder, turned on his emergency flashers, and started leaning on the horn as he sped past the stopped cars.

CHAVEZ didn't react much. Instead of looking angry or fearful, he just turned inward on himself. A small man, his body seemed to shrink even further before Clark's eyes. "Okay," he said finally, his mouth dry. "What are we doing about it?"

"Team-1 is there now, or should be. Al is running the operation. We're spectators."

"Head over?"

Clark wavered, which was unusual for him. The best thing to do, one part of his mind told him quietly, was to sit still, stay in his office and wait, rather than drive over and torture himself with knowledge that he couldn't do anything about. His decision to let Stanley run the operation was the correct one. He couldn't allow his actions to be affected by personal emotions. There were more lives at stake than his wife's and daughter's, and Stanley was a pro who'd do the right thing without being told. On the other hand, to stay here and simply listen to a phone or radio account was far worse. So he walked back to his desk, opened a drawer, and took out his Beretta .45 automatic. This he clipped to his belt at his right hip. Chavez, he saw, had his side arm as well.

"Let's go."

"Wait." Chavez lifted Clark's desk phone and called the Team-2 building.

"Sergeant Major Price," the voice answered.

"Eddie, this is Ding. John and I are going to drive over there. You're in command of Team-2."

"Yes, sir, I understand. Major Covington and his lads are as good as we are, sir, and Team-2 is suited up and ready to deploy."

"Okay, I have my radio with me."

"Good luck, sir."

"Thanks, Eddie." Chavez hung up. "Let's get going, John."

For this ride, Clark had a driver, but he had the same problem with traffic that Noonan was having, and adopted the same solution, speeding down the hard shoulder with his horn blowing and lights blinking. What should have been a ten-minute drive turned into double that.

"WHO is this?"

"This is Superintendent Fergus Macleash," the cop on the other end of the phone circuit responded. "And you are?"

"Patrick Casey will do for now," Grady answered smugly. "Have you spoken with the Home Office yet?"

"Yes, Mr. Casey, I have." Macleash looked at Stanley and Bellow, as he stood at his command post, half a mile from the hospital, and listened to the speaker phone.

"When will they release the prisoners, as we demanded?"

"Mr. Casey, most of the senior people are out of the office having lunch at the moment. Mainly, the chaps in London I spoke to are trying to track them down and get them into the office. I haven't spoken with anyone in a position of authority yet, you see."

"I suggest that you tell London to get them in quickly. I am not by nature a patient man."

"I need your assurance that no one has been hurt," Macleash tried next.

"Except for one of your constables, no, no one has been hurt—yet. That will change if you take action against us, and it will also change if you and your friends in London make us wait too long. Do you understand?"

"Yes, sir, I do understand what you just said."

"You have two hours until we begin eliminating hostages. We have a goodly supply, you know."

"You understand, if you injure a hostage, that will change matters greatly, Mr. Casey. My ability to negotiate on your behalf will be greatly reduced if you cross that line."

"That is your problem, not mine" was the cold reply. "I have over a hundred people here, including the wife and daughter of your chief counterterrorist official. They will be the first to suffer for your inaction. You now have one hour and fifty-eight minutes to begin the release of every political prisoner in Albany and Parkhurst prisons. I suggest you get moving on that immediately. Good-bye." And the line went dead.

"He's talking tough," Dr. Bellow observed. "Sounds like a mature voice, in his forties, and he's confirmed that he knows who Mrs. Clark and Dr. Chavez are. We're up against a professional, and one with unusually good intelligence. Where could he have gotten it?"

Bill Tawney looked down at the ground. "Unknown, doctor. We had indications that people were looking into our existence, but this is disquieting."

"Okay, next time he calls, I talk to him," Bellow said. "I'll see if I can calm him down some."

"Peter, this is Stanley," Rainbow Five called over his tactical radio.

"Covington here."

"What have you done to this point?"

"I have both riflemen deployed for overwatch and intelligence gathering, but I'm keeping the rest close. I'm waiting now for a building diagram. We have as yet no firm estimate of the number of subjects or hostages inside." The voice hesitated before going on. "I recommend that we consider bringing Team-2 in. This is a large building to cover with only eight men, should we have to move in."

Stanley nodded. "Very well, Peter. I will make the call."

"HOW we looking on gas?" Malloy asked, looking down as he orbited the hospital.

"A good three and a half hours, Colonel," Lieutenant Harrison answered.

Malloy turned to look into the cargo bay area of the Night Hawk. Sergeant Nance had the zip-line ropes out and hooked into the eyebolts on the floor of the aircraft. That work done, he sat in the jump seat between and behind the pilot/copilot seats, his pistol clearly visible in his shoulder holster, listening in on the tactical radio like everyone else.

"Well, we're going to be here for a while," the Marine said.

"Sir, what do you think about—"

"I think I don't like it at all, Lieutenant. Aside from that, we're better off not thinking very much." And that was a bullshit answer, as everyone aboard the Night Hawk knew. You might as well tell the world to stop turning as to tell men in this situation to stop thinking. Malloy was looking down at the hospital, figuring approach angles for a long-wire or zip-line deployment. It didn't appear all that difficult to accomplish, should it become necessary.

The panoramic view afforded from flying above it all was useful. Malloy could see everything. Cars were parked everywhere, and some trucks were close to the hospital. The police cars were visible from their flashing blue lights, and they had traffic pretty well stopped—and elsewhere the roads were clogged, at least those leading *to* the hospital. As usually happened, the roads leading away were wide open. A TV truck appeared, as though by magic, setting up half a mile or so from the hospital, on the hilltop where some other vehicles were stopped, probably rubbernecking, the Marine thought. It always happened, like vultures circling a carcass at Twentynine Palms. Very distasteful, and very human.

POPOV turned when he heard the white TV truck stop, not ten meters from the rear bumper of his rented Jaguar. It had a satellite dish on the roof, and the vehicle had scarcely halted when men stepped out. One climbed the ladder affixed to the side and elevated the oddly angular dish. Another hoisted a Minicam, and yet another, evidently the reporter, appeared, wearing a jacket and tie. He chatted briefly with one of the others, then turned, looking down the hill. Popov ignored them.

FINALLY, Noonan said to himself, pulling off the road at the other cell site. He parked his car, got out, and reached for the keys the technician had given him. Three minutes later, he uploaded his spoofing software. Then he donned his tactical radio set.

"Noonan to Stanley, over."

"This is Stanley."

"Okay, Al, I just cut off the other cell. Cell phones ought to be down now for this entire area."

"Very good, Tim. Come this way now."

"Roger, on the way." The FBI agent adjusted the headset, hanging the microphone exactly in front of his mouth and pushing the earpiece all the way in as he reentered his car and started off back toward the hospital. *Okay, you bastards,* he thought, *try using your fucking phones now.*

AS usual in emergency situations, Popov noted, you couldn't tell what was happening. At least fifteen police vehicles were visible along with the two army trucks from the Hereford base. His binoculars didn't allow him to recognize any faces, but he'd seen only one of them close-up, and that was the chief of the unit, and he'd be in some command post or other rather than visible in the open, assuming that he was here at all, the intelligence officer reminded himself.

Two men carrying long cases, probably riflemen, had walked away from the camouflage-painted trucks, but they were nowhere to be seen now, though . . . yes, he saw, using his binoculars again, there was one, just a jump of green that hadn't been there before. How clever. He'd be a sniper, using his telescopic sight to look into windows and gather information, which he'd then radio to his commander. There was another one of them around somewhere as well, but Popov couldn't see him.

"RIFLE One-Two to Command," Fred Franklin called in.

"One-Two, this is Command," Covington responded.

"In position, sir, looking down, but I don't see anything at all in the windows on the ground level. Some movement of the curtains on the third floor, like people peeking out, but nothing else."

"Roger, thank you, continue your surveillance."

"Roger that. Rifle One-Two, out." Several seconds later, Houston reported similar news. Both men were in perches, with their ghillie suits disguising their positions.

"FINALLY," Covington said. A police car had just arrived, its occupant delivering blueprints of the hospital. Peter's gratitude died in a moment, when he looked at the first two pages. There were scores of rooms, most of them on the upper levels, in any of which a man with a gun could hide and have to be winkled out—worse, all of those rooms were probably occupied with real people, sick ones, whom a flash-bang might startle enough to kill. Now that he had the knowledge, its only immediate benefit was to show him just how difficult his mission would be.

"SEAN?"

Grady turned. "Yes, Roddy?"

"There they are," Sands pointed out. The black-clad soldiers were standing behind their army trucks, only a few meters from the trucks the Irishmen had driven to the site.

"I only count six, lad," Grady said. "We're hoping for ten or so."

"It is a poor time to become greedy, Sean."

Grady thought about that for a second, then checked his watch. He'd allotted forty-five to sixty minutes for this mission. Any more, he thought, would give the other side too much time to get organized. They were within ten minutes of the lower limit. So far, things had gone according to plan. Traffic would be blocked on the roads, but only into the hospital, not away from it. He had his three large trucks, the van, and two private cars, all within fifty meters of where he was standing. The crucial part of the job was yet to begin, but his people all knew what to do. Roddy was right. It was time to wrap everything up and make his dash. Grady nodded at his subordinate, pulled out his cell phone, and hit the speed-dial button for Timothy O'Neil.

But it didn't work. Lifting the phone to his ear, all he heard was the fast-busy signal that announced that the call hadn't gone through properly. Annoyed, he thumbed END and re-dialed . . . and got the same result.

"What's this? . . ." he said, trying a third time. "Roddy, give me your phone."

Sands offered it, and Grady took it. They were all identical in make, and all had been identically programmed. He thumbed the same speed-dial command, and again got only the fast-busy response. More confused than angry, Grady nonetheless had a sudden empty feeling in his stomach. He'd planned for many things, but not for this. For the mission to work, he had to coordinate his three groups. They all knew what they were to do, but not when, not until he told them that it was time.

"Bloody . . ." Grady said quietly, rather to the surprise of Roddy Sands. Next Grady simply tried calling a mobile operator, but the same fast-busy signal resulted. "The bloody phones have stopped working."

"WE haven't heard from him in a while," Bellow observed.

"He hasn't given us a phone number yet."

"Try this." Tawney handed over a handwritten list of numbers in the hospital. Bellow selected the main ER number and dialed it on his cell phone, making sure to start with the 777 prefix. It rang for half a minute before it was picked up.

"Yes?" It was an Irish-sounding voice, but a different one.

"I need to talk to Mr. Casey," the psychiatrist said, putting the call on speaker.

"He's not here right now" was the reply.

"Could you get him, please? I need to tell him something."

"Wait," the voice answered.

Bellow killed the microphone on the portable phone. "Different voice. Not the same guy. Where's Casey?"

"Some other place in the hospital, I imagine," Stanley offered, but the answer was dissatisfying to him when no voice came back on the phone line for several minutes.

■ ■ ■

NOONAN had to explain who he was to two separate police checkpoints, but now the hospital was in sight. He called ahead on his radio, told Covington that he was five minutes away, and learned that nothing had changed.

Clark and Chavez dismounted their vehicle fifty yards from the green trucks that had brought Team-1 to the site. Team-2 was now on its way, also in another green-painted British Army truck, with a police escort to speed their way through the traffic. Chavez was holding a collection of photographs of known PIRA terrorists that he'd snatched off the intelligence desk. The hard part, Ding found, was to keep his hands from shaking—whether from fear or rage, he couldn't tell—and it required all the training he'd ever had to keep his mind on business rather than worrying about his wife and mother-in-law . . . and his unborn son. Only by looking down at the photos instead of up at the country was this possible, for in his hands he had faces to seek and kill, but the green grass around the hospital was merely empty landscape where there was danger. At times like this, the manly thing was to suck it in and pretend that you had it under control, but Chavez was learning now that while being brave for yourself was easy enough, facing danger to someone you loved was a very different situation, one in which courage didn't matter a damn, and all you could do was . . . nothing. You were a spectator, and nothing more, watching a contest of sorts in which lives dear to you were at grave risk, but in which you could not participate. All he could do was watch, and trust to the professionalism of Covington's Team-1. One part of his mind told him that Peter and his boys were as good as he and his own people were, and that if a rescue could be done, they would surely do it—but that wasn't the same as being there yourself, taking charge, and making the right things happen yourself. Sometime later today, Chavez thought, he would again hold his wife in his arms—or she and their unborn child would be taken forever from him. His hands gripped the computer-generated photographs, bending the edges, and his only comfort was in the weight of the pistol that hung in the hip-holster tucked into the waistband of his trousers. It was a familiar feeling, but one, his mind told him, which was useless at the moment, and likely to remain so.

"SO, what do I call you?" Bellow asked, when the phone line became active again.

"You can call me Timothy."

"Okay," the doctor said agreeably, "I'm Paul."

"You're an American," O'Neil observed.

"That's right. And so are the hostages you're holding, Dr. Chavez and Mrs. Clark."

"So?"

"So, I thought your enemies were the Brits, not us Americans. You know that those two ladies are mother and daughter, don't you?" He had to know it, Bellow knew, and for that reason he could point it out as though giving away information.

"Yes," the voice replied.

"Did you know that they are both Catholic, just like you?"

"No."

"Well, they are," Bellow assured him. "You can ask. Mrs. Clark's maiden name is O'Toole, as a matter of fact. She is an Irish-Catholic American citizen. What makes her your enemy, Timothy?"

"She's—her husband is—I mean—"

"He's also an Irish-Catholic American, and to the best of my knowledge he has never taken action of any kind against you or the people in your organization. That's why I have trouble understanding why you are threatening their lives."

"Her husband is the head of this Rainbow mob, and they kill people for the British government."

"No, actually, they do not. Rainbow is actually a NATO establishment. The last time we went out, we had to rescue thirty children. I was there, too. The people holding them murdered one of the kids, a little Dutch girl named Anna. She was dying, Timothy. She had cancer, but those people weren't very patient about it. One of them shot her in the back and killed her. You've probably seen it on TV. Not the sort of thing a religious person would do—not the sort of thing a Catholic would do, murdering a little girl like that. And Dr. Chavez is pregnant. I'm sure you can see that. If you harm her, what about her child? Not just a murder if you do that, Timothy. You're also aborting her unborn child. I know what the Catholic Church says about that. So do you. So does the government in the Republic of Ireland. Please, Timothy, will you please think about what you've threatened to do? These are real people, not abstractions, and the baby in Dr. Chavez's womb is also a real person, too. Anyway, I have something to tell Mr. Casey. Have you found him yet?" the psychiatrist asked.

"I—no, no, he can't come to the phone now."

"Okay, I have to go now. If I call this number again, will you be there to answer it?"

"Yes."

"Good. I'll call back when I have some news for you." Bellow punched the kill switch. "Good news. Different person, younger, not as sure of himself. I have something I can use on this one. He really *is* Catholic, or at least he thinks of himself that way. That means conscience and rules. I can work on this one," he concluded soberly but with confidence.

"But where is the other one?" Stanley asked. "Unless . . ."

"Huh?" Tawney asked.

"Unless he's not in there at all."

"Huh?" the doctor asked.

"Unless he's not bloody there. He called *us* before, but he hasn't talked to us in quite a while. Shouldn't he be doing so?"

Bellow nodded. "I would have expected that, yes."

"But Noonan has chopped the cell phones," Stanley pointed out. He switched on his tactical radio. "This is Command. Look around for someone trying to use a cellular telephone. We may have two groups of subjects here. Acknowledge."

"Command, this is Covington, roger."

"FUCK!" Malloy snarled in his circling helicopter.

"Take her down some?" Harrison asked.

The Marine shook his head. "No, up here they might not even notice us. Let's stay covert for a while."

"WHAT the hell?" Chavez observed, looking at his father-in-law.

"Inside-outside?" John speculated.

GRADY was at the point of losing his temper. He'd tried a total of seven times to make a call with his cell phone, only to find the same infuriating fast-busy response. He had a virtually perfect tactical situation, but lacked the ability to coordinate his teams. There they were, those Rainbow people, standing in a bunch not a hundred meters from the two Volvo trucks. This couldn't last, though. The local police would surely start securing the area soon. There were perhaps a hundred and fifty, perhaps as many as two hundred people now, standing in little knots within three hundred meters of the hospital. The time was right. The targets were there.

▪ ▪ ▪

NOONAN crested the hill and started driving down to where the team was, wondering what the hell he'd be able to do. Bugging the building, his usual job, meant getting close. But it was broad daylight, and getting close would be a mother of a task, probably beyond the range of possibility until nightfall. Well, at least he'd taken care of his primary function. He'd denied the enemy the chance to use cell phones—if they'd tried to, which he didn't know. He slowed the car for his approach, and saw Peter Covington in the distance conferring with his black-clad shooters.

CHAVEZ and Clark were doing much the same thing, standing still a few yards from Clark's official car.

"The perimeter needs firming up," Ding said. Where had all these vehicles come from? Probably people who happened to be in the area when the shooting started. There was the usual goddamned TV van, its satellite dish erected, and what appeared to be a reporter speaking in front of a handheld Minicam. So, Chavez thought, now the danger to his family was a goddamned spectator sport.

GRADY had to make a decision, and he had to make it now. If he wanted to achieve his goal and make his escape, it had to be now. His gun-containing parcel was sitting on the ground next to his rental car. He left it on the ground with Roddy Sands and walked to the farthest of the Volvo commercial trucks.

"Sean," a voice called from the cargo area, "the bloody phones don't work."

"I know. We begin in five minutes. Watch for the others, and then carry on as planned."

"Okay, Sean," the voice replied. To punctuate it, Grady heard the cocking of the weapons inside as he walked to the next, delivering the same message. Then the third. There were three men in each of the trucks. The canvas covers over the cargo areas had holes cut in them, like the battlements of a castle, and those inside had opened them slightly and were now looking at the soldiers less than a hundred meters away. Grady made his way back to his Jaguar. When he got there he checked his watch. He looked at Roddy Sands and nodded.

TEAM-2'S truck was starting down the hill to the hospital. Noonan's car was directly in front of it now.

■ ■ ■

POPOV was watching the whole area with his binoculars. A third military truck came into view. He looked at it and saw more men sitting in the back, probably reinforcements for the people already outside the hospital. He returned his attention to the area that already had soldiers. Closer examination showed . . . was that John Clark? he wondered. Standing away from the others. Well, if his wife were a hostage now, that made sense to let another—he had to have a second-in-command for his organization—command the operation. So, he'd just be standing there now, looking tense in his suit.

"Excuse me." Popov turned to see a reporter and a cameraman, and closed his eyes in a silent curse.

"Yes?"

"Could you give us your impressions of what is happening here? First of all, your name, and what causes you to be here."

"Well, I—my name—my name is Jack Smith," Popov said, in his best London accent. "And I was out here in the country—birding, you see. I was out here to enjoy nature, it's a nice day, you see, and—"

"Mr. Smith, have you any idea what is happening down there?"

"No, no, not really." He didn't take his eyes away from the binoculars, not wanting to give them a look at his face. *Nichevo!* There was Sean Grady, standing with Roddy Sands. Had he believed in God, he would have invoked His name at that moment, seeing what they were doing, and knowing exactly what they were thinking in this flashpoint in time.

GRADY bent down and opened his parcel, removing the AKMS assault-rifle from it. Then he slapped in the magazine, extended the folding stock, and in one smooth motion stood to straight and brought it to his shoulder. A second later he took aim and fired into the group of black-clad soldiers. A second after that, the men in the trucks did the same.

THERE was no warning at all. Bullets hit the side of the truck behind which they'd been sheltering, but before Team-1 had the time to react, the bullets came in on their bodies. Four men dropped in the first two seconds. By that time, the rest had jumped away and down, their eyes looking around for the source of the fire.

■ ■ ■

NOONAN saw them crumple, and it took a second or so of shock for him to realize what was happening. Then he spoke into his tactical radio: "Warning, warning, Team-1 is under fire from the rear!" At the same time his eyes were searching for the source—it had to be right there, in that big truck. The FBI agent floored his accelerator and dashed that way, his right hand reaching for his pistol.

MASTER Chief Mike Chin was down with a bullet in each upper leg. The suddenness only made the pain worse. He'd been totally unprepared for this, and the pain paralyzed him for several seconds, until training reasserted itself, and he tried to crawl to cover. "Chin is hit, Chin is hit," he gasped over the radio, then turned to see another Team-1 member down, blood gushing from the side of his head.

SERGEANT Houston's head snapped off his scope, and turned right with the sudden and unexpected noise of automatic-weapons fire. *What the hell?* He saw what appeared to be the muzzle of a rifle sticking out the side of one of the trucks, and he swung his rifle up and off the ground to the right to try to acquire a target.

RODDY Sands saw the movement. The sniper was where he remembered, but covered as he was in his camouflage blanket, it was hard to track in on him. The movement fixed that, and the shot was only about a hundred fifty meters. Holding low and left, he pulled the trigger and held it down, walking his rounds through the shape on the side of the hill, firing long, then pulling back down to hit at it again.

HOUSTON got one round off, but it went wild as a bullet penetrated his right shoulder, blasting right through his body armor, which was sufficient to stop a pistol round but not a bullet from a rifle. Neither courage nor muscle strength could make broken bones work. The impact made his body collapse, and a second later, Houston knew that his right arm would not work at all. On instinct he rolled to his left, while his left hand tried to reach across his body for his service pistol, while he announced over the radio that he was hit as well.

IT was easier for Fred Franklin. Too far away for easy fire from one of the terrorists' weapons, he was also well concealed under his blanket. It took him a few seconds to realize what was going on, but the screams and groans over his radio earpiece told him that some team members had been badly hurt. He swept his scope sight over the area, and saw one gun muzzle sticking out the side of a truck. Franklin flipped off his safety, took aim, and loosed his first .50-caliber round of the fight. The muzzle blast of his own weapon shattered the local silence. The big MacMillan sniper rifle fired the same cartridge as the .50-caliber heavy machine gun, sending a two-ounce bullet off at 2,700 feet per second, covering the distance in less than a third of a second and drilling a half-inch hole into the soft side of the truck, but there was no telling if it hit a target or not. He swept the rifle left, looking for another target. He passed over another big truck, and saw the holes in the cover, but nothing inside of them. More to the left—there, there was a guy holding a rifle and firing—off to where Sam was. Sergeant First Class Fred Franklin worked his bolt, loaded a second round, and took careful aim.

RODDY Sands was sure he'd hit his target, and was now trying to kill it. To his left, Sean was already back in his car, starting it for the getaway that had to begin in less than two minutes.

Grady heard the engine catch and turned to look back at his most trusted subordinate. He'd just gotten all the way around when the bullet hit, just at the base of Sands's skull. The huge .50 bullet exploded the head like a can of soup, and for all his experience as a terrorist, Grady had never seen anything like it. It seemed that only the jaw remained, as the body fell out of view, and Team-1 got its first kill of the day.

NOONAN stopped his car inches from the third of the trucks. He dove out the right-side driver's door, and heard the distinctive chatter of Kalashnikov-type weapons. Those had to be enemies, and they had to be close. He held his Beretta pistol in both hands, looked for a second at the back of the truck and wondered how to—yes! There was a ladder-handle fixture on the rear door. He slipped a booted foot into it and climbed up, finding a canvas cover roped into place. He forced his pistol into his waistband and withdrew his K-Bar combat knife, slashing at the rope loops, getting a corner free. He lifted it with his left hand, looked inside and saw three men, facing left and doing aimed fire with their weapons. Okay. It never occurred to him to say or shout anything to them. Leaning in, his left hand holding the canvas clear, he aimed with his right hand. The first round was double-action, and his finger pulled the trigger slowly, and the head nearest to him snapped to its right, and the body fell. The others were too distracted by the noise of their own weapons to hear the report of the pistol. Noonan instantly adjusted his grip on the pistol and fired off a second round into the next head. The third man felt the body hit his, and turned to look. The brown eyes went wide. He jerked away from the side of the truck and brought his rifle to his left, but not quickly enough. Noonan fired two rounds into the chest, then brought his pistol down from recoil and fired his third right through the man's nose. It exited through his brain stem, by which time the man was dead. Noonan looked hard at all three targets, and, sure they were dead, jumped back off the truck and headed forward to the next. He paused to slap in a fresh magazine, while a distant part of his mind remarked on the fact that Timothy Noonan was on autopilot, moving almost without conscious thought.

Grady floored his car, hitting the horn as he did so. That was the signal for the others to get clear. That included the men inside the hospital, whom he'd been unable to alert with his cell phone.

"JESUS Christ!" O'Neil announced when the first rounds were fired. "Why the bloody hell didn't he—"

"Too late to worry, Timmy," Sam Barry told him, waving to his brother and running for the door. Jimmy Carr was there, and the final member of the inside team joined up ten seconds later, emerging from the door to the fire stairs.

"Time to go, lads," O'Neil told them. He looked at the two main hostages and thought to wave to them, but the pregnant one would only slow them down, and there were thirty meters to his van. The plan had come apart, though he didn't know why, and it was time to get the hell out of here.

THE third military truck stopped a few yards behind Noonan's personal car. Eddie Price jumped out first, his MP-10 up in his hands, then crouched, looking around to identify the noise. Whatever it was, it was happening too bloody fast, and there was no plan. He'd been trained for this as an ordinary infantryman, but that had been twenty years ago. Now he was a special-operations soldier, and supposed to know every step before he took it. Mike Pierce came down next to him.

"What the fuck's happening, Eddie?"

Just then, they saw Noonan jump down from the Volvo truck and swap out magazines on his pistol. The FBI agent saw them, and waved them forward.

"I suppose we follow him," Price said. Louis Loiselle appeared at Pierce's side and the two started off. Paddy Connolly caught up, reaching into his fanny pack for a flash-bang.

O'NEIL and his four ran out the emergency-room entrance and made it all the way to their van without being spotted or engaged. He'd left the keys in, and had the vehicle moving before the others had a chance to close all the doors.

"WARNING, warning," Franklin called over the radio. "We have bad guys in a brown van leaving the hospital, looks like four of them." Then he swiveled his rifle and took aim just aft of the left-front tire and fired.

THE heavy bullet ripped through the fender as though it were a sheet of newspaper, then slammed into the iron block of the six-cylinder engine. It penetrated one cylinder, causing the piston to jam instantly, stopping the engine just as fast. The van swerved left with the sudden loss of engine power, almost tipping over to the right, but then slamming down and righting itself.

O'Neil screamed a curse and tried to restart the engine at once, with no result at all. The starter motor couldn't turn the jammed crankshaft. O'Neil didn't know why, but this vehicle was fully dead, and he was stuck in the open.

FRANKLIN saw the result of his shot with some satisfaction and jacked in another round. This one was aimed at the driver's head. He centered his sight reticle and squeezed, but at the same moment the head moved, and the shot missed. That was something Fred Franklin had never done. He looked on in stunned surprise for a moment, then reloaded.

■ ■ ■

O'NEIL was cut on the face by glass fragments. The bullet hadn't missed him by more than two inches, but the shock of it propelled him out of the driver's seat into the cargo area of the van. There he froze, without a clue as to what to do next.

HOMER Johnston and Dieter Weber still had their rifles in the carrying cases, and since it didn't appear that either would have much chance to make use of them, right now they were moving with pistols only. In the rear of their team, they watched Eddie Price slash a hole in the rear cover of the second Volvo truck. Paddy Connolly pulled the pin on a flash-bang and tossed it inside. Two seconds later, the explosion of the pyro charge blew the canvas cover completely off the truck. Pierce and Loiselle jumped up, weapons ready in their hands, but the three men inside were stunned unconscious from the blast. Pierce jumped all the way in to disarm them, tossed their weapons clear of the truck, and kneeled over them.

IN each of the three Volvo trucks, one of the armed men was also to be the driver. In the foremost of the three, this one was named Paul Murphy, and from the beginning he'd divided his time between shooting and watching Sean Grady's Jaguar. He saw that the car was moving and dropped his weapon to take the driver's seat and start the diesel engine. Looking up, he saw what had to be the body of Roddy Sands—but it appeared to be headless. What had happened? Sean's right arm came out of the window, waving in a circling motion for the truck to follow. Murphy slipped the truck into gear and pulled off to follow. He turned left to see the brown van Tim O'Neil had driven stopped cold in the hospital parking lot. His first instinct was to go down there and pick his comrades up, but the turn would have been difficult, and Sean was still waving, and so he followed his leader. In the back, one of his shooters lifted the rear flap and looked to see the other trucks, his AKMS rifle in his hands, but neither was moving, and there were men in black clothing there—

—ONE of those was Sergeant Scotty McTyler, and he had his MP-10 up and aimed. He fired a three-round burst at the face in the distance, and had the satisfaction to see a puff of pink before it dropped out of sight.

"Command, McTyler, we have a truck leaving the area with subjects aboard!" McTyler loosed another few rounds, but without visible effect, and turned away, looking for something else to do.

POPOV had never seen a battle before, but that was what he watched now. It seemed chaotic, with people darting around seemingly without purpose. The people in black—well, three were down at the truck from the initial gunfire, and others were moving, apparently in pursuit of the Jaguar, virtually identical with his, and the truck, now exiting the parking lot. Not three meters away, the TV reporter was speaking rapidly into his microphone, while his cameraman had his instrument locked on the events down the hill. Popov was sure it was exciting viewing for everybody in their sitting rooms. He was also sure that it was time for him to leave.

The Russian got back into his car, started the engine, and moved off, with a spray of gravel for the reporter in his wake.

"I got 'em. Bear's got 'em," Malloy reported, lowering his collective control to drop down to a thousand feet or so, his aviator's eyes locked on the two moving vehicles. "Anybody in command of this disaster?" the Marine asked next.

"MR. C?" Ding asked.

"Bear, this is Six. I am in command now." Clark and Chavez sprinted back to Clark's official car, where both jumped in, and the driver, unbidden, started in pursuit. He was a corporal of military police in the British Army, and had never been part of the Rainbow team, which he'd always resented somewhat. But not now.

It wasn't much of a challenge. The Volvo truck was powerful, but no competition for the V-8 Jaguar racing up behind it.

PAUL Murphy checked his mirror and was instantly confused. Coming up to join him was a Jaguar visually identical to the—he looked, yes, Sean was there, up in front of him. Then who was this? He turned to yell at the people in the back, but on looking, saw that one was down and clearly dead, a pool of blood sliding greasily across the steel floor of the truck. The other was just holding on.

■ ■ ■

"THIS is Price. Where is everyone? Where are the subjects?"

"Price, this is Rifle One-Two. I think we have one or more subjects in the brown van outside the hospital. I took the motor out with my rifle. They ain't going nowhere, Eddie."

"Okay." Price looked around. The local situation might even be under control or heading that way. He felt as though he'd been awakened by a tornado and was now looking at his wrecked farm and trying to make sense of what had taken place. One deep breath, and the responsibility of command asserted itself: "Connolly and Lincoln, go right. Tomlinson and Vega, down the hill to the left. Patterson, come with me. McTyler and Pierce, guard the prisoners. Weber and Johnston, get down to Team-1 and see how they are. *Move!*" he concluded.

"Price, this is Chavez," his radio announced next.

"Yes, Ding."

"What's the situation?"

"We have two or three prisoners, a van with an unknown number of subjects in it, and Christ knows what else. I am trying to find out now. Out." And that concluded the conversation.

"GAME face, Domingo," Clark said, sitting in the left-front seat of the Jaguar.

"I fuckin' hear you, John!" Chavez snarled back.

"Corporal—Mole, isn't it?"

"Yes, sir," the driver said, without moving his eyes a millimeter.

"Okay, Corporal, get us up on his right side. We're going to shoot out his right-front tire. Let's try not to eat the fucking truck when that happens."

"Very good, sir" was the cool reply. "Here we go."

The Jag leaped forward, and in twenty seconds was alongside the Volvo diesel truck. Clark and Chavez lowered their windows. They were doing over seventy miles per hour now, as they leaned out of their speeding automobile.

A hundred meters ahead, Sean Grady was in a state of rage and shock. What the devil had gone wrong? The first burst from his people's weapons had surely killed a number of his black-clad enemies, but after that—what? He'd formulated a good plan, and his people had executed it well at first—but the goddamned phones! What had gone wrong with those? That had ruined everything. But now things were back under some semblance of control. He was ten minutes away from the shopping area where he'd park and leave the car, disappear into the crowd of people, then walk to another parking lot, get in another rental car, and drive off to Liverpool for the ferry ride home. He would get out of this, and so would the lads in the truck behind him—he looked in the mirror. What the hell was that?

CORPORAL Mole had done well, first maneuvering to the truck's left, then slowing and darting to the right. That caught the driver by surprise.

In the back seat, Chavez saw the face of the man. Very fair-skinned and red-haired, a real Paddy, Domingo thought, extending his pistol and aiming at the right-front wheel.

"Now!" John called from the front seat. In that instant, their driver swerved to the left.

Paul Murphy saw the auto jump at him and instinctively swerved hard to avoid it. Then he heard gunfire.

Clark and Chavez fired several times each, and it was only a few feet of distance to the black rubber of the tire. Their bullets all hit home just outside the rim of the wheel, and the nearly-half-inch holes deflated the tire rapidly. Scarcely had the Jaguar pulled forward when the truck swerved back to the right. The driver tried to break and slow, but that instinctive reaction only made things worse for him. The Volvo truck dipped to the right, and then the uneven braking made it worse still, and the right-side front-wheel rim dug into the pavement. This made the truck try to stop hard, and the body flipped over, landed on its right side, and slid forward at over sixty miles per hour. Strong as the body of the truck was, it hadn't been designed for this, and when the roll continued, the truck body started coming apart.

Corporal Mole cringed to see his rearview mirror filled with the sideways truck body, but it got no closer, and he swerved left to make sure it didn't overtake him. He allowed the car to slow now, watching the mirror as the Volvo truck rolled like a child's toy, shedding pieces as it did so.

"Jesuchristo!" Ding gasped, turning to watch. What could only have been a human body was tossed clear, and he saw it slide up the blacktop and pinwheel slowly as it proceeded forward at the same speed as the wrecked truck.

"Stop the car!" Clark ordered.

Mole did better than that, coming to a stop, then backing up to within a few meters of the wrecked truck. Chavez jumped out first, pistol in both hands and advancing toward the vehicle. "Bear, this is Chavez, you there?"

"Bear copies," came the reply.

"See if you can get the car, will ya? This truck's history, man."

"ROGER that, Bear is in pursuit."

"Colonel?" Sergeant Nance said over the intercom.

"Yeah?"

"You see how they did that?"

"Yeah—think you can do the same?" Malloy asked.

"Got my pistol, sir."

"Well, then it's air-to-mud time, people." The Marine dropped the collective again and brought the Night Hawk to a hundred feet over the road. He was behind and down-sun from the car he was following. Unless the bastard was looking out the sunroof, he had no way of knowing the chopper was there.

"Road sign!" Harrison called, pulling back on the cyclic to dodge over the highway sign telling of the next exit on the motorway.

"Okay, Harrison, you do the road. I do the car. Yank it hard if you have to, son."

"Roger that, Colonel."

"Okay, Sergeant Nance, here we go." Malloy checked his speed indicator. He was doing eighty-five in the right outside lane. The guy in the Jag was leaning on the pedal pretty hard, but the Night Hawk had a lot more available power. It was not unlike flying formation with another aircraft, though Malloy had never done it with a car before. He closed to about a hundred feet. "Right side, Sergeant."

"Yes, sir." Nance slid the door back and knelt on the aluminum floor, his Beretta 9-mm in both hands. "Ready, Colonel. Let's do it!"

"Ready to tank," Malloy acknowledged, taking one more look at the road. Damn, it was like catching the refueling hose of a Herky Bird, but slower and a hell of a lot lower . . .

GRADY bit his lip, seeing that the truck was no longer there, but behind him the road was clear, and ahead as well at the moment, and it was a mere five minutes to safety. He allowed himself a relaxing breath, flexed his fingers on the wheel, and blessed the workers who'd built this fine fast car for him. Just then his peripheral vision caught something black on his left. He turned an inch to look—what the hell—

■ ■ ■

"GOT him!" Nance said, seeing the driver through the left-rear passenger-door window and bringing his pistol up. He let it wait, while Colonel Malloy edged another few feet and then—

—resting his left arm on his knee, Nance thumbed back the hammer and fired. The gun jumped in his hand. He brought it down and kept pulling the trigger. It wasn't like on the range at all. He was jerking the gun badly despite his every effort to hold it steady, but on the fourth round, he saw his target jerk to the right.

THE glass was shattering all around him. Grady didn't react well. He could have slammed on the brakes, and that would have caused the helicopter to overshoot, but the situation was too far outside anything he'd ever experienced. He actually tried to speed up, but the Jaguar didn't have all that much acceleration left. Then his left shoulder exploded in fire. Grady's upper chest cringed from nerve response. His right hand moved down, causing the car to swerve in that direction, right into the steel guardrail.

MALLOY pulled on the collective, having seen at least one good hit. In seconds, the Night Hawk was at three hundred feet, and the Marine turned to the right and looked down to see a wrecked and smoking car stationary in the middle of the road.

"Down to collect him?" the copilot asked.

"Bet your sweet ass, son," Malloy told Harrison. Then he looked for his own flight bag. His Beretta was in there. Harrison handled the landing, bringing the Sikorsky to a rest fifty feet from the car. Malloy turned the lock on his seat-belt buckle and turned to exit the aircraft. Nance jumped out first, ducking under the turning rotor as he ran to the car's right side. Malloy was two seconds behind him.

"Careful, Sergeant!" Malloy screamed, slowing his advance on the left side. The window was gone except for a few shards still in the frame, and he could see the man inside, still breathing but not doing much else behind the deployed air bag. The far window was gone as well. Nance reached into it, found the handle and pulled it open. It turned out that the driver hadn't been using his seat belt. The body came out easily. And there on the back seat, Malloy saw, was a Russian-made rifle. The Marine pulled it out and safed it, before walking to the other side of the car.

"Shit," Nance said in no small amazement. "He's still alive!" How had he managed not to kill the bastard from twelve feet away? the sergeant wondered.

BACK at the hospital, Timothy O'Neil was still in his van wondering what to do. He thought he knew what had happened to the engine. There was a three-quarter-inch hole in the window on the left-side door, and how it had managed to miss his head was something he didn't know. He saw that one of the Volvo trucks and Sean Grady's rented Jaguar were nowhere to be seen. Had Sean abandoned him and his men? It had happened too fast and totally without warning. Why hadn't Sean called to warn him of what he did? How had the plan come apart? But the answers to those questions were of less import than the fact that he was in a van, sitting in a parking lot, with enemies around him. That he had to change.

"LIEBER *Gott,"* Weber said to himself, seeing the wounds. One Team-1 member was surely dead, having taken a round in the side of his head. Four others right here were hit, three of them in the chest. Weber knew first-aid, but he didn't need to know much medicine to know that two of them needed immediate and expert attention. One of those was Alistair Stanley.

"This is Weber. We need medical help here at once!" he called over his tactical radio. "Rainbow Five is down!"

"Oh, shit," Homer Johnston said next to him. "You're not foolin', man. Command, this is Rifle Two-One, we need medics and we need them right the fuck now!"

PRICE heard all that. He was now thirty yards from the van, Sergeant Hank Patterson at his side, trying to approach without being seen. To his left he could see the imposing bulk of Julio Vega, along with Tomlinson. Off to the right he could see the face of Steve Lincoln. Paddy Connolly would be right with him.

"Team-2, this is Price. We have subjects in the van. I do not know if we have any inside the building. Vega and Tomlinson, get inside and check—and be bloody careful about it!"

"Vega here. Roger that, Eddie. Moving now."

Oso reversed directions, heading for the main entrance with Tomlinson in support, while the other four kept an eye on that damned little brown truck. The two sergeants approached the front door slowly, peering around corners to look in the windows, and seeing only a small mob of very confused people. First Sergeant Vega poked a finger into his own chest and pointed inside. Tomlinson nodded. Now Vega moved quickly, entering the main lobby and sweeping his eyes all around. Two people screamed to see another man with a gun, despite the difference in his appearance. He held up his left hand.

"Easy, folks, I'm one of the good guys. Does anybody know where the bad guys are?" The answer to this question was mainly confusion, but two people pointed to the rear of the building, in the direction of the emergency room, and that made sense. Vega advanced to the double doors leading that way and called on his radio. "Lobby is clear. Come on, George." Then: "Command, this is Vega."

"Vega, this is Price."

"Hospital lobby is clear, Eddie. Got maybe twenty civilians here to get looked after, okay?"

"I have no people to send you, Oso. We're all busy out here. Weber reports we have some serious casualties."

"THIS is Franklin. I copy. I can move in now if you need me."

"Franklin, Price, move in to the west. I repeat, move in from the west."

"Franklin is moving in to the west," the rifleman replied. "Moving in now."

"HIS pitchin' career's over," Nance said, loading the body into the Night Hawk.

"Sure as hell, if he's a lefty. Back to the hospital, I guess," Malloy strapped into the chopper and took the controls. Inside a minute, they were airborne and heading east for the hospital. In the back, Nance strapped their prisoner down tight.

IT was a hell of a mess. The driver was dead, Chavez saw, crushed between the large wheel and the back of his seat from when the truck had slammed into the guardrail, his eyes and mouth open, blood coming out the latter. The body tossed out of the back was dead as well, with two bullet holes in the face. That left a guy with two broken legs, and horrible scrapes on his face, whose pain was masked by his unconsciousness.

"Bear, this is Six," Clark said.

"Bear copies."

"Can you pick us up? We have an injured subject here, and I want to get back and see what the hell's going on."

"Wait one and I'll be there. Be advised we have a wounded subject aboard, too."

"Roger that, Bear." Clark looked west. The Night Hawk was in plain view, and he saw it alter course and come straight for his position.

CHAVEZ and Mole pulled the body onto the roadway. It seemed horrible that his legs were at such obviously wrong angles, but he was a terrorist, and got little in the way of solicitude.

"BACK into the hospital?" one of the men asked O'Neil.

"But then we're trapped!" Sam Barry objected.

"We're bloody trapped here!" Jimmy Carr pointed out. "We need to move. Now!"

O'Neil thought that made sense. "Okay, okay. I'll pull the door, and you lads run back to the entrance. Ready?" They nodded, cradling their weapons. "Now!" he rasped, pulling the sliding door open.

"SHIT!" Price observed from a football field away. "Subjects running back into the hospital. I counted five."

"Confirm five of them," another voice agreed on the radio circuit.

VEGA and Tomlinson were most of the way to the emergency room now, close enough to see the people there but not the double glass doors that led outside. They heard more screams. Vega took off his Kevlar helmet and peeked around the corner. Oh, shit, he thought, seeing one guy with an AKMS. That one was looking around inside the building—and behind him was half the body of someone looking outward. Oso nearly jumped out of his skin when a hand came down on his shoulder. He turned. It was Franklin, without his monster rifle, holding only his Beretta pistol.

"I just heard, five bad guys there?"

"That's what the man said," Vega confirmed. He waved Sergeant Tomlinson to the other side of the corridor. "You stick with me, Fred."

"Roge-o, Oso. Wish you had your M-60 now?"

"Fuckin' A, man." As good as the German MP-10 was, it felt like a toy in his hands.

Vega took another look. There was Ding's wife, standing now, looking over to where the bad guys were, pregnant as hell in her white coat. He and Chavez went back nearly ten years. He couldn't let anything happen to her. He backed off the corner and tried waving his arm at her.

PATSY Clark Chavez, M.D., saw the motion out of the corner of her eye and turned to see a soldier dressed all in black. He was waving to her, and when she turned the waves beckoned her to him, which struck her as a good idea. Slowly, she started moving to her right.

"You, stop!" Jimmy Carr called angrily. Then he started moving toward her. Unseen to his left, Sergeant George Tomlinson edged his face and gun muzzle around the corner. Vega's waves merely grew more frantic, and Patsy kept moving his way. Carr stepped toward her, bringing his rifle up—

—as soon as he came into view, Tomlinson took aim, and seeing the weapon aimed at Ding's wife, he depressed the trigger gently, loosing a three-round burst.

The silence of it was somehow worse than the loudest noise. Patsy turned to look at the guy with the gun when his head exploded—but there was no noise other than the brushlike sound of a properly suppressed weapon, and the wet-mess noise of his destroyed cranium. The body—the face was sprayed away, and the back of his head erupted in a cloud of red—then it just fell straight down, and the loudest sound was the clatter of the rifle hitting the floor, loosed from the dead hands.

"Come here!" Vega shouted, and she did what she was told, ducking and running toward him.

Oso grabbed her arm and swung her around like a doll, knocking her off her feet and sending her sliding across the tile floor. Sergeant Franklin scooped her up and ran down the corridor, carrying her like a toy. In the main lobby he found the hospital security guard, and left her with him, then ran back.

"Franklin to Command. Dr. Chavez is safe. We got her to the main lobby. Get some people there, will ya? Let's get these fucking civilians evacuated fast, okay?"

"Price to Team. Where is everyone? Where are the subjects?"

"Price, this is Vega, we are down to four subjects. George just dropped one. They are in the emergency room. Mrs. Clark is probably still there. We hear noises, there are civilians in there. We have their escape route closed. I have Tomlinson and Franklin here. Fred's only got a pistol. Unknown number of hostages, but as far as I can tell we're down to four bad guys, over."

"I'VE got to get down there," Dr. Bellow said. He was badly shaken. People had been shot within a few feet of him. Alistair Stanley was down with a chest wound, and at least one other Rainbow trooper was dead, along with three additional wounded, one of those serious-looking.

"That way." Price pointed to the front of the hospital. A Team-1 member appeared, and headed that way as well. It was Geoff Bates, one of Covington's shooters from the SAS, fully armed, though he hadn't taken so much as a single shot yet today. He and Bellow moved quickly.

SOMEHOW Carr had died without notice. O'Neil turned and saw him there, his body like the stem for a huge red flower of blood on the dingy tile floor. It was only getting worse. He had four armed men, but he couldn't see around the corner twenty feet away, and surely there were armed SAS soldiers there, and he had no escape. He had eight other people nearby, and these he could use as hostages, perhaps, but the danger of that game was dramatically obvious. *No escape,* his mind told him, but his emotions said something else. He had weapons, and his enemies were nearby, and he was supposed to kill them, and if he had to die, he'd damned well die for The Cause, the idea to which he'd dedicated his life, the idea for which he'd told himself a thousand times he was willing to die. Well, here he was now, and death was close, not something to be considered in his bed, waiting for sleep to come, or drinking beer in a pub, discussing the loss of some dedicated comrades, the brave talk they all spoke when bravery wasn't needed. It all came down to this. Now danger was here, and it was time to see if his bravery was a thing of words or a thing of the belly, and his emotions wanted to show the whole bloody world that he was a man of his word and his beliefs . . . but part of him wanted to escape back to Ireland, and not die this day in an English hospital.

SANDY Clark watched him from fifteen feet away. He was a handsome man, and probably a brave one—for a criminal, her mind added. She remembered John telling her more than once that bravery was a far more common thing than cowardice, and that the reason for it was shame. People went into danger not alone, but with their friends, and you didn't want to appear weak in front of them, and so from the fear of cowardice came the most insane of acts, the successful ones later celebrated as great heroism. It had struck her as the worst sort of cynicism on John's part . . . and yet her husband was not a cynical man. Could it therefore be the truth?

In this case, it was a man in his early thirties, holding a weapon in his hands and looking as though he didn't have a friend in the world—

—but the mother in her told Sandy that her daughter was probably safe now, along with her grandchild. The dead one had called after her, but now he was messily dead on the hospital floor, and so Patsy had probably gotten away. That was the best information of the day, and she closed her eyes to whisper a prayer of thanks.

"HEY, doc," Vega said in greeting.

"Where are they?"

Vega pointed. "Around this corner. Four of them, we think. George dropped one for the count."

"Talk to them yet?"

Oso shook his head. "No."

"Okay." Bellow took a deep breath. "This is Paul," he called loudly. "Is Timothy there?"

"Yes," came the reply.

"Are you okay?—not wounded or anything, I mean," the psychiatrist asked.

O'Neil wiped some blood from his face—the glass fragments in the van had made some minor cuts. "We're all fine. Who are you?"

"I'm a physician. My name is Paul Bellow. What's yours?"

"Timothy will do for now."

"Okay, fine. Timothy, uh, you need to think about your situation, okay?"

"I know what that is," O'Neil responded, an edge on his voice.

OUTSIDE, things were gradually becoming organized. Ambulances were on the scene, plus medical orderlies from the British Army. The wounded were being moved now, to the base hospital at Hereford where surgeons were waiting to treat them, and coming in were SAS soldiers, thirty of them, to assist the Rainbow troopers. Colonel Malloy's helicopter set down on the pad at the base, and the two prisoners were taken to the military hospital for treatment.

■ ■ ■

"TIM, you will not be getting away from here. I think you know that," Bellow observed, in as gentle a voice as he could manage.

"I can kill hostages if you don't let me leave," O'Neil countered.

"Yes, you can do that, and then we can come in on you and try to stop that from happening, but in either case, you will not be getting away. But what do you gain by murdering people, Tim?"

"The freedom of my country!"

"That is happening already, isn't it?" Bellow asked. "There are peace accords, Tim. And Tim, tell me, what country ever began on a foundation of the murder of innocent people? What will your countrymen think if you murder your hostages?"

"We are freedom fighters!"

"Okay, fine, you are revolutionary soldiers," the doctor agreed. "But soldiers, real soldiers, don't murder people. Okay, fine, earlier today you and your friends shot it out with soldiers, and that's not murder. But killing unarmed people *is* murder, Tim. I think you know that. Those people in there with you, are any of them armed? Do any of them wear uniforms?"

"So what? They are the enemy of my country!"

"What makes them enemies, Tim? Where they were born? Have any of them tried to hurt you? Have any of them hurt your country? Why don't you ask them?" he suggested next.

O'Neil shook his head. The purpose of this was to make him surrender. He knew that. He looked around at his comrades. It was hard for all of them to meet the eyes of the others. They were trapped, and all of them knew it. Their resistance was a thing of the mind rather than of arms, and all of their minds held doubts to which they had as yet not given voice, but the doubts were there, and they all knew it.

"We want a bus to take us away!"

"Take you away to where?" the doctor asked.

"Just get us the bloody bus!" O'Neil screamed.

"Okay, I can talk to people about that, but they have to know where the bus is going to, so that the police can clear the roads for you," Bellow observed reasonably. It was just a matter of time now. Tim—it would have been useful to know if he'd been truthful in giving out his real name, though Bellow was confident that he had indeed done that—wasn't talking about killing, hadn't actually threatened it, hadn't given a deadline or tossed out a body yet. He wasn't a killer, at least not a murderer. He thought of himself as a soldier, and that was different from a criminal, to terrorists a very important difference. He didn't fear death, though he did fear failure, and he feared almost as much being remembered as a killer of the innocent. To kill soldiers was one thing. To murder ordinary women and children was something else. It was an old story for terrorists. The most vulnerable part of any person was his self-image. Those who cared what others thought of them, those who looked in mirrors when they shaved, those people could be worked. It was just a matter of time. They were different from the real fanatics. You could wear this sort down. "Oh, Tim?"

"Yes?"

"Could you do something for me?"

"What?"

"Could you let me make sure the hostages are okay? That's something I have to do to keep my boss happy. Can I come around to see?"

O'Neil hesitated.

"Tim, come on, okay? You have the things you have to do, and I have the things I have to do, okay? I'm a physician. I don't carry a gun or anything. You have nothing to be afraid of." Telling them that they had nothing to fear, and thus suggesting that they were unnecessarily afraid, was usually a good card to play. There followed the usual hesitation, confirming that they were indeed afraid—and that meant Tom was rational, and that was good news for Rainbow's psychiatrist.

"NO, Tim, don't!" Peter Barry urged. "Give them nothing."

"But how will we get out of here, get the bus, if we don't cooperate on something?" O'Neil looked around at the other three. Sam Barry nodded. So did Dan McCorley.

"All right," O'Neil called. "Come back to us."

"THANK you," Bellow called. He looked at Vega, the senior soldier present.

"Watch your ass, doc," the first sergeant suggested. To go unarmed into the lair of armed bad guys was, he thought, not very bright. He'd never thought that the doc had such stuff in him.

"Always," Paul Bellow assured him. Then he took a deep breath and walked the ten feet to the corner, and turned, disappearing from the view of the Rainbow troopers.

IT always struck Bellow as strange, to the point of being comical, that the difference between safety and danger was a distance of a few feet and the turning of one corner. Yet he looked up with genuine interest. He'd rarely met a criminal under these circumstances. So much the better that they were armed and he was not. They would need the comfortable feelings that came with the perception of power to balance the fact that, armed or not, they were in a cage from which there was no escape.

"You're hurt," Bellow said on seeing Timothy's face.

"It's nothing, just a few scratches."

"Why not have somebody work on it for you?"

"It's nothing," Tim O'Neil said again.

"Okay, it's your face," Bellow said, looking and counting four of them, all armed with the same sort of weapon, AKMS, his memory told him. Only then did he count the hostages. He recognized Sandy Clark. There were seven others, all very frightened, by the look of them, but that was to be expected. "So, what exactly do you want?"

"We want a bus, and we want it quickly," O'Neil replied.

"Okay, I can work on that, but it'll take time to get things organized, and we'll need something in return."

"What's that?" Timothy asked.

"Some hostages to be released," the psychiatrist answered.

"No, we only have eight."

"Look, Tim, when I deal with the people I have to go to—to get the bus you want, okay?—I have to offer them something, or why else should they give me anything to give you?" Bellow asked reasonably. "It's how the game is played, Tim. The game has rules. Come on, you know that. You trade some of what you have for some of what you want."

"So?"

"So, as a sign of good faith, you give me a couple hostages—women and kids, usually, because that looks better." Bellow looked again. Four women, four men. It would be good to get Sandy Clark out.

"And then?"

"And then I tell my superiors that you want a bus and that you've shown good faith. I have to represent you to them, right?"

"Ah, and you're on our side?" another man asked. Bellow looked and saw that he was a twin, with a brother standing only a few feet away. Twin terrorists. Wasn't that interesting?

"No, I won't say that. Look, I am not going to insult your intelligence. You people know the fix you're in. But if you want to get things, you have to deal for them. That's the rule, and it's a rule I didn't make. I have to be the go-between. That means I represent you to my bosses, and I represent my bosses to you. If you need time to think it over, fine, I won't be far away, but the faster you move on things, the faster I can move. I need you guys to think about that, okay?"

"Get the bus," Timothy said.

"In return for what?" Paul asked.

"Two women." O'Neil turned. "That one and that one."

"Can they come out with me?" Bellow saw that Timothy had actually indicated Sandy Clark. This kid, O'Neil, was overwhelmed by the circumstances, and that was probably good, too.

"Yes, but get us that bloody bus!"

"I'll do my best," Bellow promised, gesturing at the two women to follow him back around the corner.

"Welcome back, doc," Vega said quietly. "Hey, great!" he added on seeing the two women. "Howdy, Mrs. Clark. I'm Julio Vega."

"Mom!" Patsy Chavez ran from her place of safety and embraced her mother. Then a pair of recently arrived SAS troopers took all of the women away.

"Vega to Command," Oso called.

"Price to Vega."

"Tell Six his wife and daughter are both safe."

JOHN was back in a truck, heading to the hospital to take charge of the operation, with Domingo Chavez next to him. Both heard the radio call. In both cases, the heads dropped for a brief moment of relief. But there were six more hostages.

"Okay, this is Clark, what's happening now?"

IN the hospital, Vega gave his radio set to Dr. Bellow.

"John? This is Paul."

"Yeah, doc, what's happening now?"

"Give me a couple hours and I can give them to you, John. They know they're trapped. It's just a matter of talking them through. There's four of them now, all in their thirties, all armed. They now have six hostages. But I've spoken with their leader, and I can work with this kid, John."

"Okay, doc, we'll be there in ten minutes. What are they asking for?"

"The usual," Bellow answered. "They want a bus to somewhere."

John thought about that. Make them come outside, and he had riflemen to handle the problem. Four shots, child's play. "Do we deliver?"

"Not yet. We'll let this one simmer a little."

"Okay, doc, that's your call. When I get there, you can fill me in more. See you soon. Out."

"Okay." Bellow handed the radio back to First Sergeant Vega. This soldier had a diagram of the ground floor pinned to the wall.

"The hostages are here," Bellow said. "Subjects are here and here. Two of them are twins, by the way, all male Caucs in their thirties, all carrying that folding-stock version of the AK-47."

Vega nodded. " 'Kay. If we have to move on them . . ."

"You won't, at least I don't think so. Their leader isn't a murderer, well, he doesn't want to be."

"You say so, doc," Vega observed dubiously. But the good news was that they could flip a handful of flash-bangs around the corner and move in right behind them, bagging all four of the fuckers . . . but at the risk of losing a hostage, which was to be avoided if possible. Oso hadn't appreciated how ballsy this doctor was, walking up to four armed bad guys and talking to them—and getting Mrs. Clark released just like that. Damn. He turned to look at the six SAS guys who'd arrived, dressed in black like his people, and ready to rock if it came to that. Paddy Connolly was outside the building with his bag of tricks. The position was isolated, and the situation was pretty much under control. For the first time in an hour, First Sergeant Vega was allowing himself to relax a little.

"WELL, hello, Sean," Bill Tawney said, recognizing the face at the Hereford base hospital. "Having a difficult day, are we?"

Grady's shoulder had been immobilized and would require surgery. It turned out that he'd taken a pair of 9-mm bullets in it, one of which had shattered the top of his left humerus, the long bone of the upper arm. It was a painful injury despite the medication given to him ten minutes before. His face turned to see an Englishman in a tie. Grady naturally enough took him for a policeman, and didn't say anything.

"You picked the wrong patch to play in today, my boy," Tawney said next. "For your information, you are now in the Hereford base military hospital. We will talk later, Sean." For the moment, an orthopedic surgeon had work to do, to repair the injured arm. Tawney watched an army nurse medicate him for the coming procedure. Then he went to a different room to speak to the one rescued from the wrecked truck.

This would be a merry day for all involved, the "Six" man thought. The motorway was closed with the two car smashes, and there were enough police constables about to blacken the landscape with their uniforms, plus the SAS and Rainbow people. Soon to be added were a joint mob of "Five" and "Six" people en route from London, all of whom would be claiming jurisdiction, and that would be quite a mess, since there was a written agreement between the U.S. and U.K. governments on the status of Rainbow, which hadn't been drafted with this situation in mind, but which guaranteed that the CIA Station Chief London would soon be here as well to officiate. Tawney figured he'd be the ringmaster for this particular circus—and that maybe a whip, chair, and pistol might be needed.

Tawney tempered his good humor with the knowledge that two Rainbow troopers were dead, with four more wounded and being treated in this same hospital. People he vaguely knew, whose faces had been familiar, two of which he'd never see again, but the profit of that was Sean Grady, one of the most extreme PIRA members, now beginning what would surely be a lifetime of custody by Her Majesty's Government. He would have a wealth of good information, and his job would be to start extracting it.

"WHERE'S the bloody bus?"

"Tim, I've talked to my superiors, and they're thinking about it."

"What's to think about?" O'Neil demanded.

"You know the answer to that, Tim. We're dealing with government bureaucrats, and they never take action without covering their own backsides first."

"Paul, I have six hostages here and I can—"

"Yes, you can, but you really can't, can you? Timothy, if you do *that,* then the soldiers outside come storming in here, and that ends the situation, and you will be remembered forever as a killer of innocent people, a murderer. You want that, Tim? Do you really want that?" Bellow paused. "What about your families? Hell, what about how your political movement is perceived? Killing these people is a hard thing to justify, isn't it? You're not Muslim extremists, are you? You're Christians, remember? Christians aren't supposed to do things like that. Anyway, that threat is useful as a threat, but it's not very useful as a tool. You can't do that, Tim. It would only result in your death and your political damnation. Oh, by the way, we have Sean Grady in custody," Bellow added, with careful timing.

"What?" That, he saw, shook Timothy.

"He was captured trying to escape. He was shot in the process, but he'll survive. They're operating on him right now."

It was like pricking a large balloon, the psychiatrist saw. He'd just let some air out of his antagonist. This was how it was done, a little at a time. Too fast and he might react violently, but wear them down bit by bit, and they were yours. Bellow had written a book on the subject. First establish physical control, which meant containment. Then establish information control. Then feed them information, bit by precious bit, in a manner as carefully orchestrated as a Broadway musical. Then you had them.

"You will release Sean to us. He goes on the bus with us!"

"Timothy, he's on an operating table right now, and he's going to be there for hours. If they even attempted to move him now, the results could be lethal—they could kill the man, Tim. So, much as you might want it, that's just not possible. It can't happen. I'm sorry about that, but nobody can change it."

His leader was a prisoner now? Tim O'Neil thought. Sean was captured? Strangely that seemed worse than his own situation. Even if he were in prison, Sean might come up with a way of freeing him, but with Sean on the Isle of Wight . . . all was lost, wasn't it? But—

"How do I know you're telling the truth?"

"Tim, in a situation like this, I can't lie. I'd just screw up. It's too hard to be a good liar, and if you caught me in a lie, you'd never believe me again, and that would end my usefulness to my bosses and to you, too, wouldn't it?" Again the voice of quiet reason.

"You said you're a doctor?"

"That's right." Bellow nodded.

"Where do you practice?"

"Mainly here now, but I did my residency at Harvard. I've worked at four different places, and taught some."

"So, your job is to get people like me to surrender, isn't it?" Anger, finally, at the obvious.

Bellow shook his head. "No, I think of my job as keeping people alive. I'm a physician, Tim. I am not allowed to kill people or to help others to kill people. I swore an oath on that one a long time ago. You have guns. Other people around that corner have guns. I don't want any of you to get killed. There's been enough of that today, hasn't there? Tim, do you enjoy killing people?"

"Why—no, of course not, who does?"

"Well, some do," Bellow told him, deciding to build up his ego a little. "We call them sociopathic personalities, but you're not one of them. You're a soldier. You fight for something you believe in. So do the people back there." Bellow waved to where the Rainbow people were. "They respect you, and I hope you respect them. Soldiers don't murder people. Criminals do that, and a soldier isn't a criminal." In addition to being true, this was an important thought to communicate to his interlocutor. All the more so because a terrorist was also a romantic, and to be considered a common criminal was psychologically very wounding to them. He'd just built up their self-images in order to steer them away from something he didn't want them to do. They were soldiers, not criminals, and they had to act like soldiers, not criminals.

"Dr. Bellow?" a voice called from around the corner. "Phone call, sir."

"Tim, can I go get it?" Always ask permission to do something. Give them the illusion of being in command of the situation.

"Yeah." O'Neil waved him away. Bellow walked back to where the soldiers were.

He saw John Clark standing there. Together they walked fifty feet into another part of the hospital.

"Thanks for getting my wife and little girl out, Paul."

Bellow shrugged. "It was mainly luck. He's a little overwhelmed by all this, and he's not thinking very well. They want a bus."

"You told me before," Clark reminded him. "Do we give it to 'em?"

"We won't have to do that. I'm in a poker game, John, and I'm holding a straight flush. Unless something screws up really bad, we have this one under control."

"Noonan's outside, and he has a mike on the window. I listened in on the last part. Pretty good, doctor."

"Thanks." Bellow rubbed his face. The tension was real for him, but he could only show it here. In with Timothy he had to be cool as ice, like a friendly and respected teacher. "What's the story on the other prisoners?"

"No change. The Grady guy is being operated on—it'll take a few hours, they say. The other one's unconscious still, and we don't have a name or ID on him anyway."

"Grady's the leader?"

"We think so, that's what the intel tells us."

"So he can tell us a lot. You want me there when he comes out of the OR," Paul told Rainbow Six.

"You need to finish up here first."

"I know. I'm going back." Clark patted him on the shoulder and Bellow walked back to see the terrorists.

"Well?" Timothy asked.

"Well, they haven't decided on the bus yet. Sorry," Bellow added in a downcast voice. "I thought I had them convinced, but they can't get their asses in gear."

"You tell them that if they don't, we'll—"

"No, you won't, Tim. You know that. I know that. *They* know that."

"Then why send the bus?" O'Neil asked, close to losing control now.

"Because *I* told them that you're serious, and they have to take your threat seriously. If they don't believe you'll do it, they have to remember that you might, and if you do, then *they* look bad to their bosses." Timothy shook his head at that convoluted logic, looking more puzzled than angry now. "Trust me," Paul Bellow went on. "I've done this before, and I know how it works. It's easier negotiating with soldiers like you than with those damned bureaucrats. People like you can make decisions. People like that run away from doing it. They don't care much about getting people killed, but they do care about looking bad in the newspapers."

Then something good happened. Tim reached into his pocket and pulled out a cigarette. A sure sign of stress and an attempt to control it.

"HAZARDOUS to your health, boy," Clark observed, looking at the TV picture Noonan had established. The assault plan was completely ready. Connolly had line charges set on the windows, both to open an entry path and to distract the terrorists. Vega, Tomlinson, and Bates, from Team-1, would toss flash-bangs at the same time and dart into the room to take the bad guys down with aimed fire. The only downside to that, as always, was that one of them could turn and hose the hostages as his last conscious act, or even by accident, which was just as lethal. From the sound of it, Bellow was doing okay. If these subjects had any brains at all, they'd know it was time to call it a day, but John reminded himself that he'd never contemplated life in prison before, at least not this immediately, and he imagined it wasn't a fun thought. He now had a surfeit of soldierly talent at his disposal. The SAS guys who'd arrived had chopped to his operational command, though their own colonel had come as well to kibitz in the hospital's main lobby.

"TOUGH day for all of us, isn't it, Tim?" the psychiatrist asked.

"Could have been a better one," Timothy O'Neil agreed.

"You know how this one will end, don't you?" Bellow offered, like a nice fly to a brook trout, wondering if he'd rise to it.

"Yes, doctor, I do." He paused. "I haven't even fired my rifle today. I haven't killed anyone. Jimmy did," he went on, gesturing to the body on the floor, "but not any of us."

Bingo! Bellow thought. "That counts for something, Tim. As a matter of fact, it counts for a lot. You know, the war will be over soon. They're going to make peace finally, and when that happens, well, there's going to be an amnesty for most of the fighters. So you have some hope. You all do," Paul told the other three, who were watching and listening . . . and wavering, as their leader was. They had to know that all was lost. Surrounded, their leader captured, this could only end in one of two ways, with their deaths or their imprisonment. Escape was not a practical possibility, and they knew that the attempt to move their hostages to a bus would only expose them to certain death in a new and different way.

"Tim?"

"Yes?" He looked up from his smoke.

"If you set your weapons down on the floor, you have my word that you will not be hurt in any way."

"And go to prison?" Defiance and anger in the reply.

"Timothy, you can get out of prison someday. You cannot get out of *death*. Please think about that. For God's sake, I'm a physician," Bellow reminded him. "I don't like seeing people die."

Timothy O'Neil turned to look at his comrades. All eyes were downcast. Even the Barry twins showed no particular defiance.

"Guys, if you haven't hurt anyone today, then, yes, you will go to prison, but someday you'll have a good chance to get out when the amnesty is promulgated. Otherwise, you die for nothing at all. Not for your country. They don't make heroes out of people who kill civilians," he reminded them once again. Keep repeating, Bellow thought. Keep drumming it in. "Killing soldiers, yes, that's something soldiers do, but not murdering innocent people. You will die for nothing at all—or you will live, and be free again someday. It's up to you, guys. You have the guns. But there isn't going to be a bus. You will not escape, and you have six people you can kill, sure, but what does that get for you, except a trip to hell? Call it a day, Timothy," he concluded, wondering if some Catholic nun in grade school had addressed him that way.

It wasn't quite that easy for Tim O'Neil. The idea of imprisonment in a cage with common criminals, having his family come to visit him there like an animal in a zoo, gave him chills . . . but he'd known that this was a possibility for years, and though he preferred the mental image of heroic death, a blazing gun in his hand firing at the enemies of his country, this American doctor had spoken the truth. There was no glory in murdering six English civilians. No songs would be written and sung about this exploit, no pints hoisted to his name in the pubs of Ulster . . . and what was left to him was inglorious death . . . life, in prison or not, was preferable to that sort of death.

Timothy Dennis O'Neil turned to look at his fellow PIRA soldiers and saw the same expression that they saw on his face. Without a spoken agreement, they all nodded. O'Neil safed his rifle and set it on the floor. The others did the same.

Bellow walked over to them to shake their hands.

"Six to Vega, move in now!" Clark called, seeing the picture on the small black-and-white screen.

□ S □ Vega moved quickly around the corner, his MP-10 up in his hands. There they were, standing with the doc. Tomlinson and Bates pushed them, not too roughly, against the wall. The former covered them while the latter patted them down. Seconds later, two uniformed policemen came in with handcuffs and, to the amazement of the soldiers, read them their legal rights. And just that easily and quietly, this day's fighting was over.

C H A P T E R 2 9

RECOVERY

THE DAY HADN'T ENDED FOR DR. BELLOW. WITHOUT so much as a drink of water for his dry throat, he hopped into a green-painted British Army truck for the trip back to Hereford. It hadn't ended for those left behind either.

"HEY, baby," Ding said. He'd finally found his wife outside the hospital, surrounded by a ring of SAS troopers.

Patsy ran the ten steps to him and hugged her husband as tightly as her swollen abdomen allowed.

"You okay?"

She nodded, tears in her eyes. "You?"

"I'm fine. It was a little exciting there for a while—and we have some people down, but everything's under control now."

"One of them—somebody killed him, and—"

"I know. He was pointing a weapon at you, and that's why he got himself killed." Chavez reminded himself that he owed Sergeant Tomlinson a beer for that bit of shooting—in fact, he owed him a lot more than that, but in the community of warriors, this was how such debts were paid. But for now, just holding Patsy in his arms was as far as his thinking went. Tears welled up in his eyes. Ding blinked them away. That wasn't part of his *machismo* self-image. He wondered what damage this day's events might have had on his wife. She was a healer, not a killer, and yet she'd seen traumatic death so close at hand. Those IRA bastards! he thought. They'd invaded *his* life, and attacked noncombatants, and killed some of his team members. Somebody had fed them information on how to do it. Somewhere there was an information leak, a bad one, and finding it would be their first priority.

"How's the little guy?" Chavez asked his wife.

"Feels okay, Ding. Really. I'm okay," Patsy assured him.

"Okay, baby, I have to go do some things now. You're going home." He pointed to an SAS trooper and waved him over. "Take her back to the base, okay?"

"Yes, sir," the sergeant replied. Together they walked her to the parking lot. Sandy Clark was there with John, also hugging and holding hands, and the smart move seemed to be to take them both to John's quarters. An officer from the SAS volunteered, as did a sergeant to ride shotgun, which in this case was not a rhetorical phrase. As usual, once the horse had escaped from the barn, the door would be locked and guarded. But that was a universal human tendency, and in another minute both women were being driven off, a police escort with them as well.

"Where to, Mr. C?" Chavez asked.

"Our friends were taken to the base hospital. Paul is there already. He wants to interview Grady—the leader—when he comes out of surgery. I think we want to be there for that."

"Roger that, John. Let's get moving."

POPOV was most of the way back to London, listening to his car radio. Whoever was briefing the media knew and talked too much. Then he heard that the leader of the IRA raiders had been captured, and Dmitriy's blood turned to ice. If they had Grady, then they had the man who knew who he was, knew his cover name, knew about the money transfer, knew too damned much. It wasn't time for panic, but it was damned sure time for action.

Popov checked his watch. The banks were still open. He lifted his cell phone and called Bern. In a minute, he had the correct bank officer on the line and gave him the account number, which the officer called up on his computer. Then Popov gave him the transaction code, and ordered the funds transferred into another account. The officer didn't even express his disappointment that so much money was being removed. Well, the bank had plenty of deposits, didn't it? The Russian was now richer by over five million dollars, but poorer in that the enemy might soon have his cover name and physical description. Popov had to get out of the country. He took the exit to Heathrow and ended up at Terminal Four. Ten minutes later, having returned his rental car, he went in and got the last first-class ticket on a British Airways flight to Chicago. He had to hurry to catch the flight, but made it aboard, where a pretty stewardess conveyed him to his seat, and soon thereafter the 747 left the gate.

"THAT was quite a mess," John Brightling observed, muting the TV in his office. Hereford would lead every TV newscast in the world.

"They were unlucky," Henriksen replied. "But those commandos are pretty good, and if you give them a break, they'll use it. What the hell, four or five of them went down. Nobody's ever pulled that off against a force like this one."

Brightling knew that Bill's heart was divided on the mission. He had to have at least some sympathy with the people he'd helped to attack. "Fallout?"

"Well, if they got the leader alive, they're going to sweat him, but these IRA guys don't sing. I mean, they *never* sing. The only pipeline they could possibly have to us is Dmitriy, and he's a pro. He's moving right now, probably on an airplane to somewhere if I know him. He's got all sorts of false travel documents, credit cards, IDs. So, he's probably safe. John, the KGB knew how to train its people, trust me."

"If they should get him, would he talk?" Brightling asked.

"That's a risk. Yes, he might well spill his guts," Henriksen had to admit. "If he gets back, I'll debrief him on the hazards involved. . . ."

"Would it be a good idea to . . . well . . . eliminate him?"

The question embarrassed his boss, Henriksen saw, as he prepared a careful and honest answer: "Strictly speaking, yes, but there are dangers in that, John. He's a pro. He probably has a mailbox somewhere." Seeing Brightling's confusion, he explained, "You guard against the possibility of being killed by writing everything down and putting it in a safe place. If you don't access the box every month or so, the information inside gets distributed according to a prearranged plan. You have a lawyer do that for you. *That* is a big risk to us, okay? Dead or alive, he can burn us, and in this case, it's more dangerous if he's dead." Henriksen paused. "No, we want him alive—and under our control, John."

"Okay, you handle it, Bill." Brightling leaned back in his chair and closed his eyes. They were too close now to run unnecessary risks. Okay, the Russian would be handled, put under wraps. It might even save Popov's life—hell, he thought, it *would* save his life, wouldn't it? He hoped that the Russian would be properly appreciative. Brightling had to be properly appreciative, too. This Rainbow bunch was crippled now, or at least badly hurt. It had to be. Popov had fulfilled two missions, he'd helped raise the world's consciousness about terrorism, and thus gotten Global Security its contract with the Sydney Olympics, and then he'd helped sting this new counterterror bunch, hopefully enough to take them out of play. The operation was now fully in place and awaited only the right time for activation.

So close, Brightling thought. It was probably normal to have the jitters at moments like this. Confidence was a thing of distance. The farther away you were, the easier it was to think yourself invincible, but then you got close and the dangers grew with their proximity. But that didn't change anything, did it? No, not really. The plan *was* perfect. They just had to execute it.

SEAN Grady came out of surgery at just after eight in the evening, following three and a half hours on the table. The orthopod who'd worked on him was first-rate, Bellow saw. The humerus was fixed in place with a cobalt-steel pin that would be permanent and large enough that in the unlikely event that Grady ever entered an international airport in the future, he'd probably set off the metal detector while stark naked. Luckily for him the brachial plexus had not been damaged by the two bullets that had entered his body, and so he'd suffer no permanent loss of use of his arm. The secondary damage to his chest was minor. He'd recover fully, the British Army surgeon concluded, and so could enjoy full physical health during the lifelong prison term that surely awaited him.

The surgery had been performed under full general anesthesia, of course, using nitrous oxide, just as in American hospitals, coupled with the lingering effects of the barbiturates that had been used to begin his sedation. Bellow sat by the bed in the hospital's recovery room, watching the bio-monitors and waiting for him to awaken. It would not be an event so much as a process, probably a lengthy one.

There were police around now, both in uniform and out, watching with him. Clark and Chavez were there, too, standing and staring at the man who'd so brazenly attacked their men—and their women, Bellow reminded himself. Chavez especially had eyes like flint—hard, dark, and cold, though his face appeared placid enough. He thought he knew the senior Rainbow people pretty well. They were clearly professionals, and in the case of Clark and Chavez, people who'd lived in the black world and done some very black things, most of which he didn't and would never know about. But Bellow knew that both men were people of order, like police officers in many ways, keepers of the rules. Maybe they broke them sometimes, but it was only to sustain them. They were romantics, just as the terrorists were, but the difference was in their choice of cause. Their purpose was to protect. Grady's was to upset, and in the difference of mission was the difference between the men. It was that simple to them. Now, however angry they might feel at this sleeping man, they would not cause him physical harm. They'd leave his punishment to the society that Grady had so viciously attacked and whose rules they were sworn to protect, if not always uphold.

"Any time now," Bellow said. Grady's vital signs were all coming up. The body moved a little as his brain started to come back to wakefulness, just minor flexes here and there. It would find that some parts were not responding as they should, then focus on them to see what the limitations were, looking for pain but not finding it yet. Now the head started turning, slowly, left and right, and soon . . .

The eyelids fluttered, also slowly. Bellow consulted the list of IDs that others had drawn up and hoped that the British police and the guys from "Five" had provided him with good data.

"Sean?" he said. "Sean, are you awake?"

"Who? . . ."

"It's me, it's Jimmy Carr, Sean. You back with us now, Sean?"

"Where . . . am . . . I?" the voice croaked.

"University Hospital, Dublin, Sean. Dr. McCaskey just finished fixing your shoulder up. You're in the recovery room. You're going to be okay, Sean. But, my God, getting you here was the devil's own work. Does it hurt, your shoulder, Sean?"

"No, no hurt now, Jimmy. How many? . . ."

"How many of us? Ten, ten of us got away. They're off in the safe houses now, lad."

"Good." The eyes opened, and saw someone wearing a surgical mask and cap, but he couldn't focus well, and the image was a blur. The room . . . yes, it was a hospital . . . the ceiling, rectangular tiles held in a metal rack . . . the lighting, fluorescent. His throat was dry and a little sore from the intubation, but it didn't matter. He was living inside a dream, and none of this was actually happening. He was floating on a white, awkward cloud, but at least Jimmy Carr was here.

"Roddy, where's Roddy?"

"Roddy's dead, Sean," Bellow answered. "Sorry, but he didn't make it."

"Oh, damn . . ." Grady breathed. "Not Roddy . . ."

"Sean, we need some information, we need it quickly."

"What . . . information?"

"The chap who got us the information, we need to contact him, but we don't know how to find him."

"Iosef, you mean?"

Bingo, Paul Bellow thought. "Yes, Sean, Iosef, we need to get in touch with him . . ."

"The money? I have that in my wallet, lad."

Oh, Clark thought, turning. Bill Tawney had all of Grady's personal possessions sitting on a portable table. In the wallet, he saw, were two hundred and ten British pounds, one hundred seventy Irish pounds, and several slips of paper. On one yellow Post-it note were two numbers, six digits each, with no explanation. A Swiss or other numbered account? the spook wondered.

"How do we access it, Sean? We need to do that at once, you see, my friend."

"Swiss Commercial Bank in Bern . . . call . . . account number and control number in . . . in my wallet."

"Good, thank you, Sean . . . and Iosef, what's the rest of his name . . . how do we get in touch with him, Sean? Please, we need to do that right away, Sean." Bellow's false Irish accent wasn't good enough to pass muster with a drunk, but Grady's current condition was far beyond anything alcohol could do to the human mind.

"Don't . . . know. He contacts us, remember. Iosef Andreyevich contacts me through Robert . . . through the network . . . never gave me a way to contact him."

"His last name, Sean, what is it, you never told me."

"Serov, Iosef Andreyevich Serov . . . Russian . . . KGB chap . . . Bekaa Valley . . . years ago."

"Well, he gave us good information on this Rainbow mob, didn't he, Sean?"

"How many did we . . . how many . . . ?"

"Ten, Sean, we killed ten of them, and we got away, but you were shot on the escape in your Jaguar, remember? But we hurt them, Sean, we hurt them badly," Bellow assured him.

"Good . . . good . . . hurt them . . . kill them . . . kill them all," Grady whispered from his gurney.

"Not quite, asshole," Chavez observed quietly, from a few feet away.

"Did we get the two women? . . . Jimmy, did we get them?"

"Oh, yes, Sean, I shot them myself. Now, Sean, this Russian chap. I need to know more about him."

"Iosef? Good man, KGB, got the money and the drugs for us. Lots of money . . . six million . . . six . . . and the cocaine," Grady added for the TV Minicam that sat on a tripod next to the bed. "Got it for us, at Shannon, remember? Flew in on the little jet, the money and the drugs from America . . .

well, think it was America . . . must have been . . . the way he talks now, American accent like the television, funny thing for a Russian, Jimmy . . ."

"Iosef Andreyevich Serov?"

The figure on the bed tried to nod. "That's how they do names, Jimmy. Joseph, son of Andrew."

"What does he look like, Sean?"

"Tall as me . . . brown hair, eyes . . . round face, speaks many languages . . . Bekaa Valley . . . nineteen eighty-six . . . good man, helped us a lot . . ."

"How we doing, Bill?" Clark whispered to Tawney.

"Well, none of this can be used in court, but—"

"Fuck the courts, Bill! How good is this? Does it match with anything?"

"The name Serov doesn't ring a bell, but I can check with our files. We can run these numbers down, and there will be a paper trail of some sort, but"—he checked his watch—"it will have to wait until tomorrow."

Clark nodded. "Hell of an interrogation method."

"Never seen this before. Yes, it is."

Just then Grady's eyes opened more. He saw the others around the bed, and his face twisted into a question. "Who are you?" he asked groggily, finding a strange face in this dream.

"My name is Clark, John Clark, Sean."

The eyes went wide for a second. "But you're . . ."

"That's right, pal. That's who I am. And thanks for spilling your guts. We got all of you, Sean. All fifteen dead or captured. I hope you like it here in England, boy. You're going to be here a long, long time. Why don't you go back to sleep now, lad?" he asked with grossly overdone courtesy. *I've killed better men than you, punk,* he thought, behind a supposedly impassive mien that in fact proclaimed his feelings.

Dr. Bellow pocketed his tape recorder and his notes. It rarely failed. The twilight state following general anesthesia made any mind vulnerable to suggestion. That was why people with high security clearances never went to the hospital without someone from their parent agencies nearby. In this case he'd had ten minutes or so to dive deep inside and come back out with information. It could never be used in a court of law, but then, Rainbow wasn't composed of cops.

"Malloy got him, eh?" Clark asked on his way to the door.

"Actually it was Sergeant Nance," Chavez answered.

"We have to get him something nice for this job," Rainbox Six observed. "We owe him for this. We got a name now, Domingo. A Russian name."

"Not a good one, it's gotta be a cover name."

"Oh?"

"Yeah, John, don't you recognize it? Serov, former chairman of KGB, back in the '60s, I think, fired a long time ago because he screwed something up."

Clark nodded. It wouldn't be the name on the guy's real passport, and that was too bad, but it was a name, and names could be tracked. They walked out of the hospital into the cool British evening. John's car was waiting, with Corporal Mole looking rather pleased with himself. He'd get a nice ribbon for the day's work and probably a very nice letter from this American pseudo-general. John and Ding got in, and the car drove to the base stockade, where the others were being kept for the time being, because the local jail wasn't secure enough. Inside, they were guided to an interrogation room. Timothy O'Neil was waiting there, handcuffed to a chair.

"Hello," John said. "My name is Clark. This is Domingo Chavez."

The prisoner just stared at them.

"You were sent here to murder our wives," John went on. That didn't make him so much as blink either. "But you fucked it all up. There were fifteen of you. There are six now. The rest won't be doing much of anything. You know, people like you make me ashamed to be Irish. Jesus, kid, you're not even an *effective* criminal. By the way, Clark is just my working name. Before that, it was John Kelly, and my wife's maiden name was O'Toole. So, now you IRA pukes are killing Irish-Catholic Americans, eh? It's not going to look good in the papers, punk."

"Not to mention selling coke, all that coke the Russian brought in," Chavez added.

"Drugs? We don't—"

"Sure you do. Sean Grady just told us everything, sang like a fucking canary. We have the number of the Swiss bank account, and this Russian guy—"

"Serov," Chavez added helpfully, "Iosef Andreyevich Serov, Sean's old pal from the Bekaa Valley."

"I have nothing to say." Which was more than O'Neil had planned to say. Sean Grady talked. Sean? That was not possible—but where else could they have gotten that information? Was the world totally mad?

" 'Mano," Ding continued, "that was *my* wife you wanted to kill, and she's got *my* baby in her belly. You think you're going to be around much longer? John, this guy ever going to get out of prison?"

"Not anytime soon, Domingo."

"Well, Timmy, let me tell you something. Where I come from, you mess with a man's lady, there's a price that has to be paid. And it ain't no little price. And where I come from, you *never, ever* mess with a man's kids. The price for that's even worse, you little fuck. Little fuck?" Chavez wondered. "No, I think we can fix that, John. I can fix him so he ain't never gonna fuck anything." From the scabbard on his belt, Ding extracted a Marine-type K-Bar fighting knife. The blade was black except for the gleaming quarter-inch edge.

"Not sure that's a good idea, Ding," Clark objected weakly.

"Why not? Feels pretty good to me right now, man." Chavez got out of his chair and walked up to O'Neil. Then he lowered his knife hand to the chair. "Ain't hard to do, man, just *flick,* and we can start your sex-change operation. I ain't a doc, you understand, but I know the first part of the procedure, y'know?" Ding bent down to press his nose against O'Neil's. "Man, you don't *ever, EVER* mess with a Latino's lady! Do you hear me?"

Timothy O'Neil had had a bad enough day to this point. He looked in the eyes of this Spanish man, heard the accent, and knew that this was not an Englishman, not even an American of the type he thought he knew.

"I've done this before, man. Mainly I kill with guns, but I've taken bastards down with a knife once or twice. It's funny how they squirm—but I ain't gonna kill you, boy. I'm just gonna make you a girl." The knife moved tight up against the crotch of the man cuffed to the chair.

"Back it off, Domingo!" Clark ordered.

"Fuck you, John! That's my *wife* he wanted to hurt, man. Well, I'm gonna fix this little fuck so he never hurts no more girls, 'mano." Chavez turned to look at the prisoner again. "I'm gonna watch your eyes when I cut it all off, Timmy. I want to see your face when you start to turn into a girl."

O'Neil blinked, as he looked deep into the dark, Spanish eyes. He saw the rage there, hot and passionate—but as bad as that was, so was the reason for it. He and his mates had planned to kidnap and maybe kill a pregnant woman, and there was shame in that, and for that reason there was justice in the fury before his face.

"It wasn't like that!" O'Neil gasped. "We didn't—we didn't—"

"Didn't have the chance to rape her, eh? Well, ain't that a big fuckin' deal?" Chavez observed.

"No, no, not rape—never, nobody in the unit ever did that, we're not—"

"You're fucking scum, Timmy—but soon you're just gonna be scum, 'cuz ain't no more fuckin' in your future." The knife moved a little. "This is gonna be fun, John. Like the guy we did in Libya two years ago, remember?"

"Jesus, Ding, I still have nightmares about that one," Clark acknowledged, looking away. "I'm telling you, Domingo, don't do it!"

"Fuck you, John." His free hand reached to loosen O'Neil's belt, then the button at the top of his slacks. Then he reached inside. "Well, shit, ain't much to cut off. Hardly any dick here at all."

"O'Neil, if you have anything to tell us, better say it now. I can't control this kid. I've seen him like this before and—"

"Too much talk, John. Shit, Grady spilled his guts anyway. What does this one know that we need? I'm gonna cut it all off and feed it to one of the guard dogs. They like fresh meat."

"Domingo, we are civilized people and we don't—"

"Civilized? My ass, John, he wanted to kill my wife and my baby!"

O'Neil's eyes popped again. "No, no, we never intended to—"

"Sure, asshole," Chavez taunted. "You had those fucking guns 'cuz you wanted to win their hearts and minds, right? Woman-killer, baby-killer." Chavez spat.

"I didn't kill anybody, didn't even fire my rifle. I—"

"Great, so you're incompetent. You think you deserve to have a dick just 'cuz you're fucking incompetent?"

"Who's this Russian guy?" Clark asked.

"Sean's friend, Serov, Iosef Serov. He got the money and the drugs—"

"Drugs? Christ, John, they're fucking druggies, too!"

"Where's the money?" John persisted.

"Swiss bank, numbered account. Iosef set it up, six million dollars—and—and, Sean asked him to bring us ten kilos of cocaine to sell for the money, we need the money to continue operations."

"Where are the drugs, Tim?" Clark demanded next.

"Farm—farmhouse." O'Neil gave them a town and road description that went into Chavez's pocketed tape-recorder.

"This Serov guy, what's he look like?" And he got that, too.

Chavez backed off and let his visible temper subside. Then he smiled. "Okay, John, let's talk to the others. Thanks, Timmy. You can keep your dick, 'mano."

IT was late afternoon over Canada's Quebec province. The sun reflected off the hundreds of lakes, some of them still covered with ice. Popov had been sleepless for the entire flight, the only wakeful passenger in first class. Again and again his mind went over the same data. If the British had captured Grady, then they had his primary cover name, which was in his travel documents. Well, he'd dispose of them that very day. They had a physical description, but he looked not the least bit remarkable. Grady had the number of the Swiss account that Dmitriy had set up, but he'd already transferred the funds to another account, one not traceable to him. It was theoretically possible that the opposition could pursue the information Grady was sure to give them—Popov had no illusions about that—perhaps even secure a set of fingerprints from . . . no, that was too unlikely to be considered a danger, and no Western intelligence service would have anything to cross-match. No Western service even knew anything about him—if they had, he would have been arrested long before.

So, what did that leave? A name that would soon evaporate, a description that fitted a million other men, and a bank account number for a defunct account. In short, very little. He did need to check out, though, very quickly, the procedures by which Swiss banks transferred funds, and whether that process was protected by the anonymity laws that protected the accounts themselves. Even that—the Swiss were not paragons of integrity, were they? No, there would be an arrangement between the banks and the police. There had to be, even if the only purpose was to enable the Swiss police to lie effectively to other national police forces. But the second account was truly a shadow one. He'd set it up through an attorney who didn't have the ability to betray him, because they'd only met over the telephone. So, there was no path from the information Grady had to where he was now, and that was good. He'd have to think very carefully about *ever* accessing the 5.7 million dollars in the second account, but there might well be a way to do it. Through another attorney, perhaps, in Liechtenstein, where banking laws were even stricter than in Switzerland? He'd have to look into it. An American attorney could guide him in the necessary procedures, also under total anonymity.

You're safe, Dmitriy Arkadeyevich, Popov told himself. Safe and rich, but it was time to stop taking risks. He'd initiate no more field operations for John Brightling. Once he got into O'Hare, he'd catch the next flight to New York, get back to his apartment, report in to Brightling, and then look for an elegant escape route. Would Brightling let him go?

He'd have to, Popov told himself. He and Henriksen were the only men on the planet who could link the executive to mass murder. He might think about killing me, but Henriksen would warn him not to. Henriksen was also a professional, and he knew the rules of the game. Popov had kept a diary, which was in a safe place, the vault of a law firm in New York, with carefully written handling instructions. So, no, that was not a real danger, so long as his "friends" knew the rules—and Popov would remind them, just in case.

Why go back to New York at all? Why not simply disappear? It was tempting . . . but, no. If nothing else, he had to tell Brightling and Henriksen to leave him alone from now on and explain why it was in their interest to do so. Besides, Brightling had an unusually good source in the American government and Popov could use that person's information as additional protection. You never had too much protection.

With all that decided, Popov finally allowed himself to relax. Another ninety minutes to Chicago. Below him was a vast world, with plenty of room to disappear in, and now he had the money for it. It had all been worth it.

"OKAY, what do we have?" John asked his senior executives.

"This name, Iosef Serov. It's not on our computer in London," said Cyril Holt of the Security Service. "What about CIA?"

Clark shook his head. "We have two guys named Serov on the books. One's dead. The other one's in his late sixties and retired in Moscow. What about the description?"

"Well, it fits this chap." Holt passed a photo across the table.

"I've seen this one before."

"He's the chap who met with Ivan Kirilenko in London some weeks ago. That fits the rest of the puzzle, John. We believe he was involved in the leak of information on your organization, as you will recall. For him, then, to show up with Grady—well, it does fit, almost too well, as a matter of fact."

"Any way to press this?"

"We *can* go to the RVS—both we and CIA have relatively good relations with Sergey Golovko, and perhaps they can assist us. I will lobby very hard for that," Holt promised.

"What else?"

"These numbers," Bill Tawney put in. "One is probably a bank account identification number, and the other is probably the control-activation code number. We'll have their police look into it for us. That will tell us something, if the money hasn't been laundered, of course, and if the account is still active, which it ought to be."

"The weapons," the senior cop present told them, "judging by the serial numbers, are of Soviet origin, from the factory in Kazan. They're fairly old, at least ten years, but none of them had ever been fired before today. On the drug issue, I forwarded the information to Dennis Maguire—he's chief of the Garda. It will be on the telly in the morning. They found and seized ten pounds of pure cocaine—by 'pure' I mean medicinal quality, almost as though it had been purchased from a pharmaceutical house. The street value is enormous. Millions," the chief superintendent told them. "It was found in a semi-abandoned farmhouse on the Irish West Coast."

"We have identification on three of the six prisoners. One has not yet been able to talk to us because of his injuries. Oh, they were using cellular phones to communicate, like walkie-talkies. Your Noonan chap did very well indeed to close the phone cells down. God only knows how many lives that saved," Holt told them.

At the far end of the table, Chavez nodded and shivered at the news. If they'd been able to coordinate their actions . . . Jesus. It would not have been a good day for the good guys. What they'd had was bad enough. There would be funerals. People would have to put on their Class-A uniforms and line up and fire off the guns . . . and then they'd have to replace the men who were gone. Not far away, Mike Chin was in a bed, a cast on one of his wounded legs because a bone was broken. Team-1 was out of business for at least a month, even as well as they'd fought back. Noonan had come through big-time, having killed three of them with his pistol, along with Franklin, who'd just about decapitated one with his big MacMillan .50, then used his monster rifle to kill the little brown truck and keep the five terrorists in it from getting away. Chavez was looking down at the conference table and shaking his head when his beeper went off. He lifted it and saw that it was his home number. He rose from his seat and called on the wall phone.

"Yeah, honey?"

"Ding, you want to come over here. It's started," Patsy told him calmly. Ding's response was a sudden flip of his heart.

"On the way, baby." Ding hung up. "John, I gotta get home. Patsy says it's started."

"Okay, Domingo." Clark managed a smile, finally. "Give her a kiss for me."

"Roge-o, Mr. C." And Chavez headed for the door.

"The timing on this thing is never good, is it?" Tawney observed.

"Well, at least something good is happening today." John rubbed his eyes. He even accepted the idea of becoming a grandfather. It beat the hell out of losing people, a fact that had yet to hammer all the way into his consciousness. His people. Two of them, dead. Several more wounded. His people.

"Okay," Clark went on. "What about the information leak? People, we've been set up and hit. What are we going to do about it?"

"HELLO, Ed, it's Carol," the President's Science Advisor said.

"Hi, Dr. Brightling. What can I do for you?"

"What the hell happened in England today? Was it our people—our Rainbow team, I mean?"

"Yes, Carol, it was."

"How did they do? The TV wasn't very clear, and—"

"Two dead, four or so wounded," the DCI answered. "Nine terrorists dead, six captured, including their leader."

"The radios we got to them, how'd they work?"

"Not sure. I haven't seen the after-action report yet, but I know the main thing they're going to want to know."

"What's that, Ed?"

"Who spilled the beans. They knew John's name, his wife and daughter's names, identities, and place of work. They had good intel, and John isn't very happy about that."

"The family members, are they okay?"

"Yeah, no civilians hurt, thank God. Hell, Carol, I *know* Sandy and Patricia. There's going to be some serious fallout over this one."

"Anything I can do to help?"

"Not sure yet, but I won't forget you asked."

"Yeah, well, I want to know if those radio gadgets worked. I told the guys at E-Systems to get them out pronto, 'cuz these guys are important. Gee, I hope they helped some."

"I'll find out, Carol," the DCI promised.

"Okay, you know where to reach me."

"Okay, thanks for the call."

CHAPTER 30

VISTAS

IT WAS EVERYTHING HE'D EXPECTED—NOT KNOWING what to expect—and more, and at the end of it Domingo Chavez held his son in his hands.

"Well," he said, looking down at the new life that would be his to guard, educate, and in time present to the world. After a second that seemed to last into weeks, he handed the newborn to his wife.

Patsy's face was bathed in perspiration, and weary from the five-hour ordeal of delivery, but already, as such things went, the pain was forgotten. The goal had been achieved, and she held her child. The package was pink, hairless, and noisy, the last part assuaged by the proximity of Patsy's left breast, as John Conor Chavez got his first meal. But Patsy was exhausted, and in due course a nurse removed the child to the nursery. Then Ding kissed his wife and walked alongside her bed as she was wheeled to her room. She was already asleep when they arrived. He kissed her one last time and walked outside. His car took him back onto the Hereford base, and then to the official home of Rainbox Six.

"Yeah?" John said, opening the door.

Chavez just handed over a cigar with a blue ring. "John Conor Chavez, seven pounds eleven ounces. Patsy's doing fine, gran-pop," Ding said, with a subdued grin. After all, Patsy had done the hard part.

There are moments to make the strongest of men weep, and this was one of them. The two men embraced. "Well," John said, after a minute or so, reaching into the pocket of his bathrobe for a handkerchief with which he rubbed his eyes. "Who's he look like?"

"Winston Churchill," Domingo replied with a laugh. "Hell, John, I've never been able to figure that one out, but John Conor Chavez is a confusing enough name, isn't it? The little bastard has a lot of heritage behind him. I'll start him off on karate and guns about age five . . . maybe six," Ding mused.

"Better golf and baseball, but he's your kid, Domingo. Come on in."

"Well?" Sandy demanded, and Chavez gave the news for the second time while his boss lit up his Cuban cigar. He despised smoking, and Sandy, a nurse, hardly approved of the vice, but on this one occasion, both relented. Mrs. Clark gave Ding a hug. "John Conor?"

"You knew?" John Terrence Clark asked.

Sandy nodded. "Patsy told me last week."

"It was supposed to be a secret," the new father objected.

"I'm her mother, Ding!" Sandy explained. "Breakfast?"

The men checked their watches. It was just after four in the morning, close enough, they all agreed.

"You know, John, this is pretty profound," Chavez said. His father-in-law noted how Domingo switched in and out of accents depending on the nature of the conversation. The previous day, interrogating the PIRA prisoners he'd been pure Los Angeles gang kid, his speech redolent with Spanish accent and street euphemisms. But in his reflective moments, he reverted to a man with a university master's degree, with no accent at all. "I'm a papa. I've got a son." Followed by a slow, satisfied, and somewhat awestruck grin. "Wow."

"The great adventure, Domingo," John agreed, while his wife got the bacon going. He poured the coffee.

"Huh?"

"Building a complete person. That's the great adventure, sonny boy, and if you don't do it right, what the hell good are you?"

"Well, you guys've done okay."

"Thanks, Domingo," Sandy said from the stove. "We worked at it pretty hard."

"More her than me," John said. "I was away so damned much, playing field-spook. Missed three Christmases, goddamnit. You never forgive yourself for that," he explained. "That's the magic morning, and you're supposed to be there."

"Doing what?"

"Russia twice, Iran once—getting assets out every time. Two worked, but one came apart on me. Lost that one, and he didn't make it. Russians have never been real forgiving on state treason. He bit the big one four months later, poor bastard. Not a good Christmas," Clark concluded, remembering just how bleak that had been, seeing the KGB scoop the man up not fifty meters from where he'd been standing, seeing the face turned to him, the look of despair on the doomed face, having to turn away to make his own escape down the pipeline he'd set up for two, knowing there was nothing else he might have done, but feeling like shit about it anyway. Then, finally, he'd had to explain to Ed Foley what had happened—only to learn later that the agent had been burned—"shopped" was the euphemism—by a KGB mole inside CIA's own headquarters building. And *that* fuck was still alive in a federal prison, with cable TV and central heating.

"It's history, John," Chavez told him, understanding the look. They'd deployed on similar missions, but the Clark-Chavez team had never failed, though some of their missions had been on the insane side of hairy. "You know the funny part about this?"

"What's that?" John asked, wondering if it would be the same feeling he'd had.

"I know I'm gonna die now. Someday, I mean. The little guy, he's gotta outlive me. If he doesn't, then I've screwed it up. Can't let that happen, can I? JC is my responsibility. While he grows up, I grow old, and by the time he's my age, hell, I'll be in my *sixties*. Jesus, I never *planned* to be old, y'know?"

Clark chuckled. "Yeah, neither did I. Relax, kid. Now I'm a"—he almost said "fucking," but Sandy didn't like that particular epithet—"goddamned *grand*father. I never planned on that, either."

"It's not so bad, John," Sandy observed, cracking open the eggs. "We can spoil him and hand him back. And we will."

It hadn't happened that way with their kids, at least not on John's side of the family. His mother was long dead from cancer, and his father from a heart attack on the job, while rescuing some children from a dwelling fire in Indianapolis, back in the late 1960s. John wondered if they knew that their son had grown up, and then grown old, and was now a grandfather. There was no telling, was there? Mortality and its attendant issues were normal at times like this, he supposed. The great continuity of life. What would John Conor Chavez become? Rich man, poor man, beggarman, thief, doctor, lawyer, Indian chief? That was mainly Domingo and Patsy's job, and he had to trust them to do it properly, and they probably would. He knew his daughter and knew Ding almost as well. From the first time he'd seen the kid, in the mountains of Colorado, he'd known that this boy had something special in him, and the younger man had grown, blossoming like a flower in a particularly tough garden. Domingo Chavez was a younger version of himself, a man of honor and courage, Clark told himself, and therefore he'd be a worthy father, as he'd proven to be a worthy husband. The great continuity of life, John told himself again, sipping his coffee and puffing on the cigar, and if it was yet one more milestone on the road to death, then so be it. He'd had an interesting life, and a life that had mattered to others, as had Domingo, and as they all hoped would, John Conor. And what the hell, Clark thought, his life wasn't over yet, was it?

GETTING a flight to New York had proven more difficult than expected. They were all fully booked, but finally Popov had managed to get himself a coach seat in the back of an old United 727. He disliked the tight fit, but the flight was short. At La Guardia, he headed for a cab, on the way out checking his inside coat pocket and finding the travel documents that had gotten him across the Atlantic. They had served him well, but they had to go. Emerging into the evening air, he surreptitiously dumped them into a trash container before walking to the cabstand. He was a weary man. His day had started just after midnight, American East Coast time, and he hadn't managed much sleep on the transatlantic flight, and his body was—how did the Americans put it?—running on empty. Maybe that explained the break with fieldcraft.

Thirty minutes later, Popov was within blocks of his downtown apartment, when the waste-disposal crew circulated past the United Airlines terminal to change the trash bags. The routine was mechanical and fairly strenuous physical labor for the mostly Puerto Rican work crew. One at a time, they lifted the metal tops off the cans and reached in to remove the heavy-gauge plastic garbage bags, then turned to dump them into wheeled containers that would later be tipped into trucks for transport to a landfill on Staten Island. The routine was good upper-body exercise, and most of the men carried portable radios to help themselves deal with the boredom of the work.

One can, fifty yards from the cabstand, didn't sit properly in its holder. When the cleanup man lifted the bag, it caught on a metallic edge and ripped, spilling its contents onto the concrete sidewalk. That generated a quiet curse from the worker, who now had to bend down and pick up a bunch of objects with his gloved hands. He was halfway through when he saw the crimson cardboard cover of what appeared to be a British passport. People didn't throw those things away, did they? He flipped it open and saw two credit cards inside, stamped with the same name on the passport. Serov, he saw, an unusual name. He dropped the whole package into the thigh pocket of his coveralls. He'd bring it by the lost-and-found. It wasn't the first time he'd discovered valuable stuff in the trash. Once he'd even recovered a fully loaded 9-mm pistol!

■ ■ ■

BY this time Popov was in his apartment, too tired even to unpack his bags. Instead he merely undressed and collapsed on the bed without even a vodka to help him off to sleep. By reflex, he turned on the TV and caught yet another story about the Hereford shoot-out. The TV was—*govno,* shit, he thought. There was the TV truck whose reporter had come close and tried to interview him. They hadn't used it, but there he was, in profile, from twenty feet away, while the reporter gave a stand-up. All the more reason to clear out now, he thought, as he drifted off. He didn't even have the energy to switch the TV off, and he slept with it on, the recurring stories entering his mind and giving him confused and unpleasant dreams throughout the night.

THE passport, credit cards, and a few other items of apparent value arrived at the waste-disposal company's Staten Island office—actually a trailer that had been towed to the spot—after the close of regular business hours. The trash collector tossed it on the correct desk and punched his time card on the way out for his drive back to Queens and his usual late dinner.

TOM Sullivan had worked late, and was now in the bar the FBI agents frequented, a block from the Jacob Javits Federal Building in lower Manhattan. His partner Frank Chatham was there, too, and the two agents sat in a booth, sipping at their Sam Adams beers.

"Anything happening on your end?" Sullivan asked. He'd been in court all day, waiting to testify in a fraud case, but had never gotten to the witness stand because of procedural delays.

"I talked with two girls today. They both say they know Kirk Maclean, but neither one actually dated him," Chatham replied. "Looks like another dry hole. I mean, he *was* cooperative, wasn't he?"

"Any other names associated with the missing girls?"

Chatham shook his head. "Nope. They both said they saw him talking to the missing one and he walked one out once, like he told us, but nothing special about it. Just the usual singles bar scene. Nothing that contradicts anything he said. Neither one likes Maclean very much. They say he comes on to girls, asks some questions, and usually leaves them."

"What kind of questions?"

"The usual—name, address, work, family stuff. Same stuff we ask, Tom."

"The two girls you talked to today," Sullivan asked thoughtfully. "Where they from?"

"One's a New Yorker, one's from across the river in Jersey."

"Bannister and Pretloe are from out of town," Sullivan pointed out.

"Yeah, I know. So?"

"So, if you're a serial killer, it's easier to take down victims with no close family members, isn't it?"

"Part of the selection process? That's a stretch, Tom."

"Maybe, but what else we got?" The answer was, not very much. The flyers handed out by the NYPD had turned up fifteen people who'd said they recognized the faces, but they were unable to provide any useful information. "I agree, Maclean was cooperative, but if he approaches girls, dumps those who grew up near here and have family here, *then* walks our victim home, hell, it's more than we have on anyone else."

"Go back to talk to him?"

Sullivan nodded. "Yeah." It was just routine procedure. Kirk Maclean hadn't struck either agent as a potential serial killer—but that was the best-disguised form of criminal, both had learned in the FBI Academy at Quantico, Virginia. They also knew that the dullest of routine investigative work broke far more cases than the miracles so beloved of mystery novels. Real police work was boring, mind-dulling repetition, and those who stuck with it won. Usually.

IT was strange that morning at Hereford. On the one hand, Team-2 was somewhat cowed by what had happened the day before. The loss of comrades did that to any unit. But on the other hand, their boss was now a father, and that was always the best thing to happen to a man. On the way to morning PT, a somewhat strung-out Team-2 Leader, who'd had no sleep at all the night before, had his hand shaken by every member of the team, invariably with a brief word of congratulations and a knowing smile, since all of them were fathers already, even those younger than their boss. Morning PT was abbreviated, in acknowledgment of his physical condition, and after the run, Eddie Price suggested to Chavez that he might as well drive home for a few hours of sleep, since he'd be of little use to anyone in his current condition. This Chavez did, crashing and burning past noon, and wakening with a screaming headache.

AS did Dmitriy Popov. It hardly seemed fair, since he'd had little to drink the day before. He supposed it was his body's revenge on him for all the travel abuse on top of a long and exciting day west of London. He awoke to CNN on his bedroom TV, and padded off to the bathroom for the usual morning routine, plus some aspirin, then to the kitchen to make coffee. In two hours, he'd showered and dressed, unpacked his bags, and hung up the clothes he'd taken to Europe. The wrinkles would stretch out in a day or two, he thought. Then it was time for him to catch a cab for midtown.

ON Staten Island, the lost-and-found person was a secretary who had this as one of her additional duties, and hated it. The items dropped on her desk were always smelly, sometimes enough to make her gag. Today was no exception, and she found herself wondering why people had to place such noxious items in the trash instead of—what? she never thought to wonder. Keep them in their pockets? The crimson passport was no exception. Joseph A. Serov. The photo was of a man about fifty, she thought, and about as remarkable to look at as a McDonald's hamburger. But it *was* a passport and two credit cards and it belonged to somebody. She lifted the phone book from her desk and called the British Consulate in Manhattan, told the operator what it was about, and got the passport control officer as a result. She didn't know that the passport-control office had for generations been the semisecret cover job for field officers of the Secret Intelligence Service. After a brief conversation, a company truck that was headed for Manhattan anyway dropped off the envelope at the consulate, where the door guard called to the proper office, and a secretary came down to collect it. This she dropped on the desk of her boss, Peter Williams.

Williams really was a spook of sorts, a young man on his first field assignment outside his own country. It was typically a safe, comfortable job, in a major city of an allied country, and he did work a few agents, all of them diplomats working at the United Nations. From them, he sought and sometimes got low-level diplomatic intelligence, which was forwarded to Whitehall to be examined and considered by equally low-level bureaucrats in the Foreign Office.

This smelly passport was unusual. Though his job was supposed to handle things like this, in fact he most often arranged substitute passports for people who'd somehow lost them in New York, which was not exactly a rare occurrence, though invariably an embarrassing one for the people who needed the replacements. The procedure was for Williams to fax the identification number on the document to London to identify the owner properly, and then call him or her at home, hoping to get a family member or employee who would know where the passport holder might be.

But in this case, Williams got a telephone call from Whitehall barely thirty minutes after sending the information.

"Peter?"

"Yes, Burt?"

"This passport, Joseph Serov—rather strange thing just happened."

"What's that?"

"The address we have for the chap is a mortuary, and the telephone number is to the same place. They've never heard of Joseph Serov, alive or dead."

"Oh? A false passport?" Williams lifted it from his desk blotter. If it were a fake, it was a damned good one. So was something interesting happening for a change?

"No, the computer has the passport number and name in it, but this Serov chap doesn't live where he claims to live. I think it's a matter of false papers. The records show that he is a naturalized subject. Want us to run that down, as well?"

Williams wondered about that. He'd seen false papers before, and been trained on how to obtain them for himself at the SIS training academy. Well, why not? Maybe he'd uncover a spy or something. "Yes, Burt, could you do that for me?"

"Call you tomorrow," the Foreign Office official promised.

For his part, Peter Williams lit up his computer and sent an e-mail to London, just one more routine day for a young and very junior intelligence officer on his first posting abroad. New York was much like London, expensive, impersonal, and full of culture, but sadly lacking in the good manners of his hometown.

Serov, he thought, a Russian name, but you could find them everywhere. Quite a few in London. Even more in New York City, where so many of the cabdrivers were right off the boat or plane from Mother Russia and knew neither the English language nor where to find the landmarks of New York. Lost British passport, Russian name.

THREE thousand four hundred miles away, the name "Serov" had been input onto the SIS computer system. The name had already been run for possible hits and nothing of value had been found, but the executive program had many names and phrases, and it scanned for all of them. The name "Serov" was enough—it had also been entered spelled as Seroff and Serof—and when the e-mail from New York arrived, the computer seized upon and directed the message to a desk officer. Knowing that Iosef was the Russian version of Joseph, and since the passport description gave an age in the proper range, he flagged the message and forwarded it to the computer terminal of the person who had originated the enquiry on one Serov, Iosef Andreyevich.

In due course, that message appeared as e-mail on the desktop computer of Bill Tawney. Bloody useful things, computers, Tawney thought, as he printed up the message. New York. That was interesting. He called the number of the Consulate and got Peter Williams.

"This passport from the Serov chap, anything else you can tell me?" he asked, after establishing his credentials.

"Well, yes, there are two credit cards that were inside it, a MasterCard and a Visa, both platinum." Which, he didn't have to add, meant that they had relatively large credit limits.

"Very well. I want you to send me the photo and the credit-card numbers over secure lines immediately." Tawney gave him the correct numbers to call.

"Yes, sir. I'll do that at once," Williams replied earnestly, wondering what this was all about. And who the devil was William Tawney? Whoever it was, he was working late, since England was five hours ahead of New York, and Peter Williams was already wondering what he'd have for dinner.

"JOHN?"

"Yeah, Bill?" Clark replied tiredly, looking up from his desk and wondering if he'd get to see his grandson that day.

"Our friend Serov has turned up," the SIS man said next. That got a reaction. Clark's eyes narrowed at once.

"Oh? Where?"

"New York. A British passport was found in a dustbin at La Guardia Airport, along with two credit cards. Well," he amended his report, "the passport and credit cards were in the name of one Joseph A. Serov."

"Run the cards to see if—"

"I called the legal attaché in your embassy in London to have the accounts run, yes. Should have some information within the hour. Could be a break for us, John," Tawney added, with a hopeful voice.

"Who's handling it in the U.S.?"

"Gus Werner, assistant director, Terrorism Division. Ever met him?"

Clark shook his head. "No, but I know the name."

"I know Gus. Good chap."

THE FBI has cordial relationships with all manner of businesses. Visa and MasterCard were no exceptions. An FBI agent called the headquarters of both companies from his desk in the Hoover Building, and gave the card numbers to the chiefs of security of both companies. Both were former FBI agents themselves—the FBI sends many retired agents off to such positions, which creates a large and diverse old-boy network—and both of them queried their computers and came up with account information, including name, address, credit history, and most important of all, recent charges. The British Airways flight from London Heathrow to Chicago O'Hare leaped off the screen—actually the faxed page—at the agent's desk in Washington.

"Yeah?" Gus Werner said, when the young agent came into his office.

"He caught a flight from London to Chicago late yesterday, and then a flight from Chicago to New York, about the last one, got a back-room ticket on standby. Must have dumped the ID right after he got in. Here." The agent handed over the charge records and the flight information. Werner scanned the pages.

"No shit," the former chief of the Hostage Rescue Team observed quietly. "This looks like a hit, Johnny."

"Yes, sir," replied the young agent, fresh in from the Oklahoma City field division. "But it leaves one thing out—how he got to Europe this time. Everything else is documented, and there's a flight from Dublin to London, but nothing from here to Ireland," Special Agent James Washington told his boss.

"Maybe he's got American Express. Call and find out," Werner ordered the junior man.

"Will do," Washington promised.

"Who do I call on this?" Werner asked.

"Right here, sir." Washington pointed to the number on the covering sheet.

"Oh, good, I've met him. Thanks, Jimmy." Werner lifted his phone and dialed the international number. "Mr. Tawney, please," he told the operator. "It's Gus Werner calling from FBI Headquarters in Washington."

"HELLO, Gus. That was very fast of you," Tawney said, half in his overcoat and hoping to get home.

"The wonders of the computer age, Bill. I have a possible hit on this Serov guy. He flew from Heathrow to Chicago yesterday. The flight was about three hours after the fracas you had at Hereford. I have a rental car, a hotel bill, and a flight from Chicago to New York City after he got here."

"Address?"

"We're not that lucky. Post office box in lower Manhattan," the Assistant Director told his counterpart. "Bill, how hot is this?"

"Gus, it's bloody hot. Sean Grady gave us the name, and one of the other prisoners confirmed it. This Serov chap delivered a large sum of money and ten pounds of cocaine shortly before the attack. We're working with the Swiss to track the money right now. And now it appears that this chap is based in America. Very interesting."

"No shit. We're going to have to track this mutt down if we can," Werner thought aloud. There was ample jurisdiction for the investigation he was about to open. American laws on terrorism reached across the world and had draconian penalties attached to them. And so did drug laws.

"You'll try?" Tawney asked.

"You bet your ass on that one, Bill," Werner replied positively. "I'm starting the case file myself. The hunt is on for Mr. Serov."

"Excellent. Thank you, Gus."

WERNER consulted his computer for a codeword. This case would be important and classified, and the codeword on the file would read . . . no, not that one. He told the machine to pick another. Yes. PREFECT, a word he remembered from his Jesuit high school in St. Louis.

"Mr. Werner?" his secretary called. "Mr. Henriksen on line three."

"Hey, Bill," Werner said, picking up the phone.

"CUTE little guy, isn't he?" Chavez asked.

John Conor Chavez was in his plastic crib-tray, sleeping peacefully at the moment. The name card in the slot on the front established his identity, helped somewhat by an armed policeman in the nursery. There would be another on the maternity floor, and an SAS team of three soldiers on the hospital grounds—they were harder to identify, as they didn't have military haircuts. It was, again, the horse-gone-lock-the-door mentality, but Chavez didn't mind that people were around to protect his wife and child.

"Most of 'em are," John Clark agreed, remembering what Patsy and Maggie had been like at that age—only yesterday, it so often seemed. Like most men, John always thought of his children as infants, never able to forget the first time he'd held them in their hospital receiving blankets. And so now, again, he basked in the warm glow, knowing exactly how Ding felt, proud and a little intimidated by the responsibility that attended fatherhood. Well, that was how it was supposed to be. *Takes after his mother,* John thought next, which meant after *his* side of the family, which, he thought, was good. But John wondered, with an ironic smile, if the little guy was dreaming in Spanish, and if he learned Spanish growing up, well, what was the harm in being bilingual? Then his beeper went off. John grumbled as he lifted it from his belt. Bill Tawney's number. He pulled his shoe-phone from his pants pocket and dialed the number. It took five seconds for the encryption systems to synchronize.

"Yeah, Bill?"

"Good news. John, your FBI are tracking down this Serov chap. I spoke with Gus Werner half an hour ago. They've established that he took a flight from Heathrow to Chicago yesterday, then on to New York. That's the address for his credit cards. The FBI are moving very quickly on this one."

THE next step was checking for a driver's license, and that came up dry, which meant they were also denied a photograph of the subject. The FBI agents checking it out in Albany were disappointed, but not especially surprised. The next step, for the next day, was to interview the postal employees at the station with the P.O. box.

"SO, Dmitriy, you got back here in a hurry," Brightling observed.

"It seemed a good idea," Popov replied. "The mission was a mistake. The Rainbow soldiers are too good for such an attack on them. Sean's people did well. Their planning struck me as excellent, but the enemy was far too proficient. The skill of these people is remarkable, as we saw before."

"Well, the attack must have shaken them up," his employer observed.

"Perhaps," Popov allowed. Just then, Henriksen walked in.

"Bad news," he announced.

"What's that?"

"Dmitriy, you goofed up some, son."

"Oh? How did I do that?" the Russian asked, no small amount of irony in his voice.

"Not sure, but they know there was a Russian involved in cueing the attack on Rainbow, and the FBI is working the case now. They may know you're here."

"That is not possible," Popov objected. "Well . . . yes, they have Grady, and perhaps he talked . . . yes, he did know that I flew in from America, or he could have figured that out, and he knows the cover name I used, but that identity is gone—destroyed."

"Maybe so, but I was just on the phone with Gus Werner. I asked him about the Hereford incident, if there was anything I needed to know. He told me they've started a case looking for a Russian name, that they had reason to believe a Russian, possibly based in America, had been in contact with the PIRA. That means they know the name, Dmitriy, and that means they'll be tracking down names on airline passenger lists. Don't underestimate the FBI, pal," Henriksen warned.

"I do not," Popov replied, now slightly worried, but only slightly. It would not be all that easy to check every transatlantic flight, even in the age of computers. He also decided that his next set of false ID papers would be in the name of Jones, Smith, Brown, or Johnson, not that of a disgraced KGB chairman from the 1950s. The Serov ID name had been a joke on his part. Not a good one, he decided now. Joseph Andrew Brown, that would be the next one, Dmitriy Arkadeyevich Popov thought, sitting there in the top-floor office.

"Is this a danger to us?" Brightling asked.

"If they find our friend here," Henriksen replied.

Brightling nodded and thought quickly. "Dmitriy, have you ever been to Kansas?"

"HELLO, Mr. Maclean," Tom Sullivan said.

"Oh, hi. Want to talk to me some more?"

"Yes, if you don't mind," Frank Chatham told him.

"Okay, come on in," Maclean said, opening the door all the way, walking back to his living room, and telling himself to be cool. He sat down and muted his TV. "So, what do you want to know?"

"Anyone else you remember who might have been close to Mary Bannister?" The two agents saw Maclean frown, then shake his head.

"Nobody I can put a name on. I mean, you know, it's a singles bar, and people bump into each other and talk, and make friends and stuff, y'know?" He thought for a second more. "Maybe one guy, but I don't know his name . . . tall guy, 'bout my age, sandy hair, big guy, like he works out and stuff . . . but I don't know his name, sorry. Mary danced with him and had drinks with him, I think, but aside from that, hey, it's too dark and crowded in there."

"And you walked her home just that one time?"

" 'Fraid so. We talked and joked some, but we never really hit it off. Just casual. I never, uh, made a move on her, if you know what I mean. Never got that far, like. Yeah, sure, I walked her home, but didn't even go in the building, didn't kiss her good night, even, just shook hands." He saw Chatham taking notes. Was this what he'd told them before? He thought so, but it was hard to remember with two federal cops in his living room. The hell of it was he *didn't* remember much about her. He'd selected her, loaded her into the truck, but that was all. He had no idea where she was now, though he imagined she was probably dead. Maclean knew what that part of the project was all about, and *that* made him a kidnapper and accessory to murder, two things he didn't exactly plan to give to these two FBI guys. New York had a death penalty statute now, and for all he knew so did the federal government. Unconsciously, he licked his lips and rubbed his hands on his slacks as he leaned back on the couch. Then he stood and faced toward the kitchen. "Can I get you guys anything?"

"No, thanks, but you go right ahead," Sullivan said. He'd just seen something he hadn't noticed in their first interview. Tension. Was it the occasional flips people got talking to FBI agents, or was this guy trying to conceal something? They watched Maclean build a drink and come back.

"How would you describe Mary Bannister?" Sullivan asked.

"Pretty, but no knockout. Nice, personable—I mean, pleasant, sense of humor, sense of fun about her. Out-of-town girl in the big city for the first time—I mean, she's just a girl, y'know?"

"But nobody really close to her, you said?"

"Not that I know of, but I didn't know her that well. What do other people say?"

"Well, people from the bar said you were pretty friendly with her . . ."

"Maybe, yeah, but not *that* friendly. I mean, it never went anywhere. I never even kissed her." He was repeating himself now, as he sipped at his bourbon and water. "Wish I did, but I didn't," he added.

"Who at the bar *are* you close to?" Chatham asked.

"Hey, that's kinda private, isn't it?" Kirk objected.

"Well, you know how it goes. We're trying to get a feel for the place, how it works, that sort of thing."

"Well, I don't kiss and tell, okay? Not my thing."

"I can't blame you for that," Sullivan observed with a smile, "but it is kinda unusual for the singles bar crowd."

"Oh, sure, there's guys there who put notches on their guns, but that's not my style."

"So, Mary Bannister disappeared, and you didn't notice?"

"Maybe, but I didn't think much about it. It's a transient community, y'know? People come in and out, and some you never see again. They just disappear, like."

"Ever call her?"

Maclean frowned. "No, I don't remember that she gave me her number. I suppose she was in the book, but, no, I never called her."

"Just walked her home only that one time?"

"Right, just that one time," Maclean confirmed, taking another pull on his drink and wishing these two inquisitors out of his home. Did they—could they know something? Why had they come back? Well, there was nothing in his apartment to confirm that he knew *any* female from the Turtle Inn. Well, just some phone numbers, but not so much as a loose sock from the women he'd occasionally brought here. "I mean, you guys looked around the first time you were here," Maclean volunteered.

"No big deal. We always ask to do that. It's just routine," Sullivan told their suspect. "Well, we have another appointment in a few minutes up the street. Thanks for letting us talk to you. You still have my card?"

"Yeah, in the kitchen, stuck on the refrigerator."

"Okay. Look, this case is kinda hard for us. Please think it over and if you come up with anything—anything at all, please call me, okay?"

"Sure will." Maclean stood and walked them to the door, then came back to his drink and took another swallow.

"HE'S nervous," Chatham said, out on the street.

"Sure as hell. We have enough to do a background check on him?"

"No problem," Chatham replied.

"Tomorrow morning," the senior agent said.

IT was his second trip to Teterboro Airport, in New Jersey, across the river from Manhattan, but this time it was a different aircraft, with HORIZON CORP. painted on the rudder fin. Dmitriy played along, figuring that he could escape from any place in the United States, and knowing that Henriksen would warn Brightling not to try anything drastic. There was an element of anxiety to the trip, but no greater than his curiosity, and so Popov settled into his seat on the left side and waited for the aircraft to start its engines and taxi out. There was even a flight attendant, a pretty one, to give him a shot of Finlandia vodka, which he sipped as the Gulfstream V started rolling. Kansas, he thought, a state of wheat fields and tornadoes, less than three hours away.

"MR. Henriksen?"

"Yeah, who's this?"

"Kirk Maclean."

"Anything wrong?" Henriksen asked, alerted by the tone of his voice.

CHAPTER 31

MOVEMENT

THE DARKNESS HID THE LANDSCAPE. POPOV stepped off the aircraft, and found a large military-type automobile waiting for him. Then he noticed the lines painted on the pavement and wondered if he'd landed on an airport runway or a country road of some sort. But, no, in the distance was a huge building, partially lit. More curious than ever, Dmitriy got into the vehicle and headed off toward it. His eyes gradually got accustomed to the darkness. The surrounding land seemed very flat, with only gentle rolls visible. Behind him he saw a fuel truck had pulled up to the business jet, perhaps to send it back to New Jersey. Well, they were expensive, and doubtless Brightling and his people wanted it back where he could use it. Popov didn't know that Horizon Corporation owned many of them; their number just increased by three from the factory outside Savannah, Georgia. He was still jetlagged, he found on entering the building. A uniformed security guard walked him to the elevator and then to his fourth-floor room, which was not unlike a medium-decent hotel room, complete with cooking facilities and a refrigerator. There was a TV and VCR, and all the tapes in the adjacent storage cupboard were—nature tapes, he saw. Lions, bears, moose, spawning salmon. Not a single feature film. The magazines on the bedside table were similarly nature oriented. How odd. But there was also a complete bar, including Absolut vodka, which was almost as good as the Russian kind he preferred. He poured himself a drink and switched on the TV to CNN.

Henriksen was being overly cautious, Dmitriy thought. What could the FBI possibly have on him? A name? From that they could perhaps develop—what? Credit cards, if they were very lucky, and from that his travel records, but none of them would have evidentiary value in any court of law. No, unless Sean Grady positively identified him as a conduit of information and funds, he was totally safe, and Popov thought he could depend on Grady not to cooperate with the British. He hated them too much to be cooperative. It was just a matter of crawling back into his hole and pulling it in after himself—an Americanism he admired. The money he'd stashed in the secondary Swiss account *might* be discoverable, but there were ways to handle that—attorneys were so useful as an institution, he'd learned. Working through them was better than all the KGB fieldcraft combined.

No, if there was any danger to him, it was to be found in his employer, who might not know the rules of the game—but even if he didn't, Henriksen would help, and so Dmitriy relaxed and sipped his drink. He'd explore this place tomorrow, and from the way he was treated, he'd know—

—no, there was an even easier way. He lifted his phone, hit 9 to get an outside line, then dialed his apartment in New York. The call went through. The phone rang four times before his answering machine clicked in. So, he had phone access to the outside. That meant he was safe, but he was no closer to understanding what was going on than he'd been during that first meeting in France, chatting with the American businessman and regaling him with tales of a former KGB field intelligence officer. Now here he was, in *Kansas,* USA, drinking vodka and watching television, with over six million American dollars in two numbered accounts in Switzerland. He'd reached one goal. Next he had to meet another. What the hell was this adventure all about? Would he find out here? He hoped so.

THE airplanes were crammed with people, all of them inbound to Kingsford Smith International Airport outside Sydney. Many of them landed on the runway, which stuck out like a finger into Botany Bay, so famous as the landing point for criminals and other English rejects sent halfway round the world on wooden sailing ships to start a new country, which, to the disbelief of those who'd dispatched them, they'd done remarkably well. Many of the passengers on the inbound flights were young, fit athletes, the pride and pick of the countries that had sent them dressed in uniform clothing that proclaimed their nations of origin. Most were tourists, people with ticket-and-accommodation packages expensively bought from travel agents or given as gifts from political figures in their home countries. Many carried miniature flags. The few business passengers had listened to all manner of enthusiastic predictions for national glory at the Olympic games, which would start in the next few days.

On arriving, the athletes were treated like visiting royalty and conveyed to buses that would take them up Highway 64 to the city, and thence to the Olympic Village, which had been expensively built by the Australian government to house them. They could see the magnificent stadium nearby, and the athletes looked and wondered if they'd find personal glory there.

"SO, Colonel, what do you think?"

"It's one hell of a stadium, and that's a fact," Colonel Wilson Gearing, U.S. Army Chemical Corps, retired, replied. "But it sure gets hot here in the summer, pal."

"It's that El Niño business again. The ocean currents off South America have changed again, and that's associated with unusually hot temperatures here. It'll be in the mid-thirties—nineties to you, I suppose—for the whole Olympiad."

"Well, I hope this fogging system works, 'cuz if it doesn't, you'll have a lot of heat-stroke cases here, pal."

"It works," the Aussie cop told him. "It's fully tested."

"Can I take a look at it now? Bill Henriksen wants me to see if it could be used as a chemical-agent delivery system by the bad guys."

"Certainly. This way." They were there in five minutes. The water-input piping was contained in its own locked room. The cop had the key for this, and took the colonel inside.

"Oh, you chlorinate the water here?" Gearing asked in semisurprise. The water came in from the Sydney city water system, didn't it?

"Yes, we don't want to spread any germs on our guests, do we?"

"Not exactly," Colonel Gearing agreed, looking at the plastic chlorine container that hung on the distribution piping beyond the actual pumps. Water was filtered through that before it went into the fogging nozzles that hung in all the concourses and ramps to the stadium bowl itself. The system would have to be flushed with unchlorinated water before delivery would work, but that was easily accomplished, and the false chlorine container in his hotel room was an exact twin of this one. The contents even looked like chlorine, almost, though the nano-capsules actually contained something called Shiva. Gearing thought about that behind blank brown eyes. He'd been a chemical weapons expert his whole professional life, having worked at the Edgewood Arsenal in Maryland and Dugway Proving Ground in Utah—but, well, this wasn't really chemical warfare. It was bio-war, a sister science of the one he'd studied for over twenty uniformed years. "Is the door guarded?" he asked.

"No, but it is alarmed, and it takes some minutes to play with the system, as you can see. The alarm system reports to the command post, and we have an ample reaction force there."

"How ample?" the retired colonel asked next.

"Twenty SAS members, plus twenty police constables, are there at all times, plus ten more SAS circulating in pairs around the stadium. The people at the CP are armed with automatic weapons. The ones on patrol with pistols and radios. There is also a supplementary reaction force a kilometer distant with light armored vehicles and heavy weapons, platoon strength. Beyond that, a battalion of infantry twenty kilometers away, with helicopters and other support."

"Sounds good to me," Colonel Gearing said. "Can you give me the alarm code for this facility?"

They didn't even hesitate. He was a former staff-grade army officer, after all, and a senior member of the consulting team for security at the Olympic Games. "One-One-Three-Three-Six-Six," the senior cop told him. Gearing wrote it down, then punched the numbers into the keypad, which armed and then disarmed the system. He'd be able to switch out the chlorine canister very quickly. The system was designed for rapid servicing. This would work just fine, just like the model they'd set up in Kansas, on which he and his people had practiced for several days. They'd gotten the swap-out time down to fourteen seconds. Anything under twenty meant that nobody would notice anything remiss in the fog-cooling system, because residual pressure would maintain the fogging stream.

For the first time, Gearing saw the place where he'd be doing it, and that generated a slight chill in his blood. Planning was one thing. Seeing where it would happen for-real was something else. This was the place. Here he would start a global plague that would take lives in numbers far too great to tally, and which in the end would leave alive only the elect. It would save the planet—at a ghastly price, to be sure, but he'd been committed to this mission for years. He'd seen what man could do to harm things. He'd been a young lieutenant at Dugway Proving Grounds when they'd had the well-publicized accident with GB, a persistent nerve agent that had blown too far and slaughtered a few hundred sheep—and neurotoxins were not a pretty death, even for sheep. The news media hadn't even bothered to talk about the wild game that had died a similar, ugly death, everything from insects to antelope. It had shaken him that his own organization, the United States Army, could make so grave an error to cause such pain. The things he'd learned later had been worse. The binary agents he'd worked on for years—an effort to manufacture "safe" poisons for battlefield use . . . the crazy part was that it had all begun in Germany as insecticide research in the 1920s and 1930s. Most of the chemicals used to kill off insects were nerve agents, simple ones that attacked and destroyed the rudimentary nervous systems in ants and beetles, but those German chemists had stumbled upon some of the deadliest chemical compounds ever formulated. So much of Gearing's career had been spent with the intelligence community, evaluating information about possible chemical-warfare plants in countries not trusted to have such things.

But the problem with chemical weapons had always been their distribution—how to spread them evenly across a battlefield, thus exposing enemy soldiers efficiently. That the same chemicals would travel downrange and kill innocent civilians had been the dirty secret that the organizations and the governments that ruled them had always ignored. And they didn't even consider the wildlife that would also be exterminated in vast quantities—and worse still, the genetic damage those agents caused, because marginal doses of nerve gas, below the exposure needed to kill, invaded the very DNA of the victim, ensuring mutations that would last for generations. Gearing had spent his life knowing these things, and he supposed that it had desensitized him to the taking of life in large quantities.

This wasn't quite the same thing. He would not be spreading organophosphate chemical poisons, but rather tiny virus particles. And the people walking through the cooling fog in the concourses and ramps to the stadium bowl would breathe them in, and their body chemistry would break down the nanocapsules, allowing the Shiva strands to go to work ... slowly, of course ... and they'd go home to spread the Shiva farther, and in four to six weeks after the ending of the Sydney Olympics, the plague would erupt worldwide, and a global panic would ensue. Then Horizon Corporation would announce that it had an experimental "A" vaccine that had worked in animals and primates—and was safe for human usage—ready for mass production, and so it would be mass-produced and distributed worldwide, and four to six weeks after injection, those people, too, would develop the Shiva symptoms, and with luck the world would be depopulated down to a fractional percentage of the current population. Disorders would break out, killing many of the people blessed by Nature with highly effective immune systems, and in six months or so, there would be just a few left, well organized and well equipped, safe in Kansas and Brazil, and in six months more they would be the inheritors of a world returning to its natural state. This wouldn't be like Dugway, a purposeless accident. This would be a considered act by a man who'd contemplated mass murder for all of his professional life, but who'd only helped kill innocent animals ... He turned to look at his hosts.

"What's the extended weather forecast?"

"Hot and dry, old boy. I hope the athletes are fit. They'll need to be."

"Well, then, this fogging system will be a lifesaver," Gearing observed. "Just so the wrong people don't fool with it. With your permission, I'll have my people keep an eye on this thing."

"Fine," the senior cop agreed. The American was really fixated on this fogging system, but he'd been a gas soldier, and maybe that explained it.

POPOV hadn't closed his shades the previous evening, and so the dawn awoke him rather abruptly. He opened his eyes, then squinted them in pain as the sun rose over the Kansas plains. The medicine cabinet in the bathroom, he found, had Tylenol and aspirin, and there were coffee grounds for the machine in the kitchen area, but nothing of value in the refrigerator. So he showered and had his coffee, then went out of the room looking for food. He found a cafeteria—a huge one—almost entirely empty of patrons, though there were a few people near the food tables, and there he went, got breakfast and sat alone, as he looked at the others in the cavernous room. Mainly people in their thirties and forties, he thought, professional-looking, some wearing white laboratory coats.

"Mr. Popov?" a voice said. Dmitriy turned.

"Yes?"

"I'm David Dawson, chief of security here. I have a badge for you to wear"—he handed over a white plastic shield that pinned to his shirt—"and I'm supposed to show you around today. Welcome to Kansas."

"Thank you." Popov pinned the badge on. It even had his picture on it, the Russian saw.

"You want to wear that at all times, so that people know you belong here," Dawson explained helpfully.

"Yes, I understand." So this place was pass-controlled, and it had a director of site security. How interesting.

"How was your flight in last night?"

"Pleasant and uneventful," Popov replied, sipping his second coffee of the morning. "So, what is this place?"

"Well, Horizon set it up as a research facility. You know what the company does, right?"

"Yes." Popov nodded. "Medicines and biological research, a world leader."

"Well, this is another research-and-development facility for their work. It was just finished recently. We're bringing people in now. It will soon be the company's main facility."

"Why here in the middle of nothing?" Popov asked, looking around at the mainly empty cafeteria.

"Well, for starters, it's centrally located. You can be anywhere in the country in less than three hours. And nobody's around to bother us. It's a secure facility, too. Horizon does lots of work that requires protection, you see."

"Industrial espionage?"

Dawson nodded. "That's right. We worry about that."

"Will I be able to look around, see the grounds and such?"

"I'll drive you around myself. Mr. Henriksen told me to extend you the hospitality of the facility. Go ahead and finish your breakfast. I have a few things I have to do. I'll be back in about fifteen minutes."

"Good, thank you," Popov said, watching him walk out of the room. This would be useful. There was a strange, institutional quality to this place, almost like a secure government facility . . . like a *Russian* facility, Popov thought. It seemed to have no soul at all, no character, no human dimension that he could identify. Even KGB would have hung a photo of Lenin on the huge, bare, white walls to give the place *some* human scale. There was a wall of tinted windows, which allowed him to see out to what appeared to be wheat fields and a road, but nothing else. It was almost like being on a ship at sea, he thought, unlike anything he'd ever experienced. The former KGB officer worked through his breakfast, all of his instincts on alert, hoping to learn more, and as quickly as he could.

"DOMINGO, I need you to take this one," John said.

"It's a long way to go, John, and I just became a daddy," Chavez objected.

"Sorry, pal, but Covington is down. So's Chin. I'm going to send you and four men. It's an easy job, Ding. The Aussies know their stuff, but they asked us to come down and give it a look—and the reason for that is the expert way you handled your field assignments, okay?"

"When do I leave?"

"Tonight, 747 out of Heathrow." Clark held up the ticket envelope.

"Great," Chavez grumbled.

"Hey, at least you were there for the delivery, pop."

"I suppose. What if something crops up while we're away?" Chavez tried as a weak final argument.

"We can scratch a team together, but you really think somebody's going to yank our chain anytime soon? After we bagged those IRA pukes? I don't," Clark concluded.

"What about the Russian guy, Serov?"

"The FBI's on it, trying to run him down in New York. They've assigned a bunch of agents to it."

ONE of them was Tom Sullivan. He was currently in the post office. Box 1453 at this station belonged to the mysterious Mr. Serov. It had some junk mail in it, and a Visa bill, but no one had opened the box in at least nine days, judging by the dates on the envelopes, and none of the clerks professed to know what the owner of Box 1453 looked like, though one thought he didn't pick up his mail very often. He'd given a street address when obtaining the box, but that address, it turned out, was to an Italian bakery several blocks away, and the phone number was a dud, evidently made up for the purpose.

"Sure as hell, this guy's a spook," Sullivan thought aloud, wondering why the Foreign Counterintelligence group hadn't picked up the case.

"Sure wiggles like one," Chatham agreed. And their assignment ended right there. They had no evidence of a crime for the subject, and not enough manpower to assign an agent to watch the P.O. box around the clock.

SECURITY was good here, Popov thought, as he rode around in another of the military-type vehicles that Dawson called a Hummer. The first thing about security was to have defensive depth. That they had. It was ten kilometers at least before you approached a property line.

"It used to be a number of large farms, but Horizon bought them all out a few years ago and started building the research lab. It took a while, but it's finished now."

"You still grow wheat here?"

"Yeah, the facility itself doesn't use all that much of the land, and we try to keep the rest of it the way it was. Hell, we grow almost enough wheat for all the people at the lab, got our own elevators an' all over that way." He pointed to the north.

Popov looked that way and saw the massive concrete structures some distance away. It was amazing how large America was, Dmitriy Arkadeyevich thought, and this part seemed so flat, not unlike the Russian steppes. The land had some dips and rises, but all they seemed to do was emphasize the lack of a real hill anywhere. The Hummer went north, and eventually crossed a rail line that evidently led to the grain silos—elevators, Dawson had called them? Elevators? Why that word? Farther north and he could barely make out traffic moving on a distant highway.

"That's the northern border," Dawson explained, as they passed into non-farm land.

"What's that?"

"Oh, that's our little herd of pronghorn antelopes." Dawson turned the wheel slightly to go closer. The Hummer bumped over the grassy land.

"They're pretty animals."

"That they are, and very fast. We call 'em the speed-goat. Not a true antelope at all, genetically closer to goats. Those babies can run at forty miles an hour, and do it for damned near an hour. They also have superb eyesight."

"Difficult to hunt, I imagine. Do you hunt?"

"They are, and I'm not. I'm a vegan."

"What?"

"Vegetarian. I don't eat meat or other animal products," Dawson said somewhat proudly. Even his belt was made of canvas rather than leather.

"Why is that, David?" Popov asked. He'd never come across anyone like him before.

"Oh, just a choice I made. I don't approve of killing animals for food or any other reason"—he turned—"not everybody agrees with me, not even here at the Project, but I'm not the only one who thinks that way. Nature is something to be respected, not exploited."

"So, you don't buy your wife a fur coat," Popov said, with a smile. He had heard about those fanatics.

"Not hardly!" Dawson laughed.

"I've never hunted," Popov said next, wondering what response he'd get. "I never saw the sense in it, and in Russia they've nearly exterminated most game animals."

"So I understand. That's very sad, but they'll come back someday," Dawson pronounced.

"How, with all the state hunters working to kill them?" That institution hadn't ended even with the demise of Communist rule.

Dawson's face took on a curious expression, one Popov had seen many times before at KGB. The man knew something he was unwilling to say right now, though what he knew was important somehow. "Oh, there's ways, pal. There's ways."

The driving tour required an hour and a half, at the end of which Popov was mightily impressed with the size of the facility. The approach road to the building complex *was* an airport, he saw, with electronic instruments to guide airplanes in and traffic lights to warn autos off when flight operations were in progress. He asked Dawson about it.

"Yeah, it is kinda obvious, isn't it? You can get a G in and out of here pretty easy. They say you can bring in real commercial jets, too, medium-sized ones, but I've never seen that done."

"Dr. Brightling spent a lot of money to build this establishment."

"That he did," Dawson agreed. "But it's worth it, trust me." He drove up the highway/runway to the lab building and stopped. "Come with me."

Popov followed without asking why. He'd never appreciated the power of a major American corporation. This could and should have been a government facility, with all the land and the huge building complex. The hotel building in which he'd spent the night could probably hold thousands of people—and *why* build such a place here? Was Brightling going to move his entire corporation here, all his employees? So far from major cities, airports, all the things that civilization offered. Why here? Except, of course, for security. It was also far from large police agencies, from news media and reporters. For the purposes of security, this facility might as easily have been on the moon.

The lab building was also larger than it needed to be, Dmitriy thought, but unlike the others, it appeared to be functioning at the moment. Inside was a desk, and a receptionist who knew David Dawson. The two men proceeded unimpeded to the elevators, then up to the fourth floor, and right to an office.

"Hi, doc," Dawson said. "This is Dmitriy. Dr. Brightling sent him to us last night. He's going to be here awhile," the security chief added.

"I got the fax." The physician stood and extended his hand to Popov. "Hi, I'm John Killgore. Follow me." And the two of them went through a side door into an examining room, while Dawson waited outside. Killgore told Popov to disrobe down to his underwear, and proceeded to give him a physical examination, taking blood pressure, checking eyes and ears and reflexes, prodding his belly to make sure that the liver was nonpalpable, and finally taking four test tubes of blood for further examination. Popov submitted to it all without objection, somewhat bemused by the whole thing, and slightly intimidated by the physician, as most people were. Finally, Killgore pulled a vial from the medicine cabinet and stuck a disposable syringe into it.

"What's this?" Dmitriy Arkadeyevich asked.

"Just a booster shot," Killgore explained, setting the vial down.

Popov picked it up and looked at the label, which read "**B-2100** 11-21-00" and nothing else. Then he winced when the needle went into his upper arm. He'd never enjoyed getting shots.

"There, that's done," Killgore said. "I'll talk to you tomorrow about the blood work." With that done, he pointed his patient to the hook his clothing hung on. It was a pity, Killgore thought, that the patient couldn't be appreciative for having his life saved.

■ ■ ■

"HE might as well not exist," Special Agent Sullivan told his boss. "Maybe somebody comes in to check his mail, but not in the past nine or ten days."

"What can we do about that?"

"If you want, we can put a camera and motion sensor inside the box, like the FCI guys do to cover dead-drops. We can do it, but it costs money and manpower to keep an agent or two close if the alarm goes off. Is this case that important?"

"Yes, it is now," the Assistant Special Agent in Charge of the New York field division told his subordinate. "Gus Werner started this one off, and he's keeping a personal eye on the case file. So, talk to the FCI guys and get them to help you cover the P.O. box."

Sullivan nodded and concealed his surprise. "Okay, will do."

"Next, what about the Bannister case?"

"That's not going anywhere at the moment. The closest thing to a hit we've gotten to this point is the second interview with this Kirk Maclean guy. He acted a little antsy. Maybe just nerves on his part, maybe something else—we have nothing on him and the missing victim, except that they had drinks and talked together at this bar uptown. We ran a background on him. Nothing much to report. Makes a good living for Horizon Corporation—he's a biochemist by profession, graduated University of Delaware, master's degree, working toward a doctorate at Columbia. Belongs to some conservation groups, including Earth First and the Sierra Club, gets their periodicals. His main hobby is backpacking. He has twenty-two grand in the bank, and he pays his bills on time. His neighbors say he's quiet and withdrawn, doesn't make many friends in the building. No known girlfriends. He says he knew Mary Bannister casually, walked her home once, no sexual involvement, and that's it, he says."

"Anything else?" the ASAC asked.

"The flyers the NYPD handed out haven't developed into anything yet. I can't say that I'm very hopeful at this point."

"What's next, then?"

Sullivan shrugged. "In a few more days we're going back to Maclean to interview him again. Like I said, he looked a little bit hinky, but not enough to justify coverage on him."

"I talked to this Lieutenant d'Allessandro. He's thinking there might be a serial killer working that part of town."

"Maybe so. There's another girl missing, Anne Pretloe's her name, but nothing's turning on that one either. Nothing for us to work with. We'll keep scratching away at it," Sullivan promised. "If one of them's out there, sooner or later he'll make a mistake." But until he did, more young women would continue to disappear into that particular black hole, and the combined forces of the NYPD and the FBI couldn't do much to stop it. "I've never worked a case like this before."

"I have," the ASAC said. "The Green River killer in Seattle. We put a ton of resources on that one, but we never caught the mutt, and the killings just stopped. Maybe he got picked up for burglary or robbing a liquor store, and maybe he's sitting it out in a Washington State prison, waiting to get paroled so he can take down some more hookers. We have a great profile on how his brain works, but that's it, and we don't know what brain the profile fits. These cases are real head-scratchers."

KIRK Maclean was having lunch just then, sitting in one of the hundreds of New York delicatessens, eating egg salad and drinking a cream soda.

"So?" Henriksen asked.

"So, they came back to talk to me again, asking the same fuckin' questions over and over, like they expect me to change my story."

"Did you?" the former FBI agent asked.

"No, there's only one story I'm going to tell, and that's the one I prepared in advance. How did you know that they might come to me like this?" Maclean asked.

"I used to be FBI. I've worked cases, and I know how the Bureau operates. They are very easy to underestimate, and then they appear—no, then *you* appear on the scope, and they start looking, and mainly they don't stop looking until they find something," Henriksen said, as a further warning to this kid.

"So, where are they now?" Maclean asked. "The girls, I mean."

"You don't need to know that, Kirk. Remember that. You do not need to know."

"Okay." Maclean nodded his submission. "Now what?"

"They'll come to see you again. They've probably done a background check on you and—"

"What's that mean?"

"Talk to your neighbors, coworkers, check your credit history, your car, whether you have tickets, any criminal convictions, look for anything that suggests that you could be a bad guy," Henriksen explained.

"There isn't anything like that on me," Kirk said.

"I know." Henriksen had done the same sort of check himself. There was no sense in having somebody with a criminal past out breaking the law in the name of the Project. The only black mark against him was Maclean's membership in Earth First, which was regarded by the Bureau almost as a terrorist—well, extremist—organization. But all Maclean did with that bunch was to read their monthly newsletter. They had a lot of good ideas, and there was talk in the Project about getting some of them injected with the "B" vaccine, but they had too many members whose ideas of protecting the planet were limited to driving nails into trees, so that the buzz saws would break. That sort of thing only chopped up workers in sawmills and raised the ire of the ignorant public without teaching them anything useful. That was the problem with terrorists, Henriksen had known for years. Their actions never matched their aspirations. Well, they weren't smart enough to develop the resources they needed to be effective. You had to live in the economic eco-structure to achieve that, and they just couldn't compete on that battlefield. Ideology was never enough. You needed brains and adaptability, too. To be one of the elect, you had to be worthy. Kirk Maclean wasn't really worthy, but he was part of the team. And now he was rattled by the attention of the FBI. All he had to do was stick to his story. But he was shook up, and that meant he couldn't be trusted. So, they'd have to do something about it.

"Get your stuff packed. We'll move you out to the Project tonight." What the hell, it would be starting soon anyway. Very soon, in fact.

"Good," Maclean responded, finishing his egg salad. Henriksen was eating pastrami, he saw. Not a vegan. Well, maybe someday.

ARTWORK was finally going up on some of the blank walls. So, Popov thought, the facility wasn't to be entirely soulless. It was nature paintings—mountains, forests, and animals. Some of the pictures were quite good, but most of them were ordinary, the kind of thing you found on the walls of cheap motels. How strange, the Russian thought, that with all the money they'd spent to build this monstrous facility in the middle of nowhere, that the artwork was second-rate. Well, taste was taste, and Brightling was a technocrat, and doubtless uneducated in the finer aspects of life. In ancient times he would have been a druid, Dmitriy thought, a bearded man in a long white robe who worshiped trees and animals and sacrificed virgins on stone altars to his pagan beliefs. There were better things to do with virgins. There was such a strange mixture of the old and the new in this man—and his company. The director of security was a "vegan," who never ate meat? What rubbish!

Horizon Corporation was a world leader in several vital new technological areas, but it was peopled by madmen of such primitive and strange beliefs. He supposed it was an American affectation. Such a huge country, the brilliant co-existing with the mad. Brightling was a genius, but he'd hired Popov to initiate terrorist incidents—

—and then he'd brought Popov here. Dmitriy Arkadeyevich thought about that as he chewed his dinner. *Why here?* What was so special about this place?

Now he could understand why Brightling had shrugged off the amount he'd transferred to the terrorists. Horizon Corporation had spent more paving one of the access roads than all the money Popov had taken from the corporate coffers and translated into his own. But this place *was* important. You could see that in every detail, down to the revolving doors that kept the air inside—every doorway he'd seen was like some sort of air lock, and made him think of a spacecraft. Not a single dollar had been spared to make this facility perfect. But perfect for what?

Popov shook his head and sipped at his tea. The quality of the food was excellent. The quality of *everything* was excellent, except the absurdly pedestrian artwork. There was, therefore, not a single mistake here. Brightling was not the sort of man to compromise on anything, was he? Therefore, Dmitriy Arkadeyevich told himself, everything here *was* deliberate, and everything fit into a pattern, from which he could discern the purpose of the building and the man who'd erected it. He'd allowed himself to be beguiled this day with his tour—and his physical examination? What the *hell* was *that* all about? The doctor had given him an injection. A "booster" he'd called it. But what for? Against what?

Outside this shrine to technology was a mere farm, and outside that, wild animals, which his driver of the day had seemed to worship.

Druids, he thought. In his time as a field officer in England he'd taken the time to read books and learn about the culture of the English, played the tourist, even traveled to Stonehenge and other places, in the hope of understanding the people better. Ultimately, though, he found that history was history, and though highly interesting, no more logical there than in the Soviet Union—where history had mainly been lies concocted to fit the ideological pattern of Marxism-Leninism.

Druids had been pagans, their culture based on the gods supposed to live in trees and rocks, and to which human lives had been sacrificed. That had doubtless been a measure exercised by the druid priesthood to maintain their control over the peasants ... and the nobility, too, in fact, as all religions tended to do. In return for offering some hope and certainty for the greatest mysteries of life—what happened after death, why the rain fell when it did, how the world had come to be—they extracted their price of earthly power, which was to tell everyone how to live. It had probably been a way for people of intellectual gifts but ignoble birth to achieve the power associated with the nobility. But it had always been about power—earthly power. And like the members of the Communist Party of the Soviet Union, the druid priesthood had probably believed that which they said and that which they enforced because—they had to believe it. It had been the source of their power, and you had to believe in that.

But these people here weren't primitives, were they? They were mainly scientists, some of them world leaders in their fields. Horizon Corporation was a collection of geniuses, wasn't it? How *else* had Brightling accumulated so much money?

Popov frowned as he piled his plates back on the tray, then walked off to deposit them on the collection table. This was oddly like the KGB cafeteria at Number 2 Dzerzhinsky Square. Good food and anonymity. Finished, he made his way back to his room, still in the dark as to what the hell had taken place in his life over the past months. Druids? How could people of science be like that? Vegans? How could people of good sense *not* want to eat meat? What was so special about the gray-brown antelopes that lived on the margins of the property? And that man, he was the director of security here, and therefore he was supposedly a man with the highest personal trust. A fucking vegetarian in a land that produced beef in quantities the rest of the world could only dream about.

What the hell was that shot for? Popov wondered again as he flipped on the television. "Booster"? Against what? Why had he been examined at all? The deeper he went, the more information he found, the more perplexing the puzzle became.

But whatever this was all about, it had to be commensurate in scope to the investment Brightling and his company had made—and that was vast! And whatever it was about, it didn't shrink at causing the death of people unknown and clearly unimportant to John Brightling. But what possible pattern did all of that fit?

Popov admitted yet again that he still didn't have a clue. Had he reported on this adventure to his KGB superiors, they would have thought him slightly mad, but they would have ordered him to pursue the case further until he had some sort of conclusion to present, and because he was KGB-trained, he could no more stop pursuing the facts to their conclusion than he could stop breathing.

■ ■ ■

AT least the first-class seats were comfortable, Chavez told himself. The flight would be a long one—about as long as a flight could be, since the destination was 10,500 miles away, and the whole planet was only 24,000 miles around. British Airways Flight 9 would be leaving at 10:15 P.M., go eleven and three quarters hours to Bangkok, lay over for an hour and a half, then another eight hours and fifty minutes to Sydney, by which time, Ding thought, he'd be about ready to pull out his pistol and shoot the flight crew. All this, plus not having his wife and son handy, just because the fucking Aussies wanted him to hold their hand during the track meet. He'd arrive at 5:20 A.M. *two* days from now due to the vagaries of the equator and the International Dateline, with his body clock probably more scrambled than the eggs he had for breakfast. But there was nothing he could do about it, and at least BA had stopped smoking on their flights—those people who did smoke would probably be going totally nuts, but that wasn't his problem. He had four books and six magazines to pass the time, plus a private TV screen for movies, and decided that he had to make the best of it. The flight attendants closed the doors, the engines started, and the captain came on the intercom to welcome them aboard their home for the next day—or two days, depending on how you looked at it.

CHAPTER 32

BLOOD WORK

"WAS THAT A GOOD IDEA?" BRIGHTLING ASKED.

"I think so. Kirk was on the travel list anyway. We can have his coworkers tell anybody who asks that he was called out of town on company business," Henriksen said.

"What if the FBI agents go back to see him?"

"Then he's out of town, and they'll just have to wait," Henriksen answered. "Investigations like this last for months, but there won't be months, will there?"

Brightling nodded. "I suppose. How's Dmitriy doing out there?"

"Dave Dawson says he's doing okay, asking a lot of touristy questions, but that's all. He had his physical from Johnny Killgore, and he's gotten his 'B' shot."

"I hope he likes being alive. From what he said, he might turn out to be our kind of people, you know?"

"I'm not so sure about that, but he doesn't know squat, and by the time he finds out, it'll be too late anyway. Wil Gearing is in place, and he says everything's going according to plan, John. Three more weeks, and then it'll all be under way. So, it's time to start moving our people to Kansas."

"Too bad. The longevity project's really looking good at the moment."

"Oh?"

"Well, it's pretty hard to predict breakthroughs, but the research threads all look very interesting at the moment, Bill."

"So we might have lived forever? . . ." Henriksen asked, with a wry smile. For all the time he'd been associated with Brightling and Horizon Corporation, he had trouble believing such predictions. The company had caused some genuine medical miracles, but this was just too much to credit.

"I can think of worse things to happen. I'm going to make sure that whole team gets the 'B' shot," Brightling said.

"Well, take the whole team out there and put 'em to work in Kansas, for crying out loud," Bill suggested. "What about the rest of the company?"

Brightling didn't like that question, didn't like the fact that more than half of the Horizon employees would be treated like the rest of humanity—left to die at best, or to be murdered by the "A" vaccine at worst. John Brightling, M.D., Ph.D., had some lingering morality, part of which was loyalty to the people who worked for him—which was why Dmitriy Popov was in Kansas with the "B"-class antibodies in his system. So, even the Big Boss wasn't entirely comfortable with what he was doing, Henriksen saw. Well, that was conscience for you. Shakespeare had written about the phenomenon.

"That's already decided," Brightling said, after a second's discomfort. He'd be saving those who were part of the Project, and those whose scientific knowledge would be useful in the future. Accountants, lawyers, and secretaries, by and large, would not be saved. That he'd be saving about five thousand people—as many as the Kansas and Brazil facilities could hold—was quite a stretch, especially considering that only a small fraction of those people knew what the Project was all about. Had he been a Marxist, Brightling would have thought or even said aloud that the world needed an intellectual elite to make it into the New World, but he didn't really think in those terms. He truly did believe that he was saving the planet, and though the cost of doing so was murderously high, it was a goal worth pursuing, though part of him hoped that he'd be able to live through the transition period without taking his own life from the guilt factor that was sure to assault him.

It was easier for Henriksen. What people were doing to the world was a crime. Those who did it, supported it, or did nothing to stop it, were criminals. His job was to make them stop. It was the only way. And at the end of it the innocent would be safe, as would Nature. In any case, the men and the instruments of the Project were now in place. Wil Gearing was confident that he could accomplish his mission, so skillfully had Global Security insinuated itself into the security plan for the Sydney Olympics, with the help of Popov and his ginned-up operations in Europe. So, the Project would go forward, and that was that, and a year from now the planet would be transformed. Henriksen's only concern was how many people would survive the plague. The scientific members of the Project had discussed it to endless length. Most would die from starvation or other causes, and few would have the capacity to organize themselves enough to determine why the Project members had also survived and then take action against them. Most natural survivors would be invited into the protection of the elect, and the smart ones would accept that protection. The others—who cared? Henriksen had also set up the security systems at the Kansas facility. There were heavy weapons there, enough to handle rioting farmers with Shiva symptoms, he was sure.

The most likely result of the plague would be a rapid breakdown of society. Even the military would rapidly come apart, but the Kansas facility was a good distance from the nearest military base, and the soldiers based at Fort Riley would be sent to the cities first to maintain order until they, too, came down with symptoms. Then they'd be treated by the military doctors—for what little good it would do—and by the time unit cohesion broke down, it would be far too late for even the soldiers to take any organized action. So, it would be a twitchy time, but one that would pass rapidly, and so long as the Project people in Kansas kept quiet, they ought not to suffer organized attack. Hell, all they had to do was to let the world believe that people were dying there, too, maybe dig a few graves and toss bags into them for the cameras—better yet, burn them in the open—and they could frighten people away from another focal center of the plague. No, they'd considered this one for years. The Project would succeed. It had to. Who else would save the planet?

THE cafeteria theme today was Italian, and Popov was pleased to see that the cooks here were not "vegans." The lasagna had meat in it. Coming out with his tray and glass of Chianti, he spotted Dr. Killgore eating alone and decided to walk over that way.

"Ah, hello, Mr. Popov."

"Good day, doctor. How did my blood work turn out?"

"Fine. Your cholesterol is slightly elevated, and the HDL/LDL ratio is a little off, but I wouldn't get very upset about it. A little exercise should fix it nicely. Your PSA is fine—"

"What's that?"

"Prostate-Specific Antibody, a check for prostate cancer. All men should check that out when they turn fifty or so. Yours is fine. I should have told you yesterday, but I got piled up. Sorry about that—but there was nothing important to tell you, and that's a case where no news really is good news, Mr. Popov."

"My name is Dmitriy," the Russian said, extending his hand.

"John," the doctor replied, taking it. "Ivan to you, I guess."

"And I see you are not a vegan," Dmitriy Arkadeyevich observed, gesturing to Killgore's food.

"Oh? What? Me? No, Dmitriy, I'm not one of those. *Homo sapiens* is an omnivore. Our teeth are not those of vegetarians. The enamel isn't thick enough. That's sort of a political movement, the vegans. Some of them won't even wear leather shoes because leather's an animal product." Killgore ate half a meatball to show what he thought of that. "I even like hunting."

"Oh? Where does one do that here?"

"Not on the Project grounds. We have rules about that, but in due course I'll be able to hunt deer, elk, buffalo, birds, everything I want," Killgore said, looking out the huge windows.

"Buffalo? I thought they were extinct," Popov said, remembering something he'd heard or read long before.

"Not really. They came close a hundred years ago, but enough survived to thrive at Yellowstone National Park and in private collections. Some people even breed them with domestic cattle, and the meat's pretty good. It's called buffalo. You can buy it in some stores around here."

"A buffalo can breed with a cow?" Popov asked.

"Sure. The animals are very close, genetically speaking, and cross-breeding is actually pretty easy. The hard part," Killgore explained with a grin, "is that a domestic bull is intimidated by a bison cow, and has trouble performing his duty, as it were. They fix that by raising them together from infancy, so the bull is used to them by the time he's big enough to do the deed."

"What about horses? I would have expected horses in a place like this."

"Oh, we have them, mainly quarter horses and some Appaloosas. The barn is down in the southwest part of the property. You ride, Dmitriy?"

"No, but I have seen many Western movies. When Dawson drove me around, I expected to see cowboys herding cattle carrying Colt pistols on their belts."

Killgore had a good chuckle at that. "I guess you're a city boy. Well, so was I once, but I've come to love it out here, especially on horseback. Like to go for a ride?"

"I've never sat on a horse," Popov admitted, intrigued by the invitation. This doctor was an open man, and perhaps a trusting one. He could get information from this man, Dmitriy Arkadeyevich thought.

"Well, we have a nice gentle quarter horse mare—Buttermilk, would you believe?" Killgore paused. "Damn, it's nice to be out here."

"You are a recent arrival?"

"Just last week. I used to be in the Binghamton lab, northwest of New York City," he explained.

"What sort of work do you do?"

"I'm a physician—epidemiologist, as a matter of fact. I'm supposed to be an expert on how diseases riffle through populations. But I do a lot of clinical stuff, too, and so I'm one of the designated family practitioners. Like a GP in the old days. I know a little bit about everything, but I'm not really an expert in any field—except epidemiology, and that's more like being an accountant than a doc, really."

"I have a sister who is a physician," Popov tried.

"Oh? Where?"

"In Moscow. She's a pediatrician. She graduated Moscow State University in the 1970s. Her name is Maria Arkadeyevna. I am Dmitriy Arkadeyevich. Our father was Arkady, you see."

"Was he a doctor, too?" Killgore asked.

Popov shook his head. "No, he was like me, a spy—an intelligence officer for State Security." Popov dropped that in to see how Killgore would react. He figured he didn't need to keep it a secret out here—and it could be useful. You give something to get something . . .

"You were KGB? No shit?" the doctor asked, impressed.

"Yes, I was, but with the changes in my country, KGB diminished in size, and I was, how you say, laid off?"

"What did you do with KGB? Can you say?"

It was as though he'd just admitted to being a sports star, Popov saw. "I was an intelligence officer. I gathered information, and I was a conduit for people in whom KGB had interest."

"What does that mean?"

"Oh, I met with certain people and groups to discuss . . . matters of mutual interest," he replied coyly.

"Like who?"

"I am not supposed to say. Your Dr. Brightling knows. That is why he hired me, in fact."

"But you're part of the Project now, right?"

"I do not know what that means—John sent me here, but he didn't say why."

"Oh, I see. Well, you'll be here for a while, Dmitriy." That had been obvious from the fax the physician had received from New York. This Popov guy *was* now part of the Project, whether he wanted to be or not. He'd had his "B" shot, after all.

The Russian tried to recover control of the conversation: "I've heard that before, project—what project? What exactly are you doing here?"

For the first time, Killgore looked uncomfortable. "Well, John will brief you in on that when he gets out here, Dmitriy. So, how was dinner?"

"The food is good, for institutional food," Popov replied, wondering what mine he'd just stepped on. He'd been close to something important. His instincts told him that very clearly indeed. He'd asked a direct question of someone who supposed that he'd already known the answer, and his lack of specific knowledge had surprised Killgore.

"Yeah, we have some good people here in food services." Killgore finished his bread. "So, want to take a ride in the country?"

"Yes, I'd like that very much."

"Meet me here tomorrow morning, say about seven, and I'll show you around the right way." Killgore walked away, wondering what the Russian was here for. Well, if John Brightling had personally recruited him, he had to be important to the Project—but if that were true, how the hell could he not know what the Project was all about? Should he ask someone? But if so, whom?

THEY knocked on the door, but there was no answer. Sullivan and Chatham waited a few minutes—they might have caught the guy on the toilet or in the shower—but there was no response. They took the elevator downstairs, found the doorman, and identified themselves.

"Any idea where Mr. Maclean is?"

"He left earlier today, carrying a few bags like he was going somewhere, but I don't know where."

"Cab to the airport?" Chatham asked.

The doorman shook his head. "No, a car came for him and headed off west." He pointed that way, in case they didn't know where west was.

"Did he do anything about his mail?"

Another headshake: "No."

"Okay, thanks," Sullivan said, heading off to where their Bureau car was parked. "Business trip? Vacation?"

"We can call his office tomorrow to find out. It's not like he's a real suspect yet, is it, Tom?"

"I suppose not," Sullivan responded. "Let's head off to the bar and try the photos on some more people."

"Right," Chatham agreed reluctantly. This case was taking away his TV time at home, which was bad enough. It was also going nowhere at the moment, which was worse.

CLARK awoke to the noise and had to think for a second or so to remember that Patsy had moved in with them so as not to be alone, and to have her mother's help with JC, as they were calling him. This time he decided to get up, too, despite the early hour. Sandy was already up, her maternal instincts ignited by the sound of a crying baby. John arrived in time to see his wife hand his newly re-diapered grandson to his daughter, who sat somewhat bleary-eyed in a rocking chair purchased for the purpose, her nightie open and exposing her breast. John turned away in mild embarrassment and looked instead at his similarly nightie-clad wife, who smiled benignly at the picture before her.

He was a cute little guy, Clark thought. He peeked back. JC's mouth was locked onto the offered nipple and started sucking—maybe the only instinct human children were born with, the mother-child bond that men simply could not replicate at this stage in a child's life. What a precious thing life was. Just days before, John Conor Chavez had been a fetus, a *thing* living inside his mother—and whether or not he'd been a living thing depended on what one thought of abortion, and that, to John Clark, was a matter of some controversy. He had killed in his life, not frequently, but not as seldom as he would have preferred, either. He told himself at such times that the people whose lives he took had deserved their fates, either because of actions or their associations. He'd also been largely an instrument of his country at those times, and hence able to lay off whatever guilt he might have felt on a larger identity. But now, seeing JC, he had to remind himself that every life he'd taken had started like this one had—helpless, totally dependent on the care of his mother, later growing into a manhood determined both by his own actions and the influence of others, and only then becoming a force for good or evil. How did *that* happen? What twisted a person to evil? Choice? Destiny? Luck, good or bad? What had twisted his own life to the good—and was his life a servant of the good? Just one more of the damned-fool things that entered your head at oh-dark-thirty. Well, he told himself, he was sure that he'd never hurt a baby during that life, however violent parts of it had been. And he never would. No, he'd only harmed people who had harmed others first, or threatened to do so, and who had to be stopped from doing so because the others he protected, either immediately or distantly, had rights as well, and he protected them and those from harm, and that settled the thoughts for the moment.

He took a step toward the pair, reached down to touch the little feet, and got no reaction, because JC had his priorities lined up properly at the moment. Food. And the antibodies that came with breast milk to keep him healthy. In time, his eyes would recognize faces and his little face would smile, and he'd learn to sit up, then crawl, then walk, and finally speak, and so begin to join the world of men. Ding would be a good father and a good model for his grandson to emulate, Clark was sure, especially with Patsy there to be a check on his father's adverse tendencies. Clark smiled and walked back to bed, trying to remember exactly where Chavez the Elder was at the moment, and leaving the women's work to the women of the house.

IT was hours later when the dawn again awoke Popov in his motel-like room. He'd fallen quickly into a routine, first turning on his coffeemaker, then going into the bathroom to shower and shave, then coming out ten minutes later to switch on CNN. The lead story was about the Olympics. The world had become so dull. He remembered his first field assignment to London, as in his hotel he'd watched CNN comment and report on East-West differences, the movement of armies and the growth of suspicion between the political groups that had defined the world of his youth. He especially remembered the strategic issues so often misreported by journalists, both print and electronic: MIRVs and missiles, and throw weight, and ABM systems that had supposedly threatened to upset the balance of power. All things of the past now, Popov told himself. For him, it was as though a mountain range had disappeared. The shape of the world had changed virtually overnight, the things he'd believed to be immutable had indeed mutated into something he'd never believed possible. The global war he'd feared, along with his agency and his nation, was now no more likely than a life-ending meteor from the heavens.

It was time to learn more. Popov dressed and headed down to the cafeteria, where he found Dr. Killgore eating breakfast, just as promised.

"Good morning, John," the Russian said, taking his seat across the table from the epidemiologist.

"Morning, Dmitriy. Ready for your ride?"

"Yes, I think I am. You said the horse was gentle?"

"That's why they call her Buttermilk, eight-year-old quarter horse mare. She won't hurt you."

"Quarter horse? What does that mean?"

"It means they only race a quarter mile, but, you know, one of the richest horse races in the world is for that distance, down in Texas. I forget what they call it, but the purse is huge. Well, one more institution we won't be seeing much more of," Killgore went on, buttering his toast.

"Excuse me?" Popov asked.

"Hmph? Oh, nothing important, Dmitriy." And it wasn't. The horses would survive for the most part, returning to the wild to see if they could make it after centuries of being adapted to human care. He supposed their instincts, genetically encoded in their DNA, would save most of them. And someday Project members and/or their progeny would capture them, break them, and ride them on their way to enjoy Nature and Her ways. The working horses, quarters and Appaloosas, should do well. Thoroughbreds he was less sure of, super-adapted as they were to do one thing—run in a circle as fast as their physiology would allow—and little else. Well, that was their misfortune, and Darwin's laws were harsh, though also fair in their way. Killgore finished his breakfast and stood. "Ready?"

"Yes, John." Popov followed him to the doors. Outside, Killgore had his own Hummer, which he drove to the southwest in the clear, bright morning. Ten minutes later they were at the horse barns. He took a saddle from the tack room and walked down to a stall whose door had BUTTERMILK engraved on the pine. He opened it and walked in, quickly saddled the horse, and handed Popov the reins.

"Just walk her outside. She won't bite or kick or anything. She's very docile, Dmitriy."

"If you say so, John," the Russian observed dubiously. He was wearing sneakers rather than boots, and wondered if that was important or not. The horse looked at him with her huge brown eyes, revealing nothing as to what, if anything, she thought of this new human who was leading her outside. Dmitriy walked to the barn's large door, and the horse followed quietly into the clear morning air. A few minutes later, Killgore appeared, astride his horse, a gelding, so it appeared.

"You know how to get on?" the physician asked.

Popov figured he'd seen enough Western movies. He stuck his left foot into the stirrups and climbed up, swinging his right leg over and finding the opposite stirrup.

"Good. Now just hold the reins like this and click your tongue, like this." Killgore demonstrated. Popov did the same, and the horse, dumb as she appeared to be, started walking forward. Some of this must be instinctive on his part, the Russian thought. He was doing things—apparently the right things—almost without instruction. Wasn't that remarkable?

"There you go, Dmitriy," the doctor said approvingly. "This is how it's supposed to be, man. A pretty morning, a horse 'tween your legs, and lots of country to cover."

"But no pistol." Popov observed with a chuckle.

Killgore did the same. "Well, no Indians or rustlers here to kill, pal. Come on." Killgore's legs thumped in on his mount, making him move a little faster, and Buttermilk did the same. Popov got his body into a rhythm similar to that of Buttermilk's and kept pace with him.

It was magnificent, Dmitriy Arkadeyevich thought, and now he understood the ethos of all those bad movies he'd seen. There *was* something fundamental and manly about this, though he lacked a proper hat as well as a six-gun. He reached into his pocket and took out his sunglasses, looked around at the rolling land and somehow felt himself to be a part of it all.

"John, I must thank you. I have never done this before. It is wonderful," he said sincerely.

"It's Nature, man. It's the way things were always supposed to be. Come on, Mystic," he said to his mount, speeding up a little more, looking back to see that Popov could handle the increased pace.

It wasn't easy to synchronize his body movements in pace with the horse, but gradually Popov managed it, and soon pulled up alongside.

"So, this is how Americans settled the West?"

Killgore nodded. "Yep. Once this was covered with buffalo, three or four great herds, as far as the eye could see . . .

"Hunters did it, did it all in a period of about ten years, using single-shot Sharps buffalo guns mainly. They killed them for the hides to make blankets and stuff, for the meat—sometimes they killed 'em just for the tongues. Slaughtered 'em like Hitler did with the Jews." Killgore shook his head. "One of the greatest crimes America ever committed, Dmitriy, just killed 'em just 'cause they were in the way. But they'll be coming back," he added, wondering how long it would take. Fifty years—he'd have a fair chance of seeing it then. Maybe a hundred years? They'd be letting the wolves and barren-grounds grizzly come back, too, but predators would come back slower. They didn't breed as rapidly as their prey animals. He wanted to see the prairie again as it had once been. So did many other Project members, and some of them wanted to live in tepees, like the Indians had done. But that, he thought, was a little bit extreme—political ideas taking the place of common sense.

"Hey, John!" a voice called from a few hundred yards behind. Both men turned to see a figure galloping up to them. In a minute or so, he was recognizable.

"Kirk! When did you get out here?"

"Flew in last night," Maclean answered. He stopped his horse and shook hands with Killgore. "What about you?"

"Last week, with the Binghamton crew. We closed that operation down and figured it was time to pull up stakes."

"All of them?" Maclean asked in a way that got Popov's attention. All of who?

"Yep." Killgore nodded soberly.

"Schedule work out?" Maclean asked next, dismissing whatever it was that had upset him before.

"Almost perfectly on the projections. We, uh, helped the last ones along."

"Oh." Maclean looked down for a second, feeling bad, briefly, for the women he'd recruited. But only briefly. "So it's moving forward?"

"Yes, it is, Kirk. The Olympics start day after tomorrow, and then . . ."

"Yeah. Then it starts for real."

"Hello," Popov said, after a second. It was as though Killgore had forgotten he was there.

"Oh, sorry, Dmitriy. Kirk Maclean, this is Dmitriy Popov. John sent him out to us a couple days ago."

"Howdy, Dmitriy." Handshakes were exchanged. "Russian?" Maclean asked.

"Yes." A nod. "I work directly for Dr. Brightling. And you?"

"I'm a small part of the Project," Maclean admitted.

"Kirk's a biochemist and environmental engineer," Killgore explained. "Also so good-looking that we had him do another little thing for us," he teased. "But that's over now. So, what broke you loose so early, Kirk?"

"Remember Mary Bannister?"

"Yeah, what about her?"

"The FBI asked me if I knew her. I kicked it around with Henriksen, and he decided to send me out a little early. I take it she's . . ."

Killgore nodded matter-of-factly. "Yeah, last week."

"So 'A' works?"

"Yes, it does. And so does 'B.' "

"That's good. I got my 'B' shot already."

Popov thought back to his injection at Killgore's hands. There had been a capital B on the vial label, hadn't there? And what was this about the FBI? These two were talking freely, but it was like a foreign language—no, it was the speech of insiders, using internal words and phrases as engineers and physicians did, well, as intelligence officers did as well. It was part of Popov's fieldcraft to remember whatever was said in front of him, however distant from his understanding, and he took it all in, despite his befuddled expression.

Killgore led his horse off again. "First time out, Kirk?"

"First time on a horse in months. I had a deal with a guy in New York City, but I never really had time to do it enough. My legs and ass are gonna be sore tomorrow, John." The bio-engineer laughed.

"Yeah, but it's a good kind of sore." Killgore laughed as well. He'd had a horse back in Binghamton, and he hoped that the family that kept it for him would let him out when the time came, so that Stormy would be able to feed himself . . . but then Stormy was a gelding, and therefore biologically irrelevant to the entire world except as a consumer of grass. Too bad, the physician thought. He'd been a fine riding horse.

Maclean stood in his stirrups, looking around. He could turn and look back at the Project buildings, but before him, and to left and right, little more than rolling prairie. Someday they'd have to burn down all the houses and farm buildings. They just cluttered the view.

"Look out, John," he said, seeing some danger forward and pointing at the holes.

"What is this?" Popov asked.

"Prairie dogs," Killgore said, letting his horse slow to a slow walk. "Wild rodents, they dig holes and make underground cities, called prairie-dog towns. If a horse steps into one, well, it's bad for the horse. But if they walk slow, they can avoid the holes."

"Rodents? Why don't you deal with them? Shoot them, poison them? If they can hurt a horse, then—"

"Dmitriy, they're part of Nature, okay? They *belong* here, even more than we do," Maclean explained.

"But a horse is—" *Expensive,* he thought, as the doctor cut him off.

"Not part of Nature, not really," Killgore went on. "I love 'em, too, but strictly speaking, they don't belong out here either."

"The hawks and other raptors will come back and control the prairie dogs," Maclean said. "No chicken farmers will be hurting them anymore. Man, I love watching them work."

"You bet. They're nature's own smart bomb," Killgore agreed. "That was the real sport of kings, training a hawk to hunt off your fist for you. I might do some of that myself in a few years. I always liked the gyrfalcon."

"The all-white one. Yeah, noble bird, that one," Maclean observed.

They think this area will be greatly changed in a few years, Popov thought. *But* what *could make that happen?*

"So, tell me," the Russian asked. "How will this all look in five years?"

"Much better," Killgore said. "Some buffalo will be back. We might even have to keep them away from our wheat."

"Herd 'em with the Hummers?" Maclean wondered.

"Or helicopters, maybe," the physician speculated. "We'll have a few of those to measure the populations. Mark Holtz is talking about going to Yellowstone and capturing a few, then trucking them down here to help jump-start the herd. You know Mark?"

Maclean shook his head. "No, never met him."

"He's a big-picture thinker on the ecological side, but he's not into interfering with Nature. Just helping Her along some."

"What are we going to do about the dogs?" Kirk asked, meaning domestic pets suddenly released into nature, where they'd become feral, killers of game.

"We'll just have to see," Killgore said. "Most won't be big enough to hurt mature animals, and a lot will be neutered, so they won't breed. Maybe we'll have to shoot some. Ought not to be too hard."

"Some won't like that. You know the score—we're not supposed to do anything but watch. I don't buy that. If we've screwed up the ecosystem, we ought to be able to fix the parts we broke, some of them anyway."

"I agree. We'll have to vote on that, though. Hell, I want to hunt, and they're going to have to vote on *that,* too," Killgore announced with a distasteful grimace.

"No shit? What about Jim Bridger? Except for trapping beaver, what did he do that was so damned wrong?"

"Vegans, they're extremists, Kirk. Their way or the highway, y'know?"

"Oh, fuck 'em. Tell 'em we're not designed to be herbivores, for Christ's sake. That's just pure science." The prairie-dog town was a small one, they saw, as they passed the last of the dirt bull's-eye'd holes.

"And what will your neighbors think of all this?" Popov asked, with a lighthearted smile. What the hell *were* these people talking about?

"What neighbors?" Killgore asked.

What *neighbors?* And it wasn't that which bothered Popov. It was that the reply was rhetorical in nature. But then the doctor changed the subject. "Sure is a nice morning for a ride."

What neighbors? Popov thought again. They could see the roofs of farmhouses and buildings not ten kilometers away, well lit by the morning sun. *What did they mean,* what *neighbors?* They spoke of a radiant future with wild animals everywhere, but not of people. Did they plan to purchase all the nearby farms? Even Horizon Corporation didn't have that much money, did it? This was a settled, civilized area. The farms nearby were large prosperous ones owned by people of comfortable private means. Where would they go? Why would they leave? And yet again, the question leaped into Popov's mind.

What is this all about?

CHAPTER 33

THE GAMES BEGIN

CHAVEZ DID HIS BEST NOT TO STUMBLE OFF THE aircraft, somewhat amazed that the cabin crew looked so chipper. Well, they had practice, and maybe they'd adapted to jet lag better than he ever had. Like every other civilian he saw, he smacked his lips to deal with the sour taste and squinted his eyes and headed for the door with the eagerness of a man being released from a maximum-security prison. Maybe traveling great distances by ship wasn't so bad after all.

"Major Chavez?" a voice asked in an Australian accent.

"Yeah?" Chavez managed to say, looking at the guy in civilian clothes.

"G'day, I'm *Lef*tenant Colonel Frank Wilkerson, Australian Special Air Service." He held out his hand.

"Howdy." Chavez managed to grab the hand and shake it. "These are my men, Sergeants Johnston, Pierce, Tomlinson, and Special Agent Tim Noonan of the FBI—he's our technical support." More handshakes were exchanged all around.

"Welcome to Australia, gentlemen. Follow me, if you please." The colonel waved for them to follow.

It took fifteen minutes to collect all the gear. That included a half dozen large mil-spec plastic containers that were loaded into a minibus. Ten minutes later, they were off the airport grounds and heading for Motorway 64 for the trip into Sydney.

"So, how was the flight?" Colonel Wilkerson asked, turning in his front seat to look at them.

"Long," Chavez said, looking around. The sun was rising—it was just short of 6:00 A.M.—while the arriving Rainbow troopers were all wondering if it was actually supposed to be setting according to their body clocks. They all hoped a shower and some coffee would help.

"Pig of a flight, all the way out from London," the colonel sympathized.

"That it is," Chavez agreed for his men.

"When do the games start?" Mike Pierce asked.

"Tomorrow," Wilkerson replied. "We've got most of the athletes settled into their quarters, and our security teams are fully manned and trained up. We expect no difficulties at all. The intelligence threat board is quite blank. The people we have watching the airport report nothing, and we have photos and descriptions of all known international terrorists. Not as many as there used to be, largely thanks to your group," the SAS colonel added, with a friendly, professional smile.

"Yeah, well, we try to do our part, Colonel," George Tomlinson observed, while rubbing his face.

"The chaps who attacked you directly, they were IRA, as the media said?"

"Yeah," Chavez answered. "Splinter group. But they were well briefed. Somebody gave them primo intelligence information. They had their civilian targets identified by name and occupation—that included my wife and mother-in-law, and—"

"I hadn't heard *that,*" the Aussie said, with wide-open eyes.

"Well, it wasn't fun. And we lost two people killed, and four wounded, including Peter Covington. He's my counterpart, commanding Team-1," Ding explained. "Like I said, wasn't fun. Tim here turned out to have saved the day," he went on, pointing at Noonan.

"How so?" Wilkerson asked the FBI agent, who looked slightly embarrassed.

"I have a system for shutting down cellular phone communications. Turns out the bad guys were using them to coordinate their movements," the FBI agent explained. "We denied them that ability, and it interfered with their plans. Then Ding and the rest of the guys came in and messed them up some more. We were very, very lucky, Colonel."

"So, you're FBI. You know Gus Werner, I expect?"

"Oh, yeah. Gus and I go back a ways. He's the new AD for terrorism—new division the Bureau's set up. You've been to Quantico, I suppose."

"Just a few months ago, in fact, exercising with your Hostage Rescue Team and Colonel Byron's Delta group. Good lads, all of them." The driver turned off the interstate-type highway, taking an exit that seemed to head into downtown Sydney. Traffic was light. It was still too early for people to be very active, aside from milkmen and paperboys. The minibus pulled up to an upscale hotel, whose bell staff was awake, even at this ungodly hour.

"We have an arrangement with this one," Wilkerson explained. "The Global Security people are here, too."

"Who?" Ding asked.

"Global Security, they have the consulting contract. Mr. Noonan, you probably know their chief, Bill Henriksen."

"Bill the tree-hugger?" Noonan managed a strangled laugh. "Oh, yeah, I know him."

"Tree-hugger?"

"Colonel, Bill was a senior guy in Hostage Rescue a few years ago. Competent guy, but he's one of those nutty environmentalist types. Hugs trees and bunny rabbits. Worries about the ozone layer, all that crap," Noonan explained.

"I didn't know that about him. We do worry about the ozone down here, you know. One must use sunblock on the beaches and such. Might be serious in a few years, so they say."

"Maybe so," Tim allowed with a yawn. "I'm not a surfer."

The door was pulled open by a hotel employee and the men stumbled out. Colonel Wilkerson must have called ahead, Ding thought a minute later, as they were fast-tracked to their rooms—nice ones—for wake-up showers, followed by big breakfasts with *lots* of coffee. As dreadful as the jet lag was, the best way for them to handle it was to gut their way through the first day, try to get a decent night's sleep, and so synchronize themselves in a single day. At least that was the theory, Ding thought, toweling off in front of the bathroom mirror and seeing that he looked almost as messed up as he felt. Soon after that, wearing casual clothes, he showed up in the hotel coffee shop.

"You know, Colonel, if somebody made a narcotic that worked on jet lag, he'd die richer 'n hell."

"Quite. I've been through it as well, Major."

"Call me Ding. My given name's Domingo, but I go by Ding."

"What's your background?" Wilkerson asked.

"Started off as an infantryman, but then into CIA, and now this. I don't know about this simulated-major stuff. I'm Team-2 commander for Rainbow, and I guess that'll have to do."

"You Rainbow chaps have been busy."

"That's a fact, Colonel," Ding agreed, shaking his head as the waiter came with a pot of coffee. Ding wondered if anyone had the Army type of coffee, the sort with triple the usual amount of caffeine. It would have come in handy right now. That and a nice morning workout might have helped a lot. In addition to the fatigue, his body was rebelling against the full day of confinement on the 747. The damned airplane was big enough for a few laps, but somehow the designers had left out the running track. Then came the slightly guilty feeling for the poor bastards who'd made the hop in tourist. They must really be suffering, Ding was sure. Well, at least it had been quick. A ship would have taken a whole month—of palatial comfort, lots of exercise opportunities, and good food. Life was full of trade-offs, wasn't it?

"You were in on the Worldpark job?"

"Yeah." Ding nodded. "My team did the assault on the castle. I was a hot hundred feet away when that bastard killed the little girl. That really wasn't fun, Colonel."

"Frank."

"Thanks. Yeah, Frank, that was pretty damned bad. But we got that bastard—which is to say, Homer Johnston did. He's one of my long rifles."

"From the TV coverage we saw, that wasn't a particularly good shot."

"Homer wanted to make a little statement," Chavez explained, with a raised eyebrow. "He won't be doing it again."

Wilkerson figured that one out instantly. "Oh, yes, quite. Any children, Ding?"

"Just became a father a few days ago. A son."

"Congratulations. We'll have to have a beer for that, later today perhaps."

"Frank, one beer and you might just have to carry my ass back here." Ding yawned, and felt embarrassment at the state of his body right then and there. "Anyway, why did you want us down here? Everybody says you guys are pretty good."

"Never hurts to get a second opinion, Ding. My lads *are* well trained, but we haven't had all that much practical experience. And we need some new hardware. Those new radios that E-Systems make, and that Global Security got for us, they're bloody marvelous. What other magic tools might you have?"

"Noonan's got something that'll knock your eyes out, Frank. I hardly believe it myself, but I don't think it'll be worth a damn down here. Too many people around. But you'll find it interesting. I promise you that."

"What's that?"

"Tim calls it the 'Tricorder'—you know the gadget Mr. Spock used all the time in *Star Trek*. It finds people like radar finds airplanes."

"How's it do that?"

"He'll tell you. Something about the electrical field around a human heart."

"I've never heard of that."

"It's new," Chavez explained. "Little company in the States called DKL, I think. That little fucker is magic, the way it works. Little Willie at Fort Bragg's in love with it."

"Colonel Byron?"

"He's the man. You said you've worked with him recently?"

"Oh, yes, splendid chap."

Chavez had a chuckle at that one. "He doesn't like Rainbow all that much. We stole some of his best people, you see."

"And gave them practical work to do."

"True," Chavez agreed, sipping his coffee. The rest of the team appeared then, dressed as their commander was, in semimilitary casual clothes. Sauntering into the coffee shop, they spotted their boss and came over.

IT was about four in the afternoon in Kansas. The morning ride had left Popov sore in unusual places. His hips especially protested the way they'd been used earlier in the day, his upper legs held out at an unusual angle. But it was a pleasant memory for all that.

There was nothing for Popov to do here. He had no assigned work, and by lunch he'd run out of things he could conveniently explore. That left television as a diversion, but TV was not one of his favorite things. A bright man, he was easily bored, and he hated boredom. CNN kept repeating the same stories on the Olympics, and while he'd always enjoyed watching that international competition, it hadn't started yet. So, he wandered the corridors of the hotel, and looked out the huge window-wall at the surrounding countryside. Another ride tomorrow morning, he thought, at least it got him outside into pleasant surroundings. After over an hour's wandering, he headed down to the cafeteria.

"Oh, hello, Dmitriy," Kirk Maclean said, just ahead of him in the line. Maclean wasn't a vegan either, the Russian saw. His plate had a large slice of ham on it. Popov remarked on that.

"Like I said this morning, we're not designed to be vegetarians," Maclean pointed out with a grin.

"How do you know that is true?"

"Teeth mainly," Maclean replied. "Herbivores chew grass and stuff, and there's a lot of dirt and grit in that kind of food, and that wears the teeth down like sandpaper. So they need teeth with very thick enamel so they won't wear out in a few years. The enamel on human teeth is a lot thinner than what you find on a cow. So either we're adapted to washing the dirt off our food first, or we're designed to eat meat for most of our protein intake. I don't think we adapted that fast to running water in the kitchen, y'know?" Kirk asked with a grin. The two men headed off to the same table. "What do you do for John?" he asked after they'd sat down.

"Dr. Brightling, you mean?"

"Yeah, you said you work directly for him."

"I used to be KGB." Might as well try it on him, too.

"Oh, you spy for us, then?" Maclean asked, cutting up his ham slice.

Popov shook his head. "Not exactly. I established contact with people in whom Dr. Brightling had interest and asked them to perform certain functions which he wished them to do."

"Oh? For what?" Maclean asked.

"I am not sure that I am allowed to say."

"Secret stuff, eh? Well, there's a lot of that here, man. Have you been briefed in on the Project?"

"Not exactly. Perhaps I am part of it, but I haven't been told exactly what the purpose of all this is. Do you know?"

"Oh, sure. I've been in it almost from the beginning. It's really something, man. It's got some real nasty parts, but," he added with a cold look in his eyes, "you don't make an omelet without breaking some eggs, right?"

Lenin said that, Popov remembered. In the 1920s, when asked about the destructive violence being done in the name of Soviet Revolution. The observation had become famous, especially in KGB, when occasionally someone objected to particularly cruel field operations—like what Popov had done, interfacing with terrorists, who typically acted in the most grossly inhuman manner and . . . recently, under his guidance. But what sort of omelet was this man helping to make?

"We're gonna change the world, Dmitriy," Maclean said.

"How so, Kirk?"

"Wait and see, man. Remember how it was this morning out riding?"

"Yes, it was very pleasant."

"Imagine the whole world like that" was as far as Maclean was willing to go.

"But how would you make that happen . . . where would all the farmers go?" Popov asked, truly puzzled.

"Just think of 'em as eggs, man," Maclean answered, with a smile, and Dmitriy's blood suddenly turned cold, though he didn't understand why. His mind couldn't make the jump, much as he wanted it to do so. It was like being a field officer again, trying to discern enemy intentions on an important field assignment, and knowing some, perhaps much, of the necessary information, but not enough to paint the entire picture in his own mind. But the frightening part was that these Project people spoke of human life as the German fascists had once done. *But they're only Jews.* He looked up at the noise and saw another aircraft landing on the approach road. Behind it in the distance, a number of automobiles were halted off the road/runway, waiting to drive to the building. There were more people in the cafeteria now, he saw, nearly double the number from the previous day. So, Horizon Corporation was bringing its people here. Why? Was this part of the Project? Was it merely the activation of this expensive research facility? The pieces of the puzzle were all before him, Popov knew, but the manner in which they fit was as mysterious as ever.

"Hey, Dmitriy!" Killgore said, as he joined them. "A little sore, maybe?"

"Somewhat," Popov admitted, "but I do not regret it. Could we do it again?"

"Sure. It's part of my morning routine here. Want to join me that way?"

"Yes, thank you, that is very kind."

"Seven A.M., right here, pal," Killgore responded with a smile. "You, too, Kirk?"

"You bet. Tomorrow I have to drive out and get some new boots. Is there a good store around here for outdoors stuff?"

"Half an hour away, U.S. Cavalry outlet. You go east two exits on the interstate," Dr. Killgore advised.

"Great. I want to get 'em before all the new arrivals strip the stores of the good outdoors stuff."

"Makes sense," Killgore thought, then turned. "So, Dmitriy, what's it like being a spy?"

"It is often very frustrating work," Popov replied truthfully.

"WOW, this is some facility," Ding observed. The stadium was huge, easily large enough to seat a hundred thousand people. But it would be hot here, damned hot, like being inside a huge concrete wok. Well, there were plenty of concessions in the concourses, and surely there'd be people circulating with Cokes and other cold drinks. And just off the stadium grounds were all manner of pubs for those who preferred beer. The lush grass floor of the stadium bowl was nearly empty at the moment, with just a few groundskeepers manicuring a few parts. Most of the track-and-field events would be here. The oval Tartan track was marked for the various distance and hurdle races, and there were the pits for the jumping events. A monster scoreboard and Jumbotron sat on the far end so that people could see instant replays of the important events, and Ding felt himself getting a little excited. He'd never been present for an

Olympic competition, and he was himself enough of an athlete to appreciate the degree of dedication and skill that went into this sort of thing. The crazy part was that as good as his own people were, they were not the equal of the athletes—most of them little kids, to Ding's way of thinking—who'd be marching in here tomorrow. Even his shooters probably wouldn't win the pistol or rifle events. His men were generalists, trained to do many things, and the Olympic athletes were the ultimate specialists, trained to do a single thing supremely well. It had about as much relevance to life in the real world as a professional baseball game, but it would be a beautiful thing to watch for all that.

"Yes, we've spent a good deal of money to make it so," Frank Wilkerson agreed.

"Where do you keep your reaction force?" Chavez asked. His host gestured and turned.

"This way."

"Hey, that feels good," Chavez said, entering the fine water fog.

"Yes, it does. It reduces the apparent temperature about fifteen degrees. I expect a lot of people will be coming here during the competition to cool down, and as you see, we have televisions to allow them to keep current on the goings on."

"That'll come in handy, Frank. What about the athletes?"

"We have a similar arrangement in their access tunnels, and also the main tunnel they will use to march in, but out on the field, they'll just have to sweat."

"God help the marathon runners," Chavez said.

"Quite," Wilkerson agreed. "We will have medical people out there at various points. The extended weather forecast is for clear and hot weather, I'm afraid. But we have ample first-aid kiosks spotted about the various stadia. The velodrome will be another place where it's sorely needed."

"Gatorade," Chavez observed after a second.

"What?"

"It's a sports drink, water and lots of electrolytes to keep you from getting heatstroke."

"Ah, yes, we have something similar here. Salt tablets as well. Buckets of the things."

A few minutes later, they were in the security area. Chavez saw the Australian SAS troops lounging in air-conditioned comfort, their own TVs handy so that they could watch the games—and other sets to keep an eye on choke points. Wilkerson handled the introductions, after which most of the troops came over for a handshake and a "G'day," all delivered with the open friendliness that all Aussies seemed to have. His sergeants started chatting with the

Aussie ones, and respect was soon flowing back and forth. The trained men saw themselves in the others, and their international fraternity was an elite one.

THE facility was filling rapidly. He'd been alone on the fourth floor the first day, Popov reflected, but not now. At least six of the nearby rooms were occupied, and looking outside he could see that the parking lot was filling up with private cars that had been driven in that day. He figured it was a two- or three-day drive from New York, and so the order to bring people out had been given recently—but where were the moving vans? Did the people intend to live here indefinitely? The hotel building was comfortable—for a hotel, but that was not the same as comfort in a place of permanent residence. Those people with small children might quickly go mad with their little ones in such close proximity all the time. He saw a young couple talking with another, and caught part of the conversation as he walked past. They were evidently excited about the wild game they'd seen driving in. Yes, deer and such animals were pretty, Popov thought in mute agreement, but hardly worth so animated a conversation on the subject. Weren't these trained scientists who worked for Horizon Corporation? They spoke like Young Pioneers out of Moscow for the first time, goggling at the wonders of a state farm. Better to see the grand opera house in Vienna or Paris, the former KGB officer thought, as he entered his room. But then he had another thought. These people were all lovers of nature. Perhaps he would examine their interests himself. Weren't there videotapes in his room? . . . Yes, he found them and slipped one into his VCR, hitting the PLAY button and switching on his TV.

Ah, he saw, the ozone layer, something people in the West seemed remarkably exercised about. Popov thought he would begin to show concern when the Antarctic penguins who lived under the ozone hole started dying of sunburn. But he watched and listened anyway. It turned out that the tape had been produced by some group called Earth First, and the content, he soon saw, was as polemic in content as anything ever produced by the USSR's state-run film companies. These people were indeed very exercised about the subject, calling for the end of various industrial chemicals—and how would air-conditioning work without them? Give up air-conditioning to save penguins from too much ultraviolet radiation? What was this rubbish?

That tape lasted fifty-two minutes by his watch. The next one he selected, produced by the same group, was concerned with dams. It started off by castigating the "environmental criminals" who'd commissioned and built Hoover

Dam on the Colorado River. But that was a *power* dam, wasn't it? Didn't people need electricity? Wasn't the electricity generated by power dams the cleanest there was? Wasn't this very videotape produced in Hollywood using the very electricity that this dam produced? Who were these people—

—and why were their tapes here in his hotel room? Popov wondered. Druids? The word came to him again. Sacrificers of virgins, worshipers of trees—if that, then they'd come to a strange place. There were precious few trees to be seen on the wheat-covered plains of western Kansas.

Druids? Worshipers of nature? He let the tape rewind and checked out some of the periodicals and found one published by this Earth First group.

What sort of name was that? Earth First—ahead of what? Its articles screamed in outrage over various insults to the planet. Well, strip mining was an ugly thing, he had to admit. The planet was supposed to be beautiful and appreciated. He enjoyed the sight of a green forest as much as the next man, and the same was true of the purple rock of treeless mountains. If there were a God, then He was a fine artist, but . . . what was this?

Humankind, the second article said, was a parasitic species on the surface of the planet, destroying rather than nurturing. People had killed off numerous species of animals and plants, and in doing so, people had forfeited their right to be here . . . he read on into the polemic.

This was errant rubbish, Popov thought. Did a gazelle faced with an attacking lion call for the police or a lawyer to plead his right to be alive? Did a salmon swimming upstream to spawn protest against the jaws of the bear that plucked it from the water and then stripped it apart to feed its own needs? Was a cow the equal of a man? In whose eyes?

It had been a matter of almost religious faith in the Soviet Union that as formidable and as rich as Americans were, they were mad, cultureless, unpredictable people. They were greedy, they stole wealth from others, and they exploited such people for their own selfish gain. He'd learned the falsehood of that propaganda on his first field assignment abroad, but he'd also learned that the Western Europeans, as well, thought Americans to be slightly mad—and if this Earth First group were representative of America, then surely they were right. But Britain had people who spray-painted those who wore fur coats. Mink had a right to live, they said. A mink? It was a well-insulated rodent, a tubular rat with a fine coat of fur. This *rodent* had a right to be alive? Under whose law?

That very morning they'd objected to his suggestion to kill the—what was it? Prairie dogs, yet another tubular rat, and one whose holes could break the legs of the horses they rode—but what was it they'd said? They *belonged* there, and the horses and people did not? Why such solicitude for a *rat?* The noble animals, the hawks and bears, the deer, and those strange-looking antelope, they were pretty, but *rats?* He'd had similar talks with Brightling and Henriksen, who also seemed unusually loving of the things that lived and crawled outside. He wondered how they felt about mosquitoes and fire ants.

Was this druidic rubbish the key to his large question? Popov thought about it, and decided that he needed an education, if only to assure himself that he hadn't entered the employ of a madman . . . not a madman, only a mass murderer? . . . That was not a comforting thought at the moment.

"SO how was the flight?"

"About what you'd expect, a whole fucking day trapped in a 747," Ding groused over the phone.

"Well, at least it was first-class," Clark observed.

"Great, next time you can have the pleasure, John. How're Patsy and JC?" Chavez asked, getting on to the important stuff.

"They're just fine. The grandpa stuff isn't all that bad." Clark could have said that he hadn't changed a single diaper yet. Sandy had seized on the ancillary baby-in-the-house duties with utter ruthlessness, allowing her husband to only hold the little guy. He supposed that such instincts were strong in women, and didn't want to interfere with her self-assumed rice bowl. "He's a cute little guy, Domingo. You done good, kid."

"Gee, thanks, Dad" was the ironic reply from ten thousand miles away. "Patsy?"

"She's doing fine, but not getting a hell of a lot of sleep. JC only sleeps about three hours at a stretch at the moment. But that'll change by the time you get back. Want to talk to her?" John asked next.

"What do you think, Mr. C?"

"Okay, hold on. Patsy!" he called. "It's Domingo."

"HEY, baby," Chavez said in his hotel room.

"How are you, Ding? How was the flight out?"

"Long, but no big deal," he lied. One doesn't show weakness before one's own wife. "They're treating us pretty nice, but it's hot here. I forgot what hot weather is like."

"Will you be there for the opening?"

"Oh, yeah, Pats, we all have security passes, courtesy of the Aussies. How's JC?"

"Wonderful" was the inevitable reply. "He's so beautiful. He doesn't cry much. It's pretty wonderful to have him, y'know?"

"How are you sleeping, baby?"

"Well, I get a few hours here and there. No big deal. Internship was a lot worse."

"Well, let your mom help you out, okay?"

"She does," Patsy assured her husband.

"Okay, I need to talk to your dad again—business stuff. Love ya, baby."

"Love you, too, Ding."

"Domingo, I think you're going to be okay as a son-in-law," the male voice said three seconds later. "I've never seen Patricia smile so much, and I guess that's your doing."

"Gee, thanks, Pop," Chavez replied, checking his U.K. watch. It was just after seven in the morning there, whereas in Sydney it was four in the hot afternoon.

"Okay, how are things there?" Clark asked.

"Good," Chavez told Rainbow Six. "Our point of contact is a short colonel named Frank Wilkerson. Solid troop. His people are pretty good, well trained, confident, nice and loose. Their relationship with the police is excellent. Their reaction plans look good to me—short version, John, they don't need us here any more than they need a few more kangaroos in the outback I flew over this morning."

"So, what the hell, enjoy the games." Bitch as he might, Chavez and his people were getting about ten grand worth of free holiday, Clark thought, and that wasn't exactly a prison sentence.

"It's a waste of our time, John," Chavez told his boss.

"Yeah, well, you never know, do you, Domingo?"

"I suppose," Chavez had to agree. They'd just spent several months proving that you never really knew.

"Your people okay?"

"Yeah, they're treating us pretty nice. Good hotel rooms, close enough to walk to the stadium, but we have official cars for that. So, I guess we're just paid tourists, eh?"

"Yep, like I said, Ding, enjoy the games."

"How's Peter doing?"

"Bouncing back okay, but he'll be out of business for at least a month, more like six weeks. The docs here are okay. Chin's legs are going to be a pain in the ass. Figure two and a half months for him to get back in harness."

"He must be pissed."

"Oh, he is."

"What about our prisoners?"

"Police are interrogating them now," Clark answered. "We're hearing more about this Russian guy, but nothing we can really use yet. The Irish cops are trying to ID the cocaine by manufacturer—it's medical quality, from a real drug company. Ten pounds of pure coke. Street value would buy a friggin' airliner. The Garda is worried that it might be the start of a trend, the IRA splinter groups getting into drugs big-time, but that's not our problem."

"This Russian guy—Serov, right?—he's the guy who gave them the intel on us?"

"That's affirmative, Domingo, but where he got it we don't know, and our Irish guests aren't giving us anything more than what we already have—probably all they know. Grady isn't talking at all. And his lawyer's bitching about how we interrogated him in the recovery room."

"Well, isn't that just a case of tough shit?"

"I hear you, Ding," Clark chuckled. It wasn't as though they'd be using the information in a trial. There was even a videotape of Grady's leaving the scene from the BBC news crew that had turned up at Hereford. Sean Grady would be imprisoned for a term defined by "the Queen's pleasure," which meant life plus forever, unless the European Union treaty interfered with it. Timothy O'Neil and the people who'd surrendered with him *might* get out around the time they turned sixty, Bill Tawney had told him the previous day. "Anything else?"

"Nope, everything's looking good here, John. I'll report in the same time tomorrow."

"Roger that, Domingo."

"Kiss Patsy for me."

"I'll even manage a hug if you want."

"Yeah, thanks, Grandpa," Ding agreed with a smile.

"Bye," he heard, and the line went dead.

"Not a bad time to be away from home, boss," Mike Pierce observed from a few feet away. "The first two weeks can be a real pain in the ass. This way, by the time you get back home, the little guy'll be sleeping four, five hours. Maybe more if you're really lucky," predicted the father of three sons.

"Mike, you see any problems here?"

"Like you told Six, the Aussies have it under control. They look like good people, man. Us bein' here's a waste of time, but what the hell, we get to see the Olympics."

"I suppose so. Any questions?"

"Do we carry?" Pierce asked.

"Pistols only, and casual clothes. Your security pass will take care of that. We pair off, you with me, and George with Homer. We take our tactical radios, too, but that's all."

"Yes, sir. Works for me. How's the jet lag?"

"How's it with you, Mike?"

"Like I been put in a bag and beat with a baseball bat." Pierce grinned. "But it'll be better tomorrow. Shit, I'd hate to think that gutting it through today won't help some tomorrow. Hey, tomorrow morning, we can work out with the Aussies, do our running on the Olympic track. Pretty cool, eh?"

"I like it."

"Yeah, it would be nice to meet up with some of those pussy athletes, see how fast they can run with weapons and body armor." At his best and fully outfitted, Pierce could run a mile in thirty seconds over four minutes, but he'd never broken the four-minute mark, even in running shoes and shorts. Louis Loiselle claimed to have done it once, and Chavez believed him. The diminutive Frenchman was the right size for a distance runner. Pierce was too big in height and across the shoulders. A Great Dane rather than a greyhound.

"Be cool, Mike. We have to protect them from the bad guys. That tells us who the best men are," Chavez observed through the jet lag.

"Roge-o, sir." Pierce would remember that one.

POPOV awoke for no particular reason he could see, except that—yes, another Gulfstream jet had just landed. He imagined that these were the really important ones for this project thing. The junior ones, or those with families, either drove out or flew commercial. The business jet sat there in the lights, the stairs deployed from their bay in the aircraft, and people walked out to the waiting cars that swiftly drove away from the aircraft and toward the hotel building. Popov wondered who it was, but he was too far away to recognize faces. He'd probably see them in the cafeteria in the morning. Dmitriy Arkadeyevich got a drink of water from the bathroom and returned to his bed. This facility was filling up rapidly, though he still didn't know why.

COLONEL Wilson Gearing was in his hotel room only a few floors above the Rainbow troops. His large bags were in the closet, and his clothing hung. The maids and other staff who serviced his room hadn't touched anything, merely checked the closet and proceeded to make up the beds and scrub the bathroom. They hadn't checked inside the bags—Gearing had telltales on them to make sure of that—inside one of which was a plastic canister with "Chlorine" painted on it. It was outwardly identical with the one on the fogging system at the Olympic stadium—it had, in fact, been purchased from the same company that had installed the fogging system, cleaned out and refilled with the nano-capsules. He also had the tools he needed to swap one out, and had practiced the skill in Kansas, where an identical installation was to be found. He could close his eyes and see himself doing it, time and again, to keep the downtime for the fogging system to a minimum. He thought about the contents of the container. Never had so much potential death been so tightly contained. Far more so than in a nuclear device, because unlike one of those, the danger here could replicate itself many times instead of merely detonating once. The way the fogging system worked, it would take about thirty minutes for the nano-capsules to get into the entire fogging system. Both computer models and actual mechanical tests proved that the capsules would get everywhere in the pipes, and spray out the fogging nozzles, invisible in the gentle, cooling mist. People walking through the tunnels leading to the stadium proper and in the concourses would breathe it in, an average of two hundred or so nano-capsules in four minutes of breathing, and that was well above the calculated mean lethal dose. The capsules would enter through the lungs, be transported into the blood, and there the capsules would dissolve, releasing the Shiva. The engineered virus strands would travel in the bloodstreams of the spectators and the athletes, soon find the liver and kidneys, the organs for which they had the greatest affinity, and begin the slow process of multiplication. All this had been established at Binghamton Lab on the "normal" test subjects. Then it was just a matter of weeks until the Shiva had multiplied enough to do its work. Along the way, people would pass on the Shiva through kisses and sexual contact, through coughs and sneezes. This, too, had been proven at the Binghamton Lab. Starting in about four weeks, people would think themselves mildly ill. Some would see their personal physicians, and be diagnosed as flu victims, told to take aspirin, drink fluids, and rest in front of the TV. They would do this, and feel better—because seeing a doctor usually did that for people—for a day or so. But they would not be getting better. Sooner or later, they'd develop the internal bleeds that Shiva ultimately caused, and then, about five weeks after the initial release of the nano-capsules, some doctor would run an antibody test and be aghast to learn that something like the famous and feared Ebola fever was back. A good epidemiology program might identify the Sydney Olympics as the focal center, but tens of thousands of people would have come and gone. This was a perfect venue for distributing Shiva, something the Project's senior members had determined years before—even before the attempted plague launched by Iran against America, which had predictably failed because the virus hadn't been the right one, and the method of delivery too haphazard. No, this plan was perfection itself. Every nation on earth sent athletes and judges to the Olympic games, and all of them would walk through the cooling fog in this hot stadium, lingering there to shed excess body heat, breathe deeply, and relax in this cool place. Then they'd all return to their homes, from America to Argentina, from Russia to Rwanda, there to spread the Shiva and start the initial panic.

Then came Phase Two. Horizon Corporation would manufacture and distribute the "A" vaccine, turn it out in thousand-liter lots, and send it all over the world by express flights to nations whose public-health-service physicians and nurses would be sure to inject every citizen they could find. Phase Two would finish the job begun with the global panic that was sure to result from Phase One. Four to six weeks after being injected, the "A" recipients would start to become ill. So, three weeks from today, Gearing thought, plus six weeks or so, plus two weeks, plus another six, plus a final two. A total of nineteen weeks, not even half a year, not even a full baseball season, and well over ninety-nine percent of the people on the earth would be dead. And the planet would be saved. No more slaughtering of sheep from a chemical-weapons release. No more extinction of species by thoughtless man. The ozone hole would soon heal itself. Nature would flourish once more. And he'd be there to see it, to enjoy and appreciate it all, along with his friends and colleagues in the Project. They'd save the planet and raise their children to respect it, love it, cherish it. The world would again be green and beautiful.

His feelings were not completely unambiguous. He could look out the windows and see people walking on the streets of Sydney, and it caused him pain to think of what would be happening to all of them. But he'd seen much pain. The sheep at Dugway. The monkeys and pigs and other test animals at Edgewood Arsenal. They, too, felt great pain. They, too, had a right to live, and people had disregarded both self-evident facts. The people down there didn't use shampoo unless it had been tested on the eyes of laboratory rabbits, held stock-still in cruel little cages, there to suffer without words, without expression at all to most people, who didn't understand animals, and cared less about them than they cared for how their burgers were cooked at the local McDonald's. They were helping to destroy the earth because they didn't care. Because they didn't care, they didn't even try to see what was important, and because they didn't appreciate what was important . . . they would die. They were a species that had endangered itself, and so would reap the whirlwind of its own ignorance. They were not like himself, Gearing thought. They didn't see.

And under the cruel but fair laws of Charles Darwin, that left them at a comparative disadvantage. And so, as one animal replaced another, so he and his kind would replace them and theirs. He was only the instrument of natural selection, after all.

THE jet lag was mainly gone, Chavez thought. The morning workout had been delicious in its sweat and endorphin-reduced pain, especially the run on the Olympic track. He and Mike Pierce had pushed hard on that, not timing it, but going as hard as they could, and on the run both had looked up at the empty stands and imagined the cheers they'd get had they been trained athletes. Then had come the showers and the grins, one soldier to another, at what they'd done, then dressing into their casual clothing, their pistols hidden under their shirts, their tactical radios jammed into pockets, and their security passes looped around their necks.

Later, the trumpets had blared, and the team of the first nation in the parade, Greece, marched out the tunnel at the far end, to the thundering cheers of the spectators in their seats, and the Sydney Olympiad had begun. Chavez told himself that as a security officer he was supposed to watch the crowd, but he found that he couldn't, without some specific danger to look at. The proud young athletes marched almost as well as soldiers, as they followed their flags and their judges on the oval track. It must have been a proud moment for them, Ding thought, to represent your homeland before all the other nations of the world. Each of them would have trained for months and years to earn this honor, to accept the cheers and hope himself to be worthy of the moment. Well, it wasn't the sort of thing you got to do as a field officer of the Central Intelligence Agency, nor a Team-2 commander of Rainbow. This was pure sport, pure competition, and if it didn't really apply to the real world, then what did that hurt? Every event would be a form of activity taken down to its essence—and most of them were really military in nature. Running—the most important martial skill was the ability to run toward battle or away from it. The javelin—a lance to throw at one's enemies. The shot put and discus—other missile weapons. The pole vault—to get one over a wall and into the enemy camp. The long jump—to get over a hole that the enemy had dug in the battlefield. These were all soldierly skills from antiquity, and the modern Games had gun sports, pistol and rifle, as well. The modern pentathlon was based on the skills needed by a military courier in the late nineteenth century—riding, running, and shooting his way to his destination, to tell his commander what he needed to know in order to command his troops effectively.

These men and women were warriors of a sort, here to win glory for themselves and their flags, to vanquish foes without bloodshed, to win a pure victory on the purest field of honor. That, Chavez thought, was a worthy goal for anyone, but he was too old and unfit to compete here. Unfit? he wondered. Well, not for one his age, and he was probably fitter than some of these people walking on the oval track, but not enough to win a single event. He felt his Beretta pistol under his shirt. That, and his ability to use it, made him fit to defend these kids against any who might wish to harm them, and that, Domingo Chavez decided, would have to do.

"Pretty cool, boss," Pierce observed, watching the Greeks pass where they were standing.

"Yeah, Mike, it sure as hell is."

C H A P T E R 3 4

THE GAMES CONTINUE

AS HAPPENS IN ALL ASPECTS OF LIFE, THINGS SET-tled into a routine. Chavez and his people spent most of their time with Colonel Wilkerson's people, mainly sitting in the reaction-force center and watching the games on television, but also wandering to the various venues, supposedly to eyeball security matters up close, but in reality to see the various competitive events even closer. Sometimes they even wandered onto the event field by virtue of their go-anywhere passes. The Aussies, Ding learned, were ferociously dedicated sports fans, and wonderfully hospitable. In his off-duty time, he picked a neighborhood pub to hang out in, where the beer was good and the atmosphere friendly. On learning that he was an American, his "mates" would often as not buy a beer for him and ask questions while watching sports events on the wall-hung televisions. About the only thing he didn't like was the cigarette smoke, for the Australian culture had not yet totally condemned the vice, but no place was perfect.

Each morning he and his people worked out with Colonel Wilkerson and his men, and they found that in *this* Olympic competition there was little difference between Australian and American special-operations troopers. One morning they went off to the Olympic pistol range, borrowing Olympic-style handguns—.22 automatics that seemed like toys compared to the .45s the Rainbow soldiers ordinarily packed—then saw that the target and scoring systems were very difficult indeed, if not especially related to combat shooting in the real world. For all his practice and expertise, Chavez decided that with luck he could have made the team from Mali. Certainly not the American or Russian teams, whose shooters were utterly inhuman in their ability to punch holes in the skinny silhouette targets that flipped full-face and sideways on computer-controlled hangers. But these paper targets didn't shoot back, he told himself, and that *did* make something of a difference. Besides, success in his form of shooting was to make a real person dead, not to hit a quarter-sized target on a black paper target card. That made a difference, too, Ding and Mike Pierce thought aloud with their Aussie counterparts. What they did could never be an Olympic sport, unless somebody brought back the gladiatorial games of Rome, and that wouldn't be happening. Besides, what they did for their living wasn't a sport at all, was it? Neither was it a form of mass entertainment in the kinder and gentler modern world. Part of Chavez admitted that he wondered what the games in classical Rome's Flavian Amphitheater had been like to watch, but it wasn't something he could say aloud, lest people take him for an utter barbarian. *Hail, Caesar! We who are about to die salute you!* It wasn't exactly the Super Bowl, was it? And so, "Major" Domingo Chavez, along with sergeants Mike Pierce, Homer Johnston, and George Tomlinson, and Special Agent Tim Noonan, got to watch the games for free, sometimes with "official" jackets to give them the cover of anonymity.

THE same was true, rather more distantly, of Dmitriy Popov, who stayed in his room to watch the Olympics on TV. He found the games a distraction from the questions that were running their own laps inside his brain. The Russian national team, naturally enough his favorite, was doing well, though the Australians were making a fine showing as hosts, especially in swimming, which seemed to be their national passion. The problem was in the vastly different time zones. When Popov was watching events live, it was necessarily an ungodly hour in Kansas, which made him somewhat bleary-eyed for his morning horseback rides with Maclean and Killgore—those had become a very pleasant morning diversion.

This morning was like the previous ten, with a cool westerly breeze, the rising orange sun casting strange but lovely light on the waving fields of grass and wheat. Buttermilk now recognized him, and awarded the Russian with oddly endearing signs of affection, which he in turn rewarded with sugar cubes or, as today, an apple taken from the morning breakfast buffet, which the mare crunched down rapidly from his hand. He had learned to saddle his own horse, which he now did quickly, leading Buttermilk outside to join the others and mounting up in the corral.

"Morning, Dmitriy," Maclean said.

"Good morning, Kirk," Popov replied pleasantly. In another few minutes, they were riding off, to the south this time, toward one of the wheat fields, at a rather more rapid pace than his first such ride.

"So, what's it like to be an intelligence agent?" Killgore asked, half a mile from the barn.

"We are called intelligence officers, actually," Popov said to correct the first Hollywood-generated misimpression. "Truthfully, it is mainly boring work. You spend much of your time waiting for a meeting, or filling out forms for submission to your headquarters, or the *rezidentura.* There is some danger—but only of being arrested, not shot. It has become a civilized business. Captured intelligence officers are exchanged, usually after a brief period of imprisonment. That never happened to me, of course. I was well trained." And lucky, he didn't add.

"So, no James Bond stuff, you never killed anybody, nothing like that?" Kirk Maclean asked.

"Good heavens, no," Popov replied, with a laugh. "You have others do that sort of thing for you, surrogates, when you need it done. And that is quite rare."

"How rare?"

"Today? Almost never I should think. At KGB, our job was to get information and pass it upwards to our government—more like reporters, like your Associated Press, than anything else. And much of the information we gathered was from open sources, newspapers, magazines, television. Your CNN is perhaps the best, most used source of information in the world."

"But what sort of information *did* you gather?"

"Mainly diplomatic or political intelligence, trying to discern intentions. Others went after technical intelligence—how fast an airplane flies or how far a cannon shoots—but that was never my specialty area, you see. I was what you call here a people person. I met with various people and delivered messages and such, then brought the answers back to my station."

"What kind of people?"

Popov wondered about how he should answer, and decided on the truth: "Terrorists, that was what you would call them."

"Oh? Like which ones?"

"Mainly European, but some in the Middle East as well. I have language skills, and I can speak easily with people from various lands."

"Was it hard?" Dr. Killgore asked.

"Not really. We had similar political beliefs, and my country provided them with weapons, training, access to some facilities in the Eastern Bloc. I was as much a travel agent as anything else, and occasionally I would suggest targets for them to attack—as payment for our assistance, you see."

"Did you give them money?" Maclean this time.

"Yes, but not much money. The Soviet Union had only limited hard-currency reserves, and we never paid our agents very much. At least I did not," Popov said.

"So, you sent terrorists out on missions to kill people?" This was from Killgore.

Popov nodded. "Yes. That was often my job. That was," he added, "why Dr. Brightling hired me."

"Oh?" Maclean asked.

Dmitriy wondered how far he could take this one. "Yes, he asked me to do similar things for Horizon Corporation."

"You're the guy who ramrodded the stuff in Europe?"

"I contacted various people and made suggestions which they carried out, yes, and so, yes, I do have some blood on my second hands, I suppose, but one cannot take such matters too seriously, can one? It is business, and it has been *my* business for some time."

"Well, that's a good thing for you, Dmitriy. That's why you're here," Maclean told him. "John is pretty loyal to his people. You must have done okay."

Popov shrugged. "Perhaps so. He never told me why he wanted these things done, but I gather it was to help his friend Henriksen get the consulting contract for the Sydney Olympics that I've been watching on TV."

"That's right," Killgore confirmed. "That was very important to us." *Might as well watch,* the epidemiologist thought, *they'll be the last ones.*

"But why?"

They hesitated at the direct question. The physician and the engineer looked at each other. Then Killgore spoke.

"Dmitriy, what do you think of the environment?"

"What do you mean? Out here? It is beautiful. You've taught me much with these morning rides, my friends," the Russian answered, choosing his words carefully. "The sky and the air, and the beautiful fields of grass and wheat. I have never appreciated how beautiful the world can be. I suppose that's because I grew up in Moscow." Which had been a hideously filthy city, but they didn't know that.

"Yeah, well, it's not all this way."

"I know that, John. In Russia—well, the State didn't care as you Americans do. They nearly killed all life in the Caspian Sea—where caviar comes from—from chemical poisoning. And there is a place just east of the Urals where our original atomic-bomb research created a wasteland. I haven't seen it, but I have heard of it. The highway signs there tell you to drive very fast to be through the zone of dangerous radiation as quickly as possible."

"Yeah, well, if we're not careful, we might just kill the whole planet," Maclean observed next.

"That would be a crime, like the Hitlerites," Popov said next. "It is *nekulturny,* the work of uncivilized barbarians. In my room, the tapes and the magazines make this clear."

"What do you think of killing people, Dmitriy?" Killgore asked then.

"That depends on who they are. There are many people who deserve to die for one reason or another. But Western culture has this strange notion that taking life is almost always wrong—you Americans cannot even kill your criminals, murderers and such, without jumping through hoops, as you say here. I find that very curious."

"What about crimes against Nature?" Killgore said, staring off into the distance.

"I do not understand."

"Well, things that hurt the whole planet, killing off whole living species, polluting the land and the sea. What about that?"

"Kirk, that is also a barbaric act, and it should be punished severely. But how do you identify the criminals? Is it the industrialist who gives the order and makes the profit from it? Or is it the worker who takes his wages and does what he is told?"

"What did they say at Nuremberg?" Killgore said next.

"The war-crimes trial, you mean? It was decided that following orders is not a defense." Not a concept he'd been taught to consider in the KGB Academy, where he'd learned that the State Was Always Right.

"Right," the epidemiologist agreed. "But you know, nobody ever went after Harry Truman for bombing Hiroshima."

Because he won, *you fool,* Popov didn't reply. "Do you ask if this was a crime? No, it was not, because he ended a greater evil, and the sacrifice of those people was necessary to restore the peace."

"What about saving the planet?"

"I do not understand."

"If the planet was dying, what would one have to do—what would be *right* to do, to save it?"

This discussion had all the ideological and philosophical purity of a classroom discussion of the Marxist dialectic at Moscow State University—and about as much relevance to the real world. Kill the whole planet? That was not possible. A full-blown nuclear war, yes, maybe *that* could have such an effect, but *that* was no longer possible. The world had changed, and America was the nation that had made it happen. Didn't these two druids see the wonder of that? More than once, the world had been *close* to loosing nuclear weapons, but today that was a thing of the past.

"I have never considered that question, my friends."

"We have," Maclean responded. "Dmitriy, there are people and forces at work today that could easily kill off everything here. Somebody has to stop that from happening, but how do you do it?"

"You do not mean simply political action, do you?" the former KGB spook observed.

"No, it's too late for that, and not enough people would listen anyway." Killgore turned his horse to the right and the others followed. "I'm afraid you have to take more drastic measures."

"What's that? Kill the whole world population?" Dmitriy Arkadeyevich asked, with hidden humor. But the reply to the rhetorical question was the same look in two sets of eyes. The look didn't make his blood go cold, but it did get his brain moving off in a new and unexpected direction. These were *fascisti.* Worse than that, *fascisti* with an ethos in which they believed. But were they willing to take action on their beliefs? Could anyone take action like that? Even the worst of the Stalinists—no, they'd never been madmen, just political romantics.

Just then an aircraft's noise disturbed the morning. It was one of Horizon's fleet of G's, lifting off from the complex's runway, climbing up and turning right, looping around to the east—for New York, probably, to bring more of the "project" people in? Probably. The complex was about 80 percent full now, Popov reflected. The rate of arrivals had slowed, but people were still coming, most by private car. The cafeteria was almost full at lunch- and dinnertime, and the lights burned late in the laboratory and other work buildings. But what were those people doing?

Horizon Corporation, Popov reminded himself, was a biotech company, specializing in medicines and medical treatments, Killgore was a physician, and Maclean an engineer specializing in environmental matters. Both were druids, both nature-worshipers, the new kind of paganism spawned in the West. John Brightling seemed to be one as well, judging by that conversation they'd had in New York. That, then, was the ethos of these people *and* their company. Dmitriy thought about the printed matter in his room. Humans were a *parasitic* species doing more harm than good to the earth, and these two had just talked about sentencing the harmful people to death—then made it clear that they thought of *everyone* as harmful. What were they going to do, kill everyone? What rubbish. The door leading to the answer had opened further. His brain was moving far more quickly than Buttermilk was, but still not fast enough.

They rode in silence for a few minutes. Then a shadow crossed the ground, and Popov looked up.

"What is that?"

"Red-tail hawk," Maclean answered, after a look. "Cruising for some breakfast."

As they watched, the raptor climbed to five hundred feet or so, then spread his wings to ride the thermal air currents, his head down, examining the surface of the land for an unwary rodent through his impossibly sharp eyes. By unspoken consent the three men stopped their horses to watch. It took several minutes and then it was both beautiful and terrible to behold. The hawk folded its wings back and dropped rapidly, then flapped to accelerate like a feathered bullet, then spread its wings wide, nosing up, its yellow talons leading the descent now—

"Yes!" Maclean hooted.

Like a child stomping on an anthill, the hawk used its talons to kill its prey, twisting and crushing, then, holding the limp tubular body in them, flapped laboriously into the sky, heading off to the north to its nest or home, or whatever you called it, Popov thought. The prairie dog it killed had enjoyed no chance, Dmitriy thought, but nature was like that, as were people. No soldier willingly gave his foe a fair chance on any battlefield. It was neither safe nor intelligent to do so. You struck with total fury and as little warning as possible, the better to take his life quickly and easily—and safely—and if he lacked the wit to protect himself properly, well, that was his problem, not yours. In the case of the hawk, it had swooped down from above and down-sun, not even its shadow warning the prairie dog sitting at the entrance to its home, and killed without pity. The hawk had to eat, he supposed. Perhaps it had young to feed, or maybe it was just hunting for its own needs. In either case, the prairie dog hung limp in its claws, like an empty brown sock, soon to be ripped apart and eaten by its killer.

"Damn, I love watching that," Maclean said.

"It is cruel, but beautiful," Popov said.

"Mother Nature is like that, pal. Cruel but beautiful." Killgore watched the hawk vanish in the distance. "That was something to see."

"I have to capture one and train it," Maclean announced. "Train it to kill off my fist."

"Are the prairie dogs endangered?"

"No, no way," Killgore answered. "Predators can control their numbers, but never entirely eliminate them. Nature maintains a balance."

"How do men fit into that balance?" Popov asked.

"They don't," Kirk Maclean answered. "People just screw it up, 'cuz they're too dumb to see what works and what doesn't. And they don't care about the harm they do. That's the problem."

"And what is the solution?" Dmitriy asked. Killgore turned to look him right in the eyes.

"Why, we are."

"ED, the cover name must be one he's used for a long time," Clark argued. "The IRA guys hadn't seen him in years, but that's the name they knew him by."

"Makes sense," Ed Foley had to admit over the phone. "So, you really want to talk to him, eh?"

"Well, it's no big thing, Ed. He just turned people loose to kill my wife, daughter, and grandson, you know? And they *did* kill two of *my* men. Now, do I have permission to contact him or not?" Rainbow Six demanded from his desk.

In his seventh-floor office atop CIA Headquarters, Director of Central Intelligence Edward Foley uncharacteristically wavered. If he let Clark do it, and Clark got what he wanted, reciprocity rules would then apply. Sergey Nikolay'ch would someday call CIA and request information of a delicate nature, and he, Foley, would have to provide it, else the veneer of amity within the international intelligence community would crumble away. But Foley could not predict what the Russians would ask about, and both sides were still spying on each other, and so the friendly rules of modern life in the spook business both did and did not apply. You pretended that they did, but you remembered and acted as though they did not. Such contacts were rare, and Golovko had been very helpful twice in real-world operations. And he'd never requested a return favor, perhaps because the operations had been of direct or indirect benefit to his own country. But Sergey wasn't one to forget a debt and—

"I know what you're thinking, Ed, but I've lost people because of this guy, and I want his ass, and Sergey can help us identify the fuck."

"What if he's still inside?" Foley temporized.

"Do you believe that?" Clark snorted.

"Well, no, I think we're past that."

"So do I, Ed. So, if he's a friend, let's ask him a friendly question. Maybe we'll get a friendly answer. The *quid pro quo* on this could be to let Russian special-operations people train a few weeks with us. That's a price I'm willing to pay."

It was ultimately a futile exercise to argue with John, who'd been the training officer to him and his wife, Mary Pat, now Deputy Director (Operations). "Okay, John, it's approved. Who handles the contact?"

"I have his number," Clark assured the DCI.

"Then call it, John. Approved," the DCI concluded, not without reluctance. "Anything else?"

"No, sir, and thank you. How are Mary Pat and the kids?"

"They're fine. How's your grandson?"

"Not too bad at all. Patsy is doing fine, and Sandy's taken over the job with JC."

"JC?"

"John Conor Chavez," Clark clarified.

That was a complex name, Foley thought, without saying so. "Well, okay. Go ahead, John. See ya."

"Thanks, Ed. Bye." Clark switched buttons on his phone. "Bill, we got approval."

"Excellent," Tawney replied. "When will you call?"

"How's right now grab you?"

"Set things up properly," Tawney warned.

"Fear not." Clark killed that line and punched another button. That one activated a cassette-tape recorder before he punched yet another and dialed Moscow.

"Six-Six-Zero," a female voice answered in Russian.

"I need to speak personally with Sergey Nikolayevich. Please tell him that this is Ivan Timofeyevich calling," Clark said in his most literate Russian.

"Da," the secretary replied, wondering how this person had gotten the Chairman's direct line.

"Clark!" a man's voice boomed onto the line. "You are well there in England?" And already it started. The Chairman of the reconfigured Russian foreign-intelligence service wanted him to know that he knew where he was and what he was doing, and it wouldn't do to ask how he'd found out.

"I find the climate agreeable, Chairman Golovko."

"This new unit you head has been rather busy. The attack on your wife and daughter—they are well?"

"It was rather unpleasant, but yes, thank you, they are quite well." The conversation was in Russian, a language Clark spoke like a native of Leningrad—St. Petersburg, John corrected himself. That was another old habit that died hard. "And I am now a grandfather."

"Indeed, Vanya? Congratulations! That is splendid news. I was not pleased to learn of the attack on you," Golovko went on sincerely. Russians have always been very sentimental people, especially where small children are concerned.

"Neither was I," Clark said next. "But it worked out, as we say. I captured one of the bastards myself."

"That I did not know, Vanya," the Chairman went on—lying or not, John couldn't tell. "So, what is the purpose of your call?"

"I need your assistance with a name."

"What name is that?"

"It is a cover identity: Serov, Iosef Andreyevich. The officer in question—former officer, I should think—works with progressive elements in the West. We have reason to believe he has instigated operations in which people were killed, including the attack on my people here in Hereford."

"We had nothing at all to do with that, Vanya," Golovko said at once, in a very serious voice.

"I have no reason to think that you did, Sergey, but a man with this name, and identified as a Russian national, handed over money and drugs to the Irish terrorists. He was known to the Irishmen from years of experience, including in the Bekaa Valley. So, I think he was KGB at one time. I also have a physical description," Clark said, and gave it.

" 'Serov,' you said. That's an odd—"

"Da, I know that."

"This is important to you?"

"Sergey, in addition to killing two of my people, this operation threatened my wife and daughter directly. Yes, my friend, this is very important to me."

In Moscow, Golovko wondered about that. He knew Clark, having met him eighteen months before. A field officer of unusual talent and amazing luck, John Clark had been a dangerous enemy, a quintessential professional intelligence officer, along with his younger colleague, Domingo Estebanovich Chavez, if he remembered right. And Golovko knew that his daughter was married to this Chavez boy—he'd just found that out, in fact. Someone had given that information to Kirilenko in London, though he couldn't remember who.

But if it were a Russian, a former *chekist* no less, who was stirring up the terrorist pot, well, that was not good news for his country. Should he cooperate? the Chairman asked himself. What was the upside and what might be the downside? If he agreed now, he'd have to follow through on it, else CIA and other Western services might not cooperate with him. Was it in his country's interest? Was it in his institution's interest?

"I will see what I can do, Vanya, but I can make no promises," Clark heard. Okay, that meant he was thinking about it at least.

"I would deem it a personal favor, Sergey Nikolay'ch."

"I understand. Allow me to see what information I can find."

"Very well. Good day, my friend."

"Dosvidaniya."

Clark punched out the tape and put it in his desk drawer. "Okay, pal, let's see if you can deliver."

THE computer system in the Russian intelligence service was not as advanced as its Western counterparts, but the technical differences were mainly lost on human users, whose brains moved at slower speed than even the most backward computer. Golovko had learned to make use of it because he didn't always like to have people doing things for him, and in a minute he had a screenful of data tracked down by the cover name.

POPOV, DMITRIY ARKADEYEVICH, the screen read, giving service number, date of birth, and time of employment. He'd retired as a colonel near the end of the first big RIF that had cut the former KGB by nearly a third. Good evaluations by his superiors, Golovko saw, but he'd specialized in a field in which the agency no longer had great interest. Virtually everyone in that subdepartment had been terminated, pensioned off in a land where pensions could feed one for perhaps as much as five days out of a month. Well, there wasn't much he could do about that, Golovko told himself. It was hard enough to get enough funding out of the Duma to keep his downsized agency operating, despite the fact that the downsized nation needed it more than ever before . . . and this Clark had performed two services that had benefited his nation, Golovko reminded himself—in addition, of course, to previous actions that had caused the Soviet Union no small harm . . . but again, those acts had helped elevate himself to the chairmanship of his agency.

Yes, he had to help. It would be a good bargaining chip to acquire for later requests to be made of the Americans. Moreover, Clark had dealt honorably with him, Sergey reminded himself, and it was distantly troubling to him that a former KGB officer had helped attack the man's family—attacks on noncombatants were forbidden in the intelligence business. Oh, occasionally the wife of a CIA officer might have been slightly roughed up in the old days of the East-West Cold War, but serious harm? Never. In addition to being *nekulturny,* it would only have started vendettas that would only have interfered with the conduct of real business, the gathering of information. From the

1950s on, the business of intelligence had become a civilized, predictable one. Predictability was always the one thing the Russians had wanted from the West, and that had to go both ways. Clark was predictable.

With that decision made, Golovko printed up the information on his screen.

"SO?" Clark asked Bill Tawney.

"The Swiss were a little slow. It turns out that the account number Grady gave us was real enough—"

"Was?" John said, thinking that he could hear the bad-news "but" coming.

"Well, actually it's still an active account. It began with about six million U.S. dollars deposited, then several hundred thousand withdrawn, and then, the very day of the attack at the hospital, all but a hundred thousand was withdrawn and redeposited elsewhere, another account in yet another bank."

"Where?"

"They say they cannot tell us."

"Oh, well, you tell their fucking Justice Minister that the next time he needs our help, we'll fuckin' let the terrorists kill off their citizens!" Clark snarled.

"They do have laws, John," Tawney pointed out. "What if this chap had an attorney do the transfer? The attorney-client privilege applies, and no country can break that barrier. The Swiss *do* have laws that govern funds thought to have been generated by criminal means, but we have no proof of that, do we? I suppose we could gin something up to get around the law, but that will take time, old man."

"Shit," Clark observed. Then he thought for a second. "The Russian?"

Tawney nodded sagely. "Yes, that makes sense, doesn't it? He set them up a numbered account, and when they were taken out, he still had the necessary numbers, didn't he?"

"Fuck, so he sets them up and rips them off."

"Quite," Tawney observed. "Grady said six million dollars in the hospital, and the Swiss confirm that number. He needs a few hundred thousand to purchase the trucks and other vehicles they used—we have records on that from the police investigation—and left the rest in place, and then this Russian chap decided they have no further use of the funds. Well, why not?" the intelligence officer asked. "Russians *are* notoriously greedy people, you know."

"The Russian giveth, and the Russian taketh away. He gave them the intel on us, too."

"I would not wager against that, John," Tawney agreed.

"Okay, let's back up some," John proposed, putting his temper back in its box. "This Russian appears, gives them intelligence information on us, funds the operation from somewhere—sure as hell not Russia, because, A, they have no reason to undertake such an operation and, B, they don't have that much money to toss around. First question: where did the money—"

"And the drugs, John. Don't forget that."

"Okay, and the drugs—come *from?*"

"Easier to track the drugs, perhaps. The Garda say that the cocaine was medical quality, which means that it came *from* a drug company. Cocaine is closely controlled in every nation in the world. Ten pounds is a large quantity, enough to fill a fairly large suitcase—cocaine is about as dense as tobacco. So the bulk of the shipment would be the equivalent of ten pounds of cigarettes. Say the size of a large suitcase. That's a bloody large quantity of drugs, John, and it would leave a gap in someone's controlled and guarded warehouse, wherever it might be."

"You're thinking it all originated in America?" Clark asked.

"For a starting point, yes. The world's largest pharmaceutical houses are there and here in Britain. I can get our chaps started checking out Distillers, Limited, and the others for missing cocaine. I expect your American DEA can attempt to do the same."

"I'll call the FBI about that," Clark said at once. "So, Bill, what *do* we know?"

"We will assume that Grady and O'Neil were telling us the truth about this Serov chap. We have a former—presumably former—KGB officer who instigated the Hereford attack. Essentially he hired them to do it, like mercenaries, with a payment of cash and drugs. When the attack failed, he simply confiscated the money for his own ends, and on that I still presume that he kept it for himself. The Russian will not have such private means—well, I suppose it could be the Russian Mafia, all those former KGB chaps who are now discovering free enterprise, but I see no reason why they should target us. We here at Rainbow are not a threat to them in any way, are we?"

"No," Clark agreed.

"So, we have a large quantity of drugs and six million American dollars, delivered by a Russian. I am assuming for the moment that the operation originated in America, because of the drugs and the quantity of the money."

"Why?"

"I cannot justify that, John. Perhaps it's my nose telling me that."

"How did he get to Ireland?" John asked, agreeing to trust Tawney's nose.

"We don't know that. He must have flown into Dublin—yes, I know, with such a large quantity of drugs, that is not a prudent thing to do. We need to ask our friends about that."

"Tell the cops that's important. We can get a flight number and point of origin from that."

"Quite." Tawney made a note.

"What else are we missing?"

"I'm going to have my chaps at 'Six' check for the names of KGB officers who are known to have worked with terrorist groups. We have a rough physical description which may be of some use for the purposes of elimination. But I think our best hope is the ten pounds of drugs."

Clark nodded. "Okay, I'll call the Bureau on that one."

"TEN *pounds,* eh?"

"That's right, Dan, and doctor-quality pure. That's a real shitload of coke, man, and there ought to be a blank spot in somebody's warehouse."

"I'll call DEA and have them take a quick look," the FBI Director promised. "Anything shaking on your end?"

"We're giving the tree a kick, Dan," John told him. "For the moment we're proceeding on the assumption that the operation initiated in America." He explained on to tell Murray why this was so.

"This Russian guy, Serov, you said, former KGB, formerly a go-between for terrorists. There weren't all that many of those, and we have some information on the specialty."

"Bill's having 'Six' look at it, too, and I've already kicked it around with Ed Foley. I talked to Sergey Golovko about it as well."

"You really think he'll help?" Director Murray asked.

"The worst thing he can say is no, Dan, and that's where we are already," Rainbow Six pointed out.

"True," Dan conceded. "Anything else we can do on this end?"

"If I come up with anything I'll let you know, pal."

"Okay, John. Been watching the Olympics?"

"Yeah, I actually have a team there."

"Oh?"

"Yeah, Ding Chavez and some men. The Aussies wanted us down to observe their security operations. He says they're pretty good."

"Free trip to the Olympics, not a bad gig," the FBI Director observed.

"I guess so, Dan. Anyway, let us know if you turn anything, will ya?"

"You bet, John. See you later, pal."

"Yeah. Bye, Dan."

Clark replaced the secure phone and leaned back in his chair, wondering what he might be missing. He was checking everything he had thought of, every loose end, hoping that somewhere someone might come up with another seemingly innocent factoid that might lead to another. He'd never quite appreciated how hard it was to be a cop investigating a major crime. The color of the damned car the bad guys drove was or could be important, and you had to remember to ask that question, too. But it was something for which he was not trained, and he had to trust the cops to do their jobs.

THEY were doing that. In London, the police sat Timothy O'Neil down in the usual interrogation room. Tea was offered and accepted.

It wasn't easy for O'Neil. He wanted to say nothing at all, but with the shock of the information given him by the police that could only have originated with Sean Grady, his faith and his resolve had been shaken, and as a result he *had* said a few things, and that was a process that once begun could not be taken back.

"This Russian chap, Serov, you told us his name was," the detective inspector began. "He flew into Ireland?"

"It's a long swim, mate," O'Neil replied as a joke.

"Yes, and a difficult drive," the police inspector agreed. "How did he fly in?"

The answer to that was silence. That was disappointing, but not unexpected.

"I can tell you something you don't know, Tim," the inspector offered, to jump-start the conversation.

"What might that be?"

"This Serov bloke set you up a numbered Swiss account for all the money he brought in. Well, we just learned from the Swiss that he cleaned it out."

"What?"

"The day of your operation, someone called the bank and transferred nearly all the money out. So, your Russian friend gave with one hand, and took away with the other. Here"—the inspector handed a sheet of paper across—"this is the account number, and this is the activation number to do transfers. Six million dollars, less what you chaps spent to buy the trucks and such. He transferred it out, to his own personal account, I'll wager. You chaps picked the wrong friend, Tim."

"That bloody fucking thief!" O'Neil was outraged.

"Yes, Tim, I know. You've never been one of those. But this Serov chappie is, and that's a fact, my boy."

O'Neil swore something at odds with his Catholicism. He recognized the account number, knew that Sean had written it down, and was reasonably certain that this cop wasn't lying to him about what had happened with it.

"He flew into Shannon on a private business jet. I do not know where from."

"Really?"

"Probably because of the drugs he brought in with him. They don't search plutocrats, do they? Bloody nobility, they act like."

"What kind of aircraft, do you know?"

O'Neil shook his head. "It had two engines and the tail was shaped like a T, but no, I do not know the name of the bloody thing."

"And how did he get to the meeting?"

"We had a car meet him."

"Who drove the car?" the inspector asked next.

"I will not give you names. I've told you that."

"Forgive me, Tim, but I must ask. You know that," the cop apologized. He'd worked hard winning this terrorist's confidence. "Sean trusted this Serov chap. That was evidently a mistake. The funds were transferred out two hours after your operation began. We rather suspect he was somewhere close, to watch, and when he saw how things were going, he simply robbed you. Russians are greedy buggers," the cop sympathized. His eyes didn't show his pleasure at the new information developed. The room was bugged, of course, and already the Police of the Metropolis were on the phone to Ireland.

THE Irish national police force, called the Garda, had almost always cooperated with their British counterparts, and this time was no exception. The senior local Gardai drove at once to Shannon to check for flight records—as far as he was concerned, all he wanted to know was how ten pounds of illegal drugs had entered his country. That tactical mistake by the IRA had only enraged the local cops, some of whom did have their tribal sympathies with the revolutionary movement to the north. But those sympathies stopped well short of drug-trafficking, which they, like most cops in the world, regarded as the dirtiest of crimes.

The flight-operations office at Shannon had paper records of every flight that arrived or departed from the complex, and with the date, the assistant operations manager found the right sheet in under three minutes. Yes, a Gulfstream business jet had arrived early in the morning, refueled, and departed soon after. The documents showed the tail number and the names of the flight crew. More to the point, it showed that the aircraft was registered in the United States to a large charter company. From this office, the Irish police officer went to immigration/customs control, where he found that one Joseph Serov had indeed cleared customs on the morning indicated. The Gardai took a photocopy of all relevant documents back to his station, where they were faxed immediately to Garda headquarters in Dublin, and then on to London, and from there to Washington, D.C.

"DAMN," Dan Murray said at his desk. "It *did* start here, eh?"

"Looks that way," said Chuck Baker, the assistant director in charge of the criminal division.

"Run this one down, Chuck."

"You bet, Dan. This one's getting pretty deep."

THIRTY minutes later, a pair of FBI agents arrived at the office of the charter company at the Teterboro, New Jersey, airport. There they soon ascertained that the aircraft had been chartered by one Joseph Serov, who'd paid for the charter with a certified check drawn on an account at Citibank that was in his name. No, they didn't have a photo of the client. The flight crew was elsewhere on another flight, but as soon as they came back they would cooperate with the FBI, of course.

From there the agents, plus some photocopied documents, went to the bank branch where Serov kept his account, and there learned that nobody at the branch had ever met the man. His address, they found, was the same damned post-office box that had dead-ended the search for his credit card records.

By this time, the FBI had a copy of Serov's passport photo—but those were often valueless for the purposes of identification, intended more, Director Murray thought, to identify the body of a plane-crash victim than to facilitate the search for a living human being.

But the case file was growing, and for the first time Murray felt optimistic. They were gradually turning up data on this subject, and sooner or later they'd find where he'd slipped up—trained KGB officer or not—because everyone did, and once you appeared on the FBI's collective radarscope, nine thousand skilled investigators started looking, and they wouldn't stop looking until told to stop. Photo, bank account, credit card records . . . the next step would be to find out how the money had gotten into his account. He had to have an employer and/or sponsor, and that person or entity could be squeezed for additional information. It was now just a matter of time, and Murray thought they had all the time they needed to run this mutt down. It wasn't often that they bagged a trained spook. They were the most elusive of game, and for that reason all the more pleasing when you could hang the head of one over the mantelpiece. Terrorism and drug-trafficking. This would be a juicy case to give to a United States Attorney.

"HELLO," Popov said.

"Howdy," the man replied. "You're not from here."

"Dmitriy Popov," the Russian said, extending his hand.

"Foster Hunnicutt," the American said, taking it. "What do you do here?"

Popov smiled. "Here, I do nothing at all, though I am learning to ride a horse. I work directly for Dr. Brightling."

"Who—oh, the big boss of this place?"

"Yes, that is correct. And you?"

"I'm a hunter and guide," the man from Montana replied.

"Good, and you are not a vegan?"

Hunnicutt thought that was pretty good. "Not exactly. I like red meat as much as the next man. But I prefer elk to this mystery meat," he went on, looking down with some distaste for what was on his plate.

"Elk?"

"Wapiti, biggest damned deer you're ever gonna see. A good one's got maybe four, five hundred pounds of good meat in him. Nice rack, too."

"Rack?"

"The antlers, horns on the head. I'm partial to bear meat, too."

"That'll piss off a lot of the folks here," Dr. Killgore observed, working into his pasta salad.

"Look, man, hunting is the first form of conservation. If somebody don't take care of the critters, there ain't nothing to hunt. You know, like Teddy Roosevelt and Yellowstone National Park. If you want to understand game, I mean *really* understand them, you better be a hunter."

"No arguments here," the epidemiologist said.

"Maybe I'm not a bunny-hugger. Maybe I kill game, but, goddamnit, I eat what I kill. I don't kill things just to watch 'em die—well," he added, "not game animals anyway. But there's a lot of ignorant-ass people I wouldn't mind popping."

"That's why we're here, isn't it?" Maclean asked with a smile.

"You bet. Too many people fucking up the place with electric toothbrushes and cars and ugly-ass houses."

"I brought Foster into the Project," Mark Waterhouse replied. He'd known Maclean for years.

"All briefed in?" Killgore asked.

"Yes, sir, and it's all fine with me. You know, I always wondered what it was like to be Jim Bridger or Jedediah Smith. Maybe now I can find out, give it a few years."

"About five," Maclean said, "according to our computer projections."

"Bridger? Smith?" Popov asked.

"They were Mountain Men," Hunnicutt told the Russian. "They were the first white men to see the West, and they were legends, explorers, hunters, Indian fighters."

"Yeah, it's a shame about the Indians."

"Maybe so," Hunnicutt allowed.

"When did you get in?" Maclean asked Waterhouse.

"We drove in today," Mark replied. "The place is about full up now, isn't it?" He didn't like the crowding.

"That it is," Killgore confirmed. He didn't, either. "But it's still nice outside. You ride, Mr. Hunnicutt?"

"How else does a man hunt in the West? I don't use no SUV, man."

"So, you're a hunting guide?"

"Yeah." Hunnicutt nodded. "I used to be a geologist for the oil companies, but I kissed that off a long time ago. I got tired of helping to kill the planet, y'know?"

Another tree-worshiping druid, Popov thought. It wasn't especially surprising, though this one struck him as verbose and a little bombastic.

"But then," the hunter went on, "well, I figured out what was important." He explained for a few minutes about the Brown Smudge. "And I took my money and hung it up, like. Always liked hunting and stuff, and so I built me a cabin in the mountains—bought an old cattle ranch—and took to hunting full-time."

"Oh, you can do that? Hunt full-time, I mean?" Killgore asked.

"That depends. A fish-and-game cop hassled me about it . . . but, well, he stopped hassling me."

Popov caught a wink from Waterhouse to Killgore when this primitive said that, and in a second he knew that this Hunnicutt person had killed a police officer and gotten away with it. What sort of people did this "project" recruit?

"Anyway, we all ride in the morning. Want to join us?"

"You bet! I never turn that down."

"I have learned to enjoy it myself," Popov put in.

"Dmitriy, you must have some Cossack in you." Killgore laughed. "Anyway, Foster, show up here for breakfast a little before seven, and we can go out together."

"Deal," Hunnicutt confirmed.

Popov stood. "With your permission, the Olympic equestrian events start in ten minutes."

"Dmitriy, don't start thinking about jumping fences. You're not *that* good yet!" Maclean told him.

"I can watch it done, can I not?" the Russian said, walking away.

"So, what's he do here?" Hunnicutt asked, when Popov was gone.

"Like he said, nothing here, exactly, but he helped get the Project going in one important way."

"Oh?" the hunter asked. "How's that?"

"All those terrorist incidents in Europe, remember them?"

"Yeah, the counterterror groups really worked good to shut those bastards down. Damned nice shooting, some of it. Dmitriy was part of that?"

"He got the missions started, all of 'em," Maclean said.

"Damn," Mark Waterhouse observed. "So, he helped Bill get the contract for the Olympics?"

"Yep, and without that, how the hell would we get the Shiva delivered?"

"Good man," Waterhouse decided, sipping his California Chardonnay. He'd miss it, he thought, after the Project activated. Well, there were plenty of liquor warehouses around the country. He would not outlive their stocks, he was sure.

CHAPTER 35

MARATHON

IT HAD BECOME SO ENJOYABLE THAT POPOV WAS waking up early, in order to relish it more. This day he woke up just after first light, and admired the orange-rose glow on the eastern horizon that presaged the actual dawn. He'd never ridden a horse before coming to the Kansas facility, and he'd found that there was something fundamentally pleasing and manly about it, to have a large, powerful animal between one's legs, and to command it with nothing more than a gentle tug on the leather reins, or even the clucking sound one made with one's tongue. It offered a much better perspective than walking, and was just . . . pleasing to him at a sub-intellectual level.

And so he was in the cafeteria early, picking his breakfast food—plus a fresh red apple for Buttermilk—just as the kitchen staff set it out. The day promised to be fine and clear again. The wheat farmers were probably as pleased as he was with the weather, the intelligence officer thought. There had been enough rain to water the crops, and plenty of sun to ripen them. The American wheat farmers had to be the most productive in all the world, Popov reflected. With this fine land and their incredible mobile equipment, that was little surprise, he thought, lifting his tray and walking to the accustomed table. He was halfway through his scrambled eggs when Killgore and the new one, Hunnicutt, approached.

"Morning, Dmitriy," the tall hunter said in greeting.

Popov had to swallow before replying. "Good morning, Foster."

"What did you think of the riding last night?"

"The Englishman who won the gold medal was marvelous, but so was his horse."

"They pick good ones," Hunnicutt observed, heading off to get his breakfast and returning in a few minutes. "So, you were a spy, eh?"

"Intelligence officer. Yes, that was my job for the Soviet Union."

"Working with terrorists, John tells me."

"That is also true. I had my assignments, and of course I had to carry them out."

"No problem with me on that, Dmitriy. Ain't none of those folks ever bothered me or anybody I know. Hell, I worked in Libya once for Royal Dutch Shell. Found 'em a nice little field, too, and the Libyans I worked with were okay people." Like Popov, Hunnicutt had piled up eggs and bacon. He needed a lot of food to support his frame, Dmitriy imagined. "So what do you think of Kansas?"

"Like Russia in many ways, the broad horizons, and vast farms—though yours are far more efficient. So few people growing so much grain."

"Yeah, we're counting on that to keep us in bread," Hunnicutt agreed, stuffing his face. "We have enough land here to grow plenty, and all the equipment we need. I may be into that myself."

"Oh?"

"Yeah, well, everybody's going to be assigned Project work to do. Makes sense, we all gotta pull together in the beginning anyway, but I'm really looking forward to getting me some buffalo. I even bought myself a real buffalo gun."

"What do you mean?"

"There's a company in Montana, Shiloh Arms, that makes replicas of the real buffalo rifles. Bought me one a month ago—Sharps .40-90—and it shoots like a son of a bitch," the hunter reported.

"Some of the people here will not approve," Popov said, thinking of the vegans, clearly the most extreme of the druidic elements.

"Yeah, well, those people, if they think they can live in harmony with nature without guns, they better read up on Lewis and Clark. A grizzly bear don't know about this friend-of-nature stuff. He just knows what he can kill and eat, and what he can't. Sometimes you just gotta remind him what he can't. Same thing with wolves."

"Oh, come on, Foster," Killgore said, sitting to join his friends. "There has *never* been a confirmed case of wolves killing people in America."

Hunnicutt thought that was especially dumb. "Oh? Well, it's kinda hard to bitch about something if a wolf shits you out his ass. Dead men tell no tales, doc. What about Russia, Dmitriy? What about wolves there?"

"The farmers hate them, have always hated them, but the state hunters pursue them with helicopters and machine guns. That is not sporting, as you say, is it?"

"Not hardly," Hunnicutt agreed. "You treat game with respect. It's *their* land, not yours, and you have to play by the rules. That's how you learn about them, how they live, how they think. That's why we have the Boone and Crockett rules for big-game hunting. That's why I go in on horseback, and I pack 'em out on horseback. You have to play fair with game. But not with people, of course," he added with a wink.

"Our vegan friends don't understand about hunting," Killgore told them sadly. "I suppose they think they can eat grass and just take pictures of the life-forms."

"That's bullshit," Hunnicutt told them. "Death is part of the process of life, and we're the top predator, and the critters out there know it. Besides, ain't nothing tastes better than elk over an open fire, guys. That's one taste I'll never lose, and be damned if I'll ever give it up. If those extremists want to eat rabbit food, fine, but anybody tells me I can't eat meat, well, there used to be a fish-and-game cop who tried to tell me when I could hunt and when I couldn't." Hunnicutt smiled cruelly. "Well, he don't bother anybody no more. Goddamnit, *I* know the way the world's supposed to work."

You killed a policeman over this business? Popov couldn't ask. *Nekulturny barbarian.* He could just as easily have bought his meat in a supermarket. A druid with a gun, surely that was an unusually dangerous sort. He finished his breakfast and walked outside. Soon the others followed, and Hunnicutt pulled a cigar from the saddlebags he was carrying and lit it as they walked to Killgore's Hummer.

"You have to smoke in the car?" the doctor complained, as soon as he saw the thing.

"I'll hold it out the fuckin' window, John. Christ, you a secondhand-smoke Nazi, too?" the hunter demanded. Then he bent to the logic of the moment and lowered the window, holding the cigar outside for the ride to the horse barn. It didn't take long. Popov saddled the affable Buttermilk, fed her the apple from the cafeteria food line and took her outside, mounted the mare and looked around the green-amber sea that surrounded the facility. Hunnicutt came out on a horse Dmitriy had never seen, a blanket Appaloosa stallion that he took to be the hunter's own. On a closer look—

"Is that a pistol?" Popov asked.

"It's an M-1873 Colt's Single-Action Army Revolver," Foster replied, lifting it from the equally authentic Threepersons holster. "The gun that won the West. Dmitriy, I never go riding without a friend," he said with a self-satisfied smile.

"Forty-five?" the Russian asked. He'd seen them in movies, but never in real life.

"No, it's a .44-40. Caliber forty-four, with forty grains of black powder. Back a hundred years ago, you used the same cartridge in your handgun and your rifle. Cheaper that way," he explained. "And the bullet'll kill just about anything you want. Maybe not a buffalo," he allowed, "but damned sure a deer—"

"Or a man?"

"You bet. This is just about the deadliest cartridge ever made, Dmitriy." Hunnicutt replaced the revolver in the leather holster. "Now, this holster isn't authentic, really. It's called a Threepersons, named for Billy Threepersons, I think. He was a U.S. Marshal back in the old days—he was a Native American, too, and quite a lawman, so the story goes. Anyway, he invented the holster late in the nineteenth century. Easier to quick-draw out of this one, see?" Foster demonstrated. It impressed Popov to see it in real life after so many movies. The American hunter even wore a wide-brim Western hat. Popov found himself liking the man despite his bombast.

"Come on, Jeremiah," Hunnicutt said, as the other two entered the corral, and with that he led them off.

"Your horse?" Popov asked.

"Oh, yeah, bought him off a Nez Percé Indian pal. Eight years old, just about right for me." Foster smiled as they walked out the gate, a man fully in his element, Popov thought.

The rides had become somewhat repetitive. Even here there was only so much land to walk and examine, but the simple pleasure of it hadn't changed. The four men went north this morning, slowly through the prairie-dog town, then close to the interstate highway with its heavy truck traffic.

"Where is the nearest town?" Popov asked.

"That way"—Killgore pointed—"about five miles. Not much of a town."

"Does it have an airport?"

"Little one for private planes only," the doctor replied. "You go east about twenty miles, there's another town with a regional airport for puddle-jumpers, so you can get to Kansas City, from there you can fly anywhere."

"But we'll be using our own runways for the Gs, right?"

"Yep," Killgore confirmed. "The new ones can hop all the way to Johannesburg from right here."

"No shit?" Hunnicutt asked. "You mean, like, we could go hunting in Africa if we want?"

"Yeah, Foster, but packing back the elephant on a horse might be a little tough." The epidemiologist laughed.

"Well, maybe just the ivory," the hunter replied, doing the same. "I was thinking lion and leopard, John."

"Africans like to eat the lion's gonads. You see, the lion is the most virile of all the animals," Killgore told them.

"How's that?"

"Once upon a time, a nature-film crew watched two males servicing a female who was in season. They *averaged* once every ten minutes for a day and a half between 'em. So, the individual males were going three times an hour for thirty-six hours. Better than *I* ever did." There was another laugh that the men all shared. "Anyway, some African tribes still believe that when you eat a body part off something you killed, you inherit the attribute of that part. So, they like to eat lion balls."

"Does it work?" Maclean asked.

Killgore liked that. "If it did, wouldn't be many male lions left in the world, Kirk."

"You got that one right, John!" And there was more general laughter that dawn.

Popov wasn't as amused by this discussion as his companions. He looked off at the highway, and saw a Greyhound bus pass by at about seventy miles per hour—but then it slowed and stopped at an odd little square building. "What's that?" he asked.

"Bus stop for the intercity buses," Mark Waterhouse replied. "They have them out here in the boonies. You sit there and wait, then you wave for the bus to stop, like the old flag stops for trains."

"Ah." Dmitriy filed that one away as he turned his horse to the east. The hawk, he saw, the one that lived around here, was up and flying again, looking down for one of those tubular rodents to eat for its own breakfast. He watched, but evidently the hawk didn't see one. They rode for another hour, then headed back. Popov ended up next to Hunnicutt.

"You been riding how long?"

"Hardly more than a week," Dmitriy Arkadeyevich answered.

"You're doing okay for a tenderfoot," Foster told him in a friendly voice.

"I want to do it more, so that I can ride better at a faster pace."

"Well, how about tonight, just 'fore sundown, say?"

"Thank you, Foster, yes, I would like that. Just after dinner, shall we say?"

"Sure. Meet me around six-thirty at the corral."

"Thank you. I will do that," Popov promised. A night ride, under the stars, yes, that should be very pleasant.

■ ■ ■

"I got an idea," Chatham said when he got to work in the Javits Building.

"What's that?"

"This Russian guy, Serov. We got a passport photo, right?"

"Yeah," Sullivan agreed.

"Let's try the flyers again. His bank, it's probably within walking distance of his apartment, right?"

"You'd think so, wouldn't you? I like it," Special Agent Tom Sullivan said with some enthusiasm. "Let's see how fast we can get that done."

"HEY, Chuck," the voice said over the phone.

"Good morning—afternoon for you, I suppose, John."

"Yeah, just finished lunch," Clark said. "Any luck with this Serov investigation?"

"Nothing yet," the assistant director for the criminal division answered. "These things don't happen overnight, but they do happen. I have the New York field division looking for this mutt. If he's in town, we'll find him," Baker promised. "It might take a while, but we will."

"Sooner is better than later," Rainbow Six pointed out.

"I know. It always is, but stuff like this doesn't happen overnight." Baker knew that he was being kicked in the ass, lest he allow this hunt to become a low-priority item. That would not happen, but this Clark guy was CIA, and he didn't know what it was like to be a cop. "We'll find the guy for you, John. If he's over here, that is. You have the British cops looking, too?"

"Oh, yeah. Thing is, we don't know how many identities he might have."

"In his place, how many would you have?"

"Three or four, probably, and they'd be similar so they're easy for me to remember. This guy's a trained spook. So, he probably has a number of 'legends' that he can change into about as easy as he changes shirts."

"I know, John. I've worked Foreign Counterintelligence before. They are elusive game, but we know how to hunt 'em. Are you sweating any more stuff out of your terrorists?"

"They don't talk all that much," the voice replied. "The cops here can't interrogate very effectively."

So, are we supposed to roast them over a slow fire? Baker didn't ask. The FBI operated under the rules established by the U.S. Constitution. He figured that CIA most often did not, and like most FBI types he found that somewhat distasteful. He'd never met Clark, and knew him only by reputation. Director Murray respected him, but had his reservations. Clark had once tortured subjects, Murray had hinted once, and that, for the FBI, was beyond the pale, however effective it might be. The Constitution said "no" on that issue, and that was that, even for kidnappers, even though that was one class of criminal that deserved it in the eyes of every special agent of the Federal Bureau of Investigation.

"Trust the Brit cops. They're damned good, John, and they have a lot of experience with IRA types. They know how to talk to them."

"You say so, Chuck," the voice responded somewhat dubiously. "Okay, anything else we get comes right to your desk."

"Good. Talk to you later if we get anything here, John."

"Right, see ya."

Baker wondered if he should visit the bathroom to wash his hands after that conversation. He'd been briefed into Rainbow and its recent activities, and while he admired the military way of doing things—like many FBI agents, he'd been a Marine officer, recruited right out of the Quantico Marine Base into the Bureau—it differed in several important areas from the Bureau's way of doing things . . . like not violating the law. This John Clark was a hardcase son of a bitch, a former Agency guy who'd done some spooky things, Dan Murray had told him, with a mixture of admiration and disapproval. But, what the hell, they were on the same side, sort of, and this Russian subject had probably initiated an operation that had gone after Clark's own family. That added a personal element to the case, and Baker had to respect that.

CHAVEZ turned in after another long day of watching athletes run and sweat. It had been an interesting couple of weeks, and though he sorely missed Patsy and JC, whom he'd hardly had a chance to meet, he couldn't deny that he was enjoying himself. But soon it would be over. Sports reporters were tallying up the medals—America had done quite well, and the Aussies had done spectacularly well, especially in swimming events—in anticipation of announcing which nation had "won" the games. Three more days and they'd run the Marathon, traditionally the last Olympic event, followed soon thereafter by the closing ceremonies and the dousing of the flame. Already the runners were walking and/or driving along the course, to learn the hills and turns. They didn't want to get lost, though that would hardly be possible, as the route would be lined with screaming fans every step of the way. And they were working out, running in the training/practice area of the Olympic Village, not so much so as to tire themselves out, but just enough to keep their muscles and lungs ready for the murderous exertion of this longest of footraces. Chavez considered himself to be in shape, but he'd never run a twenty-plus-mile course. Soldiers had to know how to run, but not *that* far, and running that distance on paved roads had to be pure murder on the feet and ankles, despite the cushioned soles of modern running shoes. Yeah, those bastards had to be in real shape, Ding thought, lying down in his bed.

From the opening-day ceremonies, when the Olympic flame had been lit, through today, the games had been wonderfully managed and run, as if the entire national soul and strength of Australia had been devoted to one task—as America had once decided to go to the moon. Everything was superbly organized, and that was further proof that his presence here was a total waste of time. Security hadn't had even a hint of a problem. The Aussie cops were friendly, competent, and numerous, and the Australian SAS backing them up were nearly as good as his own troopers, well supported and advised by the Global Security people who'd gotten them the same tactical radios that Rainbow used. That company looked like a good vendor to use, and he thought he might recommend that John talk to them along those lines. It never hurt to have an outside opinion.

About the only bad news was the weather, which had been sultry-hot for the entire Olympiad. That had kept the medics busy at their heatstroke kiosks. Nobody had died yet, but about a hundred people had been hospitalized, and thirty times that many treated and released by the firemen paramedics and Australian army medical orderlies. That didn't count the people who just sat down on the curb and tried to cool off without getting any proper medical assistance. He didn't mind the heat all that much—Chavez had never been afraid of sweat—but he also paced himself, and, like everyone else in the Olympic stadium, was grateful for that fogging system. The TV guys had even done a story about it, which was good news for the American company that had designed and installed it. They were even talking about a version for golf courses in Texas and elsewhere, where it got about this hot. Traveling from ninety-five degrees to an apparent temperature of eighty or so was a pleasant sensation indeed, not unlike a shower, and the concourses were often crowded with people in the afternoons, escaping from the blazing sunshine.

Chavez's last thought of the night was that he would not have minded having the sunblock concession. There were signs everywhere telling people to be mindful of the hole in the ozone layer, and he knew that sun-caused skin cancer wasn't a pleasant death. So, Chavez and his men liberally slathered the stuff on every morning just like everyone else. Well, a few more days and they'd go back to Britain, where their tans would be noted by the pasty-pale Englishmen, and the weather would be a good twenty degrees cooler on what the Brits called a "hot" day. Anything over seventy-five over there and people started dropping dead in the street—which made Ding wonder about the old song that claimed only "mad dogs and Englishmen go out in the noonday sun." They must have been a lot tougher back then, Chavez thought, falling off to sleep.

POPOV saddled Buttermilk at about six that evening. The sun wasn't setting yet, but that was less than an hour away, and his horse, having rested and eaten all day, was not the least bit averse to his attention—besides, he'd given Buttermilk another apple, and the mare seemed to relish them as a man might enjoy his first glass of beer after a long working day.

Jeremiah, Hunnicutt's horse, was smaller than Buttermilk, but appeared more powerful. An odd-looking animal, his light gray coat was covered from hindquarters to neck with on almost perfectly square matlike mark of deep charcoal, hence the name "blanket Appaloosa," the Russian imagined. Foster Hunnicutt showed up, hoisting his large Western-style saddle on his shoulder, and tossing it atop the blanket, then reaching under to cinch the straps in. His last act, Popov saw, was to strap on his Colt pistol. Then he slid his left foot into the left-side stirrup and climbed aboard. Jeremiah, the stallion, must have liked to be ridden. It was as though the animal transformed himself with this new weight on his back. The head came up proudly, and the ears swiveled around, waiting for the command of its rider. That was a clucking sound, and the stallion moved out into the corral alongside Popov and Buttermilk.

"He is a fine horse, Foster."

"Best I've ever had," the hunter agreed. "The App's a great all-around critter. They come from the Nez Percé Indian tribe. The Nez Percé captured the original Western horses—they were the ones who escaped from the Spanish conquistadors, and bred out in the wild. Well, the Nez Percé learned how to breed them back to the Arabian roots of the Spanish breed, and came out with these." Hunnicutt reached down to pat his horse's neck with rough affection, which the animal seemed to like. "The Appaloosa's the best horse there is, if you ask me. Smart, steady, healthy breed, not dizzy like the Arabians are, and damned pretty, I think. They aren't the best at any one thing, but they're damned good in all things. Great all-around mount. Jeremiah here's a great hunting and tracking horse. We've spent a lot of time in the high country after elk. He even found my gold for me."

"Excuse me? Gold?"

Hunnicutt laughed. "My spread up in Montana. It used to be part of a cattle ranch, but the mountains are too steep for the cows. Anyway, there's a stream coming down from the mountain. I was letting Jeremiah drink one afternoon, and I saw something shiny, okay?" Hunnicutt stretched. "It was gold, a big hunk of gold and quartz—that's the best geological formation for gold, Dmitriy. Anyway, I figure I got a fair-sized deposit on my land. How big? There's no tellin', and it doesn't matter much anyway."

"Not matter?" Popov turned in the saddle to look at his companion. "Foster, for the last ten thousand years men have killed one another over gold."

"Not anymore, Dmitriy. That's going to end—forever, probably."

"But how? Why?" Popov demanded.

"Don't you know about the Project?"

"A little, but not enough to understand what you just said."

What the hell, the hunter thought. "Dmitriy, human life on the planet is going to come to a screeching halt, boy."

"But—"

"They didn't tell you?"

"No, Foster, not that part. Can you tell me?"

What the hell, Hunnicutt thought again. The Olympics were almost over. Why not? This Russkie understood about Nature, knew about riding, and he damned sure worked for John Brightling in a very sensitive capacity.

"It's called Shiva," he began, and went on for several minutes.

For Popov it was a time to put his professional face back on. His emotions were neutralized while he listened. He even managed a smile which masked his inner horror.

"But how do you distribute it?"

"Well, you see, John has a company that also works for him. Global Security—the boss man's a guy named Henriksen."

"Ah, yes, I know him. He was in your FBI."

"Oh? I knew he was a cop, but not a fed. Anyway, they got the consulting contract with the Aussies for the Olympics, and one of Bill's people will be spreading the Shiva. Something to do with the air-conditioning system at the stadium, they tell me. They're going to spread it on the last day, see, and the closing ceremonies. The next day everyone flies home, and then, like, thousands of people all take the bug home with them."

"But what protects us?"

"You got a shot when you came here, right?"

"Yes, Killgore said it was a booster for something."

"Oh, it was, Dmitriy. It's a booster, all right. It's the vaccine that protects you against Shiva. I got it, too. That's the 'B' vaccine, pal. There's another one, they tell me, the 'A' vaccine, but that one's not the one you want to get." Hunnicutt explained on.

"How do you know all this?" Popov asked.

"Well, you see, in case people figure this out, I'm one of the guys who helped set up the perimeter security system here. So, they told me why the Project *needs* perimeter security. It's pretty serious shit, man. If anyone were to find out about what was done, hell, they might even nuke us, y'know?" Foster pointed out with a grin. "Not many people really understand about saving the planet. I mean, we do this now, or in about twenty years, hell, *everything* and *everybody* dies. Not just the people. The animals, too. We can't let that happen, can we?"

"I see your point. Yes, that does make sense," Dmitriy Arkadeyevich agreed, without choking on his words.

Hunnicutt nodded with some satisfaction. "I figured you'd get it, man. So, those terrorist things you got started, well, they were very pretty important. Without getting everybody all hot and bothered about international terrorism, Bill Hendriksen might not have got his people in place to do their little job. So," Hunnicutt said as he fished a cigar out of his pocket, "thanks, Dmitriy. You were really an important part for this here Project."

"Thank you, Foster," Popov responded. *Is this possible?* he wondered. "How certain are you that this will work?"

"It oughta work. I asked that question, too. They let me in on some of the planning, 'cuz I'm a scientist—I was a pretty good geologist once, trust me. I know a lot of stuff. The disease is a real mother. The real key to that was the genetic engineering done on the original Ebola. Hell, you remember how scary that was a year and a half ago, right?"

Popov nodded. "Oh, yes. I was in Russia then, and it was very frightening indeed." Even more frightening had been the response of the American president, he reminded himself.

"Well, they—the real Project scientists—learned a lot from that. The key to this is the 'A' vaccine. The original outbreak may kill a few million people, but that's mainly psychological. The vaccine that Horizon's going to market is a live-virus vaccine, like the Sabin polio vaccine. But they've tuned it, like. It doesn't stop Shiva, man. It *spreads* Shiva. Takes a month to six weeks for the symptoms to show. They proved that in the lab."

"How?"

"Well, Kirk was part of that. He kidnapped some folks off the street, and they tested the Shiva and the vaccines on them. Everything worked, even the first-phase delivery system that's set up to use in Sydney."

"It is a big thing, to change the face of the world," Popov thought aloud, looking north to where the interstate highway was.

"Gotta be done, man. If we don't—well, you can kiss all this good-bye, Dmitriy. I can't let that happen."

"It's a terrible thing to do, but I see the logic of your position. Brightling is a genius, to see this, to find a way of solving the problem, and then to have the courage to act." Popov hoped his voice wasn't too patronizing, but this man Hunnicutt was a technocrat, not one who understood people.

"Yep," Hunnicutt said around the cigar, as he lit it with a kitchen match. He blew the match out, then held it until it was cold before letting it fall to the ground, lest it start a prairie fire. "Brilliant scientist, and he *gets it,* you know? Thank God, he has the resources to make all this happen. Setting all this up must have cost near onto a billion dollars—hell, just this place, not counting the one in Brazil."

"Brazil?"

"There's a smaller version of the complex down there, somewhere west of Manaus, I think. I never been there. The rain forest doesn't interest me that much. I'm an open-country sort of guy," Hunnicutt explained. "Now, the African veldt, the plains there, that's something else. Well, I guess I'll get to see it, and hunt it."

"Yes, I would like to see that, to see the wildlife, how it lives and thrives in the sun," Popov agreed, coming to his own decision.

"Yep. Gonna get me a lion or two there with my H&H .375." Hunnicutt clucked and got Jeremiah to go faster, an easy canter that Popov tried to duplicate. He'd done this pace before, but now he found that he had trouble synchronizing with Buttermilk's rather easy motions. He had to switch his mind back into his body to make that happen, but he managed it, catching up with the hunter.

"So, you will transform this country to the Old West, eh?" The interstate was about two miles off. The trucks were passing by swiftly, their trailers lit in amber lights. There would be intercity buses, too, similarly lit, he hoped.

"That's one of the things we're going to do."

"And you'll carry your pistol everywhere?"

"Revolver, Dmitriy," Foster corrected. "But, yeah. I'll be like the guys I've read about, living out here in harmony with nature. Maybe find me a woman who thinks like I do, maybe build me a nice cabin in the mountains, like Jeremiah Johnson did—but no Crow Indians to worry me there," he added with a chuckle.

"Foster?"

He turned. "Yeah?"

"Your pistol, may I hold it?" the Russian asked, praying for the correct response.

He got it. "Sure." He drew it and passed it across, muzzle up for safety.

Popov felt the weight and the balance. "It is loaded?"

"Nothing much more useless than a handgun that ain't loaded. Hell, you want to shoot it? Just cock the hammer back and let go, but you want to make sure your horse is reined in tight, okay? Jeremiah here's used to the noise. That mare might not be."

"I see." Popov took the reins in his left hand to keep Buttermilk in check. Next he extended his right hand and cocked the hammer on the Colt, heard the distinctive triple click of this particular type of revolver, and took aim at a wooden surveyor's stake and pulled the trigger. It broke cleanly at about five pounds.

Buttermilk jumped slightly with the noise, so close to her sensitive ears, but the horse didn't react all that badly. And the bullet, Popov saw, grazed the two-inch stake, six meters or so away. So, he still knew how to shoot.

"Nice, isn't it?" Hunnicutt asked. "If you ask me, the Single-Action Army's got the best balance of any handgun ever made."

"Yes," Popov agreed, "it is very nice." Then he turned. Foster Hunnicutt was seated on his stallion, Jeremiah, not three meters away. That made it easy. The former KGB officer cocked the hammer again, turned and aimed right at the center of his chest, and pulled the trigger before the hunter could even be surprised by the action. His target's eyes widened, either from his unbelieving recognition of the impossible thing that was happening or from the impact of the heavy bullet, but what it was didn't matter. The bullet went straight through his heart. The body of the hunter stayed erect in the saddle for a few seconds, the eyes still wide with shock, then it fell lifelessly backward away from Popov and onto the grassland.

Dmitriy dismounted and took the three steps to the body to make sure that Hunnicutt was dead. Then he unsaddled Jeremiah, who took the death of his owner phlegmatically, and removed the bridle, too, surprised that the animal didn't bite him for what he'd just done, but a horse wasn't a dog. With that done, he smacked the stallion heavily on the rump, and it trotted off for fifty meters or so, then stopped and started grazing.

Popov remounted Buttermilk and clucked her to a northerly direction. He looked back, saw the lit windows of the Project building complex, and wondered if he or Hunnicutt would be missed. Probably not, he judged, as the interstate highway grew closer. There was supposed to be that little village to the west, but he decided that his best chance was the bus stop hut, or perhaps thumbing a ride on a car or truck. What he'd do after that, he wasn't sure, but he knew he had to get the hell away from this place, just as fast and as far as he could manage. Popov was not a man who believed in God. His education and his upbringing had not aimed him in that direction, and so for him "god" was only the first part of "goddamned." But he'd learned something important today. He might never know if there was a God, but there were surely devils—and he had worked for them, and the horror of that was like nothing he'd ever known as a young colonel of the KGB.

CHAPTER 36

FLIGHTS OF NECESSITY

THE FEAR WAS AS BAD AS THE HORROR. POPOV HAD never experienced a really frightening time as a field-intelligence officer. There had always been tension, especially at the beginning of his career, but he'd quickly grown confident in his fieldcraft, and the skills had become for him a kind of security blanket, whose warm folds had always made his soul comfortable. But not today.

Now he was in a foreign place. Not merely a foreign land, for he was a man of cities. In any such place he knew how to disappear in minutes, to vanish so completely that scarcely any police force in the world could find him. But this wasn't a city. He dismounted Buttermilk a hundred meters from the bus hut, and again he took the time to remove the saddle and bridle, because a saddled, riderless horse was sure to attract notice, but a horse merely walking about on its own probably would not, not here, where many people kept such animals for their pleasure. Then it was just a matter of easing his way through the barbed-wire fence and walking to the bus hut, which, he found, was empty. There was no schedule on the blank, white-painted walls. It was the simplest of structures, seemingly made of poured concrete, with a thick roof to stand up against the heavy winter snows, and perhaps survive the tornadoes that he'd heard about but never experienced. The bench was also made of concrete, and he sat on it briefly to work on making his shakes go away. He'd never felt like this in his life. The fear—if these people were willing to kill millions—billions—of people, surely they would not hesitate as long as a blink to end his solitary life. He had to get away.

Ten minutes after arriving at the hut, he checked his watch and wondered if there were any buses at this hour. If not, well, there were cars and trucks, and perhaps—

He walked to the shoulder and held up his hand. Cars were passing by at over a hundred thirty kilometers per hour, which left them little time to see him in the darkness, much less brake to stop. But after fifteen minutes, a cream-colored Ford pickup truck eased over to the side of the road.

"Where you headin', buddy?" the driver asked. He looked to be a farmer, perhaps sixty years of age, his face and neck scored by lines from too many afternoon suns.

"The airport in the next town. Can you take me there?" Dmitriy said, getting in. The driver wasn't wearing a seat belt, which was probably against the law, but, then, so was cold-blooded murder, and for that reason alone he had to get the hell away from this place.

"Sure, I have to get off at that exit anyway. What's your name?"

"Joe—Joseph," Popov said.

"Well, I'm Pete. You're not from around here, are you?"

"Not originally. England, actually," Dmitriy went on, trying that accent on for size.

"Oh, yeah? What brings you here?"

"Business."

"What kind?" Pete asked.

"I am a consultant, kind of a go-between."

"So, how'd you get stuck out here, Joe?" the driver asked.

What was the matter with this man? Was he a police officer? He asked questions like someone from the Second Chief Directorate. "My, uh, friend, had a family emergency, and he had to drop me off there to wait for a bus."

"Oh." And that shut him up, Popov saw, blessing his most recent lie. *You see, I just shot and killed someone who wanted to kill you and everyone you know* . . . It was one of those times when the truth simply didn't work for him or for anyone else. His mind was going at a very rapid speed, faster by a considerable margin than this damned pickup truck, whose driver seemed unwilling to pedal much harder, every other vehicle on the road whizzing past. The farmer was an elderly man and evidently a patient one. Had Popov been driving, he'd soon establish how fast this damned truck could go. But for all that, it was only ten minutes to the green exit sign with the silhouette of an airplane tacked onto one side. He tried not to pound his fist on the armrest as the driver slowly took the exit, then a right turn to what looked like a small regional airport. In another minute, Pete took him to the US Air Express door.

"Thank you, sir," Popov said, as he left.

"Have a good trip, Joe," the driver said, with a friendly Kansas smile.

Popov walked rapidly into the diminutive terminal, and then to the desk, only twenty meters inside.

"I need to get to New York," Popov told the clerk. "First class, if possible."

"Well, we have a flight leaving in fifteen minutes for Kansas City, and from there you can connect to a US Airways flight to La Guardia, Mr.? . . . "

"Demetrius," Popov replied, remembering the name on his single remaining credit card. "Joseph Demetrius," he said, taking out his wallet and handing the card over. He had a passport in that name in a safe-deposit box in New York, and the credit card was good, with a high limit and nothing charged on it in the past three months. The desk clerk probably thought he was working quickly, but Popov also needed to visit a men's room and did his best not to show that urgent requirement. It was at that moment he realized he had a loaded revolver in the saddlebags he was carrying, and he had to get rid of *that* at once.

"Okay, Mr. Demetrius, here's your ticket for now, Gate 1, and here's the one for the Kansas City flight. It will be leaving from Gate A-34, and it's a first-class aisle seat, 2C. Any questions, sir?"

"No, no, thank you." Popov took the tickets and tucked them in his pocket. Then he looked for the entrance to the departure concourse, and headed that way, stopped by a waste bin and, after quickly looking around, very carefully took the monster handgun out of the bags, wiped it, and dumped it into the trash. He checked the terminal again. No, no one had noticed. He checked the saddlebags for anything else they might contain, but they were completely empty now. Satisfied, he headed through the security checkpoint, whose magnetometer blessedly didn't beep at his passage. Collecting the leather saddlebags off the conveyor system, he looked for and found a men's room, to which he headed directly, emerging in another minute feeling far better.

This regional airport, he saw, had but two gates, but it *did* have a bar, to which Popov went next. He had fifty dollars of cash in his wallet, and five of those paid for a double vodka, which he gulped down before taking the next hundred steps to the gate. Handing the ticket to the next clerk, he was directed out the door. The aircraft had propellers, and he hadn't traveled on one of those for years. But for this flight he would have settled for rubber bands, and Popov clambered aboard the Saab 340B short-haul airliner. Five minutes later, the propellers started turning, and Popov started to relax. Thirty-five minutes to Kansas City, a forty-five-minute layover, and then off to New York on a 737, in first class, where the alcohol was free. Best of all, he sat alone on the left side of the aircraft, with nobody to engage him in conversation. Popov needed to think, very carefully, and though quickly, not too quickly.

He closed his eyes as the aircraft started its takeoff roll, the noise of the engines blotting out all extraneous noise. *Okay,* he thought, *what have you learned, and what should you do with that knowledge?* Two simple questions, perhaps, but he had to organize the answer to the first before he knew how to answer the second. He almost started praying to a God in whose existence he did not believe, but instead he stared out the window at the mainly dark ground while his mind churned away in a darkness of its own.

CLARK awoke with a start. It was three in the morning at Hereford, and he'd had a dream whose substance retreated away from his consciousness like a cloud of smoke, shapeless and impossible to grab. He knew it had been an unpleasant dream, and he could only estimate the degree of unpleasantness by the fact that it had awakened him, a rare occurrence even when on a dangerous field assignment. He realized that his hands were shaking—and he didn't know why. He dismissed it, rolled back over, and closed his eyes for more sleep. He had a budgeting meeting today, the bane of his existence as commander of Rainbow group, playing goddamned accountant. Maybe that had been the substance of his dream, he thought with his head on the pillow. Trapped forever with accountants in discussions of where the money came from and how it would be spent . . .

THE landing at Kansas City was a smooth one, and the Saab airliner pulled up to the terminal, where, presently, the propellers stopped. A groundcrewman came up and attached a rope to the propeller tip to keep it from turning while the passengers debarked. Popov checked his watch. They were a few minutes early as he walked out the door into the clean air, then into the terminal. There, three gates away from his flight at A-34—he checked to make sure it was the correct flight—he found a bar again. They even allowed smoking in here, which was unusual for an American airport, and he sniffed in the secondhand fumes, remembering the youth in which he'd smoked *Trud* cigarettes, and almost asked one of these Americans for a smoke. But he stopped short of it and merely drank his next double vodka in a corner booth, facing the wall, wanting no one to have a reason to remember him here. After thirty minutes, his flight was called. He left ten dollars on the table and walked off, carrying the empty saddlebags, then asked himself why he was bothering. But it would appear unusual for a person to board a flight carrying nothing, and so he retained them, and tucked them into the overhead bin. The best news of this flight was that 2-D was not occupied, and he took that, facing the window to make it harder for the stewardess to see his face. Then the Boeing 737 backed away from the gate and took off into the darkness. Popov declined the drink offered to him. He'd had enough for the moment, and though some alcohol helped him to organize his thoughts, too much of it muddled them. He had enough in his system to relax, and that was all he wanted.

What exactly had he learned this day? How did it fit in with all the other things he'd learned at the building complex in western Kansas? The answer to the second question was easier than the first: whatever hard data he'd learned today contradicted *nothing* about the project's nature, location, or even its decor. It hadn't contradicted the magazines by his bedside, nor the videotapes next to the TV, nor the conversations he'd overheard in the corridors or in the building's cafeteria. Those maniacs were planning to end the world in the name of their pagan beliefs—but *how the hell* could he persuade anyone that this was so? And exactly what hard data did he have to give to someone else—and to *which* someone else? It had to be someone who would both believe him and be able to take action. But who? There was the additional problem that he'd murdered Foster Hunnicutt—he'd had no choice in the matter; he'd had to get away from the Project, and that had been his only chance to do so covertly. But now they could accuse him rightfully of murder, which meant that some police force might try to arrest him, and then how could he get the word out to stop those fucking druids from doing what they said they'd do? No policeman in the known world would believe his tale. It was far too grotesque to be absorbed by a normal mind—and surely those people in the Project had a cover story or legend which had been carefully constructed to shunt aside any sort of official inquiry. That was the most rudimentary security concern, and that Henriksen fellow would have worked on that himself.

CAROL Brightling stood in her office. She'd just printed up a letter to the chief of staff saying that she'd be taking a leave of absence to work on a special scientific project. She'd discussed this matter with Arnie van Damm earlier in the day and gotten no serious objection to her departure. She would not be missed, his body language had told her quite clearly. *Well,* she thought with a cold look at the computer screen, *neither would he,* when it came to that.

Dr. Brightling tucked the letter in an envelope, sealed it, and left it on her assistant's desk for transfer into the White House proper the next day. She'd done her job for the Project and for the planet, and it was now time for her to leave. It had been so long, so very long, since she'd felt John's arms around her. The divorce had been well publicized. It had had to be. She would never have gotten the White House job if she'd been married to one of the country's richest men. And so, she'd forsworn him, and he'd publicly forsworn the movement, the beliefs they'd both held ten years before when they'd formulated the idea for the Project, but he'd never stopped believing, any more than she had. And so she'd gotten all the way inside the government, and gotten a security clearance that gave her access to literally everything, even operational intelligence, which she then forwarded to John when he needed it. Most especially, she'd gotten access to biological-warfare information, so that they knew what USAMRIID and others had done to protect America, and so knew how to engineer Shiva in such a way as to defeat *any* proposed vaccine except those which Horizon Corporation had formulated.

But it had had its own price. John had been seen in public with all manner of young women, and had doubtless dallied with many of them, for he'd always been a passionate man. It was something they hadn't discussed before their public divorce, and for that reason it had come to her as an unpleasant surprise to see him at those occasional social functions they both had to attend, always with a pretty young thing on his arm—always a different one, since he'd never formed a real relationship with anyone but her. Carol Brightling told herself that this was good, since it meant that *she* was the only woman really a part of John's life, and thus those annoying young women were merely a way for him to dissipate his male hormones. . . . But it hadn't been easy to see, and harder still to think about, alone in her home, with only Jiggs for company, and often as not weeping in her loneliness.

But set against that small personal consideration was the Project. The White House job had merely fortified her beliefs. She'd seen it all here, Carol Brightling reminded herself, from the specifications for new nuclear weapons to bio-war reports. The Iranian attempt at a national plague, which had predated her government job, had both frightened and encouraged her. Frightened, because it had been a real threat to the country, and one that could have begun a massive effort to counter a future attack. Encouraged, because she'd learned in short order that a really effective defense was difficult at best, because vaccines had to be tailored for specific bugs. And, when one got down to it, the Iranian plague had merely heightened the public's appreciation of the threat, and *that* would make distribution of the "A" vaccine the easier to sell to the public . . . and to the government bureaucrats here and around the world who would leap at the offered cure. She would even return to her OEOB office at the proper time to urge approval for this essential public health measure, and on this issue she would be trusted.

Dr. Carol Brightling walked out of her office, turned left down the wide corridor, then left again and down the steps to her parked car. Twenty minutes later, she locked the car and walked up the steps of her apartment building, there to be greeted by the faithful Jiggs, who jumped into her arms and rubbed his furry head against her breast, as he always did. Her ten years of misery were over, and though the sacrifice had been hard to endure, the reward for it would be a planet turning back to green, and a Nature restored to Her deserved Glory.

IT was somehow good to be back in New York. Though he didn't dare to return to his apartment, this was at least a city, and here he could disappear as easily as a rat in a junkyard. He told the taxi driver to take him to Essex House, an upscale hotel on Central Park South, and there he checked in under the name of Joseph Demetrius. Agreeably, there was a minibar in his room, and he mixed a drink with two miniatures of an American brand of vodka, whose inferior taste he was too anxious to be concerned about. Then, having come to his decision, he called the airline to confirm flight information, checked his watch, then called the front desk and instructed the clerk there to give him a wake-up call at the hellish hour of 3:30 A.M. The Russian collapsed into the bed without undressing. He'd have to do some quick shopping in the morning, and also visit his bank to pull his Demetrius passport out of the safe-deposit box. Then he'd get five hundred dollars out of an ATM cash machine, courtesy of his Demetrius MasterCard, and he'd be safe . . . well, if not truly safe, then safer than he was now, enough to be somewhat confident in himself and his future, such as it was, if the Project could be stopped. And if not, he told himself behind closed and somewhat drunken eyes, then at least he'd know what to avoid in order to keep himself alive. Probably.

CLARK awoke at his accustomed hour. JC was sleeping better now, after two weeks of life, and this morning he'd at least synchronized himself with the master of the house, John found, as he emerged from his morning shave to hear his grandson's first wake-up chirps in the bedroom where he and Patsy were currently quartered. Sandy was awakened by the sounds, though she'd managed to ignore the alarm on John's side of the bed, her maternal or grandmaternal instincts obviously having their own selective power. Clark headed down to the kitchen to flip on the coffee machine, then opened the front door to collect his morning copies of the *Times,* the *Daily Telegraph,* and the *Manchester Guardian* for his morning news brief. One thing about Brit papers, he'd learned, the quality of the writing was better than in most American newspapers, and the articles were rather more concise.

The little guy was growing, John told himself when Patsy came into the kitchen with JC affixed to her left breast and Sandy in tow behind. But his daughter wasn't drinking coffee, evidently fearful that the caffeine might find its way into her breast milk. Instead she drank milk herself, while Sandy got breakfast going. John Conor Chavez was fully engaged with his breakfast, and in ten minutes, his grandfather was similarly engaged with his own, the radio now on a BBC channel to catch the morning news to supplement the print in front of him. Both modalities confirmed that the world was essentially at peace. The lead story was the Olympic Games, which Ding had reported on every night for them—the morning for him, all those time zones away—the reports usually ending with the phone held to JC's little face so that his proud father might hear the mewings he occasionally made, though rarely on cue.

By 6:30, John was dressed and heading out the door, and this morning, unlike a few others, he drove to the athletic field for his morning exercises. The men of Team-1 were there, their numbers still short because of the losses at the hospital shoot-out, but proud and tough as ever. Sergeant First Class Fred Franklin led the team this morning, and Clark followed his instructions, not as ably as the younger men, but trying still to keep up, and so earn their respect if also a few disparaging looks at the old fart who thought he was something else. The also short-numbered Team-2 was at the other side of the field, led by Sergeant Major Eddie Price, John saw. Half an hour later, he showered again—doing so twice in ninety minutes almost every day had often struck him as strange, but the wake-up shower was so firm a part of his life that he couldn't dispense with it, and after working up a sweat with the troops, he always needed another. After that, dressed in his "boss's" suit, he entered the headquarters building, checked the fax machine first, as always, and found a message from FBI headquarters that told him that nothing new had developed on the Serov case. A second fax told him that a package would be couriered to him early that morning from Whitehall, without saying exactly what it was. Well, John thought, flipping on the office coffee-drip machine, he'd find out in due course.

Al Stanley came in just before eight, still showing the effects of his wounds, but bouncing back well for a man of his age. Bill Tawney was in just two minutes later, and the senior leadership of Rainbow was in place for another working day.

▪ ▪ ▪

THE phone woke him up with a jolt. Popov reached for it in the darkness, missed, then reached again. "Yes."

"It's three-thirty, Mr. Demetrius," the operator said.

"Yes, thank you," Dmitriy Arkadeyevich replied, switching on the light and swiveling to get his feet on the carpeted floor. The note next to his phone told him how to dial the number he wanted: nine . . . zero-one-one-four four . . .

ALICE Foorgate came in a few minutes early. She put her purse in a desk drawer and sat down, and began reviewing her notes on the things that were supposed to happen today. Oh, she saw, a budget meeting. Mr. Clark would be in a foul mood until after lunch. Then her phone rang.

"I need to speak to Mr. John Clark," the voice said.

"May I tell him who's calling?"

"No," the voice said. "You may not."

That made the secretary blink with puzzlement. She almost said that she could hardly forward a call under such circumstances, but didn't. It was too early in the morning for unpleasantness. She placed the incoming call on hold and punched another button.

"A call for you on line one, sir."

"Who is it?" Clark asked.

"He didn't say, sir."

"Okay," John grumbled. He switched buttons and said, "This is John Clark."

"Good morning, Mr. Clark," the anonymous voice said in greeting.

"Who is this?" John asked.

"We have a mutual acquaintance. His name is Sean Grady."

"Yes?" Clark's hand tightened on the instrument, and he punched the RECORD button for the attached taping system.

"You may know my name, therefore, as Iosef Andreyevich Serov. We should meet, Mr. Clark."

"Yes," John replied evenly, "I'd like that. How do we do it?"

"Today, I think, in New York. Take the British Airways Concorde Flight 1 into JFK, and I will meet you at one in the afternoon at the entrance to the Central Park Zoo. The redbrick building that looks like a castle. I shall be there at eleven o'clock exactly. Any questions?"

"I suppose not. Okay, eleven A.M. in New York."

"Thank you. Good-bye." The line went dead, and Clark switched buttons again.

"Alice, could you have Bill and Alistair join me, please?"

They came in less than three minutes later. "Listen to this one, guys," John said, hitting the PLAY button on the tape machine.

"Bloody hell," Bill Tawney observed, a second before Al Stanley could do the same. "He wants to meet you? I wonder why."

"Only one way to find out. I have to catch the Concorde for New York. Al, could you get Malloy awake so he can chopper me to Heathrow?"

"You're going?" Stanley asked. The answer was obvious.

"Why not? Hell"—John grinned—"it gets me out of the fucking budget meeting."

"Quite so. There could be dangers involved."

"I'll have the FBI send some people to look after me, and I'll have a friend with me," Clark pointed out, meaning his .45 Beretta. "We're dealing with a professional spook here. There's more danger to him than there is to me, unless he's got a very elaborate operation set up at the other end, and we should be able to spot that. He wants to meet with me. He's a pro, and that means he wants to tell me something—or maybe ask me something, but I'd lean the other way, right?"

"I'd have to agree with that," Tawney said.

"Objections?" Clark asked his principal subordinates. There were none. They were just as curious as he was, though they'd want good security in New York for the meeting. But that would not be a problem.

Clark checked his watch. "It's short of four in the morning there—and he wants the meet to be today. Pretty fast for this sort of thing. Why the hurry? Any ideas?"

"He could want to tell you that he had no connection with the hospital incident. Aside from that? . . ." Tawney just shook his head.

"Timing's a problem. That's a ten-thirty flight, John," Stanley pointed out. "It's now three-thirty on your East Coast. No one important will be at work yet."

"We'll just have to wake them up." Clark looked at his phone and hit the speed-dial button for FBI headquarters.

"FBI," another anonymous voice said.

"I need to talk to Assistant Director Chuck Baker."

"I don't think Mr. Baker will be in now."

"I know. Call him at home. Tell him that John Clark is calling." He could almost hear the *oh, shit* at the other end of the call, but an order had been given by a voice that sounded serious, and it would have to be followed.

"Hello," another voice said somewhat groggily a minute later.

"Chuck, this is John Clark. Something's turned on the Serov case."

"What's that?" *And why the hell can't it wait four hours?* the voice didn't go on.

John explained. He could hear the man waking up at the other end.

"Okay," Baker said. "I'll have some guys from New York meet you at the terminal, John."

"Thanks, Chuck. Sorry to shake you loose at this hour."

"Yeah, John. Bye."

The rest was easy. Malloy came into his office after his own morning workout, and called to get his helicopter readied for a hop. It didn't take long. The only headache was having to filter through the in- and outbound airliner traffic, but the chopper landed at the general-aviation terminal, and an airport security car took John to the proper terminal, where Clark was able to walk into the Speedway Lounge twenty minutes before the flight to collect his ticket. This way, he also bypassed security, and was thus spared the embarrassment of having to explain that he carried a pistol, which in the United Kingdom was the equivalent of announcing that he had a case of highly infectious leprosy. The service was British-lavish, and he had to decline the offer of champagne before boarding the aircraft. Then the flight was called, and Clark walked down the jetway and into the world's fastest airliner for Flight 1 to New York's JFK International. The pilot gave the usual preflight brief, and a tractor pushed the oversized fighter aircraft away from its gate. In less than four hours, John thought, he'd be back in the States. Wasn't air travel wonderful? But better yet, he had in his lap the package that had just been couriered in. It was the personnel package for one Popov, Dmitriy Arkadeyevich. It had been heavily edited, he was sure, but even so it made for interesting reading, as the Concorde leaped into the air and turned west for America. *Thank you, Sergey Nikolayevich,* John thought, flipping through the pages. It had to be the real KGB file, John saw. Some of the photocopied pages showed pinholes in the upper-left corners, which meant that they dated back to when KGB had used pins to keep pages together instead of staples, that having been copied from the British MI-6 back in the 1920s. It was a piece of trivia that only insiders really knew.

CLARK was about halfway across the North Atlantic when Popov awoke on his own again at seven-fifteen. He ordered breakfast sent up and got himself clean in preparation for a busy day. By eight-fifteen, he was walking out the front door, and looked first of all for a men's store that was open for business. That proved to be frustrating, until finally he found one whose doors opened promptly at nine. Thirty minutes later, he had an expensive but somewhat ill-fitting gray suit, plus shirts and ties that he took back to his hotel room and into which he changed at once. Then it was time for him to walk to Central Park.

The building that guarded the Central Park Zoo was strange to behold. It was made of brick, and had battlements on the roof as though to defend the area against armed attack, but the same walls were dotted with windows, and the entire building sat in a depression rather than atop a hill, as a proper castle did. Well, American architects had their own ideas, Popov decided. He circulated about the area, looking for the FBI agents (or perhaps CIA field officers? he wondered) who were certain to be there to cover this meeting—and possibly to arrest him? Well, there was nothing to be done about that. He would now learn if this John Clark were truly an intelligence officer. That business had rules, and Clark should follow them as a matter of professional courtesy. The gamble was a huge one on his part, and Clark had to respect it for that very reason, but he couldn't be sure. Well, one couldn't be sure of much in this world.

DR. Killgore came to the cafeteria at his accustomed hour, but surprisingly didn't find his Russian friend, or Foster Hunnicutt, there. Well, maybe they'd both slept late. He lingered over breakfast twenty minutes more than usual before deciding, the hell with it, and drove to the horse barn. There he found another surprise. Both Buttermilk and Jeremiah were in the corral, neither of them saddled or bridled. There was no way for him to know that both horses had walked back to their home on their own last night. Curious, he walked both back to their stalls before saddling up his own usual mount. He waited outside in the corral for another fifteen minutes, wondering if his friends would show up, but they didn't, and he and Kirk Maclean rode off west for their morning tour of the countryside.

THE covert side of the business could be fun, Sullivan thought. Here he was driving what appeared to be a Consolidated Edison van, and wearing the blue coveralls that announced the same employment. The clothing was baggy enough to allow him to carry a dozen weapons inside the ugly garment, but better yet it made him effectively invisible. There were enough of these uniforms on the streets of New York that no one ever noticed them. This discreet surveillance mission had been laid on in one big hurry, with no fewer than eight agents already at the rendezvous site, all carrying the passport photo of this

Serov subject, for what good it was. They lacked height and weight estimates, and that meant they were looking for an OWG, an ordinary white guy, of which New York City had at least three million.

Inside the terminal, his partner, Frank Chatham, was waiting at the exit ramp off British Airways Flight 1, in a suit and tie. His coverall outfit was inside the Con Ed van that Sullivan had parked outside the terminal. They didn't even know who this Clark guy was whom they were meeting, just that Assistant Director Baker thought he was pretty fucking important.

The aircraft got in exactly on time. Clark, in seat 1-C, stood and was the first off the aircraft. The FBI escort at the jetway exit was easy to spot.

"Looking for me?"

"Your name, sir?"

"John Clark. Chuck Baker should have—"

"He did. Follow me, sir." Chatham led him out the fast way, bypassing immigration and customs, and it was just one more time that John's passport wouldn't be stamped to celebrate his entry into a sovereign country. The Con Ed van was easily spotted. Clark went for it without being told to and hopped in.

"Hi, I'm John Clark," he told the driver.

"Tom Sullivan. You've met Frank."

"Let's move, Mr. Sullivan," John told him.

"Yes, sir." The van took off at once. In the back, Chatham sat and struggled into his blue coveralls.

"Okay, sir, what exactly is happening here?"

"I'm meeting a guy."

"Serov?" Sullivan asked, as he negotiated his way onto the highway.

"Yeah, but his real name is Popov. Dmitriy Arkadeyevich Popov. He used to be a colonel in the old KGB. I have his personnel package, read it coming across. He's a specialist in dealing with terrorists, probably has more connections than the phone company."

"This guy set up the operation that—"

"Yeah." John nodded in the front-right passenger seat. "The operation that went after my wife and my daughter. They were the primary targets."

"Shit!" Chatham observed, as he zipped his outfit up. They hadn't known *that.* "And you want to meet with this mutt?"

"Business is business, guys," John pointed out, wondering if he really believed that or not.

"So, who are you?"

"Agency, used to be, anyway."

"How do you know Mr. Baker?"

"I have a slightly different job now, and we have to interface with the Bureau. Mainly with Gus Werner, but lately I've been talking with Baker, too."

"You part of the team that took down the bad guys at the hospital over in England?"

"I'm the boss of it," Clark told them. "But don't go spreading that around, okay?"

"No problem," Sullivan replied.

"You're working the case on Mr. Serov?"

"That's one of them we've got on the desk, yes."

"What do you got on it?" John asked.

"Passport photo—I guess you have that."

"Better, I have his official KGB photo. Better than the passport one, it's like a mug shot full face and profile, but it's ten years old. What else you have?"

"Bank accounts, credit-card records, post-office box, but no address yet. We're still working on that."

"What's he wanted for?" John asked next.

"Conspiracy mainly," Sullivan answered. "Conspiracy to incite terrorism, conspiracy to traffic in illegal drugs. Those statutes are pretty broad, so that's what we use in cases where we don't have much of a clue as to what's really happening."

"Can you arrest him?"

"You bet. On sight," Chatham said in the back. "Do you want us to do that?"

"I'm not sure." Clark settled into the uncomfortable seat, and watched the approach of the New York skyline, still wondering what the hell this was all about. He'd find out soon enough, John told himself, thinking that it couldn't be soon enough to meet the fucker who'd sent armed men out after his wife and daughter. He managed a scowl at the approaching city that the FBI agents didn't notice.

POPOV thought that he had two FBI types spotted, not to mention a pair of uniformed police officers who might or might not be part of the surveillance that had to be assembling here. There was nothing for it, however. He had to meet with this Clark fellow, and that meant that the meet had to be in a public place, else he'd have to walk right into the lion's den, something he could not bring himself to do. Here he'd have some chance, just a matter, really, of walking south toward the subway station and racing down to catch a train. That would shake a lot of them off, and give him options. Dump his suit coat and change his appearance, put on the hat he had tucked into a pants pocket. He figured he had about an even chance of evading contact if he had to, and there was little danger that anyone would shoot him, not in the heart of America's largest city. But his best chance was to communicate with Clark. If he were the professional Popov believed him to be, then they could do business. They had to. There was no choice for either of them, Dmitriy Arkadeyevich told himself.

THE van crossed the East River and proceeded west through crowded streets. John checked his watch.

"No problem, sir. We'll be about ten minutes early," Sullivan told him.

"Good," John replied tensely. It was coming soon now, and he had to get his emotions totally under control. A passionate man, John Terence Clark had more than once let them loose on a job, but he couldn't allow this now. Whoever this Russian was, he had invited him to the meeting, and that meant something—what, he could not yet know, but it had to mean that *something* unusual was afoot. And so he had to set aside all thoughts of past dangers to his immediate family. He had to be stone cold at this meeting, and so, sitting there in the front seat of the Con Ed truck, Clark told himself to breathe deeply and relax, and slowly he managed to accomplish that. Then his curiosity took over. This Russian had to know that Clark knew what he'd done, and *still* he'd asked for this meeting, and insisted on having it done speedily. That had to mean something, John told himself, as they broke through traffic and turned left onto Fifth Avenue. He checked his watch again. They were fourteen minutes early. The van eased over to the right and stopped. Clark stepped out and headed south on the crowded sidewalk, past people selling used books and other gimcracks from what appeared to be portable wooden closets. Behind him the FBI agents moved the van forward, stopped it close to the meet-building and got out, carrying papers and looking around rather too obviously like Con Ed employees, John thought. Then he turned right and walked down the stairs and looked up at the redbrick building that had been someone's idea of a castle a hundred years or so before. It didn't take long.

"Good morning, John Clark," a man's voice said behind him.

"Good morning, Dmitriy Arkadeyevich," John replied, without turning at first.

"Very good," the voice said approvingly. "I congratulate you on learning one of my names."

"We have good intelligence support," John went on, without turning. "You had a pleasant flight?"

"A fast one. I've never done the Concorde before. It was not unpleasant. So, Dmitriy, what can I do for you?"

"I must first of all apologize to you for my contacts with Grady and his people."

"What about the other operations?" Clark asked as a dangle, something of a gamble, but he was in a gambling mood.

"Those did not concern you directly, and only one person was killed."

"But that one was a sick little girl," John observed too quickly.

"No, I had nothing to do with Worldpark. The bank in Bern, and the stock-trader outside Vienna, yes, those were my missions, but not the amusement park."

"So, you have implicated yourself in three terrorist operations. That is against the law, you know."

"Yes, I am aware of that," the Russian replied dryly.

"So, what can I do for you?" John asked again.

"It is more what I can do for you, Mr. Clark."

"And that is?" Still he didn't turn. But there had to be half a dozen FBI agents watching, maybe one with a shotgun microphone to record the exchange. In his haste to come over, Clark hadn't been able to get a proper recording system for his suit.

"Clark, I can give you the reason for the missions, and the name of the man who instigated it all—it is quite monstrous. I only discovered yesterday, not even twenty-four hours ago, what the purpose for all of this is."

"So, what is the objective?" John asked.

"To kill almost every human being on the planet," Popov replied.

That made Clark stop walking and turn to look at the man. The KGB file mug shot was pretty good, he saw. "Is this some sort of movie script?" he asked coldly.

"Clark, yesterday I was in Kansas. There I learned the plan for this 'project.' I shot and killed the person who told me so that I could escape. The man I killed was Foster Hunnicutt, a hunter-guide from Montana. I shot him in the chest with his own Colt forty-four pistol. From there I went to the nearest highway and managed to beg a ride to the nearest regional airport, from there to Kansas City, and from there to New York. I called you from my hotel room less than eight hours ago. Yes, Clark, I know you have the power to arrest me. You must have security watching us right now, presumably from your FBI," he said as they walked into the area with the animal cages. "And so you need only wave your hand and I will be arrested, and I have just told you the name of the man I shot, and the location where it was done. Plus you have me for inciting terrorist incidents, and I presume for drug-trafficking as well. I know this, yet I have asked for this meeting. Do you suppose that I am joking with you, John Clark?"

"Perhaps not," Rainbow Six answered, looking closely at the man.

"Very well, and in that case I propose that you have us taken to the local FBI office or some other secure place, so that I can give you the information you need under controlled circumstances. I require only your word that I will not be detained or arrested."

"You would believe me if I were to say that?"

"Yes. You are CIA, and you know the rules of the game, do you not?"

Clark nodded. "Okay, you have my word—if you're telling me the truth."

"John Clark, I wish I were not," Popov said. "Truly I wish I were not, *tovarich.*"

John looked hard into his eyes, and in them he saw fear . . . no, something deeper than fear. This guy had just called him *comrade.* That meant something, particularly under these circumstances.

"Come on," John told him, turning around and heading for Fifth Avenue.

"THAT'S our subject, guys," a female agent said over the radio circuit. "That is subject Serov all gift-wrapped like a toy from F.A.O. Schwarz. Wait. They're turning around, heading east to Fifth."

"No shit?" Frank Chatham asked. Then he saw them walking very quickly to where the van was parked.

"You got a safe house around here?" Clark asked.

"Well, yeah, we do, but—"

"Get us there, right now!" Clark ordered. "You can terminate your cover operation at once, too. Get in, Dmitriy," he said, opening the sliding door.

The safe house was only ten blocks away. Sullivan parked the van, and all four men went inside.

C H A P T E R 3 7

DYING FLAME

THE SAFE HOUSE WAS A FOUR-STORY BROWNSTONE that had been given to the federal government decades before by a grateful businessman whose kidnapped son had been recovered alive by the Federal Bureau of Investigation. It was used mainly for interviewing UN diplomats who worked in one way or another for the U.S. government, and had been one of the places used by Arkady Schevchenko, still the highest-ranking Soviet defector of all time. Outwardly unremarkable, inside it had an elaborate security system and three rooms outfitted with recording systems and two-way mirrors, plus the usual tables, and more comfortable chairs than normal. It was manned around the clock, usually by a rookie agent in the New York field division whose purpose was merely that of doorman.

Chatham took them to the top-floor interview room and sat Clark and Popov down in the windowless cubicle. The microphone was set up, and the reel-to-reel tape recorder set to turning. Behind one of the mirrors, a TV camera and attendant VCR was set up as well.

"Okay," Clark said, announcing the date, time, and place. "With me is Colonel Dmitriy Arkadeyevich Popov, retired, of the former Soviet KGB. The subject of this interview is international terrorist activity. My name is John Clark, and I am a field officer of the Central Intelligence Agency. Also here are—"

"Special Agent Tom Sullivan—"

"And—"

"Special Agent Frank Chatham—"

"Of the FBI's New York office. Dmitriy, would you please begin?" John said.

It was intimidating as hell for Popov to do this, and it showed in the first few minutes of his narrative. The two FBI agents showed total incredulity on their faces for the first half hour, until he got to the part about his morning rides in Kansas.

"Maclean? What was his first name?" Sullivan asked.

"Kirk, I think, perhaps Kurt, but I think it ended with a K," Popov replied. "Hunnicutt told me that he'd kidnapped people here in New York to be used as guinea pigs for this Shiva sickness."

"Fuck," Chatham breathed. "What does this guy look like?"

Popov told them in very accurate terms, down to hair length and eye color.

"Mr. Clark, we know this guy. We've interviewed him in the disappearance of a young woman, Mary Bannister. And another woman, Anne Pretloe, disappeared under very similar circumstances. Holy shit, you say they were murdered?"

"No, I said they were killed as test subjects for this Shiva disease that they plan to spread at Sydney."

"Horizon Corporation. That's where this Maclean guy works. He's out of town now, his coworkers told us."

"Yes, you will find him in Kansas," Popov told them, with a nod.

"You know how *big* Horizon Corporation is?" Sullivan asked.

"Big enough. Okay, Dmitriy," Clark said, turning back, "exactly how do you think they will spread this virus?"

"Foster told me it was part of the air-cooling system at the stadium. That is all I know."

John thought about the Olympics. They were running the marathon today, and that was the last event, to be followed by the closing ceremonies that evening. There wasn't time to think very much further than that. He turned, lifted the telephone, and dialed England. "Give me Stanley," he told Mrs. Foorgate.

"Alistair Stanley," the voice said next.

"Al, this is John. Get hold of Ding and have him call me here." John read the number off the phone. "Right now—immediately, Al. I mean right the hell now."

"Understood, John."

Clark waited four and a half minutes by his watch before the phone rang.

"You're lucky he got me, John. I was just getting dressed to leave and watch the mara—"

"Shut the hell up and listen to me, Domingo," Clark said harshly.

■ ■ ■

"YEAH, John, go ahead," Chavez answered, getting out a pad to take some notes. "Is this for real?" he asked after a few seconds.

"We believe it to be, Ding."

"It's like something from a bad movie." Was this something concocted by SPECTRE? Chavez wondered. What was the potential profit in it for anybody?

"Ding, the guy giving this to me is named Serov, Iosef Andreyevich. He's here with me now."

"Okay, I hear you, Mr. C. When is this operation supposed to take place?"

"Around the time of the closing ceremonies, supposedly. Is there anything else today besides the marathon?"

"No, that's the last major event, and we ought not to be too busy 'til the race ends. We expect the stadium to start filling up around five this afternoon, and then they have the closing ceremonies, and everybody goes home." *Including me,* he didn't have to add.

"Well, that's their plan, Ding."

"And you want us to stop it."

"Correct. Get moving. Keep this number. I'll be here all day on the STU-4. From now on, all transmissions will be secure. Okay?"

"You got it. Let me get moving, John."

"Move," the voice told him. "Bye."

Chavez hung up, wondering how the hell he'd do this. First he had to assemble his team. They were all on the same floor, and he went into the corridor, knocked on each door, and told the NCOs to come to his suite.

"Okay, people, we got a job to handle today. Here's the deal," he began, then spun the tale for about five minutes.

"Christ," Tomlinson managed to say for all of them. The story was quite incredible, but they were accustomed to hearing and acting upon strange information.

"We have to find the control room for the fogging system. Once we do that, we'll put people in there. We'll rotate the duty. George and Homer, you start, then Mike and I will relieve you. Call it two-hour rotation inside and outside. Radios will be on at all times. Deadly force is authorized, people."

Noonan had heard the briefing, too. "Ding, this whole thing sounds kinda unlikely."

"I know, Tim, but we act on it anyway."

"You say so, man."

"Let's move, people," Ding told them, standing.

■ ■ ■

"THIS IS the day, Carol," John Brightling told his ex-wife. "Less than ten hours from now, the Project starts."

She dropped Jiggs on the floor and came to embrace him. "Oh, John!"

"I know," he told her. "It's been a long time. Couldn't have done it without you."

Henriksen was there, too. "Okay, I talked with Wil Gearing twenty minutes ago. He'll be hooking up the Shiva dispenser right before they start the closing ceremonies. The weather is working for us, too. It's going to be another hot one in Sydney, temperature's supposed to hit ninety-seven degrees. So, people'll be camping out under the foggers."

"And breathing heavily," Dr. John Brightling confirmed. That was another of the body's methods for shedding excess heat.

CHAVEZ was in the stadium now, already sweating from the building heat and wondering if any of the marathon runners would fall over dead from this day's race. So Global Security, with whose personnel he'd interfaced briefly, was part of the mission. He wondered if he could remember all the faces he'd seen in the two brief conferences he'd had, but for now he had to find Colonel Wilkerson. Five minutes later, in the security-reaction hut, he found the man.

"G'day, Major Chavez."

"Hey, Frank. I got a question for you."

"What's that, Ding?"

"The fogging system. Where's it come from?"

"The pumping room's by Section Five, just left of the ramp."

"How do I get in there?"

"You get a key to the door and the alarm code from me. Why, old boy?"

"Oh, well, I just want to see it."

"Is there a problem, Ding?" Wilkerson asked.

"Maybe. I got to thinking," Chavez went on, trying to formulate a persuasive lie for the moment. "What if somebody wanted to use it to dispense a chemical agent, like? And I thought I might—"

"Check it out? One of the Global people beat you to that one, lad. Colonel Gearing. He checked out the entire installation. Same concern as you, but a bit earlier."

"Well, can I do it, too?"

"Why?"

"Call it paranoia," Chavez replied.

"I suppose." Wilkerson rose from his chair and pulled the proper key off the wall. "The alarm code is one-one-three-three-six-six."

Eleven thirty-three sixty-six, Ding memorized.

"Good. Thanks, Colonel."

"My pleasure, Major," the SAS lieutenant colonel replied.

Chavez left the room, rejoined his people outside, and headed rapidly back to the stadium.

"Did you tell 'em about the problem?" Noonan asked.

Chavez shook his head. "I wasn't authorized to do that. John expects us to handle it."

"What if our friends are armed?"

"Well, Tim, we *are* authorized to use necessary force, aren't we?"

"Could be messy," the FBI agent warned, worried about local laws and jurisdictions.

"Yeah, I suppose so. We use our heads, okay? We know how to do that, too."

KIRK Maclean's job at the Project was to keep an eye on the environmental support systems, mainly the air-conditioning and the over-pressurization system, whose installation he didn't really understand. After all, everyone inside the buildings would have the "B" vaccine shot, and even if Shiva got in, there wasn't supposed to be any danger. But he supposed that John Brightling was merely being redundant in his protective-systems thinking, and that was okay with him. His daily work was easily dealt with—it mainly involved checking dials and recording systems, all of which were stuck in the very center of normal operating ranges—and then he felt like a ride. He walked into the transport office and took a set of keys for a Project Hummer, then headed out to the barn to get his horse. Another twenty minutes, and he'd saddled his quarter horse and headed north, cantering across the grassland, through the lanes in the wheat fields where the farm machines turned around, taking his time through one of the prairie-dog towns, and heading generally toward the interstate highway that formed the northern edge of the Project's real estate. About forty minutes into the ride, he saw something unusual.

Like every rural plot of land in the American West, this one had a resident buzzard population. Here, as in most such places, they were locally called turkey buzzards, regardless of the actual breed, large raptors that ate carrion and were distinctive for their size and their ugliness—black feathers and naked red-skinned heads that carried large powerful beaks designed for ripping flesh off the carcasses of dead animals. They were Nature's garbage collectors—or Nature's own morticians, as some put it—important parts of the ecosystem, though distasteful to some. He saw about six of them circling something in the tall grass to the northeast. Six was a lot—then he realized that there were more still, as he spotted the black angular shapes in the grass from two miles away. Something large had evidently died, and they had assembled to clean—eat—it up. They were careful, conservative birds. Their circling and examination was to ensure that whatever they saw and smelled wasn't still alive, and hence able to jump up and injure them when they came down to feed. Birds were the most delicate of creatures, made mostly for air, and needing to be in perfect condition to fly and survive.

What are they eating? Maclean wondered, heading his horse over that way at a walk, not wanting to spook the birds any more than necessary, and wondering if they were afraid of a horse and rider. Probably not, he thought, but he'd find out about this little bit of Nature's trivia.

Whatever it was, he thought five minutes later, the birds liked it. It was an ugly process, Maclean thought, but no more so than when he ate a burger, at least as far as the cow was concerned. It was Nature's way. The buzzards ate the dead and processed the protein, then excreted it out, returning the nutrients back to the soil so that the chain of life could proceed again in its timeless cycle of life-death-life. Even from a hundred yards away, there were too many birds for him to determine what they were feasting on. Probably a deer or pronghorn antelope, he thought, from the number of birds and the way they bobbed their heads up and down, consuming the creature that Nature had reclaimed for Herself. What did pronghorns die of? Kirk wondered. Heart attacks? Strokes? Cancer? It might be interesting to find out in a few years, maybe have one of the Project physicians do a postmortem on one—if they got there ahead of the buzzards, which, he thought with a smile, ate up the evidence. But at fifty yards, he stopped his horse. Whatever they were eating seemed to be wearing a plaid shirt. With that he urged his horse closer, and at ten yards the buzzards took notice, first swiveling their odious red heads and cruel black eyes, then hopping away a few feet, then, finally, flapping back into the air.

"Oh, fuck," Maclean said quietly, when he got closer. The neck had been ripped away, leaving the spine partly exposed, and in some places the shirt had been shredded, too, by the powerful beaks. The face had also been destroyed, the eyes gone and most of the skin and flesh, but the hair was fairly intact, and—

"Jesus . . . Foster? What happened to you, man?" It required a few more feet of approach to see the small red circle in the center of the dark shirt. Maclean didn't dismount his horse. A man was dead, and, it appeared, had been shot dead. Kirk looked around and saw the hoofprints of one or two horses right here . . . probably two, he decided. Backing away, he decided to get back to the Project as quickly as his horse could manage. It took fifteen minutes, which left his quarter horse winded and the rider shaken. He jumped off, got into his Hummer and raced back to the Project and found John Killgore.

THE room was grossly nondescript, Chavez saw. Just pipes, steel and plastic, and a pump, which was running, as the fogging-cooling system had started off from its timer a few minutes before, and Chavez's first thought was, *what if the bug's already in the system—I just walked through it, and what if I breathed the fucking thing in?*

But here he was, and if that were the case . . . but, no, John had told him that the poisoning was to start much later in the day, and that the Russian was supposed to know what was going on. You had to trust your intelligence sources. You just had to. The information they gave you was the currency of life and death in this business.

Noonan bent down to look at the chlorine canister that hung on the piping. "It looks like a factory product, Ding," the FBI agent said, for what that was worth. "I can see how you switch them out. Flip off the motor here"—he pointed—"close this valve, twist this off with a wrench like the one on the wall there, swap on the new one, reopen the valve and hit the pump motor. Looks like a thirty-second job, maybe less. Boom-boom-boom, and you're done."

"And if it's already been done?" Chavez asked.

"Then we're fucked," Noonan replied. "I hope your intel's good on this, partner."

The fog outside had the slight smell of chlorine, Chavez told himself hopefully, like American city water, and chlorine was used because it killed germs. It was the only element besides oxygen that supported combustion, wasn't it? He'd read that somewhere, Domingo thought.

"What do you think, Tim?"

"I think the idea makes sense, but it's one *hell* of a big operation for somebody to undertake, and it's—Ding, who the hell would do something like this? And *why,* for Christ's sake?"

"I guess we have to figure that one out. But for now, we watch this thing like it's the most valuable gadget in the whole fucking world. Okay." Ding turned to look at his men. "George and Homer, you guys stay here. If you gotta take a piss, do it on the floor." There was a drainage pit there, they all saw. "Mike and I will handle things outside. Tim, you stay close, too. We got our radios, and that's how we communicate. Two hours on, two hours off, but never more than fifty yards from this place. Questions?"

"Nope," Sergeant Tomlinson said for the rest. "If somebody comes in and tries to fool with this? . . ."

"You stop him, any way you have to. And you call for help on your radios."

"Roge-o, boss," George said. Homer Johnston nodded agreement.

Chavez and the other two went back outside. The stadium had filled up, people wanting to see the start of the marathon . . . and then what? Ding wondered. Just sit here and wait for three hours? No, about two and a half. That was about the usual championship time, wasn't it? Twenty-six miles. Forty-two kilometers or so. One hell of a long way for a man—or woman—to run, a daunting distance even for him, Chavez admitted to himself, a distance better suited to a helicopter lift or a ride in a truck. He, Pierce, and Noonan walked to one of the ramps and watched the TVs hanging there.

By this time the runners were assembling for the crowded start. The favorites were identified, some of them given up-close-and-personal TV biographies. The local Australian commentary discussed the betting on the event, who the favorites were, and what the odds were. Smart money seemed to be on a Kenyan, though there was an American who'd blown away the record for the Boston Marathon the previous year by almost half a minute—evidently a large margin for such a race—and a thirty-year-old Dutchman who was the dark horse among the favorites. Thirty, and a competitor in an Olympic competition, Chavez thought. Good for him.

"Command to Tomlinson," Chavez said over his radio.

"I'm here, Command. Nothing much happening 'cept this damned pump noise. I'll call you if anything happens, over."

"Okay, Command out."

"So, what do we do now?" Mike Pierce asked.

"Wait. Stand around and wait."

"You say so, boss," Pierce responded. They all knew how to wait, though none of them especially liked it.

"CHRIST," Killgore observed. "You sure?"

"You want to drive out and see?" Maclean asked heatedly. Then he realized that they'd have to do that anyway, to collect the body for proper burial. Now Maclean understood Western funeral customs. It was bad enough to see vultures pick a deer's body apart. To see the same thing happening to a human being whom you knew was intolerable, love for Nature or not.

"You say he was shot?"

"Sure looked like it."

"Great." Killgore lifted his phone. "Bill, it's John Killgore. Meet me in the main lobby right away. We have a problem. Okay? Good." The physician replaced the phone and rose. "Come on," he said to Maclean.

Henriksen arrived in the lobby of the residential building two minutes after they did, and together they drove in a Hummer north to where the body was. Again the buzzards had to be chased off, and Henriksen, the former FBI agent, walked up to take a look. It was as distasteful as anything he'd seen in his law-enforcement career.

"He's been shot, all right," he said first of all. "Big bullet, right through the X-ring." The wound had been a surprise for Hunnicutt, he thought, though there wasn't enough of the man's face left to tell, really. There were ants on the body as well, he saw. Damn, Henriksen thought, he'd been depending on this guy to help with perimeter security once the Project went fully active. Somebody had murdered an important Project asset. But who?

"Who else hung out with Foster?" Bill asked.

"The Russian guy, Popov. We all rode together," Maclean answered.

"Hey," Killgore said. "Their horses were out this morning, Jeremiah and Buttermilk were both in the corral. Both unsaddled and—"

"Here's the saddle and bridle," Henriksen said, fifteen feet away. "Okay, somebody shot Hunnicutt and then stripped the tack gear off his horse . . . okay, so nobody would see a riderless horse with a saddle on it. We have a murder here, people. Let's find Popov right now. I think I need to talk to him. Anybody see him lately?"

"He didn't show up for breakfast this morning like he usually does," Killgore revealed. "We've been eating together for a week or so, then taking a morning ride. He liked it."

"Yeah," Maclean confirmed. "We all did. You think he—"

"I don't think anything yet. Okay, let's get the body into the Hummer and head back. John, can you do a post on this?"

This seemed a cold appellation for a dead colleague, Killgore thought, but he nodded. "Yeah, doesn't look like it'll be too hard."

"Okay, you get the feet," Bill said next, bending down and trying to avoid touching the parts the buzzards had feasted on. Twenty minutes later, they were back in the Project. Henriksen went up to Popov's fourth-floor room and used his passkey to get in. Nothing, he saw. The bed hadn't been slept in. He had a suspect. Popov had killed Hunnicutt, probably. But why? And where the hell was that Russian bastard now?

It took half an hour to check around the Project complex. The Russian was nowhere to be found. That made sense, since his horse had been found loose that morning by Dr. Killgore. Okay, the former FBI agent thought. Popov had killed Hunnicutt and then skipped. But skipped where? He'd probably ridden to the interstate highway and thumbed a ride, or maybe walked to a bus stop or something. It was a mere twenty-five miles to the regional airport, and from there the bastard could be in Australia by now, Henriksen had to admit to himself. But why would he have done any of that?

"John?" he asked Killgore. "What did Popov know?"

"What do you mean?"

"What did he know about the Project?"

"Not much. Brightling didn't really brief him in, did he?"

"No. Okay, what did Hunnicutt know?"

"Shit, Bill, Foster knew everything."

"Okay, then we think Popov and Hunnicutt went riding last night. Hunnicutt turns up dead, and Popov isn't anywhere to be found. So, could Hunnicutt have told Popov what the Project is doing?"

"I suppose, yes," Killgore confirmed with a nod.

"So, Popov finds out, gets Foster's revolver, shoots him, and bugs the hell out."

"Christ! You think he might—"

"Yes, he might. Shit, man, anybody *might.*"

"But we'd got the 'B' vaccine in him. I gave him the shot myself!"

"Oh, well," Bill Henriksen observed. *Oh, shit,* his brain went on. *Wil Gearing's going to initiate Phase One* today*!* As if he could have forgotten. He had to talk to Brightling right away.

Both Doctors Brightling were in the penthouse accommodations atop the residence building, overlooking the runway, which now had four Gulfstream V business jets on it. The news Henriksen delivered wasn't pleasing to either of them.

"How bad is this?" John asked.

"Potentially it's pretty bad," Bill had to admit.

"How close are we to—"

"Four hours or less," Henriksen replied.

"Does he know that?"

"It's possible, but we can't know for sure."

"Where would he have gone?" Carol Brightling asked.

"Shit, I don't know—CIA, FBI, maybe. Popov's a trained spook. In his position I'd go to the Russian embassy in D.C., and tell the *rezident.* He'll have credibility there, but the time zones and bureaucracy work for us. KGB can't do *anything* fast, Carol. They'll spend hours trying to swallow whatever he tells them."

"Okay. So, we proceed?" John Brightling asked.

A nod. "Yeah, I think so. I'll call Wil Gearing to give him a heads-up, maybe?"

"Can we trust *him?*" John inquired next.

"I think so, yes—I mean, hell, yes. He's been with us for years, guys. He's *part* of the Project. If we couldn't trust him, we'd all be fucking in jail now. He knows about the test protocols in Binghamton, and nobody interfered with that, did they?"

John Brightling leaned back in his chair. "You're saying we can relax?"

"Yeah," Henriksen decided. "Look, even if the whole thing comes apart, we're covered, aren't we? We turn out the 'B' vaccine instead of the 'A' one, and we're heroes for the whole world. Nobody can trace the missing people back to us unless someone cracks and talks, and there're ways to handle that. There's no physical evidence that we've done anything wrong—at least none that we can't destroy in a matter of minutes, right?"

That part had been carefully thought through. All of the Shiva virus containers were a two-minute walk from the incinerators both here and at Binghamton. The bodies of the test subjects were ashes. There *were* people with personal knowledge of what had happened, but for any of them to talk to the authorities meant implicating themselves in mass murder, and they'd all have attorneys present to shield them through the interrogation process. It would be a twitchy time for all involved, but nothing that they couldn't beat.

"Okay." John Brightling looked at his wife. They'd worked too hard and too long to turn back. They'd both endured separation from their loves to serve their greater love for Nature, invested time and vast funds to do this. No, they couldn't turn back. And if this Russian talked—to whom, they couldn't speculate—even then, could those he talked to stop the Project in time? That was scarcely possible. Husband-physician-scientist traded a look with wife-scientist, and then both looked at their Director of Security.

"Tell Gearing to proceed, Bill."

"Okay, John." Henriksen stood and headed back to his office.

■ ■ ■

"YES, Bill," Colonel Gearing said.

"No big deal. Proceed as planned, and call me to confirm the package is delivered properly."

"Okay," Wil Gearing replied. "Anything else I have to do? I have plans of my own, you know."

"Like what?" Henriksen asked.

"I'm flying up north tomorrow, going to take a few days to dive the Great Barrier Reef."

"Oh, yeah? Well, don't let any sharks eat you."

"Right!" was the laughing reply, and the line cut off.

Okay, Bill Henriksen thought. *That's decided.* He could depend on Gearing. He knew that. He'd come to the Project after a life of poisoning things, and he, too, knew the rest of the Project's activities. If he'd ratted to anybody, they would not have gotten this far. But it'd have been so much better if that Russian cocksucker hadn't skipped. What could he do about that? Report Hunnicutt's murder to the local cops, and finger Popov/Serov as the likely killer? Was that worth doing? What were the possible complications? Well, Popov could spill what he knew—however much or little that might be—but then they could say that he was a former KGB spy who'd acted strangely, who'd done some consulting to Horizon Corporation—but, Jesus, started terrorist incidents in Europe? Be serious! This guy's a murderer with imagination, trying to fabricate a story to get himself off a cold-blooded killing right here in Middle America . . . Would that work? It might, Henriksen decided. It just might work, and take that bastard right the hell out of play. He could say anything he wanted, but what physical evidence did he have? Not a fucking thing.

POPOV poured a drink from a bottle of Stolichnaya that the FBI had been kind enough to purchase from a corner liquor store. He had four previous drinks in his system. That helped to mellow his outlook somewhat.

"So, John Clark. We wait."

"Yeah, we wait," Rainbow Six agreed.

"You have a question for me?"

"Why did you call me?"

"We've met before."

"Where?"

"In your building in Hereford. I was there with your plumber under one of my legends."

"I wondered how you knew me by sight," Clark admitted, sipping a beer. "Not many people from your side of the Curtain do."

"You do not wish to kill me now?"

"The thought's occurred to me," Clark replied, looking in Popov's eyes. "But I guess you have some scruples after all, and if you're lying to me, you'll soon wish you were dead."

"Your wife and daughter are well?"

"Yes, and so is my grandson."

"That is good," Popov announced. "That mission was a distasteful one. You have done distasteful missions in your career, John Clark?"

He nodded. "Yeah, a few."

"So, then, you understand?"

Not the way you mean, sport, Rainbow Six thought, before responding. "Yeah, I suppose I do, Dmitriy Arkadeyevich."

"How did you find my name? Who told you?"

The answer surprised him. "Sergey Nikolay'ch and I are old friends."

"Ah," Popov managed to observe, without fainting. His own agency had betrayed him? Was that possible? Then it was as if Clark had read his mind.

"Here," John said, handing over the sheaf of photocopies. "Your evaluations are pretty good."

"Not good enough," Popov replied, failing to recover from the shock of viewing items from a file that he had never seen before.

"Well, the world changed, didn't it?"

"Not as completely as I had hoped."

"I do have a question for you."

"Yes?"

"The money you gave to Grady, where is it?"

"In a safe place, John Clark. The terrorists I know have all become capitalists with regard to cash money, but thanks to your people, those I contacted have no further need of money, do they?" the Russian asked rhetorically.

"You greedy bastard," Clark observed, with half a smile.

THE race started on time. The fans cheered the marathon runners as they took their first lap around the stadium, then disappeared out the tunnel onto the streets of Sydney, to return in two and a half hours or so. In the meantime, their progress would be followed on the Jumbotron for those who sat in the stadium seats, or on the numerous televisions that hung in the ramp and concourse areas. Trucks with remote TV transmitters rolled in front of the lead runners, and the Kenyan, Jomo Nyreiry, held the lead, closely followed by Edward Fulmer, the American, and Willem terHoost, the Dutchman, the leading trio not two steps apart, and a good ten meters ahead of the next group of runners as they passed the first milepost.

Like most people, Wil Gearing saw this on his hotel room TV as he packed. He'd be renting diving gear tomorrow, the former Army colonel told himself, and he'd treat himself to the best diving area in the world, in the knowledge that the oceanic pollution that was harming that most lovely of environments would soon be ending. He got all of his clothing organized in a pair of Tumi wheeled suitcases and set them by the door of the room. He'd be diving while all the ignorant plague victims flew off to their homes across the world, not knowing what they had and what they'd be spreading. He wondered how many would be lost to Phase One of the Project. Computer projections predicted anywhere from six to thirty million, but Gearing thought those numbers conservative. The higher the better, obviously, because the "A" vaccine had to be something that people all over the globe would cry out for, thus hastening their own deaths. The real cleverness of it was that if medical tests on the vaccine recipients showed Shiva antibodies, they'd be explained away by the vaccine—"A" was a live-virus vaccine, as everyone would know. Just a little more live than anyone would realize until it was a little too late.

IT was ten hours later in New York, and there in the safe house Clark, Popov, Sullivan, and Chatham sat, watching network coverage of the Olympic games, like millions of other Americans. There was nothing else for them to do. It was boring for them all, as none were marathoners, and the steps of the leading runners were endlessly the same.

"The heat must be terrible to run in," Sullivan observed.

"It's not fun," Clark agreed.

"Ever run in a race like this?"

"No." John shook his head. "But I've had to run away from things in my time, mainly Vietnam. It was pretty hot there, too."

"You were there?" Popov asked.

"A year and a half's worth. Third SOG—Special Operations Group."

"Doing what?"

"Mainly looking and reporting. Some real operations, raids, assassinations, that sort of thing, taking out people we really didn't like." Thirty years ago, John thought. Thirty years. He'd given his youth to one conflict, and his manhood to another, and now, in his approaching golden years, what would he be doing? Was it really possible, what Popov had told him? It seemed so unreal, but the Ebola scare had been real as hell. He remembered flying all over the world about that one, and he remembered the news coverage that had shaken his country to its very foundations—and he remembered the terrible revenge that America had taken as a result. Most of all, he remembered lying with Ding Chavez on the flat roof of a Tehran dwelling and guiding two smart-bombs in to take the life of the man responsible for it all, in the first application of the President's new doctrine. But if this were real, if this "project" that Popov had told them about were what he said it was, then what would his country do? Was it a matter for law enforcement or something else? Would you put people like this on trial? If not, then—what? Laws hadn't been written for crimes of this magnitude, and the trial would be a horrid circus, spreading news that would shake the foundations of the entire world. That one corporation could have the power to do such a thing as this . . .

Clark had to admit to himself that his mind hadn't expanded enough to enclose the entire thought. He'd acted upon it, but not really accepted it. It was too big a concept for that.

"Dmitriy, why did you say they are doing this?"

"John Clark, they are druids, they are people who worship nature as though it were a god. They say that the animals belong in places, but people do not. They say they want to restore nature—and to do that they are willing to kill all of mankind. This is madness, I know, but it is what they told me. In my room in Kansas, they have videotapes and magazines that proclaim these beliefs. I never knew such people existed. They say that nature hates us, that the planet hates us for what we—all men—have done. But the planet has no mind, and nature has no voice with which to speak. Yet they believe that they do have these things. It's amazing," the Russian concluded. "It is as if I have found a new, mad religious movement whose god requires our deaths, human sacrifice, whatever you wish to call it." He waved his hands in frustration at his inability to understand it.

"DO we know what this guy Gearing looks like?" Noonan asked.

"No," Chavez said. "Nobody told me. I suppose Colonel Wilkerson knows, but I didn't want to ask him."

"Christ, Ding, is this whole thing *possible?*" the FBI agent asked next.

"I guess we'll know in a few hours, man. I know something like this happened once before, and I know John and I helped take out the bastard who did it to us. On the technical side, I'd have to ask Patsy about it. I don't know biology. She does."

"Jesus," Noonan concluded, looking over at the entrance to the pump room. The three of them headed over to a concession area and got half-liter cups of Coca-Cola, then sat down to watch the blue-painted door. People walked past it, but nobody actually approached it.

"Tim?"

"Yeah, Ding?"

"Do you have arrest powers for this?"

The FBI agent nodded. "I think so, conspiracy to commit murder, the crime originated in America, and the subject is an American citizen, so, yes, that should hold up. I can take it a step further. If we kidnap his ass and bring him to America, the courts don't care how somebody got there. Once he's in front of a United States District Court judge, how he came to be there doesn't interest the court at all."

"How the hell do we get him out of the country?" Chavez wondered next. He activated his cell phone.

CLARK picked up the STU-4's receiver. It took five seconds for Ding's encryption system to handshake with his. A computerized voice finally said *Line is secure,* followed by two beeps. "Yeah?"

"John, it's Ding. I got a question."

"Shoot."

"If we bag this Gearing guy, then what? How the hell do we get him back to America?"

"Good question. Let me work on that."

"Right." And the line went dead. The logical place to call was Langley, but, as it turned out, the DCI was not in his office. The call was routed to his home.

"John, what the hell is going on down there, anyway?" Ed Foley asked from his bed.

Clark told the DCI what he knew. That took about five minutes. "I have Ding staking out the only place this can be done, and—"

"Jesus Christ, John, is this for real?" Ed Foley asked, somewhat breathlessly.

"We'll know if this Gearing guy shows up with a package containing the bug, I suppose," Clark replied. "If he does, how do we get Ding, his people, and this Gearing guy back to the States?"

"Let me work on that. What's your number?" John gave it to him and Ed Foley wrote it down on a pad. "How long have you known about this?"

"Less than two hours. The Russian guy is right here with me. We're in an FBI safe house in New York City."

"Is Carol Brightling implicated in this?"

"I'm not sure. Her ex-husband sure as hell is," Clark answered.

Foley closed his eyes and thought. "You know, she called me about you guys a while back, asked a couple of questions. She's the one who shook the new radios loose from E-Systems. She talked to me as though she was briefed in on Rainbow."

"She's not on my list, Ed," John pointed out. He'd personally approved all of the people cleared into the Rainbow compartment.

"Yeah, I'll look at that, too. Okay, let me check around and get back to you."

"Right." Clark replaced the receiver. "We have an FBI guy with the Sydney team," he told the others.

"Who?" Sullivan asked.

"Tim Noonan. Know him?"

"Used to be tech support with HRT?"

Clark nodded. "That's the guy."

"I've heard about him. Supposed to be pretty smart."

"He is. He saved our ass in Hereford, probably my wife and daughter, too."

"So, he can arrest this Gearing mutt, nice and legal."

"You know, I've never worried all that much about enforcing the law—mainly I enforce policy, but not law."

"I suppose things are a little different with the Agency, eh?" Sullivan asked, with a smile. The James Bond factor never really goes away, even with people who are supposed to know better.

"Yeah, some."

GEARING left his hotel, carrying a backpack like many of the other people on the street, and flagged a cab just outside. The marathon was about half an hour from its conclusion. He found himself looking around at the crowded sidewalks and all the people on them. The Australians seemed a friendly people, and what he'd seen of their country was pleasant enough. He wondered about the aborigines, and what might happen to them, and the Bushmen of the Kalahari Desert, and other such tribal groupings around the world, so removed from normal life that they wouldn't be exposed to Shiva in any way. If fate smiled upon them, well, he decided, that was okay with him. These kinds of people didn't harm Nature in any way, and they were insufficiently numerous to do harm even if they wanted to, which they didn't, worshipping the trees and the thunder as the Project members did. Were there enough of them to be a problem? Probably not. The Bushmen might spread out, but their folkways wouldn't allow them to change their tribal character very much, and though they'd increase somewhat in number, they'd probably not even do much of that. The same with the "abos" of Australia. There hadn't been many of them before the Europeans had arrived, after all, and they'd had millennia to sweep over the continent. So the Project would spare many people, wouldn't it? It was vaguely comforting to the retired colonel that Shiva would kill only those whose lifestyles made them the enemies of Nature. That this criterion included everyone he could see out the cab windows troubled him little.

THE taxi stopped at the regular drop-off point by the stadium. He paid his fare plus a generous tip, got out, walked toward the massive concrete bowl. At the entrance, he showed his security pass and was waved through. There came the expected creepy feeling. He'd be testing his "B" vaccine in a very immediate way, first admitting the Shiva virus into the fogging system, and then walking through it, breathing in the same nano-capsules as all the other hundred-thousand-plus tourists, and if the "B" shot didn't work, he'd be condemning himself to a gruesome death—but he'd been briefed in on that issue a long time ago.

"THAT Dutchman looks pretty tough," Noonan said. Willem terHoost was currently in the lead, and had picked up the pace, heading for a record despite the weather conditions. The heat had taken its toll of many runners. A lot of them slowed their pace to get cold drinks, and some ran through pre-spotted water showers to cool off, though the TV commentators said that these had the effect of tightening up the leg muscles and were therefore not really a good thing for marathoners to do. But they took the relief anyway, most of them, or grabbed the offered ice-water drinks and poured them over their faces.

"Self-abuse," Chavez said, checking his watch and reaching for his radio microphone. "Command to Tomlinson."

"I'm here, boss," Chavez heard in his earpiece.

"Coming in to relieve you."

"Roger that, fine with us, boss," the sergeant replied from inside the locked room.

"Come on." Ding stood, waving for Pierce and Noonan to follow. It was just a hundred feet to the blue door. Ding twisted the knob and went inside.

Tomlinson and Johnston had hidden in the shadows in the corner opposite the door. They came out when they recognized their fellow team members.

"Okay, stay close and stay alert," Chavez told the two sergeants.

"Roge-o," Homer Johnston said on his way out. He was thirsty and planned to get himself something to drink, and on the way out he placed his hands over his ears, popping them open to rid himself of the pump noise.

The sound was annoying, Chavez realized in the first few minutes. Not overly loud, but constant, a powerful deep whirring, like a well-insulated automobile engine. It hovered at the edge of your consciousness and didn't go away, and on further reflection made him think of a beehive. Maybe that was the annoying part of it.

"Why are we leaving the lights on?" Noonan asked.

"Good question." Chavez walked over and flipped the switch. The room went almost totally dark, with just a crack of light coming in from under the steel fire door. Chavez felt his way to the opposite wall, managed to get there without bumping his head, and leaned against the concrete wall, allowing his eyes to adjust to the darkness.

GEARING was dressed in shorts and low-cut hiking boots, with short socks as well. It seemed the form of dress the locals had adopted for dealing with the heat, and it was comfortable enough, as was his backpack and floppy hat. The stadium concourses were crowded with fans coming in early for the closing ceremonies, and he saw that many of them were standing in the fog to relieve themselves from the oppressive heat of the day. The local weather forecasters had explained ad nauseam about how this version of the El Niño phenomenon had affected the global climate and inflicted unseasonably hot weather on their country, for which they all felt the need to apologize. He found it all rather amusing. Apologize for a natural phenomenon? How ridiculous. With that thought he headed to his objective. In doing so, he walked right past Homer Johnston, who was standing, sipping his Coke.

"ANY other places the guy might use?" Chavez worried suddenly in the darkness.

"No," Noonan replied. "I checked the panel on the way in. The whole stadium fogging system comes from this one room. If it's going to happen, it will happen here."

"If it's gonna happen," Chavez said back, actually hoping that it would not. If that happened, they'd go back to Lieutenant Colonel Wilkerson and find out where this Gearing guy was staying, and then pay a call on him and have a friendly little chat.

GEARING spotted the blue door and looked around for security people. The Aussie SAS troops were easily spotted, once you knew how they dressed. But though he saw two Sydney policemen walking down the concourse, there were no army personnel. Gearing paused fifty feet or so from the door. The usual mission jitters, he told himself. He was about to do something from which there was no turning back. He asked himself for the thousandth time if he really wanted to do this. There were fellow human beings all around him, people seemingly just like himself with hopes and dreams and aspirations—but, no, those things they held in their minds weren't like the things he held in his own, were they? They didn't get it, didn't understand what was important and what was not. They didn't see Nature for what She was, and as a result they lived lives that were aimed only at hurting or even destroying Her, driving cars that injected hydrocarbons into the atmosphere, using chemicals that found their way into the water, pesticides that killed birds or kept them from reproducing, aiming spray cans at their hair whose propellants destroyed the ozone layer. They were *killing* Nature with nearly every act they took. They didn't care. They didn't even try to understand the consequences of what they were doing, and so, no, they didn't have a right to live. It was his job to protect Nature, to remove the blight upon the planet, to restore and save, and that was a job he must do. With that decided, Wil Gearing resumed his walk to the blue door, fished in his pocket for the key and inserted it into the knob.

"COMMAND, this is Johnston, you got company coming in! White guy, khaki shorts, red polo shirt, and backpack," Homer announced loudly into everyone's ear. Beside him, Sergeant Tomlinson started walking in that direction, too.

"Heads up," Chavez said in the darkness. There were two shadows in the crack of light under the door, and then the sound of a key in the lock, and then there was another crack of light, a vertical one as the door opened, and a silhouette, a human shape—and just that fast, Chavez knew that it *was* all real after all. Would the lights reveal an inhuman monster, something from another planet, or . . .

. . . just a man, he saw, as the lights flipped on. About fifty, with closely cropped salt-and-pepper hair. A man who knew what he was about. He reached for the wrench hanging on the wall-mounted pegboard, then shrugged out of his backpack, and loosened the two straps that held the flap in place. It seemed to Chavez that he was watching a movie, something separated from reality, as the man flipped off the motor switch, ending the whirring. Then he closed the valve and lifted the wrench to—

"Hold it right there, pal," Chavez said, emerging from the shadows.

"Who are you?" the man asked in surprise. Then his face told the tale. He was doing something he shouldn't. He knew it, and suddenly someone else did, too.

"I could ask you the same thing, except I know who you are. Your name is Wil Gearing. What are you planning to do, Mr. Gearing?"

"I'm just here to swap out the chlorine canister on the fogging system," Gearing replied, shaken all the more that this Latino seemed to know his name. How had that happened? Was he part of the Project—and if not, then what? It was as if someone had punched him in the stomach, and now his entire body cringed from the blow.

"Oh? Let's see about that, Mr. Gearing. Tim?" Chavez gestured for Noonan to get the backpack. Sergeant Pierce stayed back, his hand on his pistol and his eyes locked on their visitor.

"Sure looks like a normal one," Noonan said. If this was a counterfeit, it was a beaut. He was tempted to open the screw top, but he had good reason not to. Next to the pump motor, Chavez took the wrench and removed the existing canister.

"Looks about half full to me, pal. Not time to replace it yet, at least not with something called Shiva. Tim, let's be careful with that one."

"You bet." Noonan tucked it back into Gearing's pack and strapped the cover down. "We'll have this checked out. Mr. Gearing, you are under arrest," the FBI agent told him. "You have the right to remain silent. You have the right to have an attorney present during questioning. If you cannot afford an attorney, we will provide you with one. Anything you say can be used against you in a court of law. Do you understand these rights, sir?"

Gearing was shaking now, and turned to look at the door, wondering if he could—

—he couldn't. Tomlinson and Johnston chose that moment to come in. "Got him?" Homer asked.

"Yep," Ding replied. He pulled his cell phone out and called America. Again the encryption systems went through the synchronization process.

"We got him," Chavez told Rainbow Six. "And we got the canister thing, whatever you call it. How the hell do we get everybody home?"

"There's an Air Force C-17 at Alice Springs, if you can get there. It'll wait for you."

"Okay, I'll see if we can fly there. Later, John." Chavez thumbed the END button and turned to his prisoner. "Okay, pal, you're coming with us. If you try anything stupid, Sergeant Pierce here will shoot you right in the head. Right, Mike?"

"Yes, sir, I sure as hell will," Pierce responded in a voice from the grave.

Noonan reopened the valve and turned the pump motor back on. Then they went back out into the stadium concourse and walked to the cabstand. They ended up needing two taxis, both of which headed to the airport. There they had to wait an hour and a half for a 737 for the desert airport, a flight of nearly two hours.

ALICE Springs is in the very center of the continental island called Australia, near the Macdonnell mountain range, and a strange place indeed to find the highest of high-tech equipment, but here were the huge antenna dishes that downloaded information from America's reconnaissance, electronic intelligence, and military communications satellites. The facility there is operated by the National Security Agency, NSA, whose main site is at Fort Meade, Maryland, between Baltimore and Washington.

The Qantas flight was largely empty, and on arrival, an airport van took them to the USAF terminal, which was surprisingly comfortable, though here the temperature was blisteringly hot, heading down from an afternoon temperature of 120.

"You're Chavez?" the sergeant in the Distinguished Visitors area asked.

"That's right. When's the plane leave?"

"They're waiting for you now, sir. Come this way." And with that they entered another van, which rolled them right to the front-left-side door, where a sergeant in a flight suit gestured them aboard.

"Where we going, Sarge?" Chavez asked on his way past.

"Hickam in Hawaii first, sir, then on to Travis in California."

"Fair enough. Tell the driver he can leave."

"Yes, sir." The crew chief laughed, as he closed the door and walked forward.

It was a mobile cavern, this monster transport aircraft, and there seemed to be no other passengers aboard. Gearing hadn't been handcuffed, somewhat to Ding's disappointment, and he behaved docilely, with Noonan at his side.

"So, you want to talk to us about it, Mr. Gearing?" the FBI agent asked.

"What's in it for me?"

He'd had to ask that question, Noonan supposed, but it was a sign of weakness, just what the FBI agent had hoped for. The question made the answer easy:

"Your life, if you're lucky."

CHAPTER 38

NATURE RESORT

IT WAS JUST TOO MUCH FOR WIL GEARING. NOBODY had told him what to do in a case like this. It had never occurred to him that security would be broken on the Project. His life was forfeit now—how could that have happened? He could cooperate or not. The contents of the canister would be examined anyway, probably at USAMRIID at Fort Dietrick, Maryland, and it would require only a few seconds for the medical experts there to see what he'd carried into the Olympic stadium, and there was no explaining that away, was there? His life, his plans for the future, had been taken away from him, and his only choice was to cooperate and hope for the best.

And so, as the C-17A Globemaster III transport climbed to its cruising altitude, he started talking. Noonan held a tape recorder in his hand, and hoped that the engine noise that permeated the cargo area wouldn't wash it all away. It turned out that the hardest part for him was to keep a straight face. He'd heard about extreme environmental groups, the people who thought killing baby seals in Canada was right up there with Treblinka and Auschwitz, and he knew that the Bureau had looked at some for offenses like releasing laboratory animals from medical institutions, or spiking trees with nails so that no lumber company would dare to run trees from those areas through their sawmills, but he'd never heard of those groups doing anything more offensive than that. This, however, was such a crime as to redefine "monstrous." And the religious fervor that went along with it was entirely alien to him, and therefore hard to credit. He wanted to believe that the contents of the chlorine canister really was just chlorine, but he knew that it was not. That and the backpack were now sealed in a mil-spec plastic container strapped down in a seat next to Sergeant Mike Pierce.

"HE hasn't called yet," John Brightling observed, checking his watch. The closing ceremonies were under way. The head of the International Olympic Committee was about to give his speech, summoning the Youth of the World to the next set of games. Then the assembled orchestra would play, and the Olympic Flame would be extinguished . . . just as most of humanity would be extinguished. There was the same sort of sadness to it, but also the same inevitability. There would be no next Olympiad, and the Youth of the World would not be alive to hear the summons? . . .

"John, he's probably watching this the same as we are. Give him some time," Bill Henriksen advised.

"You say so." Brightling put his arm around his wife's shoulders and tried to relax. Even now, the people walking in the stadium were being sprinkled with the nano-capsules bearing Shiva. Bill was right. Nothing could have gone wrong. He could see it in his mind. The streets and highways empty, farms idle, airports shut down. The trees would thrive without lumberjacks to chop them down. The animals would nose about, wondering perhaps where all the noises and the two-legged creatures were. Rats and other carrion eaters would feast. Dogs and cats would return to their primal instincts and survive or not, as circumstances allowed. Herbivores and predators would be relieved of hunting pressure. Poison traps set out in the wild would continue to kill, but eventually these would run out of their poisons and stop killing game that farmers and others disliked. This year there would be no mass murder of baby harp seals for their lovely white coats. This year the world would be reborn . . . and even if that required an act of violence, it was worth the price for those who had the brains and aesthetic to appreciate it all. It was like a religion for Brightling and his people. Surely it had all the aspects of a religion. They worshiped the great collective life system called Nature. They were fighting for Her because they knew that She loved and nurtured them back. It was that simple. Nature was to them if not a person, then a huge enveloping idea that made and supported the things they loved. They were hardly the first people to dedicate their lives to an idea, were they?

"HOW long to Hickam?"

"Another ten hours, the crew chief told me," Pierce said, checking his watch. "This is like being back in the Eight-Deuce. All I need's my chute, Tim," he told Noonan.

"Huh?"

"Eighty-Second Airborne, Fort Bragg, my first outfit. All the way, baby," Pierce explained for the benefit of this FBI puke. He missed jumping, but that was something special-ops people didn't do. Going in by helicopter was better organized and definitely safer, but it didn't have the *rush* you got from leaping out of a transport aircraft along with your squadmates. "What do you think of what this guy was trying to do?" Pierce asked, pointing at Gearing.

"Hard to believe it's real."

"Yeah, I know," Pierce agreed. "I'd like to think nobody's that crazy. It's too big a thought for my brain, man."

"Yeah," Noonan replied. "Mine, too." He felt the mini tape recorder in his shirt pocket and wondered about the information it contained. Had he taken the confession legally? He'd given the mutt his rights, and Gearing said that he understood them, but any halfway competent attorney would try hard to have it all tossed, claiming that since they were aboard a military aircraft surrounded by armed men, the circumstances had been coercive—and maybe the judge would agree. He might also agree that the arrest had been illegal. But, Noonan thought, all of that was less important than the result. If Gearing had spoken the truth, this arrest might have saved millions of lives. . . . He went forward to the aircraft's radio compartment, got on the secure system, and called New York.

Clark was asleep when his phone rang. He grabbed the receiver and grunted, "Yeah?" only to find that the security system was still handshaking. Then it announced that the line was secure. "What is it, Ding?"

"It's Tim Noonan, John. I have a question."

"What's that?"

"What are you going to do when we get there? I have Gearing's confession on tape, the whole thing, just like what you told Ding a few hours ago. Word for fucking word, John. What do we do now?"

"I don't know yet. We probably have to talk to Director Murray, and also with Ed Foley at CIA. I'm not sure the law anticipates anything this big, and I'm not sure this is something we ever want to put in a public courtroom, y'know?"

"Well, yeah," Noonan's voice agreed from half a world away. "Okay, just so somebody's thinking about it."

"Okay, yeah, we're thinking about it. Anything else?"

"I guess not."

"Good. I'm going back to sleep." And the line went dead, and Noonan walked back to the cargo compartment. Chavez and Tomlinson were keeping an eye on Gearing, while the rest of the people tried to get some sleep in the crummy USAF seats and thus pass the time on this most boring of flights. Except for the dreams, Noonan discovered in an hour. They weren't boring at all.

"HE still hasn't called," Brightling said, as the network coverage went through Olympic highlights.

"I know," Henriksen conceded. "Okay, let me make a call." He rose from his seat, pulled a card from his wallet, and dialed a number on the back of it to a cellular phone owned by a senior Global Security employee down in Sydney.

"Tony? This is Bill Henriksen. I need you to do something for me right now, okay? . . . Good. Find Wil Gearing and tell him to call me immediately. He has the number . . . Yes, that's the one. Right now, Tony . . . Yeah. Thanks." And Henriksen hung up. "That shouldn't take long. Not too many places he can be except maybe on the way to the airport for his flight up the coast. Relax, John," the security chief advised, still not feeling any chill on his skin. Gearing's cell phone could have a dead battery, he could be caught up in the crowds and unable to get a cab back to his hotel, maybe there weren't any cabs—any one of a number of innocent explanations.

DOWN in Sydney, Tony Johnson walked across the street to Wil Gearing's hotel. He knew the room already, since they'd met there, and took the elevator to the right room. Defeating the lock was child's play, just a matter of working a credit card into the doorjamb and flipping the angled latch, and then he was inside—

—and so were Gearing's bags, sitting there by the sliding mirror-doors of the closet, and there on the desk-table was the folder with his flight tickets to the Northeast Coast of Australia, plus a map and some brochures about the Great Barrier Reef. This was odd. Wil's flight—he checked the ticket folder—was due to go off in twenty minutes, and he ought to be all checked in and boarding the aircraft by now, but he hadn't left the hotel. This was very odd. *Where are you, Wil?* Johnson wondered. Then he remembered why he was here, and lifted the phone.

▪ ▪ ▪

"YEAH, Tony. So, where's our boy?" Henriksen asked confidently. Then his face changed. "What do you mean? What else do you know? Okay, if you find out anything else, call me here. Bye." Henriksen set the phone down and turned to look at the other two. "Wil Gearing's disappeared. Not in his room, but his luggage and tickets are. Like he just fell off the planet."

"What's that mean?" Carol Brightling asked.

"I'm not sure. Hell, maybe he got hit by a car in the street—"

"—Or maybe Popov spilled his guts to the wrong people and they bagged him," John Brightling suggested nervously.

"Popov didn't even know his name—Hunnicutt couldn't have told him, he didn't know Gearing's name either." But then Henriksen thought, *Oh, shit. Foster* did *know how the Shiva was supposed to be delivered, didn't he? Oh, shit.*

"What's the matter, Bill?" John asked, seeing the man's face and knowing that something was wrong.

"John, we may have a problem," the former FBI agent announced.

"What problem?" Carol asked. Henriksen explained, and the mood in the room changed abruptly. "You mean, they might know? . . ."

Henriksen nodded. "That is possible, yes."

"My God," the Presidential Science Advisor exclaimed. "If they know that, then—then—then—"

"Yeah." Bill nodded. "Then we're fucked."

"What can we do about this?"

"For starters, we destroy all the evidence. All the Shiva, all the vaccines, all the records. It's all on computer, so we just erase it. There shouldn't be much in the way of a paper trail, because we told people not to print anything up, and to destroy any paper notes they might make. We can do that from here. I can access all the company computers from my office and kill off all the records—"

"They're encrypted, all of them," John Brightling pointed out.

"You want to bet against the code-breakers at Fort Meade? I don't," Henriksen told them. "No, those files all have to go, John. Look, you beat a criminal prosecution by denying evidence to the prosecutors. Without physical evidence, they can't hurt you."

"What about witnesses?"

"The most overrated thing in the world is an eyewitness. Any lawyer with half a brain can make fools out of them. No, when I was working cases for the Bureau, I wanted something I could hold in my hand, something you could pass over to the jury so they could see it and feel it. Eyewitness testimony is pretty useless in court, despite what you see on TV. Okay, I'm going to my office to get rid of the computer stuff." Henriksen left at once, leaving the two Brightlings behind him.

"My God, John," Carol said in quiet alarm, "what if people find out, nobody'll understand . . ."

"Understand that we were going to kill them and their families? No," her husband agreed dryly, "I don't think Joe Sixpack and Archie Bunker will understand that very well."

"So, what do we do?"

"We get the hell out of the country. We fly down to Brazil with everyone who knows what the Project is all about. We still have access to money—I have dozens of covert accounts we can access electronically—and they probably can't make a criminal case against us if Bill can trash all the computer files. Okay, they may have Wil Gearing under arrest, but he's just one voice, and I'm not sure they can come after us legally, in a foreign country, on the word of one person. There are only fifty or so people who really know what's happening—all of it, I mean—and we have enough airplanes to get us all to Manaus."

IN his office, Henriksen lit up his personal computer and pulled open an encrypted file. It had telephone numbers and access codes to every computer in Horizon Corporation, plus the names of the files relating to the Project. He accessed them via modem, looked for the files that had to go, and moved them with mouse-clicks into trash cans that shredded the files completely instead of merely removing their electronic address codes. He found that he was sweating as he did so, and it took him thirty-nine minutes, but after that time was concluded, he was certain that he'd completely destroyed them all. He checked his list and his memory for the file names and conducted another global search, but no, those files were completely gone now. Good.

Okay, he asked himself, what else might they have? They might have Gearing's Shiva-delivery canister. That would be hard to argue with, but what, really, did it mean? It would mean, if the right people looked at it, that Gearing had been carrying a potential bio-war weapon. Gearing could tell a U.S. attorney that it had come from Horizon Corporation, but no one working on that segment of the Project would ever admit to having done it, and so, *no,* there would be no corroborating evidence to back up the assertion.

Okay, there were by his count fifty-three Horizon and Global Security employees who knew the Project from beginning to end. Work on the "A" and

"B" vaccines could be explained away as medical research. The Shiva virus and the vaccine supplies would be burned in a matter of hours, leaving no physical evidence at all.

This was enough—well, it was almost enough. They still had Gearing, and Gearing, if he talked—and he *would* talk, Henriksen was sure, because the Bureau had ways of choking information out of people—could make life very uncomfortable for Brightling and a lot of other people, including himself. They would probably avoid conviction, but the embarrassment of a trial—and the things that the revelations might generate, casual comments made by Project members to others, would be woven together . . . and there was Popov, who could link John Brightling and himself to terrorist acts. But they could finger Popov for murdering Foster Hunnicutt, and that would pollute whatever case he might try to make . . . the best thing would be to be beyond their reach when they tried to assemble a case. That meant Brazil, and Project Alternate in the jungles west of Manaus. They could head down there, sheltered by Brazil's wonderfully protective extradition laws, and study the rain forest . . . yes, that made sense. Okay, he thought, he had a list of the full-Project members, those who knew everything, those who, if the FBI got them and interrogated them, could hang them all. He printed this list of the True Believers and tucked the pages in his shirt pocket. With the work done and the alternatives analyzed, Henriksen went back to Brightling's penthouse office.

"I've told the flight crews to get the birds warmed up," Brightling told him when he came in.

"Good." Henriksen nodded. "I think Brazil looks pretty good right now. If nothing else, we can get all of our critical personnel fully briefed on how to handle this, how to act if anyone asks them some questions. We can beat this one, John, but we have to be smart about it."

"What about the planet?" Carol Brightling asked sadly.

"Carol," Bill replied, "you take care of your own ass first. You can't save Nature from inside Marion Federal Penitentiary, but if we play it smart, we can deny evidence to anyone who investigates us, and without that we're safe, guys. Now"—he pulled the list from his pocket—"these are the only people we have to protect. There's fifty-three of them, and you have four Gulfstreams sitting out there. We can fly us all down to Project Alternate. Any disagreement on that?"

John Brightling shook his head. "No, I'm with you. Can this keep us in the clear legally?"

Henriksen nodded emphatically. "I think so. Popov will be a problem, but he's a murderer. I'm going to report the Hunnicutt killing to the local cops before we fly off. That will compromise his value as a witness—make it look like he's just telling a tale to save his own ass from the gallows, whatever they use to execute murderers here in Kansas. I'll have Maclean and Killgore tape statements we can hand over to the local police. It may not be enough to convict him, but it will make him pretty uncomfortable. That's how you do this, break up the other guy's chain of evidence and the credibility of his witnesses. In a year, maybe eighteen months, we have our lawyers sit down and chat with the local U.S. attorney, and then we come home. Until then we camp out in Brazil, and you can run the company from there via the Internet, can't you?"

"Well, it's not as good as what we planned, but . . ."

"Yes," Carol agreed. "But it beats the hell out of life in a federal prison."

"Get everything moving, Bill," John ordered.

"SO, what do we do with this?" Clark asked, on waking up.

"Well," Tom Sullivan answered, "first we go to the Assistant Director in Charge of the New York office, and then we talk to a United States attorney about building a criminal case."

"I don't think so," Clark responded, rubbing his eyes and reaching for the coffee.

"We can't just put the arm on them and whack 'em, you know. We're cops. We can't break the law," Chatham pointed out.

"This can never see the light of day in a court. Besides, who's to say that you'll win the case? How hard will this be to cover up?"

"I can't evaluate that. We have two missing girls they probably murdered—more, if our friend Popov is right—and that's a crime, both federal and state, and, Jesus, this other conspiracy . . . that's why we have laws, Mr. Clark."

"Maybe so, but how fast do you see yourself driving out to this place in Kansas, whose location we don't know yet, with warrants to arrest one of the richest men in America?"

"It will take a little time," Sullivan admitted.

"A couple of weeks at least, just to assemble the case information," Special Agent Chatham said. "We'll need to talk with experts, to have that chlorine jar examined by the right people—and all the while the subjects will be working to destroy every bit of physical evidence. It won't be easy, but that's what we do in the Bureau, y'know?"

"I suppose," Clark said dubiously. "But there won't be much element of surprise here. They probably know we have this Gearing guy. From that they know what he can tell us."

"True," Sullivan conceded.

"We might have to try something else."

"What might that be?"

"I'm not sure," Clark admitted.

THE videotaping was done in the Project's media center, where they'd hoped to produce nature tapes for those who survived the plague. The end of the Project as an operational entity hit its members hard. Kirk Maclean was especially downcast, but he acted his role well in explaining the morning rides that he, Serov, Hunnicutt, and Killgore had enjoyed. Then Dr. John Killgore told of how he'd found the horses, and then came Maclean's explanation of how the body was found, and the autopsy Killgore had personally performed, which had found the .44 bullet that had ended Foster Hunnicutt's life. With that done, the men joined the others in the lobby of the residence building, and a minibus ferried them to the waiting aircraft.

It would be a 3,500-mile flight to Manaus, they were told on boarding, about eight hours, an easy hop for the Gulfstream V. The lead aircraft was nearly empty, just the doctors Brightling, Bill Henriksen, and Steve Berg, lead scientist for the Shiva part of the Project. The aircraft lifted off at nine in the morning local time. Next stop, the Amazon Valley of central Brazil.

IT turned out that the FBI *did* know where the Kansas site was. A car and two agents from the local resident agency drove out in time to see the jets lift off, which they duly reported to their base station, and from there to Washington. Then they just parked at the side of the road, sipped at their drinks, ate their McDonald's burgers and watched nothing happening at all at the misplaced buildings in the middle of wheat country.

THE C-17 switched crews at Hickam Air Force Base in Hawaii, then refueled and lifted off for Travis in northern California. Chavez and his party never even departed the aircraft, but watched the new crew arrive with box lunches and drinks, and then settled in for the next six hours of air travel. Wilson Gearing was trying to explain himself now, talking about trees and birds and fish and stuff, Ding overheard. It was not an argument calculated to persuade the father of a newborn, and the husband of a physician, but the man rambled on. Noonan listened politely and recorded this conversation, too.

THE flight south was quiet on all the aircraft. Those who hadn't heard about the developments in Sydney guessed that something was wrong, but they couldn't communicate with the lead aircraft without going through the flight crews, and they had not been briefed in on the Project's objectives—like so many of the employees of Horizon Corporation, they had simply been paid to do the jobs for which they were trained. They flew now on a southerly course to a destination just below the equator. It was a trip they'd made before, when Project Alternate had been built the previous year. It, too, had its own runway sufficient for the business jets, but only VFR daylight capable, since it lacked the navigation aids in Kansas. If anything went wrong, they would bingo to the Manaus city airport, ninety-eight miles to the east of their destination, which had full services, including repairs. Project Alternate had spare parts, and every aircraft had a trained mechanic aboard, but they preferred to leave major repairs to others. In an hour, they were "feet-wet" over the Gulf of Mexico, then turned east to fly through the international travel corridor over Cuba. The weather forecast was good all the way down to Venezuela, where they might have to dodge a few thunderheads, but nothing serious. The senior passengers in the lead aircraft figured that they were leaving the country about as fast as it could be done, disappearing off the face of the planet they'd hoped to save.

"WHAT'S that?" Sullivan asked. Then he turned. "Four jets just left the Kansas location, and they headed off to the south."

"Is there any way to track them?"

Sullivan shrugged. "The Air Force maybe."

"How the hell do we do that?" Clark wondered aloud. Then he called Langley.

"I can try, John, but getting the Air Force hopping this quick won't be easy."

"Try, will you, Ed? Four Gulfstream-type business jets heading south from central Kansas, destination unknown."

"Okay, I'll call the NMCC."

▪ ▪ ▪

THAT was not a difficult thing for the Director of Central Intelligence to do. The senior duty officer in the National Military Command Center was an Air Force two-star recently rotated into a desk job after commanding the remaining USAF fighter force in NATO.

"So, what are we supposed to do, sir?" the general asked.

"Four Gulfstream-type business jets took off from central Kansas about half an hour ago. We want them tracked."

"With what? All our air-defense fighters are on the Canadian border. Calling them down wouldn't work, they'd never catch up."

"How about an AWACS?" Foley asked.

"They belong to Air Combat Command at Langley—ours, not yours—and well, maybe one's up for counter-drug surveillance or maybe training. I can check."

"Do that," Ed Foley said. "I'll hold."

The two-star in blue went one better than that, calling the North American Aerospace Defense Command in Cheyenne Mountain, which had radar coverage over the entire country, and ordering them to identify the four Gs. That took less than a minute, and a computer command was sent to the Federal Aviation Administration to check the flight plans that had to be filed for international flights. NORAD also told the general that there were *two* E-3B AWACS aircraft aloft at the moment, one 300 miles south of New Orleans doing counter-drug operations, and the other just south of Eglin Air Force Base, conducting routine training with some fighters based there in an exercise against a Navy flight out of Pensacola Naval Air Station. With that information, he called Langley Air Force Base in the Virginia Tidewater, got Operations, and told them about the DCI's request.

"What's this for, sir?" the general asked Foley, once the phone lines were properly lashed up.

"I can't tell you that, but it's important as hell."

The general relayed that to Langley Operations, but did not relay the snarled response back to CIA. This one had to be kicked to the four-star who ran Air Combat Command, who, conveniently, was in his office rather than the F-16 that came with the job. The four-star grunted approval, figuring CIA wouldn't ask without good reason.

"You can have it if you need it. How far will it be going?"

"I don't know. How far can one of those Gulfstream jets go?"

"Hell, sir, the new one, the G-V, can fly all the way to friggin' Japan. I may have to set up some tanker support."

"Okay, please do what you have to do. Who do I call to keep track of the shadowing operation?"

"NORAD." He gave the DCI the number to call.

"Okay, thank you, General. The Agency owes you one."

"I will remember that, Director Foley," the USAF major general promised.

"WE'RE in luck," Clark heard. "The Air Force is chopping an AWACS to us. We can follow them all the way to where they're going," Ed Foley said, exaggerating somewhat, since he didn't understand the AWACS would have to refuel on the way.

THE aircraft in question, a ten-year-old E-3B Sentry, got the word fifteen minutes later. The pilot relayed the information to the senior control officer aboard, a major, who in turn called NORAD for further information and got it ten minutes after the leading G departed U.S. airspace. The steer from Cheyenne Mountain made the tracking exercise about as difficult as the drive to the local 7-Eleven. A tanker would meet them over the Caribbean, after lifting off from Panama, and what had been an interesting air-defense exercise reverted to total boredom. The E-3B Sentry, based on the venerable Boeing 707-320B, flew at the identical speed as the business jets made in Savannah, and kept station from fifty miles behind. Only the aerial tanking would interfere with matters, and that not very much. The radar aircraft's call-sign was Eagle Two-Niner, and it had satellite radio capability to relay everything, including its radar picture, to NORAD in Colorado. Most of Eagle Two-Niner's crewmen rested in their comfortable seats, many of them dozing off while three controllers worked the four Gulfstreams they were supposed to track. It was soon evident that they were heading somewhere pretty straight, five minutes or about forty-one miles apart, attempting no deception at all, not even wavetop flying. But that, they knew, would only abuse the airframes and use up gas unnecessarily. It didn't matter to the surveillance aircraft, which could spot a trash bag floating in the water—something they regularly did in counter-drug operations, since that was one of the methods used by smugglers to transfer their cocaine—or even enforce the speed limit on interstate highways, since anything going faster than eighty miles per hour was automatically tracked by the radar-computer system, until the operator told the computer to ignore it. But now all they had to look at were commercial airliners going and coming in routine daily traffic, plus the four Gulfstreams, who were traveling so normal, straight, and dumb that, as one controller observed, even a Marine could have taken them out without much in the way of guidance.

■ ■ ■

BY this time, Clark was on a shuttle flight to Reagan National Airport across the river from Washington. It landed on time, and Clark was met by a CIA employee whose "company" car was parked outside for the twenty-minute ride to Langley and the seventh floor of the Old Headquarters Building. Dmitriy Popov had never expected to be inside this particular edifice, even wearing a VISITOR—ESCORT REQUIRED badge. John handled the introductions.

"Welcome," Foley said in his best Russian. "I imagine you've never been here before."

"As you have never been to Number 2 Dzerzhinsky Square."

"Ah, but I have," Clark responded. "Right into Sergey Nikolay'ch's office, in fact."

"Amazing," Popov responded, sitting down as guided.

"Okay, Ed, where the hell are they now?"

"Over northern Venezuela, heading south, probably for central Brazil. The FAA tells us that they filed a flight plan—it's required by law—for Manaus. Rubber-tree country, I think. A couple of rivers come together there."

"They told me that there is a facility there, like the one in Kansas, but smaller," Popov informed his hosts.

"Task a satellite to it?" Clark asked the DCI.

"Once we know where it is, sure. The AWACS lost a little ground when it refueled, but it's only a hundred fifty miles back now, and that's not a problem. They say the four business jets are just flying normally, cruising right along."

"Once we know where they're going . . . then what?"

"Not sure," Foley admitted. "I haven't thought it through that far."

"There might not be a good criminal case on this one, Ed."

"Oh?"

"Yeah," Clark confirmed with a nod. "If they're smart, and we have to assume they are, they can destroy all the physical evidence of the crime pretty easily. That leaves witnesses, but who, you suppose, is aboard those four Gs heading into Brazil?"

"All the people who know what's been happening. You'd want to keep that number low for security reasons, wouldn't you—so, you think they're going down there for choir practice?"

"What?" Popov asked.

"They need to find and learn a single story to tell the FBI when the interrogations begin," Foley explained. "So, they all need to learn the same hymn, and learn to sing it the same way every time."

"What would you do in their place, Ed?" Rainbow Six asked reasonably.

Foley nodded. "Yeah, that's about it. Okay, what should we do?"

Clark looked the DCI straight in the eye. "Pay them a little visit, maybe?"

"Who authorizes that?" the Director of Central Intelligence asked.

"I still draw my paychecks from this agency. I report to you, Ed, remember?"

"Christ, John."

"Do I have your permission to get my people together at a suitable staging point?"

"Where?"

"Fort Bragg, I suppose," Clark proposed. Foley had to yield to the logic of the moment.

"Permission granted." And with that Clark walked down the narrow office to a table with a secure phone to call Hereford.

ALISTAIR Stanley had bounced back well from his wounds, enough so that he could just about manage a full day in his office without collapsing with exhaustion. Clark's trip to the States had left him in charge of a crippled Rainbow force, and he was facing problems now that Clark had not yet addressed, like replacements for the two dead troopers. Morale was brittle at the moment. There were still two missing people with whom the survivors had worked intimately, and that was never an easy thing for men to bear, though every morning they were out on the athletic field doing their daily routine, and every afternoon they fired their weapons to stay current and ready for a possible call-up. This was regarded as unlikely, but, then, none of the missions that Rainbow had carried out had been, in retrospect, very likely. His secure phone started chirping, and Stanley reached to answer it.

"Yes, this is Alistair Stanley."

"Hi, Al, this is John. I'm in Langley now."

"What the bloody hell's been happening, John? Chavez and his people have fallen off the earth, and—"

"Ding and his people are halfway between Hawaii and California now, Al. They arrested a major conspirator in Sydney."

"Very well, what the devil's been going on?"

"You sitting down, Al?"

"Yes, John, of course I am, and—"

"Listen up. I'll give you the short version," Clark commanded, and proceeded to do that for the next ten minutes.

"Bloody hell," Stanley said when his boss stopped talking. "You're sure of this?"

"Damned sure, Al. We are now tracking the conspirators in four aircraft. They seem to be heading for central Brazil. Okay, I need you to get all the people together and fly them to Fort Bragg—Pope Air Force Base, North Carolina—with all their gear. Everything, Al. We may be taking a trip down to the jungle to . . . to, uh, deal decisively with these people."

"Understood. I'll try to get things organized here. Maximum speed?"

"That is correct. Tell British Airways we need an airplane," Clark went on.

"Very well, John. Let me get moving here."

IN Langley, Clark wondered what would happen next, but before he could decide that he needed to get all of his assets in place. Okay, Alistair would try to get British Airways to release a spare, reserve aircraft to his people for a direct flight to Pope, and from there—from there he'd have to think some more. And he'd have to get there, too, to Special Operations Command with Colonel Little Willie Byron.

"TARGET One is descending," a control officer reported over the aircraft's intercom. The senior controller looked up from the book he was reading, activated his scope, and confirmed the information. He was breaking international law at the moment. Eagle Two-Niner hadn't gotten permission to overfly Brazil, but the air-traffic-control radar systems down there read his transponder signal as a civilian air-cargo flight—the usual ruse—and nobody had challenged them yet. Confirming that information, he got on his satellite radio to report this information to NORAD and, though he didn't know it, on to CIA. Five minutes later, Target Two started doing the same. Also both aircraft were slowing, allowing Eagle Two-Niner to catch up somewhat. The senior controller told the flight crew to continue on this heading and speed, inquired about fuel state, and learned that they had another eight hours of flight time, more than enough to return to their home at Tinker Air Force Base outside Oklahoma City.

IN England, the British Airways card was played, and the airline, after ten minutes of checking, assigned Rainbow a 737-700 airliner, which would await their pleasure at Luton, a small commercial airport north of London. They'd have to go there by truck, and those were whistled up from the British army's transport company at Hereford.

IT looked like a green sea, John Brightling thought, the top layer of the triple-canopy jungle. In the setting sun, he could see the silvery paths of rivers, but almost nothing of the ground itself. This was the richest ecosystem on the planet, and one that he'd never studied in detail—well, Brightling thought, now he'd be able to, for the next year or so. Project Alternate was a robust and comfortable facility with a maintenance staff of six people, its own power supply, satellite communications, and ample food. He wondered which of the people on the four aircraft might be good cooks. There would be a division of labor here, as at every other Project activity, with himself, of course, as the leader.

AT Binghamton, New York, the maintenance staff was loading a bunch of biohazard-marked containers into the incinerator. It was sure a big furnace, one of the men thought—big enough to cremate a couple of bodies at the same time—and, judging by the thickness of the insulation, a damned hot one. He pulled down the three-inch-thick door, locked it in place, and punched the ignition button. He could hear the gas jetting it and lighting off from the sparkler-things inside, followed by the usual *voosh*. There was nothing unusual about this. Horizon Corporation was always disposing of biological material of one sort or another. Maybe it was live AIDS virus, he thought. The company did a lot of work in that area, he'd read. But for the moment he looked at the papers on his clipboard. Three sheets of paper from the special order that had been faxed in from Kansas, and every line was checked off. All the containers specified were now ashes. Hell, this incinerator even destroyed the metal lids. And up into the sky went the only physical evidence of the Project. The maintenance worker didn't know that. To him container G7-89-98-00A was just a plastic container. He didn't even know that there was a word such as Shiva. As required, he went to his desktop computer—everyone here had one—and typed in that he'd eliminated the items on the work order. This information went into Horizon Corporation's internal network, and, though he didn't know it, popped onto a screen in Kansas. There were special instructions with that, and the technician lifted his phone to relay the information to another worker, who relayed it in turn to the phone number identified on the electronically posted notice.

■ ■ ■

"OKAY, thank you," Bill Henriksen replied upon hearing the information. He replaced the cabin phone and made his way forward to the Brightlings.

"Okay, guys, that was Binghamton. All the Shiva stuff, all the vaccines, everything's been burned up. There is now no real physical evidence that the Project ever existed."

"We're supposed to be happy about that?" Carol demanded crossly, looking out her window at the approaching ground.

"No, but I hope you'll be happier than you'd be if you were facing an indictment for conspiracy to commit murder, doctor."

"He's right, Carol," John said, sadness in his voice. So close. So damned close. Well, he consoled himself, he still had resources, and he still had a core of good people, and this setback didn't mean that he'd have to give up his ideals, did it? Not hardly, the chairman of Horizon told himself. Below, under the green sea into which they were descending, was a great diversity of life—he'd justified building Project Alternate to his board for that very reason, to find new chemical compounds in the trees and plants that grew only here—maybe a cure for cancer, who could say? He heard the flaps lower, and soon thereafter, the landing gear went down. Another three minutes, and they thumped down on the road-runway constructed along with the lab and residential buildings. The aircraft's thrust-reversers engaged, and it slowed to a gradual stop.

"OKAY, Target One is down on the ground." The controller read off the exact position, then adjusted his screen's picture. There were buildings there, too? Well, okay, and he told the computer to calculate their exact position, which information was immediately relayed to Cheyenne Mountain.

"THANK you." Foley wrote the information down on a pad. "John, I have exact lat and longe for where they are. I'll task a satellite to get pictures for us. Should have that in, oh, two or three hours, depending on weather there."

"So fast?" Popov asked, looking out the seventh-floor windows at the VIP parking lot.

"It's just a computer command," Clark explained. "And the satellites are always up there." Actually, three hours struck him as a long time to wait. The birds must have been in the wrong places for convenience.

■ ■ ■

RAINBOW lifted off the runway at Luton well after midnight, British time, looping around to the right over the automobile-assembly plant located just off the airport grounds and heading west for America. British Airways had assigned three flight attendants to the flight, and they kept the troopers fed and supplied with drink, which all the soldiers accepted before they settled down as best they could to sleep most of the way across. They had no idea why they were going to America. Stanley hadn't briefed them in on anything yet, though they wondered why they were packing *all* of their tactical gear.

SKIES were blessedly clear over the jungles of central Brazil. The first KH 11D went over at nine-thirty in the night, local time. Its infrared cameras took a total of three hundred twenty frames, plus ninety-seven more in the visible spectrum. These images were immediately cross-loaded to a communications satellite, and from there beamed down to the antenna farm at Fort Belvoir, Virginia, near Washington. From there they went by landline to the National Reconnaissance Office building near Dulles Airport, and from there via another fiber-optic line to CIA headquarters.

"This looks pretty vanilla," the senior duty photoanalyst told them in Foley's office. "Buildings here, here, here, and this one here. Four airplanes on the ground, look like Gulfstream Vs—that one's got a longer wing. Private airfield, it's got lights but no ILS gear. I expect the fuel tanks are here. Power plant here. Probably a diesel generator system, by the look of this exhaust plume. This building looks residential from the window-light pattern. Somebody build a nature resort we're interested in?" the analyst asked.

"Something like that," Clark confirmed. "What else?"

"Nothing much for a ninety-mile radius. This here used to be a rubber-tree plantation, I'd say, but the buildings are not warmed up, and so I'd have to say it's inactive. Not much in the way of civilization. Fires down this way"—he pointed—"campfires, maybe from indigenous people, Indian tribes or suchlike. That's one lonely place, sir. Must have been a real pain in the ass to build this place, isolated as it is."

"Okay, send us the Lacrosse images, too, and when we get good visual-light images, I want to see those, too," Foley said.

"We'll have a direct-overhead pass on another bird at about zero-seven-twenty Lima," he said, meaning local time. "Weather forecast looks okay. Ought to get good frames from that pass."

"How wide is this runway?" Clark asked.

"Oh, looks like seven thousand feet long by three hundred or so wide, standard width, and they've cut the trees down another hundred yards—meters, probably, on both sides. So, you could get a fair-sized airplane in there if the concrete's thick enough. There's a dock here on the river, it's the Río Negro, actually, not the Amazon itself, but no boats. I guess that's left over from the construction process."

"I don't see any telephone or power lines," Clark said next, looking closely at the photo.

"No, sir, there ain't none. I guess they depend on satellite and radio comms from this antenna farm." He paused. "Anything else you need?"

"No, and thanks," Clark told the technician.

"Yes, sir, you bet." The analyst walked out to take the elevator for his basement office.

"Learn anything?" Foley asked. He himself knew nothing about running around in jungles, but he knew that Clark did.

"Well, we know where they are, and we know about how many of 'em there are."

"What are you planning, John?"

"I'm not sure yet, Ed" was the honest reply. Clark wasn't planning much, but he was starting to think.

THE C-17 thumped down rather hard at Travis Air Force Base in California. Chavez and his companions were rather seriously disoriented by all the travel, but the walk outside the aircraft was, at least, in pleasantly cool air. Chavez pulled out his cell phone and speed-dialed Hereford, then learned that John was in Langley. He had to dredge that number up from his memory, but remembered it after twenty seconds or so, and dialed.

"Director's office."

"This is Domingo Chavez calling for John Clark."

"Hold, please," Foley's receptionist replied.

"Where are you now, Ding?" John asked, when he got on the line.

"Travis Air Force base, north of 'Frisco. Now where the hell are we supposed to go?"

"There should be an Air Force VC-20 waiting for you at the DV terminal."

"Okay, I'll get over that way. We don't have any of our gear with us, John. We left Australia in a hurry."

"I'll have somebody take care of that. You get the hell back to D.C., okay?"

"Yes, sir, Mr. C," Ding acknowledged.

"Your guest, what's his name—Gearing?"

"That's right. Noonan sat with him most of the way. He sang like a fuckin' canary, John. This thing they planned to do, I mean if it's real—*Jesuchristo, jefe.*"

"I know, Ding. They've bugged out, by the way."

"Where to, do we know?"

"Brazil. We know exactly where they are. I have Al bringing the team across to Fort Bragg. You get to Andrews, and we'll get organized."

"Roge-o, John. Let me go find my airplane. Out." Chavez killed the phone and waved for a blue USAF van that took them to the Distinguished Visitors' lounge, where they found yet another flight crew waiting for them. Soon thereafter, they boarded the VC-20, the Air Force version of the Gulfstream business jet, and aboard they found out what time it was from the food that the sergeant served them. Breakfast. It had to be early morning, Chavez decided. Then he asked the sergeant for the correct time and reset his watch.

C H A P T E R 3 9

HARMONY

IT STRUCK NOONAN AS TERRIBLY ODD THAT HE WAS traveling with a confessed attempted-mass-murderer in an aircraft without the man's being in handcuffs or a straitjacket or some sort of restraint. But, as a practical matter, what was he going to do, and where was he going to go? It might be possible to open the door and jump out, but Gearing didn't strike the FBI agent as a suicide risk, and Noonan was damned sure he wasn't going to hijack this aircraft to Cuba. And so Tim Noonan just kept an eye on the prisoner, while considering that he'd arrested the mutt on another continent, in a different time zone and hemisphere, and on the far side of the International Dateline. He'd been in on the Fuad Yunis takedown in the Eastern Mediterranean ten or eleven years before, but he figured this might be the FBI's all-time distance record for arresting a subject and bringing the mutt home. Close enough to twelve thousand miles. Damn. The price had been the air travel, which had his body thoroughly wrecked and crying out for exercise. He changed the time setting on his watch, then wondered if the day was the same—but, he decided, while you could ask the USAF sergeant flight attendant for the time, you'd look like a total fucking idiot to have to ask the date. Maybe he'd get it from a copy of *USA Today* back in the States, Noonan thought, pushing his seat back and locking his eyes on the back of Wil Gearing's head. Then he realized: He'd have to turn his prisoner in when they got to Washington, but to whom, and on what charge?

"OKAY," Clark said. "They get into Andrews in two hours, and then we'll take a puddle-jumper to Pope and figure out what to do."

"You've got a plan already, John," Foley observed. He'd known Clark long enough to recognize that look in his eyes.

"Ed, is this my case to run or isn't it?" he asked the DCI.

"Within reason, John. Let's try not to start a nuclear war or anything, shall we?"

"Ed, can this ever come to trial? What if Brightling ordered the destruction of all the evidence? It's not hard to do, is it? Hell, what are we talking about? A few buckets of bio-gunk and some computer records. There're commercial programs that destroy files thoroughly enough that you can't recover them ever, right?"

"True, but somebody might have printed stuff up, and a good search—"

"And then what do we have? A global panic when people realize what a bio-tech company can do if it wants. What good will that do?"

"Toss in a senior presidential advisor who violated security. Jesus, that would not be very helpful for Jack, would it?" Foley paused. "But we can't *murder* these people, John! They're U.S. citizens with *rights,* remember?"

"I know, Ed. But we can't let them go, and we probably can't prosecute them, can we? What's that leave?" Clark paused. "I'll try something creative."

"What?"

John Clark explained his idea. "If they fight back, well, then, it makes things easier for us, doesn't it?"

"Twenty men against maybe fifty?"

"My twenty—actually, more like fifteen—against those feather merchants? Give me a break, Ed. It may be the moral equivalent of murder, but *not* the legal equivalent."

Foley frowned mightily, worried about what would happen if this ever made the media, but there was no particular reason that it should. The special-operations community kept all manner of secrets, many of which would look bad in the public media. "John," he said finally.

"Yeah, Ed?"

"Make sure you don't get caught."

"Never happened yet, Ed," Rainbow Six reminded him.

"Approved," said the Director of Central Intelligence, wondering how the hell he'd ever explain this one to the President of the United States.

"Okay, can I use my old office?" Clark had some phone calls to make.

"Sure."

"IS that *all* you need?" General Sam Wilson asked.

"Yes, General, that should do it."

"Can I ask what it's for?"

"Something covert," he heard Clark reply.

"That's all you're willing to say?"

"Sorry, Sam. You can check this out with Ed Foley if you want."

"I guess I will," the general's voice rumbled.

"Fine with me, sir." Clark hoped the "sir" part would assuage his hurt feelings.

It didn't, but Wilson was a pro, and knew the rules. "Okay, let me make some phone calls."

The first of them went to Fort Campbell, Kentucky, home of the 160th Special Operations Aviation Regiment, whose commanding officer, a colonel, made the expected objection, which was expectedly overridden. That colonel then lifted a phone of his own and ordered an MH-60K Night Hawk special-operations helicopter ferried to Pope Air Force Base, along with a maintenance crew for some TDY to a place he didn't know about. The next phone call went to an Air Force officer who took his notes and said, "Yes, sir," like the good airman he was. Getting the pieces in place was mainly an exercise in electronics, lifting encrypted phones and giving spooky orders to people who, fortunately, were accustomed to such things.

CHAVEZ reflected that he'd come three quarters of the way around the world, most of it in the last twenty-two hours, and was landing at an airfield he'd used only once before. There was Air Force One, the VC-25A version of the 747 painted in a scheme known all over the world, and with him was someone who'd planned to kill all the people who'd known it. He'd learned years before not to reflect too much on the things that he did for his country and the $82,450 per year that he now earned as a mid-level CIA employee. He had a master's degree in international relations, which he jokingly defined as one country fucking another—but now, it wasn't a country, it was a *corporation.* Since when did *they* start to think they could play games at this level? he wondered. Maybe it was the New World Order that President Bush had once talked about. If that's what it was, it didn't make sense to the commander of Team-2. Governments were selected, by and large, by the citizens, and answered to them. Corporations answered—if they did so at all—to their shareholders. And that wasn't quite the same thing. Corporations were supposed to be overseen by the governments of the countries in which they were domiciled, but everything was changing now. It was private corporations that developed and defined the tools that people across the world were using. The changing technological world had given immense power to relatively small organizations, and now he was wondering if that was a good thing or not. Well, if people depended on governments for progress, then they'd still be riding horses and steamships around the world. But in this New World Order things had little in the way of controls at all, and that was something somebody should think about, Chavez decided, as the aircraft came to a halt on the Andrews ramp. Yet another anonymous blue USAF van appeared at the stairs even before they were fully deployed.

"BUILDING up those frequent-flyer miles, Domingo?" John asked from the concrete.

"I suppose. Am I sprouting feathers yet?" Chavez asked tiredly.

"Only one more hop for now."

"Where to?"

"Bragg."

"Then let's do it. I don't want to get too used to standing still if it's just temporary." He needed a shave and a shower, but that, too, would have to wait until Fort Bragg. Soon they were in yet another Air Force short-haul aircraft, lifting off and heading southwest. This hop was blessedly short, and ended at Pope Air Force Base, which adjoins the home of the 82nd Airborne Infantry Division at Fort Bragg, North Carolina, also home of Delta Force and other special-operations units.

For the first time, someone had thought what to do with Wil Gearing, Noonan saw. Three military policemen carted him off to the base stockade. The rest of the people on the trip ended up in Bachelor Officers' Quarters, more colloquially known as "the Q."

Chavez wondered if the clothing he stripped off would ever be clean enough to wear again. But then he showered, and set on the sink in the bathroom was a razor that allowed him to scrape off a full day's accumulation of black blur on his—he thought—manly face. He emerged to find clothing laid out.

"I had the base people run this over."

"Thanks, John." Chavez struggled into the white boxers and T-shirt, then selected the forest-pattern Battle Dress Uniform—BDU—items laid on the bed, complete to socks and boots.

"Long day?"

"Shit, John, it's been a long *month* coming back from Australia." He sat down on the bed, then on reflection lay down on the bedspread. "Now what?"

"Brazil."

"How come?"

"That's where they all went. We tracked them down, and I have overheads of the place where they're camped out."

"So, we're going to see them?"

"Yes."

"To do *what,* John?"

"To settle this thing out once and for all, Domingo."

"Suits me, but is it legal?"

"When did you start worrying about that?"

"I'm a married man, John, and a father, remember? I have to be responsible now, man."

"It's legal enough, Ding," his father-in-law told the younger man.

"Okay, you say so. What happens now?"

"You get a nap. The rest of the team arrives in about half an hour."

"The rest of what team?"

"Everybody who can move and shoot, son."

"Muy bien, jefe," Chavez said, closing his eyes.

THE British Airways 737-700 was on the ground for as little time as possible, refueled from an Air Force fuel bowser and then lifted off for Dulles International Airport outside Washington, where its presence would not cause much in the way of comment. The Rainbow troopers were bused off to a secure location and allowed to continue their rest. That worried some of them slightly. Being allowed to rest implied that rest was something they'd need soon.

Clark and Alistair Stanley conferred in a room at Joint Special Operations Command Headquarters, a nondescript building facing a small parking lot.

"So, what gives here?" asked Colonel William Byron. Called "Little Willie" by his uniformed colleagues, Colonel Byron had the most unlikely sobriquet in the United States Army. Fully six-four and two hundred thirty pounds of lean, hard meat, Byron was the largest man in JSOC. The name dated back to West Point, where he'd grown six inches and thirty pounds over four years of exercise and wholesome food, and ended up a linebacker on the Army football team that had murdered Navy 35–10 in the autumn classic at Philadelphia's Veterans Stadium. His accent was still south Georgia despite his master's degree in management from Harvard Business School, which was becoming favored in the American military.

"We're taking a trip here," Clark told him, passing the overheads across the table. "We need a helo and not much else."

"Where the hell is this shithole?"

"Brazil, west of Manaus, on the Río Negro."

"Some facility," Byron observed, putting on the reading glasses that he hated. "Who built it, and who's there now?"

"The people who wanted to kill the whole fucking world," Clark responded, reaching for his cell phone when it started chirping. Again he had to wait for the encryption system to handshake with the other end. "This is Clark," he said finally.

"Ed Foley here, John. The sample was examined by the troops up at Fort Dietrick."

"And?"

"And it's a version of the Ebola virus, they say, modified—'engineered' is the term they used, as a matter of fact—by the addition of what appears to be cancer genes. They say that makes the little bastard more robust. Moreover, the virus strands were encased in some sort of mini-capsules to help it survive in the open. In other words, John, what your Russian friend told you—it looks like it's fully confirmed."

"What did you do with Dmitriy?" Rainbow Six asked.

"A safe house out in Winchester," the DCI replied. It was the usual place to quarter a foreign national the CIA wanted to protect. "Oh, the FBI tells me that the Kansas State Police are looking for him on a murder charge. Supposedly he killed one Foster Hunnicutt from the state of Montana, or so he has been accused."

"Why don't you have the Bureau tell Kansas that he didn't kill anybody. He was with me the whole time," Clark suggested. They had to take care of this man, didn't they? John had already made the conceptual leap of forgetting that Popov had instigated an attack on his wife and daughter. Business, in this case, was business, and it wasn't the first time a KGB enemy had turned into a valuable friend.

"Okay, yes, I can do that." It was a little white lie, Foley agreed, set against a big black truth. In his Langley, Virginia, office, Foley wondered why his hands weren't shaking. These lunatics had not only *wanted* to kill the whole world, but they'd also had the *ability* to do so. This was a new development the CIA would have to study in detail, a whole new type of threat, and investigating it would be neither easy nor fun.

"Okay, thanks, Ed." Clark killed the phone and looked at the others in the room. "We just confirmed the contents of the chlorine canister. They created a modified form of Ebola for distribution."

"What?" Colonel Byron asked. Clark gave him a ten-minute explanation. "You're serious, eh?" he asked finally.

"As a heart attack," Clark replied. "They hired Dmitriy Popov to interface with terrorists to set up incidents throughout Europe. That was to increase the fear of terrorism, to get Global Security the consulting contract for the Australians, and—"

"Bill Henriksen?" Colonel Byron asked. "Hell, I *know* that guy!"

"Yeah? Well, his people were supposed to deliver the bug through the fogging-cooling system at the Olympic stadium in Sydney, Willie. Chavez was there in the control room when this Wil Gearing guy showed up with the container, and the contents were checked out by the USAMRIID guys at Fort Detrick. You know, the FBI could almost make a criminal case out of this. But not quite," Clark added.

"So, you're heading down there to . . ."

"To talk to them, Willie," Clark finished the statement for him. "They have the aircraft scrubbed yet?"

Byron checked his watch. "Ought to."

"Then it's time for us to get moving."

"Okay. I have BDUs for all your people, John. Sure you don't need a little help?"

"No, Willie. I appreciate the offer, but we want to keep this one tight, don't we?"

"I suppose, John." Byron stood. "Follow me, guys. Those folks you're going to see in Brazil?"

"Yeah?" Clark said.

"Give them a special hello for JSOC, will ya?"

"Yes, sir," John promised. "We'll do that."

THE major aircraft sitting on the Pope Air Force Base ramp was an Air Force C-5B Galaxy transport, which the local ground crew had been working on for several hours. All official markings had been painted over, with HORIZON CORPORATION painted in the place of the USAF roundels. Even the tail number was gone. The clamshell cargo doors in the rear were being sealed now. Clark and Stanley got there first. The rest of the troops arrived by bus, carrying their personal gear, and they climbed into the passenger compartment aft of the wing box. From that point on, it was just a matter of having the flight crew—dressed in civilian clothing—climb up to the flight deck and commence start-up procedures as though they were a commercial flight. A KC-10 tanker would meet up with them south of Jamaica to top off their fuel tanks.

■ ■ ■

"OKAY, so that's what seems to have happened," John Brightling told the people assembled in the auditorium. He saw disappointment on the faces of the other fifty-two people here, but some relief was evident as well. Well, even true believers had consciences, he imagined. Too bad.

"What do we do here, John?" Steve Berg asked. He'd been one of the senior scientists on the Project, developer of the "A" and "B" vaccines, who'd also helped to design Shiva. Berg was one of the best people Horizon Corporation had ever hired.

"We study the rain forest. We have destroyed everything of evidentiary value. The Shiva supply is gone. So are the vaccines. So are all the computer records of our laboratory notes, and so forth. The only records of the Project are what you people have in your heads. In other words, if anybody tries to make a criminal case against us, you just have to keep your mouths shut, and there will be no case. Bill?" John Brightling gestured to Henriksen, who walked to the podium.

"Okay, you know that I used to be in the FBI. I know how they make their criminal cases. Making one against us will not be easy under the best of circumstances. The FBI has to play by the rules, and they're strict rules. They *must* read you your rights, one of which is to have a lawyer present during questioning. All you have to say is, 'Yes, I want my lawyer here.' If you say *that,* then they can't even ask you what the time is. Then you call us, and we get a lawyer to you, and the lawyer will tell you, right in front of the case agents, that you will not talk at all, and he'll tell the agents that you will not talk, and that if they try to make you talk then they've violated all sorts of statutes and Supreme Court decisions. That means that *they* can get into trouble, and anything you might say cannot be used anywhere. Those are your civil protections.

"Next," Bill Henriksen went on, "we will spend our time here looking at the rich ecosystem around us, and formulating a cover story. That will take us some time and—"

"Wait, if we can avoid answering their questions, then—"

"Why concoct a cover story? That's easy. Our lawyers will have to talk some with the United States attorneys. If we generate a plausible cover story, then we can make them go away. If the cops know they can't win, they won't fight. A good cover story will help with that. Okay, we can say that, yes, we were looking at the Ebola virus, because it's a nasty little fucker, and the world needs a cure. Then, maybe, some loony employee decided to kill the world—but *we* had nothing to do with that. Why are we here? We're here to do primary medical research into chemical compounds in the flora and fauna here in the tropical rain forest. That's legitimate, isn't it?" Heads nodded.

"Okay, we'll take our time to construct an ironclad cover story. Then we'll all memorize it. That way, when our lawyers let us talk to the FBI so that we can be cooperative, we give them only information which cannot hurt us, and will, in fact, help us evade the charges that they might hit us with. People, if we stand together and stick to our scripts, we can't lose. Please believe me on that. We *can't lose* if we use our heads. Okay?"

"And we can also work on Project 2," Brightling said, resuming the podium. "You are some of the smartest people in the world, and our commitment to our ultimate goal has *not* changed. We'll be here for a year or so. It's a chance for us to study nature, and learn things we need to learn. It will also be a year of working to find a new way to achieve that to which we have dedicated our lives," he went on, seeing nods. There were already alternate ideas he could investigate, probably. He was still the chairman of the world's foremost biotech company. He still had the best and brightest people in the world working for him. He and they still cared about saving the planet. They'd just have to find something else, and they had the resources and the time to do so.

"Okay," Brightling told them, with a beaming smile. "It's been a long day. Let's all bed down and get some rest. Tomorrow morning, I'm going out in the forest to see an ecosystem that we all want to learn about."

The applause moved him. Yes, all of these people cared as much as he did, shared his dedication—and, who knew, maybe there was a way for Project 2 to happen.

Bill Henriksen came up to John and Carol during the walk to their rooms. "There is one other potential problem."

"What's that?"

"What if they send a paramilitary team here?"

"You mean like the Army?" Carol Brightling asked.

"That's right."

"We fight them," John responded. "We have guns here, don't we?"

And that they did. The Project Alternate armory had no fewer than a hundred German-made G-3 military assault rifles, the real sort, able to go full-automatic, and quite a few of the people here knew how to shoot.

"Yes. Okay, the problem with this is, they can't really arrest us legally, but if they do manage to apprehend us and get us back to America, then the courts won't care that the arrests were illegal. That's a point of American law—once you're in front of the judge, that's all the judge cares about. So, if people show up, we just have to discourage them. I think—"

"I think our people won't need much in the way of encouragement to fight back after what those bastards did to the Project!"

"I agree, but we'll just have to see what happens. Damn, I wish we'd gotten some radar installed here."

"Huh?" John asked.

"They will come, if they come, by helicopter. Too far to walk through the jungle, and boats are too slow, and our people think in terms of helicopters. That's just how they do things."

"How do they even know where we are, Bill? Hell, we skipped the country pretty fast and—"

"And they can ask the flight crews where they delivered us. They had to file flight plans to Manaus, and that narrows it down some, doesn't it?"

"They won't talk. They're well paid," John objected. "How long before they can figure all that out?"

"Oh, a couple of days at worst. Two weeks at best. I think we ought to get our people trained in defense. We can start that tomorrow," Henriksen proposed.

"Do it," John Brightling agreed. "And let me call home and see if anybody's talked to our pilots."

The master suite had its own communications room. Project Alternate was state-of-the-art in many ways, from the medical labs to communications. In the latter case the antenna farm next to the power-generating facility had its own satellite-phone system that also allowed e-mail and electronic access to Horizon Corp.'s massive internal computer network. Immediately upon arriving in his suite, Brightling flipped on the phone system and called Kansas. He left instructions for the flight crews, now most on the way back home, to inform Alternate if anyone tried to interrogate them regarding their most recent overseas trip. That done, there was little else left to do. Brightling showered and walked into the bedroom and found his wife there.

"It's so sad," Carol observed in the darkness.

"It's goddamned infuriating," John agreed. "We were so fucking close!"

"What went wrong?"

"I'm not sure, but I think our friend Popov found out what we were doing, then he killed the guy who told him about it and skipped. Somehow he told them enough to capture Wil Gearing down in Sydney. Damn, we were within *hours* of initiating Phase One!" he growled.

"Well, next time we'll be more careful," Carol soothed, reaching to stroke his arm. Failure or not, it was good to lie in bed with him again. "What about Wil?"

"He's going to have to take his chances. I'll get the best lawyers I can find for him," John promised. "And get him the word to keep his mouth shut."

GEARING had stopped talking. Somehow arriving back in America had awakened in him the idea of civil rights and criminal proceedings, and now he wasn't saying anything to anybody. He sat in his aft-facing seat in the C-5, looking backward at the circular seal that led into the immense void area there in the tail, while these soldiers mainly dozed. Two of them were wide awake, however, and looking right at him all the way while they chatted about something or other. They were loaded for bear, Gearing saw, lots of personal weapons evident here and others loaded into the cargo area below. Where were they going? Nobody had told him that.

Clark, Chavez, and Stanley were in the compartment aft of the flight deck on the massive air-lifter. The flight crew was regular Air Force—most such transports are actually flown by reservists, mainly airline pilots in civilian life—and they kept their distance. They'd been warned by their superiors, the warnings further reinforced by the alteration in the aircraft's exterior paint job. They were civilians now? They were dressed in civilian clothes so as to make the deception plausible to someone. But who would believe that a Lockheed Galaxy was civilian owned?

"It looks pretty straightforward," Chavez observed. It was interesting to be an infantryman again, again a Ninja, Ding mused, again to own the night—except they were planning to go in the daylight. "Question is, will they resist?"

"If we're lucky," Clark responded.

"How many of them?"

"They went down in four Gulfstreams, figure a max of sixteen people each. That's sixty-four, Domingo."

"Weapons?"

"Would you live in the jungle without them?" Clark asked. The answer he anticipated was, not very likely.

"But are they trained?" Team-2's commander persisted.

"Most unlikely. These people will be scientist-types, but some will know the woods, maybe some are hunters. I suppose we'll see if Noonan's new toys work as well as he's been telling us."

"I expect so," Chavez agreed. The good news was that his people were highly trained and well equipped. Daylight or not, it would be a Ninja job. "I guess you're in overall command?"

"You bet your sweet ass, Domingo," Rainbow Six replied. They stopped talking as the aircraft jolted somewhat, as they flew into the wake-turbulence of the KC-10 for aerial refueling. Clark didn't want to watch the procedure. It had to be the most unnatural act in the world, two massive aircraft mating in midair.

Malloy was a few seats farther aft, looking at the satellite overheads as well, along with Lieutenant Harrison.

"Looks easy," the junior officer opined.

"Yeah, pure vanilla, unless they shoot at us. Then it gets a little exciting," he promised his copilot.

"We're going to be close to overloading the aircraft," Harrison warned.

"That's why it's got two engines, son," the Marine pointed out.

It was dark outside. The C-5's flight crew looked down at a surface with few lights after they'd topped off their tanks from the KC-10, but for them it was essentially an airliner flight. The autopilot knew where it was, and where it was going, with waypoints programmed in, and a thousand miles ahead the airport at Manaus, Brazil, knew they were coming, a special air-cargo flight from America which would need ramp space for a day or so, and refueling services—this information had already been faxed ahead.

It wasn't yet dawn when they spotted the runway lights. The pilot, a young major, squirmed erect in his front-left seat and slowed the aircraft, making an easy visual approach while the first-lieutenant copilot to his right watched the instruments and called off altitude and speed numbers. Presently, he rotated the nose up and allowed the C-5B to settle onto the runway, with only a minor jolt to tell those aboard that the aircraft wasn't flying anymore. He had a diagram of the airport, and taxied off to the far corner of the ramp, then stopped the aircraft and told the loadmaster that it was his turn to go to work.

It took a few minutes to get things organized, but then the huge rear doors opened. Then the MH-60K Night Hawk was dragged out into the predawn darkness. Sergeant Nance supervised three other enlisted men from the 160th SOAR as they extended the rotor blades from their stowed position, and climbed atop the fuselage to make sure that they were safely locked in place for flight operations. The Night Hawk was fully fueled. Nance installed the M-60 machine gun in its place on the right side and told Colonel Malloy that the aircraft was ready. Malloy and Harrison preflighted the helicopter and decided that it was ready to go, then radioed this information to Clark.

The last people off the C-5B were the Rainbow troopers, now dressed in multicolor BDU fatigues, their faces painted in green and brown camouflage makeup. Gearing came down last of all, a bag over his head so that he couldn't see anything.

It turned out that they couldn't get everyone aboard. Vega and four others were left behind to watch the helicopter lift off just at first light. The blinking strobes climbed into the air and headed northwest, while the soldiers groused at having to stand in the warm, humid air close to the transport. About that time, an automobile arrived at the aircraft with some forms for the flight crew to fill out. To the surprise of everyone present, no special note was made of the aircraft type. The paint job announced that it was a large, privately owned transport, and the airport personnel accepted this, since all the paperwork seemed to be properly filled out, and therefore had to be true and correct.

IT was so much like Vietnam, Clark thought, riding in a helicopter over solid treetops of green. But he was not in a Huey this time, and it was nearly thirty years since his first exposure to combat operations. He couldn't remember being very afraid—tense, yes, but not really afraid—and that struck him as remarkable, looking back now. He was holding one of the suppressed MP-10s, and now, riding in this chopper to battle, it was as though his youth had returned—until he turned to see the other troops aboard and remarked on how young they all looked, then reminded himself that they were, in the main, over thirty years of age, and that for them to look young meant that he had to be old. He put that unhappy thought aside and looked out the door past Sergeant Nance and his machine gun. The sky was lightening up now, too much light for them to use their night-vision goggles, but not enough to see very well. He wondered what the weather would be like here. They were right on the equator, and that was jungle down there, and it would be hot and damp, and down there under the trees would be snakes, insects, and the other creatures for whom this most inhospitable of places was indeed home—and they were welcome to it, John told them without words, out the door of the Night Hawk.

"How we doing, Malloy?" John asked over the intercom.

"Should have it in sight any second—there, see the lights dead ahead!"

"Got it." Clark waved for the troops in the back to get ready. "Proceed as planned, Colonel Malloy."

"Roger that, Six." He held course and speed, on a heading of two-nine-six, seven hundred feet AGL—above ground level—and a speed of a hundred twenty knots. The lights in the distance seemed hugely out of place, but lights they were, just where the navigation system and the satellite photos said they would be. Soon the point source broke up into separate distinct sources.

"Okay, Gearing," Clark was saying in the back. "We're letting you go back to talk to your boss."

"Oh?" the prisoner asked through the black cloth bag over his head.

"Yes," John confirmed. "You're delivering a message. If he surrenders to us, nobody gets hurt. If he doesn't, things'll get nasty. His only option is unconditional surrender. Do you understand that?"

"Yeah." The head nodded inside the black bag.

The Night Hawk's nose came up just as it approached the west end of the runway that some construction crew had carved into the jungle. Malloy made a fast landing, without allowing his wheels to touch the ground—standard procedure, lest there be mines there. Gearing was pushed out the door, and immediately the helicopter lifted back off, reversing course to the runway's east end.

Gearing pulled the bag from his head and oriented himself, spotted the lights for Project Alternate, a facility he knew about but had never visited, and headed there without looking back.

AT the east end, the Night Hawk again came into hover a foot or so off the ground. The Rainbow troops leaped out, and the helicopter immediately climbed up for the return trip to Manaus, which would be made into the rising sun. Malloy and Harrison put on their sunglasses and held course, keeping a close watch on their fuel state. The 160th Special Operations Aviation Regiment maintained its helos pretty well, the Marine thought, flexing his gloved hands on the controls. Just like the Air Force pukes in England.

NOONAN was the first to get set up. All the troops ran immediately into the thick cover a scant hundred yards from the thick concrete pavement of the runway and headed west, wondering if Gearing had noted their separate arrival here. It took fully half an hour for them to make their way over a distance that, had they run it, would have taken scarcely ten minutes. For all that, Clark thought it was good time—and now he remembered the creepy feeling that came from being in the jungle, where the very air seemed alive with things hoping to suck one's blood and give you whatever diseases would take your life as slowly and painfully as possible. How the hell had he endured the nineteen months he'd spent in Vietnam? Ten minutes here and he was ready to leave. Around him, massive hardwood trees reached two or three hundred feet to the sky to form the top canopy of this fetid place, with secondary trees reaching about a third that height, and yet another that stopped at fifty or so, with bushes and other plants at his feet. He could hear the sound of movement—whether his own people or animals he couldn't be sure, though he knew that this environment supported all manner of life, most of it unfriendly to humans. His people spread out to the north, most of them plucking branches to tuck under the elastic bands that ran around their Kevlar helmets, the better to break up the outline of their unnatural shapes and improve their concealment.

THE front door of the building was unlocked, Gearing found, amazed that this should be so. He walked into what appeared to be a residential building, entered an elevator, punched the topmost button and arrived on the fourth floor. Once there, it was just a matter of opening one of the double doors on the corridor and flipping on a light in what had to be the master suite. The bedroom doors were open, and he walked that way.

John Brightling's eyes reported the sudden blaze of light from the sitting room. He opened them and saw—

"What the hell are you doing here, Wil?"

"They brought me down, John."

"*Who* brought you down?"

"The people who captured me in Sydney," Gearing explained.

"What?" It was a little much for so early in the morning. Brightling stood and put on the robe next to the bed.

"John, what is it?" Carol asked from her side of the bed.

"Nothing, honey, just relax." John went to the sitting room, pulling the doors closed as he did so.

"What the fuck is going on, Wil?"

"They're here, John."

"*Who*'s here?"

"The counterterror people, the ones who went to Australia, the ones who arrested me. They're *here,* John!" Gearing told him, looking around the room, thoroughly disoriented by all the traveling he'd done and not sure of much of anything at the moment.

"Here? Where? In the building?"

"No." Gearing shook his head. "They dropped me off by helicopter. Their boss is a guy named Clark. He said to tell you that you have to surrender—unconditional surrender, John."

"Or else what?" Brightling demanded.

"Or else they're going to come in and get us!"

"Really?" This was no way to be awakened. Brightling had spent two hundred million dollars to build this place—labor costs were low in Brazil—and he considered Project Alternate a fortress, and more than that, a fortress that would have taken months to locate. Armed men—here, right now—demanding his surrender? What was this?

Okay, he thought. First he called Bill Henriksen's room and told him to come upstairs. Next he lit up his computer. There was no e-mail telling him that anyone had spoken with his flight crews. So, nobody had told anyone where they were. So, how the hell had anyone found out? And who the hell was here? And what the hell did they want? Sending someone he knew in to demand their surrender seemed like something from a movie.

"What is it, John?" Henriksen asked. Then he looked at the other man in the room: "Wil, how did you get here?"

Brightling held up his hand for silence, trying to think while Gearing and Henriksen exchanged information. He switched off the room lights, looked out the large windows for signs of activity, and saw nothing at all.

"How many?" Bill was asking.

"Ten or fifteen soldiers," Gearing replied. "Are you going to do what they—are you going to surrender to them?" the former colonel asked.

"Hell, no!" John Brightling snarled. "Bill, what they're doing, is it legal?"

"No, not really. I don't think it is, anyway."

"Okay, let's get our people up and armed."

"Right," the security chief said dubiously. He left the room for the main lobby, whose desk controlled the public-address system in the complex.

"OH, baby, talk to me," Noonan said. The newest version of the DKL people-finding system was up and running now. He'd spotted two of the receiver units about three hundred yards apart. Each had a transmitter that reported to a receiving unit that was in turn wired to his laptop computer.

The DKL system tracked the electromagnetic field generated by the beating of the human heart. This was, it had been discovered, a unique signal. The initial items sold by the company had merely indicated the direction of the signals they received, but the new ones had been improved with parabolic antennas to increase their effective range now to fifteen hundred meters, and, by triangulation, to give fairly exact positions—accurate to from two to four meters. Clark was looking down at the computer screen. It showed blips indicating people evenly spaced in their rooms in the headquarters/residential building.

"Boy, this would have been useful in Eye-Corps back when I was a kid," John breathed. Each of the Rainbow troopers had a GPS locator built into his personal radio transceiver, and these, also, reported to the computer, giving Noonan and Clark exact locations for their own people, and locations also on those in the building to their left.

"Yeah, that's why I got excited about this puppy," the FBI agent noted. "I can't tell you what floor they're on, but look, they've all started moving. I guess somebody woke them up."

"Command, this is Bear," Clark's radio crackled.

"Bear, Command. Where are you?"

"Five minutes out. Where do you want me to make my delivery?"

"Same place as before. Let's keep you out of the line of fire. Tell Vega and the rest that we are on the north side of the runway. My command post is a hundred meters north of the treeline. We'll talk them in from there."

"Roger that, Command. Bear out."

"This must be an elevator," Noonan said, pointing at the screen. Six blips converged on a single point, stayed together for half a minute or so, then diverged. A number of blips were gathering in one place, probably a lobby of some sort. Then they started moving north and converged again.

"I like this one," Dave Dawson said, hefting his G3 rifle. The black German-made weapon had fine balance and excellent sights. He'd been the site-security chief in Kansas, another true believer who didn't relish the idea of flying back to America in federal custody and spending the rest of his life at Leavenworth Federal Penitentiary—a part of Kansas for which he had little love. "What do we do now, Bill?"

"Okay, we split into pairs. Everybody gets one of these." Henriksen started passing over handheld radios. "Think. Don't shoot until we tell you to. Use your heads."

"Okay, Bill. I'll show these bastards what a hunter can do," Killgore observed, liking the feel of his rifle as well and pairing off with Kirk Maclean.

"These, too." Henriksen opened another door, revealing camouflage jackets and pants for them to wear.

"What can we do to protect ourselves, Bill?" Steve Berg asked.

"We can kill the fuckers!" Killgore replied. "They're not cops, they're not here to arrest us, are they, Bill?"

"Well, no, and they haven't identified themselves, and so the law is—the law is unclear on this one, guys."

"And we're in a foreign country anyway. So those guys are probably breaking the fucking law to be here, and if people want to attack us with guns we can defend ourselves, right?" Ben Farmer asked.

"You know what you're doing?" Berg asked Farmer.

"Ex-Marine, baby. Light weapons, line-grunt, yeah, I know what's happening out there." Farmer looked confident, and was as angry as the rest of them at the upset of their plans.

"Okay, people, *I* am in command, okay?" Henriksen said to them. He had thirty armed men now. That would have to be enough. "We make them come to us. If you see somebody advancing toward you with a weapon, you take the bastard out. But be *patient!* Let them in close. Don't waste ammo. Let's see if we can discourage them. They can't stay here long without supplies, and they only have one helicopter to—"

"Look!" Maclean said. A mile and a half away, the black helo landed at the far end of the runway. Three or four people ran from it into the woods.

"Okay, be careful, people, and *think* before you act."

"Let's do it," Killgore said aggressively, waving to Maclean to follow him out the door.

"THEY'RE leaving the building," Noonan said. "Looks like thirty or so." He looked up to orient himself on the terrain. "They're heading into the woods—figuring to ambush us, maybe?"

"We'll see about that. Team-2, this is Command," Clark said into his tactical radio.

"-2 Lead here, Command," Chavez replied. "I can see people running out of the building. They appear to be armed with shoulder weapons."

"Roger that. Okay, Ding, we will proceed as briefed."

"Understood, Command. Let me get organized here." Team-2 was intact, except for the absence of Julio Vega, who'd just arrived on the second helicopter delivery. Chavez got onto his radio and paired his people off with their normal partners, extending his line northward into the forest, and keeping himself at the hinge point on the southern end of the line. The Team-1 people would be the operational reserve, assigned directly to John Clark at the command post.

Noonan watched the Team-2 shooters move. Each friendly blip was identified by a letter so that he'd know them by name. "John," he asked, "when do we go weapons-free?"

"Patience, Tim," Six replied.

Noonan was kneeling on the damp ground, with his laptop computer sitting on a fallen tree. The battery was supposed to be good for five hours, and he had two spares in his pack.

PIERCE and Loiselle took the lead, heading half a kilometer into the jungle. It wasn't a first for either of them. Mike Pierce had worked in Peru twice, and Loiselle had been to Africa three separate times. The familiarity with the environmental conditions was not the same thing as comfort. Both worried about snakes as much as the armed people heading their way, sure that this forest was replete with them, either poisonous or willing to eat them whole. The temperature was rising, and both soldiers were sweating under their camo makeup. After ten minutes, they found a nice spot, with a standing tree and a fallen one next to it, with a decent field of fire.

"They've got radios," Noonan reported. "Want me to take them away?" He had his jammer set up already.

Clark shook his head. "Not yet. Let's listen in to them for a while."

"Fair enough." The FBI agent flipped the radio scanner to the speaker setting.

"This is some place," one voice said. "Look at these trees, man."

"Yeah, big, ain't they?"

"What kind of trees?" a third asked.

"The kind somebody can hide behind and shoot your ass from!" a more serious voice pointed out. "Killgore and Maclean, keep moving north about half a mile, find a place, and sit still there!"

"Yeah, yeah, okay, Bill," the third voice agreed.

"Listen up everybody," "Bill's" voice told them. "Don't clutter up these radios, okay? Report in when I call you or when you see something important. Otherwise keep them clear!"

"Yeah."

"Okay."

"You say so, Bill."

"Roger."

"I can't see shit," a fifth responded.

"Then find a place where you can!" another helpful voice suggested.

"They're in pairs, moving close together, most of 'em," Noonan said, staring down at his screen. "This pair is heading right for Mike and Louis."

Clark looked down at the screen. "Pierce and Loiselle, this is Command. You have two targets approaching you from the south, distance about two-fifty meters."

"Roger, Command. Pierce copies."

SERGEANT Pierce settled into his spot, looking south, letting his eyes sweep back and forth through a ninety-degree arc. Six feet away, Loiselle did the same, starting to relax as far as the environment was concerned, and tensing with the approach of enemies.

DR. John Killgore knew the woods and knew hunting. He moved slowly and carefully now, with every step looking down to assure quiet footing, then up and around to examine the landscape for a human shape. They'd be coming in to get us, he thought, and so he and Maclean would find good spots to shoot them from, just like hunting deer, picking a place in the shadows where you could belly up and wait for the game to come. Another couple of hundred yards, he thought, would be about right.

THREE hundred meters away, Clark used the computer screen and the radios to get his people moving to good spots. This new capability was incredible. Like radar, he could spot people long before he or anyone else could see or hear them. This new electronic toy would be an astounding blessing to every soldier who ever made use of it . . .

"Here we go," Noonan said quietly, like a commentator at a golf tournament, tapping the screen.

"Pierce and Loiselle, this is Command, you have two approaching targets just east of south, approaching at about two hundred meters."

"Roger, Command. Can we engage?" Pierce asked. At his perch, Loiselle was looking at him instead of his direct front.

"Affirmative," Clark replied. Then: "Rainbow, this is Six. Weapons-free. I repeat, we are weapons-free at this time."

"Roger that, I copy weapons-free." Pierce acknowledged.

"LET'S wait till we can get both of 'em, Louis," Pierce whispered.

"D'accord," Sergeant Loiselle agreed. Both men looked to their south, eyes sharp and ears listening for the first snapped twig.

THIS wasn't so bad, Killgore thought. He'd hunted in worse country, far noisier country. There were no pine needles here to make that annoying swishing sound that deer could hear from half a time zone away. Plenty of shadows, little in the way of direct sunlight. Except for the bugs, he might have even been comfortable here. But the bugs were murder. The next time he came out, he'd try to spray some repellent, the physician thought, as he moved forward slowly. The branch of a bush was in his way. He used his left hand to move it, lest he make noise by walking through it.

THERE, Pierce saw. A bush branch had just moved, and there wasn't a breath of wind down there to make that happen.

"Louis," he whispered. When the Frenchman turned, Pierce held up one finger and pointed. Loiselle nodded and returned to looking forward.

"I have a visual target," Pierce reported over his radio. "One target, a hundred fifty meters to my south."

MACLEAN was less comfortable on his feet than he would have been on horseback. He did his best to mimic the way John Killgore was moving, however, though both keeping quiet and keeping up were proving to be incompatible. He tripped over an exposed root and fell, making noise, then swearing quietly before he stood.

"BONJOUR," Loiselle whispered to himself. It was as though the noise had switched on a light of sorts. In any case, Sergeant Loiselle now saw a man-shape moving in the shadows, about one hundred fifty meters away. "Mike?" he whispered, pointing to where his target was.

"Okay, Louis," Pierce responded. "Let them get closer, man."

"Yes."

Both men shouldered their MP-10s, though the range was a little too far as yet.

IF there was anything larger than an insect moving, Killgore thought, he couldn't hear it. There were supposed to be jaguars in this jungle, leopard-size hunting cats whose pelts would make a nice throw rug, he thought, and the 7.62mm NATO round this rifle fired should be more than adequate for that purpose. Probably night hunters, though, and hard to stalk. But what about the capybaras, the largest rat in the world, supposed to be good to eat despite its biological family—they were supposed to feed during the day, weren't they? There was so much for his eyes to see here, so much visual clutter, and his eyes weren't used to it yet. Okay, he'd find a place to sit still, so that his eyes could learn a pattern of light and darkness and then note the change in it that denoted something that didn't belong. *There's a good spot,* he thought, a fallen tree and a standing one . . .

"COME on in, sweetheart," Pierce whispered to himself. At one hundred yards, he thought, that would be close enough. He'd have to hold a little high, like for the target's chin, and the natural drop of the bullet would place the rounds in the upper chest. A head shot would be nicer, but the distance was a little too far for that, and he wanted to be careful.

KILLGORE whistled and waved to Maclean, pointing forward. Kirk nodded agreement. His initial enthusiasm for this job was fading rapidly. The jungle wasn't quite what he expected, and being out here with people trying to attack him didn't make the surroundings any more attractive. He found himself, strangely, thinking of that singles bar in New York, the darkened room and loud dance music, such a strange environment . . . and the women he'd found there. It was too bad, really, what had happened to them. They were—had been—people after all. But worst of all, their deaths had not had any meaning. At least, had the Project moved forward, their sacrifice would have counted for something, but now . . . but now it was just a failure, and here he was in the fucking jungle holding a loaded rifle, looking for people who wanted to do to him what he'd done. . . .

■ ■ ■

"LOUIS, you got your target?"

"Yes!"

"Okay, let's do it," Pierce called in a raspy voice, and with that he tightened his grip on the MP-10, centered the target on the sights, and squeezed the trigger gently. The immediate result was the gentle *puff-puff-puff* sound of the three shots, the somewhat louder metallic sound of the cycling of the submachine gun's action, and then the impact of all three rounds on the target. He saw the man's mouth spring open, and then the figure fell. His ears reported similar sounds from his left. Pierce left his spot and ran forward, his weapon up, with Loiselle in close support.

Killgore's mind didn't have time to analyze what had happened to him, just the impacts to his chest, and now he was looking straight up into the treetops, where there were small cracks of blue and white from the distant sky. He tried to say something, but he wasn't breathing very well at the moment, and when he turned his head a few inches, there was no one there to see. Where was Kirk? he wondered, but found himself unable to move his body to—he'd been shot? The pain was real but strangely distant, and he lowered his head to see blood on his chest and—

—who was that in camouflage clothing, his face painted green and brown?

And who are you? Sergeant Pierce wondered. His three rounds had sprinkled across the chest, missing the heart but ripping into the upper lungs and major blood vessels. The eyes were still looking, focused on him.

"Wrong playground, partner," he said softly, and then life left the eyes, and he bent down to collect the man's rifle. It was a nice one, Pierce saw, slinging it across his back. Then he looked left to see Loiselle holding an identical rifle in one hand and waving his hand across his throat. His target was bloodily dead, too.

"HEY, you can even tell when they get killed," Noonan said. When the hearts stopped, so did the signals the DKL gadget tracked. Cool, Timothy thought.

"Pierce and Loiselle, this is command. We copy you took down two targets."

"That's affirmative," Pierce answered. "Anything else close to us?"

"Pierce," Noonan replied, "two more about two hundred meters south of your current position. This pair is still moving eastward slowly, they're heading toward McTyler and Patterson."

"Pierce, this is Command. Sit tight," Clark ordered.

"Roger, Command." Next Pierce picked up the radio his target had been carrying, leaving it on. With nothing else to do, he fished into the man's pants. So, he saw a minute later, he had just killed John Killgore, M.D., of Binghamton, New York. *Who were you?* he wanted to ask the body, but this Killgore fellow would answer no more questions, and who was to say that the answers would have made any sense?

"OKAY, people, everybody check in," the citizens band walkie-talkie said over Noonan's scanner unit.

HENRIKSEN was just inside the treeline, hoping that his people had the brains to sit still once they found good spots. He worried about the incoming soldiers, if that's what they were. The Project people were a little too eager and a little too dumb. His radio crackled with voices acknowledging his order, except for two.

"Killgore and Maclean, report in." Nothing. "John, Kirk, where the hell are you?"

"THAT'S the pair we took out," Pierce called into Command. "Want me to let him know?"

"Negative, Pierce, you know better than that!" Clark replied angrily.

"No sense of humor, our chief," Loiselle observed to his partner, with a Gallic shrug.

"WHO'S closest to them?" the voice on the radio asked next.

"Me and Dawson," another voice answered.

"Okay, Berg and Dawson, move north, take your time, and see what you can see, okay?"

"Okay, Bill," yet another voice said.

"More business coming our way, Louis," Pierce said.

"Oui," Loiselle agreed. He pointed. "That tree, Mike." It had to be three meters across at the base, Pierce saw. You could build a house from the lumber from just that one. A big house, too.

"Pierce and Loiselle, Command, two targets just started moving towards you, almost due south, they're close together."

▪ ▪ ▪

DAVE Dawson was a man trained in the United States Army fifteen years before, and he knew enough to be worried. He told Berg to stay close behind him, and the scientist did, as Dawson led the way.

"COMMAND, Patterson, I have movement to my direct front, about two hundred meters out."

"That's about right," Noonan said. "They're heading straight for Mike and Louis."

"Patterson, Command, let 'em go."

"Roger," Hank Patterson acknowledged.

"This isn't very fair," Noonan observed, looking up from his tactical picture.

"Timothy, 'fair' means I bring all my people home alive. Fuck the others," Clark responded.

"You say so, boss," the FBI agent agreed. Together, he and Clark watched the blips move toward the ones labeled L and P. Five minutes after that, both of the unidentified blips dropped off the screen and did not return.

"That's two more kills for the our guys, John."

"Jesus, this thing's magic," Clark said after Pierce and Loiselle called in to confirm what the instrument had already told them.

"Chavez to Command."

"Okay, Ding, go," Clark responded.

"Can we use that instrument to move in on them?"

"I think so. Tim, can we steer our guys in behind them, like?"

"Sure. I can see where everybody is, just a question of keeping them well clear until we bend 'em around and bring them in close."

"Domingo, Noonan says he can do this, but it'll take time to do it right, and you guys'll have to use your heads."

"I'll do the best I can, *jefe,*" Chavez called back.

IT was twenty minutes before Henriksen tried to raise Dawson and Berg, only to find that they were not answering. There was something bad happening out there, but he didn't have a clue. Dawson was a former soldier, and Killgore an experienced and skilled hunter—and yet they'd fallen off the earth without a trace? What was happening here? There were soldiers out there, yes, but *nobody* was that good. He had little choice but to leave his people out there.

■ ■ ■

PATTERSON moved first, along with Scotty McTyler, heading west-northwest for three hundred meters, then turning south, moving slowly and silently, blessing the surprisingly bare ground in the forest—the ground got little sunlight to allow grass to grow here. Steve Lincoln and George Tomlinson also moved as a team, steering around two bad-guy blips to their north, and maneuvering right behind them.

"We have our targets," McTyler reported in his Scottish burr. On Noonan's screen they appeared to be less than a hundred meters away, directly behind them.

"Take 'em down," Clark ordered.

BOTH men were facing east, away from the Rainbow troopers, one sheltering behind a tree and the other lying on the ground.

The standing one was Mark Waterhouse. Patterson took careful aim and loosed his three-round burst. The impacts pushed him against the tree, and he dropped his rifle, which clattered to the ground. That caused the lying one to turn, and grip his own rifle tighter when he was hit, and the reflexive action of his hand held the trigger down, resulting in ten rounds fired on full-automatic into the forest.

"Oh, shit," Patterson said over the radio. "That was mine. His rifle must've been set on rock-and-roll, Command."

"WHAT was that, what was that—who fired?" Henriksen called over the radio.

IT only made things easier for Tomlinson and Lincoln. Both of their targets jumped up and looked to their left, bringing both into plain view. Both went down an instant later, and a few minutes after that the command voice on the enemy radio circuit called for another status check. It now came up eight names short.

BY this time, Rainbow was more behind than in front of Henriksen's people, steered into place by Noonan's computer-tricorder rig.

"Can you get me on their radio?" Clark asked the FBI agent.

"Easy," Noonan replied, flipping a switch and plugging a microphone in. "Here."

"Hi, there," Clark said over the CB frequency. "That's eight of your people down."

"Who is this?"

"Is your name Henriksen?" John asked next.

"Who the hell is this?" the voice demanded.

"I'm the guy who's killing your people. We've taken eight of them down. Looks like you have twenty-two more out here. Want I should kill some more?"

"Who the fuck are you?"

"The name's Clark, John Clark. Who are you?"

"William Henriksen!" the voice shouted back.

"Oh, okay, you're the former Bureau guy. I suppose you saw Wil Gearing this morning. Anyway." Clark paused. "I'm only going to say this once: Put your weapons down, walk into the open, and surrender, and we won't shoot any more of you. Otherwise, we'll take down every single one, Bill."

There was a long silence. Clark wondered what the voice on the other end would do, but after a minute he did what John expected.

"Listen up, everybody, listen up. Pull back to the building right now! Everybody move back right now!"

"Rainbow, this is Six, expect movement back to the building complex right now. Weapons are free," he added over the encrypted tactical radios.

The panic in Henriksen's radio call turned out to be contagious. Immediately they heard the thrashing sound of people running in the woods, through bushes, taking direct if not quiet paths back toward the open to which many ran without thinking.

That made an easy shot for Homer Johnston. One green-clad man broke from the trees and ran down the grassy part next to the runway. The weapon he carried made him an enemy, and Johnston dispatched a single round that went between his shoulder blades. The man took one more stumbling step and went down. "Rifle Two-One, I got one north of the runway!" the sniper called in.

It was more direct for Chavez. Ding was sheltering behind a hardwood tree when he heard the noises coming his way from two people he'd been stalking alone. When he figured they were about fifty meters away, he stepped around the tree trunk, to see that they were heading the other way. Chavez sidestepped left and spotted one, and brought his MP-10 to his shoulder. The running man saw him and tried to bring up his rifle. He even managed to fire, but right into the ground, before taking a burst in the face and falling like a sack of beans. The man behind him skidded to a stop and looked at where Chavez was standing.

"Drop the fucking rifle!" Ding screamed at him, but the man either didn't hear or didn't listen. His rifle started coming up, too, but as with his companion, he never made it. "Chavez here, I just dropped two." The excitement of the moment masked the shame of how easy it had been. This was pure murder.

IT was like keeping score for Clark, like some sort of horrid gladiatorial game. The unknown blips on the screen of Noonan's computer started disappearing as their hearts stopped and with them the electronic signals they generated. In another few minutes, he counted four of the thirty signals they'd originally tracked, and those were running back to the building.

"CHRIST, Bill, what happened out there?" Brightling demanded at the main entrance.

"They slaughtered us like fucking sheep, man. I don't know. I don't know."

"This is John Clark calling for William Henriksen," the radio crackled.

"Yeah?"

"Okay, one last time, surrender right now, or else we come in after you."

"Come and fucking get us!" Henriksen screamed in reply.

"VEGA, start doing some windows," Clark ordered in a calm voice.

"Roger that, Command," Oso replied. He lifted the shoulder stock of his M-60 machine gun and started on the second floor. The weapon traced right to left, shattering glass as the line of tracers darted across the intervening distance into the building.

"Pierce and Loiselle, you and Connolly head northwest into the other buildings. Start taking stuff down."

"Roger, Command," Pierce replied.

THE survivors from the forest party were trying to shoot back, mainly at empty air, but making noise in the lobby of the headquarters building. Carol

Brightling was screaming now. The glass from the upstairs windows cascaded like a waterfall in front of their faces.

"Make them stop!" Carol cried loudly.

"Give me the radio," Brightling said. Henriksen handed it to him.

"Cease firing. This is John Brightling, cease firing, everybody. That means you, too, Clark, okay?"

In a few seconds, it stopped, which proved harder for the Project people, since Rainbow had only one weapon firing, and Oso stopped immediately on being ordered to.

"Brightling, this is Clark, can you hear me?" the radio in John's hand crackled next.

"Yes, Clark, I hear you."

"Bring all of your people into the open right now and unarmed," the strange voice commanded. "And nobody will get shot. Bring all of your people out now, or we start playing really rough."

"Don't do it," Bill Henriksen urged, seeing the futility of resistance, but fearing surrender more and preferring to die with a weapon in his hands.

"So they can kill us all right here and right now?" Carol asked. "What choice do we have?"

"Not much of one," her husband observed. He walked to the reception desk and made a call over the building's intercom system, calling everyone to the lobby. Then he lifted the portable radio. "Okay, okay, we'll be coming out in a second. Give us a chance to get organized."

"Okay, we'll wait a little while," Clark responded.

"This is a mistake, John," Henriksen told his employer.

"This whole fucking thing's been a mistake, Bill," John observed, wondering where he'd gone wrong. As he watched, the black helicopter reappeared and landed about halfway down the runway, as close as the pilot was willing to come to hostile weapons.

PADDY Connolly was at the fuel dump. There was a huge above-ground fuel tank, labeled #2 Diesel, probably for the generator plant. There was nothing easier or more fun to blow up than a fuel tank, and with Pierce and Loiselle watching, the explosives expert set ten pounds of charges on the opposite side of the tank from the generator plant that it served. A good eighty thousand gallons, he thought, enough to keep those generators going for a very long time.

"Command, Connolly."

"Connolly, Command," Clark answered.

"I'm going to need more, everything I brought down," he reported.

"It's on the chopper, Paddy. Stand by."

"Roger."

JOHN had advanced to the edge of the treeline, a scant three hundred yards from the building. Just beyond him, Vega was still on his heavy machine gun, and the rest of his troops were close by, except for Connolly and the two shooters with him. The elation was already gone. It had been a grim day. Success or not, there is little joy in the taking of life, and this day's work had been as close to pure murder as anything the men had ever experienced.

"Coming out," Chavez said, his binoculars to his eyes. He did a fast count. "I see twenty-six of 'em."

"About right," Clark said. "Gimme," he said next, taking the glasses from Domingo to see if he could recognize any faces. Surprisingly, the first face he could put a name on was the only woman he saw, Carol Brightling, presidential science advisor. The man next to her would be her former husband, John Brightling, Clark surmised. They walked out, away from the building onto the ramp that aircraft used to turn around on. "Keep coming straight out away from the building," he told them over the radio. And they did what he told them, John saw, somewhat to his surprise.

"Okay, Ding, take a team and check the building out. Move, boy, but be careful."

"You bet, Mr. C." Chavez waved for his people to follow him at a run for the building."

Using the binoculars again, Clark could see no one carrying weapons, and decided that it was safe for him to walk out with five Team-1 troops as an escort. The walk took five minutes or so, and then he saw John Brightling face-to-face.

"I guess this is your place, eh?"

"Until you destroyed it."

"The guys at Fort Dietrick checked out the canister that Mr. Gearing there tried to use in Sydney, Dr. Brightling. If you're looking for sympathy from me, pal, you've called the wrong number."

"So, what are you going to do?" Just as he finished the question, the helicopter lifted off and headed for the power-plant building, delivering the rest of Connolly's explosives, Clark figured.

"I've thought about that."

"You killed our people!" Carol Brightling snarled, as though it meant something.

"The ones who were carrying weapons in a combat zone, yeah, and I imagine they would have shot at my people if they'd had a chance—but we don't give freebies."

"Those were good people, people—"

"People who were willing to kill their fellow man—and for what?" John asked.

"To save the world!" Carol Brightling snapped back.

"You say so, ma'am, but you came up with a horrible way to do it, don't you think?" he asked politely. It didn't hurt to be polite, John thought. Maybe it would get them to talk, and maybe then he could figure them out.

"I wouldn't expect you to understand."

"I guess I'm not smart enough to get it, eh?"

"No," she said. "You're not."

"Okay, but let me get this right. You were willing to kill nearly every person on earth, to use germ warfare to do it, so that you could hug some trees?"

"So that we could save the world!" John Brightling repeated for them all.

"Okay." Clark shrugged. "I suppose Hitler thought killing all the Jews made sense. You people, sit down and keep still." He walked away and got onto his radio. There was no understanding them, was there?

Connolly was fast, but not a miracle worker. The generator room he left alone. As it turned out, the hardest thing to take care of was the freezer in the main building. For this he borrowed a Hummer—there were a bunch of them here—and used it to ferry two oil drums into the building. There being no time for niceties, Connolly simply drove the vehicle through the glass walls. Meanwhile, Malloy and his helicopter ferried half the team back to Manaus and refueled before returning. All in all, it took nearly three hours, during which time the prisoners said virtually nothing, didn't even ask for water, hot and uncomfortable as it was on the frying-pan surface of the runway. Clark didn't mind—it was all the better if he didn't have to acknowledge their humanity. Strangest of all to him, these were educated people, people whom he could easily have respected, except for that one little thing. Finally, Connolly came striding over to where he was standing, holding an electronic box in his hand. Clark nodded and cued his tactical radio.

"Bear, Command."

"Bear copies."

"Let's get wound up, Colonel."

"Roger that. Bear's on the way." In the distance, the Night Hawk's rotor started turning and Clark walked back to where the prisoners were sitting.

"We are not going to kill you, and we are not going to take you back to America," he told them. The surprise in their faces was stunning.

"What, then?"

"You think we should all live in harmony with nature, right?"

"If you want the planet to survive, yes," John Brightling said. His wife's eyes were filled with hatred and defiance, but also curiosity now.

"Fine." Clark nodded. "Stand up and get undressed, all of you. Dump your clothes right here." He pointed at a corner joint in the runway.

"But—"

"Do it!" Clark shouted at them. "Or I will have you shot right here and right now."

And slowly they did. Some disrobed quickly, some slowly and uncomfortably, but one by one they piled their clothing up in the middle of the runway. Carol Brightling, oddly, wasn't the least bit modest about the moment.

"Now what?" she asked.

"Okay, here's the score. You want to live in harmony with nature, then go do it. If you can't hack it, the nearest city is Manaus, about ninety-eight miles that way—" He pointed, then turned. "Paddy, fire in the hole."

Without a word, Connolly started flipping switches on his box. The first thing to go was the fuel tank. The twin charges blew a pair of holes in the side of the tank. That ignited the diesel fuel, which blew out of the tank like the exhaust from a rocket, and propelled the tank straight into the power house, less than fifty meters away. There the tank stopped and ruptured, pouring burning #2 diesel fuel over the area.

They couldn't see the freezer area in the main building go, but here as well, the diesel fuel ignited, ripping out the wall of the freezer unit and then dropping part of the building on the burning wreckage. The other buildings went in turn, along with the satellite dishes. The headquarters-residence building went last, its poured concrete core resisting the damage done by the cratering charges, but after a few seconds of indecision, the core snapped at the ground-floor level and collapsed, bringing the rest of the building down with it. Over a period of less than a minute, everything useful to life here had been destroyed.

"You're sending us out into the jungle without even a knife?" Hendriksen demanded.

"Find some flint rocks and make one," Clark suggested, as the Night Hawk landed. "We humans learned how to do that about half a million years ago.

You want to be in harmony with nature. Go harmonize," he told them, as he turned to get aboard. Seconds later, he was strapped into the jump seat behind the pilots, and Colonel Malloy lifted off without circling.

You could always tell, Clark remembered from his time in 3rd SOG. There were those who got out of the Huey and ran into the bush, and there were those who lingered to watch the chopper leave. He'd always been one of the former, because he knew where the job was. Others only worried about getting back, and didn't want the chopper to leave them behind. Looking down one last time, he saw that all the eyes down there were following the Night Hawk as it headed east.

"Maybe a week, Mr. C?" Ding asked, reading his face. A graduate of the U.S. Army's Ranger School, he didn't think that *he* could survive very long in this place.

"If they're lucky," Rainbow Six replied.

EPILOGUE

NEWS

THE *INTERNATIONAL TRIB* LANDED ON CHAVEZ'S desk after the usual morning exercise routine, and he leaned back comfortably to read it. Life had become boring at Hereford. They still trained and practiced all their skills, but they hadn't been called away from the base since returning from South America six months earlier.

Gold Mine in the Rockies, a front-page story started. A place in Montana, the article read, owned by a Russian national, had been found to contain a sizable gold deposit. The place had been bought as a ranch by Dmitri A. Popov, a Russian entrepreneur, as an investment and vacation site and then he'd made the accidental discovery, the story read. Mining operations would begin in the coming months. Local environmentalists had objected and tried to block the development in court, but the federal district court judge had decided in summary judgment that laws from the 1800s governing mineral exploration and exploitation were the governing legal authority, and tossed the objections out of court.

"You see this?" Ding asked Clark.

"Greedy bastard," John replied, checking out the latest pictures of his grandson on Chavez's desk. "Yeah, I read it. He spent half a million to buy the place from the estate of Foster Hunnicutt. I guess the bastard told him more than just what Brightling was planning, eh?"

"I suppose." Chavez read on. In the business section he learned that Horizon Corporation stock was heading back up with the release of a new drug for heart disease, recovering from the loss in value that had resulted from the disappearance of its chairman, Dr. John Brightling, several months earlier, a mystery that remained to be solved, the business reporter added. The new drug, Kardiklear, had proven to reduce second heart attacks by fully 56 percent in FDA studies. Horizon was also working on human longevity and cancer medications, the article concluded.

"John, has anybody gone back to Brazil to—"

"Not that I know of. Satellite overheads show that nobody's cutting the grass next to their airport."

"So, you figure the jungle killed them?"

"Nature isn't real sentimental, Domingo. She doesn't distinguish between friends and enemies."

"I suppose not, Mr. C." Even terrorists could do that, Chavez thought, but not the jungle. So, who was the real enemy of mankind? Himself, mostly, Ding decided, setting the newspaper down and looking again at the photo of John Conor Chavez, who'd just learned to sit up and smile. His son would grow into the Brave New World, and his father would be one of those who tried to ensure that it would be a safe one—for him and all the other kids whose main tasks were learning to walk and talk.